SEVENTH

A NOVEL OF THE LAST DAYS

SEAL

SEVENTH

A NOVEL OF THE LAST DAYS

SEAL

a novel

JESSICA DRAPER
RICHARD D. DRAPER

Covenant Communications, Inc.

Published by Covenant Communications, Inc.
American Fork, Utah

Printed in United States of America
First Printing: April 2003

10 09 08 07   13 12 11 10 9 8 7

ISBN 1-59156-190-6

The doctrines and prophecies cited in this book are real, but the events in the story bear no intentional resemblance to any current or future persons, institutions, or events (it's a novel, not a prediction). As for reality, whatever actually happens, God is in charge, and everything will come out right.

Epigraph

Only the spiritually sensitive heard the cry of pain. It wasn't quite a voice, more a feeling that translated itself into words coming from deep within the Earth: "Wo, wo is me, the mother of men; I am pained, I am weary, because of the wickedness of my children. When shall I rest, and be cleansed from the filthiness which is gone forth out of me?"

PROLOGUE

On the last day of winter, 252,801 babies were born, and 252,357 people died. 78,676 babies were aborted, which didn't contribute to either statistic. 253 people were killed in terrorist strikes; 165 died in retaliatory raids for previous attacks.

Stocks rose for the fourth straight day on all major indexes, with biochemical and genetics giant MedaGen leading the charge; personal-futures shares fell slightly, as the American Psychological Association's annual "Human Reliability Report" projected increasing unemployment and demotivation among the workforce.

Honors students in First World countries sweated over placement and achievement tests that would let them get the corporate scholarships and cushy jobs they needed to support their expected lifestyles; their underachieving peers traded boasts, taunts, pills, and cigarettes in the parking lots.

Virginia Diamante's music video "All for Me" climbed to the top of the charts. Famine deepened in Asia, insurgent battles heated up in South America, and disease decimated countless villages in Africa. The most sophisticated weather forecasts, as usual, were only 50 percent accurate, though all the reports were right about it being the end of winter and a full moon.

On March 20, spring officially arrived, and the Sixth Seal closed with a bang.

CHAPTER 1

The three earthquakes hit simultaneously. Incredible pressure building along tectonic fault lines all over the world suddenly released as millions of tons of rock shuddered, groaned, and slipped far underground. The seismic shift discharged massive waves of energy, rippling through the earth's crust and warping the surface of the land. Compression waves spread outward from the epicenters of the quakes, contracting and expanding solid ground like ripples in a still pond.

The ripples rushed through actual water, too. With the first massive shockwave rising from the deep-hidden seafloor, the ocean suddenly sucked away from the beaches on the easternmost Philippine islands. Inland, the crowds jostling through the city streets—haggling, bargaining, jockeying for position—came to a standstill after the first shudder whispered through the ground beneath their feet. They had just enough time to realize that something had gone very wrong indeed when the full force of the quake hit. The ground bucked and heaved, throwing people from their feet and buildings from their foundations. Palm trees shivered and lashed in the still air. Sidewalks and roads cracked, chunks of concrete tossed upward, meeting their cousins falling from the buildings above. Multistory apartment buildings, hurriedly thrown up to house the immigrants pouring into the cities, collapsed in on themselves, story after story compressed into concrete, wood, and blood laminate. Geysers of water plumed into the air as underground water mains exploded under the twisting pressure. Geysers of flame followed as pipelines ripped and power lines fell, their sparks igniting volatile fumes. The inhabitants fled, screaming, crying, begging for mercy, praying, as the earth heaved beneath them. Some paused to help others as they stumbled; many shoved the unlucky out of their way; all struggled to escape the terrible avalanches of brick, wood, and cement cascading down man-made cliffs.

Those closer to the shoreline abandoned their hovels or hotels for the beach, where a vast expanse of wet sand greeted their astonished gazes. The first series of shocks faded, the sounds of destruction gradually dying into the howls of the wounded and bereft, the thunder of explosions—and a dim, distant roaring that began at the very edge of hearing, then grew. Sunlight, slightly dimmed by smoke and dust, glittered from a distant whitecap, glinted from the foaming crest of a gigantic wave. It swept over the tide pools the water had abruptly deserted before, then hit the beach, sweeping the earthquake's survivors back into the broken buildings they had abandoned, uprooting trees, and dousing the fires glowing in the ruins under a frothing, hissing tide.

The tide in Central China needed no mighty whitecaps or curling crests of waves. The earthquakes ripping through the deep mountain faults spread into the deep topsoil of the plains and weakened and crumbled the mighty dams and dikes that held the Yellow River in its enforced course. Millions of acre-feet of water spilled out, the floodwaters inexorably fanning out in all directions. Fields, factories, villages, and roads all fell under the rolling, tumbling currents spreading through the countryside. Peasants lucky enough to have some warning of the watery doom rapidly converging on them jammed the roads; others, closer to the dikes and dams, lost their lives as well as their farms in the ochre-colored floods. Their cries merged with those of city dwellers lost in a nightmare of crashing masonry, twisted girders, and yawning pits where subway tunnels had run.

Pits yawned through downtown San Francisco as well, cracks raggedly bisecting streets, parks, and buildings. The taller skyscrapers swayed, the ground twisting and shifting under their massive foundations. Some, built to withstand only lesser quakes—or built with substandard materials—groaned, shivered, and finally tumbled, smashing into the smaller buildings surrounding them. Glass exploded outward in glittering cascades, showering the streets below with lethal shards. Freeways slithered like snakes on their supports and then crashed down, one, two, six layers deep, overpasses meeting the underpasses in catastrophic embraces. Subway tunnels collapsed under avalanches of dirt, rocks, and substandard materials. Power lines writhed and snapped, sending hissing sparks arcing into the night air. Beach houses built like cliff dwellings tumbled, rolling into the ravenous ocean below. Nightmare darkness crashed into the city on a wave of extinguished lights, subsonic rumbles replaced with the din of sirens, screams, and car alarms.

* * *

In the cramped, plastic-smelling confines of the International Space Station, another alarm rang, its persistent buzzing finally driving the nighttime crew to action.

"Jim. Jim. James. Hey, Hideyoshi! Wake up!" Ivana poked the tectonic specialist sleeping in the hammock, then poked him again when all she got was a half-conscious grunt in response. "Rise and shine, sleeping beauty. Your infernal buzzers are beeping."

"Buzzers beeping?" Hideyoshi stirred, the words filtering through his uneasy dreams of falling through seemingly solid ground. He sat up abruptly, the motion setting the hammock thumping against its supports in the weightless environment of the space station. "The alarm on the geologic lasers? Why didn't you tell me?"

"I did," Ivana pointed out, watching her crewmate struggle with the zipper and straps that snugged him into the sleeping cocoon. She grinned. "Hate to say it, Jimbo, but it doesn't take a rocket scientist to figure out a slumber bag."

Hideyoshi finally gave up on the zipper and simply unhooked the bag from its wall fastenings. He launched himself down the round corridor toward the laser-detection module, wearing the slumber bag like a half-shed skin. "Obviously, it doesn't take a tectonic specialist, either," he shot back over his shoulder.

Ivana grinned and glided after him. "So, what's up with all the alarms? The sonar detectors catch something big going on?"

"No, not the sonar. It's the InSAR system alert," Hideyoshi said, his fingers dancing over the console controls. "Remember? I told you about it last week."

Ivana rolled her eyes. "Right. Like I remember all the acronyms you throw at me. I'll stick with my own bag of tricks for trying to calculate the butterfly effect." She glanced at the readouts. "Still, this looks interesting, now that it's screaming. Which experiment is this again?"

"This one's satellite-borne radar imaging. We're using it to keep an eye on the Three Sisters in Oregon. Got Becker down there, running surface tests for outgassing and salinity levels in the lakes around the volcanic sites." Data scrolled down the screens, and topographical maps zoomed in to show a definite rise in the low dome between the taller, more sharply defined cones of the mountains around it. "Crust deformation, terrain rise—wow, 27 inches! What the heck is going on . . ." His voice trailed off.

"Outgassing? Sounds like something Captain Nakima would be involved in," Ivana observed. "What are you chasing with training lasers at the ground between a bunch of volcanoes? What does 27 inches mean?"

"It means incipient volcanic activity," Hideyoshi said, after his crewmate smacked his shoulder to get his attention. His eyes remained glued on the readouts, a deep frown line growing between his straight, black brows. "InSAR keeps track of the rising ground over a big magma chamber. They detected a buildup of pressure underground back in the '90s, higher levels of carbon dioxide in the air, more dissolved minerals in the water. All signs of incipient volcanic activity—"

"Whoa!" Ivana exclaimed, staring at another screen across the tiny room that housed the terrestrial-science module. (The astronomers and physicists got the comparatively large, luxurious suites near the station's powerful telescopes; the biologists had more room, too, but it was full of rats, monkeys, and for one very long mission, vocalizing bullfrogs.)

"Whoa is right," Hideyoshi agreed. "We thought we had a baby volcano back then, but with these readings—Ivana, what's wrong?"

"James!" she exclaimed at the same time, her voice higher and more frightened than his. "Not your baby volcano—something else. Look!"

Hideyoshi dragged his eyes away from his readouts to follow Ivana's pointing finger. The scene on the TV monitor tuned to the news channels chilled them both: screaming crowds running from onrushing water, walls collapsing in aftershocks, fires roaring through ruins, graphics showing the spreading waves of destruction around the earthquakes' epicenters.

"Dear Heaven," Ivana whispered, the words she used so casually on other occasions taking on the tones of prayer.

The images of catastrophe reflected in their eyes, blue and brown irises around ebony pools of horror. The InSAR alarm sounded again, its urgent tones cutting through the muted sound from the satellite-news broadcast.

Hideyoshi looked at it vaguely, then gasped. He launched himself across the room, grabbing a handhold to keep himself from bouncing off the wall. Activation lights blossomed on the sat-phone's face as he ripped it out of its cradle and stabbed at its buttons. "Becker, answer, answer, answer," he chanted tightly. "Answer, answer—Becker!"

"Jim? What—it's nearly1:00 A.M.! I know there's no nighttime in space, but some of us need our sleep."

"Becker, get off that mountain," Hideyoshi ordered.

"What? Why?" The geologist's voice sounded less upset than excited.

"Get in your truck, turn on the radio, and listen to the news—as you drive as fast as you can off that mountain!" Hideyoshi repeated. "InSAR's going nuts. The dome's risen nearly *three feet* in the last three hours, and there's been an earthquake along at least two Northern California faults. Becker, our baby volcano's about to be born—"

"And I'm standing right in the delivery room!" Becker finished the thought. Thuds, crashes, and whispered grunts came through the open connection, followed by the sound of rushing air abruptly cut off with the slam of a truck door. "Jim, you still there?" Becker asked as the engine roared to life.

"Still here, Andre, costing the taxpayers thousands of dollars in connect fees while you skip around camp wasting valuable time," Hideyoshi reminded him.

"Wind's kicked up," the geologist informed him. "Trees are shaking like crazy." Static, then the professionally unruffled voice of a news announcer filled the spaces between his words. "Had a crazy dream about sleeping on a mother-lode pile of JELL-O—but that's more along your line, isn't it?"

"What?" Hideyoshi asked, his gaze fixed on InSAR's readouts. The topographical representation changed abruptly from burnt orange to glowing red as the lasers detected another ground surge.

"JELL-O, Mormons, you know, Jim, that's what you folks are famous for," Becker informed him. "You haven't—Cripes!"

"What?" Ivana and Hideyoshi both yelped.

"Steam," Becker shouted. "Ground's shaking. Road's bucking like a trawler deck."

The geologist kept up a running commentary for about twenty minutes, objective observations interspersed with decidedly subjective yelps. He raced his truck down the mountain road, dodging falling tree limbs, dislodged boulders, and terrified wildlife.

Far behind him, Becker's seismograph registered each successive shock, its sensitive needle swinging in wider and wider arcs across the blue-lined paper. Suddenly, it stopped, then quivered slightly. The tent Becker had abandoned shivered, then went still as the wind abruptly died. The night seemed to hold its breath, then a sigh rippled through the dark woods. The sky having said its piece, the ground took over. The sound began too low for anything but giants to hear, then gradually rose into the audible range as the magma and gasses beneath the dome reached critical pressure and erupted into the night, spewing a million tons of glowing molten rock, superheated steam, and suffocating cinders.

The InSAR console went silent as the lasers lost their lock on the now-vanished ground. Becker's satellite phone caught one last, "Whoa!" and fell silent as well. The dust cloud rolled upward and outward in great billowing gouts, smashing through the lowest layer of clouds and spreading across the thinner layers of the sky in a huge plateau of choking talc, lit from beneath like the roof of the Inferno. The superheated dust cloud flowed horizontally as well, blasting through the trees, vaporizing the tender needles and spring buds, laying flat the trunks of forest giants. Steam erupted from meadows, and boiling water bubbled through streams and ponds, killing plants and animals alike. Flows of molten rock followed, glowing ebony scarlet as it oozed in ever-widening streams out of the rents ripped deep in the ground, gouts of it spattering in sluggish fountains as the flows piled and mounted in the deep pit.

A shoulder of a hill shielded the main access road from the first blast wave, but it couldn't dampen the vibration through the ground. As the explosion hit, Becker's truck bounded off the road, careened through the trees, and landed hard in the creek below. The geologist tumbled out of the vehicle, kicking the door open and falling into the frighteningly warm and muddy water. He pushed toward the shore through the chest-high water, keeping his feet until another explosion threw him into the stream. He surfaced, spluttering—until the surface of the water bloomed into red-gold highlights. Chunks of half-melted rock crashed out of the sky, annihilating the disabled truck and lighting fires through the still-standing trees and underbrush. He dove and surfaced once again, considered the flames blossoming along the creek's shoreline, and swam as quickly as he could downstream, riding the increasingly turbulent, debris-choked flow.

The creek widened into a ford about the same time that the water became too wild—and too hot—for comfort. Becker pulled himself up and waded toward the moving lights on the shore, stumbling over the rocks barely submerged in the roiling flood. Hands reached down to help him climb the steep bank. He looked up to see Bob Fox, the owner of the bait shop/general store beside the ford, and two rangers. A small group of other people huddled behind them, frightened, dirty, and sporting temporary bandages.

"Glad you got out, Becker," Fox said. "You were up there pretty far."

"You're the geologist?" one of the rangers asked. When Becker said yes, he checked off an entry on his clipboard. "Still twenty-six missing," he informed his colleague, stepping away to bark an update into his radio. The reply was buried in static from the electrical charges in the dust.

"Thought you were keeping an eye on that volcano." The ranger looked at Becker.

"We were," Becker said, beginning to shake as the real danger he'd so narrowly escaped sank in, replacing the mixture of scientific interest and blind panic that had carried him through his mad flight down the mountain. Good thing he hadn't set up camp right on top of the dome!

"Didn't get a lot of warning," Fox commented.

Becker took a deep breath. "As my Mormon colleague on the ISS would say, Bob, nobody knows the time or season for an act of God. Even if we keep trying to figure it out."

A light dusting of ash fell from the sky, thickening into drifting, feather-sized flakes. The full moon had vanished behind a curtain of ash-filled clouds.

* * *

In the week before the earthquake hit, two hundred and twenty-two LDS missionaries left the Mission Training Center in Provo, Utah, for their mission assignments in the Orient. The quake knocked out transmission stations in many areas, including those in Taiwan. The missionaries' parents anxiously waited for word of their children's well-being. Among them were Chinedu Ojukwu, an administrator in the Church Educational System in Salt Lake City, and his wife, Adaure. Their youngest son, Chisom, was assigned to the Taiwan Taipei West Mission. Unable to sleep, Chinedu stepped out onto his back porch, glancing up as the silvery full moon slid behind a bank of clouds.

* * *

The moon electronically reappeared over the shoulder of a shaken reporter in San Francisco. Above the glow of the fires burning throughout the city, the moon hung like a rusty coin, its silver bright-ness dimmed into bloody shadow. "Casualty reports are still coming in; estimates from FEMA put the death toll at 7,000 and rising, just five hours after the earthquakes. Aftershocks still rock this area, terri-fying the traumatized survivors of what many insurance-investment specialists are calling the most destructive and expensive natural disaster in human history." Crawls along the bottom and sides of the screen augmented the news with cold, hard statistics: damages, deaths, injuries, hotline numbers to call to check on survivors, and promos for private investigation and tracking businesses, hospitals, and ambulance services.

The scene in the center of the screen panned away from the reporter, capturing the empty, frightened faces and staring eyes of the people crowding around the Red Cross emergency station. Some wore bandages, slings, and other obvious signs of injury; for the rest, the hurt hovered behind their eyes, their once-firm belief in an equally firm world shaken as violently as their neighborhoods.

"The human toll is horrific, and damage reports are equally high, with billions of dollars lost in the quakes, floods, and fires," the reporter continued, his voice shaking as he read the latest reports from the PDA screen the cameraman held up. "Estimates are coming in from communities hundreds of miles from the epicenter. The US Geological Survey reports that the effects of the quake in Central California were felt as far away as Canada and New Mexico."

A map filled the screen, animated ripples flowing from the crimson target showing the center of the quake. The whiter light from the graphic lit the small, bare room where the expensive monitor leaned against the wall, the wires from its speakers trailing over the threadbare carpet. The carpet matched the cracks in the wall and the cardboard pane in the south-facing window; it did not, however, match the expensive console—or the stereo, computer, random bits of electronic equipment, and firearms on the makeshift, sagging shelves. A collection of music discs had tumbled onto the floor when the foundation shook; they lay in a spray of rainbow plastic, along with the pile of library books and empty cola cans that Dove had stacked on the shelf beside them the night before.

The light from the screen also lit Dove's face as he watched the report sideways from his position on the floor. Dove's given name was Salvatore, but Benny had taken to calling him *Hasbìdì*—Navajo for dove—because of the cooing noises he'd made as a baby. The nickname had modified into English because none of their friends could properly pronounce the tone-dependent Navajo version. It had stuck when Dove grew up, too, but for different reasons. Now, the other members of the borderland gang called him Dove because things got really peaceful after he'd been around. Other gangs laughed about the name, until they'd seen what he could do with a gun—or a knife, in a pinch. Not that he had to enforce his reputation much anymore, not since those first years when he and Benny had just come off Grandpa's sheep ranch on the Rez and joined *Abuelo's* army. The enforcers, dealers, and thugs that made up the underside of society on both sides of the U.S. and Mexican border respected *Abuelo's* territory, and they knew that Dove and Benny were big men in his outfit. They earned that reputation, just like they earned the payback that bought the expensive toys in the rundown house on the edge of town.

The *Brujos* were the first bunch in a long time who'd come to challenge *Abuelo's* domination of the runner and backup business in this section of Amexica, as the pundits had christened these border-lands between the United States and Mexico. So far, they hadn't pulled any direct offensives, just the usual chest-thumping routine— short brawls, trespassing on *Abuelo's* shooting ranges in the hills, and leaving their chop spray-painted on the cliffsides. Rumor whispered that they had heavy backing from a new player in the never-ending skirmishes between various drug lords and smugglers who had popped up since the weakening of both American and Mexican police power in the area. The same rumors said that they had something bigger than .38s in their armory—military surplus munitions, including anti-aircraft guns and shoulder-mounted grenade launchers.

That thought—and the extra calculus homework the teacher at the alternative high school had assigned—had kept Dove awake until just before midnight, when the combination of derivative equations and caffeine withdrawal had finally knocked him out. The shud-dering had brought him back to consciousness too soon and had shaken loose the worry in his head again. "People got bigger prob-lems," he said softly to himself, watching the stunned faces on the screen. He uncurled from under the blanket, shivering slightly in the early spring chill, and padded into Benny's room.

"Benny," he said softly. "Benny, it was an earthquake."

"Huh?" His brother stirred and turned over in the big, tousled bed, running a hand through his equally tousled hair. "Have a bad dream, *Hasbidi*?"

"No, Benny. It was an earthquake," he repeated. "Not the *Brujos* setting off grenades."

"You hear that Dolores?" Benny asked, poking the feminine lump in the bed beside him. The earth really did move."

"Whatever, *chico*," Dolores muttered, swatting his hand away and burrowing back under the covers.

Benny pulled the covers up to her shoulders and slid out of the bed on the other side. "News?" he asked, as he headed for the door, pausing to grab his jeans and Dove before he closed the door behind him.

"Jealous?" Dove asked, watching Benny pull on his jeans. "Think I'm making a move on Dolores?"

"Just trying to keep you pure, little brother," Benny assured him, teeth glinting in the light from the screen showing firefighters rushing to contain a propane-explosion blaze in a trailer park. "You wanna get messed up with the chicks I bring home, you're nuts. Dolores'd take your head off, *chico*."

"Lancelot and Galahad," Dove commented.

"What?" Benny asked absently, watching the disasters scroll by in real time.

"Lancelot was a knight who slept with his *jefe's chiquita*," Dove explained. "Cheated on his own old lady doing it. Comes later on, his old lady has a kid. Lancelot decides *chiquito's* gonna be the perfect knight, not like his papa. Named the kid Galahad; he grew up the ultimate knight, wicked righteous the whole way down. So perfect he got the Holy Grail. But he didn't get the girl."

"Knights? As in old-time Anglo knights?" Benny looked at him in disbelief. "I ever tell you that you read too much?"

Dove grinned at him. "Nah, you tell me to read more—go to school, *Hasbìdì*, do your homework, be a good boy, learn stuff from your teachers or I'll smack you into next week, keep out of the tequila, get that cig out your mouth, don't look at Dolores or the other *chiquitas*—"

Benny laughed. "*Callarse*, Dovey. You read 'cause you're looking for heroes."

"I got a hero, Benny," Dove said, giving his brother an exaggerated worshipful look. This time he laughed as Benny smacked his head, the impact turning into a rough but affectionate ruffle of Dove's thick, raven hair. His laugh didn't last long, though, as the grim newscast caught their attention again.

"It'll be OK," Benny said softly, rubbing his little brother's shoulder, reflexively comforting him. They were still sitting in front of the screen when Dolores emerged from the bedroom, blinking and yawning in the yellowed light of the dusty, smoky sunrise.

CHAPTER 2

Dear Chisom,

Good morning to you. Your mother and I were delighted to finally get your e-mail with the attached Vid. The Mission Office phoned as soon as the transmission stations were running to tell us you were alright, but it's still good to hear from you personally. It was good to see your new companion too. I chuckled at your description of how conspicuous you feel. I can imagine. It is not every day that the Taiwanese meet a six-foot-six (or is it seven?) inch, black Mormon missionary who speaks nearly fluent Chinese. Peoples' curiosity will get you into quite a number of doors which might not have been opened otherwise. Take good advantage of it. I'm sure having a native Taiwanese as your trainer will really help you get into the culture more quickly. Was he surprised at how well you already spoke Mandarin?

I am amazed how real these three-dimensional pictures look. Vids are wonderful. They are so lifelike they make me feel like I can just reach into the screen and touch things. And, I might add, you're looking good too. I must say, your letter brought us both joy and sorrow; joy because we now know that you arrived safely in the mission field (with the transmissions interrupted for a few days, we were a bit worried), and sorrow because of the devastation you described and recorded for us. Though the news continues to cover the aftermath of the earthquake, it touches us more with you there. I still find the damage caused by the monster unbelievable. Never before has history recorded an earthquake with three epicenters and ground movement above 8 points on the Richter scale at all three. It literally shook the whole earth. Taiwan is fortunate that it was hundreds of miles from the center of the quake that rocked Asia. It is disheartening to know, as you described, that many buildings, even newer ones, were damaged so badly they will need to be torn down. On the other hand, I am grateful so few lives were lost. That is not the case with those places at or near the epicenter in China, the Philippines, and the U.S. west coast. What we see on TV breaks our hearts. There are miles where the land is broken, heaved, or sunken with all life destroyed.

As I watch the news, I am reminded of the havoc nature wrought among the Lamanites and Nephites at the time of the Lord's death. In 3 Nephi it tells how great cities were burned with fire while others sank into the sea and some were covered with earth. That is exactly what the news is showing us.

What is sad is that the current devastation results from the same circumstances as those described in the Book of Mormon. There we read that the destructions came because the majority of people turned from God and began persecuting the Saints, even attempting to kill the prophets. I fear the same thing is happening today. Did you know that the Church is closing three more missions due to lack of conversions and growing opposition? What an odd world. In some places the Church grows rapidly, and in others we are pulling out our missionaries.

As I see it, God has been using the forces of nature as a tool for conversion since the Church was organized, but especially in the last half century. The hardships we are seeing are God's way of trying to wake people up and bring them to Him. In Doctrine and Covenants 43, the

Lord says He will use thunder and lightning, earthquakes and hailstorms as His means of crying repentance. But, He warns, if the world does not respond, He will unleash His wrath. I fear we are living in the transition period between God's coaxing the world to repent and His preparing to cleanse it of all wickedness.

Yes, the world is paying for the rejection of the gospel by many leaders of state, many peoples' manifest hatred of the Brethren (evidenced by the ever-increasing threats and attempts on their lives—for example, the two assassination attempts on Area Authority Seventy, one in the Philippines and the other in Venezuela), and attacks on our chapels and members in some areas. I might just share one more frightening item in that vein. It has not been confirmed yet, but there is some talk that these attempts are not random acts by "some crazies." Our insiders are telling the Brethren that the methods used by the assassins looked very professional and Providence was all that saved our people. The police fear the attempts suggest an organized group has targeted the Church and its leaders. I hope that does not prove true. Time will tell. I'll keep you posted.

On the bright side, the Church has been able to account for all its missionaries and, apart from some broken bones, stitches, and bruises, all seem to have survived quite well. Thank goodness the Mission Presidents heeded the Prophet's warnings! That gives your Mother and me confidence you will be protected during these troubled times. We need that confidence, knowing that the earth is just at the beginnings of the sorrows of the End Time. Obedience will be your shield. That's what saved our Elders. Don't forget that.

I'm going to let your Mom fill you in on family matters. I'll close by answering the question you posed in your e-mail, "Was this the prophesied earthquake?" It depends on what you mean. Prophecy mentions many earthquakes and there will be one that will make this one look like a BB gun compared to a howitzer. That one will be associated with the Lord's coming. At that time, God will rearrange the land masses to conform to conditions before the great division in the days of Peleg. If that is the earthquake you have in mind, then no, this is not the prophesied earthquake.

However, this one is mentioned specifically. In Revelation chapter 6, John saw, as part of the devastation of the sixth seal, "a great earthquake; and the sun became black as sackcloth of hair, and the moon became as blood." The world's eyes confirm the reality of John's prediction. There are some areas where the dust clouds are beginning to block out sunlight and volcanoes spew deadly smoke. Over ever-increasing areas of the earth, where the ash and dust clouds are massing, the moon glows blood red. I find it highly ironic that the wicked are hardening their hearts against righteousness in full view of one of the greatest signs of the last days, namely, the bloody moon and dusky sun. Instead of responding to our message of hope and assurance with delight and acceptance, they turn to death for security. Suicide rates have skyrocketed. Even among many of the believers, the pessimism is extreme, but I should not be surprised. Again, John saw it and warned us that at the time many would want the mountains to cover them so they would not have to face God's wrath. How literally we see this scripture fulfilled as people of all races and classes have expressed a desire to die before conditions get worse. Notice, my son, that the distress of the close of sixth seal does not increase righteousness among these people but the desire to die. Further, they ask the right question: "Who will be able to stand?" We have the answer, but they will not hear. How sad.

God revealed to Joseph Smith that the sixth seal represents events to take place during that period of earth's history before the second coming when the days of the Gentiles, as they are called, are about to close. If you're interested, look at Revelation 6:12–17 in light of D&C 77:7, 10. As I read the scriptures, I am forced to believe that we have witnessed the closing of the sixth seal and the fulfilling of the days of the Gentiles. That means the seventh seal is now opening. If that is the case, then this is not a good time for the wicked whom the scriptures leave without hope.

As for the righteous, how different the story. This period promises to be the greatest in earth's history. I will admit we are in for a bit of a rough time, but these are but the birth pangs of the coming glory. I'm so thankful we can be a part of it all and I know we have prophets who will get us through. Let your light shine brightly that people may see it and be drawn to God and saved both spiritually and temporally. And may the red hues of the hazy moon remind you and testify to them that the time is short.

Love,
Your dad,
Chinedu

* * *

"The volume of ash in the air will visibly affect the color of the sky for several months," Hideyoshi explained, indicating the readouts for the camera. "The scattering effect of the dust is why the moon looks red and the sun seems a lot dimmer than usual over the last two weeks. Our computer projections show that the ash and dust will affect the weather, too. Historical accounts of volcanic explosions—such as the Krakatoa eruption during the nineteenth century—show that ash prevents sunlight from reaching the surface of the earth, which leads to cooler temperatures and less predictable weather patterns. Our climatologist, Dr. Ivana Mir, can explain the kinds of weather effects we'll see."

"As Dr. Hideyoshi said," Ivana regarded the camera with the same expression she'd use on a semibright undergraduate student in a beginning meteorology course, "the dust and ash in the air will cause a decided cooling effect in the northern hemisphere. Wind patterns will cause the dust to continue to drift in a northeasterly direction, over Northern Canada. This will cause an increased *La Niña* effect, causing—"

"Get ready to cut it short, Kim." Monk, the producer for Channel 8 News, sat back in his seat with a sigh. "The audience really digs Hideyoshi—a cute Japanese fella cuts a lot of ice with the females 18 to 35. Did you see the ratings spike when he came on? But Corporate's gotta find another female lead. That Dr. Mir can take the temperature down to below freezing with a single look. Between her and the hard science, we've lost six rating points locally in the last 30 seconds. It can't play any better in flyover country, either. The earthquakes are getting to be old news." He sighed, checking his monitors for promising stories on the incoming feeds. Riots, famines, terrorist attacks, epidemics, political skullduggery, Virginia's latest affair—nothing big enough to unseat the earthquakes as the lead story. "But it looks like we're stuck with it for awhile. Time to spice things up. Ready with the human-interest angle?"

Kim nodded and adjusted her headset, sending the "wrap it up" signal to the anchor and sending the green light to the next field crew in the queue. The signal—and its attendant ads, promos, and supplementary materials—slipped into place, waiting for channel space.

"That's the view from Dr. James Hideyoshi, tectonic specialist at the International Space Station," the anchor intoned. "Relating the cosmic consequences of the worldwide catastrophe. We can't do anything about the ash in the sky, but here on earth the cleanup efforts continue. Clara Cortez, our economics correspondent, was in Manila to cover the latest meeting of the Worldwide Growth Association. Obviously, the events of the last two weeks have interrupted the controversial meeting of international corporate leaders—and our reporter's scheduled interviews. Now, Clara is live with a Channel 8 Aftermath Report." The logo for Channel 8's exclusive series of man-on-the-street interviews flashed on the screen.

"This is Clara Cortez, live from the earthquake zone here in the Philippines." The scene switched to show the economics reporter, dressed down in khakis and a windbreaker, standing in a devastated street. In the background, wailing mourners and shell-shocked victims wandered amid the rubble of their homes.

The red light on the studio camera flicked to amber. The anchor broke her professional freeze and threw down her prop script. "'Cosmic consequences of the worldwide catastrophe'? Who writes this stuff?! I can't say lines like that on the air! My credibility will be shot!"

"Calm down, Hairdo, we'll take care of it," Monk intoned over the studio speakers. Monk never bothered to learn anchors' names; they came and went as the ratings rose and fell, a series of interchangeable hairstyles and Miss America smiles. He cut the intercom to the studio as she screamed, "For the third time today, my name is KATHY!" The anchor's manager rushed from the wings, petting and reassuring, promising to make the studio pay when her contract negotiations came up again.

"Note to copy writers," Monk growled at Kim. "No more of that alliteration. I don't care what kind of muse strikes when they hear the name 'Clara Cortez.' Even if it was funny."

Kim nodded, grinning.

The old lady Clara was interviewing grinned too, showing the last few enamel holdouts between the gaps in her smile. The reporter had thrust a microphone into her face, asking "As you look at the devastation from the earthquake, including your own home of 40 years, how do you feel?"

A younger woman—daughter or neighbor—stared at Clara in disbelief. But even standing amid the cracked ruins of her home, the older lady radiated a calm that could've been either shock or unshakeable inner serenity. Her smile just grew broader as she answered the reporter's question, then turned her back on the camera and continued gathering up pieces of her belongings. The translator couldn't match her delivery, but did get the words: "At least when the wave came, it put out the fires."

"Others here in the Philippines aren't taking their losses so calmly," Clara observed. The scene shifted to a large crowd of shouting, wailing people. "Earlier today, protesters converged on the few undamaged buildings in the center of the capital, including the United States Embassy. Last week, corporate security forces battled protesters who gathered to raise their objections to the WGA's policies in the Third World." Stock footage showed protesters in a running battle against helmeted, armored private troops—tear gas, high-pressure hoses, and rubber bullets flying in all directions. "Now, the business leaders have gone, but the crowds have grown." Another scene change, and now the camera showed waves of chanting, crying people, some carrying pictures of loved ones lost in the quake, others bearing signs or effigies demonizing the WGA and Philippine leaders. "The more radical elements in this crowd are blaming the wickedness of the West for releasing God's wrath on their nation. Others are protesting the lack of international aid and the internal corruption that led to the deaths of so many in the poorer areas, where unenforced building codes and dishonest contractors led to catastrophic building collapses. Reports have come in that bullets fired in a superstitious effort to frighten off the earthquakes have caused injuries as well. The casualty figures continue to rise, as rescuers continue their efforts. With every hour that passes, however, hope fades." A baby doll, dirty and half buried under the fall of rubble from an apartment building, filled the screen before the camera focused on the reporter once again. "From Manila, this is Clara Cortez."

"Rescue efforts continue here at home as well." Anchor Kathy regained her seat and her composure in time to smile sadly at the camera. (She hadn't given such a convincing performance since her last movie audition.) "However, even here in California, the aftermath of the quakes is not without controversy. For a regional report, we go to Anne O'Neal in San Jose."

"Thank you, Kathy," Anne said, her calm belying her racing heart. "We're here in San Jose, where cleanup efforts are continuing." Busy workers crossed the field of view behind her. Volunteers handed out sack lunches to other volunteers who were tired and hungry from their efforts digging out and hauling away rubble from the badly damaged homes and apartment buildings in the worst-hit neighborhoods. "As you can see, many of these volunteers are wearing bright yellow T-shirts with 'Walnut Springs Stake' on them. They're Mormons, or members of The Church of Jesus Christ of Latter-day Saints, as they prefer to be called. Pedro Hernandez, the elders quorum leader for one of the groups of volunteers, is here with me. Mr. Hernandez, can you tell us about your volunteer efforts—and what an elders quorum leader is?"

"An elders quorum is a group of men without enough to do at home, and I'm the one with the phone list," Hernandez smiled.

"Seriously, the elders quorum is an organization in each ward—congregation—that most of the adult men belong to. The Relief Society's here, too—they're the ladies, and the ones who really do all the organizing. After the quake, we started making calls, and people turned out."

"They sure did," Anne said, as the camera panned over the scene, volunteers, victims, and rescue workers blending in surprisingly organized chaos. "What do you say to the charges that the Mormons are grandstanding here, taking over from state-appointed aid agencies?"

Hernandez's smile only wavered slightly. "We're working with the Red Cross and state agencies. In fact, we're just like any other volunteers here, ready to do whatever is needed for whoever needs it. We're just here to help."

"Mormons have a reputation for taking care of their own," Anne observed.

"Of course, I'm not an official spokesman," Hernandez pointed out. "The earthquakes hit everybody, Mormons included. My own house got a small crack in the foundation from the aftershocks, but at least I've got a house—unlike these folks. Everybody deserves a hand up. It's a chance to be Good Samaritans. We're here to help anybody who needs it."

"And you've certainly got the organization to do it," Anne said. "Thank you, Mr. Hernandez." He nodded, smiled again, and stepped back, picking up his shovel. Anne turned back to her camera man. "Over 300 volunteers from The Church of Jesus Christ of Latter-day Saints have descended on this area, the most impressive turnout of any volunteer agency. As you can see, they're well organized, hard working, and prepared for anything. Unfortunately, they're also at the center of a charitable feud."

A group of unhappy-looking people standing around a Red Cross station appeared on camera as Anne continued, "Representatives from the United Baptist churches in the area have refused to join the cleanup efforts as long as the Red Cross allows the Mormons to help. I spoke with the Red Cross representative, Shauna Hall, earlier today, and while she declined to appear on camera, she stated that she appreciated the assistance from The Church of Jesus Christ of Latter-day Saints and hoped that the Baptists would not let their doctrinal differences affect these much-needed volunteer efforts.

"Unfortunately, today's events are yet another eruption of the simmering hostility between the two communities, especially on the United Baptist side. The conflict between the Mormons and Evangelical Christians has grown more fierce since the Mormons moved their headquarters from Salt Lake City, Utah, to Independence, Missouri." The scene changed to show the new Church Headquarters in Independence, with its gray granite walls and exquisite flowerbeds. "The United Baptist Convention has reiterated its charge that Mormons are not Christian, and it has stepped up its missionary efforts in the Midwest to combat what prominent evangelist Tommy Gibbs calls 'the encroaching scourge of unbelief.'" Stock footage of Tommy Gibbs appeared on screen, the handsome, silver-haired preacher smiling as he addressed the crowd at his latest, highly successful revival.

Anne, regaining the eye of the camera, smiled. "From what I've seen today, there is plenty of belief on both sides. The question is, will those beliefs help or hinder rescue efforts? Despite the debate, the Mormons are here, now, shovels in hand and sack lunches ready. This is Anne O'Neal, in San Jose." She smiled, professionally poised, as the broadcast ended.

"Nice one," Leon, her cameraman, commented. "You going for a little ratings-building controversy, or you got it in for the Baptists?"

Anne unhooked her mike pin, glancing over at the busy volunteers. A cheer went up as they unearthed a tear-stained young woman's wedding album, one of the motherly looking Mormon volunteers handing the keepsake to the new bride with a hug. "Let's just say that what's good for the news could be good for me, too."

"And going to Notre Dame?" Leon persisted, as he took the mike from Anne and finished packing his camera equipment.

"What can I say? Once a Catholic-school student, always afraid of nuns." Anne climbed into the nondescript Channel 8 car. "I'm definitely not afraid of Baptists, even if some of them do think that the Pope is the devil."

"Him and Walt Disney," Leon agreed, driving carefully around the piles of rubble in the street.

"What's that girl's current status?" Monk asked as the local religion reporter signed off, filing the report for replay later in the day. "She's got potential."

Kim keyed up the local reporter's file, sending it to Monk's console. Her head shot, career stats (journalism degree from Notre Dame, local-news experience, feature writing), and current resumé appeared on the producer's console.

"Definitely got potential," he repeated.

"Thank you, Anne," Kathy said, hesitating only slightly over the local reporter's name before she settled into the national-news crawl on the prompter again. "And the Mormon Church has other problems as well, with one of their Twelve Apostles missing and suspected dead in the Philippines. We'll be back later with the update on the earthquake-recovery efforts in that area." She smiled, shifting emotional gears as the set colors and screen graphic behind her changed to the jazzy design of the upcoming World Music Awards logo. "Now, let's go with a lighter note from our entertainment reporter, Garrett de Long, with the latest scoop on the star who's setting off earthquakes of her own in the music world."

"Thanks ever so, Kathy," Garrett gushed as the scene switched to show him at the informal, light-intensive Entertainment Desk.

The crawls along the bottom of the screen changed, too, from running totals of damage estimates and casualty reports interspersed with promos for emergency-preparedness, survivalist, and military-supply Web sites to the latest chart-topping music videos, singles, box-office totals, gossip blurbs, and promos for Web sites devoted to selling all of the above. The center screen split, showing Garrett and his melon-pink couch on one side, a voluptuously writhing female singer on the other. Out of deference to the early hour and open-channel subscription rules, discreet video blurring hid the most vital bits of her anatomy, although a crawl along the bottom of the picture advertised uncensored access for a "nominal" fee and a promise that the viewer was at least 18 years old. Nothing censored the lyrics, though, and her breathy entreaties to a lover (or possibly attacker) sighed and fluttered atop the background beat.

"And earthquakes make a good comparison for the performing style of Virginia Diamante!" Garrett exclaimed. "Or, as she told this reporter . . ." Here, the screen opposite him filled with Virginia's heart-shaped, perfectly made-up face, coils of platinum and ebony hair, and deeply obvious cleavage as she said, "My friends call me Virgin—it's kinda like nicknaming the tallest guy in the room Tiny." She finished with a lascivious lick of her lips and a tinkling giggle. The playback returned to her video, even more blurred now with the introduction of one—or possibly two—more underclothed participants.

"Whew!" Garrett exclaimed, wiping imaginary sweat from his own made-up brow, "Virginia or Virgin—and we're not even guessing—this girl is hot, hot, hot! And so's her latest album, *All for Me*, the week's top seller." He didn't need to add a disclosure statement warning viewers that Channel 8's owner, Universal Media, owned the label sponsoring the album in question—the crawl at the bottom of the screen did that for him. It also posted the Web site and order number for the album, the video, and the lingerie collection Virginia had worn for the clip.

"Rumor has it that the video, available at midnight tonight from all Universal Entertainment locations, features Virginia in outfits that have to be seen to be believed," Garrett continued, waggling his eyebrows as the non-singing Virginia appeared on the monitor again, wearing another example of the outfits Garrett referred to. "Named on the Ten Worst-Dressed Celebrities list?" she cooed. "Baby, that doesn't bother me." Another giggle and a flirt of diaphanous scarf ended the clip.

That earned a replay of Garrett's trademark brow-wiping gesture. "Whew! Keep your fingers off that touchpad, boys and girls!" (He paused to let the audience appreciate the double entendre.) "Rumor also has it that the Diamond didn't just simulate the saucy moves from the video—if you know what I mean."

"I *never* fake it!" Virginia purred from her pretaped position on the back panel.

"I believe it," Garrett informed her, and turned back to the audience. "Check out the uncensored version now," the screen flashed the access numbers and credit-card registration code, "and we'll be back later in this broadcast with more Virginia, live from Singapore!"

* * *

"Oh, shut UP!" Merry ordered, zapping the smarmy entertainment reporter and his gushing report about the latest nanobot-cosmetic trend with a well-aimed blast from her remote stylus.

Garret, exclaiming over "Tattoos that shift under your skin to show your mood—and when you're IN the mood!" along with the obligatory pictures, promos, and statistics on the numbers of people in each state who'd fallen for the new fad, abruptly disappeared.

Merry glanced at Missy, playing happily on her blanket in the book-avalanche disaster area that had been a well-ordered office/library three weeks ago. "Kiddo, if I ever catch you lisping like that—or dancing around on TV in your underwear—I'll revoke your allowance and driving privileges until the end of time," she informed her daughter.

Missy, with an 18-month-old's blissfully self-assured love of attention, looked up, waved her stuffed bumblebee, blew spit bubbles, and laughed.

"Yeah, you laugh, you cute girl!" After a brief break to blow on Missy's tummy and tumble around on the cluttered rug, Merry sighed and went back to work straightening the mess that resulted when the—comparatively mild—aftershocks brought the makeshift shelves down with all their contents. "Three weeks after the quake, and I'm still trying to get stuff back on the shelves. I never realized how much time being a mom takes—or how little I come in here, now that I'm not doing research anymore." She gathered a two-year run of scientific journals from the chair and desk where they'd fallen. "Guess it's a good idea I wasn't in here at the time—these would've brained me when the shelves let go of the walls. Your daddy's a genius geneticist, baby doll, but he's definitely not a carpenter."

She restacked a tall pile of scientific journals, then picked up a plastic disc case, brushing her fingers over the embossed label. *Techniques for Detecting Telomere Degeneration in Multi-generation Germ Cell Development* by Meredith Steinem Anthony. Her dissertation. That had cost two years of painstaking research, excruciating examinations, long nights, endless cups of coffee—and then an equal number of long nights without coffee, after she met a couple of missionaries whose deep conviction of the truth had shone through their teenage awkwardness to illuminate a place in her soul that she hadn't even realized needed light.

"Everything changed that year, Miss-Miss," she said softly, rubbing a finger over the date blazoned on the case. "I got baptized, got this done, and got married." A wry smile pulled at the corner of her mouth. "Sidney—your grandmother—couldn't decide whether to throw me a party for getting my degree or throw a fit for getting married—and to a Mormon, of all things! She doesn't care about religion one way or another—she figured it was a passing fad, like my vegetarian period—but Sidney's got very progressive ideas about marriage. Bit of advice—don't get her started on 'the patriarchy.' Still, compared to me joining a primitive Christian cult and changing my name to my husband's, she'd probably prefer it if I were strutting around on TV in my underwear."

The thought of her deeply womanish mother having to make the choice between the two options made Merry grin. She put her dissertation onto the stack with Chris's. That cover proclaimed its contents to be *Genetic Factors Contributing to Decay in Pancreatic Protein Synthesis* by Christopher Galen—he'd joked that his parents' laziness would save him from any high Church calling, because they hadn't given him a middle initial. "Christopher Galen," she said aloud.

Missy looked up and waved her bee again at the sound of her father's name, shouting, "Dad a dad a dad a dad!" Her actual first word had been "pretty" (said while looking in a mirror, of course), but she'd rapidly made up for it by christening Chris "dad a dad" in as many repetitions as she felt like at the time.

"Yup, that's him," Merry affirmed. "Your Dad. Never to appear on the stand at General Conference, welcoming the world to the Conference Center in lovely Independence, Missouri." The thought reminded her of the more serious part of the newscast, slowly moving away from intensive coverage of the earthquakes to more exciting events than mere rebuilding efforts, and she shuddered slightly. Used to be that a major tragedy would bring the world to a complete halt—Sidney still went on about the events of September 11, 2001—but now the global catastrophes just served as opportunities for ratings stunts and advertising. Kidnappings didn't rate much of a mention, even when they involved the ordained leaders of one of the world's fastest growing and least understood religions.

"I hope Elder Stacy's okay," she told Missy. She remembered him from the last General Conference broadcast—a small, sturdy man with a beautiful deep voice and an even deeper conviction of God's love for all his children, Latter-day Saint or not. He'd been sent to the Philippines to preside at the Pacific Rim General Conference, and had disappeared on his way to the airport after the conference. No one had asked for a ransom.

The baby looked up, a serious line between her little eyebrows. "Okay," she repeated.

Merry nodded. "OK."

The doorbell rang. "Ha!" Merry exclaimed, sweeping up Missy. "We are saved from this drudgery by the ringing of yonder bell!" She sprinted down the hallway and flung open the door. "Carmen! Just in time! I was starting to talk about social politics and worldwide tragedies with an eighteen month old."

Carmen Callatta, Merry's best friend (besides Chris, of course) hiked her own bundle of joy higher on her substantial hip and grinned. Gianni echoed the grin; he was a curly-haired moppet a year older than Missy—their very, very, very last one, Carmen asserted to anyone who'd listen. "Me, too—I needed an excuse to get out of my house and go sit in somebody else's for awhile. Somebody with more to talk about than trucks." On cue, Gianni waved his favorite toy, a brightly colored plastic dumptruck.

"That would be me. We're heavy into bumblebees right now. Come in," Merry invited, stepping back from the door.

"Ah, it's not a formal visit," Carmen assured her. "Just came by to make sure you're all right, with all that shaking going on." She looked around the tidy, if somewhat bare, living room. "But as usual, you're on top of it. My place still looks like a disaster area. Not that it takes an earthquake for that to happen."

"I'm still working on the library," Merry admitted.

"Let's get back there, then," Carmen suggested. "We'll talk about how the world's going to heck in a handbasket while we straighten up your bookshelves."

"Bad as it looks," Merry commented, surveying the avalanche from the fallen shelves, "it could be a lot worse. At least San Diego didn't get hit by a tidal wave!"

"And you don't have anybody sticking a microphone in your face, asking you how you feel about losing everything and a couple of family members, too," Carmen agreed, settling Gianni onto the blanket next to Missy. They regarded each other solemnly for a moment, then went back to playing with their respective toys, Gianni vrooming his car over the blankets and Missy chewing on her bumblebee while making soggy buzzing noises.

"You saw that bit, too, huh?" Merry asked.

"What bit?" Carmen laughed. "They *all* do that. Which bit are you talking about?"

"Some economics reporter in the Philippines asking a little old lady who lost her house how she felt at the moment," Merry told her, shuffling a pile of papers together. (They were Chris's notes on his latest project; he was so enthusiastic about finding a cure for diabetes that he could never leave work at work. Plus, he tended to have inspirations in the shower.) "The lady held her own, though—told the reporter that at least the tidal wave put out the fire."

"Good one," Carmen agreed.

"Yeah, but it's not all funny. Did you hear about what's up in San Francisco? The Baptists are refusing to volunteer because the Mormons got there first!" Merry shook her head disgustedly. "Talk about petty. At least the reporter there didn't seem to agree with them, and the first guy they talked to—some poor elders quorum president—came across well."

"I always like it when our team acts like they know what they're doing," Carmen said. "Where does this beast go?" She hefted a huge looseleaf stuffed with handwritten sheets.

"Oh, those are my notes from my undergrad days. I never really know where to put them, but I can't seem to throw them away." Merry took the binder and gazed at it as if it could tell her what to do with it. "All that ink, all those hours—all that neat handwriting! Graduate school is pure death on penmanship."

"Just like having kids'll kill your figure," Carmen added, "and watching the TV will kill your opinion of the human race. Did you see that report on the idiots looting through earthquake zones? They're threatening to sue the store they were robbing because an aftershock made the roof collapse on them before they could get out!"

Merry shoved her note-filled folder onto the corner of the bottom shelf—they could just stay there for now, helping prop up the other shelves—and rolled her eyes. "I saw the 'entertainment' report, now that the network's tired of running earthquake stories and needs to sell some more product. Some cheap-looking femme displaying her assets to the world. Somehow, pixelating the nudity just makes it worse. And that's the news, for crying out loud! The promos are even worse."

Carmen sighed. "When I was little, I remember a bunch of mothers throwing a fit and making supermarkets put plastic thingies over magazine racks to keep dirty headlines away from childrens' tender eyes. Wonder what they'd think of getting full-frontal on the evening news?"

"They've probably all had strokes and died by now," Merry sighed, too. "I keep looking at that, looking at Missy, and wondering how to explain it to her."

"We've considered dumping our set right in the trash," Carmen told her, beginning to gather a slithery pile of magazines. "But then the kids would just go over to their friends' houses to see it—or downtown, or on the train, or in school, or wherever."

"It's pervasive, all right," Merry agreed. She picked up her wedding pictures from the mounds on the floor, Chris beaming out of the topmost photo, dizzy with happiness and great expectations, Merry smiling shyly at her new mother-in-law behind the camera, wondering what she'd gotten herself into but at the same time feeling more secure than she'd ever felt in her life. They hadn't hired a professional photographer—or a professional anything else, for that matter. It had been a very restrained affair, even by Mormon standards, so a double handful of snapshots commemorated their wedding day, immortalizing Chris's parents, brother, sisters, and grandmothers in photographic freeze-frame along with the happy couple. No one but Merry represented the bride's side of the family.

Sidney hadn't come, and since she had custom-selected Merry's father out of an exclusive list of sperm-bank donors rather than the traditional dating scene, there was no ex-husband to invite. She'd told Merry that her principles simply would not let her condone her daughter's "conforming to an outmoded form of female oppression and throwing away all that education and potential."

She hadn't appreciated Merry's snide rebuttal: "Hmm. So you respect everyone's right to make choices about their lifestyles—unless those choices aren't ones you'd make?"

Chris's mother hadn't said a thing about Sidney's absence, other than a single, "She certainly missed seeing a lovely bride." Grandma Galen seemed to regard Merry as an orphan, and promptly opened her heart and home to her new granddaughter. Merry both deeply appreciated the love and acceptance Chris's family so freely offered and felt overwhelmed when they were near. Though she would never admit it, Benson Bioceuticals' job offer had been a relief, taking her and Chris across the desert to San Diego, within visiting distance of the Galen clan in Provo but not close enough for weekly visits from his mother (whom Merry could not quite call Mom, though she would've liked to). Still, it had been wonderful when she came out for a week after Missy was born, offering moral support, advice about everything from diapers to dusting, and an unfailing sense of humor. Sidney had called from Chicago to remind Merry of the excellent child-care facilities available from Benson Bioceuticals and the state of California, then sent a blue, unisex jumper and a storybook featuring families whose only commonality was the lack of a traditional mother and father. She still hadn't actually met Missy.

Merry sighed silently and shook herself back to the current topic of conversation, putting the small pile of photos back into the shoebox where they lived. She might have betrayed Sidney's ideals by marrying and embracing a primitive, literalist Christianity, but she hadn't succumbed to scrapbooking. "Remember when you could get phone service that just included actually making phone calls, without broadband cable and Web access?"

Carmen had noticed Merry's sad expression as she looked at the wedding photos, but wisely decided to go with the conversation Merry felt more comfortable with at the moment. What some people did to their kids! "Ah, we've got a better deal now. And I figure if I'm there, and Tony's there, watching with the kids, we can jump in with 'is that how *we* do things?' and 'what do you think of that?' comments to keep them on their toes."

"Ah, that old 'involved parenting' thing," Merry said, nodding solemnly. "I've heard of that. Know what they're watching, talk about values, teach 'em critical thinking by example, that stuff."

"Works better than letting the boob tube give 'em role models," Carmen informed her.

"Role models," Merry snorted. "Don't get me started on role models. Sidney called again, telling me all about how I'm failing Missy while sending me about 50 pages of articles on gender-role modeling and the importance of encouraging daughters to act on their aggressive instincts."

"Sounds like she's gathering material for her next set of seminars," Carmen observed.

Merry nodded, stacking paperbacks along the baseboard. They'd have to wait for a permanent home until she and Chris put up the shelves again—with professional instructions this time. "You'd think feminism's been around long enough that people wouldn't need seminars to get the hang of it. Especially with the amount of money they pay, just to hear the same old 'out of the kitchen and into the factory or office or military or whatever' rant—"

A wicked little giggle interrupted Merry's own standard rant about her mother's professional feminism. "Ercake!" Missy shouted, knocking over the stack of magazines Carmen had gathered. The slippery things slithered all over the floor. Gianni laughed and clapped, getting into the act by tossing a couple of books to the floor.

"Hey, hey, let's not contribute to the natural disasters in here!" Carmen swept up both kids. "You want an earthquake? I'll *give* you an earthquake," she growled teasingly, shaking them around in her arms. The kids flailed and laughed, Missy demanding "More ercake!" when Carmen stopped.

Carmen laughed and nosed her, then kissed Gianni's head. "Ah, poor thing. She just doesn't know how great it is in the kitchen."

"Never gave it a shot," Merry agreed, more soberly than she'd meant to. She reached over to pet Missy's flyaway curls. "I must admit, though, sometimes I can see her point." She looked around at the library and laughed. "Taking off for the office right now sounds pretty good, with all this mess! Leave it for the maid, come back to a tidy house, a hot dinner—"

"And a baby who missed you like crazy," Carmen added. She put down the kids and patted Merry's shoulder. "It's tough. That's why I'm here. And you've got Chris."

"Oh, sure, the deserter, off in the lab and far away from this mess and strained peas and conversations without the proper complement of syllables in them," Merry mock-complained. "Expecting a hot dinner when he gets home!" She relented. "Not that he expects it. I really do appreciate how much he pitches in around here. Especially when I'm feeling overwhelmed. And I really appreciate you, too. Carmen, you're just a natural."

"Only my hairdresser knows for sure," Carmen assured her, then shrugged. "Speaking of overwhelmed, it looks like Tony's on the pink list down at SpielTech again. You wouldn't think there'd be so much turnover in the video game biz, but I guess the kids are off on another craze right now. Anyway, as long as he's on half-time, we're going to be tight, especially with Giovanni off on a mission."

"Oh, Carmen, I'm sorry," Merry said, touching Carmen's shoulder. "Can't he go somewhere else? He's a terrific artist."

"Ah, he really likes what he's doing—and when it pays, it pays really well. We've talked it over 'til we're blue in the face, but he really feels like he's where he needs to be. Says he can make sure that at least some of the games are decent. He did get another offer, but neither of us felt really good about that—don't you hate it when fasting and praying gives you the answer you knew but didn't really want? So we're where we're supposed to be for now." Carmen patted Merry briskly. "Hey, don't put on that long face—tall girl like you doesn't need to get any longer. We got the solution: I'm setting up a daycare. Tony'll be there to help out half-time, I've got my primary-education certificate, I'll cut my daughter Donna in for minimum-wage plus experience for the old resumé, and we're set."

"You'll be great at it," Merry reassured her. "Want to practice on Missy?"

Carmen laughed. "Much as I love the Melissa-girl, I get plenty of practice as it is." She handed the kid in question back to Merry as her watch alarm went off. "Oops, time to go pick up Lucrezia. She's got math practice after school these days, of all the crazy things. But you keep an eye out for somebody who needs a good daycare, and tell Chris, too. It won't be cheap, but it'll be full service. Kids guaranteed to know their colors, numbers, and letters by the time they're two!"

"And the Articles of Faith by six?" Merry teased.

"I do what I can," Carmen batted her eyelashes modestly. She hugged Merry, neatly adjusting the kids. Her tone grew serious as she added, "And so do you. It'll all work out in the end," then lightened. "Unless we're late picking up your sister," she informed Gianni. "That'll just ruin her whole day. Big hugs to Chris." The two of them rushed off down the steps, Carmen bouncing more than necessary as she ran to make Gianni laugh. They piled into the car. Carmen could very easily make two a pile, but she could also neatly arrange a half dozen kids in under a minute.

Merry and Missy waved from the doorway, Missy waiting until Gianni wasn't looking to shout, "Bye, bye, Janny!"

"That's Carmen," Merry informed Missy as she closed the door front. "Armed for all occasions with moral support, common sense, extra sippy cups, and an all-terrain minivan."

CHAPTER 3

"Be prepared, *Hasbidi*." Grandfather's voice ran in Dove's memory, the mental tape wowing slightly from being replayed so often. The metallic snap of the shotgun closing over a shell remained clear as Grandfather neatly loaded his gun and drew a bead on the big German Shepherd leading the dog pack harassing their small flock of sheep. "You can't expect the unexpected, so you have to be ready for it when it happens." The gunshot from his memory blended with the one that blew the corner off the crate he crouched behind. The dogs had savaged four lambs, but at least they hadn't shot back.

He slipped around the smashed crates of cocaine, gun at the ready, eyes out for any hostile movement in the powdery fog. The first couple of shots had blown the lights in the huge warehouse—either Benny knocked them out to provide cover for *Abuelo's* team, or the *Brujos* killed the lights to save their own tails, leaving everybody stumbling around in the dim sunset light filtering through the high windows. Either way, it complicated things. So did the thick dust filling the air. Dove held his breath behind the handkerchief over his face, trying not to breathe enough cocaine to affect his judgment—or his aim. A movement through the darkness caught his attention, then one of the *Brujos* sprinted across an open space between the ranks of crates. Dove fired just once, leading his target just as Grandfather had taught; the drug runner fell, disappearing in a cloud of cocaine.

A fusillade of shots followed, as *Abuelo's* gang and the *Brujos* opened fire indiscriminately. None of the *Brujos* have a clear target, Dove thought, holding his gun against his chest, and they're not really aiming. Why waste ammunition, firing without a good chance to make it count? That meant cover fire. What were they covering?

Cesare and Rico, *Abuelo's* lieutenants, had decided on a full-on assault through the front of the warehouse, and they were leading the rest of the strike team spreading through the interior. The *Señor* (the generic term for the borderlands crime bosses) who owned this section of the border didn't welcome competition in any of his rackets—drug running, smuggling, gambling, bribing INS agents, selling fake IDs and passports, and whatever else could turn a profit in the Wild West of Amexica. Rumor, backed up with a lot of swaggering from a formerly minor-league gang, said the *Brujos* had signed on with another outfit coming up from South America. The cocaine filling the warehouse and clogging the *Señor's* supply channels proved the rumors well enough for him to tell *Abuelo* to take care of it. The point wasn't necessarily total annihilation of the opposing forces— just a strong show of force, a bloody warning to the *Brujos* about the danger of stepping into claimed territory. As usual, Rico had assigned Dove and Benny to back-up detail, providing cover fire at the rear instead of heading the charge. Dove listened to the racket, trying to make out directions in the chaos of gunfire as he held his own position. Lots of noise from the front, a bit from one side, but nothing from the back of the warehouse.

The sounds of explosions in the hills came back to Dove over the sharper cracks of bullets. The *Brujos* had some major firepower behind them, and other rumors hinted that their new masters weren't just smuggling temporary euphoria. He tossed a shattered chunk of molded cocaine "pottery" at Perro's arm. The other soldier whirled, his gun coming up until he realized it was Dove, not another attack. Dove waved the barrel off, pointed toward the back of the warehouse, signaled that he was going to go look for something, and slunk around the rows of crates, heading down the quiet side, away from the firefight.

Perro swore under his breath. Dove was off on another one of his nutty hunches. He hesitated momentarily, remembering Rico's orders to stay at the front of the warehouse, then sighed and crawled after Dove. Crazy as they were, Dove's hunches usually paid off.

The noise of the firefight, more sporadic now, receded behind him. Dove hit the perimeter of the big building, ran along the wall keeping low and quiet, then took up cover behind the last row of crates just in time to see two of the *Brujos* run past, heading for the back door. They hit the floor, rolling to take up covering positions, their guns pointed toward the front of the warehouse, as three more huffed up the aisle, carrying a heavy box between them.

The *Brujos* set the box down—very carefully—and popped the lid. Dove saw the glitter of metal and spray of colored wires inside the box. Perro hit the dirty floor beside him, gun at the ready. "What is it?" he whispered.

"Looks like a bomb," Dove answered back.

"Andele!" the blond *Brujos* hissed, smacking the third man on the arm. The gunshots were getting louder as the firefight came closer.

"Vamos time," the third said. He put his fingers to his lips and whistled, loud and long, four times. The two who had covered for them rose and ran for the door, heaving open the service access and disappearing into the night outside.

Immediately, the noise of the firefight intensified near the center of the warehouse. From the sound of it, somebody either had a submachine gun or had turned on the spray mode of an illegal AK or Uzi. Two more *Brujos*, one carrying a bulging bag of cash, ran out of the warehouse.

That's way too many bullets for serious shooting, Dove thought. *They're running, firing behind them as they go. Covering a retreat.*

"They're coming," Dove informed Perro. "Tell Benny they're heading out the back door."

Perro nodded, flicking on his cell phone. Dove dismissed the whispered conversation as he drew bead on the forehead of the kneeling man. He exhaled and squeezed the trigger.

The other two *Brujos* whirled as the bomb expert jerked backward and fell into the crates behind him, red splattering them and the case. One hit the deck, the other shot back from where he stood. Bullets splintered out of the crate in front of Dove, releasing a smell of cordite and bananas. He rose out of concealment suddenly, snapping off a shot that took the standing Brujo in the neck, then threw himself flat again as the last one returned fire and four more burst out of the darkness. One took a single look at the bodies sprawled around the case and sprinted for the exit, leaping the last of his fallen comrades in his haste to get out of there. He didn't make it—one of his gang mates shot him in the back, then snapped an order to the remaining two, turning to lay a line of punctures in the increasingly shattered line of crates shielding Dove and Perro. The leader, a slick-looking, young man with cold eyes, kept up the barrage, advancing slowly. His two companions held their ground, adding their efforts to the annihilation of their attackers' disintegrating cover.

"Madre!" Perro exclaimed.

"Is it lit? Where's Benny? Is it lit?" Dove asked, popping up to catch a glimpse of the case and the *Brujos* surrounding it. Nobody was touching it. He got off a shot that winged one of them, then flattened again, muttering viciously, "Blue-streaking whack-a-mole game."

The last crate exploded in a fountain of splinters. Perro yelled and scuttled for cover farther down the aisle. He yelled again as a bullet hit his shoe. Dove launched himself forward, rolling fast under the Brujo's line of fire, and came up standing almost within arm's reach of them, his gun pointing at the case. Metal and wires glittered in the soft light, a tangle of high-tech jewelry around an ugly cube of putty. The digital timer glowed neutrally, showing all zeros on its face.

Dove grinned whitely at the *Brujos*, who had recovered from their surprise and trained their guns on him. "Think you can hit me before I hit it?" he asked. "Think it likes bullets?"

They hesitated momentarily, the two soldiers glancing at the bomb, then at each other. The leader matched Dove's grin. "It doesn't, it takes you out, too," he observed.

"It does, you do, what's the difference?" Dove shrugged, keeping his grin, internally screaming for Benny.

The leader gave it a second's more consideration, sizing Dove up. He opened his mouth—and one of his soldiers lurched forward to fall over the box, blood spewing from his mouth. The sound of the shot hit at the same moment, as Benny tore out of the maze of boxes, Rico, Cesare, and the rest of the team behind him. The *Brujos'* leader hesitated only a second, then spat a curse and sprinted away, diving outside and slamming the door behind him. Bullets inscribed braille insults on the metal surface of the door and eliminated the last couple of *Brujos* who got the retreat order too late.

Rico ordered a sound-off, then detailed a team to sweep the warehouse as he flicked on his cell phone to report their success to *Abuelo*.

Perro managed a weak grin at Dove, standing hesitantly as blood puddled out of his shoe. He glanced at the caseful of plastique. "Call you *perro, chiquito*—bomb-sniffing dog."

Suddenly, the warehouse seemed very calm.

Benny, noticing it, kicked one of the mush-oozing crates (this one was marked "Bananas"—truthfully, as it happened) and grinned. "*Hasbìdì*, we gotta get you one of them olive leafs. Things always get real peaceful when you're around."

"Branches, Benny. Olive branches," Dove growled, but he couldn't help grinning as Benny ruffled his hair, releasing several puffs of expensive dust.

"Kid, you need a shower—or a hundred-dollar bill!" Benny turned suddenly and smacked an unopened cellophane of drugs out of Perro's hands. "And you need a brain transplant as well as a new sneaker if you go messing with that. Let's get out of here."

Dove agreed, catching Perro's arm and helping him limp toward the exit. Rico and Cesare counted them off again, checking their soldiers for booty—though Dove noted that they didn't pat each other down, and that Rico's pockets looked a lot heavier than spent clips could account for. They piled into the two vans, as sirens began to sound in the far-off center of town. The *Señor's* bribes ensured that the local law enforcement would arrive in time to catalog the damage, but not quickly enough to catch the perpetrators.

Benny was the last one to reappear, silhouetted against the rising flames as the warehouse went up in a toxic smoke signal to the *Brujos'* backers. That would show them, trying to use the *Brujos* to move into the territory *Abuelo* controlled for the *Señor*. If that's what they were doing. The weight dragging on his arm made him wonder exactly what the *Brujos'* backers had in mind. He brushed off the slight worry, though, as he jumped into the waiting van. They won, they got out, and that's all that mattered. Why try to read the *Brujos'* coke-soaked minds?

He grinned at Dove and heaved the too-familiar metal case into the van as he swung in and slammed the door. "Think I'd forget and leave this in when we torched the place?"

* * *

The case made a disturbing centerpiece for the victory party, until *Abuelo* appeared and told Benny to "Take that witches' box out of here." The absence of the bomb didn't hurt Benny's spirited recounting of the battle—or the admiring gleam in Dolores's eyes, as she cataloged the worshipful glances of the other women in the room. Dove grinned at that, raising his glass of *horchata* (on Benny's orders) with the others every time Benny said "shot," but as the sun rose, the darkness of the warehouse threw a shadow over his party mood. He left shortly after dawn, checked on Perro ("Hey, who else loses a little toe in a battle? Lots of pretty pity for the Dog"), and went home to hit the shower

He stood in the steaming flow, turned hot as his skin could stand it, and resolutely did not throw up. He closed his eyes against the memory of the bomb tech's face, glad the man's eyes had been hidden beneath the brim of his cap. *The Brujos are animals*, he reminded himself, over and over again. *Less than animals, who do nothing to deserve to die. Evil is evil, and good is—Benny*. And Grandpa, before he died and they had to leave the sheep camp (because even on the Navajo Reservation there hadn't been any family members to take them in). *And doing a job with honor*. He brushed aside the voice inside his heart that asked whether anyone could do a dishonorable job with honor. *We don't run drugs*, he told the voice for the millionth time; *we work for Abuelo. Abuelo* worked for the *Señor*, and if the *Señor* ran drugs and guns across the border, he also kept the peace, making it possible for the mamas and papas and babies to live day to day without ending up prey for bandits and corrupt *federales* on both sides of the border. The high, clear view from the sheep camp came vividly into his head, no corruption, no violence, no drugs—and no people, no one to help when he and Benny had come home to find Grandfather slumped in the rutted driveway.

Dove pushed away the last image of his grandfather, dead where he'd fallen as he stumbled out of the house. He'd left the house to avoid leaving his ghost there, but he'd left a Navajo-shaped hole in Dove's soul, which he tried to fill with reading and studying other cultures, other ideas of honor. Benny tried to fill it by making him go to school and be a good boy, pushing Dove to be better than the border trash thug he always said he himself was. And then he'd grin.

Benny was grinning as he opened the shower curtain and he caught Dove's hand. He was drunk, as he usually was after a fight, but it hadn't slowed his reflexes much yet. "Good thing you don't carry a blade in the shower," he noted, then his voice softened. "It's okay, *Hasbìdì*. You did good today. You okay?"

"Okay, Benny," Dove agreed, willing it to be true.

* * *

"Okay, okay! Whoa! Stay, stay, stay," Merry ordered frantically, catching the wobbly end of a shelf and trying to hold it up with one hand while balancing Missy on her hip with the other arm. She was finally down to the last bit of cleaning up the earthquake mess in the office, trying to set the shelves back up, reinforced this time. Everything had gone fine until she'd figured that she could shore up the still-standing shelf by slipping another bracket in underneath it. It looked simple—she'd just boost the shelf up a tiny bit, then slide the brace in. The fact that she had to hold Missy during the operation didn't really occur to her until she'd already started. Then she realized that she actually needed three hands. The bracket tumbled to the floor, as did a couple of the books on the shelf.

"Good evening, Merry, Miss!" a voice called cheerfully from the hall. "Where are my favorite girls in the whole world?"

"Chris! In here!" Merry shouted. "Help!"

"Ercake!" Missy added at the top of her lungs. "Elp! Elp!"

Chris bounded into the room, catching the shelf as Merry finally lost her grip on it. A couple more books thumped to the floor, but the rest stayed put as he lifted the unsecured end of the long board. Merry retrieved the bracket from the floor, swooping Missy down to pick it up. She ducked the bracket as Missy enthusiastically swung it in a wide arc and gently removed it from her daughter's grip.

"Okay," Merry said, much less frantically this time. "Lift it up just a touch more, and I'll click this into place." She moved in close, snuggling under his upraised arm, then paused, looking up into his eyes. "On the other hand, maybe I like you stuck right there where you can't get away," she said, following up that observation with a kiss.

Chris returned it, then laughed as Missy nosed her little head in for a share of the action. He gave her a big kiss on the cheek and grinned at Merry. "Why would I want to get away? 'There's nowhere I'd rather be,'" he sang, then winced. "Except maybe in a position with my arms around you rather than up at shoulder height."

"Wimp," Merry laughed, but quickly slid the bracket into place.

Chris let the shelf go, testing its reinforced stability with a gentle shake. "Not bad, not a bad idea at all. Trying to do it yourself one handed, on the other hand—"

"All right, point conceded. The only excuse I have is that it sounded like a good idea at the time," Merry informed him, then grinned. "And you, lucky man, don't even have to listen to my prepared spiel about brilliant minds that can't follow simple directions about putting the screws for the bookshelves into the studs, not just through the wallboard."

"Oops," Chris said. He surveyed the much neater room, looking at the holes where the screws had pulled through the walls during the quake. "Guess this really shows that my theory about being able to tell where the studs were by the sound differences of knocking on the walls isn't applicable to real-life situations." He grinned, a bit abashed. "That's what you get for marrying a geneticist instead of a handyman. Still, it looks a lot better in here—which is what I get for marrying a geneticist."

"Yeah, learning how to clean up after an experiment in the lab really helps with the occasional household disaster," Merry said, surprising herself with the edge in her tone. She smiled to soften it.

Missy launched herself with a squeal of "Dad-a-dad!" through the short expanse of thin air between her parents. Chris caught her with practiced ease, swinging her up to sit on his shoulders. He tickled his daughter's feet and smiled at his wife. "I got this on the way home." He rummaged in his jacket pocket and held up a flashlight-sized electronic device.

"Ooh, neat," Merry said. "An electronic device!"

"A stud finder," Chris informed her, waggling his eyebrows.

"Don't even start," Merry warned him, then grinned. "I don't need one of these to find that kind of stud." She kissed him, then examined the box. "Looks like it does work on your sound-differential theory—it's just got better calibrated ears." Running the box over the wall quickly elicited a beep, indicating the presence of solid wood behind the paint and compressed chalk. "Though your ears aren't too far off—look, you missed this one by just two inches."

Chris laughed. "Diplomatic of you." He swung Missy down into his arms and squeezed her gently. "I promise to do a much better job this time—no estimations, just hard data. I even bought anchor screws, which the guy at the hardware store said would do the trick. And I'll have plenty of time to put the shelves up, too, since MedaGen just bought out Benson Bioceuticals."

"MedaGen?" Merry repeated, then exclaimed, "Oh, no, not them! They're the ones who started off as the makers of those super chickens, aren't they? Now they're heavy into human stem-cell research—and they have those really obnoxiously sappy promos all over the TV and Web. You can't work for them—can you?"

"I don't know—in fact, at this point, I don't even know if I'm still on the employed list. They're doing a 'consolidation' to eliminate redundant positions now. I'll find out at the end of the week if they're still going to honor my contract," Chris explained, then sighed. "None of us have access to the lab or the network until they figure it out. Just when Protocol 4 was looking promising, too."

Merry rubbed his shoulder, taking a deep breath to smooth the panicked jag that fluttered through her stomach. Not now, not when they had a baby, a pediatrician, a house payment! The earthquake had rocked her physical house—was this going to be a disaster for her financial house as well? For the second time (the first being Missy's birth), she realized how dependent she was on Chris—financially, physically, emotionally. Obeying the prophet's guidance in leaving her own career to be a full-time mother had been harder than she'd anticipated. Sidney had objected, of course—vociferously and repeatedly—and her colleagues had looked at her like she'd completely lost her mind, but Merry prided herself on making her own path, whatever anyone else thought. The idea of giving up two incomes to depend on a single paycheck was a lot harder for her to feel comfortable about. Especially in today's job market.

MedaGen prided itself on its "progressive" policies, which meant the company, like so many others, didn't have employees in the traditional sense of the word anymore. Instead, they had "contractors," individually bargaining with people who had the skills and talents they needed. SpeilTech did the same thing, and as Carmen had told her, the policy made every job into seasonal employment—the season depending not on weather but on market conditions. According to the analysts, this let people use market forces to find the perfect situation, unencumbered by long-term employment agreements or non-competition clauses. They touted the benefits of competition driving up pay scales for valuable workers and weeding out the deadwood that had choked corporate rolls for so long. In Merry's opinion, it was all a fancy way of getting around the laws and (increasingly outmoded) traditions that demanded employers take care of their people, a loophole companies used so they didn't have to pay benefits or regular raises or severance packages to anyone but their most permanent personnel.

Chris squeezed Merry, held her close, wordlessly acknowledging what she was thinking, but (like her) unwilling to say the worst aloud. Missy laid her head on his other shoulder, not understanding why her parents were concerned, but very aware that her daddy was sadder than he'd sounded. Her sweet empathy and innocence of troublesome economic realities shook her parents out of their mournful reverie.

Merry squeezed Chris and rubbed Missy's back. "If Protocol 4 is promising, a couple of days in cold storage won't hurt it," she reassured them all. "And if storage does hurt it, it wasn't actually all that promising. You, on the other hand, are definitely the most promising young geneticist in the field. In fact, I wouldn't be surprised if MedaGen bought Benson just to get their claws on your contract!"

"I think it was the chance to get closer to the fabulous Meredith Galen," Chris informed her. "They're probably counting on me to recruit you to their cause when you complete your current, groundbreaking, devastatingly cute project." He kissed Missy on the head, then did the same to Merry.

"That's the stuff," Merry approved. "And when they get back with their terrific offer, we'll consider whether we want to be associated with a high-rolling, multinational biotech outfit like them. We'll probably have to dodge dump trucks of money, fleets of corporate cars, and other blandishments."

"At least we have a choice," Chris said lightly. "Poor Errol—Humphrey, you remember him, the lab manager? He's been sold right over to the new masters, along with the office furniture and land-scaping service."

"Hate to say it," Merry informed Chris, "but he deserves it. Gambling on floating loans backed up by home equity is bad enough. Gambling on floating loans based on a share of your personal net worth is just stupid. Especially when you get too greedy for cash and don't remember to retain enough shares to keep a controlling interest on the board! Mr. Humphrey put himself on the stock market, couldn't supply the rate of return he'd promised, and now they own his contract permanently. He's just lucky that they can't sell him for parts."

"Being a biotech company and all," Chris finished for her, raising his eyebrow. "There's an idea. Nah, they'll just cut his salary and reduce his grade to junior supervisor. He'll complain about it, but at least it's job security."

"That kind of job security we can do without," Merry said firmly. "I owe my soul to you, Missy, and God—and MedaGen can butt right out. In fact, in honor of our status as free citizens of this corporate paradise, I suggest that we go out for a big bucket of free-range chicken with all the fixings."

"Chicken!" Missy exclaimed happily—and very clearly. Chicken was one of her favorite foods, and thus one of her favorite words. Why she liked the word "trapezoid" so much wasn't as clear.

Chris laughed. "Excellent—we'll celebrate possible stormy straits ahead in the financial seas by spending some of our hard-earned nest egg on a luxurious chicken dinner." He nosed Missy. "And when we're done, we'll come right back here to update my vita on the Web. The early bird catches the worm, and this worm's going to make sure there are plenty of birds lined up."

* * *

Dear Chisom,

    We have enjoyed receiving your Vids via computer link. We enjoyed especially your pictures of those beautiful birds eating in the park. I wish the Vids could hold more than three minutes of 3-D material. Even so, they are wonderful. I enjoy the first hand look you give us of how things are going in Taiwan. I appreciate your diligence in sending these to us weekly, especially in these last weeks after the earthquake. Your dear Mother worries every time she anticipates a letter and one does not come. Transmissions are still a bit unreliable.

    We wish the world would be able to recover faster from the quake, but we understand it will be months if not a whole year before conditions are near normal again. I am glad to hear that the situation is stable in Taiwan. China, the Philippines, and the west coast have really taken a pounding. According to reports, there are places, especially in China, where civil strife is mounting. I hate to see the bloodshed. Losing so many people in the earthquake was bad enough, but to think the survivors are turning on each other is horrible. China is not the only place there is civil unrest. Internal strife is looming in many lands. I fear the destabilization of weak govern-ments triggered in part by the earthquake will bring the planet even more war than she already has. Wars and rumors of wars dominate the news.

    I note that, because of the amount of debris in the air, some fear the weather patterns are shifting and the food-growing areas may not get the water they need for their crops. Certainly, we have seen some unusual and even harsh weather in some areas. Tornadoes have been ripping up the Plains States as never before and the East Coast is bracing for a hurricane of real power.

    I must admit, seeing the dimmed sun day after day and particularly the moon rise blood red does get to me.

Still, let me assure you, it is all part of the Lord's plan. He warned us clearly in Doctrine and Covenants 87 that "with the sword and by bloodshed the inhabitants of the earth shall mourn; and with famine, and plague, and earthquake, and the thunder of heaven, and the fierce and vivid lightning also, shall the inhabitants of the earth be made to feel the wrath, and indignation, and chastening hand of an Almighty God, until the consumption decreed hath made a full end of all nations." We are now in the midst of that prophecy.

I am glad most of the Saints have stored food and funds, for I fear that soon the time is coming when we will need them. Even so, I know that God is at the helm. He has given us clear warning that such would be the case and promised, "if ye are prepared ye shall not fear" (D&C 38:30).

I close this letter with interesting but what you may consider sad news. You will not be returning home to Salt Lake. What do you think of that? The Brethren have asked me to leave the Church Education System and move to Church Headquarters in Jackson County, Missouri. I have been asked to take George Richards' place as director of the Church's public-relations department. I guess the Lord decided since he gave me the gift of languages (which you seem to have inherited in doubles), He was going to put me to work. I have enjoyed the gift and thought that being able to help get seminaries going in a number of countries and then translating and disseminating educational materials may have been the reason the Lord so blessed me. Now I wonder if helping the Church at headquarters might be it. Maybe it's all of these.

Since the Brethren want me to start working as soon as I can, your mother and I will be flying to Missouri next week to start looking for housing. I'm sure she will keep you posted on what we find.

In the meantime, keep sending us your Vids and we will do the same. We're very interested in what is

*happening in your life, with the Church, and in the Far
East.*
> *Much Love,*
> *Your father*
> *Chinedu*

* * *

"That's it, Doctor." A weary lab assistant held out a thick folder.
She couldn't bring herself to look through it again. "The file on the
last subject in the control group. The electronic copies are in the
project folder."

"Let's see." Dr. Twilley took the file, flipping through it.
Everything in order, a complete record of the subject's reaction to the
experimental treatment, laid out in cool tables and graphs. "A bit
premature, isn't it? We don't have exact time of death yet." He nodded
toward the one-way window.

Beyond the glass, in a sealed room, a man lay bonelessly on a thin
cot. Almost literally boneless in some places, Twilley thought.
Fascinating, how the immune system in different subjects reacted in
different ways to the same immune-system acceleration. This one had
developed a raging case of joint degenerative arthritis, as well as total
liver failure and the lung-tissue breakdown that was killing him as the
research team watched. As if reading the doctor's thoughts, the
monitor above the subject's bed flickered, the heart-rate line spiking
erratically.

"Looks like this might be it," another lab assistant observed.
"Finally," he added. The guy had hung on for a week longer than
anybody thought he would; they'd even had to scrap the original set of
dates for the lab pool, since nobody had chosen a day beyond that week.

A long, plaintive tone replaced the staccato beeping. The heart
line flattened completely, running in a straight green stream. One by
one, the other monitors did the same, until finally even the delta
waves on the EEG machine disappeared into a simple line.

"And that's it for Xavier Chaudry," Twilley announced. "Time of
death, 10:24 A.M. Note that in the file."

"And then knock off for some shut-eye?" the second lab assistant
asked, hopefully.

"And then clean up the lab," Twilley said sharply. "Dispose of the body. Don't bother with a death certificate; with so many casualties from the earthquake and victims still unaccounted for, people will just assume he's gone missing. I'll report the final findings to Dr. Christoff at Headquarters." He paused at the door. "Oh—dump the unused stem cells, too, and the strains that didn't work. We've found our solution."

"We'd better get a big bonus out of this, too," muttered the second assistant, as their boss disappeared. "Since you can bet we won't get credit on the patent. The big bosses take all the real plums for themselves. Man, when I get my own lab, you can bet I'm grabbing every success that comes down the pike, no matter what." He rambled on, through the evening, until the last microscopic evidence of Xavier Chaudry's existence was cleared from the cage-like cell.

She nodded occasionally, saying nothing at all. She knew it was irrational, but she didn't think she'd sleep much tonight, no matter how tired she was. When she did, she woke again, her dreams haunted by the image of bodies, full grown and never born, both tossed out like garbage, burning in an incinerator that gaped like the maw of Moloch in the old, mythological stories her grandmother had told her.

*   *   *

"Of course. Last month, tsunamis blast out of the Pacific, so he simply must defy the elements by visiting the beach." Ms. Zelik, Chief Operations Officer for the multinational pharmaceutical firm MedaGen, stepped out of her sleek, silver car into the hot Southern California sunshine.

She stepped out of her shoes (no use ruining them in the damp sand) and strode across the wooden deck to where Abbott lay. The new CEO of MedaGen had taken the weekend at the corporate-owned beach house, where he lay beside the waves, sunning himself in the company of this week's over-bosomed bimbo.

Abbott blinked, raising his sunglasses as Zelik's shadow fell across him. He gazed up at the COO, then smiled. "My word, you do exist outside a conference room!"

"Surprise," she said dryly. Dry fit her, cool and sweatless even under the noon sun, making her perfectly tailored suit work for her instead of against her, in contrast with his stupid little Speedo. "It's this sort of thing that made me wonder if you existed in one. Before I became acquainted with your work ethic, of course."

"And then the doubt was confirmed?" Abbott sat up, swinging his legs over the edge of the beach chair, still smiling. Cami—or Leslie? He couldn't remember offhand—instantly leaned over (way over) to rub suntan lotion onto his back.

The two regarded each other narrowly behind the casual banter, still circling warily. It hadn't been long—just eight months—since Abbott accepted the position of CEO at MedaGen and Zelik promptly tried to destroy him. She'd succeeded with two previous CEOs, dynamiting their corporate careers when they threatened her tidy internal empire, but Abbott had proved more slick and better connected than she'd thought. The two top corporate predators had reached an uneasy *détente,* both coming to the conclusion that for the moment it was easier to collaborate on exterminating lesser predators in MedaGen's power structure than waste their energy fighting each other. The truce meant that they exchanged information, respect, and a certain level of confidence. It didn't mean they had to like it.

"We have confidential matters to discuss." Zelik cut the chatter with her usual abruptness.

Abbott's smile didn't twitch, even as his eyebrows did. "Babycakes, could you leave us alone for a minute? Go in, chill down for later." The bimbo giggled and jiggled her way to the beach house.

"You didn't need to do that," Zelik commented, her tone a crystal of frozen acid as she settled fastidiously into the chair the bimbo had vacated. "She couldn't understand anything we said, anyway, let alone pass it along to someone who could."

"Why don't you like women?" Abbot asked. He didn't bother to defend Leslie—or Cami?

"Why do you like stupid women?" she asked, with a smile of her own. "Because they're nonthreatening?"

"Do you like smart men?" he pursued, giving her a calculating look.

"I don't know," she said. "I'll tell you when I meet one."

Abbott laughed appreciatively. "Maybe you have. I've been able to counter your ploys pretty effectively. Even that maneuver with Tang Chen. What does that say for my intelligence—or yours?" Recognizing that he'd scored a palpable hit, he brushed off the question before she could answer. "So, what's this confidential matter we absolutely need to discuss?"

"The human trials are over." She handed him the data, an innocuous disc. "We got the report from Twilley this morning. The Corinth protocol is working perfectly, destroying a broad range of existing diseases and preventing new ones."

"Side effects?" he asked, turning the disc over in his hands.

She didn't shrug, didn't show any sign of the smug satisfaction under her emotionless expression. "Just one, but it's major—and it's the one we planned for. If a subject who's been vaccinated doesn't get another dose of a slightly modified version of the protocol, he dies of massive immune-system overload. Usually within three weeks of the onset of initial symptoms."

He whistled softly, keeping the flicker of greedy excitement out of his own face as he waited for the other conversational shoe to drop.

"But that's not bad," she noted, after a moment's pause to see whether he'd lose his cool enough to ask. He didn't. She reluctantly gave him a self-control point. "The booster's also a complete success. One hundred percent fatality rate without it, one hundred percent survival rate with it."

"Yes!" He sat up straight, grinning broadly. Their feasibility consultants hadn't been confident when Abbott had proposed a two-stage "solution" to ensure the vaccine's total success, but it looked like the research team had pulled it off after all. "Perfect. Jackpot! Talk about building customer loyalty. Forget branding—we've got literally lifelong consumers."

She almost smiled at that, but the expression never made it past her sunglasses. "We have just one potential problem: Dr. Christoff, the head of the project, seems to be getting cold feet."

Abbot's eyes narrowed, giving his conventionally handsome face a sharpness that he never showed for company photos. "So up his pay—and remind the good doctor that we can not only raise his pay, we can liquidate . . . his pay." The slight pause hovered over the words.

"I've already got the paperwork in process." Zelik rose, reflexively brushing at the imaginary sand particles clinging to her from the chair.

"Have you also got the paperwork for MedaGen's final acquisition of Benson Bioceuticals in process?" Abbott watched her. Such a pity—she had a great body.

"I do," she said flatly, ignoring his lingering look.

"Now's not the time for a security leak," he reminded her. "The last thing we want is for BritPharm to find out about the Corinth protocol—or our other projects."

"That's not going to be a problem." She adjusted her sunglasses, a hint of smugness filtering through the surface ice. "The new management at Benson is re-interviewing all employees with complete background checks and upgrading security as well. We're bringing in Wilson's best teams, from Corp Headquarters."

"And all that hardware you love?" Abbott asked.

She ignored the suggestion in his comment. "Yes. Cameras, retinal scanners, tight network firewalls—and a new security staff. Nothing will happen in that building without me knowing about it. Absolutely nothing."

"That's good," Abbott conceded.

"It is." She gazed down at him from what seemed to be Olympian heights. "Your office is coming along nicely, too. See you Monday."

He watched her glide over the sand and back to her car, taking her warning. "Note to me," he said into his personal digital device, "Have the new office swept for bugs first thing. Wouldn't want anybody sneaking a peek into my office in the middle of the night."

* * *

"This reminds me of the last months of graduate school," Merry told Chris. "Slaving over our resumés in the middle of the night; half thrilled to finally finish with school, half terrified of the future."

Chris leaned away from the screen to nuzzle her ear. "And thinking that for a medical geek, you sure look hot in computer light."

"Just for a medical geek?" she asked, raising an eyebrow. Well, trying to; Chris could raise just one. Merry always ended up raising two, but you could tell she put in extra effort.

He grinned. "Well, there was that one liberal arts major . . ."

"I'm going to give you a chance to make up for that statement— later. What've we got so far?"

She punched his shoulder and matched the grin with one of her own.

"Education, work history, goal statement, research list, bibliography," Chris read out, scrolling through the pages. "All that's left is personal interests, and that's easy enough." He typed quickly, saying the words aloud as they appeared on screen. "Cooking, rock climbing, cute brunettes wearing fuzzy red sweaters with degrees in cellular genetics."

"You can't post that!" Merry protested as Chris hit the "Submit" button.

"Just did," he informed her smugly, pulling her over to him. "Why not? It's all true."

"Because it's a misplaced modifier," she informed him, plopping down on his lap and snuggling in. "Makes it sound like the sweater's got a degree in genetics."

"It's a very talented sweater," he whispered.

The blue glow from the screen lit the remains of their fast-food chicken feast, the white containers glowing pale aqua, their red stripes darkened into ominous black. The shadows from the ever-changing promos running across the screen turned the empty shelf brackets into abstract art on the walls.

The Web site where Chris and Merry posted their personal digital information had promos, as all Web sites did. However, because they bought their online access from a Web company closely associated with The Church of Jesus Christ of Latter-day Saints, the ever-changing display at the top and sides of the screen didn't include the usual run of ads for liquor, pornography, electronic casinos, cosmetic surgery, online contests, get-rich-quick schemes, personal escorts, surveillance cameras, and semi-legal pharmaceuticals. Instead, the brightly colored banners and pictures spread pro-family messages, inspirational quotes, online cards with gospel messages, and other Church-related items—along with the inevitable ads for preparedness supplies, online library services, cooking sites, and craft stores.

When the Mormon-oriented (but not officially Church-owned or promoted) services first came online, many analysts, commentators, and business people (inside and outside of the Church) made dire predictions about the future for Mormon-owned and operated Web service providers. They'd warned that creating "Happy Valley" Web communities would result in the formation of "electronic ghettos," isolating members of the Church from the real, lively life of the Internet. As time went on, however, the providers' philosophy of "be in the world but not of the world" actually paid off. People outside the Church, looking for freedom from the ever-deepening tide of dreck swamping the Web in a tidal wave of splash and pop-up ads, turned to the Mormon-hosted services in record numbers.

In a completely practical sense, the Mormon resumé sites had proved a huge hit as well. Far from cutting job possibilities for their participants, the Latter-day Saint employment boards boasted a much higher than average rate of placements for their members. (Chris's brunette-mentioning resumé joined many thousands of others in just such a worldwide employment bazaar.) Employers surfed the Mormon sites for workers they knew they could depend on for integrity, work ethic, linguistic skills, and a staggeringly high average level of education. "Tough job? Get Mo!" was the tongue-in-cheek but effective slogan of one heavily LDS job board. On the downside, some companies hired Mormons strictly on a contractual basis, wanting to tap into their well-known work ethic but officially disapproving of the Church's "intolerant" stands on political and social issues (abortion, domestic-partner benefits, gay adoptions, etc.). Despite the explosive growth of the Church and the ever-increasing media coverage its policies received—or perhaps because of them—a certain social stigma was still attached to being publicly known as a Mormon. For many of the members of the Church, however, being "out" as a Mormon had become a personal statement, a challenge to detractors and a declaration of independence from the social expectations of Babylon.

At least that's what Chris told Merry when he set up their joint virtual identity on MoWeb—primarily to post their resumés, but also to register for wedding presents. (Sidney had completely disapproved of that, too, though not quite as much as she disapproved of the wedding itself.) Merry nodded solemnly and called him "Comrade Brother" for a week. Primarily, though, she appreciated the service for its content filters (the service automatically hid any blatantly violent, pornographic, blasphemous, or racist content) on both Web sites and the ubiquitous ads.

The Net news scrolls that decorated the bottom of their personal home page were dedicated to Church-related info, too. When Chris flicked off the screen the latest news off the Bonneville Communications wire happily announced the recent dedication of the 1,000th temple in Kuala Lampur. The Church had hit 25 million members, and had earned the official title of the fastest-growing denomination—a distinction indeed in a world where conventional wisdom held that organized religion was in decline, or at the very least barely relevant to modern concerns.

* * *

Of course, just because one set of pundits declared religion dead didn't mean that others weren't willing to haul out the ol' corpse to see if there was still life in it—especially if it was a Sunday morning or afternoon and there wasn't much else to boost ratings. At least Channel 8 was willing to give it a try.

"Welcome to *Sunday Morning*, the program that investigates the news you care about," the announcer's confident introduction boomed over the title graphics and theme music. The music tried for upbeat but serious at the same time; it wound up somewhere between game show and soap opera. "And here's your host, Darren McInnes, star of *Newsroom* and Oscar-winning actor."

Darren turned to the camera, putting his leading-man, bland handsomeness and professionally perfect gravitas to good use. "Good morning, and welcome to *Sunday Morning*. Today, we look at a topic that has become more important after this month's devastating natural disasters: faith. Some see the earthquakes that devastated the western United States, central China, and the Philippine islands as just another incident in a long string of disasters, just another evidence of God's absence or nonexistence. Others see a divine hand shaking the earth—either to punish evildoers or give believers a sign that the end is near. What's the real story? Can faith make a comeback in an increasingly secular world? We'll dive into the debate today—and give you the answers you're looking for."

Images filled the screen, a visual documentary of the devastation the earthquakes wreaked: collapsed buildings, upturned trees, broken and disconnected roads, collapsed dikes. "The earthquakes wreaked unthinkable damage, destroying property, interrupting services, tearing away the thin fabric of security in the victims' everyday lives." The scenery shots gave way to more personal ones: families digging through the rubble of their homes, desperate rescue efforts to save buried victims, shell-shocked survivors, sobbing children clutching ragged toys. "And the earthquakes are only the most recent disasters. The famines sweeping through Asia, the horrible epidemics wreaking havoc in Africa, the violent revolutions convulsing South and Central America, all spread chaos and pain in their wake." Pictures illustrated each point, traversing the globe in a litany of attractively photographed tragedy. "When that fabric disappears, where can we turn for comfort, for security? Everyone, it seems, has a different answer."

A montage of expertly edited snippets followed—snippets of crying worshippers, preaching clergymen, and awe-inspiring religious architecture.

"And earthquakes, and mists of darkness, and pillars of smoke and fire will chasten the unbelievers, the blasphemers, the revilers of all that is holy!" Rafael Sanbourne, a Southern reverend to the tips of his polished shoes, declaimed to a swaying, Hallelujah-shouting congregation. His rhythmic accent wrapped the semiscriptural words in homegrown poetry.

"Allah calls for repentance among his people," one Muslim cleric, a well-known moderate, entreated in subtitles.

"Allah calls for jihad against the unbelievers and the Great Satan!" another thundered from his headquarters bunker in a secure and secret location.

"Mother Earth cries out to us, her children, to understand her pain, to heal her hurts, to be one with her once more," an earnest, flower-bedecked woman billed as Mona Moonflower assured her sandaled listeners as she lit a stick of incense. "If we will but meditate on our responsibility to all of her children."

"Brother Light will lead us from the snares of the wicked," another flower-bedecked woman swooned, as the object of her devotion, a short, dark man surrounded by ardent devotees, slipped past the cameras lurking for him in the debris-strewn streets of Manila. The scene switched to an obviously amateur video of a candlelit service, the soft beat of drums and wailing of pipes underscoring but not overwhelming the low, rich voice of the speaker. The crawl under the screen identified him as Rashi Janjalani, now known as Brother Light.

"God's love is unconditional," Tommy Gibbs boomed to a sellout audience at the latest Universal Church of Christ revival/crusade. "No matter what happens in your life, if you have the faith to say, 'I'll give this to you, Jesus,' He'll take it. No matter what burden, what pain, whatever is happening in your life. Give it to Jesus! These earthquakes are just another demonstration of God's almighty power, another demonstration that Jesus is the only way we can make it. They're the opening of the seventh seal, the time when God moves to cleanse the world of its wickedness. The disasters around the world stand as a warning to Christ's people that His time is nigh at hand. We, His children, faithful followers, must get our houses in order. And how do we do that? By loving Jesus and accepting him as our personal Savior."

"The key to understanding this life is to remember that individual existence comes from desire, and desire causes suffering," a saffron-robed, Buddhist monk intoned. "Acceptance, patience, and faith in the compassion of Maitreya Buddha will salve the emotional wounds of living in violent, traumatic times as we relinquish all desire."

"Our hearts go out to all who have lost homes, livelihoods, and loved ones in the recent disasters. Our hearts go out to you, and we beg you, 'Do not lose hope.' We have the Savior's promise, repeated multiple times in all dispensations: 'If ye are prepared, ye shall not fear.' We know that Heavenly Father loves His children, and that He knows what is best for us," President Smith softly but confidently reassured the international audience for General Conference, broadcast for the first time from the new Conference Center in Independence, Missouri.

The scene returned to Darren, smiling archly in the *Sunday Morning* set. "Others don't see things through the same faithful lenses. Skeptics, agnostics, and atheists all have their own opinions."

Again a montage filled the screen. "Earthquakes are earthquakes," Andre Becker asserted confidently. "I wouldn't presume to tread on holy territory, but I know what causes earthquakes and what they do. Molten rock and superheated gasses from the earth's core make their way up through the crust along faults in the tectonic plates. The increased pressure pushes on the rock around the fault lines, the plates slide past each other, and we get a whole lotta shakin' going on."

"How can anyone believe in a benevolent God with all the horrible suffering going on in the world?" a young woman exclaimed, waving her handmade "Christians Go to Hades, Not to Seattle" poster as a protest against the United Baptist Convention's annual meeting (held in Seattle that year).

"Humans have abused and polluted the environment with carbon dioxide, sulfur compounds, biotoxins, antibiotics, overgrazing, deforestation, strip mining, and a host of other selfish, short-sighted practices," Cosheen Hall ("noted environmental expert and activist," according to the subtitle) said tightly. "And now we're suffering the consequences. It's very typical of human nature to want to place the blame—and the responsibility—on the shoulders of some fictional deity."

"I don't have the data to comment definitively on divine interventions," James Hideyoshi informed the camera carefully, "I'm here as a climatologist. I personally believe that God is well aware of what's going on and will act where He wants to. But even if the volcanic explosion happening at the same time as the earthquakes is simply coincidence, it's a good time to think about life and death and how much good you're doing in the world."

"A valid point, if not a particularly scientific one," Darren observed, as the camera showed him again. This time, it pulled back to reveal a panel of experts sitting around the crescent-shaped table in front of him. "Obviously, there's plenty to say on both sides. Here at *Sunday Morning*, we've assembled a panel of religious experts to get to the bottom of the debate."

He introduced the spokespeople for the debate: Hindu, Buddhist, Muslim, Hasidic Jew, and Wiccan, along with the token Christian and atheist. They were a group of individuals representing the widest demographic possible, each carefully selected to appeal to the largest number of viewers—and for the properly combative attitudes to start the arguments ("lively discussions") that earned higher ratings, even in a soft time slot like Sunday 10:00 A.M.

Monk nodded, satisfied, from the control room, as Kim slid the latest numbers to him. "There's a sucker born every minute," he quoted. "Why watch this stuff when you could kick back with a nice cup of coffee, a box of donuts, and the funnies?"

Kim just shook her head.

What the verbal brawl lacked in finesse it made up in enthusiasm. The Wiccan made the one slam-dunk of the segment, hotly deploring the prevailing Christian-centric viewpoint and its ignorant millennialism. Several other panelists fervently agreed, and the program ended with the "fundamentalist" Christian panelist fuming and foaming as the atheist deployed postmodern irony and sarcasm. Darren thanked them—shouting through the ongoing slugfest, as planned.

"Obviously, this is a topic that raises blood pressure as well as hopes and fears." He stated the obvious with blank-faced ease. "But we don't have to go far for words of wisdom. As I learned in my personal, exclusive interview with Sondra van Dash, Oscar-winning actress and humanitarian, there's a silver lining to every cloud—or earthquake."

The segment ended with Sondra herself, graduated from ingenue to devoted New Age guru, filmed in soft light and the living room of her Malibu mansion, soothingly explaining, "The world is entering the Tenth Age; the earthquakes are simply the birthing pains of a glorious future" as Darren listened attentively. (The interview, as expected, segued into advertisements for her latest book, *Living in the Tenth Age*.)

The scene returned to Darren in the studio. He smiled and summed up the segment, "Clearly, in times of stress, people want to believe in something, and prayer gives them that—whatever they're praying to" over a scene of a group of Hindus worshiping a cow. "I'm Darren McInnes, and this is *Sunday Morning*. Have a good day." He didn't apologize for the false advertising that promised answers at the top of the show.

"What's up next?" Monk asked Kim as the credits and promos rolled.

She tweaked up the computer, pointing to the schedule.

"Affiliates' choice for 15 minutes, huh?" Monk considered for a second, then came to his decision with the speed that made him a legend among local-news producers. "That Anne O'Neal's a religion reporter, isn't she? See what we've got from her." He leaned back in his chair as Kim's fingers flew on the keyboard. "I like the way her earrings swing when she talks, and I bet a lot of 18- to 35-year-old guys do too."

Much to Monk's disappointment, Anne wore small, pearl-button earrings for her opening speech. In a conservative, gray suit and tastefully lacy white blouse to go along with the pearls, she fit beautifully among the groomed flowerbeds and splashing fountains in front of the vast, marble façade of the building. The building itself managed to look discreet and dignified without being overwhelming, which, given its truly juggernaut size, it should've been.

"This is Anne O'Neal, Channel 8 religion correspondent, with a special report from Independence, Missouri, the newly established headquarters of The Church of Jesus Christ of Latter-day Saints, popularly known as the Mormons. The Church of Jesus Christ, as they prefer to be known, is the fastest-growing Christian denomination in the world. In fact, according to the latest study from Washington State University, it may be the fastest-growing denomination of any religion. As amazing as that may seem, this Church is accustomed to exceeding expectations. This impressive conference center, the largest completely enclosed auditorium in North America, houses a world-class communications network, including a fully functioning satellite broadcasting station." Footage of the cavernous interior of the Conference Center scrolled across the screen, diving down into the back hallways and into a control room that put NASA's Mission Control to shame.

"The Church's holdings extend from pecan groves in Georgia to wheat farms in Nebraska." Pictures of lush farmland and leafy orchards accompanied that statement.

"The Church refuses to divulge full information about their financial holdings, but preliminary investigations point to a financial empire rivaling that of the most powerful multinational corporations.

'MedaGen,' in the words of one analyst who requested anonymity, 'got nothin' on this outfit.' Church members pay an annual tithe of ten percent of their income, and the Church's investments have been extremely successful—if not divinely inspired." Unrelated but impressive shots of elegant, Neoclassical banks, Wall Street firms, and frantic stock-pit traders underlined the analysts' speculations, then segued into a shot of the Twelve Apostles filing into the Conference Center for its inaugural meeting. The context underlined their suit-and-tie, businesslike appearance.

"Success, however, often breeds enemies, and that has certainly happened in the case of this Church." A crowd of Muslims protesting the building of the Mormon temple in Kuala Lumpur illustrated this comment. "The Church's conservative stances on social issues and unorthodox doctrines have drawn fire from both left and right. Evangelical Christians do not officially recognize Mormons as Christians, preferring instead to label the Church as a cult or pagan organization." The scene changed to show angry protesters picketing that same inaugural conference, Christian protesters carrying signs and shouting slogans against the un-Christian cult gathering inside the huge building.

"At the same time, progressive organizations such as the Women's Council on Human Rights denounce the Church for its oppression of women, condemnation of gays and lesbians, and emphasis on conservative values." The Christian protest melded into another, this one a San Francisco march against Mormon intolerance.

"Lately, however, the old protests have taken on a new, more violent character. Unknown vandals have targeted Mormon churches throughout the Southwest, burning chapels and leaving spray-painted warnings on the walls of homes." Fire pouring from the broken windows of a church house sent thick smoke into the sky, obscuring the deep blue and high desert clouds before wafting over the camera's lens. The smoke cleared as the camera switched to the crude, misspelled graffiti on the beige stucco walls and cedar fence of an otherwise pleasant-looking house.

"In addition, rumors of organized mobs targeting Mormons spread as the Church moved its headquarters from its traditional location in Salt Lake City to its former capital in Independence, Missouri. The move was a symbol of triumph, a vindication for the Mormons' forced departure from the state of Missouri in the 1830s. Mobs had killed Joseph Smith, the founder and first 'prophet' of the Church, and the members fled west under the leadership of Brigham Young." Portraits of Joseph Smith and Brigham Young filled the screen, then a panoramic shot of the Salt Lake Valley, which smoothly transitioned into an equally panoramic view of the new headquarters. "Now, they have returned, buying land from the financially strapped Independence municipal government, establishing a growing presence throughout the state where a former governor once signed an extermination order against them. Despite some residents' misgivings, however, the Mormons are here to stay—fulfilling, some say, Joseph Smith's prophecy that the Saints would claim this promised land as their birthright from the Gentiles before spreading their gospel truth to the entire world."

A flurry of clips followed, showing anti-Mormon demonstrators in all areas of the world: French government officials revoking official recognition of the Church, Philippine devotees of Brother Light burning President Smith in effigy, Chinese police rounding up members of the Church in Siankang, Senator Garlick fulminating against Mormon interference with pro-business legislation, a lesbian tearfully decrying her excommunication—all ending with another shot of smoke against desert sky.

The scene returned to Anne, standing in the sunlight in front of the headquarters building. She regarded the camera solemnly. "The only question now is whether the world is ready to hear it—or whether the Rocky Mountains of the Church's traditional headquarters are tall enough to shield the Saints from their enemies this time."

* * *

Dear Chisom,

I am so glad the situation in Taiwan has improved a bit over the last couple of weeks so that you can spend more time doing formal missionary work than giving temporal assistance. Don't down play the latter, however. I know you were a bit frustrated not being able to get right into teaching. Remember, you are there to do good, and by showing real love and concern, I'm sure the spirit you carry with you opened hearts. Those will eventually open doors. I am even more pleased to find out that there has been, as I suspected, a good deal of interest in your message. I am intrigued that tragedy often leads to humility and a quest for answers. As I told you before, you will find many attracted to what you have to say because you do have the answers.

Since your mother filled you in on all the incidents on our move to Jackson County, I'll just share a few personal observations. Like her, I am pleased with the house we were able to find. Due to the drought and recession that hit the area over the past few years, a lot of people have moved out, leaving houses and land available at bargain prices. Of course the Church has been purchasing property here, at Far West and at Adam-ondi-Ahman, among other places, for well over a half century. As a result, when the Brethren decided to move the headquarters of the Church here and build the office building and temple, the land was already secured. Then, with the natural disaster and economic problems that occurred, other land has become available, and many Saints have moved into the area. The Brethren, however, are not calling for a general Church gathering to Jackson county. The Saints, as Joseph Smith said, will remain a strong people in the Rocky Mountains until the Lord comes. The Brethren will continue to call only those who are needed here. So don't worry about the faithful Saints in Taiwan. The Lord promised that God will protect his people both in Zion and her stakes from the storm of his wrath, and that includes those in your area. (See D&C 115 for the full quote.)

The Church is strong here, but only in pockets. I suspect there will always be a strong non-Mormon (and sometimes anti-Mormon) population in the state. Missionary work, however, is doing well here in spite of the Universal Baptists' opposition, I am pleased to say. I find it fascinating even yet, that it is members living their religion who are still the best missionaries. That's what attracted your grandfather and grandmother to the Church so many years ago in Nigeria. I will be ever grateful to those good Saints who modeled a Christlike life and thereby attracted your grandparents to the gospel.

Work in the Church's central office is keeping me very busy. As I mentioned in an earlier letter, the Church is shutting down more missions all the time (mostly in Europe; France has bluntly shut its doors against us), but opening some in other places—such as India, where the Church is really growing. We should have over 26 million members world wide by the end of the year! The rapid growth of the Church keeps the Brethren running, but with the seventh quorum of seventy now functioning, there is plenty of help to keep the Church strong and well led.

The rapid growth of the Church is also causing a lot of opposition in some areas. Though other churches are growing due to recent events, ours has really picked up membership. Further, the Church has a lot of political power, and by flexing its civil muscle on moral issues, it has brought the ire of some powerful but amoral people upon us. We had three of our chapels firebombed in one night in the deep South, and many of the faithful Saints there are being harassed. We may be shutting down missions in that area before long if the situation worsens. It just shows that, in spite of all that has happened, Babylon is the big winner for now. Men and women still fall for her seductive promises and are fighting even harder against God and His people.

I mentioned before the concern some have expressed that there may be an actual organization that has targeted the Church for destruction. It is looking more and more like that may be the case. If it is, we are in for it, because so many sectarians are angry with us and continue to spread their lies. Anti-Mormonism continues to be big business. We know for sure that hate groups are forming in some areas here and in South America. Their leaders may not have a hard time recruiting members if their lies continue. I fear for our Latin American brothers and sisters.

I am reminded of a scripture in 1 Nephi 14 where the prophet says he saw the Church in the last days, "and its numbers were few, because of the wickedness and abominations of the whore who sat upon many waters; nevertheless, I beheld that the church of the Lamb, who were the saints of God, were also upon all the face of the earth." That part of the prophecy has certainly come true. Nephi goes on to say that he saw that the great "mother of abominations did gather together multitudes upon the face of all the earth, among all the nations of the Gentiles, to fight against the Lamb of God." That's where it looks like we are headed. I have no fear, however, because Nephi goes on to say that, though the saints were scattered upon all the face of the earth, "they were armed with righteousness and with the power of God in great glory." Even now, I see God's hand upon His people. Nephi goes on to say that in response to "the whore's objectives, the Lord will allow war to increase among the Gentiles. Thus, the prophet declared that "the wrath of God was poured out upon that great and abominable church, insomuch that there were wars and rumors of wars among all the nations . . . of the earth." (See 1 Nephi 14:10–17 on this.) How ironic that the Lord will use war as a means to initially distract and eventually destroy those who would war against His Church!

In all, I see that never has the world needed to hear the message of the gospel more than now. Be diligent and work hard that you may bring those Chinese people who will hear into the fold.

Well that is enough for now. I am very proud of you. Love,
Your father,
Chinedu

* * *

CHAPTER 4

"There's no way that barrel's good enough cover to use as a shield," Benny informed Cesare. "No way, *chico*."

"Shut up, Benny," Cesare hissed, blasting away with his computer generated rail gun around the barrel in question.

Sure enough, the mercenary femme Cesare was shooting at Rose out of her own pile of industrial debris, her assets bouncing in a way calculated to distract her opponents, and returned fire with two howitzer-sized hand cannons. The barrel disappeared into independent atoms, and Cesare's ego went down in a burst of crimson glop that completely obscured his vision. Cheers, vulgar comments, and laughter erupted from the peanut gallery: Perro, Calvin, and the other *compadres* sprawled around the room after a long night of pixilated combat. The gang tended to gather at Benny's for after-hours entertainment, mostly because he was the only one who used his share of *Abuelo's* protection-money take to actually buy a house. The others burned their bonuses in booze, broads, and bangles.

As Perro joked, "What do you call Rico when he's broken up with his girlfriend? Homeless!" He was still limping along on crutches (more ostentatiously when he thought he could get attention from the *chicas*), but the loss of his toe hadn't slowed his mouth down at all.

"I tell you, or what?" Benny asked, thumping Cesare on the shoulder.

"Shut up, Benny," Cesare repeated, returning the thump with a hard left and throwing the game controller at him. "You're so slick, you take out that b—"

"News!" Perro interrupted, using the end of his crutch to disconnect the game console and flip on the television instead. "Let's see if we got some channel time on this one. Maybe they've figured out who pulled the warehouse raid by now."

"Not likely," Dove snorted, but he edged in closer too, leaving off making breakfast and coming into the room from the kitchen to get a look at the screen. Benny gave him a disgusted look, taking back the bowie knife Dove had been using to cut apples. Dove shrugged, holding up three fingers. (That was code for argument #3: "Dove, don't use weapons as kitchen implements!" "Benny, I use weapons because we don't have any kitchen implements!")

Benny shook his head and grinned. He reached for Dolores as she wandered in from the bedroom, half wrapped in a silky kimono. She neatly avoided his hand, and went past him into the kitchen— Dolores's way of letting Benny know she didn't appreciate him staying up all night with his buddies playing video games. She did manage to brush up against Cesare, though. (Sure, he was playing, too, but he wasn't ignoring her to do it.) Benny's grin got sharper. Dove sighed silently. *Here we go again; it's going to be Juanita all over.*

Much to Perro's disappointment, the morning's edition of the local news didn't lead with an in-depth profile of *Abuelo's* gang and its most charismatic (and limping on crutches) member. "Nah, couldn't be that. Nobody interviewed me, Perro," Dove informed him and grinned.

Much to his delight, however, the local news did a follow-up report on last week's hot story. A long shot showed archive footage of the smoldering ruins of the warehouse in the background, as a warehouse supervisor denied any knowledge about what had been in the warehouse, about what may have caused a fire in the warehouse, or who might have been in the warehouse when the fire happened. Given half a chance, he probably would've denied any knowledge of the very existence of any warehouse at all. However, since the reporter had already confirmed the fact that his official job description read "Warehouse Supervisor" for the building now smoldering in ashes, it was a little late for plausible deniability. So he went for professing complete ignorance instead, probably under the assumption that it was safer under the circumstances to be an idiot than an incompetent.

"Sheriff Pizarro's office has issued a statement denying that they have any definite leads on the mysterious fire, despite rumors that a local gang has claimed responsibility. Law enforcement sources will say only that the investigation is continuing. Whoever is responsible, the warehouse is a total loss, due to an officially unexplained but probably arson-caused fire," the reporter informed the perpetrators. "But given the lack of information about what was in the warehouse, there are no estimates of damages." He smiled sardonically. "Looks like life as usual on the border, Lupe."

That's why Dove liked the early morning news—all local, and sometimes the actual personality bubbled through the thick layer of TV professionalism.

"Thanks, Mike." Lupe turned to the camera as the World Report logo appeared over her shoulder. "In national news, a massive shootout between rival gangs in Trenton left 56 people dead and many more wounded." A "sensitive viewer" warning scrolled across the bottom of the screen. Video, shaky, handheld, and shot from what looked like a fire escape, showed figures tearing through an alleyway, the muzzle flashes of their guns standing out starkly in the dusk. One of the men, slightly slower than the others, suddenly stiffened, jerked forward, and fell into his companions. They fought free, leaving the wounded man lying in the alley. Another group of men ran up and clustered around the wounded figure. Their arms raised and fell. The scene abruptly cut off.

Lupe reappeared. Her journalistic impartiality hadn't completely displaced her humanity yet, and the camera caught her swallowing hard. "The spokesman for the Trenton police says that a running gun battle erupted when members of the gangs met to discuss disagreements over drugs and territory in the inner city." Again, the scene shifted, showing a crowd of shouting, sign-carrying citizens parading in front of a line of warily watching police. "Protesters have besieged the police department, asking why the police didn't do more to stop the incident. The answers, like so much else in our modern cities, are unclear."

"Unclear!" Cesare laughed. "It's clear—the guys with the biggest guns are going to win, and the cops are staying out of it, taking their cut off the top."

The scene changed again, showing crying kids and weeping mothers against graffiti-spattered tenements riddled with bullet holes. Funeral processions with dark coffins and dull flowers followed. The voice-over poetically likened the chaos in America's inner cities to the tide of violence spreading through once-secure areas all over the world—much to the edification of the audience gathered around Benny's television set, who cheered every new set of rebels, gang lords, and religious fanatics. Every shot that included heavy-duty military hardware (rocket launchers, grenades, laser sites) got a chorus of whistles, compliments, and "I have *got* to get me some of that!"

The commentator, oblivious, nattered on about race riots, strikes, and murders among migrant workers in Europe; African nations' dissolution into disease and disaster; Egyptian semi-stability in the erupting viper pit of the Near East; Chinese warlords imitating ancient models as they slashed and burned through the far provinces; military coups, drug lords' wars, and rebel uprisings in South America. Each statement came with its own images—overwhelmingly focusing on innocent victims and bloody aftermaths.

"Same story all over," Benny agreed. "Legitimates going bent, punks taking over, and little kids losing mamas and papas."

"International chaos is not simply international, anymore," a professorial talking head intoned.

"Oh, tell us all about it, teacher!" Perro hooted.

"We see this in the increasing isolation of individuals in our worldwide society, the lack of ties reflected in the increasing breakdown of law and order in the United States. Talk of the global economy focuses on the lack of local resources, but that is only half the story. The United States military has been overextended across the globe, and has had to pull in its resources to protect itself. Even so, it has run into difficulties, because the National Guard and police cannot control the inner cities or outlying areas where corruption scandals are rampant."

More pictures followed, police handcuffed and handcuffing, packages of money and unknown substances changing hands in evidence rooms, tarnished badges. The voice-over began again: "L.A., New York, Des Moines—all over this country, cops taking bribes, sheriffs charging 'tolls' for safe passage, and INS agents joining the coyotes in smuggling paying customers across the borders. What can the federal government do about it? Can the United States remain united? And at what cost? Watch Channel 8 News for the full report at 10:00 tonight."

"Full report tonight at 10:00. Why bother? We just got to go down the road to get all the bent cop we need," Benny snorted.

"What's the matter, Benny? You don't like our buddy Pizarro?" Rico asked, coming in without knocking. Stripes and Marco, his ever-present shadows, followed him through the door.

"What's not to like about Pizarro?" Benny shrugged. "He's so bent he's come round full circle."

"Fzzt—speak of the devil," Perro stage whispered.

Sure enough, the door opened again to frame the expansive bulk of Sheriff Pizarro himself. Like Rico, he had a couple of deputies shadowing him. Unlike Rico, he wore his gun in full view. He hooked his thumbs into the gun belt straining around his thick waist and grinned at the suddenly expressionless faces of *Abuelo's* soldiers. "Howdy, boys," he said. "Been up to some big doin's in the last week or so?"

Enrique Pizarro was the local law enforcement in the gang's sprawling section of Amexica, the wide swath of the desert country that had regressed to a "Wild West" state with time, an ever-growing population, and insufficient oversight from the Federal agencies assigned to keep peace. The areas around the bigger cities that circled Pizarro's playground—Las Cruces, Ciudad Juarez, even Roswell—still maintained their grip on mainstream society. So did the tightly patrolled confines of the military installations (White Sands, Alamagordo, and the other top-secret testing and proving grounds). However, between the outposts of civilization, new towns sprang up around sources of water and well-traveled roads, while old towns fell off the grid and into the control of local authorities. The city, county, and state police and sheriff's departments sometimes cooperated and sometimes conflicted, their policies ranging from simply trying to keep the peace to actively collaborating with the forces of chaos surrounding them.

The philosophy of most of the borderlands' residents came down to live and let live—as in, "I'll just mind my own business and live

my life, and I'll pay you a significant bribe if you'll let me live it."
They were here to make a profit, cut a deal, settle on a few acres, or
get away from outstanding warrants in other areas, and they didn't
have the inclination to argue with deputies who shot first and asked
questions later. Besides, they knew they were probably better off
keeping quiet. Fully half the population had no official permission to
live and work where they did, and another quarter had official papers
that wouldn't stand up to an expert's appraisal. Thus, the civilians
weren't likely to make an official complaint to the *federales* when the
drug runners, gangs, or police officers overstepped their authority.
The man with the gun to your head, after all, has a lot more clout
than the one sitting behind a desk a hundred miles away—who'd only
work to get you deported or jailed if he knew about your existence at
all. This situation meant that anybody with a healthy dose of self-
confidence and a willingness to use "whatever means necessary" to
make his point rose to the top very quickly. Guys like Enrique
Pizarro, for instance.

Pizarro came up from Tijuana more years ago than Dove could
remember directly, but rumor said that he'd been running from a
murder rap on a protection racket gone wrong. Whatever he'd done
back in Mexico had taught him a few things about discretion, and his
ability to organize a posse and scrape up introduction money had
impressed the local *Señor* enough to underwrite Pizarro's campaign
for sheriff. With that kind of backing, the citizens immediately threw
their support behind the newcomer as well. Thus, the sheriff was not
just part of the local law enforcement, he *was* local law enforcement.
He ran for sheriff on a very simple platform: "A Vote for Pizarro Is a
Vote Not to Have Your Car Confiscated, Your House Burned Down,
and Your Tail Tossed in the Clink Until Doomsday." It was a long
slogan, but a very effective one.

Pizarro took full advantage of the weakened central control that the
talking heads on the news bemoaned from a safe distance. Federal laws,
naturalization-service regulations, and police procedures on either side of
the border threw a lot less weight than a posse of well-paid, better-armed,
and deeply amoral deputies—especially when the deputies stopped a
"suspect" on a lonely, dirt road a long way from town. Pizarro tolerated
Abuelo's gang and the few others operating in his self-appointed jurisdic-

tion in return for a cut of their profits. (Protection for a protection racket, as Dove called it.) On the upside, he took care of paying off the judges, too. Which service he took the opportunity to remind them of.

"Good thing Cap Muntabi down the fire station needs a couple new tires on the department car. Turns out he can't get out to investigate arsons 'til he gets 'em replaced." The sheriff fixed Benny, then Rico, with a meaningful glance. "I'm sure your boss, *Abuelo*, can see his way clear to making a contribution to the fireman's ball, eh? Wouldn't want firebugs running around loose, would we?"

Dove growled under his breath. Benny shot him a warning look. Rico just grinned, all easy agreeability. "No problem, *Gordo*. We love the fire department. You think Cap would want whitewalls or steel-belted radials?"

"Don't go fancy," Pizarro advised, shaking a cigar out of its silver-gilded tube and snicking the end off with an equally flashy cigar cutter. "Cap's a simple man. I, on the other hand," he stowed the cutter and lit the cigar with the lighter that was the final piece in the monogrammed set, "appreciate the good things in life."

"Tough on a sheriff's salary," Dove muttered under his breath to Perro. Perro grinned.

Pizarro didn't glance that direction; maybe he hadn't heard. "Life's not worth living without the freedom," he hit the word hard, one hand jingling the cuffs at his belt, "to kick back once in awhile." He blew a thick cloud of smoke, leered at Dolores, and announced, "You boys be good—I'm gonna go see your grandpa, and I'd hate to have to tell him anything that'd disappoint him. Like you all not buying tickets to the policeman's ball this year."

"Right, Henry," Rico's smile acquired harder glints. "*Abuelo's* got our contribution for this month's debutante ball, just like usual."

"Going the extra mile, collecting donations yourself," Benny observed.

"You got yourselves a full-service sheriff here, boys," Pizarro said with a gold-capped smile. His two deputies added their own dental displays under their deep-tinted sunglasses. They kept the glasses turned toward Rico and Benny as Pizarro rolled out to his Cadillac squad car and all three of them rolled away in a purr of expensive engine noise and a muffled salsa beat. *Abuelo's* gang watched him go.

Dove growled. "Crooked cops oughta be shot with their own pieces."

Perro made an unprintable joke about that idea, but Calvin and a couple of the other guys—especially the younger ones—nodded, their expressions darkening.

Rico glanced from them to Dove and did some growling of his own. "Like we need a bunch of *federales* whomping down on us around here." He grabbed the front of Dove's shirt and shook him. "You think *Abuelo's* not taking care of you? You think you could do better?"

Dove met his eyes steadily, not resisting but not giving an inch, either. "I think cops shouldn't be stealing from the people they're supposed to protect—and they shouldn't be taking bribes off the guys they're supposed to be hauling in."

"And that would be us?" Rico hissed. "You want to see *Abuelo* rotting in some cell? Or your *major hermano* Benny? You're talking treason." He let Dove go, aiming a hard slap at the kid's face.

Dove rode the blow, then caught his wrist as Rico went for the backhand return, tossing his hand back at him. "I don't want to see anybody in jail but Pizarro."

"Why should we pay a cut to Fat Henry anyway?" Perro wondered aloud.

Rico snorted, taking a bottle of beer from Scruffy. (Scruffy sighed and went back to the kitchen to get another one.) "Maybe we shouldn't." He took a deep swallow. "Maybe it's time to kick Fat Henry's fat head over the mesa. Maybe the *Brujos* have the right idea. I've heard about this General down in Sudamerica wiping out corrupt governments, giving his guys a piece of the real action."

"Anybody who'd hire the *Brujos* is just looking for cannon fodder," Dove snapped. "They're a bunch of stupid mooks. So hey, Rico, you'd be perfect for them."

Calvin and Perro laughed, Cesare and Marco glowered, Rico gave Dove a vicious grin, and Benny tossed a brown bag at Dove's head. Perro and Scruffy automatically ducked. Rico blinked, slow and reptilian. Dove caught the bag reflexively. Everybody looked at Benny.

"All right, shut up, everybody. Go to school, Dove, you got your lunch," he ordered.

Dove hesitated just long enough to read the warning in Benny's eyes. "Going, going." He kicked the stool out from under Perro. "Come on, *chicos*. We got time to get there 'fore Miz Frog pastes us with a detention again."

Perro sighed, accepted Dove's offered hand, and heaved himself up. He and Dove collared Calvin, and the three of them piled into Perro's Dogmobile. The cloud of blue oil smoke marked their passage, while the noise from the dead muffler gave fair warning of their approach.

"Schoolboys," Rico scoffed, turning his cold gaze on Benny. "We need soldiers."

Benny turned from the door to meet Rico's eyes. He shot *Abuelo's* second in command a stare that reminded Rico that Benny had earned the respect the rest of the gang gave him. "Better they go to school than end up coked, drunk, or dead—like you're going to be, if you keep up the jabber."

"That a threat, Benny?" Rico asked.

"No, Rico, that's a promise," Benny assured him mildly. He looked at the window, where the exhaust from the Dogmobile was slowly dissipating. "We gather them, we teach them to fight for us, and we keep them off the streets until they end up dying for us. Maybe being homeless is better."

"Ask them," Rico advised, "if they'd rather starve than fight. And ask them if they want to follow that little brother of yours to the devil, 'cause that's where he's going if he disses me again." He went to the door, Stripes and Marco obediently following. "They'll tell you— better breathing than not, better under *Abuelo's* roof than none at all."

* * *

"Riots in Manila got worse today, as thousands of people were left homeless after the earthquakes took to the streets of the capital," Kathy intoned, reading the morning news from the scanners. "They called for help, funding, aid—anything to make their situation better after a month of neglect, disease, and destitution. The government deployed riot police to break up the crowd, which only fueled the riot further. Damage and casualty reports are climbing. In other news, the search continues for the missing Mormon authority, Elder Thomas J. Stacy. A militant group, the Children of the Light, have claimed responsibility for his disappearance, but the reports are still unconfirmed. Now, let's turn to business news. How's the stock market today, Tom?"

"The results were mixed today, Kathy, with—" The screen went dark. The strains of a Celtic ballad replaced the tight patter of the newscast.

Chris nodded, satisfied, and walked across the kitchen from the TV monitor. He leaned over and kissed Merry's neck as she stirred the lumps out of a pan of cracked wheat cereal. "Enough with the doom and gloom, huh?"

Merry smiled and leaned against him for a moment before handing him the spoon. "Sure, enough with doom and gloom. Why worry about riots in the Pacific when we've got the big interview today?" She rescued the box of cereal packets from Missy, then picked her up and settled her into the high chair. "And offers rolling in from the Web resumés, I take it?"

"Just one this morning, but it's early days yet. Can't expect much after just a week and a bit, not in this economy. And, just in case, we've got the interview covered," Chris assured her lightly, dishing them bowls of mush and liberally drizzling them with honey before adding splashes of milk. "I'll dazzle our new overlords with the patented Galen charm, and we'll be sitting pretty." He set the bowls on the table.

He and Merry joined hands and bowed their heads. After a giggle at her parents' reminder that "it's prayer time," Missy did too. True, she held the pose for only a couple of seconds (roughly through "we thank thee"), but she refrained from banging her spoon on her tray until Merry said "Amen" (mostly because Chris reached over and gently caught her hands). Merry used the momentary silence to put in a sincere request for Heavenly Father to be with Chris that day as he reinterviewed for his job, and to inspire the human-resource person at MedaGen and the headhunters combing the Web to see his excellent qualities and realize how much their companies needed him. She hesitated only slightly before amending the request with a "or please help us to find the situation where we need to be." It was a lot easier to ask Him to help those searching for Elder Stacy, and for the safety of the missionaries around the world.

When she finished, Chris added his "Amen" to hers and let Missy go.

"And in the very unlikely chance that the patented Galen charm blows a gasket?" Merry pressed, popping a spoonful of mush into Missy's mouth.

Chris paused in his expert breakfast-shoveling technique. "Then we say we didn't really want to work for MedaGen anyway and make the runner-up extremely happy." Suddenly, he looked worried. "Why? Do you know something I don't?"

"No!" Merry exclaimed. "No, Chris, you'll do great! I didn't mean—" She broke off as he started laughing. She threw a napkin at him. "Pull my chain, will you? Here I am, understandably wanting to confirm our plans to secure our future, and you're teasing. Make yourself useful and read scriptures to us."

He did, managing to catch Missy's interest by doing different voices for Alma, Amulek, Zeezrom, and the heckling crowd. Merry spooned mush into Missy until it started coming back, then dug into her own cereal while she listened. Missy added a soundtrack of spoon drumming and squeals.

"And that's it for today's episode," Chris announced, closing the Book of Mormon. "Will Alma and Amulek escape? Will Zeezrom see the error of his ways? Tune in tomorrow!"

"For some reason, Amulek really works as a Scot," Merry told him. She lifted Missy out of the high chair and applied a warm washcloth to her face. "Prophecy sounds good in a Celtic accent."

"And thank you for that, lass," Chris told her in his Amulek voice. He shrugged on his jacket and swept Missy up in his arms for a big hug. "You be good, munchkin." He set her down on the floor and caught Merry up in an emphatic hug. "And don't you worry. It'll all work out. I promise."

"We just need to have faith?" Merry asked, smiling. Her smile faded slightly. "Chris, what if it doesn't? Things don't turn out right all the time, not in reality. Look at those people Alma and Amulek converted—they end up barbecued! What if MedaGen doesn't keep you, or they're too scummy to work for, and you can't find another job?" The incessant barrage of news boiled back into her mind. "What if that preacher is right and these disasters really are the beginning of the end of the world?"

"Then when we go out tonight to celebrate my continued employment, we'll eat dessert first. Merry, it's not the end of the world yet. And even if it were, I figure President Smith is as good an authority as Tommy Gibb, and he said that things will work out right. Eventually, if not right now. We've covered our bases, we've got our food storage, we're willing to do whatever God wants us to, and we'll get through it." He kissed her, pulled back, and looked deeply into her eyes. "I love you."

"I love you, too," she told him, kissing him back and straightening his lapels. She took a deep breath and summoned a smile. It wasn't as hard as she feared. "And if that patented Galen charm doesn't convince them to keep you, they just don't deserve to have such a terrific geneticist on their payroll. You'll have to rub it in during your Nobel acceptance speech."

"There's the spirit," he told her. "Thanks for the boost. I'll call you from my desk or on this." He waved his cell phone. "And we'll celebrate either way."

"We will!" Merry exclaimed, sweeping up Missy and following him to the door. She opened it for him with a flourish. "Go get 'em! Knock 'em dead! Good luck! Not that you'll need it!"

"Gud luk!" Missy shouted. "Gud luk! Gud luk!"

He blew them both kisses as he settled into the driver's seat and pulled the car out of the garage. They waved until he turned out of sight. "Good thing we agreed a long time ago that only one of us could go to pieces at a time," he said to himself. "Did you do that intentionally, to take the stress off me, letting me be strong for her?" he prayed. "And, Galen charm aside, please help," he finished. "Yup, I'm nervous, all right," he admitted to himself. "Buck up, bucko! You've got a family to support." He took a deep breath and turned on the radio, avoiding the news.

The never-ending coverage of the repercussions of the earthquakes—like media aftershocks bubbling up through the morass of advertising as a disconcerting reminder that life didn't necessarily go on—hadn't gotten under his skin like it had Merry's, but he sympathized with her unease. It was tough enough to know that their financial situation might drastically change, but to know that and not be able to do anything directly about it must be maddening. Merry wasn't used to not being in control. He smiled, thinking about the intense, confident, quiet girl in his graduate lab—the one who knew all the answers, could figure out how to run any piece of equipment, and for some reason didn't realize how attractive she was. Fortunately, also for reasons he didn't understand, the other guys in the lab didn't seem to realize it either.

One night, as they collaborated on an experiment, he finally cranked up the nerve to ask her if she'd like to go to dinner with him. She'd thought about it, glanced at the timer on the incubator where their latest batch of proteins cooked, replicating under accelerated conditions, and told him they had about 20 minutes—she'd be glad to run over and pick something up from the local taco stand if he were hungry. When he clarified that he meant out to dinner with him when they had time to enjoy it, not now ("As in a date, Merry"), she blinked, gave him a narrow-eyed appraisal, and said, "Why?" He laughed and told her he liked her company, found her attractive, and wanted to see her socially as well as at the lab. She continued that long look for another few seconds, and finally said, "I believe you. But since you're thinking that way, we seriously need to talk."

They hadn't actually done that dinner date for another four months, but they had talked about everything but their experiments: her goals, his plans for the future, her distrust of conventional social relationships, his very traditional family, her mother's rabid womanism, his devotion to eradicating the diabetes that plagued his father, her feeling of rootlessness in a world where morality was negotiable depending on the situation at the moment, his deep-seated testimony of Christ and the restored gospel. He still joked that she fell in love with what the missionaries taught before she fell in love with him; she assured him that getting his company for eternity was a nice side bonus to going to the temple for the first time.

Even after they were married, she often grilled him on some bit of scripture or doctrine—"Was this Mormon-culture, custom, or actual Church law?" she would often ask—like wanting complete clarification of what Paul meant when he said that women should keep silent in church. He explained as best he could—their library of scriptural reference works had certainly expanded exponentially from his small stash of recommended resources for missionaries—comparing the eternal principle of the need for order and the role of the priesthood in presiding during meetings with the situation Paul wrote to correct.

"It's not that women shouldn't teach or pray or speak in church," he'd assured her. "It's that the Relief Society president shouldn't try to take over the bishop's role."

She gave him one of her calculating looks, then led him on a chase through other scriptures and commentaries to confirm what he told her. The thought and work she put into learning the gospel had amazed, then embarrassed Chris. He'd grown up in the Church and pretty much took things for granted as "the way it is." He had occasional questions or doubts—especially in his teenage years—but the idea that the gospel might not be true had never really occurred to him. His mission broadened his doctrinal horizons considerably while reinforcing his underlying testimony, but it had been listening to Merry wrestle with the concepts and their implications that had made him take a hard look at his own assumptions. That was a distinctly uncomfortable experience; he never expected to have to intellectually confront the stark reality of God, good, evil, agency, and consequences along with someone whose scalpel-sharp mind sliced through the missionary discussions as easily as it dissected the principles of genetics. His testimony not only survived the experience but developed the ice-crystal sheen of certainty on more than one point, when the doctrines not only stood up to Merry's inquisition but had an answer for almost every question she posed. In the process, he grew to love her more than he thought possible, not the least for the fact that all of her questions came from an honest desire to know, to understand, and, ultimately, to believe. Her humility to accept some things on faith and put her trust in God and prayer made her even more beautiful to him. The Saturday he baptized and confirmed her was one of the happiest days of his life; he felt that they'd both been through the water and fire and walked away cleansed.

Not that the questions had stopped after she'd joined the Church and, a little over a year later, went through the Temple. She still pushed him and herself and God for answers. Her probing, and her intensity about it, had frightened him at first, but when he realized she wasn't looking for an excuse to disbelieve, he learned to enjoy their debates and the sometimes surprising, sometimes reassuring understanding of concepts that came from them. He even began to bring up his own concerns or speculations, watching her slice them into causes and effects, standards and variables, then apply the same thorough research and logic to them as she expected him to do for her questions. (He told her she'd drag him all the way to qualifying for Heaven if she kept this up. She sighed and told him she and Jesus had to get him there *somehow*.) That didn't mean they always found answers, but she learned to deal with that too. She applied the formula of "search, debate, pray"—and if that strategy didn't yield the answer she wanted, she would finally growl that even if she didn't understand something, even if it chafed her logical, feminist, Western-rational mind, she'd trust that God knew what He was doing—even if she was going to have to talk to Him about it later.

Like quitting her research to stay home with Missy, for instance. That decision had involved many late-night discussions, much research, and even more praying, but she finally decided that if she was going to be a mother, she was going to do it right, even if "being a real mom" didn't come as easily for her as she thought it should. (In Chris's opinion, she was a great mom, but while she appreciated the sentiment, she considered him a biased observer.) It didn't come easy for her to completely depend on Chris, either, for economic as well as emotional support, but she did that, too. She channeled all the professional competence and enthusiasm she couldn't use right then into caring for and educating Missy and into supporting Chris right back; in fact, she pretty much moral-supported the heck out of him.

* * *

"Consider it moral support, Keyes. An incentive." Zelik's liquid-nitrogen stare passed from one tech to the other, leaving the men shivering in its wake. "Double the fee if you get it up and running by tomorrow morning. And you pay half your fee if it doesn't work—or if we have to call you back to stamp out bugs."

"You couldn't find anybody else who'd take that deal, but we will," Keyes, the lead tech informed MedaGen's Chief Operations Officer, his resilient geek pride rebounding slightly. He'd just started his own security-installation business, and a job like this one could really make his reputation. (He didn't want to add the inevitable corollary: it could really break his reputation, too—and, with that kind of penalty, break his company's credit rating as well.)

"Confident of you," she noted. "Let's all hope it's well founded."

The techs watched her leave, closing the door behind her with a precise, threatening click.

"All right, let's get this puppy up and running," Keyes snapped at his assistant. They dove again into their toolkits, boxes, and webs of multicolored wire.

"Weird kind of security system," the apprentice tech observed, screwing a panel into place.

"Huh?" Keyes, contemplating what he could do with double MedaGen's already high commission as he rapidly ran a system check, didn't even look over.

"Yeah, weird." The kid moved to the next panel. All the lights on his transmission tester flashed green, and he began screwing the front plate into place. "Sure. You notice, we got outside cameras, and sure we got motion detectors in the parking lot, and we got the door security, but most of it's not about people breaking in from outside. More like people trying to break out from the inside." He motioned around with his screwdriver at the video monitors ringing them. "We got cameras in every room, audio monitors, phone tappers, you name it. Sitting in this room tomorrow morning, we could see everything anybody was doing in the whole building—and listen in on them, and check out what they were doing on their computers, too."

"Yeah," Keyes shrugged off the kid's curiosity. "That's what they're paying us buckets of cash to do. They're a big biotech firm. They got lots of stuff they want to keep top secret. Now, quit yapping and keep testing. We got a lot to do tonight."

One more panel, one more series of green lights. Network taps up and running. The younger tech glanced around at the blank eyes of the monitors. "Keeping things top secret—or just hidden," he muttered.

"Yeah, like the dead bodies of slowpoke techs," Keyes growled, as a fountain of sparks hissed off a live connection. He sighed, glancing at his watch. "We're gonna need all the luck we can get."

* * *

"Good luck," Chris said out loud, as he pulled into his usual parking spot (out by one of the spindly trees in the Benson parking lot, well away from the hotly contested places near to the doors). "Not that you'll need it." He headed for his interview (one of the sad facts of modern corporate life was that you ended up interviewing for the same job multiple times, usually well after you'd gotten the job in the first place) whistling the insanely infectious theme song from one of Missy's cartoons.

The whistling got him a grin from one of the technicians installing some kind of equipment beside the smoked-glass doors of the building. "Good morning," he said. "How old's your kid?"

Chris grinned back. "She's nearly two—19 months. Yours?"

"He's three. Man, does that song get under your skin or what?" The tech's badge proclaimed "MedaGen" in large letters, the company's logo glittering from the holograph square in the corner; his name (Nick Tatopolous), rank (Technician), and serial number (53N82T).

"Under my skin, into my head, right through my ears, you name it," Chris agreed, glancing from Nick to the piles of boxes, wires, and other shiny bits to the other technician (who didn't seem interested in joining the conversation). "What's up?"

"Security arrangements," Nick told him, hefting one box. "This here's a retinal scanner. We'll put it right up there, inside the first door, 'bout head height. You walk up, put your card into the slot," he flicked his own ID card to illustrate, "look into the box, and it runs a laser over your eyeball. Takes a real detailed picture. Compares it to the picture they've got on file for you in the database. If it matches, the door unlocks, and you're in."

"And if it doesn't match?" Chris asked, looking at the pieces of the scanner. "Iron bars fall from the ceiling? Poison gas fills the space between the doors? Dobermans erupt from the floor?"

Nick laughed. "Wouldn't that be sweet? Nah—you just don't get in, and some receptionist chick hauls herself over here from the security desk to give you a crusty look and tell you to try it again. No big deal— if anybody gets real insistent about getting in, she calls security, and then the tough guys come to take you away. MedaGen's real serious about security." He leaned in confidentially. "There's a lot of that industrial espionage stuff goes on in the big leagues. They even got us installing those voice printers on the labs in here for extra measures."

"Don't those things have problems occasionally?" Chris asked, picturing himself locked out of his lab. "Like not recognizing your voice if you have a cold or something?"

"You don't get that much with the real top-of-the line models," Nick told him, then grinned again, elbowing Chris's arm. "Good reason to call in sick, though."

"You could'a called in sick, all the work you're getting done," the other tech growled. "Stop gabbing and start unpacking."

"Lighten up, Bob," Nick advised him. "We're on company time."

Chris smiled at both of them and went through the (for the moment) open doors. The argument faded behind him as he crossed the lobby into the neutral glare of a pair of unfamiliar security guards standing to either side of the reception desk. The bronze letters that had spelled out "Benson Bioceuticals" were already gone from the wall, leaving faded shadows behind. Another workman was busy extracting the silver-hologram MedaGen logo sign from its packing materials.

The receptionist herself hadn't changed, though her usual smile was tighter around the corners than usual. He laid his old Benson Bioceuticals ID on the desk for her. "Hi, Chris. Thanks," she said, taking his old access card and sliding a piece of laminated paper across the shiny surface in front of her. "Here's your temporary badge."

"Hi, Naomi. I see they've already got you rebranded," he observed, clipping the badge to his lapel.

Naomi touched her own badge, an official plastic card on a lanyard around her neck, its MedaGen logo glittering. She managed a more relaxed smile. "Yes, I had my interview at 7:00 this morning, first thing. They decided to keep me."

"Smart of them," Chris told her. "You're the life of the office. I've got mine in ten minutes."

"Let me buzz you through to Humphrey's office," she said. "All the interior doors are locked down, and since nobody has badges yet, you can't get into the labs until this afternoon."

"Nobody?" he asked, surprised. "But I've got to run the simulations for Protocol 4. It's been cooking, and the replications should be complete by now."

One of the security guards leaned in, uncrossing his massive arms. His badge didn't have a name, just a number and a larger MedaGen logo. With his impassive face, shaved head, and black uniform, he didn't really need an official "Security Guard" note on his badge, either. "Nobody gets into the labs today. You've been buzzed through. Get going."

Chris looked at him, contemplating a smart remark, then caught Naomi's frightened expression out of the corner of his eye. What did MedaGen think they had to hire these polished-up thugs to protect—or to hide? The thought tossed goose bumps along his arm. He shrugged off the irrational reaction and grinned at Naomi, ignoring the big man. "See you later, Naomi."

She smiled back. "See you later, Chris. Good luck!" She hit the button, opening the interior door.

"Not that I'll need it," he said jauntily, tossing her a salute and walking confidently into the administrative wing—Mahogany Row, as the secretaries called it.

Most of the doors to the executives' offices were still closed, the soft murmurs of confidential conversations leaking around the mid-level soundproofing. (Nick would probably get the work order for upgrading that to Level 10 SilentGuard by the end of the week, Chris thought.) The doors that stood open revealed hastily vacated desks, the shelves and desktops still littered with books, plants, ornaments, and files that the departing employees hadn't valued enough to bring home—or that the security personnel who packed the office hadn't bothered to include in the "personal effects" boxes.

Humphrey's door was open. Boxes, half filled, covered the desk and spilled onto the floor. So did stacks of files, manuals, certificates, all the detritus that accumulates in five years of living in an office. A low, continuous stream of irritated commentary came from the man packing them. Occasionally, as he tossed something onto the already overflowing trash can, the words rose toward audible levels. They definitely weren't pleasant.

"Careful, there—I think the sprinklers nearly heard you that time," Chris said. "At least they're letting you pack your own stuff instead of having one of those security gorillas do it for you."

Errol Humphrey looked up. He had the kind of face that advertising people and casting agents saw and instantly thought "business executive" or "prosecuting attorney"—square jaw, heavy brows, almost handsome but not quite. His mother may have caught a glimpse of that handsomeness when she named him Errol, hoping great things for her boy. His personality, however, had betrayed him, fitting far better with his last name. He had enough ambition to try to become his own boss through selling stock on his plans for future accomplishments, but not enough self-control to actually accomplish any of them.

Now he didn't have a boss so much as a landlord—as in the old feudal system that gave a lord rights over his land and the serfs that lived on them. If the land changed hands, so did the people, doing the same work for a different lord, forbidden from moving away on their own. Of course, the United States had outlawed chattel slavery a long time ago, and nobody actually owned Humphrey; they just owned his contract, a "noncompetition" clause that prevented him from changing jobs without their clearance. Everything he earned and produced for the rest of his life, less a thin allowance for living expenses and slender savings plan, belonged to them—until he accumulated enough capital to buy back a controlling share in his future from the Board. Benson Bioceuticals had bought Humphrey's services from PersonalSecurity, Inc., the company that had pioneered the future-stock market.

PersonalSecurity had started up years ago, buying life-insurance policies from people with terminal illnesses, paying out the face value of the policy up front, then collecting the actual money when the person finally died. AIDS patients had jumped for the service, spending their windfalls living luxuriously for the few months they thought they had left. With the improvement in AIDS and cancer treatments, however, these supposedly terminal patients found themselves with a lot more life left—and PersonalSecurity found itself holding policies for a lot longer than they'd wanted to. Through a combination of slick lawyering, lobbying, and the pervasive influence of business in government and law, PersonalSecurity won a series of court cases that established a precedent for buying stock not in a person's current productivity but future expectations of earnings. The example of a couple of pop stars who sold stock in the royalties from their future hits only bolstered PersonalSecurity, Inc.'s position, and business had boomed.

They gave Humphrey the advance on his personal stock that was supposed to help him set up a vastly profitable business. Instead, he spent the money on office furniture, expensive "business trips," and lavish parties to "impress future investors." He was less surprised than he expected when he got the official letter telling him that because the return on his stocks was less than projected in a three-year cycle, the Board had bought out his controlling interest.

PersonalSecurity arranged for him to work at Benson Bioceuticals, and now MedaGen, as a mid-level manager, seeing him as simply another company resource to be deployed to best effect to boost the company's bottom line. He produced at an acceptable (court-set) rate for them, so they let him walk around outside of jail. MedaGen accepted the deal because PersonalSecurity provided Humphrey's health insurance, guaranteed his performance, and demanded a lower rate of pay for him than they'd have to shell out for a free-agent employee. To Humphrey's credit, both his employer and the Board got most of their money's worth. He was an efficient, if uninspired, middle manager, and seemed resigned to working for the Board in return for a higher level of job security than he'd have otherwise. His three years of high living had at least taught him that he didn't have the drive to hustle jobs as a free agent. Accepting a lower pay rate and Big Brother leaning over his shoulder seemed a fair trade off, compared to the freedom to succeed—or starve. Of course, that didn't mean he didn't complain about it.

"Security gorillas," Humphrey snorted. "It's all the same no matter where you go. Get a college degree, pile up management experience, and you still get some goon with a high-school diploma ordering you around. Telling you to get out of the office that you earned—that you clawed your way up the ladder to get, no thanks to you—to clear it out for some MedaGen bigwig who won't even use it most of the time. Stuffing me in a cubicle down by the labs. Siddown, Galen. Might as well get down to business."

Chris settled into the visitor chair and raised an eyebrow at his manager. "Gee, down by the labs like the rest of us. How are you ever going to survive?"

Humphrey gave him an irritated look and flopped into the leather executive chair. He had to move a box aside on his desk to see Chris. "Get smart with me because you know they're keeping you around, huh?" He tossed a contract across the desk to Chris. "Laugh it up, Wonderboy. You may be one of the hottest guys in genetic-marker research, but there's always somebody coming up the ladder, snapping at your heels." He sighed. "For now, though, you're gold. MedaGen's heavy into that whole stem-cell research that's blowing up a storm in Europe; they got their pet senator to pass an exclusion for them. They need your team to unravel all that protein spaghetti and make them a billion dollars finding a cure for obesity, impotence, and saggy a—"

"Which is why I don't know if I want to sign this," Chris interrupted, riffling through the contract. It was a pretty standard independent contract, offering a set salary, possible bonuses for patents, a thin line of insurance, and the option to renegotiate in a year's time, if either party didn't terminate the contract first.

Humphrey rolled his eyes. "What? You like fat broads? I thought your wife was a skinny—"

"Don't mention my wife," Chris interrupted again, this time with a lot more heat. "That's over the line, Errol." He waited until Humphrey shrugged and nodded in half apology before he continued. "I'm serious here. I don't like stem-cell research—I think it's an expensive dead end, compared to other methods of genetic therapy. Plus, according to the article one of their researchers published in the *Frontiers of Genetics* journal last year, they're still committed to using stem cells from aborted babies. I won't do that." He glanced at the contract. "Not even for what they're offering."

"Listen to the rational, empirical scientist talking," Humphrey said sarcastically, then leaned forward, his voice still sharp but more serious. "Chris, pull your head out. MedaGen's the biggest game in town. You've got the brains they know they need, and you may be really on to something with the research you've been doing around here. You want somebody to put muscle behind all those protocols you're fiddling with, they're the ones who can do it. You think Myriad Genetics can provide the lab equipment and assistants you need? Like fun they can. So tell the new bosses you won't work with stem cells if you have to, but don't walk away from a fat contract and the chance to make a real difference. Butch up about all that teenage idealism. You're a grown-up now—with a family to support and all. Don't be more of an idiot than Mormons can help, throwing it out over some theoretical fetuses you couldn't save anyway."

Chris looked at Humphrey for a long minute, neither of them moving. Finally, he leaned back in his chair. "And that's why they keep you on, isn't it? When are you going to pull your own head out and buy your contract back?"

"What, and miss out on all the perks of being an indentured servant?" Humphrey's sarcasm snapped back in place. "Go ahead and take a day off to 'consider the offer.' I'll keep your badge warm for you. Maybe you'll even get lucky and they'll get spooked enough to add another zero to the salary they're throwing out. But don't count on it. This whole business sector is shaking down, consolidating, and it's all under MedaGen's big, happy umbrella. Believe me, they bought Benson Bioceuticals as part of an overall power play upstairs. This is just the beginning of MedaGen's bid for total world domination. Things are really going to heat up from here."

* * *

Dear Chisom,

With the exception of the early heat wave we're suffering, life is going well here in Missouri. Along the West Coast over the past month, the situation is improving in much the same way as you report in Taiwan. The government will soon be pulling out the National Guard from parts of California and removing the restraints of martial law. I still can't believe that people took advantage of the period of chaos to loot and rob. And the estimated numbers of looters—staggering. What a wicked world we live in!

In contrast, I must say that I am pleased you are able to spend so much of your time teaching the gospel. I am not a bit surprised that the missionaries are finding many doors opening. The earthquake shattered more than houses. It also shattered old ways of thinking and, thus, forced people to take a hard look at their belief systems. That in turn caused them to ask new questions. The Church will see growth in the Far East because of this.

I was pleased with your report that the temple sustained little damage and was back in full service a week ago. The news out of San Francisco is sad. Reports tell of startling discoveries concerning the collapse of a number of supposedly earthquake-resistant complexes. Investigators have found that certain contractors and inspectors had joined together secretly agreeing to use substandard materials and short-cut methods to make higher profits. Well, they made their money at the expense of hundreds of lives lost in those buildings. Many are wondering what buildings in other cities are unsafe as well. I tell you, son, Babylon is alive—as the news shows. The Church's insistence on using top-grade materials, its own contractors and inspection teams, as well as following building codes, (along with a little divine help) has really paid off this time.

You asked about the Great and Abominable Church of the Devil as found in 1 Nephi 13 and 14 and if this is the same as Babylon the Great, the Mother of Harlots referred to in Revelation 17 and 18. The simple answer is, Yes. These are just different names for Satan's church. The word church, however, has a broader meaning than you may think. The word translates an ancient term that designated more than a religious congregation. It described any association where people are bound together by mutual interest and cause. What Nephi saw was an assemblage of people bound together by the devil to promote that which God hates. The scriptures use the term Babylon to symbolize such assemblages (for there is more than one) and what they do.

Nephi gives a clear description of her major characteristics. Babylon dominates the world (14:11); early in her career, she excised important truths and covenants from the Bible (13:26–29); after that she moved on to influence governments and businesses; she promotes sexual immorality (13:7); she seeks wealth and luxury (13:7–8); and finally, she persecutes and, when she can, destroys the righteous and innocent (13:5). All in all, she is the arch enemy of God and His kingdom.

As you noted, in chapter 14:10, Nephi clearly states, there are save two churches only; the one is the church of the Lamb of God, and the other is the church of the devil. So how can there be only two if Babylon is but one among many? The answer is that chapter 13 is talking about an actual historical institution, while chapter 14 uses the term symbolically. According to Nephi's symbolism, there can be only one true Church, the one with the saving keys. All other churches must be false because they cannot deliver on their promise to bring one to eternal life.

What you must get clear, however, is that association with one or the other is determined by loyalty rather than by membership. There are Latter-day Saints whose lifestyle shows a loyalty to Satan and who, therefore, belong to the church of the devil. Conversely, there are those not yet in our Church who, due to their love and loyalty to the Lord, are members of the Church of the Lamb. These are the ones who will hear the Master's voice calling through you. Your task is to find them and get them into the formal institution where they can thrive in a fullness of truth.

The scriptures dealing with her are a bit frightening—knowing that right now Babylon is alive and well, growing in strength and power, ever seducing more to her cause, and willing to destroy any who get in her way.

I hope this helps you with these chapters and also allows you to see the importance of your work. We offer counterpoint to her seductions and can bring people hope and joy. I'll return to the subject of Babylon in a later letter. For now, know of my love and respect.

Your father,

Chinedu

* * *

Random chatter filled the conference room where the MedaGen Board held its meetings. The deep-pile carpet, hand-worked tapestry hangings, and smooth leather upholstery—along with the state-of-the-art, sound-dampening material in the walls and ceiling—absorbed and softened the voices of the Assistant Vice Presidents, Vice Presidents, and other corporate officers milling around the big room speculating on their superiors' plans. The same kind of thing happened in every corporate meeting at every level of any company: the boss calls the meeting, the employees gather on time or close to it, gossip, sound out coworkers, jockey for position, and trade company rumors while they wait for the boss to arrive. Each of the occupants of the conference room usually played the superior role in this play, supposedly too important or busy to get to their own meetings on time, thus providing nervous subordinates with plenty of time to stew over possible developments. Only a couple of the executives currently waiting in the room were aware enough of it to appreciate the irony, however.

At last, two solemn attendants opened both sides of the double door. This caused a sudden flurry of activity, as MedaGen's administrative corps dropped their small talk and hurried to take their places at the long, obsidian-black table running down the center of the room like a sheet of frozen ink. A man and a woman appeared in the doorway, back lit by the light from the wall of windows in the reception area.

"Ah, here they are at last, Alpha and Omega," snided Whittier, a relatively new member of the board. He'd discreetly assisted in MedaGen's hostile takeover of the company at which he had been

Vice President, and in reward he received the appointment to run his former business as a subsidiary of MedaGen.

His neighbor, Abdullah, a veteran of MedaGen's boardroom wars, merely smiled blandly. "Speak directly into the sprinklers, Whittier." (Actually, the audio pickups studding the room were hidden in the mother-of-pearl buttons studding the soundproofing hangings on the walls. The backup video cameras lurked next to the fire-control sprinklers.)

Abbott, CEO of MedaGen, strode into the room with glinting, dominant smiles for everyone. From the top of his perfectly waved, just slightly graying head to the toes of his mirror-polished, tooled-leather boots, he exuded the kind of elegant confidence that MedaGen marketed almost as much as their actual genetically based medical products. He patted a select few on the shoulder, greeting them by name, ensuring their continued rise up the corporate ladder; nodded to others whose work merited their continuance with the company, if not the favor of his official recognition; and cut one unfortunate (and incompetent) board member dead. That man, recognizing the corporate equivalent of the Black Spot and knowing his days in MedaGen's employ were numbered, summoned enough courage to keep from breaking down in front of everyone. His neighbors slid their chairs a little further from his, as if to edge away from contagion. They resolutely avoided glancing in his direction.

Only Zelik, MedaGen's Chief Operations Officer, bucked the trend of shunning the marked man. She stopped beside his chair, laid one long-fingered, long-nailed hand on his shoulder, and gave him a smile that had all the tender warmth of a display of enamel-handled scalpels. "Come see me after the meeting, Kerr. We'll talk."

She continued down the table to her place at the foot, a small pocket of chilled silence spreading around her as she passed. The clicking of her (untrendy but evocative) spiked heels disappeared into the carpet but echoed in everyone's minds. She spoke to no one else, settling into her chair and flicking on the digital display under the table's surface with a sharp tap of one equally sharp nail. She sat back, steepled her fingers, and regarded Abbott's empty chair below the MedaGen logo with a steady, freezing gaze down the length of the table. No one tried to catch her eye.

Abbott at last worked his way around the room, his warm voice booming through the quiet as he tossed off comments, asked after families, reminded his listeners of the importance of their projects to the company. After thus reminding each of his subordinates that he knew what was going on in their divisions (departments, labs, and personal lives) and bestowing his marks of favor on the current favorites, he came to a stop beside his own leather-upholstered throne. Before sitting, however, he swept the assembled executives with a bright smile and regaled them with the obligatory scandalous joke about a politician opposing MedaGen interests. He got the expected (practically required) laugh, which he joined in.

"Now, remember, boys and girls, if anybody objects to my using such language in a professional setting," he assured them, "he or she is welcome to talk to Ms. Zelik about it."

Another titter, this one distinctly nervous, greeted that suggestion.

"So, if we have no objections, are we ready to begin?" Abbott asked.

"If you've finished entertaining the troops," Zelik told him, the words lightly etched in acid.

"I've warmed them up for you," Abbott responded with a smile. "Go ahead and administer the *coup de grace*." (Well-hidden winces greeted that turn of phrase; Whittier grinned.)

"If you will check your readouts," Zelik ordered, "you will see that our takeover of Benson Bioceuticals is officially complete. The Federal Securities and Exchange Commission approved the sale two days ago, and the final transfer of ownership took effect last night at midnight. Benson Bioceuticals was the third-largest biotech research and development company in the United States, and they are now a division of MedaGen."

Scattered applause greeted this news, along with whispers up and down the table.

"The acquisition will affect the structure of the current Research & Development arm. New organizational charts and tables of authority will arrive in your e-mail boxes shortly." She favored them with a new-moon smile.

"That can't be good," Whittier whispered to his neighbor, "if the Ice Queen's smiling about it."

"Shh," Abdullah hissed, not looking at the younger man. Zelik's glance did flick his way, however.

"Congratulations to all involved in the Benson Bioceuticals victory," Abbott proclaimed. "And congratulations also to Reiko Ishihara and her European operations team!" The executive in question smiled and nodded as the board politely applauded her. "Thanks to their tireless efforts—we'll slip a little extra into your budget to cover all those bribes, Reiko" (he winked at his audience, receiving an appreciative laugh in return) "—our penetration into the European market is going very well; as of last week, we've got the BritPharm people officially on the run. If Reiko's team keeps up its sterling work, it'll hand us the contract as exclusive hospital suppliers for all of Europe. Just more proof, boys and girls, that a socialized system can't stand up to the determined assault of capitalism."

"Getting market share in Europe is great," Whittier observed when the applause died down. "But my division does domestic R&D. What about the opposition to our research here in the United States? We've had protesters picketing outside our lab in San Jose every day this week."

Abbott sized him up with a long look, then grinned expansively. "Whittier, isn't it? New on the team since you sold out your grandpa's drug company. That hairstyle does a lot for you, lad—the gel helps cover up the water behind your ears."

Whittier kept his wry smile in place as the laughter wore itself out. "I may be new to MedaGen, but I know a PR problem when I see one. If the pro-life brigades keep this up, we're going to have a hard time getting our stem-cell exemption extended."

"It's not the pro-lifers that are the main problem," Zelik corrected. "They've got a bad reputation and less respect with the moderate voter—and the moderate voter's politician."

"Exactly," Abbott said, his voice dropping to drive home the seriousness of the point he was about to make. "The most delicate problem facing us now is the opposition of various Luddite groups to most advances in bio-genetic research. An organized, competent protest group could foreseeably interfere with our plans to roll out our latest breakthrough, the Corinth vaccine. We'll need dependable, strong political backing to implement our solution to the world's epidemics, which means we'll have to outsmart and out-maneuver potential opponents."

He tapped the table to display a list of those potential opponents. Thanks to MedaGen's aggressive acquisition policies, no other biotech companies appeared on the list. All possible competitors had been devoured or weakened badly enough to represent no threat.

"The Universal Baptists and others are vocal," he noted, highlighting the fourth entry in the list, The Church of Jesus Christ of Latter-day Saints. "But it's this one, the outfit most of the media's been dismissing as a wacko cult, that's the biggest and most organized threat."

"A wacko cult doesn't sound like much of a threat," Whittier remarked.

Abbott shot him another sharp smile. "Lesson two, junior—don't buy your own propaganda. This outfit has deep pockets, a historic aversion to progressive social legislation, and a whole stable full of smart and competent people. Blast their hides." His exaggerated, Southern-accented curse undercut the Church's potential for causing trouble and got him another laugh.

Zelik clicked the table with her talons again, bringing up the Church's Web site. For a second, the image of Christ glowed through the MedaGen logo reflected in the table. Next to the Church's site, results from polls in six states showed results of opinion surveys on abortion, euthanasia, gay marriage, and other examples of what Abbot called "progressive legislation."

"As you can see from these results," Zelik stated, "the Church exerts a significant political influence on the more ignorant voter. Unfortunately, their members usually *are* voters, unlike most other populations who historically oppose our industry. The Church also has expanded its holdings in recent years to include pharmaceutical plantations and processing plants. So, as a company, we made certain—overtures—to the Church's Board of Trustees, offering them opportunities for research partnerships, rain-forest property, and other necessary industries—"

"But the Church won't play," Abbott finished for her, earning a cool look. He glared around the room, then smiled smugly. "Let them try to gather all the grass-roots support they'd like among the fundamentalist crowd. We, due to my own efforts, have an ace in the hole. Senator Howard W. Garlick, senior member of the Senate, key man on several committees vital to our interests, and long-time political game player, is in our pocket. Thanks to some brilliant negotiations—and detective work—by our own Ms. Zelik, the good senator has agreed to help MedaGen achieve the federal recognition and support we need to successfully roll out the Corinth vaccine."

"Now we can just hope he's an honest politician—meaning he stays bought," Whittier observed to Abdullah during the applause.

"Yes, yes, that's a coup," Abbott agreed. "But we've got more. After we sweep the governmental roadblocks out of the way, all we have to do is sell the product. And we've got the perfect new ad campaign, guaranteed to send our profits—and stock prices—through the roof." With a flourish, he unveiled the posters. Virginia Diamante pouted smolderingly up into the executives' faces, slithering seductively over satin pillows, running scantily clad through a field of flower-studded grass, as the narrator extolled the virtues of "living free." The ad ended with a close-up of Virginia (starting at belly level and rising slowly to her face) as she whispered, "Consequences? Never!"

She got a bigger round of applause than the Senator had (though, to be fair, they hadn't seen a video of him—which, considering the type of video Madison Avenue liked to use, that was probably a good thing). Abbott beamed, preening with the triumph and his subordinates' adoration. Zelik rolled her eyes, whether at Virginia herself, the ads, or the male executives' reaction to both, she gave no indication. Neither of the other women sitting at the table visibly echoed her reaction, however.

Abbott let the applause and excited chatter go until just before the reaction got cold, then brought his hands together in a resounding clap. "That's it, boys and girls—we're poised to blow the competition out of the water forever. Get out there and make it happen! Make me proud of you—and don't disappoint Ms. Zelik!" He bestowed a brilliant smile on them and strode out of the room, the liveried attendants opening the double door for his dramatic exit.

Whittier clapped for the exit. Abdullah closed his eyes wearily, while a few others glanced at Whittier with wide eyes. No one laughed.

Zelik simply smiled, showing her arctic-white teeth, as she rose to her feet. (The executives quickly followed, gathering their briefcases and PDDs for a quick getaway.) She paused as she drew even with Whittier. "You're still new here," she noted.

"First board meeting," he agreed, trying to look casual in his seat as she stood over him, just close enough to make him crane his neck to look up at her.

"Ignorance, as the police say, is no excuse," she snapped. "Nobody here is impressed by insubordination. Keep a professional demeanor, Mr. Whittier, or you won't need to send in a resignation." She gazed at him, judging the effect of her threat, driving the point home with her cold eyes and a final question. "Is that clear?"

"Crystal," he said, but a slight catch in his throat marred the flippancy of the crisp military reply. So did the slight hunch of his shoulders as he scuttled back to his own cozy headquarters, the office that used to belong to his grandfather.

CHAPTER 5

Abuelo's official headquarters wasn't much to look at (definitely no carpets, carvings, or cameras), but it always smelled good. The aroma of fresh-made tortillas, chili peppers, and hot meat enveloped Dove as he slipped into the kitchen entrance of Mama Rosa's. From the front, the restaurant *Abuelo* adopted as his office/home away from home looked like any other run-down taco joint in town; from the kitchen, it looked exactly like the small slice of Mexican-flavored heaven it was. The actual Mama Rosa, if there had been a real woman behind the clichéd name, had died a long time ago. Her smiling portrait on the sign outside showed a plump, often-retouched testament to her legendary existence, but now Franklin kept the stove fire—and the restaurant's secret recipes—hot. Franklin wasn't an official member of *Abuelo's* gang, but he didn't mind the extra security that came from having a dozen or so of the toughest *muchachos* in town as regular customers. Nobody ever got in Franklin's face, let alone robbed the restaurant, and *Abuelo* paid him enough to make up for any mooching.

Dove slid a hot tortilla off the tray, got a white-and-silver smile from the cook, and settled down on the rickety chair beside the stove to read his own book instead of doing homework.

"School go all right?" Franklin asked, his long, dark hands slapping another set of tortillas onto the sizzling oil-drum cooker.

"Talked my way out of detention," Dove told him. "Dogmobile got us there late. Again."

"You oughta take that bike of yours, save you being late and talking your way out of hot water. That where your buddies are? Detention?" Franklin's expression indicated the empty chairs around

Dove, the lack of fellow homework shirkers. "Thought you'd get them off, too."

Dove grinned. "I did. Then Calvin and Perro couldn't keep their mouths shut, and they both got tossed."

"Yeah, maybe they'll get their assignments done, unlike you. What trash you reading now?" Franklin nodded toward the book in Dove's lap.

"Without me, they wouldn't be in school *or* do homework," Dove said. "And hey, this stuff is research for a Social Studies paper—one on Current Themes, too."

"And what's that?" Franklin asked, angling for a look at the cover. "How the world's going to —— in a handbasket? How the Rez got more drunks than the border's got druggies? How it's the White Man holding all us colored folk down?"

Dove's eyes got even darker. "Yeah, something like that. Teacher don't like us saying we gotta stop being victims and blaming the Man for all our problems. Makes 'em nervous when we think for ourselves. Makes 'em think maybe we don't need their help to get strong." He opened the book, flipping to the page he'd marked with a twenty-dollar bill, part of his share from burning the *Brujos* out of the warehouse.

Franklin shrugged, turning back to tossing chopped jalapenos into his enchilada filling. "At least you're reading something real. That King Arthur and all your Japanese soldiers are far out already—it's that Batman stuff got me worried."

The noise of boots and voices in the back room jarred Dove out of his research (though *The Warrior in Traditional Navajo Ritual and Religion: Harmony in War* wasn't exactly what his social-studies teacher had in mind when she gave the assignment to the class to find out about their "traditional values") a few minutes later. The noise itself wasn't unusual; it just meant that *Abuelo* had come in for the night. The unusual bit was the lack of joking, arguing, and general banter. From the sound of it, most of the senior soldiers had come in, and they'd come in serious. The scrape of chairs came through the kitchen door clearly, through the odd silence.

Dove put the book back in his backpack and slipped over to the storeroom door. Mama Rosa's storeroom was *Abuelo's* Oval Office, the place where all professional negotiations and nonlethal diplomacy took place. And from the look of it, negotiations were about to begin. Serious negotiations, too; *Abuelo's* glittering, demanding arm candy, Sasha, wasn't included in the group. Neither were Dolores or the other girls, just *Abuelo's* top lieutenants and soldiers. Dove wasn't technically a senior soldier—more like a valuable but unpredictable young pup—but he had no intention of being left out. He slipped through the door.

Abuelo, all of 37 years old and veteran of more street fights, gang wars, and run-ins with *federales* than his younger followers could imagine, presided over the borderland gang like the domineering patriarch they expected him to be. He lacked the gentle kindness of Dove's real grandfather, but the gang members all knew he cared about them, even if he saw them more as tactical assets than family members. The sight of him sitting across the table from a slick-looking stranger brought Dove up short. The overall scene fit the usual parameters: the two big dogs regarding each other over a pair of glasses and a single bottle, each with tense lieutenants ranged behind him. The thing that hit him like a brick was the identity of the visiting dignitary: the *Brujos'* smooth-combed, cold-eyed leader from the warehouse.

"What the—" he yipped, protesting before he even thought of something coherent to say.

Slick looked at him, a flicker of icy smile breaking his impartial expression as he recognized Dove, too. *Abuelo* didn't smile or even look over. Benny did that, giving his little brother the eye. Rico gave him a hard look too, but it was Benny's wordless warning that made Dove back out of the room, swallowing both questions and objections.

Franklin glanced at him as he dropped his bag by the chair and raced into the *baño*. He leaned against the graffiti-covered wall next to the sink, his eye in line with the crack beside the mirror. The eaves-dropper's post was intentional; occasionally, *Abuelo* dealt with people who couldn't be trusted not to bring assassins to the meeting, so *Abuelo* made sure he had his own assassins ready when necessary. From this angle, Dove couldn't see much of what happened on the table itself, just possible targets—the back of *Abuelo's* head, Benny's denim-covered shoulder, Slick's full face and torso—but the Spanglish negotiations came through clearly.

"*El General* is looking for soldiers," Slick informed *Abuelo*. "You have a reputation that makes him think you may be the ones he needs."

"How much is he paying?" Rico asked. "And what's the job?"

"What do we know about this General?" Benny cut through Rico's mercenary questions. "You tell us who we're talking about, we maybe think about it."

The incipient argument between Benny and Rico ended abruptly, as *Abuelo* coolly, dispassionately, and thoroughly cussed them both out in Navajo. Rico didn't understand as many of the words as Benny did, but they both got the point and shut up.

"We're soldiers," *Abuelo* conceded. "But we don't fight unless it's worth our time."

"Soldiers have no reason to live without a war," Slick pointed out. "The General wants men with the courage and cleverness to make his missions successful."

"Or die for his cause, like the *Brujos*?" Benny asked.

Slick shrugged, his open hand brushing the *Brujos* off as a subject not worth his consideration. "The *Brujos* are thugs, muscle without brains. Good enough for grunt work but not much else—as you found out for yourselves. The General needs professionals for specialized operations. Your raid against the *Brujos* impressed him."

"Professionals work for pay," *Abuelo* informed him. "And right now, *Señor* pays us to fight his battles. If your General can offer more, we may work for him. If not, you'll find out how impressed the General's going to be with our raids."

Slick nodded. "Practical." He slid an envelope across the table and rose to his feet, straightening his leather jacket. "An initial offer—and token of the General's appreciation for your reputation. Plus a test, to see if you have the brains he's looking for. I'll be back for your answer and to drop off the practical portion of the exam." He saluted *Abuelo* and sauntered out, his men falling in behind him.

Abuelo waited until Slick's polished boots had clicked out through Mama Rosa's swinging doors, then shoved the envelope over to Stripes. Stripes flicked out his knife and slit the manila flap, carefully sliding out the papers within, wary of possible booby traps. A bomb was unlikely, given the thinness of the envelope, but poison—

either straight out or bacterial—was always a possibility. A thin sheaf of photos, maps, and printouts spread over the table, without a trace of suspicious powder. *Abuelo* perused them slowly, as Benny and Rico restrained themselves from crowding in to read over his shoulder.

Finally, *Abuelo* put the General's proposal down, shoving the pages toward his lieutenants. "Pretty much like the *Señor's* deal," he told them. "Protection, peacekeeping, turf guarding."

"Some smuggling stuff over the border," Benny added, tapping the paper. "Maybe some smuggling people over the border. We're not drug runners—or coyotes."

"He's paying better than the *Señor*," Rico pointed out. "Twice more. And he's promising better supplies, too—and weapons. Look at this list!" He passed the catalog sheet to Marco, who whistled.

"For what?" Benny asked. "You ask me, this looks like a cartel move. This General's a dust runner for sure. The *Señor's* not clean, but he's not that dirty."

"Clean, dirty, what does it matter?" Rico snorted.

"It matters," Dove burst into the storeroom. "We don't work for dusters or coyotes."

"Call you cockroach, not dove," Rico growled. "Jumping out of dark corners to run where you're not wanted."

"Big weapons just mean big money, not smarts or honor," Dove informed *Abuelo*—and, more importantly, Perro and Calvin, who had finally arrived back at Mama Rosa's from detention and found themselves in the middle of another of Dove and Benny's confrontations with Rico and his coterie.

"Honor?" Rico rolled his eyes. "What's honor?"

"Bushy do," Perro attempted to clarify, with his usual tin ear for sarcasm. "Like them Japanese guys—"

"*Bushido*," Dove corrected. "The code of the samurai."

"You're a border rat!" Rico exploded. "You're a Navajo border rat. You *got* no honor! You got nothing but what *Abuelo* gives you! And you'll shut up and thank him for it!"

"How do I thank anybody if I shut up?" Dove snapped back, his hands (like Rico's) coming up to defend or attack. They faced each other in thick silence, Rico taller and more experienced, Dove faster and young enough to be reckless. The rest of the gang held back, most of them withholding judgment for the moment. Perro and Calvin, however, watched with excitement in their eyes, while Marco and Stripes followed the exchange disdainfully.

Abuelo didn't look at either of them; he flicked through the papers again, then gazed steadily at Benny.

"Cool it, *Hasbìdì*," Benny stepped between his little brother and Rico. It didn't earn him kind looks from either one. "Chill, Rico. Japanese guys got nothing to do with this."

"South Americans do," Calvin observed, looking up from the papers he'd slipped over to peruse when he realized that tonight wasn't the night that Dove would take Rico down. "Rich ones, too."

"South Americans got nothing to do with us," Perro said, attempting to light a cigarette. Dove snatched it from him and flicked him with it.

"South Americans got as much to do with us as the *Señor*," Marco pointed out.

Everybody else jumped in too, arguing for or against Slick's proposal. Benny and Dove (with about a third of the gang) argued against getting mixed up with an unknown dust runner who'd already hired the *Brujos*. Rico argued just as loudly (and more profanely) that he'd heard that the General was going places, and they could either go with the next wave or get drowned. Besides, he argued, this proved that the General recognized that he could either fight them or hire them—and he'd rather not fight them. That got a round of satisfied nods and oaths in agreement.

"Enough!" *Abuelo* brought his hands down on the table with a crack that brought everyone's eyes back to him. "We could use the cash. Expenses have been up. I've also heard the General has major operations going down. We play this right, we can get a piece of it. He plays this right, he maybe gets a piece of us. Let him come back with the job. I'll tell you if we go for it. Got it?" He looked around the room, locking eyes with each of them. Satisfied with what he saw, he sat back in his chair. "Looks like we got that all clear now."

Marco swept up the packet and tucked the papers back into the envelope as *Abuelo* shouted, "Franklin! Get your lazy tail in here with the enchiladas!"

* * *

"Yup, that's pretty much clear as bells," Merry sighed, as she tossed the glossy company prospectus onto the table. "They're up to their elbows in using babies as ingredients in their products, all right." She shuddered. "How they can sit there with straight faces and explain that they're not killing anybody is totally beyond me."

Chris rubbed her shoulder as he paced by her chair. He'd been circling the kitchen table for the last half hour, as they leafed through MedaGen's business plan, advertisements, latest shareholder report, Web site, employee packet, and selected news transcripts. "It's not all that hard, really," he told her. "The official line is that an embryo's not a person, just a set of cells with the potential to become a person. Once you separate being from becoming, you're nearly home free. Add on the argument that you're using that potential to decrease current suffering without actually causing suffering, and it's pretty well all roses."

"It's Babylon, is what it is," Merry growled. "Turning people into profit. This is just more direct than usual." She reached down to pet Missy's hair. Missy had co-opted a pile of discarded ads and was happily reducing them to paper wads, singing to herself.

Chris nodded, flopped into the other chair, and sighed. "Okay, that's it—I go back tomorrow and toss this employee handbook right back in Humphrey's face. Game over."

"Don't resign yet," Merry said slowly.

"No?" Chris raised an eyebrow. "I thought we just agreed that MedaGen was the next closest thing to the Devil's own playground, babies to bucks and all."

"Don't get sarcastic," Merry cautioned. "I know I'm coming down on them really hard, but Chris, look. You've got two other offers, only one of which is even serious. Humphrey, much as I hate to admit it, was right about one thing: since MedaGen bought out Benson Bioceuticals, there really isn't anybody else in the US who can support the kind of research you're doing, and BritPharm is clear over in Scotland. Not that you wouldn't make a lovely Scotsman—"

"And I thank you for that, m'dear," Chris told her, using the Amulek accent.

She grinned, then sobered again. "Seriously, with how destabilized Europe's getting, I'd rather not go there. At least here we've still got a reasonable chance of making a living. And with MedaGen, you've got a better than reasonable chance of actually coming up with a permanent cure for diabetes. You'll still be working on your own gene therapy, not with their new cell lines, and when you succeed, you'll show them that they don't have to work with aborted embryos to get results that really work."

"So you're advocating the old 'worm your way in and effect change from the inside' ploy, huh?" he asked. "It's a strange day when you start to sound like Humphrey, and when I find myself agreeing with both of you. Merry, are you sure about this?"

"Study it out in your mind, then ask," Merry paraphrased. "I'm ready to ask if you are."

* * *

"That's the problem with asking," Chris told her the next day, as he picked up Missy and gently removed her socks from her hands. She laughed and waved the freed digits, grabbing for her daddy's nose. He got hers first and tickled her before handing her off to her mommy so he could straighten his tie. "Sometimes you get the most inconvenient answers." He sighed and looked at Merry with big, Bambi eyes. "Are you sure I have to do this? I'd really rather stay home and make cookies with you and Missy. Or I could be the house husband and hang around with Missy eating bonbons, taking bubble baths, and reading novels until you brought home the bacon."

Merry grinned. "Sorry, bucko, no bonbons in your future. Somebody's got to be the breadwinner around here, and you're officially elected. Get out there and use that professionally trained mind to make the world a better place while Missy and I work on learning colors." She swallowed the mixed emotions that rose in the back of her mind and continued lightly, "Tell you what—we'll make cookies today so you'll have some when you get home. In the meantime," she swung Missy over and handed him a brown paper sack, "here's your lunch. Go get 'em."

"Lunch," Missy sang. "Lunch, dad a dad a dad!"

"What more do I need to face the world, besides lunch and kisses from my ladies?" Chris asked, collecting both.

By the time he had spent a half hour on the road, however, Chris figured out the other thing he needed to face the world: a better route to work. The cars in front of him abruptly slowed to a crawl, then to a complete stop. Far down the road, he could see flashing lights clustered around the downtown exit. Great. First day of work—well, so to speak—and he was stuck in a traffic jam. He flicked on the radio, scanning through the stations to find a traffic report.

"Another bomb threat against the Mayor, police chief, and city government officials has closed all access to the Mayor's Office, the City Council chamber, and all of City Hall. Looks like homegrown wackos this time, with a crayoned note protesting the government's discrimination against crackers," the traffic bunny informed him, her tone right between newswoman professional and radio-sidekick sarcastic. "The police department is still open, though, so better be careful about speeding through any roadblocks. There's been a complete security lockdown of all the main entry points, and the normal traffic has been diverted off onto the freeways and surface streets. Looks like slow to dead traffic in all directions. If you can, take an alternate route—"

"And what if we're already stuck in the dead traffic?" Chris asked her.

"And if you can't, take a toke of whatever you're smoking, 'cause you're going to be there for awhile," she answered—not Chris, of course, but the DJ, who'd asked the same question. He thought her answer was a lot funnier than Chris did.

After he caught his breath from laughing, the DJ bade the traffic girl good-bye (she was already giving the same report on another station—suitably edited for an "adult contemporary" format, of course), and continued, "Speaking of smoking, we're back to Southern California's favorite show, the Top 7 at 7. We've got our number one up next, Virginia's chart-busting single, 'Leave It, Love Me.'" The song queued up, its sinuous beat winding under the DJ's blathering on. "Remember, the Top 7 at 7—and Virginia herself—are sponsored by Sexcape Records. Be ready to call in *en flagrante*—if you know what I mean—for tickets to—"

"Gack!" Chris said, hitting the scan button. Stupidly vulgar radio contests were bad enough, but the combination of that with pop's most recent Delilah was just too much. Virginia, in voice or visual, just didn't appeal to him. Oh, sure, she appealed to his hormones—the "natural man," as his dad had euphemistically put it—but the whole package (sex, selfishness, and a wantonness that came across as cruelty) gave him a sick knot in his stomach. That knot got tighter when he thought about what Missy might learn from creatures like Virginia. It was bad enough to know that Merry already had to deal with society's presold ideal of the "perfect" body and "free" behavior Virginia represented.

"Love—love of neighbor, but also love of self," exhorted the preacher femme on the next channel. "Love thy neighbor as thyself, said the Lord. Doesn't that mean that we need to love ourselves? And doesn't that mean accepting ourselves? God loves you, and you should love you, too—'

Great, Chris thought. *One extreme to the other, from total selfishness and lust to total selfishness and pride, and neither one comes close to the truth.* He hit the scan button again automatically. Commercials poured into his ears, unnoticed, as another thought occurred to him. Real truth, teaching—yipes! He'd better get hold of his home-teaching families.

He turned off the radio and flicked on the voice-activated PhoneWeb connection in the car. "Call the Simpsons, Hollises, and Sanchez family," he directed the phone. It beeped once to register that it understood and waited for further instructions. "Have their machine call my machine when they're home and tell me that they're available to take a call." The light on the dash glowed green, then settled into a softly pulsing throb, letting him know that it was biding its time in the electronic ether until it could fulfill his command.

"Computers," he said aloud, quickly adding, "No, not you! No command," when the connection glowed yellow again, waiting for him to tell it to do something else. "Pretty amazing."

The change at Benson Bioceuticals was also pretty amazing. Friendly Nick and his silent partner had vanished, but the black-glass entrance bore vivid testimony to their efforts: the retinal scanner stood silent sentry duty between the doors, at once innocuous and deeply threatening. Inconvenient, too—the specs had probably told Nick to place the reader at eye level for "the average person of 5'8", which meant that Chris, slightly taller at 6'1", had to scrunch down a bit to look directly into the target. It ran its laser-beam sensor over Chris's iris, comparing that record to the one registered for his temporary employee ID.

"Access granted." The text display below the scanner spelled out the words as an impersonal, androgynous voice spoke them aloud. "Doctor Christopher Galen. You have two grace instances before your temporary employee ID expires. See the receptionist to register for a permanent ID."

The door whooshed open, allowing him into MedaGen's newest temple. Naomi handed over his permanent ID with a smile. The security guards, still standing stiffly in their intimidating MedaGen uniforms, didn't even acknowledge his presence, their gimlet eyes focused on the doorway.

"Have you fed them today, Naomi?" Chris asked under his breath. "They're watching that door like they're expecting a doughnut delivery at any minute." He caught a flicker of spark in the mustachioed guard's eye, all professional malice. "Or maybe something from the butcher's," he amended.

Naomi gave him a worried smile. "Hope you have a good day, Chris," she hinted.

"You too, Naomi," he told her, taking the hint and clipping the hook for his permanent employee badge to his lapel. The MedaGen logo glinted in holographic rainbows. "There. Just like new. Welcome to the family!" He tossed a jaunty salute to the guards, neatly swiped his card through the scanner on the door to the lab areas, and strode confidently into his own inner sanctum.

His grin faded slightly at the voice printer guarding access to his own work area, but the machine accepted both his name and his vocal chords as belonging to the real Chris Galen. The trusty computer console in his lab, however, still had Missy's crayon artwork stuck to its sides and didn't pretend it couldn't recognize him without six new kinds of authorization. That helped dispel the slight gloom he'd been feeling since he walked in, and he began whistling softly as he typed in his account name—ChrisG, as usual—and password.

Even the message informing him that his password had been reset and asking him to specify a new one didn't dent his increasingly good mood. He typed in the next permutation of his usual password (CLUVM2) with a flourish and watched the system accept the change with no hiccups.

The whistling ("Onward Christian Soldiers" in this case, which puzzled him slightly) faded away, however, as he scanned the list of files the computer presented for him. "Protocol 4" appeared nowhere on the screen, its attendant database, reports, charts, and illustrations nowhere in evidence. His e-mail box had somebody else's messages in it. Even the background of his computer screen had changed, from the blue/green fractal pattern he liked to a barren-looking moonscape.

"What the heck?" he muttered, reaching for the phone to call the network techs and politely request that they put his electronic desktop back the way he left it.

He never completed the gesture, though; the word "vaccine" caught his eye and stopped his hand. A vaccine, huh? Intriguing. He'd heard rumors about the new vaccine MedaGen had devoted heavy-duty resources to developing. According to their whisper campaign—strictly confidential for now, nothing actually stated in any journals or advertising—it was supposed to be the next-generation super treatment, a vaccine so powerful that it could kickstart the human immune system into defeating even rapidly mutating, highly contagious viruses. He'd snorted at the rumors; it seemed like the classic example of blue-sky dreaming, a deal far too good to be true. And yet, here he was, in MedaGen's computer files, looking at a file marked "Corinth vaccine."

For a second, he hesitated, politeness and professionalism warring with curiosity, but rationalization came to his rescue. After all, he'd logged in as usual, with his own username, which should mean that he could see only the files that he should see. Maybe this was MedaGen's way of getting new employees up to speed on the current projects. That explanation held up just long enough for him to open the files, spreading the reports, data, and charts describing the Corinth vaccine over his monitor. After that, rationalization took a back seat to surprise—and sheer scientific fascination. He could no more close those files than stop breathing.

Data filled his vision, relating immune-system responses to specific genetic markers, antigens to physiological reactions, mouse experiments to human trials. Result after result pointed to the vaccine's complete effectiveness against a wide variety of illnesses: AIDS, influenza, encephalitis, ebola—the list went on and on. As he read, however, the chill fingers of doubt began to scratch at his initial absorption. Questions bubbled just under the rosy surface of the data. With immune-system levels that high, wouldn't severe side effects become evident? Allergic reactions, for instance, or the kind of self-destruction that ravaged joints in rheumatoid arthritis? Where had MedaGen conducted these human trials, without having to answer hard questions first? International companies often used labs in countries outside the United States and European Union to avoid the FDA's stringent controls on new medical treatments, and MedaGen was certainly rich and powerful enough to get around regulations it found inconvenient. But if they'd gone overseas for their tests, how did they expect to get the results past the domestic watchdogs? What good did it do them to create a vaccine that they could never sell in the world's richest markets? Of course, there was an outside chance that they didn't intend to sell it at all, but to donate it to help quell the devastating scourges of disease ripping through the Third World.

"And if you believe that, I have some nice oceanfront property in New Mexico I'd like to sell you," Chris said aloud, finishing the thought as vague but definitely dark speculations loomed in his imagination. "What are you people doing?"

The sudden chime of the phone startled him. He snorted at the sudden feeling of getting caught doing something he shouldn't and pulled his hand back from the "shut down" button, half guilty and half annoyed at feeling guilty.

"Chris Galen here," he answered, only a slight crack in his cheerful tone.

"Gregor Christoff here," the voice on the other end of the line informed him tightly. At the same moment, the video-conference window on Chris's screen lit. It showed a thin-faced, nervous-looking man, all long nose, large eyes, and wild hair.

Chris resisted the urge to run a hand over his own short hair, suddenly aware that it'd been awhile since he had it cut. What a pair of mad scientists they must look! "Hello, Gregor," he said with a smile toward the camera mounted atop his console. "Nice to meet a MedaGen veteran. How can I help you?"

"You can get out of my files," Christoff informed him. The flat sentence came across as more matter of fact than hostile. "And you can tell me how you got into them in the first place."

Chris blinked. "Well, I just logged in as usual—"

"Get out of the files, then tell me how you got in," Christoff interrupted urgently.

"All right," Chris told him, swept along by the other man's fierce insistence. He clicked "Log Out" and watched the moonscape, with its cargo of mysterious vaccine data files, vanish under the generic MedaGen log-in screen. "What's the hurry?"

"What are you doing at work so early? How did you get into my files?" Christoff asked, only slightly less tense now that Chris had closed the files.

Boy, this guy has a bad case of the single-mind blues, Chris thought. He briefly considered letting Christoff's manner get under his skin, but decided to practice some Christian charity—in honor of both of their names, if nothing else. Besides, if he alienated the guy, he'd never find out what was going on. He smiled again. "I've got a daughter who's one and a half, and she's definitely a morning person. I figure if I'm already up at 5:00, why not get a jump on the day? That way I can get things done before the rest of the lab critters come in to toss monkeys at me, and I get home earlier, too, which—"

"How did you get into my files?" Christoff interrupted again.

Chris sighed silently. "I'm not sure exactly myself. I just logged on with my usual ID, ChrisG—"

"And changed the password when it told you to," Christoff nodded rapidly in the monitor picture, his tendrils of hair waving wildly. "Yes, yes, that makes sense. What's the password you changed it to? And don't do it again."

"What, change my password?" Chris asked. "I'm definitely going to change it if I've given it to you. Why not? Why should I tell you? What's going on?"

Christoff hesitated a moment, his eyes darting around the room Chris couldn't see. "You're not the only ChrisG in the company anymore," he finally said. "That's me, Christoff, Gregor: ChrisG. I asked the techs when my account didn't ask me for my password like it should've. They said you were logged in as me—your console was logged in as me. They're changing all the network IDs and passwords, from the merger. All the lab personnel got new ones. Just bad luck you got mine by accident. Now, I need your password so I can get into my own files. I don't want to tell the techs. Save us both trouble if you just give me yours. They won't even know you saw anything. Better that way. You're GalenC. Log on with that name, and set your password to something else if you want. You'll get to your files. Not mine."

"Thanks," Chris said, still taken aback by Christoff's intense manner. "But I have a couple of questions. I mean, the research you're doing looks really good—unbelievably good, actually—so much so that I don't see how you managed to gather that data. This looks totally experimental—"

Christoff had gotten more agitated as Chris talked, and he burst into a flurry of speech, his hands blurring in the video-conference window. "No, no, don't ask questions. It's very, very confidential— top secret, eyes-only, need to know, nondisclosure. Get out and stay out. Forget it. Don't worry about it." Suddenly, he leaned forward into the camera. The lens emphasized the bags under his eyes, the wrinkles at their corners. "It could be the end—it could be the end of all of us!" he whispered.

Chris leaned forward, too, amazed at the other man's reaction. "Gregor, it's OK. Listen, my password's CLUVM2. Go ahead and use it, I'll think of something else—"

Christoff suddenly sat back, regaining his self possession as if someone had doused him with cold water (or rationality). He rapidly typed the password in, watched his files come up, and fixed Chris with a sober eye and stern expression. "Good, thanks. It's fine," he said coolly. "I've heard promising things about your research too. Time for you to get back to it. Perhaps we'll meet at the company retreat this summer and talk about what you're doing. For now, remember that you're GalenC. I'll reset my password. You choose another one too." With that, he cut the connection, leaving Chris staring at a blank screen.

"Welcome to MedaGen," Chris muttered aloud. "They turn the place into a fortress overnight, but can't get their network connections right." He logged on to his console again. The familiar blue/green mathematical lace of his fractal wallpaper greeted him, all the Protocol 4 files shining from their places in its spiraling arms. So did the e-mail, informing him that his username was GalenC, and that he should use it to log on and immediately change his password. He snorted. "Well, lookee here. They've sent me a message telling me how to log in. Of course, I have to log in to *get* the message."

He set about changing his password, this time to "MryChrsMss!" (short for "Merry, Chris, Miss," the greeting his mother loved to use on them—he and Merry hadn't thought that through when they named their daughter Melissa). "There, that should do it. We're all fine, and nobody gets a demerit from the technical-support people," he informed the now-dark conference window on his monitor.

Still, Christoff's extreme reaction tickled at the back of his mind. Were the techs at the home office really that snarky? What did he mean by, "It could be the end of all of us?" That sounded ominous enough and he looked scared, but it smacked more of paranoia—or better, dealings under the table, Chris decided. Like the corporate shenanigans Humphrey's always talking about (and dabbling in). Christoff's probably worried that somebody's going to figure out that he's falsified his research results before he can massage them to look a lot more realistic than that vaccine's looking now.

That explanation fit the other man's extreme insistence that Chris get out of his data, sounded like a good reason for his reaction. Once a scientist got a reputation for being unreliable, he could kiss his productivity, grants, and career a sad good-bye. "It could be the end of all of us." That might go for MedaGen as a whole, if they publicized breakthroughs that hadn't actually happened yet and terminally wounded their image in the minds of potential consumers, even if that was less likely. Still, as he reviewed the latest files for his own Protocol 4, Chris couldn't help wondering about the glimpses he'd seen of Christoff's human-trial results—and his extremely nervous reaction. Was this the kind of behavior he could expect from a company with a long track record of playing at the far edges of acceptable scientific ethics? Welcome to MedaGen indeed. Merry was going to love hearing about this.

* * *

Dear Chisom,

I'm not sure you're going to love hearing this, but my work has kept me very busy—along with my new calling as an assistant in our ward's High Priests group—and it will probably get busier as time goes on. As a result, I may not be quite so faithful writing to you for the next little while. Sorry about that. I'm glad your mother writes you regularly. She and I are pleased that you are finding enough people to teach that you have little time to tract. Tracting was never the highlight of my days as a missionary. I am also glad to hear how effective the members are at being missionaries. I can tell you that reports here show your success is common in Japan, Korea, and Mongolia. The Church is also growing in the Philippines, but opposition is getting stronger there and that hurts the work.

I was interested in your report that a disproportionate number of earthquake-damaged buildings were built by a company that used substandard materials and paid off inspectors to look the other way. I wonder if they could possibly be the same group I told you about whose buildings failed in San Francisco.

Which brings me to your request that I expand on what I told you in my last e-mails about Babylon. Let me first give you some background. As the Lord has set up His kingdom on earth so, too, has Satan. The scriptures use the name of the ancient Mesopotamian capital, Babylon, to symbolize it. That city was the center of commerce, trade, and immorality in Isaiah's day. It was very wealthy, sophisticated, immoral, and idolatrous.

Today, spiritual Babylon is found where any government (local or national), church, businesses, company, or institution plays by its rules. We find those rules in the fifth chapter of Moses. There we read how Satan taught Cain the great secret of how to murder *and get gain. With Satanic inspiration, Cain formed a brotherhood (in his case, with real brothers) that worked together to promote the aims of his secret society. (We see an offshoot in the Book of Mormon in the form of Gadiantonism.) It worked and still works on what others have called the Mahanic Principle: the rules by which human life is turned into property. How does Babylon do it?*

An excellent example would be the tobacco companies still flourishing today. They have known since the middle part of the last century that nicotine was addictive and tars caused cancers, but hid their findings and pitched their wares through advertising, often directed at teenagers. Their researchers learned that the earlier people start smoking, the harder it is for them to break the addiction. Even when the companies were caught and the U.S. sued their socks off and forced certain regulations on them, they continued to advertise abroad, especially in the Middle East. Nothing shows more clearly their total disregard for human life and love for property.

Of course, the worst offenders are the drug cartels, dealers, and pushers who still have success giving away free samples to hook the unwary, then charge them sky-high prices once they are addicted. What is amazing is that they have been using this technique for decades and it still works. Of course, the legalization of marijuana and softening of attitudes towards other drugs like "ecstasy" ("Hey, it's just for parties," as they say,) has not helped. Too many people equate legal with moral. The result is a society that plays word games (as the modern damnable proverb says, It depends on what the meaning of 'is' is") and thereby feels moral.

The Mahanic Principle works. Babylon has amassed an obscene amount of property and seduces people to sell people to share in it. Look at Revelation 18 to see her stores. There we also find that she trades in slaves and the souls of men. Can you imagine that—she thrives in the brisk business of making money by selling people!

Don't get the idea that this is just the slave trade, though I notice that in spite of the decimation of Africa due to AIDS and civil war, a brisk slave trade still continues there. Imagine, Africans raiding tribal foes to capture, enslave, and sell them. How sick and sad. But that is not the only place she works. Every once in awhile we see glimpses on the news of unscrupulous, hard, unfeeling people treating other humans not just as animals but as objects to be used for their own gain.

Know this, son, nothing good ever comes out of Babylon. She always trades in human futures. She has succeeded in seducing much of the world into her camp, especially its leaders. You see, what she is at the core is a philosophy that many, especially top brass in companies and rulers of peoples, find impossible to resist. They buy into her ways because she promises happiness, security, and prosperity. She especially promises power and, ultimately, salvation. She teaches people how to make outrageous amounts of money by turning wants into needs. She has even learned how to create wants where there were none so she can turn them into needs. She does this through expert and sustained advertising. She uses many mediums and many fronts, always appealing to the desires, dreams, and fantasies of the natural man.

A good example you may not know about is a new 3-D computer craze that has scandalized many. By putting on the special gloves, suit, and goggles, a person cannot only see but feel what the computer program projects. The idea behind the engineering was to create a new and effective teaching tool, but Babylon got hold of it and tied it to sexy videos that are pitched to young males. Now you can do more than just watch scantily clad females gyrate before your very eyes, you can reach out and touch them. (Come to think of it, maybe I should not have brought up that kind of imagery to a young missionary. Well, it's all right to know about it, just don't dwell on it, okay?)

My point is, once again, Babylon has turned a good thing into something sordid. She has sold virtue for pennies (albeit, billions of them). In the process, she has abused, distorted, and degraded the view of many younger men toward females and not only marginalized but also objectified women. But that is what Babylon, Mother of Harlots, does—makes human beings objects to be bought, sold, used, drained, and discarded—all for profit.

She is the direct cause of much of the opposition the Church faces. Her captains are continually moving more openly and aggressively against the Church (which has been prophesied, see 1 Nephi 13:8–9).

From the picture I have painted, I hope you can see that she is a philosophy, or should I say theology, that institutions buy into. She supplies the direction, they supply the muscle. Between the two, the players get the capital or power they want. Those who do not play by her rules get squashed. The Church has yet to face her might. Still, the Saints will prevail (see 1 Nephi 22:14). Even so, I fear we will be in for a bit of a rough time; therefore, prepare your people well. Make sure they are converted and their testimonies are strong. If they are, they will endure well what is coming.

I have gone on way too long. You're probably thinking that this letter is just like family home evenings when Dad has the lesson, never ending.

I love you. Keep spreading God's word.

Your father,

Chinedu

* * *

"It's bad karma, trading one boss for another. Things get messed up," Dove informed Perro. "The *Señor's* going to blow a stack when he finds out Rico's delivering another boss's box across the river. Think he wants us doing freelance jobs? We signed on to him, we ought to stay signed until we tell him we're breaking contract."

Above their heads, acid-green neon ran through the outline of palm fronds swaying in the nonexistent evening breeze. The green turned into equally acid yellow as it gushed through the tubes spelling out Carlito's—the name of the strip club that the sign dominated as much as it decorated. The strip bar had been here for years—probably had "saloon" written over the doors back when the parking meters had been hitching posts and the town still had a whimsical Western nickname like Elephant Butte. Since then, the old building had seen half as many renovations as new owners, and probably almost that many little-fish soldiers collecting "insurance" like Dove and Perro were doing.

Perro shifted his backpack from one shoulder to the other. He was tired of the whole argument, back and forth, General this, *Brujos* that, for the last week and a half. Whatever *Abuelo* decided, that should be good enough—and right now, *Abuelo* was judiciously playing both sides of the fence. Perro just objected to working on a Friday. Sure, Dove and Benny were probably right about it all, but why fight about it? He shrugged at Dove as he gawked at the posters promoting this week's new girls. "Yeah, messed up," he agreed, grinning.

Dove smacked his shoulder, pushing him through the doors. "You know what I mean."

Trujo, the bouncer, loomed out of the darkness of the entryway. "IDs?" he demanded. The flickering lights reflecting from the small stage behind him played over his bald head and equally hard, equally hairless arms. Tattoos more than made up for his lack of natural pelt, covering him thickly from scalp to waist.

"Hey, Trujo," Perro said, the flickering lights from the stage just out of sight turning his teeth white-pink-yellow in time to the thumping beat. "How about closing your eyes for a couple seconds? We could slip right on by, and you could ignore us for a couple hours."

The bouncer's reply was unprintable—partly because of content, partly because to print something, one would have to know how to spell it. He didn't budge.

Dove rolled his eyes at Perro. "Bark up another tree, Perrito," he advised. "We got no time to stay. *Abuelo* sent us to find out if Carlito still wants to renew his insurance policy."

Trujo growled, one massive fist coming up in a blur of ink and skin. Dove's hand moved even faster, the blade that appeared in one of them tossing glints back toward the disco lights. Both stopped suddenly, the knife and tattoos within millimeters of each other, as the two locked eyes.

"We got no trouble with you or Carlito," Dove said softly. "*Abuelo* don't make trouble. You say go, we go—and Pizarro comes down to take his own cut. And the *Brujos* think maybe you're a good target. And the *Señor* asks what's the matter, you don't like his wine for this place no more? Me and Perro, we don't care which way it goes. We're just messenger boys. So you tell us what to do."

* * *

"Ain't no way I would do what he said, even if I could," Perro informed Dove as they clattered down the alleyway beside Carlito's, the backpack heavier by another monthly dues payment to *Abuelo*—and from him to the *Señor*. They emerged onto the main street again, heading for the Dogmobile through the slowly thickening Friday crowd on the cracked sidewalks. The stream parted for them—not as swiftly as it would have for Rico or Benny, or *Abuelo* himself, but it parted.

The drunk who bounced off Dove swore—then choked, when Perro gave him a hard look, backed up with the glitter of a wrist knife. He kept his eye on them as he retreated—until he bumped into another pair of young men, these two much better dressed, but definitely harmless looking in their white shirts. They got the full profanity treatment and dirt kicked at their dress shoes, but they didn't pull knives, just stepped aside to let him pass.

"Trujo's just proving he's still got something 'sides tattoos under his jeans," Dove sighed. He detested tax collecting; shooting *Brujos*, dusters, and raiders on the *Señor's* orders hit him hard afterwards, but shaking down storekeepers and bartenders for the *Señor* didn't even have a sheen of honor about it. Benny's explanation that they were providing a good service for the money by keeping the trash out of those same stores and bars didn't feel right, even though it made sense on the surface.

"Yeah, you're probably right," Perro agreed, then grinned at Dove. "And that's your problem. *Chico*, you think too much! Honor this, good guys that, yakka yadda. Come on, let's get Calvin, and *do* something tonight. Like getting together with Consuela and her girls and getting high enough to forget all that feather-head algebra junk you been stuffing in my head all week."

Dove grinned. "Stick to the math, Perrito—you got a better chance being a rocket scientist than spending time with Consuela or her girls!"

"I'll just get high as a rocket," Perro informed him. "I got the scratch, and going blind on fumes sounds good."

He pointed at the advertisement smiling from the digital billboards lining the bus station. The lush visuals of a whiskey ad disappeared; images of a gauze-covered female torso replaced them. "Bliss," the woman's husky, seductive voice whispered. "The designer pharmaceutical designed just for you. Higher highs, no lows, perfect for that party atmosphere. And shh," she winked over pursed, full, glossy lips, "it's still almost illegal!"

"You got enough water behind your ears," Dove said, "without liquefying your brains, too."

* * *

"I know it's a cliché, Kathy, but I can't help saying this: when it rains, it pours." On the evening news broadcast, Clara Cortez stood in the wet green of the Philippine jungle, the ever-present damp and melancholy scene dampening even her blow-dried perfection. "After the earthquakes and tidal waves, we'd hope for peace for the citizens of this beleaguered island country. God—or some of God's more radical followers—seem to have a different plan, however."

The camera panned slowly away from her, its gaze sending the devastated scene into homes and businesses all over the world. A tiny village stood under the dripping trees and heavy sky, utterly silent except for the vague sound of running water. Unlike previous images of the devastation wrought by natural disasters, all the shabby buildings in this scene stood intact—but utterly lifeless. In the distance, far from the camera, figures in full-body environment suits prowled through the empty paths and rooms. They carried scanners, detectors, and stretchers weighed down with rain-slicked body bags.

Clara reappeared on screen, the sudden shift in focus betraying the fact that she stood several yards away from the eerie scene. "This is—was—a leper colony, run by nuns of the Order of St. Theresa of Bombay. Just four days ago, it was home to an estimated 56 patients, with five nurses who belonged to the order. Now, however, the village is completely empty. All the people who lived here have been wiped out. Aguilar Corazon, an infectious-disease specialist from the Ministry of Health, is here with me now. Dr. Corazon, can you tell us what's happened here?"

The bright eye of the worldwide public fastened onto the slender, older man standing beside Clara, his rumpled clothes and tired eyes testifying to his official capacity. Dr. Corazon regarded the camera with a steady, weary gaze. "We have reason to believe," he said solemnly in barely accented English, "that the inhabitants here were killed not by leprosy but by a virus that entered the colony as a contaminant in a crate of medicines. When the nurses injected the patients with what they thought were antibiotics, they actually injected them with deadly infection."

"We have reports about that," Clara jumped in. "Specifically, that a note was found in the crate. Can you tell us the contents of that note?"

"I cannot," Dr. Corazon said shortly. "You will excuse me now?" He didn't wait for her permission; he simply nodded politely and disappeared in the direction of the village, meeting a pair of investigators who came toward him at a run, shrugging half out of their protective suits. They went into a huddle with the doctor, clustered around a small pile of equipment.

Clara went to follow, but the impassive guard who appeared out of the foliage to block her path deterred her with a purposefully displayed machine gun. She stopped and turned to the camera again. "As you can see, the government has sealed this area, putting it under quarantine for the safety of others. But will that be enough? If terrorists have begun to use biological weapons, are any of us safe?"

"Watch it, girlie," Monk cautioned Clara from the blue-lit darkness of the producer's nest thousands of miles away. "Sell it, but don't oversell it. We want ratings, not panic or eye-rolling."

Kim nodded, hand poised over the kill switch that would transfer the broadcast back to Kathy.

"In this case, however," Clara continued smoothly, Monk's caution and her own journalistic instincts warning her away from completely scaring off her home-viewer audience, "it seems that the culprits have a definite target in mind. Unfortunately, Dr. Corazon could not confirm or deny the existence of a note accompanying the tainted medicine. According to our sources, however, such a note did exist. It said, 'the unclean are now cleansed, welcomed back to the ever-loving bosom of God; so all those infected with unclean thoughts can look forward to their ultimate salvation in death, while the obedient inherit a purified world.' It wasn't signed."

"Do the authorities have any idea who might be behind this attack?" Kathy asked (as prompted from Monk's control booth).

After a split-second's delay (even satellite transmissions couldn't overcome small gaps in conversations between people on different sides of the earth), Clara nodded. "Obviously, a fringe religious group is the prime suspect. Again, according to sources who prefer to remain anonymous, several groups have claimed responsibility: a splinter group of Islamic Jihad, the Asian Liberation Army, the Al-Aqsa Front, and others. So far, however, the CIA does not officially acknowledge any of those claims."

"Have we seen something like this anywhere else?" Kathy shot her next scripted question into the ether, using her "concerned newscaster" face and voice.

"Actually, yes," Clara responded—again as coached; Kim quickly sent the backup data to her to read from the small prompter built into the camera. "It may be related to the sudden epidemic that wiped out an isolated mining community in South America. Speculation suggests it's the same bug. This incident may also be related to the disappearance of Elder Stacy, the Mormon Apostle."

"Thank you, Clara," Kathy told her. Clara nodded and then disappeared as a still photo of the missing Apostle appeared over Kathy's designer-clad shoulder.

The scrolling information bar at the bottom of the screen read out pertinent details of Elder Stacy's life: birth, mission, marriage—and death. "And now, in related news, we have confirmed reports that Thomas J. Stacy of The Church of Jesus Christ of Latter-day Saints has been found and confirmed dead.

While specific details are not available at this time, it appears that he was executed soon after his abduction." The display over her shoulder ran through a montage of clips of Elder Stacy: speaking at General Conference, waving to cheering crowds in South Africa, arriving to dedicate the temple in Belize, answering questions during a Japanese press interview.

"Again, no credible claim of responsibility has come to the authorities pursuing the case," Kathy continued. "However, it seems likely that this incident is related to the growing hostility toward the Mormon Church in this part of the world. Combined with anti-American sentiment, these protests have often resulted in violence." This time the montage showed shouting, screaming protesters, their faces distorted with hate, throwing stones and bottles, burning American flags and copies of the Book of Mormon outside a mission home and then in front of the American Embassy.

"That makes caution all the more necessary. Elder Stacy's body will be shipped home as soon as it's through quarantine," Kathy finished. "And speaking of quarantine, we have an update on the potential for biological and chemical attacks on civilians around the world—and here at home."

Kim queued up the appropriate report.

"The official policy from the Homeland Security Agency emphasizes the potential for violence to any American—and now the possible specter of biological attacks hangs over innocent civilians everywhere." An unseen reporter narrated the segment, taking visitors on a tour through the offices of the Homeland Security administration, focusing on the competent but tense expressions of staffers walking purposefully down halls and into offices. Posters of the color-coded levels of threat hung on the walls.

The Homeland Security Advisor appeared on screen, serious but self-assured as she answered the narrator's unheard question. "All the government's watchdog agencies, on both law-enforcement and public-health sides, are sharing information that will help us respond to any kind of attack, including those that utilize biological or chemical agents."

"But can the government prevent a terrorist attack, or respond quickly enough to stop an epidemic unleashed on the public?" the reporter pressed—but not to the Secretary herself. Instead, he addressed that question to a series of "regular Americans" caught on the street of a large city.

"I'm stocking up on penicillin, just in case," a blowsy-looking woman assured the camera.

"Gov'mint ain't never moved fast 'nough to do me no good," a baseball-capped man asserted.

"We need more help and information about these attacks, and we're not getting it," an elderly lady informed the reporter. "Something like air-raid sirens, to tell us when to put on our gas masks."

"Like, how do we know it's not the CIA making people sick?" a teenage tattoo display inquired.

"I can hardly even go outside anymore, for worrying about anthrax or bubonic plague," a nervous young mother stammered, clutching her young child. "And I don't want Chelsea touching anything on a public playground. You just never know."

"You just never know," the narrator repeated. "All over America—indeed, all over the world—citizens already pushed to the brink now find another possible threat lurking in something as seemingly innocent as a medicine bottle." A close-up of a bottle followed, the prescription label artfully blurred, the bottle itself backlit to look ominous.

Kathy regained center stage. "An alarming report on threats to the health of Americans. Does the federal government need to step in to protect Americans from the burgeoning threat of biological warfare and potential epidemics? Or would that lead to restrictions on medical care and invasions of privacy? Stay tuned, as an all-star panel debates the question of medical privacy and ethics, right here on Channel 8."

"And cut to the talking heads," Monk ordered. He grinned, tapping the ratings display on his screen. "That report got 'em stirred up. Nothing like Homeland Security and terrorist attacks to catch peoples' attention. Put the nerves into 'em, and they'll listen to just about anything until they slouch off to the kitchen for a snack. Even political speeches."

CHAPTER 6

The trumpet prelude to an "Important Special Report" blared through the kitchen. Missy laughed and warbled along with it, enthusiastically missing most of the notes. Merry laughed and leaned over to rub noses with her. She glanced at the TV, displaying a patriotic montage of the Capitol, the Flag, and what looked at first glance like Mom's apple pie.

"Oh, here we go again. Somebody has something important to tell us." She sighed and ruffled Missy's hair. Missy showed her a dinosaur toy and growled. "I know I shouldn't subject you to the news. It's biased, heavily based on advertising, and sensationalistic, but at least it's a way to keep up on all these depressing events in the world while I fold this mountain of laundry you generate."

Missy laughed and threw her dinosaur at the screen. It bounced off the special report logo behind Kathy's shoulder as she did a quick intro for the Very Important Person who'd called the press conference.

"We all know of the threats of heinous terrorist conspiracies and rogue nations across the globe," Senator Howard W. Garlick intoned, solemnly facing the cameras that crowded around the Senate steps. (His aides had worked the phones well—all the major networks and cable outlets had sent representatives.) "Suicide bombers, hijackings, cyber threats, have all unfortunately become commonplace. Now, the threat of new weapons of mass destruction, chemical and biological weapons, looms over our free country."

Merry growled (Missy imitated the sound). "Yeah, we know—what are you doing about it?"

Garlick's deep frown disappeared suddenly, as he bestowed a triumphant smile on his (unseen) audience. The sun broke through the clouds at just the right moment, throwing watery light over the moisture-speckled, white-marble façade behind the podium full of audio pickups—and the white-haired, distinguished-looking politician behind the small forest of mikes. "I am here to proclaim the dawning of a brave new beginning for America!" he announced confidently, the sunlight making a halo around him.

"In conjunction with the National Health Coalition, the Centers for Disease Control, and patriotic private companies, I have the privilege of announcing the creation of a new weapon in the war against terror." A discreetly attractive aide sent a series of bullet-point and chart slides to the networks' Web sites as she set up the posterboard versions beside Garlick's podium. They gave what passed for the full dump; the Senator himself covered only the most exciting and politically advantageous parts of the plan. (Even the slides, however, left out the inconvenient hard-science bits.) They also prominently sported MedaGen's logo watermarked into the backgrounds and listed the company as "sponsor" at the end.

MedaGen had provided more than just their logo. They'd also sent a multimedia program to the networks along with Senator Garlick's invitation to the press conference. The networks obligingly spliced it into their computers and modified the live broadcast using the multimedia to make the political speech more lively and keep those ratings up. The pulsing beat of "Leave It, Love Me," Virginia's certified dance-floor hit, began its bump-and-grind thump under the broadcast of Garlick's speech.

"AllSafe is the ultimate weapon in the war against terrorism. It is a brave new beginning for America, the solution to the national health-care crisis and the threat of biological attacks," Garlick summarized. "This vaccine completely shields its users from all biological weapons—anthrax, smallpox, all the rest. In initial trials, AllSafe also prevents the scourges that, while not capable of being created in weapons-grade versions, infect and kill thousands of Americans every year. AIDS, ladies and gentlemen, is a thing of the past!"

Images of Virginia and her troupe of underdressed but extremely flexible dancers underscored that point, sharing a split screen with the Senator's Washington pinstripes.

"But how much will the vaccine cost, Senator?" a reporter asked, just as on cue as the sunshine, but much more scripted.

"We strongly believe that all Americans should benefit from the amazing medical breakthroughs that made this vaccine possible," Garlick assured him. "I have introduced a bill that will ensure that no American, regardless of race, age, gender, sexual orientation, or income, will be left behind. Unless our opponents in the Senate and House kill the measure—and with it uncounted thousands of citizens—the Federal Government will be able to offer this vaccine to every American at a minimal cost. In fact, for most of our citizens, it will be covered by existing health plans, including Medicare."

A burst of cheering and clapping—some of it from the assembled journalists, more from the crowd gathered behind them—blended with the applause recorded on Virginia's dance track.

"Oh, great, so we get to pay for it indirectly, with taxes and insurance premiums," Merry muttered. "And you're using all these nice little reporters as extras in your political commercial, putting pressure on all those nasty-bad opponents on the Hill. They probably don't even see it as a breach of their journalistic ethics. Pay them enough, promise them ratings, and they'll do anything."

"Pay 'nuff," Missy observed.

Merry chuckled. "Oh, my cynical, world-weary baby!"

The slick split-screen effect disappeared, however, as Garlick got to the second part of his speech. "And because this vaccine will protect us all against the evil plots of terrorists, I also propose that we use this weapon to short-circuit those plots before they can even begin. Anyone who has not been vaccinated must not be allowed to visit Washington, D.C.—or to move freely about the country—spreading contagion. We have increased security measures to prevent suicide bombings; this vaccine allows us to implement measures that will put a stop to suicide infections as well!"

"What?" Merry stared at the screen in disbelief.

This time, more than a smattering of applause interrupted him; the paid crowd loudly whistled and clapped their approval for the Senator's safety-first idea. The Senator beamed and waved, completely ignoring the semi-independent reporters' further (unscripted) questions. The press conference broke up as each reporter turned to his or her own camera to breathlessly comment on the Senator's amazing, shocking, groundbreaking proposal, but all the commentaries quickly gave way to the staple of modern, electronic democracy: the online poll. Statistics, charts, and fluctuating poll numbers filled TV screens and Web sites, along with even more commentary.

"As we can see, Kathy," Channel 8's political correspondent needlessly pointed out, "self-identified libertarians have registered their strong resistance to the idea of mandatory vaccinations, while health-care professionals are overwhelmingly in favor of Senator Garlick's plan."

"And the numbers are still coming in for the Channel 8 Web poll," Kathy noted, equally redundantly, before turning a bright smile on the viewers at home. "Are you for or against vaccinations to prevent epidemics from biological terrorist attacks? Now is your chance to cast your vote in our electronic democracy. How else will the peoples' elected representatives know how to serve you best? Make your voice heard!" The crawl at the bottom of the screen gave the standard information: participation in "electronic democracy" cost only $1.99 per vote.

"Chris!" Merry called, disbelief and anger thickening her voice. "Chris, are you hearing this?"

"I'm hearing this," Chris said tightly from right behind her—he'd come from the library office into the kitchen without her noticing. "And I'm not liking it."

"Is this AllSafe thing that vaccine you told me about, that Corinth project? The one Dr. Christoff acted so weird about?" Merry asked. "Did that senator just seriously propose a law to make everybody take it?"

"I don't know what he seriously proposed," Chris said. "Who knows how much they mean and how much they're just saying to further their own agendas? But I think the vaccine he's talking about is that Corinth project of Christoff's. A one-size-fits-all solution for any disease." He glanced at the hammer he'd been using to put up the bookshelves (anchoring them firmly to the wall studs this time) and shook his head. "Can you imagine the kind of profits MedaGen's looking at if the government does decide to make that vaccination mandatory? You can bet they won't let it go cheap, no matter what the Senator says about making it affordable."

"Could he do that?" Merry asked. "You said they hadn't even run refereed tests here, that the FDA hadn't even approved it yet."

Chris looked thoughtful. "No, he can't actually get it into circulation without the FDA passing off on it. Not in this country, anyway. And that process can take years." *Unless they move the human trials overseas*, he thought silently. *And bribe the FDA reviewers to overlook possible side effects. But even MedaGen wouldn't do that. Right?*

Merry rescued a clean but now soggy sock from Missy's mouth. "So this whole press-conference thing, and the bill, could they be just leverage to try to push the FDA into approving it early? How much did MedaGen contribute to his campaign, anyway?"

"Who's to say? If they did it right—so to speak—the money's spread through several organizations and a couple of party funds," Chris thought aloud. "I think he's got a bigger audience in mind than just his peers on the Hill. The way he's selling it, this vaccine was much more than a preparedness tool for people paranoid about possible terrorist attacks. Look at the list of diseases it's targeting— STDs, half of them. He's not just pushing disaster prevention, he's selling freedom from medical consequences."

"Oh, great," Merry said. "So now you can buy your way out of the inconvenient side effects of sleeping around. Don't want a baby? Get an abortion. Don't want a disease? Get vaccinated."

"Get vaccinated," Chris repeated. "With the Corinth vaccine. Somebody on that project has a black sense of humor—and has been reading either the New Testament or Roman history, since they used to use 'Corinthize' as a slang term for sleeping around, among other things. But how does the vaccine work? I haven't seen any of this stuff published, not even a hint of it."

"MedaGen is a private company," Merry pointed out. "Universities publish their findings to get credit for them and angle for more grant money. Companies don't publish their findings until they have the patents locked down, and don't have to tell everybody what they're researching even then, since they're out to sell it. The legal value of intellectual property and all that. They don't have to tell any more than they want to, not publicly."

"Still, I'd like to know," Chris told her. "If it's not just hot air, nothing but advertising or political maneuvering, how did they do that? Christoff must be a flaming genius."

"Well, you did say he had Einstein hair," Merry said.

"Is that the key to genius?" he asked, laughing. "Wild white hair?"

"Hmm—must not be," Merry observed, abandoning her laundry folding to stand up and run her hands through Chris's thick locks. She got a kiss for that.

Missy took advantage of the momentary parental distraction to knock the basket of folded clothes off the couch.

* * *

"The Big Sister, as we're calling the mountain now, thanks to Andre Becker, the geologist in charge of the survey team—anyway, the volcano is building its cone now," Hideyoshi said. Becker had risked his life to get a video camera close enough to capture the images of the mountain that underscored his words, close-up photos of a volcano in progress. "In addition to spouting the plumes of gas, ash, and dust that have darkened Oregon skies and prevent us from getting a clear satellite shot of the volcano, it's pumping out thousands of tons of lava every day. As the molten rock cools, it solidifies and builds up in layers and waves. The original explosion opened a huge vent in what used to be a shallow valley between the original Three Sisters volcanoes. Now, due to seismic action and the magma flows, the three mountains are well on their way to becoming one. According to our InSAR computers, the mountain is growing at an average rate of ten feet per day."

"How has the dust affected the space station?" the news reporter asked inanely.

Hideyoshi managed to keep his expression stoic—but his eyebrows quirked. "We're far enough above the atmosphere to escape any direct effects," he managed to say with a straight face.

* * *

The uniformed Legitimates guarding the nominal border checkpoint marking the boundary between the Mexico and American sides of Amexica weren't as kind. "*Estupida*," was the mildest of the comments that greeted the reporter's question.

Dove slipped past the checkpoint at a discreet distance, taking advantage of the deputies' distraction, walking his dirt bike so the sound of it wouldn't alert them. He had plenty of practice finding his way around the guard posts on the dirt roads far from the highways and lights. Sure, the deputies stationed out here tended to shoot first and ask questions later, but they also didn't keep much of an eye out for people trying to sneak *into* Mexico. The video cameras caught Dove as a shadowy figure slipping past the razor-wire and infrared-sensor fences, but the picture went nowhere in particular, with the set turned to Hideyoshi's volcano update. Even if the monitors had been tuned to the correct station, nobody would have paid much attention—they'd been paid not to. The *Señor* had his own reasons for wanting lax security along this section of the border, and the *federales* had long since realized that it was much cheaper to let the locals take care of the illegal alien problem. Anyone who crossed the border without paying the entrance fee would find himself (or herself) getting the sharp end of the *Señor's* immigration policies. Skulls piled along the coyotes' formerly favorite routes through the back country testified to those policies' effectiveness.

Of course, Dove had the credentials he needed to walk right through the checkpoint—and being an employee of the firm, so to speak, he wouldn't even have to pony up the usual fee. However, since he was out on *Abuelo's* business without the *Señor's* approval, he preferred not to attract the attention of his fellow employees while he still had the General's packet in his bag along with his books.

That packet had thumped into his chest earlier that evening. He'd come into Mama Rosa's from school, as usual, chaffering with Perro, Calvin, and a couple of *Abuelo's* other soldiers, also as usual. What wasn't usual was bouncing off Slick. Dove recovered, coming to a halt nearly nose to nose with the General's recruiter. He got a close look at his own reflection in Slick's sunglasses before one of the *Brujos* behind Slick planted a hand on his shoulder and moved him out of the way. Dove let himself swing around on one heel, like a door, and watched the trio of them (Slick and his two muscle-bound thugs) get into a Land Rover with black-tinted windows.

"There is *way* too much window tint on that thing," Perro advised.

"There is way too much slime inside that thing," Dove said, pushing open the swinging doors to Franklin's dining room.

That's when the package hit him. He caught it with both hands, reflexively using it as a shield as he looked over it at Rico's sneer.

"Time for you to earn your keep, bird boy," he informed Dove.

"You finally decided you need tail-kicking lessons?" Dove asked him. Perro and Calvin laughed.

Benny didn't—and neither did *Abuelo*. That sobered up Dove's cheering section in a hurry.

"Take that out to Blanca Hacienda and deliver it to the men in the old ranch house," *Abuelo* told him. "By midnight, no later. No bodies. And don't get distracted."

Dove's reaction to getting handed one of Slick's errands got no further than "But—" before Benny snarled, "Get moving, *Hasbìdì*. You better run to beat moonrise."

So Dove watched the moon rise from the Mexican side of the border, getting his bearings before gunning his bike down the dirt road and over the hill. He didn't have far to go before the wrought-iron gate arch leading to the old ranch house loomed before him. He stopped the bike and rolled it off the track, hiding it behind the massive outcropping of boulders that marked the ranch's outer boundary. Blanca Hacienda had been the headquarters of the *Señor's* predecessor, Recho Ojo. He'd made his reputation early, back when success in the borderland drug and slavery business depended on a talent for lunatic cruelty—and a willingness to build an empire with as much blood and charred bone as necessary. Or more than necessary, which is where Recho Ojo excelled. He'd exemplified the philosophy that if killing a man was effective, killing his entire family had to work even better. The sand-drifted foundations of Mayorsville were still an eloquent testimony to that, the burned-out remnants of a town whose police chief had arrested one of Ojo's lieutenants and actually brought him to trial.

The *Señor* was like the Romans to Recho Ojo's Huns; he hit his rivals hard until they swore fealty, then cut them in for a share of the profits. Rumor had it that he'd finagled official backing on both south and north sides of the border, as the local governments finally realized that they couldn't count on the *federales* to stop the chaos spreading through the deserts. *Señor* put a stop to the coyotes, all right, and Recho Ojo's Huns, too, starting at the top. After the battle, Ojo ended up as an extra decoration, swinging from the archway until his skeleton fell apart.

Mere death hadn't been enough to destroy the horrific reputation Ojo had left behind, however. Ghost stories about Ojo's victims still sent shivers down the spines of the kids (and most of their elders) in the towns around the border: the girl who wandered, crying and bleeding from the gash in her neck, pleading for someone to save her big brother from Ojo's men; the old woman who appeared out of dark alleys, her shawl still smelling of smoke, her face half burned away; the young man who carried his head by its hair, looking for the man who cut it off; the gunfighter who challenged drunk soldiers to duels in the dead hours before morning, only to laugh as their bullets passed through the holes already drilled into his torso. Even Ojo himself made an appearance in some stories, a vengeful ghost sporting a skull in which only one sullen eye still gleamed (the right one, of course). The *Señor*, cannily, built the stories into his own reputation, promoted them to help "his" citizens remember the reasons they paid his dues. Nobody could tell a ghost story like Benny, and the fact that his talent paid off for the gang was all gravy.

Slick's men must be foreigners, recruits from the same far-off South American killing fields that spawned their General leader, or they wouldn't be easy about making the old Blanca Hacienda their hideout— or even sleeping there after midnight, Dove thought. The rope that legend said broke Ojo's neck still swayed in the thin breeze as he headed up the winding drive, shadowed by the skeletal branches of desiccated lilac bushes.

It could've been the whispering breeze, or the rattle of dead twigs, or the ghost stories, or the thought of walking into an ambush that sent prickles through the hair on Dove's neck. It wasn't. It was the package in his backpack, probably full of cash to pay off the boys running the General's operations on the southern side. Delivering mysterious packages wasn't unusual; *Abuelo's* gang ran packets fairly often, usually messages and cash for the drug dealers or gang bosses, and Dove had played courier from ten years old on up. What made this trip different wasn't the cargo or the loneliness of the drop location—it was the customer. He didn't like Slick. His dislike of the General's spokesman came from the vivid memory of Slick shooting the Brujo soldier in the warehouse, putting a bullet into his own man without a flicker of conscience or even anger. *Abuelo* could be ruthless when he had to be, and he'd dealt plenty of blows to his soldiers, even killed a couple of them when they tried a mutiny a few years ago. But when he had to skin his own cats, he did it out of fury and regretted it afterwards. Enough to get drunk, anyway. Slick hadn't even blinked. The guy—and his unseen but somehow looming General—felt nastier than even Recho Ojo. Stupid, crazy mean was bad enough; smart, psychotic mean was worse.

Sudden brilliance blossomed around Dove, casting the dead bushes into high relief, pinning him in the high-intensity beams of a car's headlights. The vehicle was pulled into the last turn of the drive, backed right up under the remains of the lilacs, just waiting for somebody to get too wrapped up in philosophizing and walk right into its view. Dove swore under his breath. Don't get distracted! He squinted into the light, discarding his first impulse to run even before a voice ordered him to freeze. Where would he go? The dead bushes barred both sides of the narrow driveway behind him, the car blocked the way forward. Besides, he recognized the voice.

Sure enough, Pizarro's expansive bulk appeared, sauntering up beside the car. The light glinted off the whiter parts of his teeth as he grinned around his cigar. "Well, look what we have here. I'd heard that *Abuelo's* boys had been jumping the border lately, and sure enough, here you are. What's little Pigeon up to now, out so late on a school night? And with his homework, too." He reached for Dove's backpack.

Dove dodged, swinging the pack out of the way. "Science project," he informed Pizarro. "I'm out collecting leaves and rocks for a diorama display on our desert environment. What're you doing outside your jurisdiction?"

Pizarro's smile got hard. "Jurisdiction? That's a big word for a border rat like you—you learn that in school? My 'jurisdiction' includes your thick skull, boy. Now, you can give that over, or you can find out what else my jurisdiction includes." His right hand hovered over the pistol in its holster at his belt.

Again, Dove dodged the sheriff's grab, but the big man caught one strap of the backpack and used it to swing Dove around hard, into the side of the car's hood. Dove slid off, down the side of the car, away from the blow Pizarro aimed at his head, and dodged around the back, still holding the strap tightly. They tussled over control of the pack, but not too hard; Dove had no desire to get shot over a shipment of Slick's. Instead, when Pizarro slammed him into the car's back door, Dove pulled sharply upward on the strap he still held, sending the backpack's contents spilling to the dusty road.

Pizarro settled for thumping Dove hard in the chest to back him off and muttering an obscene comment about Dove's klutziness, then shoved him violently away. Dove recovered his balance as Pizarro got distracted by the books that had fallen out of the backpack.

"What's a half-breed loser want with military history—and some stupid Chinese stuff?" he snorted, throwing one of the volumes at Dove's head.

"It's the *Daodejing*," Dove told him, estimating his chances of grabbing the backpack before Pizarro pulled Slick's package out of the bottom of it. "Dao means 'way,' like how to live." Not good—especially not after Pizarro pulled his gun.

"Ain't that sweet, the idiot trying to figure out how to live. I got a hint for you—be smart and just concentrate on breathing. That's the way to stay alive." He laid the backpack on the car's trunk, rifling through it while keeping a bead on Dove's torso. With practiced ease, he found the fastenings for the pack's false bottom and pulled out the paper-wrapped packet. "Well, look at this. Kid's brought a lunch on his little science expedition. How about I take a share of this? You can eat what I don't want later."

He ripped into the package, setting his gun meaningfully beside the backpack. Instead of the wad of shrink-wrapped bills Dove had expected, however, the sheriff exposed a hard-plastic case, black with silver hinges and lips around its clamshell opening. He popped it open, and Dove caught the flash of something shiny between Pizarro's thick fingers. Clearly, the sheriff had expected cash too, or at least something smokable. "What the—"

Three glass vials popped out of the velvet-lined hollows inside the case and fell into the sand at the side of the drive as Dove hit Pizarro low, his shoulder hitting the sheriff under the man's overhang of belly, driving the wind out of him. Dove caught his belt and heaved, keeping the bigger man off balance, and swung open the car's door. Another hard kick, and the sheriff fell into the back seat of his police car. Dove slammed the door on him, dodging low around the car (just in case the sheriff decided to fire through the windows), swept up the pack, and grabbed the vials, stuffing them and their case into the bag as he pelted around the car, heading for the Hacienda. Sure enough, he barely had time to make the final turn in the ranch's long driveway before a shot and the sound of shattering glass broke the silence behind him.

Dove ran, wishing he knew more effective cuss words, both for himself and for the sheriff. Pizarro would make trouble for him later over this, but he couldn't bring himself to let the sheriff take the packet from him. He didn't care about Slick, but he did care about *Abuelo's* opinion of him—and he detested crooked cops. Hypocrisy grated on him even worse than outright villainy. Dove knew *Abuelo* was a criminal, but at least he made no bones about it; Pizarro was supposed to be a good guy.

The ranch house loomed in front of him, its empty windows looking like the sockets in Ojo's ghost-story skull. No lights shone through them, no vehicles parked in the tumbleweed-decorated yard. Dove's spine itched, anticipating the next shot from Pizarro's gun. Where were they? He had to deliver this package of glass bottles and get out of there, preferably without getting lead poisoning from the sheriff. On cue, a figure rose out of the darkness of the hacienda's wrap-around porch. At least four flashlights and yet another pair of headlights blinded Dove in their beams.

On the subject of villains, he thought, skidding to a halt as a quartet of scruffy, nervous-looking men burst out of the ranch house. They came to a halt within the circle of light, so he could see them as more than silhouettes. He held up his hands, the backpack dangling from one, the plastic case in the other. "*Abuelo* sent me," he told them, taking care not to make any sudden moves. They looked nervous as cats.

"What's the shooting?" one of them demanded. The others stood behind him, twitching around their rifles and gazing into the darkness.

"Sheriff from over the border," Dove told them. "He had his car pulled in down the driveway. You guys expecting a visit from the not-very legitimates?"

"He followed you?" the guy growled. This time, the rifle barrel swung up to point at Dove's head.

"No," Dove repeated. "Like I said, he'd pulled in already. Been scoping you out for the *Señor*, probably, since he's alone and on the wrong side of the border."

The man didn't have any better swear words than Dove did, but that didn't stop him from using them. He grabbed the case from Dove, spitting at his comrades, "Get him before—"

"Too late," Dove noted, as the sound of the patrol car's engine gunning down the driveway faintly reached their ears.

"Good thing this job isn't C.O.D.," he added a moment later, watching the four of them burst out of a lean-to shed in their own badly dented pickup and blaze down the road after Pizarro.

Shots exploded in the distance. Dove didn't wait to see whether the four had reinforcements still hiding in the ranch house; he left Blanca Hacienda at a run and retrieved his bike from the rocks. Keeping well off the roads, he got past the border without bringing a bullet home as a souvenir.

Instead, uneasiness followed him into the front room, along with the first slivers of dawn. Vials. Not money, but vials—and not enough vials to mean a drug shipment. Maybe a sample of some new merchandise, the rational side of his mind suggested. Maybe some nasty new poison like those guys on the news are always jawing about, the paranoid side suggested. Both agreed on the main point, however. "Benny," he said, spotting his brother slumped on the couch, "There's no way we should be running stuff for the General, no matter what *Abuelo* says."

Benny looked up, eyes slowly focusing on Dove. He sighed, shaking his head and running a weary hand over his face. "*Hasbìdì*, don't start."

"Pizarro knew," Dove informed him urgently. "Maybe not exactly, but he knew. Benny, he was there, waiting by Blanca Hacienda. Hid back in the bushes, and must've been there for a few hours, 'cause I didn't see him pass me. The *Señor*'s getting suspicious. He didn't know what I was carrying, but—"

"*Abuelo's* made a decision, and we have to stick to it," Benny told him, his voice flat. "He tells us what to do, and we do it. Let him worry about what the *Señor* knows and doesn't know." He sighed again, gazing at the bottle in his hand like he didn't see it. Then he laughed bitterly. "What else are we gonna do, *Hasbídí*?" He took a long pull at the bottle.

When his eyes came up again, they were hard. "And you better watch your mouth better. You go nay saying *Abuelo* much more, and Rico will take you down."

"*Abuelo* swore loyalty to the *Señor*, like we swore it to him. So what about honor, Benny? What about what's right?" Dove asked, fear and anger making his voice sharp.

Benny's eyes lost their diamond glint as he slumped back into the beat-up couch. "Way things are, we don't got a lot of options for standing up, *Hasbídí*. We gotta be practical instead of right."

The slump of his shoulders and the dull defeat in his voice finally registered in Dove's whirling brain. So did the absence of Dolores's pantyhose hanging on the shower curtain rod he could see through the bathroom door, the space where her makeup case had been, the empty cigar box where Benny's rainy-day money usually was, and the tequila bottle on the floor by Benny's feet. It was as empty as Benny's eyes.

Dove flopped onto the couch beside Benny and leaned his head against his big brother's shoulder. "I'm sorry, Benny," he said softly. "She didn't make you happy anyway."

That got a short laugh from Benny. "Yeah. See why I told you not to get messed up with her?" He took another drag on the bottle. "You know they're poison, but it still hurts when they leave."

* * *

Thumpa, thumpa, thumpa. "Leave her! Love me! Leave him! Love me! Leave it! Love me!"

"Gack," Chris said, hitting the scan button on the car radio.

"Weather report brought to you by the Smoking Gun. Get all your *exotic* smoking supplies—"

"Gack again." Scan.

"I mean that there is just too much hatred in the world today. Why can't people accept Sam and me for what we are? They just see two guys holding hands, and they think they have to take our son away—" Scan. "Vitamin supplements from China, guaranteed to—" Scan. "And the Lord saith that all who bow down to Babylon shall be destroyed, so send your love offering—" Scan. "The FBI has confirmed today that Elder Thomas J. Stacy of the—" Scan. Wait. Back up.

"—Christ of Latter-day Saints was executed by a militant religious group in the Philippines. Calling themselves the Children of Light, the extremists have issued a statement saying that they intend to 'drive the infidels into the sea,' beginning with the Mormons. While their exact religious affiliation is unknown, the FBI spokesman did confirm that they are not part of any known terrorist organization. The spokesman for The Church of Jesus Christ has said that the Church is taking the threat seriously, and it has issued a warning to its members and may be pulling out its American missionaries in the Philippines."

"Wow," Chris whispered. He stared at the blue sky above the street light, thinking a quick prayer for Elder Stacy's family—and the other families facing an unknown, violent threat. He vividly remembered the families he'd taught in Ecuador, their strength in the face of persecution from both their Catholic neighbors and the suspicious police. *Please help them*, he thought. *Please help all of us.*

"In other news, the political repercussions from Senator Howard Garlick's surprise announcement of the AllSafe vaccine continue to ripple through the halls of both the House and the Senate. Al Eisenstadt, Republican representative from Montana, denounced the promise of federal funding for the vaccine as 'liberal demagoguery,' while Senator Cofi Bellowes of Virginia has strongly stated her support for Senator Garlick's proposal, calling opponents—"

"Like she even knows what he's proposing!" Chris growled, turning off the radio in disgust. "I've really got to start bringing my own music." Or join a ride-sharing program to save on the horrendous cost of gas. But that came down to the old dilemma: saving money by joining a car pool or taking mass transit meant giving up independence and conforming to somebody else's schedule.

The car pool versus driving question had faded away by the time Chris arrived at work, obediently bowing to the visual scanner, waving to Naomi, and stating his name for his lab door. What hadn't faded was the lingering fish smell of Senator Garlick's promotion of the Corinth vaccine.

Chris waved at the other early-bird lab workers, John and Lia Ping, trading the usual greetings. ("Good morning, Chris. Missy up early again?" "You know it—why are you already here?" "Hey, I'm STILL here from last night!" "John Boy, you've got to work smarter, not harder.") Settling into his own cubicle, he turned on his monitor. The familiar log-in screen came up—and so did a sudden impulse. "I bet he didn't change that password." Before he could talk himself out of it, Chris entered "ChrisG" as the account name, following it with CLUVM2 as the password.

Sure enough, after chewing on them for a few seconds, the network accepted Christoff's credentials. The Corinth files appeared on Chris's screen, just as they'd done before. This time, however, each file icon also had a tiny, red dot in the corner. That meant they were obsolete or unused files, marked for "garbage disposal" as part of server maintenance. Chris quickly copied as many of the files as he could, downloading them to his own account, before the computer deleted them off the server as the detritus files of a defunct account. He watched the timer bar crawl up, measuring the copying process, as a new message appeared on screen: "Warning: This account will be disabled and deleted at 10:30 A.M. If you are still authorized to use this account or need access for administrative reasons, contact Tech Support at extension 5-4321. Please have your employee ID number ready."

Chris had seen that kind of message before, both here at MedaGen and back at Benson Bioceuticals; it was common practice to set an intern's or contractor's account to expire on a particular day or time. But why would Christoff's user account be marked as inactive? By all indications, he was a senior employee—and with AllSafe all over the news, his project had taken off like a nuclear Roman candle!

The files finished copying to his account, alerting him to their arrival with a soft chime. He quickly logged back off, resigning as Gregor Christoff and logging back in as himself. He chuckled softly as he resisted the urge to look warily over his shoulder as he did. Spy versus spy—or, in this case, geneticist versus network security. Sometimes, he had to admit, it felt like the same thing.

Still, what happened to Christoff? He keyed in a search in the MedaGen employee directory and newsletter for "Christoff, G." Had the guy's paranoia finally given him a stroke? The grin faded from Chris's face as the search came back. No, not a stroke, a car accident. The obituary had made the employee newsletter two days ago; Chris, who didn't bother reading the company propaganda, hadn't seen it. "Gregor Christoff, Senior Genetic Analyst, Dies in Crash." The story underneath explained that Christoff had died in a car accident over the weekend. It quoted his supervisor as saying that he had been a valuable member of the team and that they would miss him. It listed his accomplishments at the company (with the exception of the Corinth project) but mentioned no survivors (even his dog died in the crash). Beside the story, Christoff's thin, lined face stared out under its shock of Einstein hair.

"What are you doing? Looking for your long-lost grandfather?" The sudden question in Humphrey's voice made him jump. Darn these cubicles that forced you to sit with your back to the door! He'd have to be more alert to the smell of coffee wafting from Humphrey's cup.

Chris hid the sudden adrenaline rush and firmly reined in his impulse to close the newsletter window. Instead, he half turned in his chair to grin at Humphrey. "Hey, boss. Adjusting to life down here in Cubicle-ville with us peons?" he asked.

Humphrey groaned, taking a gulp of the hot liquid in his ever-present mug. "Rub it in, Galen. You know as well as I do that I'm just a project manager around here. A paper pusher. A clock watcher." His tone changed just slightly, suspicion replacing self-pity. "Speaking of which, how's that Protocol 4 coming? Your prelim report on that is due next Friday. You going to have it ready for the review board?"

"Have I ever been late with a prelim?" Chris asked, all wounded innocence.

Humphrey grunted through another swallow of coffee. (*Why don't they put an addiction-warning label on that stuff?* Chris wondered for the thousandth time.) "When you've been in the trenches as long as I have," he informed Chris, "you know there's always a first time for everything."

"Not this time," Chris assured him. "Things are actually looking pretty good. I think we'll be ready to start the large-scale sampling and sequencing right on time. This could be a real step forward. Maybe not as big as this AllSafe thing in the news, but pretty good anyway." He glanced speculatively at his monitor, then at Humphrey. "What do you know about that, by the way? All the company newsletter's saying is that MedaGen is proud and pleased to do its patriotic duty in saving all Americans—and, presumably, any friendly foreigners with the cash to pay for it—from the vile schemes of terrorists with biological weapons. They're not giving any hints about how it actually works." As evidence, he keyed up the current issue of the newsletter, sending up a silent prayer of thanks when his blue-sky improvising about the lead story's contents proved accurate.

Humphrey rolled his eyes. "How it actually works. You science types always want to know that. What does it matter? MedaGen's got the fat federal contract, and everybody's stock options are going to go right through the roof. Except mine. Indentured servants don't get nice Christmas presents like the rest of the family does."

"They also don't get thrown into the snow when Daddy and Mommy decide they have too many mouths to feed," Chris reminded him.

"Nah, they just get their rations cut back to bread and water," Humphrey shot back. "While the children get swept up out of the snow by the next pair of rich parents that come along."

"Things are tough all over," Chris agreed. "So you haven't heard anything about this new AllSafe vaccine they're so thrilled about?"

"Persistent, aren't you?" Humphrey shrugged. "The top bosses are scrambling to get the FDA to approve it, and Corporate's put a fairy-tale ending on the whole business. If you're going to insist on talking about work, I'm leaving."

"Fairy-tale ending?" Chris asked, puzzled.

"Yeah," Humphrey said over his shoulder as he left in search of more congenial conversation topics. (And to prod along Lia Ping on her own prelim report. The company didn't keep Humphrey around just for his taste in ties.) "Like the old story about the girl on the glass mountain and the king who wants princes to try to climb it. The guy who gets the approval wins the princess's hand and half the kingdom—and if he doesn't get the approval, he's a foot shorter. Starting at the head."

"Whack," Chris said softly. He clicked the newsletter closed and checked his e-mail box—nothing important, as usual—then wandered over to the clean-room observation window. He stood there, watching the robot arms neatly sorting the sample of gene sequences, the numbers for Protocol 4 scrolling down the screen. It really did look good, and he already had the preliminary report almost ready to go; he'd written it yesterday. So nobody should mind if he took a little of his time today to take a look at the company's latest glass mountain. He went back to his cubicle, brought up his prelim report, ready to jump it to the front of the screen at a moment's notice, and pulled open the copies he'd rescued from Christoff's account. More numbers scrolled down the screen, as well as reports, lab notes, research logs—everything, it looked like, except Christoff's own prelim and final reports. Now, why would those be missing? They were standard procedure that no one, not even the most busy or lazy, overlooked if they wanted further funding. They should be part of the package . . . unless someone took them out. But why?

CHAPTER 7

"I don't understand what's going on with Christoff's data," Chris told Merry with a sigh. He pushed the palmtop away, its screen still displaying the grids outlining the protein molecules that made up the active ingredients in Christoff's vaccine viruses.

"Where does it lose you?" Merry asked, retrieving Missy's cup from her tray. Missy didn't object to the loss of one of her favorite playthings; she was happily banging her plastic dinosaur against a tiny fighter jet.

"Most of it is pretty clear," Chris told her, stacking their plates and silverware for easier transportation to the sink. "The carrier virus itself is pretty basic, a lot like the one they modified to insert genes for immune-response cells into babies' bone marrow."

"The 'bubble baby' thing," Merry remembered aloud. "Right. And this vaccine is supposed to defeat a wide spectrum of diseases, so it makes sense to use a virus to boost immune responses."

Chris nodded. "Right. So far, so good. The delivery mechanism is straightforward—direct blood delivery, a standard injection. The carrier's transparent. But what the gene therapy actually does inside the cells, there's where things go south in a hurry. I've been through his data summary twice, but the ingredients just don't seem to add up to the final product. On the surface, it looks like we've got a case of two plus two equaling five here." He slipped the dishes into their spots in the dishwasher.

"I can't believe that MedaGen would try to hoodwink the government with a vaccine that totally didn't work," Merry said skeptically, wetting a washcloth with warm water. "That's way too high profile a con to play. Hold still, sweetie—time to clean your face."

Missy scrunched up the face in question, but submitted to the procedure with relative grace. She then demanded that her dinosaur and jet go through the same treatment.

"It can't be a con," Chris agreed, leaning against the sink. "And I admit that I didn't get all of Christoff's data. Some of it had already been deleted as obsolete. Obviously, somebody's got a full copy somewhere, but they'd hardly give me access to their top-secret, high-profile new project just for the asking."

Merry laughed, releasing Missy from her high chair. "Especially not if you walk in and say, 'Humphrey, be a sport and hand me the password to the Ultimate Vaccine files, would you? I strongly suspect that it's bogus, but I'd like to be sure before I kick up a huge fuss with the FDA approvals.' That'd get you a long way."

"That'd probably get me shot," Chris informed her, only half joking. "Or wrapped around a lamp post."

She glanced up at the sober undertone in his voice. "What?"

"Nothing—really, Merry, nothing. It's just that finding out Christoff was working on MedaGen's biggest breakthrough since—I don't know, the smallpox vaccine—when he got killed in a car accident, and his files so promptly marked for deletion, and Humphrey suddenly appearing over my shoulder as I was looking at them . . . it just felt sinister." He shrugged at his own overstatement, smiling to take the urgency out of the imagined dire possibilities. "I'm probably still unconsciously resenting them for buying out Benson Bioceuticals, or something goofy like that, building on MedaGen's reputation for ruthlessness. That and their voice printers and retina scanners and top-level priority clearance and tech support that practically asks for a tissue sample to do DNA checks before they grant access to the data-crunching computers. It's enough to make anybody a little paranoid."

"Parnoid," Missy repeated.

"Yeah, paranoid," Chris laughed, sweeping her up. "Pair of noids—that's your mom and me, Miss Missy. You keep up with all this precocious talking, and you're going to be a nerd, too." He rubbed noses with her. "Not that that's a bad thing. Actually pays pretty well, once you're out of high school."

"And once you manage to find a man who isn't intimidated by your brains," Merry added.

Chris waggled his eyebrows at her. "Not just unintimidated—downright turned on! There's nothing sexier than a girl who breezes right through leading a study session on molecular genetics while smelling like heaven."

"Which this particular little girl doesn't at the moment." Merry grinned back at him and appropriated the baby. "Time for your bath, Miss."

"Bath!" Missy eagerly agreed.

Chris followed his ladies into the bathroom, perching on the sink with the data blinking and scrolling across the screen in his hand while Merry handled the tiny tsunami generator in the tub. He had to dodge a particularly well-aimed gout of water, but caught it on his shirt instead of the palmtop. "Hmm," was his only reaction.

"Here," Merry said finally, presenting him with a squirming, slick Missy and the little hooded towel. "Trade ya." She neatly appropriated the palmtop.

Chris did more tickling and chasing the baby than efficient drying, but between the towel and evaporation, Missy got dried off. Merry followed them out of the bathroom more sedately, examining Christoff's files for herself.

"Chris, is this all the data you could download?" she asked.

"Yup, all of it," he affirmed, neatly sticking Missy into her diaper and fluffing her little nightgown over her head. "From what I've been able to tell, I got all the raw files, all the uncrunched data. The reports are what's missing, the ones that make sense of the raw data." He paused to blow on Missy's tummy, much to her delight. "The problem is that I don't know what measures or constants Christoff was using to chart the data, and I don't have time to figure it out. Protocol 4 is going into first-round testing, and I'm going to need my total share of compute cycles to handle that."

"Plus, running the top-secret Corinth vaccine data through the computer on your shifts is going to look suspicious at least," Merry finished the thought. "Hey, tell you what. Why don't I check it out here? We've got the raw data right here, and while our computer's not as fast as those behemoths you've got down at the lab, it's also all ours—we can crunch the data on it for days if we need to."

He looked up at her, surprised, then grinned. "And you're hands down the expert on reverse-engineering somebody else's constants from their results."

"I'm decent at it," Merry agreed, matching his grin and catching the plastic dinosaur that flew toward his head. "Watch it—she's getting to be a dead eye with that thing."

"Dead eye," Missy said smugly.

"Time for bed, Dead eye," Merry told her. "Kiss the daddy and ask nice for a story. Mommy's going to un-sog the bathroom."

Missy did both, and Chris hauled her off to bed and performed a spirited rendition of "Little Red Riding Hood."

He used the Big Bad Wolf voice when he caught Merry from behind and nibbled her neck too. "My, what a great brain you have." The next sentence came out in his own voice, however. "Merry, do you really want to take a crack at Christoff's data?"

She turned in his arms, putting her own arms around his neck. "Yes," she said decisively. "I've been feeling like I need to get back into practice. It feels weird—research was my whole life for years, and I haven't touched a byte of it in nearly two years. It's like my whole Ph.D. is just rotting away in my head."

"Not a chance," he said decisively. "Even without Christoff's data. From the sound of it, though, I deduce that your mother called today."

Merry sighed and thumped her forehead into his shoulder. "Yes. And Sidney ran through her standard list of complaints: I got married. I married a fundamentalist fanatic. I'm a fundamentalist fanatic myself. I quit my well-paying, respectable job. I'm wasting my education while providing a bad example for my daughter. I'm a complete atavistic throwback to the unenlightened, doormat-shaped women of olden times. And the oldie but goodie, if I wanted to get married, why couldn't I find some nice girl?"

Chris petted her hair. "And where would that leave me?" he asked, keeping the amusement out of his voice with a sincere (if only partly successful) effort.

She pulled away enough to look into his eyes and give him the roguish grin that brought out her dimple. "Why, as the best man at a lovely beach wedding—assuming California follows Oregon's lead and legalizes same-sex marriages, of course," she laughed.

"Why not?" he rejoined, chuckling. "Look at the great things that happened when they followed Oregon's lead and legalized marijuana."

"What, triple the advertisements, and all the kids thinking that Mary Jane's as unhip as their parents and champagne cocktails?" Merry guessed.

"And packs of marijuana cigarettes having an official Surgeon General's warning on them," Chris reminded her. "'This product can kill your brain cells *and* give you cancer.'"

"All the fun stuff's bad for you," Merry mock pouted.

"Not *all* of it," Chris reminded her with a wink.

* * *

Dear Chisom,

Let me report that the response to the Church in those areas affected by the quake and other disasters over the last few weeks has certainly been as positive as the Brethren expected. Quite a number of the General Authorities have been sent as administrators to those areas where the response has been especially warm. That is one of the reasons you have seen an increase in the number of Seventies in your mission. Some members wondered why Pres. Smith built up the last two Quorums so rapidly. Now we see his inspiration.

Of course that is not the only thing that has made some wonder. Those who are tradition bound have had a hard time accepting his restoration of the office of Associate President and Pres. Smith's call of Elder Rojas to that position. Don't get me wrong. People do not seem to object to Pres. Rojas. It's the new office. What the members fail to realize is that Joseph Smith established the office in December 1834. He called it the office of assistant president and appointed Oliver Cowdery to that position. He held it until his apostasy in 1838. In 1841, the Lord called Hyrum Smith to take Oliver's place, saying that "I appoint unto him that he may be a prophet, and a seer, and a revelator unto my church, as well as my servant Joseph; That he may act in concert also with my servant Joseph" (D&C 124:94–95).

Joseph explained that the Assistant, or as our current Prophet calls the office, the Associate President, is to assist in presiding over the whole Church, and to officiate in the absence of the President. Further, according to Joseph, the Associate President is to act as spokesman for the Church. The scriptural example comes from Exodus 4, where the Lord appointed Aaron to be the spokesman to Pharaoh and the Hebrews.

It is of note that it was Joseph and Hyrum, those who jointly held the office of president, who were martyred at Carthage. The two acted as joint witnesses leaving behind a binding testimony. From that time to this, that office has not functioned. Now, with the added burden of a bourgeoning worldwide Church, the Lord has instituted it once more. If you're curious about this office, you can read Joseph Fielding Smith's book, Essentials in Church History, pages 179–180.

Pres. Rojas has certainly filled the position well. He is very good-looking, dignified, fearless, and an articulate spokesman for the Lord's Church. His work with the media and in other venues has freed Pres. Smith to concentrate on the spiritual development and guidance of the kingdom.

Due to Pres. Rojas's wonderfully articulated pro-life stand, the pro-choice movement has taken the opportunity to do some serious protesting against the Church. I am intrigued at how righteous, sophisticated, and modern they sound. The rampant sacrificing of innocents that they advocate is, however, nothing short of very ancient Molech worship, albeit in modern guise. Molech, by the way, was an Old Testament idol to which worshipers sacrificed children in order to get assistance and blessings from the gods. The Lord called the practice an abomination and told His *prophets that its practice was a major reason why the Canaanites forfeited their right to the land. Israel later worshiped the same idol and they too were punished. (See 2 Chronicles 28:2 and 33:2.)*

Many Bible readers shudder at the practice of februation (passing children through blazing fire as a means of sacrifice) and wonder how a people could be so barbaric, godless, cruel, and unloving. The irony is that, even among these sensitive souls, few raise an eyebrow at abortion. They cannot see that the worship of Molech is alive and well today, but with new names: Materialism, Selfishness, and Convenience being the leading three. These gods are, in reality, nothing more than Babylon in yet another of her guises. Why is it that animals' rights have caught on among so many, yet the rights of unborn children have not? We live in an upside-down world when people get upset over the mistreatment of animals and yet condone the slaughter of innocent children. It appears that a just God is going to quickly put an end to this insanity.

Well, that's a pretty gloomy note to end this transmission on, but I cannot back away from my feelings. As you know I don't back down from what I feel the Lord wants. Your mother has teased me often saying that my parents did well to name me "Chinedu" because it translates as "the Lord is my leader." But His words heighten my appreciation for how desperately the world needs the message that you and your fellow missionaries are there to give. Be strong, testify, love the people, and bring those who are willing to come out of Babylon into the gospel light. You and your companions are literally the saviors of the people.

Love,
Your father,
Chinedu

* * *

"And—fade to commercial," Monk intoned.

Kim neatly slid the prerecorded messages into the player, while on the desk set, Kathy dropped her on-air smile like a cheap china dish and had another meltdown, this time about the long hours she had to work. "I deserve *more* than this!" she shouted. "I am a valuable asset around here! I am *sick* to *death* of getting the late-night shift and the weekends and every lame story that comes out of Podunk, Nowhere—"

"Valuable, my fat—paycheck," Monk snorted. "Better watch it, baby, you're replaceable." He glanced at Kim, then at the clocks arranged across the production booth's wall. "Speaking of which. We ready with our correspondent out in Hawaii?"

Kim nodded, opening the satellite link. Audio and visual tests scrolled across the screen and through the producers' headsets. The picture flickered, and a pleasant, unobtrusively elegant hotel room came into focus, all beige, cream, and tasteful gilt accents. The only thing that hinted at the room's tropical location was the spray of brilliantly colored blooms on the desk—and the equally brilliantly colored but definitely less tasteful pattern on the cameraman's shirt. Leon, the cameraman in question, looked up, checked the monitor for the feedback image, saw his own psychedelically colored self, and grinned widely, giving Monk the thumbs-up signal.

"Link's hot, Anne," Leon informed the reporter over his shoulder. Then he got out of the way to monitor the camera from his accustomed position behind it and gave her a reassuring thumbs-up signal.

Anne O'Neal smiled, practicing the expression for the camera, listening to the test tone in her earpiece as Kim sent the frequencies. "We're receiving," she said. She took a deep breath, calming herself for the interview. She hadn't expected the call from the network brass, giving her the assignment to interview President Rojas of The Church of Jesus Christ of Latter-day Saints—tomorrow, and in Hawaii. Leon had taken it as a great step forward, her big break, official recognition from the Big Brass, the start of a grand and wonderful career. She'd laughed it off, but she had to admit, in the darkest parts of her ego, that she thought so too. That added an unaccustomed dose of adrenaline to the morning's proceedings.

The dark, distinguished man beside her didn't move, his handsome head bowed, his hands clasped but relaxed in his lap. The conservative suit he wore fit him perfectly—and emphasized the playfulness of the brilliantly colored tie he wore with it. He looked contemplative, but certainly not nervous. Then again, he was used to addressing hundreds of thousands, if not millions, of Church members, facing down protesters, and negotiating with heads of state all over the world. Answering questions from an ambitious cub reporter wouldn't shake him.

"And we're live in five," Monk informed them, "four, three . . ."

"Good morning. I'm Anne O'Neal, religion specialist for Channel 8 News. I'm here in Hawaii this morning, and with me is Richard M. Rojas, formerly one of the Twelve Apostles and now the Associate President of The Church of Jesus Christ of Latter-day Saints." She turned her attention to her guest. "Good morning, President Rojas. I understand that the M in your name stands for Moroni. Is that right?"

President Rojas looked up, and Monk's apprehension about a dull interview promptly receded. The guy knew how to face a camera, and ready intelligence showed through his expression. His well-cut face lightened in a quick, white smile. "Good morning, Anne. It is indeed. Moroni is my middle name."

"For those of our viewers unfamiliar with Mormon scriptures—" Anne started.

"And that would be a majority of them," Rojas interjected, "but they're certainly more than welcome to check out the lds.org Web site if they would like to know more—"

"Moroni was the angel who delivered the Golden Book to Joseph Smith, wasn't he?" Anne did the interrupting herself this time and firmly took back the reins of the conversation.

"He was indeed," Rojas agreed. "And more than that, he was a prophet who lived more than a thousand years ago here in the Americas. He left us a powerful testimony of the love and power of Jesus Christ in the Book of Mormon, and in the 1800s gave that record to Joseph Smith."

"Thus founding The Church of Jesus Christ of Latter-day Saints, popularly known then and now as the Mormons, after that same Book of Mormon," Anne informed him—and, more to the point, her viewers. "And it is about your Church and its activities that I'd like to talk to you."

"Fire away," Rojas invited, settling comfortably but attentively back in his chair. "Figuratively speaking, of course."

"All right," Anne said. "First, let me extend sincere condolences from all of us here at Channel 8 for the loss of your fellow Apostle, Elder Stacy. I understand that you are on your way to Manila now to escort his body back to the United States?"

"That's right, Anne," Rojas said. "Thank you for your sympathy. We all loved and respected Elder Stacy very much, and we'll surely miss him. But we know that he, like so many before him, died doing our Heavenly Father's work, and he is not lost to us forever. Thanks to the great Atonement of our Savior, Jesus Christ, we know that we will meet again."

"Happiness in the hereafter is a comforting thought," Anne agreed. "At the same time, however, we have to deal with what happens here and now. And, unfortunately, your Church has come under fire lately on a wide range of topics. I'd like to show you just a few clips from the interviews I've done in the last month, then have you comment on them, if you would."

Rojas nodded, a smile twinkling in his eyes but not showing on his lips. "Roll on, Anne. We'll both see what I have to say."

Clips of the interviews replaced the sunlit hotel room. Under rainy skies outside the new Church Headquarters in Independence, Missouri, a vociferous group of anti-Mormon protesters waved signs and chanted slogans decrying the Church as a non-Christian cult. "We just don't like these people coming in, spreading their anti-Christ message, pushing themselves in where they're not wanted," a woman exclaimed. "This is the Bible belt, and they don't even believe in the Bible. They've taken over the City Council, and now they're trying to grab the election for mayor, too. We won't let them!"

Another protest replaced the Christian political rally; the signs were the same, the slogans on the signs changed. "The Mormons are homophobic bigots who try to push their fundamentalist agenda by pouring money into illegal political pressure!" a gay-rights protester snarled. The triangle tattoo on his forehead distorted as he scowled. "Look what they did in California—and Hawaii, too—using their members to defeat the human-rights initiatives that would acknowledge the universal human right to marry and adopt children!"

An equally incensed spokesperson, this time for a "pro-choice" group, replaced him. "Oh, yes, we know the Mormons. They're behind most of the abortion clinic bombings and assassinations of innocent medical professionals simply trying to give women the healthcare they desperately need." In response to Anne's question, she tossed her head. "We don't have any *proof* that they're behind it, but we know they support domestic terrorism, just like the other right-wing, Christian-fundamentalist fanatics."

"We do not support fanatics of any kind," a United Nations spokesperson said next. "Of course, people should be able to worship what and how they want to. However, we strongly believe that international cooperation on religious rights should be directed toward crafting resolutions that give widespread endorsement to the idea of freedom of belief, not on proselytizing for specific religions. The Church of Jesus Christ of Latter-day Saints, by its aggressive presence, inflames the sensibilities of the residents of many countries who do not appreciate its hard-line missionary tactics. Really, it smacks of the worst kind of cultural imperialism." Images of shouting, stone-throwing mobs and a burning chapel underscored his point.

The burning faded, replaced by the calm picture of Anne and Rojas. She looked at the Apostle, who looked serious but not distressed. "As you can see, President Rojas, many activists and others are upset at your Church's presence and influence on a variety of political and social issues, from gay rights to free speech to abortion to international cooperation on religious rights. Does this opposition worry you?"

Rojas smiled, sitting forward, easily bringing the camera (and thus the viewer) into the conversation. "Actually, Anne, I would be more worried if we didn't run into opposition. Opposition, as the quote goes, shows that what we're doing is making a difference. We stand up for what we know is right, and our members live what they believe. We know the truth, we gladly share it, and we hold to it. That has never been a recipe for worldly success and popularity, from ancient times right through to today."

"Still, sometimes that opposition can get very strong," Anne pointed out. "In fact, the attacks on The Church of Jesus Christ have been growing, both in numbers and in violence. Some sources have said that your Church's increased visibility and activity was the reason for Elder Stacy's assassination."

"I would sincerely regret it if that were so," Rojas told her. "But even if it were, we cannot stop sharing our message of hope, life, and love with all Heavenly Father's children. If we have to 'waste away our lives,' what better way to do it than in service to the Savior?"

"According to some statements, President Rojas, the Church does a lot more than just share its message," Anne said. "Several critics contend that the leadership of the Church tells its members how to vote as well."

Rojas shook his head. "That's been the rumor ever since the 1840s," he told her. "It's as false now as it was then—if not even more so! I want to emphasize that every individual member of The Church of Jesus Christ of Latter-day Saints, in every country and state on the globe, is completely free to vote as his or her conscience dictates, and the Church absolutely encourages him or her to do so! The active, heartfelt, and sincere involvement of members of the Church is vitally important, especially in matters that strike directly at the heart of the family and morality—such as the sacredness of marriage, the value of life, and the freedom of all people in this world to worship how, when, and what they may without fear of persecution."

"That openness to community involvement does not seem to extend to the Church's internal matters, however," Anne pointed out. "In fact, if I may cite a recent example, your unprecedented appointment as Associate President of the Church has caused a controversy that divided the ranks of the Church itself."

"Unlike the common process in many Protestant denominations," Rojas reminded her gently, "we believe that revelation from Jesus Christ Himself does not need to go through a committee of mortals for approval. As a Church, we sustain the word of the Prophet, indicating that we understand and agree to accept and support the revealed policy. So it was with my appointment—which is not completely unprecedented, by the way. Hyrum Smith, the Prophet Joseph Smith's brother, held the position of Associate President until his death. I am deeply sorry that so many of my brothers and sisters have allowed the change to shake their testimonies, and I hope that they will take the time to sincerely examine their feelings and seek a witness through prayer of its appropriateness. The Church is not a static entity, holding to ancient traditions. We believe in, we *live* in, a vital, living Church and actively seek divine guidance as we move forward."

"The Church seems to move too fast for some, and much too slowly for others," Anne noted. "The controversy over your appointment seems to be the mirror image of the controversies over the official stance on other social issues, which have caused intellectuals and other moderates to leave the Church."

Rojas fixed her with his dark eyes and smiled sadly. "Again, the Church regrets the loss of any of our members—of anyone, member or not, who refuses to heed the truth. But the real head of the Church is Jesus Christ, and what He says, goes."

"Thank you, President Rojas," Anne said. "You've been very open with us. I'm sure we all, regardless of personal convictions, can agree that actively pursuing good is an admirable thing. Best wishes for improved health to President Smith." She paused for a split second, then added, "We have just a few seconds more. Is there any message you'd like to leave with our viewers?"

"Thank you, Anne," Rojas said graciously. "Yes, there is." He looked deeply into the camera, his dark eyes seeming to look through the lens into the eyes of the millions of his brothers and sisters. "Remember that our Savior, Jesus Christ, calls all to come to Him for peace, which you can find nowhere else. No matter who feels uncomfortable about this, whoever wishes it were different, wickedness never was happiness. And it never will be."

"Thank you, President Richard M. Rojas," Anne said hurriedly, discomfited by his simple statement, and even more troubled by the fact that it did make her uncomfortable. "This is Anne O'Neal, Channel 8 News."

"And we're clear," Monk informed her through the satellite link. "Good job, Anne." He clicked off the live feed, and looked at the image of President Rojas, shaking Anne's hand before the video transmission ended. "And we'd better watch that guy—he's got some slick to him."

Kim nodded, cueing up the next report. The overly familiar bump-and-grind beat filled Monk's headphones as the spotlights flicked on in the studio, illuminating the second-string anchor. The guy smiled under his blow-dried hairdo. "Well, Anne, I don't know about all that happiness business—but 'wickedness' is about to get a whole lot less contagious." The smirk quotient in his smile went up several notches. "In fact, the hot question for our panel of sexperts is: With the upcoming FDA approval of MedaGen's AllSafe vaccine, which promises complete freedom from sexually transmitted diseases, is the age of 'safe sex' finally over? Tune in at 11:00 for our panel's passionate discussion on this hot topic!"

* * *

The sun beat down on the broken tiles of Blanca Hacienda's roof, pouring out of a permanently hazy sky. The slight amber glow of sunlight, filtered through a thin scarf of high-altitude volcanic ash, lent the ramshackle building a soft elegance that it certainly didn't deserve. The flattering light didn't do anything for the building's inhabitants, however.

"I can see them from here, sir," Slick said coolly into a compact satellite phone. He held a pair of binoculars to his eyes, assessing the situation at the makeshift camp hidden behind the hacienda's walls. "Apart from living like the pigs they are, they don't appear to be doing well. One of the locals delivered the plague culture to them two days ago, on schedule, and it looks like the symptoms have started. Yes, they're coughing hard, and two of them haven't stirred despite the kicks of their leader. Looks like the research team's latest vaccine didn't work. The coyotes have all caught the plague."

The two soldiers beside Slick traded glances. One, Omerta, subtly held up two fingers. The other, Butch, shook his head, then held up three fingers, raising the bet. Omerta thought about that, then nodded.

"I agree, Sir," Slick said. "It's a waste of resources—but sacrificing incompetents doesn't hurt as much as losing real soldiers. Besides, this way, we keep the expenses down to a minimum while we hope for better luck with the vaccine next time. At least we know the plague virus itself works extremely well." A sharp smile flicked under his sunglasses. "Yes, sir, that's why you love me."

He put the phone away with a practiced flick and stowed the binoculars in the glove compartment of the truck. "Let's go pay off our *compadres*," he informed his deputies.

They both grinned at that, opening the back of the bed to pull out a pair of rifles.

"Not real sneaky about being out here, are they?" Butch asked. He pointed down at the hacienda's yard, the truck parked in plain view beside the sagging porch.

"No loss, then," Omerta snorted. Other than his bet to Butch, of course, but he didn't mention that to Slick.

"Ready?" Slick asked, bored with their comments.

"Ready," Omerta agreed, adjusting his own sunglasses.

Butch settled for chambering a round in the rifle and climbing into the large Ford. He called shotgun, of course.

Omerta parked the big vehicle in the thin shade from the dead lilac bushes. The three of them walked blatantly toward the hacienda, stopping in the middle of the yard, dust and bits of tumbleweed blowing over their boots.

The campers came out to meet them. "Hey, Slick, man, we expected you two days ago!" *Gordo* yelled. "We got the shakes bad from that crap medicine you gave us, and we're running out of smokes. 'Bout time you coughed up our money and we got out of here!"

"Not feeling well?" Slick called back.

"We're fine," *Gordo* bluffed, pausing to cough. The guys behind him weren't even that good at bluffing; one of them stumbled and had to catch the badly leaning pole not quite holding up the porch to keep from falling over himself.

"Mainly, we're sick of sitting out here burning our butts off sitting on that pile of junk you ordered," *Gordo* informed Slick. He took a step off the porch. "So how about you come across with the cash, and we cruise?"

Slick lit a cigarette, took a drag, and gazed at *Gordo* through his sunglasses. "Actually, *Gordo*, seems to me you're mainly just sick."

"What's that supposed to mean?" *Gordo* growled. His camp mates echoed both his growl and his lowering brows. They came off the porch with as much menace and determination as they could, despite the fact that for most of them, the world felt as if it were pitching like a ship in a typhoon.

"It means we've got your payment right here," Slick assured him, reaching into his pocket. His hand blurred as he pulled the pistol from the holster built into his jacket.

Gordo went down before he even realized he'd been shot. His buddies had more of a clue, since it took a fraction of a second longer for Omerta and Butch to limber up their guns, but they didn't have a lot of time to stew about it. They hit the ground, the porch, and, in one case, the wall of the hacienda amid colorful, if monochrome, crimson splatters.

Slick nodded, tucking his pistol back into its den. "And we're done here." He shot that ice-cold grin at his deputies, retrieving the packet of cash *Gordo* had died for out of his pocket. "Bonuses all around."

Omerta flinched slightly as the packet arced toward his chest, but caught it neatly as Slick turned away. Butch smacked his shoulder and grabbed the bag of cash.

"You want us to bury the mess?" Omerta asked Slick.

Slick gave him a long look. "Think about it, *estupido*. Do I want you to walk through contaminated blood, pick up infectious corpses, breathe air filled with the most deadly virus ever created? And then do I want you to get into the same truck I'm in, breathing the same air?"

"Guess not," Omerta admitted, after processing the pattern.

"Get in the truck," Slick snarled. "And because you're not completely useless, when I want you dead, I won't make you dig any grave but your own."

Omerta got into the truck, ignoring Butch's grin. He stared intently out the windshield as he navigated the truck down the narrow drive between the dead bushes. "No graves, no cleanup, cocaine in camp. So what happens when the cops get out here and find 'em?"

Slick flicked his cigarette butt out of the window. It hit the packed dirt, then rolled under the dead bushes and came to a stop in a thin drift of parchment-dry leaves. The embers glowed as the heat started to spread. "Fire will kill the bugs fast enough and burn out the obvious evidence. Nobody's coming out here, not for days, not for weeks, not for months. That's why we chose a haunted house, remember? Who's going to come here? It's all been picked over. And the local sheriff—Pizarro—won't get out here anytime soon. He's lived long enough to have good instincts about what's healthy and not."

"What about somebody else? Like the *federales*," Butch suggested.

"If the *federales* ever see this nice piece of work, it'll be long after the bug's died off. They'll see charred, gunshot skulls and figure it's drug runners busting the *Señor's* territory. He gets his chops busted, we don't show up on the radar." Slick dismissed that concern. Behind them, he noticed, a thin curl of smoke rose in the rear-view mirror. He didn't draw the others' attention to it, just flicked a razor-sharp smile to himself.

"Yeah, but say somebody does get here, and they go walking through all them viruses and whatever before they kick off," Omerta persisted, turning on to the dirt road that led away from the hacienda. "And they get sick, then what happens?"

"Then they better hope that AllSafe stuff's as good as the gov'mint's saying it is," Slick informed him. *That would be an interesting test*, he thought. *Maybe the General won't have to keep depending on those idiot researchers to find an effective vaccine after all. Maybe MedaGen has done it for us.*

* * *

"So it does just what they say it does." Chris sighed.

"With a twist," Merry agreed.

They both solemnly regarded the screen of their office computer. Chemical matrices, statistics, DNA strands, and projected models for immune-system response glowed back at them. Merry's painstaking (and sometimes banana-stained) analysis of Christoff's raw data files had proved quite straightforward, once she pinned down the gene sequences the experiment used. Now, shining in full color from the flat screen, was the secret of AllSafe. The "vaccine" did indeed guard a normal, healthy human from almost every known human-infectious virus and bacteria. It worked by using stem cells (harvested, as Merry suspected, from cloned human embryos) to exponentially heighten the immune system to such a pitch that the white blood cells in the body immediately attacked and destroyed any unfamiliar invader they encountered. "Shoot first, ask questions later," Merry had told Missy. However, the simulated tests Merry ran suggested that the vaccine's effectiveness is actually a double-edged sword. The first dose heightened the immune system, providing all the stated benefits—but if the patient didn't get another dose within six months, the immune system went into overdrive and began attacking the body's own tissues. In longer-range simulations, the stem cell based medicine actually started causing a total, fatal breakdown of the immune system. It essentially burned itself out, taking the rest of the body with it.

"Just goes to show what happens when you try to push too hard. I'd like to get at least a couple of real-life trials in to be absolutely, 110 percent sure," Merry said.

"Not likely, with the new regulations," Chris snorted. "They make permits for animal research just slightly easier to get than licenses to store spent nuclear fuel rods."

"Oh, no, I meant human trials. Those are tons easier to get approved," Merry informed him sarcastically. "Seriously, though, the computer model they're using is pretty tight. I think we can trust that we've figured out how MedaGen's new Corinth vaccine works. And why they're so eager to roll it out all at once and as quickly as possible."

"Maybe they don't know about the long-range effects," Chris suggested, still staring at the screen, wishing he could disbelieve what the data were telling him.

Merry snorted cynically. "Like fun they don't. If you ask me, they're more interested in guarding their bottom line than helping humanity. Bunch of pushers—only the first one's free."

"You're letting Sidney get to you," Chris told her, breaking his morbid fascination with the monitor to stroke her hair and grin at her. "Suspecting everybody of underhanded dealings."

"Not everybody," Merry assured him. "Only the patriarchy!"

"Dad-a-dad-a-dad!" Missy called from her bedroom. "Dad-a-dad-a-dad!"

"Guess that makes you part of the patriarchy," Merry said, saving her analysis to a backup disk.

"Guess it does," Chris agreed. "And I don't trust MedaGen either. But still, we should give them a chance to do the right thing."

"I hope you have better success convincing them to show you why AllSafe's really safe than we do actually getting Missy to go to bed on time," Merry sighed. "Four extra kisses tonight. This is getting ridiculous."

"Dad-a-dad!" Missy shouted again. "Kiss!"

* * *

"Kiss!" Virginia breathed, then took a deep breath for the benefit of the camera panning down her torso. "Live!" she cooed, throwing a bump and grind in at the appropriate moment. The blue-green jewel in her navel glittered in time to the beat, morphing into a pool as the camera dove closer. "Free!" her voice urged as she undulated through the aqua water, bursting to the surface under a waterfall that morphed into a shower of pink, red, and white rose petals barely hiding the parts of her anatomy that standard-broadcast customers had to pay extra to see. "AllSafe," she intoned, blowing a petal-storm kiss at the camera. The floral blizzard blanked the screen; for a moment, the MedaGen logo shone in dark crimsons amid the variegated reds.

"What's that?" Chris asked, coming up behind Humphrey. The manager was watching Virginia's latest merchandising porn on the large screen that dominated the lab's one large conference room.

"Like you can't tell?" Humphrey swiveled around in the high-backed, faux-leather chair at the head of the conference table and shot Chris a sardonic look. "It's the sucker ad for AllSafe, Dr. Geneticist. And they call you a genius. I just downloaded it off the leak site."

"Quite . . . colorful, if you count skin tones as colors," Chris noted, then looked from the screen to Humphrey. "Sucker ad? Leak site?"

"They really do keep you under a rock, don't they?" Humphrey said with mock sympathy. "A sucker ad's the one you put out before the real ad, to drive up attention and mindshare."

"FDA regulations prohibit advertising new drugs until the approval process is complete," Chris said reflexively, his notes from the required Medicine and the Law course springing back into mind.

Humphrey nodded, tapping his temple sagely. "Well, looks like you have a little marketing savvy after all, even if you got the wrong perspective on it. No, MedaGen can't officially advertise until they jump though federal hoops. That's what a leak site's for. Plenty of lonely geeks out there want to get a look at Virginia before anybody else does. They go looking for the inside scoop, going to spoiler Web sites. We leak our sucker ad to the spoiler site, they put it out like it's top secret, and boom! Our mindshare blasts through the roof—and we haven't released the ad." He smiled smugly. "We've even got the logs that show unauthorized downloads from the company's computers. Anybody asks about it, we're the innocent victims of a bunch of hackers."

"And when the vaccine passes FDA approval, MedaGen puts out an entirely different ad, proving their good faith." Chris filled in the final details.

"Right." Humphrey nodded, reaching for the controls. "Want to see the legit ad? It's got even more 'color' than this one. Marketing had a hard time keeping it off Virginia's own leak site. Her people wanted maximum exposure—and in this case, they got it. You've never seen so much—"

"Humphrey," Chris interrupted, stepping forward and flicking off the screen. "I'm married."

Humphrey rolled his eyes, all jaded boredom. "Oh, yeah, I forgot. You're married. Can't be watching anything the little wifey wouldn't approve of."

"Close, but not quite. I meant that I'm married, so I've not only seen that much, but far better." Chris grinned at him. "A steady relationship has all kinds of benefits, Humphrey. You ought to try it sometime."

"Can it, Galen," Humphrey growled. "Why are you even here this late, instead of home with that steady relationship? It's got to be something besides rubbing my nose in a solo Friday night."

"Actually, it has more to do with that ad than Friday nights," Chris said. "Errol, I managed to get a look at Gregor Christoff's data."

"Christoff—the guy in the car wreck? Why would you care—" The light of realization dawned suddenly in Humphrey's face. He rose from his chair abruptly, all sarcasm erased. "Christoff was working on the Corinth vaccine before he got pancaked. How did you get into his files?"

Chris took a deep mental breath. "Does that really matter? A network glitch. I got a copy before the techs erased his user folder. What's important is what that data suggest. It looks like the vaccine works not just effectively but too well—AllSafe tunes up the immune system so high that it ends up eating itself to death from the inside, unless you get another dose to moderate the effects."

"Can you prove that?" Humphrey demanded tightly.

"No, I can't prove that, but the FDA trials will do that and more," Chris told him. "Maybe I can save MedaGen some embarrassment, if nobody's thought to run the long-term simulations yet. I just need full access to the vaccine data to double check."

"Full access to the vaccine data, when you've already cracked into top-secret files?" Humphrey snarled. "Like —— you will. You're already treading thin ice, Galen. You want to add criminal prosecution to the pink slip you're asking for? One word from MedaGen, and you'll never work in the biotech sector again—when you finally get out of prison after serving the maximum sentence for industrial espionage. You're lucky that I'm the only one here, or you'd be canned for sure!" His voice rose, as he repeated the same essential ideas, his language getting worse with each repetition.

Chris waited, looking steadily at the manager, until Humphrey's threats burned themselves out. "Listen, Errol, I'm not grandstanding here. If what I've seen is true, then either MedaGen's criminally incompetent or willfully negligent. Or actively pushing a substance that makes addiction look like nothing."

"And I'm not kidding here," Humphrey told him. "You don't want to get into this, Chris, if you don't want to get snapped like a twig."

"I don't want to get into this?" Chris exclaimed. "Maybe you didn't hear me. If whoever's on this team hasn't found a way to chill that vaccine—and I don't see how they can and still keep it effective—people are going to *die* if they don't get follow-up shots for their rest of their lives!"

Humphrey pulled the slightly ragged edges of his careless attitude around himself again. "Even if you're right, what does it matter? Shot's free to employees. Better to live than die."

"Better to die than live in bondage," Chris countered.

"Dramatic, aren't you?" Humphrey grinned. The smile dropped abruptly. "Galen, I like you. You're a smart kid and a good egg. So do yourself and that nice wife of yours a big favor. Let the project team and the FDA worry about making sure the vaccine's safe. Go home—and if you don't mention this to anybody, I won't either."

"But—" Chris began.

"In fact, as far as I'm concerned, I didn't see you tonight," Humphrey continued, sweeping his immaculately tailored jacket off the back of the chair. "And because I was home getting blind drunk, you didn't see me, either. No matter who asks," he walked to the door, tossing on the jacket. "You and I were never here, and we sure as rain in Seattle didn't have this conversation." He looked at Chris. "Remember what I told you about idealism? Add this: nobody becomes a martyr to common sense."

"No, just martyrs to other peoples' greed and pride," Chris informed the door, but Humphrey let it close without reacting to Chris's parting shot. He whirled, glaring at Virginia, still pouting at three times life size from the screen. "Common sense!"

Chris watched him go, arguments bubbling up unspoken. Common sense screamed that taking poison is stupid, no matter what the guy selling you the poison said. Common sense argued that it's better to perfect precautions that prevented infections than employ drastic measures to beat diseases afterward. Common sense also says that the MedaGen Board isn't going to welcome anybody stomping in and shouting about AllSafe being anything but safe. What was the likelihood that they'd somehow missed the vaccine's long-term effects? How much was he willing to bet that they'd appreciate him pointing out the horribly convenient downside to their potential golden goose? Was he willing to bet his job—his family's living—that this was all just a dire but well-intentioned mistake?

Chris slumped into a chair, rocking slowly back and forth. The casters squeaked in time to the movement. A succession of thoughts raced through his mind, each with its associated images: Protocol 4, gene after gene slotting neatly into the deactivated pancreatic cells of mice, reactivating the delicate process that made insulin, driving diabetes and all its insidious damage into retreat. The scientific journals that already invited him to share his findings, his name in discreet but oh-so-satisfying black and white on their prestigious pages. Charges of industrial espionage, a deadly accusation in the eyes of the business-friendly courts, and the iron gray bars of a white-collar prison. Merry's grim face as she told him what her analysis suggested, and the simulation's vivid depiction of an immune system, driven amok by AllSafe, tearing into the body's own tissues. General Moroni, fighting the rebels in his own country in defense of their families and freedoms, willing to stand up for the right no matter what the cost. Missy's wide smile and bright eyes, her coppery curls wafting in the cold wind of the street after her daddy lost his job and went to prison as a spy. Missy again, crying in pain as her immune system ate her from the inside out, MedaGen (in the form of Virginia's half-naked self) demanding that he and Merry cough up an exorbitant fee to save their baby.

"No!" Chris lurched out of his chair, glaring at Virginia's projected image. "Not Missy, and not anybody else's child! This cure is worse than any disease—and I'm not going to let you do it!" He stabbed the remote viciously, dissolving Virginia's suggestive pose as the Channel 8 News broadcast replaced her image on the screen.

"—and that was the scene in Washington just a few minutes ago," Kathy informed him, "as protesters converged to protest the FDA's evaluation of MedaGen's AllSafe vaccine. Spokespeople for the protesters argue that every day the FDA delays the vaccine means more needless deaths. Senator Howard Garlick agrees."

A shot of Senator Garlick glowering at reporters dissolved as shouting protesters filled the screen behind Kathy. Police moved in, keeping riot shields between themselves and the crowd, throwing tear-gas canisters, shooting barrages of pepper balls into the writhing mass of humanity. The mob finally broke and ran, as the soft-core anarchists among them decided they'd had enough of the pepper's sting. A few sign-waving zealots held their ground, shouting slogans that the bedlam around them reduced to half-audible gibberish. The slogans on their signs mentioned AIDS in a dozen colors; it seemed a good bet that they were against it. The transmission ended abruptly as a pepper ball splatted against the camera lens.

That ended the live report (and the camera man's shift for the evening), but statistics still ran along the crawl bar beneath Kathy: 7

officers hurt in the fracas, 157 protesters injured to some degree, $180,000 in property damage. The numbers updated with each repetition, fluctuating up and down with the latest reports. So did the poll numbers from the "electronic democracy" that Channel 8 touted so avidly. From the numbers, the crowd in the online coliseum was giving a thumbs-down to the forces of law and order.

"And speaking of AllSafe," Kathy said, turning on the "everything's okay now" smile that newspeople learned to use early in their careers, "Channel 8's Web sources have secured a sneak preview of the latest ad—"

Chris used a word that he definitely didn't want Missy hearing (let alone repeating) and stabbed the Power button on the console. Silence flooded into the room, leaving him alone with the echoes of shouted slogans. Needless deaths, indeed. Protesting the FDA's attempts to keep a potentially deadly "medicine" out of the public's hands! "Wait a minute," he exclaimed aloud. "The FDA!"

He sprinted down to his own office through the darkened hallways. Lia Ping was still here, he noted absently, watching the gene sequencers work. Other than her unobtrusive presence, however, the lab cubicles were deserted. He slowed slightly, considering enlisting her help, but kept moving. Better to take it to the top right away, and worry about securing local support later.

A few moments' flicking through his electronic address book found the phone number he needed. Elizabeth Gessler, the contact at the FDA for his Benson Bioceuticals projects, might know about the AllSafe eval. The computer dialed as he held the phone to his ear, half holding his breath, half whispering, "Please, Elizabeth, be there. I know you're busy, I know you're working. I know—"

"Hello?" She sounded tired and wary, skittish as if she expected the phone to bite her.

Or the person on the other end of the line, Chris corrected the thought. "Elizabeth, hello. It's Chris Galen, out at Benson's—I mean, MedaGen's San Diego office."

"Oh," her voice lost the burring edge of paranoia. "Chris! How's it going? You got that diabetes cure ready for our review yet?"

"Not yet," he told her. "But soon, if everything works out. Listen, Elizabeth, I need to talk to the head of the team doing the evaluation for AllSafe—"

"Chris, don't," she interrupted. "Please. Don't even bring it up. You know I can't talk about an ongoing eval. Especially not that one!"

"Elizabeth," Chris took a deep breath and sent a quick but heartfelt prayer for inspired cooperation heavenward. "Just give me a name and a number. I've got information from Gregor Christoff, the guy who developed the stuff in the first place. I just need to get it to the right person. You know me, Elizabeth. I don't play politics. This is important—no, not important. It's absolutely critical."

The pause on the line went on so long that Chris's imagination filled in crickets chirping. He realized it was the sound of her typing. At last, she said, "Christoff's on the list, all right. Listen, I can't give you the name or the number, but tell you what—I'll transfer you down there. They can decide whether or not they want the data."

"Thanks, Elizabeth," Chris said. "I owe you more than you know."

"You sure do, and don't think I won't collect in full," she returned. Her voice disappeared in a series of electronic beeps as she transferred the call.

"Hello?" Once again, the voice was female, tired, and wary—and utterly unfamiliar.

"Hello. This is Chris Galen, from MedaGen. I have data on AllSafe from Gregor Christoff that may not have been included in the evaluation information," Chris said, keeping his voice level with effort.

A soft shuffling came through the line, then she said, "I don't see your name on the list of project-team members. What is this data?"

"It's the raw simulation data for the Corinth vaccine," Chris told her. "I can send it to you right now, if you'll give me your e-mail address."

"Not likely," she informed him. "I'll believe you are who you say you are, since your phone location checks out as MedaGen San Diego, but this is a high-security matter. If you have information that bears on the evaluation, send it in an official amendment to the packet we have."

"But that requires going through MedaGen's project team for the vaccine, and I have reason to believe that someone is deliberately suppressing this data," Chris told her. "From Christoff's data, it appears that a single dose of the vaccine causes an extreme heightening of the immune system that is ultimately fatal if the patient doesn't get regular follow-up doses."

Again, a flickering silence filled the airwaves—but this one didn't last as long and came to a much less satisfactory conclusion. "I really don't want to talk about it," she finally said. "We're busy right now, with AIDS activists and who knows what other protesters marching outside. They're throwing Molotov cocktails at the building to protest the vaccine going through the approval process at all. Everybody from the Senator on down wants this stuff available yesterday!"

"Which is why you should be extra cautious and careful about evaluating the tar out of it!" Chris almost shouted. "Can't you see that they're trying to shove it down your throat?"

"I can see as well as you can—even better," she told him sharply. "And now, I'm going to tell you, officially, to back off. We're working on it, it's confidential, and it's not your place to ask about it. If there is something wrong with the vaccine, if there are unwanted side effects, we'll find them. Now, you can break the connection immediately and keep out of an official evaluation, or I'll file an official complaint with MedaGen."

She didn't wait for him to choose; she simply hung up, leaving him holding a dead receiver. He sighed, resisting the urge to pound his head against the desk. After a moment, however, his optimism reasserted itself. Pride was the cardinal sin, sure, but it also came in handy occasionally. Ms. FDA hadn't sounded a bit pleased at the idea that MedaGen had held out on her. Maybe that push was all she needed to do a really thorough evaluation and turn up the same results that Merry had. Feeling more confident, he tapped into his home computer through his lab workstation, entering his password to gain access to Christoff's data files and Merry's simulation. By the time he'd e-mailed them to Elizabeth, asking her to make sure they got to Ms. FDA, he was practically whistling.

Of course, there would be trouble if Humphrey found out he'd sent Christoff's files to the FDA, but he felt more secure about even that confrontation now. Humphrey was right—if he confronted the AllSafe project team or (heaven forbid) MedaGen's Board directly, they'd just fire him. This way, he had an outside witness—and a government agency at that—to back up his assertions. And if they proved him wrong, he hadn't given the information to anybody but the people charged with doing the evaluation, which is just what you'd expect from a conscientious employee. Besides, there were laws that protected whistle blowers, right?

Chris flicked off the computer and walked out through the darkened corridors, waving to Lia Ping as he left. He didn't wave to the surveillance camera that swiveled to watch him go. He didn't even see it. The screen that showed him leave didn't accompany the image with the usual border of advertisements and inducements. Its only decoration was the silver MedaGen logo in the upper corner.

CHAPTER 8

"My child just wasn't being challenged in school. She wasn't accomplishing as much as my friends' kids," said the perfectly coiffed mother, looking deeply concerned.

"Homework was just taking her way too long," a blue-collar but clearly upwardly mobile father explained, leaning in earnestly.

"How could we expect him to get into a good preschool when he didn't know his colors yet?" asked an anxious grandmother.

"At EduStart centers across the nation, children get the help and encouragement they need to excel," the invisible announcer reassured everyone, as the scenes changed to show parents and children happily consulting EduStart counselors. Kids presenting multimedia slide shows, award-winning science-fair projects, and one-act plays underscored the point as the rates for personal-tutoring service scrolled across the screen. "Why trust your child's education to failing public schools?" the tagline asked.

Dove snorted. "'Cause nobody but rich people got to worry about Junior getting into an exclusive preschool," he informed the screen. The full-page ad disappeared, receding into the constant crawl of advertising that ran down the side of the computer's screen. (Of course, since it was a library's system, all the ads had to be at least slightly educational in content, if not in product—and the liquor companies' logos were smaller.)

Perro laughed. "Yeah, rest of us do just fine with juvie halls—the scenery ain't much, but the grub's free."

The laugh earned him a glower from one of the librarians. She'd stationed herself near the public-access computers when the boys came in, keeping a sharp eye on them as she sorted through late-return slips.

"Hey, it's a free country," Perro growled.

"Nothing's free in this country," Dove corrected, smacking Perro's shoulder and keeping his voice down. "Even libraries got to run ads on their computers before you can do any research. And you keep up the racket, she'll have Pizarro down here to bust our tails."

"For what?" Perro demanded. "Trying to kyfe one of these old-time boxes here?" He tapped the side of the computer's housing, securely bolted to the equally heavy table and covered with Plexiglas.

Calvin grinned sharply. "Sure. They'll let us download porn, but they don't trust us." He stretched. "How much longer we got to hang here, *Hasbìdì*? I'm starved. And thirsty. And bored."

"And heading for a fat F on your paper. Then what happens? You want to go back to juvie for busting your probation?" Dove asked. "Now, pay attention, and I'll show you how to find the stuff for the paper. You got to know how to work the system, Calvin, or you're going to end up ignorant like Perro."

"Hey!" Perro objected. "At least I'm good looking."

Calvin shrugged his opinion of that statement, but he did lean forward again.

"It's not hard—I figured it out awhile ago." Dove showed them the basic rules for the search engine, then turned the controls over to Perro and Calvin, settling for smacking them when the noise level got too high. Apart from that, though, he pretty much tuned out the discussion as they argued over the best way to find information on "swimsuit model photography" (their chosen job to report on for the Professional Skills portion of their probation-mandated "life skills training"). He didn't bother to contribute to the debate of the advantages of photographing swimsuit-clad models ("Beautiful women, man! And trips to Cancun, *ese!*"). Across the room, the librarians' conversation had caught and held his attention.

"I saw it on the news at noon," the elder lady informed the one who stood closer to the terminals. "A whole family found dead in a little farmhouse, right down by the border."

"Which side?" the younger one asked, finishing with her late-return slips and beginning to enter some kind of library-related information into her own computer.

"Mexico side," Old Librarian said, in a tone that made it clear such things were only to be expected on the south side of the street. "A whole bunch of them, grandpa down to a baby, with all kinds of uncles and cousins—you know how it is." They both nodded, and she continued, "But the oddest thing is that none of them had a mark on them. Guy at the last-chance station down there said one of them had come in to get cold medicine last week, then nobody heard anything from them again. Until some deputies came out to pick up one of the cousins—outstanding warrant on him—and found them all just lying around."

"Hantavirus, maybe?" Young Librarian suggested.

"Hantavirus doesn't work that quickly," Old Librarian said decisively, her tone declaring that library training made her an expert on long-distance medical diagnoses as well as shushing people. "You ask me, it was like those villages down further south where everybody ended up dead—terrorists spreading poison. Or another drug cartel moving in. Or some kind of natural disaster—poison gas out of the ground."

"That's as likely as the other two," Young Librarian said, looking over her half glasses at the older woman with a slightly disguised version of the same disdain she'd shot at Perro. "There's no earthly reason for terrorists to poison a bunch of poor dirt farmers out in the desert, just like there's no reason for a drug cartel to do it. And poison gas doesn't simply erupt out of the ground."

Old Librarian sniffed. "You may have a fancy university degree, Linda, but you don't know everything. Right on the news yesterday, that nice Oriental doctor on the Space Station and that strange geology man in Oregon said that poison gasses came right up out of cracks in the ground around by that big volcano. And in China, too, after the big quake. Venting, they said it was called."

"Out of a *volcano*, Cora. Or an earthquake zone. Not just out of the desert," Young Librarian informed her. "And you ought to take the news with a dose of salt. They're just out for ratings. They'd do a story blaming the ghosts at Blanca Hacienda for things, if they thought it would get more people to watch."

"Some people are saying it *was* Ojo's dead men, cursing those people," Old Librarian said. She glanced at her coworker, judging her reaction to that, then adopted a superior expression. "These country people will believe just about anything."

That said, both librarians dropped their interpersonal tension to unite in common eye-rolling over the superstitions of the unwashed masses, then hopeful appraisal of the new vaccine the government was sponsoring. However, the glittering memory of a plastic case full of vials crowded their chatter out of Dove's head. He pushed his chair back, taking another computer, and typed in a quick search. Sure enough, a teaser clip of the newscast showed Intrepid Reporter Mike standing in the scrub-covered desert, telling Lupe (and the viewers) that the authorities had discovered the entire family dead—under suspicious circumstances. In the distance, behind Mike, behind the huddle of farm buildings, behind the teams in HazMat suits investigating the mystery, rose the dramatic outcropping of rock that marked the entrance to Blanca Hacienda. That farm couldn't be more than a couple of miles away from the old ranch house.

A cold wash of foreboding and incipient guilt chilled Dove. He left the Channel 8 Web site screaming headlines to itself as he rose, swinging his backpack on, and headed for the door.

"Hey, man, where you going?" Perro called, looking up from the antique video game they'd gotten sidetracked into. Flashes of light erupted from the machine gun cradled in the arms of the impossibly buxom heroine, blasting an inexplicably animated stone statue into bits.

"Yeah, you're supposed to be helping us on this research stuff," Calvin reminded him.

Dove shook his head, forcing a teasing smile. "I told you everything I know. Now you'll have to follow the Force, Grasshopper." He glanced at Young Librarian and added, more for her benefit, "And try to keep it down, would you?"

* * *

The bike's engine fluttered, then purred into silence as Dove pulled into the shadow of a long, low mesa. He slithered through the cheat grass, climbing the slope until he topped the rise overlooking the farm in the news report. He'd avoided the dry ruts of the road that led to the place, along with the haphazard "Hazard" signs that dotted the area. Official vehicles had swarmed into the area, throwing another curtain of dust into the ashy sky. Teams of investigators in environment suits walked slowly through the yard and buildings, using machines that looked like metal detectors to sweep the place for contaminants. Farther out, beyond the yellow "caution" and "police" tapes, uniformed officers stood around, talking to each other and a couple of guys in suits—oh, and a *femme*, too, coming around the ambulance. Probably FBI agents, or Homeland Security officers, come to find out if the news reports hyperventilating about terrorist biological attacks had any truth to them. Dove spotted Pizarro's bulk easily. The sheriff leaned against a dusty, black SUV, shaking his head as he listened to one of the suits.

Yeah, like he's going to get a straight answer out of Pizarro, Dove thought scornfully. Pizarro would do whatever the *Señor* told him to—and cooperating with the *federales* had never been high on the *Señor's* "To Do" list, for today or any day. That meant the sheriff wouldn't be telling the suits about meeting Dove out at Blanca Hacienda, or about the vials that spilled out of the plastic case.

That thought brought Dove's attention back to the yard itself. Sure enough, the truck parked in the farmhouse yard looked familiar—not out of place amid the rest of the dented and rusted equipment—but definitely not belonging there. It looked too much like the one his contacts had piled into to go tearing off in pursuit of Pizarro to be coincidence.

But how had the people in the farmhouse known to go looking for a pickup at Blanca Hacienda? Or had the guys waiting at the ranch house sold it to them? Despite the sun beating out of the yellowed sky, that nasty chill returned across the back of Dove's neck. What were those vials for? Did the desperados sell the farmer and his family a lot more than just a truck, then back off and wait to see what happened?

Boiling fury blasted through Dove's veins, evaporating the chill. They'd used him to knock off a bunch of civilians—with poison! He scuttered back down the hillside with enough speed to leave his own thin dust trail in the air. Orders from *Abuelo* didn't cover this kind of operation. Shooting somebody who could shoot back was one thing, shaking down bouncers for a share of their racket fell barely within bounds, but killing unarmed—and probably completely unaware—farmers crossed the line that Dove hadn't consciously drawn for himself. The bike's engine roared to life again, its tires throwing up a more definite dust trail as he drove around the clumps of chamisa and juniper for Blanca Hacienda.

His rage had cooled enough for tactics by the time he got there. Once again, he parked the bike in the shadow of the boulders and slipped up the long drive. This time, however, he jumped the crumbling rock wall and kept to the outside of the line of dead lilacs, looking through the bare branches for any sign of life. Abruptly, the lilacs thinned and disappeared, a long section of them burned into charcoal sticks. Footprints and violently disturbed sand circled the area around the blackened bushes, showing where someone—a bunch of someones—had stamped and smothered out the fire. No sign of water, of course, just the shovel marks and piles of sand marking the spot where the fire had stopped. Dove looked toward the ranch house, puzzled. Nothing moved, no sound of voices came to his straining ears, but the thin wail of a circling raptor drew his attention skyward. A half dozen black birds circled low to the ground, crows by the look and sound of them. The falcon he'd heard suddenly plummeted through them, scattering the black birds as it came in for a landing in the hacienda's front drive. Not something it would be likely to do with people around.

Dove bent to look around the last lilac bush before the burned-out gap. A thin breeze brought a sickly sweet, rotten, altogether too familiar smell through the dead branches. The only sound and movement in the courtyard came from the birds. Another falcon had already landed, and the two raptors occasionally screamed at the crows, but that was more out of instinct than need. There was plenty of carrion to go around. He caught sight of the red-checkered shirt the outfit's leader had worn and the white cowboy hat of another man. Feeling sicker than he had at the farmhouse, Dove took a deep breath, gagged, and steeled himself. Pulling his bandana over his mouth and nose, he carefully stepped through the ashes of the lilacs.

The birds fluttered and screamed at him, warning him away from their dinner, but they didn't need to. Sure enough, these were the guys he'd delivered the packet to, sprawled around the yard, dead as the lilacs but a lot more grisly. From what he could tell, they'd been plugged neatly from a safe distance. Of course, he couldn't be absolutely sure, on a long-distance inspection, but the remembered glitter of crystal and the environment suits prowling the farmhouse kept him from coming close enough to double check his initial estimate. The farmers had come here to check out the smoke from a fire—and found a bunch of dead desperados. Since they were strangers, and since out here the smart money was always on minding your own business, the farmers had put out the fire and left, taking the truck with them as salvage. Only this time, the smart money was on leaving even a good piece of equipment to the ghosts.

Dove glanced around, checking the ground at the entrance to the driveway. A warm glitter shone from under the lilacs. A brass shell casing lay with a couple dozen of its mates, around a set of sharp-pressed boot tracks. The tracks (nice, new boots, not the worn ones the desperados wore) led to another set of tracks, these from new, probably expensive, all-terrain tires. The older, worn tracks of the salvaged truck crossed them in several places, leading back down the drive—to home and death. Dove followed the tracks down the drive, across the road—and right into the library and the news reports again.

* * *

Empty villages in Chile, Peru, and Ecuador filled the library screens, making a mockery of the ads extolling the virtues of technical degrees, investment opportunities, and personal tutoring services. Every piece told the same story, using the same ghastly illustrations: bodies sprawled unattended or packed into biohazard bags; streets whose only movement came from the slow flight of heavy, black flies; unattended dishes, ploughs, and toys. Dove quickly gave up replays of the television news stories. Broadcast news had picked up the tale, of course, running a whole series of "special reports," each more dramatic than the last, but short on facts and petering out quickly after the first barrage of "Terrorists have struck—and you're next! Tune in at 10:00 for the full story!" However, after the images ceased to shock (amazing as it seems, even grisly death becomes old hat after repeated exposures) and the ratings fell, the producers quickly turned to the next breaking scandal. (In this case, the riots over the FDA's investigation of AllSafe.) Deep in the reaches of the Web, however, a few in-depth newspapers took up the tale, magazines devoted to covering world events for an ever-thinning group of subscribers who paid for details the television didn't bother to include. For the moment at least (until the next round of cuts for public services), the public library appeared on that list.

After a series of ever-tightening searches, Dove found more in-depth coverage of the unexplained extinctions wiping out jungle villages in South America. What he didn't find was a solid answer about what happened, how it happened, who did it—or even who the victims were. Of course, some answers were obvious: the dead men, women, and children in a stricken village were the people who lived in the village. What got fuzzy, however, is what they did and how they might have become targets. Frightened people from neighboring villages talked openly of rebels using the wasted villages as bases of operations to stage antigovernment raids, but they whispered of curses lashed down by offended jungle gods or vengeful saints. Amid rational declarations that the dead had worked for a cartel, synthesizing drugs out of poisonous ingredients that somehow contaminated the air or water, frightened eyes hinted at more apocalyptic scenarios. Local priests urged their congregations to pray for deliverance from sin, temptation—and the wrathful hand of God. "He sends earthquakes to warn us, the Curse of Egypt to stir us unto repentance, volcanoes to remind us of the fires of Hades awaiting the sinner," cried an itinerant preacher. Another priest barely escaped with his life, after rumors of his consorting with the witches responsible for the curses ran through the town; the "witches" weren't so lucky, or forewarned in time. Disease, poison, drugs, curses, mob violence: death had become contagious, its bony hand anointing young and old with its ashen mark.

Dove rubbed his eyes, death and horror thick in his head. What had he carried to Blanca Hacienda? What new ghosts walked the desert now, coughing out soul contagion? Dead souls, dead eyes— Slick's cool face and reflective sunglasses—turned in Dove's memory, the sickle smile showing skull teeth. Slick had given *Abuelo* that case, a packet to deliver for the General, who would pay well for accomplished soldiers. The General, a man to watch, gathering power and influence in the South—far beyond Mexico.

It took only a moment to turn the search from medical to political news. New images replaced the plague-empty villages, but the theme continued: new villages equally empty, but smoldering in ashes, pocked with bullet holes, marred by blackened bomb craters. Growing slowly but surely, out of the ruin of Central American economies and deep jungles, a new order had begun to emerge. It grew on a rising tide of blood, survivors gasping out the same tale: every soldier in a platoon or hornet's nest dead, rumors of jungle camps wiped out, rebel armies suddenly becoming a lot more efficient and well armed. Where disorganized militias had battled back and forth over military coups, strike teams sporting black and green uniforms now carried out precision operations with the smooth efficiency of the old German Wehrmacht—or Caesar's Legions. Some local authorities officially recognized the new power, extending hands of friendship, formally requesting assistance in cleaning out rebels, drug runners, and other insurgents. They paid in gold, supplies, and munitions, sending their peace offerings to the leader of the *Liberacion* forces.

Those forces, better armed and more ruthless than the corrupt or intimidated governmental troops, exploded from the jungle to topple corrupt regimes, wipe out rebels, and destroy cartel lords, leaving a sickening trail of carnage in their wake. A single reporter had managed to interview the right-hand man of the General himself, the "tactical genius" who had forged a modern military out of an ever-growing horde of gangs, police, and soldiers. The spokesman, Johann Brindermann, categorically denied the overheated charges of ethnic cleansing, genocide, or biological warfare. General Garza, he stated in a clipped, European accent, did only what was necessary, no more, and certainly no less. "One does not request that a snake refrain from biting. One uses a machete to cut off its head."

"And chop its body into tiny pieces?" the journalist persisted.

"If necessary, yes," Brindermann said flatly, motioning to the silent soldiers on either side.

They deposited the reporter, shaken, blindfolded, but undamaged, outside a Catholic church. The townsfolk proved even less talkative than the General's lieutenant. Clearly, the reporter concluded, the General's forces had intimidated the natives into silence, which explained their hesitation to speak out. However, they also replaced even bloodier chaos with comparative peace. Were the Liberacionistas, under the iron-fisted command of General Garza, the only viable future of Latin America?

Images filled Dove's mind as he stared not so much at as through the screen: uniforms vs. shabby denims, machine guns vs. shotguns, bales of marijuana vs. thin plastic cases of glittering vials. Coughing, shaking delivery boys stumbling out of the dilapidated ranch house, only to get shot by Slick and his two thugs. And over them all, a blurry portrait of a proud profile above a black, quasi-military jacket—the General, Andrea Cesar Garza.

* * *

"Who's that military guy? And why's the picture so fuzzy?" Senator Garlick demanded, storming through the frosted-glass doors into Abbott's luxurious office. He came to an abrupt halt on the hand-tied Oriental rug at the far side of Abbott's obsidian-topped desk and tossed his briefcase impatiently into a less-luxurious visitor's chair.

Abbott neatly twisted the slender screen away from the intruding politician's line of sight, swiveling his deep, leather chair to put its back between them. "Thank you, Johann. I'll have our people check into things and get back to you on the negotiations," he said smoothly, not acknowledging the interruption—or the peremptory tone. With a flick of his finger, he broke the connection, dissolving the image of the man on the far end of the line.

When he turned back to face his unannounced guest, however, the irritation showed clearly in his set expression. "Senator. To what do we owe this unexpected pleasure?"

"Impatience," Zelik suggested. She walked through the door that Garlick had left open behind him, pulling it shut after her. She gave the senator an icy, appraising look. "Or incompetence."

Garlick bristled. "You're hardly in a position to be talking about incompetence," he snarled. "I want a progress report on that vaccine, and I want it now. What's the hold up? The FDA should've approved it two days ago, and we're still in testing? Do you want to explain that?"

Abbott sighed. "These things take time, Senator. Science cannot be rushed."

"The —— it can't!" Garlick informed him. "You think the guys down at Los Alamos took their own sweet time about building the bomb?"

"Appropriate analogy," Zelik said, crossing her legs as she settled into the visitor chair not currently supporting the Senator's briefcase.

Abbott shot her a quelling glance. "I'd hardly call AllSafe a bomb," he remonstrated. "It's the future of medicine." A satisfied smile crossed his face. "And it's ours."

"It's late, is what it is," Garlick reminded him. "I've paid more than enough to bribe off the FDA, and I need this vaccine approved *now* if I want to solidify my chance at becoming chief of Homeland Security."

"How are you going to handle the stresses of ensuring homeland security, if a little delay like this sends you into apoplexy?" Zelik asked. "In politics, as in war, campaigns never go quite like you expect them to."

"Don't lecture me on politics," Garlick snapped back. "I know more about campaigns than you ever will. The key to a successful campaign is to out-spend, out-think, and out-lie the other guy—and, if necessary, to out-muscle him, too. And if you can't help me on that, I have other—allies—who will, without being particular about who they have to apply that muscle to. You're playing in the big leagues now. Much bigger than just pushing drugs—I mean, selling pharmaceuticals. I'm helping you into the biggest monopoly the world's ever seen, when that vaccine hits the streets. In return, I expect you to deliver that vaccine, as promised. Or I'll do a lot more than file a complaint with the Better Business Bureau." He glowered at the two MedaGen executives, leaving the sentence hanging in the incense-scented air of the office.

"You want us to be intimidated by your rumored Mob ties? When we're running a multinational corporation with ties to more governments than you can count? Is that your idea of a threat?" Zelik asked, bored. She picked a paperweight off Abbott's desk, turning the crystal-encased strand of magnified DNA in her fingers as she stared back at the senator.

Her lack of concern did more than Abbott's unruffled, "No need for that kind of talk" to make Garlick pull in his horns. Still, the senator didn't completely deflate. He turned his glare on Abbott instead. "Back to my original question. What's the holdup with the FDA approval?"

Abbott sighed, leaning back in his chair, hands behind his head as he looked at the ceiling. "One thing MedaGen has always prided itself on is the quality of its Research and Development department."

"What does—" Garlick began, but Abbott's sitting forward in his chair and bringing his hands down on his desk with an audible slap stopped him.

"What does the quality of our employees have to do with holding up the FDA approval?" Abbott finished for him. "I'll *tell* you what it has to do with it—and with your half-lobed strategy for spreading bribes around a federal agency. Apparently, one of our conscientious researchers managed to get his hands on the original source data for the Corinth project, and he considerately sent that data to his own contact at the FDA. Your well-bribed team leader called *us* in a panic, wondering how to cover up the mess."

Garlick paled. "Mess? You promised that the vaccine would be medically perfect, that any adverse effects wouldn't show up in the final report or tests."

Abbott sat back again, smiling reassuringly. "It is, and they don't. Don't worry, Senator. We've sent the correction to the data set. The FDA will be able to run their tests without any embarrassing results. In a way, this could even be helpful—when the time comes to announce that everybody will need consistent booster shots, we can point out that the FDA considered the possibility of continued dosages and considered it fair in light of AllSafe's exceptional protective qualities. It's all in the wording of the report—which we can expect in another few days."

Garlick shot a suspicious glance from Abbott to Zelik and back.

Abbott smiled at him. "Relax, Howard. We're all on the same side here, remember? We want the FDA approval just as much as you do. Maybe more. It'll happen. For now, get out there, put your dignified mug on camera, and deplore the political maneuverings delaying the country's last, best hope of defeating evil, terrorist plots. That's even a good line for the speech—accuse the FDA holdouts of being terrorists." He rose and walked around the desk, picking up the senator's briefcase and pressing its handle into his hand, then putting an arm around the senator's shoulders and walking him to the doors. "Do your convincing Father Knows Best act, and stir up a bit of street protest. That always goes over big."

At the doors, he shot Garlick his own million-dollar smile. "And Senator, never, *ever* come here without an appointment again. There's too much at stake to throw it away because you can't wait for a secure meeting." He opened the door into the plush reception area.

The secretary, a young, intellectually pretty thing, looked up attentively. So did the two men sitting on the leather couch, their beautifully tailored suits not quite straining over their urban-gladiator muscles. The two *consigliore* stood, waiting for a signal from Garlick, their faces impassive, their hands hovering casually at their perfectly pressed lapels.

Their presence put some of the spark back into Garlick's eyes as he turned to smile at Abbott. "Thanks for the consultation on such short notice," he said, the powerful man showing his *noblesse oblige* to a useful retainer. "I'll expect a full report as soon as the FDA process is complete."

"You'll have one," Abbott assured him. "Good day, Senator. It's a pleasure working with you."

"Likewise," Garlick said benevolently. He couldn't quite keep the stalk out of his walk as he headed for the elevator, the secretary scurrying ahead to catch the door and the two muscle boys falling in behind.

Abbott's smile disappeared the moment his office doors closed again. "It will be so good not to need idiots like him anymore." He turned on Zelik. "And what about our 'conscientious employee'? What is he asking for? More importantly, how much longer will we need him?"

Zelik set the paperweight down on the desk with a crystalline click. "He's not asking for anything."

"Not asking for anything?" Abbott looked at her, then puzzlement gave way to a grudging admiration. "Holding out to see what we offer first? Not bad for a scientist."

"No." Zelik shrugged away that idea. "He's not asking for anything because he's not trying to shake us down. From what his supervisor said, this guy figures somebody on the Corinth team just made a mistake and forgot to include the right data. With Christoff's . . . *accident* and all." She emphasized the word to make the point.

"Christoff's accident," Abbott repeated. He gazed at the original Picasso hanging above his desk. The broken lines and disjointed limbs of the figure fit his mood. "First, there's a crisis of conscience for the lead researcher on the Corinth project team, and now we have a boy scout running around. We have prospects, future bargains that don't need the attention of someone who lets his concern for humanity overcome his common sense and company loyalty. More immediately, I just reassured the Senator that we'd have FDA approval next week. I hope his money and our data will take care of that."

Zelik rose from the chair and smoothed her severe, straight skirt. Her dead expression never flickered as she said, "I'm sure they will, and I'm sure we'll find a way to deal with our conscientious employee, too."

"Yes, as soon as possible," Abbott said, not looking at her as she moved to the doors. "In fact, you did such a good job with Christoff, why don't *you* take care of it?"

* * *

Dear Chisom,

So, telling you my name means the Lord is my leader has raised your curiosity about the meaning of the names of the other members of the family. Yes, each name has a meaning. That's why your mother and I picked them. All your names are from the Nigerian Ido dialect. Your name means God is with me. Your mother's name means daughter of pride, in the good sense, of course. When you get home, I'll tell you why we named the other children what we did.

On a sad note, the Church here has been shocked by the martyrdom of Elder Stacy and the two young Elders. I suspect you're feeling it over there too. He was an Apostle of love, compassion and understanding if ever there was one. As one of the Church's ambassadors to the nations, he has been most effective. He would have made a big difference for the Church in the Philippines. He will be missed. It is interesting that his martyrdom has really bothered some of the Saints. Some have even asked where God was or wondered if Elder Stacy was listening to the Spirit.

Both positions make wrong assumptions. Those who hold them do not look to our own history. A number of our leaders have been killed, for example, Joseph and Hyrum Smith, Parley P. Pratt, during the nineteenth century, and Hosang Sui here in the twenty-first. Some Saints do not seem to understand what God shared with John the Revelator. As John viewed the fifth seal (his own day), he saw those who had been slain for the word of God, and for the testimony which they held (Revelation 6:9). They cried to God to avenge their deaths, but he asked for patience, assuring them that it would come, but they should rest yet for a little season, until their fellowservants also and their brethren, that should be killed as they were (v. 11). Elders Sui and Stacy along with the missionaries Anderson and Johnson are four of these fellowservants. I fear they will not be the last.

Even so, the Church moves forward as never before. The strength of the Saints is marvelous. Those Brethren who have returned from their various assignments bring encouraging word. The Spirit rests upon God's people and they are doing His work.

I pray the Lord to direct your work that you may take care of His children.

With love,
Your father,
Chinedu

* * *

"Here, babykins, let me take care of that for you," Merry told Missy, washing the globs of pureed plums off her daughter's face.

Missy giggled, turning her face so her ear got a good scrubbing instead, then happily reapplied the layer of sticky purple from the copious supply on her highchair's tray. "Pitty!" she announced. "Yip dik!"

"Pretty lipstick, huh?" Merry laughed. "I'd buy that a bit better if you kept it even in the remote vicinity of your actual mouth, kiddo. This isn't makeup, it's food." She glanced into the bottle, then had to admit, "Even if it doesn't look like it. Still, I'm sure there are starving children in China who'd eat it instead of wearing it."

The cliché, trite as it was, set off a reminder in Merry's head: China, starving, news coverage. "Speaking of which," she said looking at her watch, then turning on the TV, "let's see if the FDA has realized that their AllSafe vaccine isn't actually a vaccine." She applied the cloth to Missy's face again, then extricated the baby from the high chair for a more thorough washing.

On the screen behind her, a commercial for "family" vacations (separate accommodations for Mom and Mom's girlfriend, Dad and his new wife, and each of the kids) faded into the first installment of the evening's news reports. Vacation spots and luxury living gave way abruptly to a scene of well-worn devastation. Many of the sharp corners had worn off the broken bricks in the hills of rubble that still stood in earthquake-devastated cities, as weather, wind, and half-hearted cleanup efforts picked at them. The piles themselves had taken on a more natural contour, flattening somewhat as scavengers took what they could to build secondary shelters, broadening as cleanup crews shoveled remaining debris into larger piles to clear spaces for new dwellings.

Kids swarmed over the mounds, too, looking for anything usable, anything interesting, playing King of the Hill and hide-and-seek amid the ruins. The camera focused on the ragged, busy children as the reporter introduced the scene, rattling off Chinese and Philippine village names, casualty numbers that had once been shockingly high and now seemed almost routine. Just as time had dulled the jagged edges of the metal and concrete blocks, exposure and repetition had taken the horror out of the numbers: "Hundreds have been killed, thousands hurt, tens of thousands left homeless by the earthquakes and the floods that followed. With their homes destroyed, many of these people now face a struggle for survival, as food and clean water are as scarce as undamaged houses."

The scene changed, showing weeping women, empty-eyed men, and serious children corralled into long lines, waiting for aid workers to give them a thin ration of rice, a bag of beans, an altogether too small container of water to tide them and their families over for another day. "Donations have poured into the affected areas from all around the world," yet another reporter assured the viewers. "The United Nations, UNICEF, and the Red Cross have been working at top capacity since the earthquakes. Private and religious organizations, especially the Catholic Relief efforts and The Church of Jesus Christ of Latter-day Saints, have contributed food, clothing, medicine, and other much-needed supplies. However, it's just not enough for everyone."

Crowds swarmed around supply trucks entering the quake-devastated areas, reaching and begging for a share of the precious cargo. Exhausted aid workers could only repeat, "One per family, please, one per family," as blank-faced soldiers stood guard, weapons ready. Riots had broken out in three refugee camps, as rumors of shortages and favoritism ignited the smoldering rage and helplessness into wildfires of violence. The camera caught the violence, desperate people fighting tooth and claw over the precious crates. A barrel of rice, upset in the brawl, toppled, its contents spilling into the dust of the roadway, trampled underfoot by people who needed it so much. A child, slipping between the milling legs, tried to scoop as much of the dirt and rice as she could into her skirt. The camera rocked as the milling mob enveloped it, then went black.

"Unfortunately, while the worst of circumstances sometimes brings out the best in people," the original reporter had reappeared, far away in space and time from the riot at the aid station, "it also brings out the worst. Opportunists have taken advantage of the disrupted transportation systems to sell necessities at inflated prices."

The scene shifted again, this time to a makeshift bazaar. A hard-looking man presided over a table piled high with packets of emergency rations, each marked clearly with the logo of the United Nations. He bargained hard with a thin woman over the price of two packets, while his two beefy, well-armed sons stood guard on either side of the table. At another booth, a smiling woman assured two men that she had salvaged the crates of canned goods from a smashed truck at great risk to herself and her daughters, so she could not possibly part with them for less than the price she'd posted (the equivalent of a day's wages). A group of uniformed soldiers hustled the cameraman away, as the lens caught a glimpse of a supply truck being diverted away from an aid station.

"Sadly, opportunism doesn't stop at the border," observed Kathy, as the scene switched to show the anchorwoman behind her desk. A new graphic logo, indicative of a general breakdown of societal order, glowed above her shoulder. "Just outside San Francisco, gas stations have hiked prices to $10 per gallon. In this case, however, they are the ones who paid the price. Angry mobs descended on the stations, protesting the price hike." Footage from the protests appeared, illustrating her words. Plate-glass windows shattered under a barrage of bricks, stones, and pieces of forcibly dismantled gasoline pumps. A cashier huddled inside her bullet-proof booth as furious protesters rocked it off its deep-set concrete foundation.

"At one station, protesters actually set the pumps on fire, causing a series of explosions," Kathy continued. The fireballs exploded in molten colors on cue, black-masked anarchists amid the shouting crowd cheering on the fires. They blocked the driveway, refusing to let a fire truck near the blaze. Across the street, police stood by, watching but making no move to intervene.

"We don't have to put up with this!" barked a furious man, identified as a gas-company spokesman. "Law-abiding companies shouldn't be targets of mob violence while the police stand idly by! This is extortion, pure and simple. They let us burn because our company wouldn't pay the bribes they demanded!"

"We don't want to get involved in a civilian protest," explained the police captain to the microphone shoved in his face. The reflective surface of the riot-shield made his expression hard to read. "It's hard to justify using force on a protest rally."

"The San Francisco Police Department is reviewing the policy on protests, but their spokesman informs Channel 8 that the officers' behavior conformed to the latest Supreme Court rulings," Kathy informed the viewers, as ads for SFPD merchandise (pro and con) ribboned under her. "In other news, protests continue over the FDA review of the AllSafe vaccine. Senator Howard W. Garlick, sponsor of the bill that would make the AllSafe vaccine available to every American, appeared at the site of the protests to reassure voters."

Sign-waving, shouting crowds gave way to a press-conference tent as Senator Garlick took the podium. The crowds booed as he said, "I understand your frustration with typical Washington bureaucracy— and I'm frustrated too!" They cheered as he said, "But I assure you that in this case, even Washington bureaucracy can't interfere with the good of the American people! I have assurances from the leader of the review team that the review is going very well. AllSafe will pass final approval very soon. And if any bureaucrat tries to delay it further, they'll find out exactly what the American people think of bureau- cracy!" Even more enthusiastic cheers rang out. The Senator held his triumphant pose, fist raised as he basked in the warm glow of the video lights and mob adoration.

"What?" Merry yelped, running into the room with a half-dressed and still damp Missy over her shoulder. "Final approval? How in the h—" Missy's echoing "how?" cut through long-fought habit and high stress, forcing a last-second edit. "How did that happen? We *told* them what it would do! We *told* you!"

"Maybe we didn't."

Merry whirled at the sound of Chris's dejected voice. He had come in while she was busy yelling at the television, and now slumped tiredly against the doorframe. She hurried over to him, handing him Missy so she could give him a hug. "What happened?" she asked again, but much more quietly this time.

Chris squeezed her back, kissed Missy's head, and pulled them both with him as he flopped onto the couch. "I tried to call Elizabeth back when I got to work this morning, to see if she'd been able to pass along your data analysis and Christoff's original information. Her phone just rang and rang at first, no voicemail or anything. Then, an hour or so later, it rang just once, and a recording kicked in. It said Elizabeth had been put on indefinite leave. I held on for the operator and got somebody I've never worked with before. She steadfastly refused to acknowledge that she'd ever heard of Elizabeth or anybody else I've worked with and wouldn't put me through to anybody at all. She just kept telling me that I wasn't in the database."

He sighed, rubbing his eyes, then glared at the television, which was blathering on about the latest poll results showing huge mounds of popular support for AllSafe, Senator Garlick, and increased amounts of chocolate chips in a popular brand of cookie. Missy sighed too, leaning against her daddy's chest. He rubbed her back.

"That doesn't sound good," Merry said, thinking aloud. "'Indefinite leave' sounds kind of dire."

"More than just kind of," Chris told her solemnly. "Merry, I think I'm in serious trouble. After I got off the phone with Miss Unhelpful, I went to look up some project-related information and found out that my privileged-file access had disappeared. When I called tech support, the guy at the end of the line transferred me to security."

"Security?" Merry repeated, a chill rippling over the hair on her arms.

"Security," Chris affirmed. "The officer—and he sounded like an officer, too, or one of those sunglassed soldiers of fortune they've got guarding the lobby—took down my name, rank, and serial number, then told me that they were investigating a security leak. They'd get back to me with more information about my account when they had it, and in the meantime, I wasn't to leave town."

"He said that?" Merry asked. "Don't leave town?"

Chris grinned tiredly. "Keep your hands in plain sight, and hand over your belt and shoelaces. No, he didn't actually say it, but from the tone in his voice, he definitely considered me a suspect of some kind. So does Humphrey. He came into my office, halfway between blazing and weaseling. Between ripping me for getting him in trouble with his bosses, he tried to pump me for information about how office-politically contagious I am and how likely it is to spread to him in particular when they decide to can my tail."

"There are plenty of other companies out there who'd kill to get you on staff!" Merry said staunchly. "Just that one week when MedaGen took over, you got three bites off our Web site. Let MedaGen get rid of you—they're just cutting their own throats!"

"According to Humphrey's wild imagination, they're not above getting rid of me by cutting *my* throat," Chris told her. He shook his head, snuggling Missy and Merry a bit closer. "Guy's completely paranoid. But he's been around long enough to be a pretty good judge of the human-resources situation. They're going to toss me out as soon as they can figure out how to claim Protocol 4 as their own and forbid me from working on it."

Suddenly, he slammed a fist down on the arm of the couch. Missy jumped with a distressed squeak. He apologized wordlessly, giving her a squeeze and continuing the interrupted slow rub on her little back. He continued, more quietly but no less intensely, "Merry, they're going to throw me out for doing the right thing, saving lives instead of bolstering their bottom line. And even worse, they're going to push that vaccine into production and that idiot senator is going to cajole, threaten, and bribe everybody he can think of to make it mandatory. We have *got* to find a way to make the FDA listen to the facts and stop this!"

"Sounds like Garlick's already gotten to the FDA," Merry observed. "Or someone has. Poor Elizabeth! And here's the stupid reporter, going on about how great it is that AllSafe's getting closer to approval all the time, with the lame-brained protesters out there jumping up and down with glee. Look at that!" She pointed to the TV screen, where the online poll numbers glowed public approval for AllSafe. Her eyes reflected the bright colors of the chart, then seemed to glaze over slightly.

"But how do we do it?" Chris asked. "Going through channels obviously didn't work. It's like that stupid horse and water saying. I can send copies of Christoff's data and your analysis until my fingers fall off. How can we force anybody with the right expertise to actually look at the evidence?"

Merry blinked, breaking her morbid fascination with the TV screen. She looked at Chris, the beginnings of a smile starting to play around her mouth. "How about we threaten to firebomb them?"

"Merry, get serious," Chris remonstrated, surprised. "We can't—" His protest died off abruptly; this time it was his turn to stare at the TV, where Kathy was doing her 30-second recap of the day's news, to a montage of appropriate images—including pro-AllSafe picketers shouting slogans and threats. "Firebombs," he echoed.

"They don't have the expertise, but if you tell a bunch of people that something's dangerous enough times, they'll at least start thinking something might be wrong," Merry said, excited. "Look at what happened with genetically modified foods years ago—propaganda based on prejudice and misunderstanding turned the public against any produce that had even the faintest whiff of mutation around it."

"And in that case, it took legitimate researchers years and amazing amounts of effort to reclaim the reputation of certain products," Chris told her. "Even so, people still go on about it."

"Right," Merry hugged him, then bounced on the couch cushion. "And this time we've got right on our side from the first. What's that saying? 'The truth will out'? Well, now's the time for Truth to leave the closet, in the gaudiest clothes she can find! Even if people don't get the science straight, they'll understand that this vaccine is nothing they want to jump into blindfolded. Then we'll see how far the senator and his pet researchers get!"

Her enthusiasm cooled a little, however, as Virginia's writhing figure replaced Kathy on the screen. The sucker ad had indeed broken big—MedaGen's decoy mind-share mannequin had made its worldwide debut as part of the news, and they didn't have to pay a cent.

"The only problem is, how do we get the word out to the protesters?" Merry settled back into the crook of Chris's arm, prepared to put some heavy thinking into the problem.

He grinned at her and gave her a kiss on the nose. "Well, finally I get to come up with a solution. Look carefully at the screen, Merry my girl. What do you see?"

"A silicone-enhanced version of what I see in the mirror when I get out of the shower," Merry shot back.

"Hardly enhanced," Chris contradicted, giving her a sultry look. "However, I'm not going to get distracted remembering that scene right now. Look lower—at the screen crawl."

"Statistics for MedaGen's stock-market price," Merry summarized, wondering what Chris was getting at. "Statistics on Virginia's latest album sales. Why does anybody buy those things? Weather reports for everywhere but where we live. Headlines. Requests for local-interest news stories to fill in the gaps in their 24-hour programming. Ads for news-related merchandise—" She stopped as the realization hit her. "Requests for local-interest news stories!"

"With the Web site and toll-free number," Chris agreed. "I knew you'd catch on quick. So, Merry Galen, girl detective, shall we put this babe to bed and make a cub reporter's day?"

"You know it!" Merry laughed softly. She quickly wrote down the number, then gathered Missy's blanket, currently favorite toy car, and ever-present dinosaur as Chris carried the tired baby into her room.

"Do you think somebody will be there at this hour?" Chris asked, settling Missy into her crib.

"This hour?" Merry leaned over to kiss Missy, then kissed Chris. "Have you forgotten how most of the world runs—besides us, since we're old, boring, married people now? All the ambitious young bucks are still at their desks, on their phones, chomping at the bit to get ahead. It's not even seven o'clock yet!"

Chris grinned. "Oh, yeah. Boy, am I glad that my ambitious young buck days are over." He ruffled Missy's hair. "Ready for prayers, Miss Missy?"

"Amen," Missy said, yawning.

"Not quite yet, kiddo," Chris told her. "But you're catching on."

Merry watched, feeling warm, happy, and safe as Chris led Missy through a simple prayer. She repeated the words with her usual uncanny precision for such a little girl, then ended with a sudden flourish of words that neither of them could understand before capping off the prayer with an emphatic "Amen!"

"Amen!" Chris said, snuggling her down in her blankets. "Good night, Missy."

"Night, Dadadad," Missy agreed. "Night, Mama."

"Good night, my Miss," Merry said, turning off the light. The bluebird of happiness that Carmen had given Missy as a baby-shower present glowed sky colored under the switch.

"Did you catch that last bit?" Chris asked, as he followed Merry into the living room.

"The Missy-ese part, you mean?" Merry smiled. "Nope, but some of them sounded familiar. Sometimes I don't know if she's trying English words that don't work out, or if she's making up her own as she goes along."

"My grandpa used to say babies spoke the original Adamic tongue," Chris said.

"Not a chance," Merry shook her head decisively, picking up the phone and entering the news hotline number. "Can you imagine commanding the elements to organize themselves, or even sounding dignified, in a language that depended quite that heavily on ba-ba and la-la sounds?" She offered the phone to Chris.

He looked at it, swallowing against the nervousness. "I'll settle for trying to sound dignified in any language at all right now."

"Give 'em the Dr. Galen treatment," Merry advised, jumping up slightly to sit on the counter and rub his back supportively. "Not pushy, just knowledgeable."

"And trustworthy. Yes, ma'am," he finished for her, then jumped slightly as a marginally bored voice answered the other end of the line. "Oh, hello, Lee Yuan. My name is Chris Galen—Dr. Christopher Galen. I'd like to speak with someone there about a potential problem with MedaGen's AllSafe vaccine."

"You and a dozen other people," Yuan told him. "I'm sorry, Dr.—Galen, right?—but this hotline is for news, not for editorials. I can give you the number for the editor's desk, if you'd like. Or you can e-mail your comments right to the Channel 8 Web site. The address is—"

"I'm not talking about an editorial," Chris interrupted. "I have looked at the original research data that went into developing the AllSafe vaccine—the project's name was Corinth at MedaGen—and it looks like there are serious problems with it."

"The original research data?" Yuan sounded slightly more interested, but still wary. "How did you get hold of that kind of information?"

"I work at MedaGen," Chris told him. "I spoke with Dr. Gregor Christoff, the former team lead on the Corinth project, and got his notes. Then, when we analyzed the projections, we realized that the vaccine has very serious, even potentially deadly, side effects."

"What was your name again?" Yuan asked. "Galen, right? How do you spell that?"

"Checking the MedaGen Web site directory for me?" Chris asked, grinning. He spelled his name, last and first, then added, "The picture shows me wearing a white lab coat, blue shirt, and tie with sunflowers on it. My daughter gave it to me for my birthday a couple of months ago. She's not quite two, and is already displaying a very bold fashion sense."

Yuan laughed. "That's quite a tie, all right."

"But anybody can describe the picture," Chris finished for him. "It's public access. That's not the point. I'd really appreciate the chance to come down and talk to you about the projections for AllSafe."

"Dr. Galen—Chris," Yuan said patiently. "The FDA is looking into it. There are protesters all over—maybe you've seen the reports on the news? If there's something wrong with it, they'll find it."

"Lee, I've seen the news—and that's what's got me worried," Chris informed him. "Look at the situation with suspicious reporter's eyes. There are a lot of powerful people with a big stake in making this go through. I have no idea what all the ins and outs are, but I know I've tried going through proper channels, and hit brick walls at every turn. We've got to make somebody take this seriously, even if they find out that our analysis is wrong and there's no danger. In fact, I'd rather get this out there and be wrong than let it go if we're right."

The sincerity and urgency in Chris's voice caught the reporter's attention. He hesitated, then said, "You've got copies of this data? Can you send it to me?"

Chris breathed a silent sigh of relief—and a quick prayer. "Yes, I've got it, but I'd rather not send it. It's too complicated for anybody not trained in genetics to understand it right off—and it's still MedaGen's intellectual property. I don't want copies of it just running around loose out there. However, I can show it to you. I'm not sure how much you'll understand, even with my explanation, but if you can get someone else with experience in genetic medicine, you'll have another expert witness to back up our story."

"That's a good idea," Yuan agreed. "OK, tell you what. Can you come down to the station at 9:30 tomorrow? Bring your data, and I'll see if I can get one of our science or medicine consultants to come over. We'll check it out."

"We'll be there at 9:30, data in hand," Chris said.

"Remember, I'm not saying we're going to run the story," Yuan cautioned. "I'm just saying that it sounds worth a look. That's it."

"That's all we expect," Chris told him. "Thanks for being willing to look."

Yuan considered that, then added, "Listen, Dr. Galen, it's not that I don't believe *you* specifically. It's just that big stories get all kinds of nuts coming out of the woodwork. The last woman who called me about this was just about hysterical. According to her, AllSafe is the Mark of the Beast, something out of the original Apocalypse."

"Interesting idea," Chris admitted. "But I promise not to go Biblical on you. We'll see you tomorrow."

"Who's we?" Yuan asked, his reporter's instincts kicking in.

"Me, my wife Meredith Galen, also a doctor of genetic medicine, and our daughter, Melissa," Chris said.

"She got a degree, too?" Yuan asked.

"Not yet," Chris told him, "but we're expecting great things."

"I'll settle for expecting you tomorrow," Yuan said.

Chris bade him a good evening and hung up. He leaned back against Merry, holding her arms around him. "Whew. Well, we got somebody in the media to maybe listen to us. Here we go. I hope it's not too late."

Merry squeezed him. "It's not too late. Even if the FDA approves it tonight, there's still all kinds of hoops to jump through before Garlick's team gets it legally required for everybody. And you can bet they're not going to start giving it to select populations before they've got their nationwide rollout ready. If we're right—and I'm betting we are—they don't want anybody to realize how many 'booster' shots we're talking about until just about everybody's already been vaccinated once."

"You're sexy when you're cynical," Chris told her. "So this can wait until morning, huh?"

"Yeah, it can wait until morning," Merry assured him.

Both of them, however, had a hard time waiting until morning. Merry woke several times, aware that Chris had done the same, but both of them pretended to let the other sleep. The nervousness didn't come from feeling that they were doing the wrong thing, Chris decided, after plenty of wakeful opportunities to consider the question. He knew, deep down, that they had the responsibility—even the obligation—to get their concerns about AllSafe out there. No, the shivers of apprehension grew out of the idea that a major company could be so callous, that a well-respected Senator would literally bargain for political power with people's lives. All his life, Chris had been a team player, more interested in the ultimate goal than who got the credit, and he didn't like circumventing the system—or the implications that made him feel he absolutely had to. He hoped, but not quite prayed, that the Corinth team's half-cocked analysis had come from careless impatience, not arrogant calculation. He did pray that he and Merry would be able to present their case, that Yuan and his expert would listen and understand—that it would all come out for the best.

Merry's thoughts whirled around similar paths, but with different stops on anxiety's Stations of the Cross. She had a low opinion of Humphrey personally, but suspected that he did know his way around office politics. Could they hurt Chris professionally—she refused to consider the outlandish idea that MedaGen might try to actually hurt him—could they torpedo his brilliant career? Was she right in her analysis? What if she'd missed something, despite the hours she'd spent poring over the numbers, and her mistake cost Chris everything? But what if they were right, and they didn't say anything? "Love thy neighbor" certainly took on some weird shapes at times—though she had to admit that she was much more interested in protecting Missy than the faceless crowd. She fell into unsettled dreams, racing around to bat away the DNA spiral-code snakes that threatened to coil around Missy and Chris.

Both of them were more than happy to get up when Missy's usual morning greetings came singing through their bedroom door.

They hustled through the morning routine, out of an excess of nervous energy rather than any actual need for speed. Missy caught the excitement too, squeaking and tossing her dinosaur around, not knowing whether she was hyper or worried. Merry tried to take a deep breath and calm down, as she checked and double-checked the downloaded data for Yuan. Base data—present. Analysis—accounted for. Simulations—ready. Projected effects—rolling. She snapped the palmtop closed and tucked it securely into the diaper bag.

"Ready?" Chris asked, adjusting his tie for the sixth time.

"Ready?" Missy asked, leaning against his leg.

"Ready," Merry agreed. She hefted the bag and took Chris's hands, smiling at him. "The tie is fine, you look like the epitome of scientific trustworthiness, and your socks match. Everything will be all right."

"And you look businesslike and lovely at the same time," Chris said, tucking a curl behind her ear. "I'd believe you if you told me the sky was purple."

"How about we keep our case to what we can actually back up with evidence?" Merry suggested, laughing.

"Oh, well, if you insist," Chris conceded. "Come on, Miss, prayer time."

They knelt, Chris then Merry taking turns to ask for divine guidance on their mission. Missy added her enthusiastic "Amen!" several times—including at the end of the prayers.

They bundled Missy into her car seat, then strapped themselves in, pulling out into the light Saturday traffic. Merry acted as navigator as usual, repeating directions from the digital map on the dashboard.

"OK, so one more turn, and we're there," Chris said, pulling into the intersection as their light turned green.

"Right," Merry said. A flash of light and streak of motion caught her eye. She looked up to see the grille of a truck barreling toward them. "Chris! Watch out!"

He'd already seen it, fighting the wheel to turn their little car out of the way, swerving desperately to keep the truck from hitting the passenger side where Missy and Merry sat.

Tires screeched, metal groaned, and the grinding, screaming sound of the collision ripped through Merry's ears. The smashing pressure hit a second later, the force throwing her against her door, her head hitting hard enough to crack the window. Everything slowed in front of Merry's half-blinded eyes, jagged bits of debris sparkling as they arced gently through the air to bounce on the pavement. Through the detached haze of disbelief and pain, she heard Missy take a breath, then begin to wail.

"Missy," she breathed, her first flare of panic subsiding even as she felt pieces of something moving in her chest when she inhaled. Another jag quickly followed. "Chris?" she called.

"Merry," his voice came from far away, thickened. He coughed, then said clearly, "I love you."

"I love you too. Can you get Missy out of her seat?" she whispered, before the world went dark.

CHAPTER 9

The thick, rose-musk dimness gave way to a soft yellow glow as Dove turned on the bedside light. Benny rolled over, shielding his eyes with one hand. The girl next to him murmured something incoherent and muffled, pulling the pillow over her head.

"*Hasbidi*? What is it?" Benny asked, sliding his pistol back onto the shelf on the headboard as his eyes adjusted to the light.

"I've got to talk to you," Dove said softly.

"Now?" Benny looked from the clock to the mound of long hair, dark skin, and blankets beside him.

"Now," Dove said flatly.

Benny sighed. "All right already. Kill the light and wait for me in the front room."

Dove turned off the lamp and moved to the door. He didn't actually walk down the hall until he heard Benny get out of bed. The black and gray whirl of his thoughts didn't stop him from giving Benny a jaundiced glance when his brother finally appeared, yawning and hiking on a pair of sweats. "In bed at seven o'clock, huh? Looks like you got over Dolores pretty quick. So who's this one?"

"Sharice," Benny said. "She's come down to work at the truck factory over the border." He looked like he couldn't decide whether to be annoyed at the question (and the tone) or not.

Dove helped him along by saying, "And that ain't all she's working. This is getting pretty old, you telling me to stay true while you do as you please all over the barrio."

Benny smacked him hard. Dove knew he deserved it and didn't duck, but he didn't break eye contact, either. Benny's hand, raised for another blow, slowly relaxed. He ran it through his tousled hair instead, looking sad, exasperated, and guilty. "Listen, I told you, it's like cigarettes—"

"They'll get you sick and make you wish you never started on them," Dove finished the lecture. He touched Benny's shoulder, half apologetically. "I know. I've listened. And watching you keep coming back to get your heart ripped out and your b—"

"Enough already," Benny interrupted. "You really get me out of a real nice spot to bust my chops about my girlfriends? Or just Sharice?"

"No. I didn't know about Sharice. I hope she works out," Dove said. He caught Benny's arm, pushing him onto the couch. "Listen—" He started to say something, reconsidered, then started pacing.

Benny watched his little brother wrestle with whatever it was, then finally stuck out a foot as Dove went past. "What already?"

Dove skipped to keep from tripping, then stopped. "Benny, the General, General Garza, he's a terrorist or something, using sickness to kill people down South and now around here, too. That package *Abuelo* had me deliver for Slick—it was germs or something. Viruses. Some kind of disease, all in little glass vials."

"What?" Benny looked at him. "Where you coming up with that? Did you open the box? You're not supposed to do that, not ever. They put dye packs in there sometimes, booby traps—even bombs! You could've taken your head off! And if *Abuelo* finds out, he'll take your head off for you!"

"No, I didn't open it. It kind of fell open, by accident. Like I told you, Pizarro was there waiting for me. He grabbed my backpack, and the box opened when we were fighting over it. I saw the little bottles then, but I figured it was just designer go-juice. I handed it over, figured if those guys wanted to toast their brains, that's their business, and nothing to do with me."

"Right," Benny agreed. "So you delivered it and left. So now leave it alone."

"I delivered it, yeah." Dove swallowed hard. "And I killed them— the guys who took it and some farmer types down the road, too."

Benny reached over, caught Dove's jacket, and pulled him down to kneeling. He took Dove's face in his hands and looked into his little brother's eyes. "*Hasbìdì*, just tell me what you saw, what you found out. Tell it in order, like I taught you. Don't try to explain it to me."

Dove took a deep breath, leaning into Benny's hands, then nodded. He settled back on his haunches. "I delivered that box, with the vials in it, like I told you, and came back. I stayed out of Pizarro's way, just in case, kept low, went to school. The teacher gave us a paper, something about social problems, like she's so hot on. I got my stuff, then I was helping Perro and Calvin get theirs at the library when the girls there started talking about a bunch of farmers dead down by the border. They said it was hantavirus or something, but then they started jabbering about Ojo's ghosts down at Blanca Hacienda. Just for kicks, I looked up the news clip, and saw the farm's close to the big rocks down there. That got me wondering, since there's all those cops down there, and I wondered about those bottles, so I went to check it out."

"You've always had good instincts," Benny said as he paused. "Woman's intuition," he added, grinning.

Dove rolled his eyes, but the pressure to get the story out superseded the need to insult Benny back. "Serious, Benito. I got there, pulled up out of sight. They got the FBI, cops, even Pizarro, and I didn't want them seeing me. I could see them, though—and I could see a truck in the yard, looked just like the one Slick's friends had that night. Then it hit me that Slick's friends maybe killed off the farmers, poisoned them with what I brought. I jumped back on my bike to go over—"

"And do what, *Hasbìdì*? Lay a guilt trip on them?" Benny interrupted, his eyes wide and furious. "Taking on you don't know how many guys with you don't know how many guns, all by yourself! You know better—"

"Benny, you said you'd let me tell it," Dove interrupted, grabbing Benny's head this time and shaking him. "Let me! I don't know what I was going to do, I just went, okay?" He let go, took a breath, and the rest came in a rush. "I got there, and the guys were all dead— looked like Slick had shot them all from too far away to touch. I found the shell casings by more tire tracks. There were birds around, too, and a big burned place in those old bushes. Looks like a fire started after the desperados were dead, the farmer came to see about it, and kyfed the truck. Only he walked around the dead guys and got whatever they got, and came home and gave it to his family, and they died of whatever was in that box I delivered."

He looked up at Benny, making sure his brother was following. Benny nodded silently, motioning him to go on. "I burned it back to the library and checked out the stories—whole villages wiped out down South, everybody dead down to the dogs and rats, and nobody knows what's happened. They're saying it's terrorists, but terrorists don't kill farmers nobody cares about. Some of the stories said that the dead people worked for drug runners down there, or helped out revolutionaries, and that's why they got whacked. So I checked out revolutionaries, and all the reports talked about that General Garza, the one Slick works for, the one with the big guns and money who's recruiting gangs like the *Brujos*—and us. He's got an army down south, helping out the presidents who'll hire him, chasing out the drug runners. But Benny, I think he's using the viruses, too, and now he's spreading out up here, just across the border. And he's using us to help him." Dove paused, opened his mouth, then shut it, realizing he didn't have any more to say.

Benny sat back against the couch cushions. He wiped a hand over his face, staring at the shadowed ceiling. "You put all this together from the library?" he finally said. "Then you're not the only one knows it. Let the Legitimates take care of this one—if you know, the *federales* know."

"I don't know they do," Dove said, more sure than not. "They don't know Slick wanted me to deliver medicine-looking stuff to the guys at Blanca Hacienda, or where that truck came from. They're thinking it's hantavirus, or maybe something like those towns down south, but they don't know it's from Slick and that Slick works for this General Garza."

"So say they don't know," Benny conceded for argument's sake. "Why's a big-shot general from down south messing around with viruses up here? They're bad news enough. Why use a germ when a bullet does the job just as well—and without coming back on you?"

"Maybe they're trying to find a cure, like that AllSafe stuff on the news," Dove suggested, remembering the lead desperado's eager grab for the box. "Those guys were real happy to get the bottles. Maybe they thought it'd make them immune or something."

"Maybe. It's thin, Dove, really thin." Benny looked thoughtful, then stood up abruptly. "But woman's intuition or not, you ain't been wrong much about stuff." Now it was his turn to pace. "I gotta think about this."

Dove pulled his legs out of the way. "Okay, maybe the virus side is thin—even if I don't think so. But think about this too, Benny. Slick and those two shadows of his shot the desperados out at Blanca Hacienda, point blank shot them with no warning. They weren't hiding, not crouching behind stuff, not shooting back. He called 'em out, they came out thinking they were safe, and they got shot to bits. Bird food. You think Slick's going to treat us different when he's done with us? Look what he did to the desperados—and to the *Brujos*, too. That General's got his own game going, and he'll run over anybody he wants to win it. You want to be the henchman in the movie, Benny, the one who gets shot by his boss if the hero doesn't finish him off first?"

Benny stopped pacing, looking down at Dove. He grinned tightly. "All right, so now you're starting to make sense, even if it's coming out of all those movies. Told you they'd rot your brain."

Dove watched him walk back down the hall, uncertain about what that comment meant. He grinned too, though, as Benny came back in and tossed his jeans and shirt on the couch. He pulled off the sweats, ordering, "Go get my boots. You might be up in the night—" he chuckled. "I guess we both are. But whatever's up, we're going to tell *Abuelo* about it. Crazy as you sound sometimes, you ain't been completely wrong yet."

* * *

The burnt-cocoa smell of Franklin's molé hit them as soon as they walked into Mama Rosa's, the smooth syncopation of a classic tango blending with the smell and the dim light glowing from the candles on the tables. Rico looked up from his cards, rolled his eyes, and muttered "Little *chiquito's* out late on a school night," to his buddies. They sniggered. Marco glanced at Dove, looked at Rico, and upped the bet, tossing a handful of battered tokens into the middle of the table. Cesare snorted, appreciating the implication.

Benny caught Dove's belt loop and pulled him past. "You want to talk to *Abuelo*, talk to him. Let the losers get on with losing." He said that last out loud, earning him a dark look from Rico.

Abuelo looked up from the newspaper spread over the table, his hands still busy with the intricate pieces of the motorcycle model he was painting. Sasha glanced over too, then returned her attention to the magazine she was reading. His eyes went from Benny to Dove, then back again. "What?"

"Dove's got something to tell you," Benny said.

"It's about Slick," Dove told him. "Him and his General—they're using us to run viruses for them."

That caught *Abuelo's* attention—and the attention of everybody else in the room. Perro and Calvin, who'd left their low-rank spot by the door to drift after Dove and Benny, looked at each other with wide eyes. Rico glowered; Marco and Cesare, like the half-dozen other of *Abuelo's* gang, just waited.

"Heavy talk about somebody paying us." *Abuelo* put down his paint brush.

"I can back it up," Dove said. He quickly summarized the story he'd told Benny: vials in the box, dead farmers, stolen truck, murdered desperados, plague-emptied villages and the General's reputation down south. "We work for the *Señor*," he finished, "not some southerner who spreads disease and shoots his own soldiers. Running drugs is low, but the customers know what they're getting. When you run viruses, everybody dies."

Rico barked a laugh, breaking the morbid spell Dove's explanation had woven around *Abuelo's* gang. "So we're low? And now you know more than *Abuelo* and the rest of us, 'cause you got a library card. Looks like little Pigeon's got more problems with his 'honor.' You forget what I told you?" His voice dropped, a snarl replacing the sneer. "You got no honor. You're a border rat—no matter how much you go to school or read those stupid books. If you had any guts, you'd get drunk, get over yourself, and leave the thinking to the big wolves."

"You mean leave the thinking to you?" Benny growled back. "What you going to think with, Rico? We all know your head doesn't even work as a hat rack."

Rico swung at him, tight and hard, all deadly intent. Benny blocked his fist, caught the follow-up in the ribs, and got off a shot of his own that glanced off Rico's pulled-up shoulder. Marco and Cesare tensed, while the rest of the gang instinctively backed off, giving the combatants room. Dove thought a vicious curse at Rico, watching the lieutenant's hands carefully, waiting for the flash of a blade. Neither Benny nor Rico ever went unarmed.

Abuelo's sharp "Cut it," broke the panting dead silence of a serious fight. He gestured authoritatively with the sawed-off, pistol-grip shotgun he'd neatly retrieved from beside his chair.

Dove leapt forward, catching Benny's off elbow on the backswing, and pulled his brother back, away from Rico—but without getting in his way or binding his arms, just in case. Marco hesitated a moment longer, but stepped in as Rico lunged toward Benny again. Rico bounced off the big man's chest, pushing off him to come to a stop by Cesare, who put a restraining hand on his shoulder. The crowd cleared, the seasoned soldiers breaking their ring around the fighters to move into *Abuelo's* corner—carefully out of the line of fire. Perro and Calvin, physically caught between Rico's *compadres* and the rest of the gang, but with loyalty tugging them in a third direction, shot agonized looks at Dove and Benny.

"You work for me," *Abuelo* informed them coldly. "You bust it up when I tell you to. And only when I tell you to, or you don't worry about the likes of Slick shooting you." He regarded them for a moment more, his eyes as flat and deadly as the dull shine of the hand cannon, before laying the gun on the paint-streaked newspaper next to the delicate pieces of the model. "Rico."

"*Abuelo?*" Rico said, barely adding the question mark.

"Can it." The order to shut up carried just a hint of the brimstone and acid in *Abuelo's* face. "*Hasbidi?*"

"*Abuelo?*" Dove kept the break out of his voice with an effort; deference came easily.

"Your brother better teach you proper respect," *Abuelo* observed, not even glancing at Benny, "or he'll be the only one left in his family. We got one captain here, one boss, one papa. That's me. I brought you into this family, and if you disrespect me, I will take you out. Understand?"

"Yes," Benny and Dove said in unison. Benny took it with an expression as impassive as *Abuelo's*. Dove, however, looked like he wanted to spit.

Abuelo gazed into the distance, his fingers tapping the butt of the gun. His eyes came down to lock, laserlike, on the ex-combatants, but he spoke to everyone in the room. "Listen to this. I'll decide if we hook up with Slick and the General—and you'll do what I say. The *Señor* ain't been giving us what we deserve, so he'll get what he deserves. And so will we."

The gang relaxed slightly as *Abuelo* drove his point home with that long stare, then picked up his brush again. Sasha rolled her eyes and went back to her gossip rag. The jukebox chose that moment to start an old country spoof song, lamenting the difficulty of finding a barber when you're out of town. Perro sang along with the chorus, ruffling Calvin's hair, avoiding Dove's eye. Chairs scraped as card games—and dinner—resumed, everyone acting elaborately casual, throwing off the tension.

Dove glanced at Benny, who shrugged after a moment, then grinned and poked Marco away from the fifth chair around the poker game. He caught Dove's eye and nodded toward Perro and Calvin. "So who's winning?" he asked, glancing at the other players. His smile got sharper, showing his canines. "Or who *was* winning?"

Rico advised Cesare to be ready to do something vulgar to Benny, and dealt him in.

Proving we're still in the family, Dove thought, *saving face*. He choked down his fury and embarrassment, casually wandering across the room to slouch against the table nearest the jukebox, where Perro and Calvin sat.

Perro shot him a sideways, noncommittal look. Calvin, less attuned to the social tension or more bluntly direct, poked Dove's chest. "See? Libraries get you in Dutch every time. Better off ducking school."

"And winding up like Rico?" Dove laughed, pointing to the game, where Benny had already won a hand. "Mean, broke, *and* stupid?"

"Mean, maybe," Perro suggested. "That can come in handy sometimes."

Dove snagged a taco from Perro's plate. "Mean and smart beats mean and dumb every time." His eyes strayed to *Abuelo*, calmly painting serial numbers on a replica plane. Frustration boiled again, the stolen taco losing its spice as he thought of the vials glinting in their case. "But honorable and smart beats mean and smart. You can't pull backhanded maneuvers and expect it to come out all right at the last—"

"Hey, back off that," Perro warned, interrupting him. "You want a faceful of lead? *Abuelo* says drop it, we drop it. You and Benny want your hides dried, keep it up."

"You want your hides dried, you won't get those papers done," Dove riposted, realizing with a sinking feeling that even his friends weren't willing to back him on this one. "What'd you guys find on the library's Net?"

After token protests from Perro and Calvin, they settled down to the mundane task of outlining their term papers on contemporary social problems. Only Dove had even the faintest inkling that Mama Rosa's, filled with outlaw enforcers for the local crime boss, made an ironic setting for such an endeavor.

At last, Benny had proved his point and rose from the game, taking leave of *Abuelo* and motioning Dove to follow as he walked to the door. Dove saluted their leader and fell in beside him, feeling shaken, relieved, and betrayed—not so much by *Abuelo* as by Perro and Calvin, by the other members of the gang who ignored his warning. He pushed the door hard as he went through.

The slam didn't quite happen, however. Rico caught the door, his silhouette darkening the streak of yellow light as he followed. Marco and Cesare's bulk tripled the shadow.

"Leaving already?" Rico asked.

"Why stay?" Benny shot back with a hard glare. "I never liked molé."

Rico shook his head, the flash of his teeth in the dark showing in an expression that wasn't a smile. "You never liked lots of stuff, Benito. But sometimes you don't have to like it. Garza's got big things going, and some of us decided we're not gonna be border trash forever."

"You're going to be plague trash instead?" Dove asked. "You want to sell out to General Garza? Forget border rats—maybe you'll get to be the next lab rats for Slick to try his poison on."

"Maybe you better stop worrying about Slick and start listening to *Abuelo*—for as long as he's talking to you." Once again, Rico didn't quite smile at them. "*Buenos noches, chicos.* Watch where you're walking on the way home. Be sad if you got hit in the dark."

Benny shrugged casually, turning away from the trio, his hand on Dove's neck, bringing him along. "*Buenos noches, hijos.* And Rico, I did get hit once." He grinned over his shoulder at them. "Earned me a hot stripe of road rash. But you should'a seen the other truck."

* * *

A battered truck, its grille smashed and hanging, its front axle broken, filled the screen. "Police reports confirm that Rusty Larue was driving while impaired when he ran a red light and hit a compact car in the intersection," the reporter noted, as the scene changed to show partying rednecks clashing beer mugs and inhaling deeply on thick, doctored stogies before staggering out to other trucks. "This accident was one of three DWI accidents last night. It is also the fourth fatal crash in as many months that involve a suspect who admitted to smoking pot before getting behind the wheel. That's a trend that has, unfortunately, gone up since the decriminalization of marijuana. Looks like it's time to add a new slogan: don't toke and drive."

"Time indeed. Thanks, Tom," the anchor said, switching easily from concern to light-hearted amusement, as the crawl at the bottom of the screen combined statistics on DWI convictions with ads for the liquor and marijuana companies that sponsored them. The top of the screen showed a couple holding an outrageously dressed dog. "And you may wonder what these pet owners were thinking—or smoking—when they entered their pets into this contest!" Poodles in bikinis paraded across a poolside stage with amused commentary from the anchor. The obligatory funny pets story over, the local news switched to the national.

Channel 8's nationwide logo replaced the local channel's call sign, then faded into a shot of gray, rain-weeping sky. "This is Anne O'Neal, for Channel 8 News. I'm standing outside the Independence, Missouri, headquarters of The Church of Jesus Christ of Latter-day Saints. And, as you can see, the weather fits the solemn occasion. Today, the Church bids formal farewell to one of its Apostles, Thomas J. Stacy. Elder Stacy, along with two young missionaries who had accompanied him, was ambushed, kidnapped, and shot point-blank by unknown assailants during an official visit to the Church's conference in the Philippines." Images of thick, green jungle plants shifting in the hot breeze suggested ambushes and worse.

"Thousands of mourners turned out in Manila to see the bodies off on their journey home." The plane appeared, sitting on the tarmac, as a sea of quietly resolute onlookers watched dark-suited pallbearers carry three coffins into the cargo hold. As Elder Stacy's coffin disappeared, the strains of "We Thank Thee, O God, for a Prophet" filled the air. "They expressed their continued love and support for a Church that has made amazing strides not only in the Philippines but throughout the world."

Scenes of the Salt Lake Temple, photos of the new headquarters in Independence, demographic charts of worldwide membership growth, portraits of Joseph Smith and Brigham Young, shots of Mormon congregations from Cape Town to Helsinki, and pictures of smiling missionaries teaching in their own neighborhoods accompanied Anne's recital as she briefly listed the Church's accomplishments just during Elder Stacy's lifetime. "Membership in The Church of Jesus Christ has increased dramatically in the last twenty years. You can find Mormons in almost every country in the world, and many governments previously opposed to foreign churches have officially recognized the Mormons—if not for their religion, for their work ethic, dedication to education, and unfailing humanitarian aid. This growth has been promoted by an ever-growing and increasingly native missionary force. It is also backed by impressive economic and financial power. The Church owns businesses, financial networks, and property all over the world. In fact, you can find Mormon temples and temple communities in almost every country, province, and state.

"However, the Church's dramatic growth throughout the world has also caused less positive—even destructive—ripples." The lovely landscaping and happy faces of local LDS members disappeared, replaced by an even more menacing scene: rioters, masked with kerchiefs, tossing Molotov cocktails at chapels, waving fists and shouting outside the gates of the Manila Temple. Speakers shouted denunciations of the Church from pulpits and street corners, the camera catching one brief glimpse of the Most Reverend Rashi Janjalani, an especially charismatic preacher better known as Brother Light. "In fact, unconfirmed reports speculate that it's likely that the assassins who killed Thomas Stacy are affiliated with the growing anti-Mormon movement spreading through the Philippine islands. Local religious leaders have denounced The Church of Jesus Christ. Members have experienced death threats, beatings, and vandalism of their property and buildings—and now, the murder of two missionaries and one of the Church's Apostles."

Anne reappeared, the rain still falling softly around her. "Today, The Church of Jesus Christ bids farewell to that Apostle. Heads of state, government officials, business leaders, and celebrities have come to pay their respects. This Church, for all its conservatism, attracts a disproportionate number of ambitious, prominent, and powerful people." A montage of head shots followed, luminaries filing solemnly through the broad doors in the wake of the coffin. "And, of course, almost the full complement of the Church's own leadership is here, led by Richard M. Rojas, the newly appointed Associate President, an office first and last seen in the early days of the Church. His unusual appointment caused a schism that resulted in some members leaving the Church, but the majority of its membership has stood behind both President Smith and President Rojas."

The camera followed the coffin into the conference room, focusing on the flower-bedecked pulpit. "And thousands of those faithful have come here to celebrate the life and mourn the death of one of their own, under the leadership of their newly appointed leader."

President Rojas appeared behind the pulpit, his warmly passionate voice filling the conference room and the airwaves with heartfelt conviction and comfort. "We gather on this solemn occasion to bid farewell to President Thomas Jared Stacy, a friend, a leader, and a righteous, kind-hearted man. He died sealing his testimony, reaching out to our brothers and sisters in the Philippines. We deeply regret his death and miss his gentle sense of humor, his unwavering testimony. We do not mourn, however, because we know that Jesus Christ, our

Savior, has triumphed over death. Through the miracle of His Atonement, we are not consigned forever to the bands of death . . ."

* * *

"Nice funeral," Leon observed, wrapping up his camera cords.

"I said, 'nice funeral,'" Leon repeated. "These guys are always so upbeat about it. You notice that hardly anybody even wore black? It's not quite a New Orleans brass band, but they don't get all down about it. Wouldn't mind having that Rojas guy do *my* eulogy." He stowed his gear in the back of the semiofficial Channel 8 vehicle, kicking the door open for Anne and giving her a wink. "Bet you wouldn't either, huh?"

"Wouldn't what?" she asked.

"Wouldn't mind Rojas doing your eulogy—or doing anything else for you." He pulled the van away from the curb, merging into the heavy (but remarkably well-behaved) traffic.

"Cut it out, Leon. We're talking about a Mormon Church president." Anne sighed. "Yes, he's charming and handsome—but it's like he's a priest or something."

"Aura of sanctity?" Leon suggested.

Anne looked at him, surprised. "Where'd you get that?"

Leon shrugged, turning onto the freeway. "Heard it somewhere. Besides, the guy's married with six kids. Not exactly priest material."

"Not until the Vatican gives in or the American College of Cardinals takes the bit in their teeth and finally renounce celibacy permanently," Anne told him.

"That'll be a story," Leon grinned. "And the way you've got old Monk up at Channel 8 all over you, they might send you to Rome to cover it."

"So long as it's not another funeral," Anne said. "Good or not, they always get me down."

* * *

There were no dignitaries, politicians, celebrities, or reporters at Christopher Galen's funeral, just a soft-spoken bishop reassuring the Galen family and the few ward members who came to the graveside service.

"We know that families are forever. And we know that whatever it was, Chris fulfilled his mission on Earth. We all got to know his quick sense of humor, his compassion, and his willingness to serve—he was certainly a fine ward clerk." Bishop Michelsen knew how lame that sounded, but he sincerely meant it. His voice wavered, then cracked as he fought tears.

Merry smiled encouragingly at him, silently urging him on. Missy chose that moment to loudly protest "No! Tired! Go!" She'd had it with this whole church in the middle of the week thing. Merry patted her, but couldn't do more, the pain in her side preventing anything but the gentlest of movements. Grandma Galen took over, picking Missy up and gently rocking her until she forgot her boredom for the moment. Merry shot her mother-in-law a quick, grateful smile.

"It's hard to understand God's timing," Bishop Michelsen recovered and went on. "But He loves all His children and watches over them. He sees even a sparrow fall."

He sees it, but he doesn't catch it, Merry thought. For a moment, the cold numbness filling her chest threatened to crack, but she took a deep breath, concentrating on the pain from her badly bruised ribs until the numbness returned. The pleasant, neutral expression on her face never wavered, and her eyes stayed dry through the graveside service. She leaned lightly against Grandpa Galen's arm, touching him only enough to take some of the strain off her right side. Somehow, she couldn't believe that the shiny box they were lowering into the ground actually had anything to do with Chris.

She was still here, wasn't she? Banged and bruised, true, with a healing concussion and aches that made her exquisitely aware of her body from ankles to ears, but alive. She hurt too much to be dead. Chris should be here, sympathizing, gagging on painkillers with her—he never could swallow pills on the first try. And he never would. She stumbled slightly, knowing that Grandpa Galen had steadied her but not feeling it through the pain.

Memories mixed together, confused bits of the hospital, the accident scene, the ambulance ride. The doctors' explanations replayed in her head, technical terms for the horrendous damage Chris had suffered when the heavy iron supports for the "poacher lights" on the truck's grille broke loose from their poor welds. In the collision, they had smashed through the window and into his head. "He didn't know what hit him," "He didn't suffer," "There's nothing we could do," the nurse had said apologetically, trying to reassure Merry when she woke from her second blackout in the ambulance to find herself in the hospital. "He shouldn't've died," the investigating cop muttered as he took Merry's statement about the accident, adding a pungent assessment of Rusty Larue, pothead drivers, and incompetent welders for good measure. Merry had patted his shoulder awkwardly, recognizing his pain more clearly than she felt her own.

The words of the prayer came through the protective haze between her and reality, dedicating the box and the ground around it to wait in peace until the glorious Resurrection. She mechanically threw a handful of dirt into the grave, belatedly wondering if that were something Mormons did. The tiny stones rattled on the lid of the coffin that didn't have anything to do with Chris.

Missy happily tossed another couple of handfuls down; she always loved playing outside. Merry ruffled her hair, casting around for something that could keep Missy from tearing off through the gravestones. None of them were in any shape to chase her down. "Come on, Miss Missy, let's get some lunch."

"Lunch?" Missy looked up from the big hole, interested. "Tatoes?"

"Yes, I'm sure there are tatoes," Merry agreed.

"Tatoes, tatoes, tatoes," Missy sang. She kept up the happy singsong chant as they left the cemetery, supplementing it with an occasional "Where's tatoes? There's tatoes!" before continuing the refrain.

"There are always tatoes," Grandma Galen said, a hint of smile breaking through her solemn expression as she picked Missy up and walked back to the car.

"Chris never did like funeral potatoes," Grandpa Galen observed, after the funeral cortege had wound its way back through the streets to the church. Efficiently compassionate Relief Society ladies had set out a buffet and waited with friendly but solemn smiles to replenish any dish, part of the scene but not really part of the funeral.

Carmen broke ranks and leaned forward over the table. "That's why we didn't make all the usual kind," she said confidentially, tapping the side of her own baking dish with a smile. "Try this one. It's got a little zip to it."

"A little zip sounds good about now," Merry told her, glancing at the sheer number of containers on the table. "And from the looks of it, you could supply a little zip to a big army!"

"We knew you'd have teenage nephews coming," Carmen told her, gesturing toward the boys filing down the table, filling their plates and beginning to relax from the enforced formality of the service. "Always better to have more than less, especially when you're dealing with hungry boys."

"Tatoes!" Missy exclaimed happily, as Grandma Galen dished her a spoonful on a plate.

Merry felt the aroma of the food—including the cheesy, peppery smell of the potatoes—try to slither down her throat, past the wall of ice. She swallowed, taking another breath. "You always come through, Carmen."

"I just recommended recipes. Alana took care of the tough stuff." Carmen assured Merry, nodding toward the Compassionate Service leader. "She's the one who really came through." Her expressive eyes darkened as she blurted, "I wish your mother had come through—or just come at all!"

The words crashed into one of those inconvenient pauses in the general chatter. Carmen's hands flew to her mouth. "Oh, Merry, I'm so sorry! I don't know what I'm saying—"

"Just the truth," Merry interrupted, reaching to pat Carmen's shoulder. Her hand felt dead, clumsier than usual. Touches had always come so easily to Chris—so easily to her when she was with him. Now she felt unmoored, detached from everyone, every feeling, awkward and hesitant inside a bubble of Novocain. The worst part was that the bubble seemed stretched thin, about to burst. And if that happened, pain would overwhelm her, drown her completely, make her break down and lose control, and—she focused on the other emotion behind the bubble's thin skin. Anger honed her voice into a razor's edge. "Sidney had a conference to go to. It's her once in a lifetime chance to address the International Organization of Women. Funerals don't help anyone, don't promote necessary social change. Besides, she feels certain that I'll be fine. This was just a starter marriage anyway."

She became aware of eyes on her, realized that her voice had risen to easily audible levels on the last phrase. Alana and her Compassionate Service Corps pretended they hadn't heard, melting back into the wallpaper—or in this case, the paneled walls of the gym. The bishop tried to shoot her a reassuring glance, but looked too worried about her to really carry it off. Carmen's husband, the first counselor, did better, settling for sympathetic—but he knew the whole story. Chris's sister didn't know about Sidney's history; she looked furious, turning away to catch her four-year-old son as he barreled past.

"See why I don't call you Mom?" Merry asked Chris's mother, as lightly as she could, trying to make a joke of it. "You're much better than any connotations of that word."

A tear trickled down Grandma Galen's cheek. She wiped it away and matched Merry's smile with one much sweeter. "Sweetie, you can call me whatever you'd like. You'll always be my girl."

Carmen came around the table and hugged Merry, as tightly as she dared around the bandages. "Sorry I even brought it up—my big mouth. You've got a real mom here, a real family, and a forever marriage. Chris will always love you. How could anybody not? Now, you settle down off those bruises and see if you can eat something. Like these 'tatoes."

Merry graciously accepted a lightly stacked plate and sat down, equally graciously accepting the murmured condolences of the guests, who filed past as they left. She didn't manage more than a bite of the potatoes, but they stayed with her, right in the hollow of her throat. She had to keep swallowing to keep them there, blocking the lump that threatened to rise past them. The lump stayed down and the lip stayed steady as the family gathered and dispersed into cars, as Grandpa Galen strapped Missy into her car seat, as they saw everyone off to their various cars and lodgings, even as they walked back into the house that seemed so empty despite all the familiar things.

Like the single snapshot of their wedding, Chris smiling happily with his arm around her. It drew her eye irresistibly to meet his steady, confident gaze, the white steeple of the temple rising behind them, pointing toward eternity, toward heaven—toward where Chris was now, where she couldn't reach.

"Where Daddy?" Missy asked, rubbing her eyes tiredly, repeating a question she'd reflexively asked all week. "Where Daddy?"

"Daddy has gone to be with Jesus," Merry said softly, kneeling despite the screaming from her bruises. She hugged Missy. "He's got things he needs to do there, but he's waiting for us. We just need to be brave right now."

"Oh. Brave," Missy sighed. She dismissed the unimportant bits. "I want Daddy."

"I know, sweetie. I do too," Merry told her, keeping her voice level with an increasingly desperate effort. Inside the bubble, under the lump, she could hear the crying start: He's dead, he's gone, he's not here, he's not coming back; you are alone, you are utterly alone.

Grandma Galen's voice came through the roaring in Merry's ears. "Come over here, darling, let's get you a bath and jammies." She swept up Missy, paused to gently kiss Merry's cheek. "I'll take care of her, honey. You take a pain pill and go lie down. It's been a long day."

It's been a long day for you too, Merry thought, but the words wouldn't come. Instead, the tears did, welling up behind her eyes. She stumbled up the stairs as they spilled over, filling her head with salt water that instantly soaked through her pillow as she fell into bed. This time, the physical pain didn't even come close. She sobbed, deep, gasping, wracking breaths that wordlessly screamed the question spinning like a razor-edged, black-hued kaleidoscope inside her: "Why? Why Chris? Why Missy? Why me? Why?"

* * *

"Why keep it in a vault, instead of putting it where people can see it?" asked Virginia, blinking wide eyed at the sculpted nymph and faun twined sinuously around each other. She was practicing sweet-voiced wonderment, but her natively shrewd, sharp tone pricked through the words. Her dress and the nymph's looked like they'd come from the same designer: short on fabric, long on revealing.

The recently crowned Sexiest Celebrity, along with an exclusive selection of MedaGen's board, senior stockholders, and allies (including the ever-present Senator Garlick) had come to Abbott's art-appreciation soiree to celebrate the debut of MedaGen's full-media ad campaign. The entertainer—since Virginia billed herself as singer, actress, model, and media producer—as always, dressed to make an impression. Her vividly colored dress and glitter-powdered skin stood out like a phoenix in a rookery in the small crowd of perfectly tailored but conservatively cut suits. Her outrageously flirtatious, completely confident manner and crystalline giggle, as much as her dress (or the lack thereof), caught the undivided attention of every male in the room and provoked uneasy or outright hostile reactions from the few female executives. She immediately discerned who dominated the gathering and attached herself to Abbott, devoting the lion's share of attention to her current employer and best chance for furthering her future plans.

Julian, Virginia's tall, slender, red-headed secretary—more formally, "personal administrative assistant," which Julian thought sounded rather too close to "personal digital assistant"—hovered at a discreet distance from her, doing everything but adjusting the lights for best effect.

The other four members of Virginia's entourage were standard-issue muscle boys, officially present as bodyguards, but with a habit of preening and posing that clearly identified them as aspiring actors and models themselves. The executives and senator had quickly disregarded them as anything but mobile statuary, equally sculpted but probably with less average intelligence than the Greco-Roman masterpieces ranked along the vault room's silk-covered walls. The senator's well-armed escorts, as beautifully tailored as the executives but with the inescapable aura of hard boiling, gave Virginia's bodyguards harder looks, but the chief of the security delegation warned them away from having any fun at the bejewelled pretty boys' expense. Both contingents watched each other across the room as their employers wandered among Abbott's collection of priceless, and supposedly lost, artifacts, including the marble faun and nymph piece that had provoked Virginia's question.

"Not everyone chooses to put everything they have on display," Zelik observed looking directly at Virginia, careless malice dripping from her tone.

"Because then people would know he's got it, instead of whatever national treasury it came from," Whittier whispered in an aside to Julian. Whittier had taken an instant liking to Julian. Almost as instant as the hatred that flared between Zelik and their latest spokesmodel.

"Sure, like the ones who should be wearing bags over their heads," Virginia shot back, all the cotton candy in her voice turned to steel wool. "What did you say, Julian, about that?"

Julian instantly glided to Virginia's side, smoothly stroking a strand of Virginia's hair into place and making a minute adjustment to the gauzy folds of her dress while saying mildly, "'Modesty is the virtue of the unattractive.' It's a quote from Oscar Wilde."

Virginia tossed her head, not enough to shake off Julian's primping, just enough to send a cascade of her currently blonde hair tumbling over one shoulder. "Make that shorter, we could put it in my next song." She sneered at Zelik and shimmied, singing, "If you don't got it, don't flaunt it."

"With the right beat, maybe it could fly," Julian equivocated, glancing at the frozen face of MedaGen's Chief Operating Officer. Watching Virginia sharpen her spoon-sharp wit against the short-skirted corporate genius probably couldn't hurt their long-term success, but Zelik's unsmiling, unimpressed cool and the way the men in the room watched her with flickers of fear in their eyes marked her as a dangerous enemy. Julian caught Virginia's eye and tried to convey that information in a subtle head shake.

"Dedicated to Ms. Zelik, you know," Virginia persisted, disregarding her assistant's diplomatic warning. "And all the other skinny a—"

"We're all dedicated to Ms. Zelik around here," Whittier declared, interrupting Virginia's expanded catalog and raising his glass of altogether too expensive champagne in his superior's direction.

Julian shot him a grateful glance, followed up with a slow wink. An extra flush joined the heat that the champagne sent into Whittier's face.

"Of course," Abbott agreed amiably, stroking a hand down Virginia's back and catching Zelik's eye. "We love all our ladies."

Virginia snuggled into his touch, giving him the Bambi eyes, then shot Zelik a look that was anything but doelike from under her long, glitter-tipped lashes. Zelik settled for turning a withering glare on Abbott for putting her in the same category as Virginia—and for calling her a lady.

"But she is right, Virginia, about keeping the best parts for members only," he continued, gesturing with his free hand around the room, where each sculpture, painting, piece of jewelry, and artifact rested in its own case in a halo of precisely directed light. "All of these lovely things vanished a long time ago, from poorly guarded museums, private collections of bankrupt tycoons, badly managed archaeological digs." He smiled, relishing the fact that they had come to rest in his very exclusive collection, the visible symbols of his dominance over all the other avid, wealthy, powerful collectors in the world. "I've been amazingly lucky in finding them, being able to bring them here where they are preserved for posterity. The public had their chance to look, but they also left them out where irresponsible people could steal them. They're much safer here. And this way, we get to enjoy them right up close."

Virginia smiled up at him, appreciating the double entendre. His hand began to drop lower to emphasize the "close" bit, but she caught it and returned it to him with a flirtatious giggle. "You want that close, you better pony up some pretty things yourself. Like this one."

Abbott quickly caught her hand before her fingertips touched the velvet-lined case containing a magnificent golden Egyptian pectoral and pendant. He kissed her fingers as she turned a narrow-eyed, stormy look on him. "Careful, my dear. Just as you don't travel without body-guards, that necklace is well protected." He nodded at the guard standing unobtrusively to attention at the door of the vault room.

The guard flicked two switches. The overhead lamps and spot-lights dimmed dramatically. Thin blue and red threads of light glowed through the darkness, outlining every case with lambent lines of energy. "Laser motion detectors," Abbott explained smugly. "All the cases are wired. The slightest touch sets off silent alarms and signals every security guard in the building. It also closes and locks the vault door until someone enters the authorized password into the keypad in my office. And the only person who has that password is me."

"So don't touch anything, Julian," Virginia deflected the momen-tary embarrassment onto her assistant, "or you'll be in here long enough that even you'll be worth something."

"Oh, be nice," Julian purred back, nuzzling Virginia while auto-matically thinking, *Old movie reference. Will she never come up with an original insult? Or remember that while a little taste of cattiness combined with a hint of exhibitionistic lesbianism appeals to the audi-ence, nastiness puts them off?*

"So don't touch anything, Miss Diamante, or you'll lock us in until we all turn into artifacts," Zelik added, as nasty as she wanted to be, with no points to make with the guys in the room. She glanced from the laser-guarded artifact cases to the foot-thick vault door. She raised an eyebrow at Abbott. "Unless you have a secret exit from the vault you can use to get to the keypad in your office?"

Abbott colored slightly, hiding his reaction well, but still deflated and furious at the disdainful tilt of her eyebrow—and his architects' lack of foresight. Outwardly, however, he laughed heartily, refusing to acknowledge the mistake. "Of course I do—and I'm not going to show it to you." He ended the comment on a light note that got a laugh from the party. He smiled back and gestured sharply at the guard; the lights came back up.

Virginia laughed too, tapping Abbott's nose with one long, lacquered fingernail. "Oh, I think I can get all your secrets out of you, sooner or later. Like what's this?" She pointed to the bulbous figure of a featureless, overwhelmingly voluptuous clay statuette hanging like a collection of terracotta spheres against the black-velvet backdrop. "Other than a 'before' shot of Ms. Zelik?"

"It's a figure of a fertility goddess," Abbott told her. "From a newly discovered dig in Columbia. It's one of the newest pieces in my collection. A new . . . business associate sent it."

Virginia dismissed the piece as needing a session at the liposuction clinic and moved on to the cases containing jewelry. Most of the party followed, more for the view Virginia's sequin-studded costume afforded than for the decidedly unsparkling (but plentifully crude) conversation she promoted.

Senator Garlick, however, held back as the rest of the mob wandered on. He caught Zelik's arm. "Columbia, huh? MedaGen looking to put up a branch office down in South America?"

Zelik removed her arm from his grasp and gave him a Vulcan stare. "If the company were considering such a move, all information concerning it would be strictly confidential until the official announcement."

"Don't get coy," he growled. "Abbott's been taking a lot of calls from a satellite service running out of Bogota. What's going on?"

"Business," she informed him shortly.

"There's a strict embargo against Columbia until they use all that aid money to clean up their drug trade," the Senator reminded her.

"There's also a law against wiretapping without cause, even if your credentials give you full access to the Justice Department's eavesdropping equipment," Zelik reminded him. She shrugged slightly, the motion barely stirring her perfectly tailored jacket. "Not that laws bother you overmuch."

That remark hit its target. Garlick's iron-gray brows drew together thunderously, before suddenly clearing. He smiled, his white teeth glinting. "Laws, like rules, keep the idiots in line. You just got to know when to break them." The smile got sharper as he added, "And how to cover it up when you do. For all the security around here, you've got some big holes, besides the vault door that'll close down on you if that blonde bombshell goes off."

"Oh?" Zelik sipped the mineral water in her glass.

"Oh." Garlick gave her a hard look. "What's happened with that little leak you people had, the one that's going to put a big crimp in the AllSafe project? You said you'd handle it."

"We did," she told him, a flicker of smile crossing her own thin features.

"Discreetly?" Garlick dropped his voice, glancing aside at a pair of MedaGen stockholders examining the delicate impressions of an archaeopteryx fossil. "No blowback? No tracks?"

"Untraceable," she assured him. "The pest problem resolved itself before the exterminator even got there."

"We should always be so lucky," Garlick said.

"You can't depend on luck to come through every time," Zelik corrected. "It did this time, but we already had measures in place. I never leave anything important to chance." Her sliver of smile disappeared, leaving only a sub-zero glint in her eyes. "And if you ever tap MedaGen's phone records again, you'll have a chance to test the effectiveness of my measures for yourself."

Garlick tossed back his champagne and met her stare. "Is that a threat?"

She took his glass, placing it neatly on the tray of a deaf-mute server walking past. "A promise. And a reminder to never underestimate your allies, Senator." With a sidelong look at Whittier talking earnestly to Julian, she added, "Or take them at face value."

CHAPTER 10

It sounded like a simple job; take a box out to Tsossie's ranch, leave it in the old shearing shed, come back with the envelope another runner had hidden under the watering trough. Benny took the assignment as a peace-offering job after a couple of tense weeks, proof that he and Dove had managed to get back into *Abuelo's* good graces. Dove had obeyed Benny's stern advice and shut up about diseases, the General, and anything else before he got them both jumped out of the gang, maybe fatally. Benny had a point; more talk cast a shadow on *Abuelo*, which didn't make them any points in the leader's book. Thus, he'd mostly kept his distaste for Slick to himself, but the more he thought about it, the more he worried about the gang's future—and theirs. Perro and Calvin had picked up Dove's uneasiness; it made Calvin quieter and Perro louder and earned them both static from Rico as well as warning smacks from Benny.

Despite the simmering conflict, *Abuelo* had called Benny over to Mama Rosa's early that Saturday morning, tossing him a well-wrapped package and an equally opaque stare as he said, "Do the right thing, Benny. For you and *Hasbìdì*."

Benny caught the package and (he figured) the hint, and packed up Dove for a drive through the badlands.

Dove's anti-Slick civil disobedience and complete lack of enthusiasm for the desert run irritated Benny, who'd read him the riot act on the way out, reminding him that they were better off with *Abuelo* than not, and to shape up his snarky attitude or Benny would beat it out of him—if *Abuelo* didn't do it first. The lecture, punctuated with pauses for Dove to fill with his unconditional agreement and promises to do better (most of them had gone unfilled), had made for a long drive, even during a long drive. Lunch at Silver City hadn't been any more comfortable, but at least sitting in a restaurant within earshot of a middle-class Anglo family and a whole herd of preschoolers having a birthday party had shut Benny up for a few minutes.

"I still don't like it," Dove informed Benny when they climbed back into the car.

"You still worried that we're shipping supergerms out to the middle of nowhere?" Benny growled. Dove's silence was all the answer he needed. Spitting curses in three languages, Benny grabbed the package out of the smuggler's well inside the back seat. He threw it hard at Dove. "You think *Abuelo's* gonna get mixed up in that? You think he's gonna send us out with plague? All right, bust the seal and check it out. It's party favors for the *Señor's* Northern buddies or it's payoff for the Feds. You can eat crow now, with me, and when we get back, with *Abuelo*. Maybe that'll fill your mouth so you can't complain."

Dove looked from the box to Benny, hesitating for the second it took to remember the vials spilling out of the case in his backpack and the FBI boys in EVA suits walking around the farm by Blanca Hacienda. He flicked out his knife and neatly levered up the layers of duct tape. Plastic wrap came next, blurring the outlines of the next layer. Traces of light green and dirty white showed through the cellophane.

"It's not germs or drugs, Benny. It's money," Dove said, removing the plastic and riffling the neat stacks of banded bills. "A lot of money." He looked past his brother, staring at the low, dry hills beyond the parking lot. "*Abuelo* told you to do the right thing? For both of us?"

"Yeah," Benny shrugged, reaching over to take out a deck and fanning it expertly. No sign of counterfeit, no off-color ink, no smell of drugs. Just a quarter million in $100 bills. He looked up, studying Dove's profile, and sighed. "So what?"

"I think he wants us to take the money and run," Dove said quietly.

Benny snapped something unprintable and tossed the money back into his little brother's lap. He started the engine and peeled out of the parking space. Having to abruptly brake to avoid slamming into a minivan filled with preschoolers in party hats really took the drama out of the dramatic gesture. He settled for whistling between gritted teeth as they waited for the van to lumber out of the way.

"Benny, it's a payoff," Dove repeated. "*Abuelo* wants us out of here."

"*Abuelo's* family," Benny informed him. "He gave us a job when nobody else looked at us, put us up, got us money, took care of us. He's our *Señor*. No way I'm taking off with his *dinero*."

"How about Slick's?" Dove asked. "*Abuelo's* our *Señor*, but he's in a tough spot, between his *Señor* on one side, Slick and the General on the other—with Rico pushing hard. *Abuelo* likes you, Benny. He doesn't want to hurt you, or hurt me, 'cause that would hurt you. So he gives us a wad of Slick's money and an excuse to head North. We get out of his hair, Slick loses face with the General and maybe Rico, and he's off the hook."

This time it was Benny's turn to look into the distance, watching the road scroll away in front of them. Finally, he shrugged away the doubts. "How'd you get so cynical so young?"

"Maybe it's the people I run around with," Dove muttered.

"I'm the one supposed to be complaining about the younger generation." Benny grinned, reaching over to tousle Dove's hair. Dove thought about dodging, but leaned into his touch instead. "*Hasbidí*, you been watching too many movies. Yeah, Rico's shooting off his mouth, but *Abuelo's* not going to fall for some General way down south who sends a coyote like Slick up here. He's got a handle on it. This might be Slick's money, but it's not for us to take. More like he's sending a present up north, maybe to Toyoshi or Gonzalez. The *Señor's* going down, but *Abuelo* will land on his feet. So will we."

He went quiet, watching the road. "Besides, I never toasted a job in my life. And I never stole anything, neither." He couldn't quite keep a straight face on that one. "Well, nothing from my boss, anyway."

"And you ask why I'm cynical," Dove said. He rolled his eyes at Benny.

"Ah, shut up," Benny told him, reaching over to turn on the radio.

The desert miles rolled by in brown, dry, rocky waves. Neither brother had anything more to say, but plenty to think about.

"Looks like rain," Benny finally noted, gesturing out the Jeep's window at the storm clouds mounting into the blue and orange desert sky.

Dove eyed the clouds, their spreading tops and sparkling white in the setting sun, their blue-black bottoms trailing thin curtains of water droplets that evaporated before they hit the ground. "Maybe," he conceded, "but you can't trust clouds like that. They'll probably just pass over."

"Knowing our luck, it'll only rain enough to pull that ash slop out of the air and all over my car," Benny agreed. He pulled to the side of the road, the dust from the wheels blowing forward around them as the Jeep stopped on the shoulder of the dirt track. "That's it—the gate out to Tsossie's old sheep ranch. Got it? Let's go."

"Got it," Dove said unenthusiastically, as he reached into the back seat to haul out the anonymous, shoebox-sized package *Abuelo* had sent them to deliver. He'd already resecured the tape and plastic.

They'd driven farther out of *Abuelo's* territory than Dove had been before, traveling north out of the borderlands and into the big stretch of high desert that nobody had officially claimed as territory yet. Well, unless you counted the Tribal Police agencies and the rare FBI or BLM agent. Clearly, they weren't on *Abuelo's* business this far north. All Dove's original doubts crashed down on him again, despite Benny's confidence—and this time they brought relatives with them. What if this job wasn't a setup from *Abuelo?*

"*Hasbídí,* move your tail or I'll kick it out of the car," Benny growled. "I want to drop this and get home!"

Big-brotherly threats didn't make Dove move any faster, however, especially since he realized that the important thing was that the money in the package belonged to Slick—or, more accurately, to Slick's General.

A glint of setting sun off mirror shades drew Dove's attention and confirmed his new theory.

Slick strolled out of the shearing shed, Butch slouching along behind him. At the same moment, an engine cranked into life. Pizarro's undercover-marked sheriff mobile rolled out from behind the ruins of the old house and pulled to a stop at eleven o'clock. More dust blew across the yard, but the thin, rust-colored cloud didn't dim the slash of a smile on Slick's face—or the shine of the shotgun barrel Butch cradled in both huge fists.

"Benny," Dove whispered, backing a step. "Ambush, Benny."

"Vamos, *Hasbìdì*," Benny said quietly. "Back to the Jeep, then—"

"Too late," Dove said, glancing back.

Rico stood in the drive by the Jeep, Marco behind him, Cesare on the other side. Rico didn't bother to smile. His hand came up, the silver pistol sending hard shards of light into Dove's eyes.

"Down!" Dove shouted, throwing himself aside, and throwing the package hard at Rico's head.

Rico dodged the flying box, his shot cracking over Dove's head to kick up a puff of dust by the tire of Pizarro's car. Marco threw himself to the ground, out of the line of fire, reaching for the box. Dove rolled, pulling his own pistol. He heard Rico's furious curse at Cesare (telling him to wake up and fire) and two more shots, but saw only the hard shine of Cesare's gun swinging toward Benny. Images of Cesare—in their home, playing video games with Benny, growling at the younger guys' horsing around, following Rico like a Great Dane—darkened and vanished into the gun's narrow, iron throat. In Dove's eyes, Cesare seemed pinned in place, slowly spinning against the ochre-stained sky as the world turned right-side up. The glint of Dove's gunsight merged with the snarl on Cesare's face—which promptly disappeared in a haze of chunky crimson mist.

The noise of the shot crashed against his ears a split second later, and the crushing barrage of explosions filled his head. Shouts ran between the shots like the melody in a scream-core song: Rico swearing as Cesare slid bonelessly down the side of the Jeep; Marco's disbelieving "Cesare!"; Pizarro reflexively yelling "Freeze! Drop it!" as he retreated behind the unmarked patrol car; Slick calmly instructing Butch to "slag both of them." Only one voice was absent.

"Benny!" Dove called. He squeezed off two more shots, making Butch and Slick duck behind the rapidly disintegrating ruins of the shearing shed.

Rico was coming around the Jeep toward them, keeping low, shooting as he ran, dodging Benny's shots.

Dove looked wildly around, then jumped as he felt a hand close around his ankle and pull.

"Get to the Jeep," Benny hissed, ignoring the gun muzzle in his face as Dove hit the ground next to him. "Marco won't shoot us."

Dove didn't have a chance to argue. Benny surged to his feet at a flat run. Marco, looking up from the ruin of Cesare, saw him coming and froze, just as Benny had predicted, the barrel of his shotgun wavering uncertainly. Benny kept coming, giving Rico's left-hand man no time to think, or to readjust to the idea of shooting at someone in his own gang. "Marco, move your fat—" He never finished the sentence.

Butch's shotgun didn't waver at all. The blast took Benny in the back, throwing him forward and smashing him to the ground. Dove screamed Benny's name, emptying his gun with vicious accuracy. Once again, Butch and Slick had to dodge bullets as one smashed off Slick's sunglasses, spraying sharp-edged shards into the dimming sunlight. Dove grabbed Benny's boot, pulling frantically at his brother's body—the dead weight sliding slowly backward as Dove tried to move him, haul him to the questionable safety of the open door of Pizarro's car. He lost his grip as a bolt of fire ripped into his shoulder and down his back.

The momentum of the shot hit like a baseball bat, striking him out. He fell into the black whirlpool that threatened to block out his sight, landing heavily in the dust. Benny's brown eyes, wide but empty, shone through the darkness, staring sightlessly into his own through a thin fringe of dry grass. Hot tears filled his eyes, burning like the blood flowing over his arm and ribs. The image of Slick's tooled-leather boots smeared through the pain and saline, their satiny shine wavering like a mirage, stepping around the ruts, stopping at the edge of Dove's vision.

"Make sure of them," Slick instructed.

Butch laughed, the gravel in his voice roughening his vulgar assessment of their chances. The toes of his work boots didn't gleam as he tromped toward Dove—but a quicksilver glisten shone beside Benny's left hand, still half under his body. "*Hasbidi*, get to the Jeep," his brother's voice whispered from a million miles away—and inside Dove's head and heart.

"Gracias, Benito," Dove whispered, lying still, watching through his eyelashes as Butch came closer. *That's right, you hijo de puta, closer—but not too close.* Now, if his hands would only obey him, despite the lightning tearing through him.

Butch stopped beside Benny's shoulder, one of those boots coming up to thump heavily into Benny's unresisting ribs. It drew back stained with streaks of red. So did the barrel of the shotgun, which prodded heavily into Dove's back. The blow unleashed another wave of sickening pain.

"They're dead," Butch called over his shoulder. "Dog meat."

"Make sure," Slick's cool, vindictive voice came back, as if from a long distance.

It didn't matter—nothing mattered but what lay within a foot of those stained boots. Dove's hand shot out, closing on the slim steel blade of Benny's hideout knife, whipping it around. The hilt slapped into his palm, his fingers closing hard around it, turning it blade up as he rolled onto his good side. The knife ripped through Butch's jacket and slid to the hilt in the big man's ribs. Butch gasped, breath driven out of his mouth, bubbling through the wound. Dove lurched to his feet and caught Butch with both hands, half holding him up, half using him for support. They swung around, off balance, Butch fighting for breath, Dove fighting to keep the thug between him and Slick.

Dove stumbled backward, retreating toward the open door of Pizarro's patrol car. Butch fought the pull, more curses bubbling from his bloody lips. Dove kept his grip, then felt two shots hit Butch's back, sending them both sprawling. Dove fell halfway into the patrol car, Butch landing heavily on his legs. Dove kicked free, slithering across the seat. He caught a glimpse of Pizarro's face, mouthing words that couldn't penetrate the roaring in his ears. The key turned under his slippery fingers; the engine roared to life as he crushed the gas pedal to the floor. Pizarro's face went by in a white blur as he leaped out of the way, flashes of light springing from his gun. By the time Dove thought to veer to hit Slick, he was already past, navigating down the dirt track requiring all his attention.

He hauled on the steering wheel as Rico and the Jeep suddenly loomed in front of him, forcing the patrol car's right wheels up onto the bank beside the road. Dove grimly accelerated, feeling as much as hearing the grinding scream as the car and Jeep scraped past each other. Rico blasted two more bullets into Pizarro's patrol car, but he couldn't aim and drive at the same time. The two vehicles finally broke apart—and with the sudden release, Rico nearly ran over Slick himself. He skewed the Jeep around, fighting the momentum in a cloud of dust. Dove caught a glimpse of Tsossie's shed collapsing as the Jeep skidded into it. Then a thick curtain of dust and distance obscured the picture in the rearview mirror.

The car jounced out of the deep ruts and onto the roughly graded surface of the dirt road. Every bump sent pain shooting through Dove's side, weakening his hands. He held on, gritting his teeth against the tears and pain, keeping the gas pedal to the floor, feeling the hot wash of blood flowing across his leg. He barely caught the turn onto the asphalt surface of the highway, wrestling with the uncooperative wheel until the car leveled out. Straight, flat road stretched in front of him, leading north, darkening in the last light of sunset— and the growing shadow behind Dove's eyes. He drove through the twilight until darkness flowed down to overwhelm him. He dimly felt the car bounding over tussocks of grass, before it came to a halt nose-first in a stand of junipers. He seemed to float lightly toward the windshield, the spider-webbed pattern of a bullet hole filling his vision before he tumbled into the warm, ebony space between the shining webs.

Through the darkness, rain finally began to fall.

* * *

Black webs hid the doorway, shifting shadows of menacing velvet that billowed and withdrew as Merry tried to brush them aside. Through a sudden break in the folds, she caught sight of a winding stairway. Missy's cries echoed in the stone-walled stairwell, the plaintive sobs coming from all directions at once.

"Missy! Missy, I'm coming!" Merry called.

The blowing curtains muffled her words, throwing them back into her ears, and distorting them into the harsh squawking of the seagulls that circled under the clouded sky over the endless stairs. She pushed through, running down the infinite flights, but the stairs curved up and away, leading her farther from her weeping baby. Fear, misery, and loneliness overwhelmed her, heavy as the mists that rose from the worn stone steps sweeping horizontally in a mind-bending twist. Merry sank to her knees on those impossible steps, crying helplessly despite her frantic efforts to keep calm. Her tears sparkled like opals, falling in perfect globes into the abyss in front of her.

She watched them fall, then leapt off the stairs herself. The tear globes grew into huge spheres as she tumbled past them, images flickering on their surfaces: Virginia with a snake twined around her torso, laughingly offering an apple; Humphrey dressed in a maitre d's tuxedo, offering a tray full of genetically altered viruses wrapped in hundred-dollar bills; Grandma and Grandpa Galen as the couple from *American Gothic*, with a Book of Mormon and a rifle at the ready to repel the screaming mob bearing down on their farmhouse; Sidney addressing a conference, the gaudy banner "Ending Gender in Postmodern Culture" flashing with starlights behind her; Elder Stacy riding his flower-strewn coffin and waving to the crowds of mourners, the bullet holes in his back still oozing. The images reached out for Merry, trying to pull her into the bubbles. She thrust away from them, swimming through the air that felt like thick syrup. Her breaths came in chest-aching gasps. She didn't have time for this! Missy needed her!

One last push, and she emerged into Missy's room, rushing to the crib to gather up her sobbing daughter. A fever burned through Missy's little nightgown, her hair plastered in wet curls to her head as she cried. The vaccine ran through her veins, glowing blue and red as her heart beat, the genetically enhanced immune responses eating into Missy's own body. "Dadadad," she whispered, worn out from crying, pleading for help.

Merry held her close, knowing that her daughter was desperately ill, knowing that she needed a blessing—and knowing that Chris wasn't there, would never be there to give it. Cold despair flooded her heart as she exclaimed, "Chris, why? How could you leave us?"

"I didn't have a lot of choice at the time," Chris said with a rueful half smile.

"Chris?" Merry stared at him in the dim, pale-blue glow of Missy's night light. Hope surged into her throat, choking off the mad tornado of questions tearing through her head. Why was he here? How could he be? Could he—could anyone—be back, from Paradise or wherever he'd gone? Was she having a vision?

"No, Merry." He stepped closer, lightly touching her face. "No vision, no return from the dead." The old Chris smile flickered across his face, sympathetic but mischievous. "You're just not the vision type."

"So you won't be followed by three ghosts who show me the error of my ways?" Merry asked, smiling herself, despite the disappointment that washed through her.

Missy had stopped crying, falling peacefully asleep in her crib again, holding her dinosaur. She receded, the light growing around Merry and Chris until they stood in the sun-dappled quad where they'd met for lunch back in graduate school. Lunch and endless debates over literature, music, politics, culture—and then over Christianity, the New Testament, Mormonism, scriptures, the Plan of Salvation, the First Vision, the idiosyncrasies of 19-year-old missionary boys, planning a baptism. Chris had proposed to her under this tree, going down on one knee like her one true love in a storybook story (as the song went). She'd blamed the reflections of sunlight off the ring for the tears that filled her eyes.

The warmth from that blazing sun matched the heat of the fury that rose in Merry's chest. Why not a vision? Didn't she deserve it? Didn't Missy deserve a father? Didn't Chris deserve some divine protection after all he'd done? What happened to the scriptures promising the righteous had no need to fear?

Chris shook his head, as if he felt her anger, pain, and grief. "No more ghosts. No ghosts at all. I'm not really here, sweetheart, but you'll trust the dream image of me enough to listen to what you know is true, even when you're in too much pain to acknowledge it. There's another scripture, too—the one that says that 'all these things shall give you experience.' That includes persecution, pain, sickness, trials, heartache, and car accidents, and it applies to everybody from martyred prophets on down." He brushed a lock of hair away from her face, his touch so insubstantial that she saw more than felt it. "Merry, it's not fair—it's just life. Heavenly Father loves us and wants the best for us. That's the only guarantee we've got."

"So the 'best' is for you to die, to leave us?" Merry spat back, the sky darkening to burnt crimson between the withering leaves. "What about the importance of families? What about the good we were trying to do? Is this what we get for trying to do right—our lives destroyed by a drunk and amateur welder?"

The sunlight crept back with Chris's smile. "Merry, think about it," he chided gently. "Death is not the worst thing that can happen, not by a long way. Yes, it's hard right now—I miss you, you miss me, it hurts. But it's not the end! We are sealed together forever, and we'll have each other and Missy for eternity. We haven't lost anything but a tiny slice of time—and we'll have all the time in the universe to make up for it."

"For now, though, you've left *me* to deal with the whole life thing alone—not just raising Missy, not just learning to sleep in a cold bed, not just facing everybody's freaked-out expressions of pity as they stand there wondering what to say, what to do about the poor little widow—" She took a breath, stopping the torrent of words. "It leaves me to confront the problem that got you killed—the Corinth vaccine."

"Yes, it does," Chris agreed solemnly. "You're the only one who can explain the evidence—if you choose to do it. Rocky Larue smoked away his agency and took me with it. That's the other guarantee in this world: everybody has to choose what to do with what life throws at her."

Politically correct pronoun, Merry noted. "Free agency, huh? So Rocky Larue's whiskey and pot binge can destroy your life—my life, Missy's life, your parents' lives—all because we get to make our own choices? So what happens at the Battle of Armageddon when the good guys hire a careless mechanic and have a blowout on the way to the valley and don't get there in time? God's entire plan, the Triumph of Heaven, depends on everybody making the best possible choices, all because of free agency? What happened to the hand of God, Chris? What happened to parting the Red Sea? What happened to angels rolling the stone away? What happened to arrows failing to hit the guy on the wall?" Her voice cracked, tears spilling down her cheeks again.

"What happened to Abinadi testifying as he burned? What happened to Peter crucified upside down or Elder Stacy being martyred? What happened to legions of heaven protecting the Son of God? The 'good guys' won't fight at Armageddon—they will rejoice in the safety of Zion as Evil destroys itself and the angels bind Satan in the pit," Chris said softly, his voice deeper and more resonant as the light grew around them, emerald and molten gold. "God knows the end from the beginning. He is the Master of heaven and earth, stars and sky; His path is one eternal round—and He holds the keys to both Heaven and Hell. His Plan is reality, and it will come out just as it should. Trust in that, and trust in Him. If one avenue closes, He'll make sure another one opens. The only question is how we use our agency, for Him or against Him. It doesn't matter who does the work, as long as the work gets done. We all have the decision to make, Merry. What are you going to decide?"

"Chris," Merry whispered, as the brilliance filled her sight. "I love you."

"I love you," he said, just as he'd said it in the car that day, the last words he said to her. Darkness curtained down, the light disappearing down a long, lonely tunnel.

Missy's voice called through the black. Merry's eyes flew open. "Not again," she said aloud, startling herself into realizing that she had woken up at last. The image of Chris still burned in the back of her eyes, his tousled hair a wild halo in the leaf-shadowed sunlight.

"Chris," she whispered, the loss rising through her chest to choke her. Anger got there first, however, and set her tongue on fire. "What decision will I make?" she shouted. "I'll *tell* you what I think about your blue-streaking decisions!" She did so, at length, using every word she could remember from Sidney's "power vocabulary" lessons. She cussed out Chris, Rocky Larue, MedaGen, free agency, luck, and God, vividly and at length. When her breath finally ran out, she flopped face-down on the bed.

The hot words had exorcised the anger—at least temporarily—leaving an aching hole in her heart. To her surprise, however, it didn't hurt as fiercely as it had before, the knife-edged sting mellowing into a deep-bruise ache. A tiny sparkle of green-gold sunlight flickered in the darkness and remained.

Merry took a deep breath, slithering off the bed to land on her knees. The clock measured off several silent minutes before the words finally came. "Heavenly Father," she said at last, "I'm sorry. I know you've heard worse, but not from me. I miss Chris—but you know that, too." Anger rose again; she swallowed it down. "Please. I'm going to trust you. Thee. I'm going to trust that Chris is okay, that we'll be okay. And I'm going to trust Thee to show me how to do what we both felt we needed to. But I'm going to need help doing it. Please help."

Those two words, "please help," repeated again and again, as the rest of the words dissolved into a heartfelt plea for understanding and strength. She didn't hear any voices, didn't see Chris, didn't feel the pain disappear. But when she did hear Missy's voice really coming through the door, she had the strength to stand, brush her hair back, and wipe the tears from her cheeks. She even managed a watery smile at Grandma Galen, who met her in the hallway with Missy.

"Looks like you're feeling better," Chris's mother noted, handing Missy over.

Merry shifted Missy and gave her mother-in-law a heartfelt hug. "I'm feeling something, which is probably good, even if I don't like it."

Grandma Galen patted her arm. "Feeling is better than not, even if it hurts at the moment."

"And you know that as well as I do," Merry said, tears starting again. She didn't hide them this time. "It wasn't just me who lost Chris. Thank you—Mom." The title came out sounding a little strange, but it came out, freeing another gush of tears, this time from Grandma Galen.

Merry said it again at the airport as she and Missy saw Chris's—her—family off to Provo, adding "Dad" for Chris's father. She assured them that she didn't need any help but would call every day. She and Missy waved until the grandparents disappeared through the security checkpoint.

Missy kept waving all the way home, much to the amusement of the other drivers on the road, singing, "Bye, bye, hello," over and over again. The song finally ended with "Bye, bye Grandma. Bye, bye Grandpa. Bye, bye, Dadadad. Hello, Mommy. Hello, Missy. Hello, house," as they walked into the silent living room.

"Bye, bye," Merry repeated, feeling the loneliness permeating the house, threatening to drown the spark of light in her heart. *Please, Heavenly Father, help.*

"How about 'hello, Carmen'?" a bright voice suggested from the doorway.

"Hello, Carmen," Merry said.

Missy happily repeated it, Gianni picking up the refrain. They chased each other through the kitchen, laughing like little loons.

"Nothing like the thunder of little paws to chase the lonely away," Carmen noted with satisfaction, giving Merry a careful but comforting hug.

* * *

> *Dear Chisom,*
>
> *I continue to be extremely busy at work and, therefore, have neglected to write you for awhile. Everyone is putting in long hours, especially the Brethren. I can't believe that Pres. Smith at his age can work such long hours. Yet, he seems to be thriving. Even so, it is a very good thing he has Pres. Rojas and Presidents Marquis and Hansen, two excellent councilors, to assist him. The Twelve are scattered over the globe carrying out assignments and keeping the Church moving. It may be months before they're all back.*
>
> *It is hard for me to believe how polarized the world is becoming. And the Church is being greatly affected by it. In some areas the Church is seeing success like never before, and in others the opposition not only continues to mount, but is getting meaner. Chapels in South America, Mexico, and even in the American southwest have been badly damaged or burned down and members harassed. Thank goodness, we have no reports of any deaths yet. We had a chapel broken into and extensively damaged in North Carolina for the first time. On the other hand, the Church is doing well here in the Midwest and the Utah missions continue to baptize many. Salt Lake City is experiencing some problems. With the members being only a third of the population there, they can't control the evil influences that have*

come in. Gangs are getting worse and worse in some areas and sections of the city are like the worst urban ghettoes. Downtown is still nice and relatively safe, but as a whole, Salt Lake is not much different than many big cities. Thank goodness the membership remains high in all other areas of the state and has been very successful in shutting out much of the evil.

As you may have assumed, I attended the funeral service for Elder Stacy. I found it touching, informative, and full of the Spirit. Still, I know I will miss his cheerful, energetic ways. I still cannot imagine anyone who would be so twisted as to take his life or that of any of the Brethren. Yet security here and everywhere the Brethren go is very tight.

On a brighter note, I do not know if you heard that Dr. Robert Nabil has been called to replace Elder Stacy in the Quorum of the Twelve. I am very pleased. You may remember how impressed I was with the good doctor when he successfully treated your mother for cancer a few years ago. What you may not know is why I was so impressed. He is one of the leading researchers in the world in the field of molecular medicine, specializing in cancer research. He was one of the reasons I was happy to get your mother into the University of Utah medical center. What I did not realize until I got to know him was that he is not only a man of science but also a man of faith. I remember that in our last meeting before your mother went into the hospital, he asked about our beliefs concerning priesthood blessing and when I assured him we would see that it happened, he requested that we also pray for him and he would do the same for us. Here was a world-renowned doctor who wanted to make sure the Spirit was with all of us. What a Saint. I have seen him briefly but twice since he's been here. I was pleased he remembered me, but then how many six foot, four inch, two hundred and fifty pound Nigerians do they have around here? Even so, he greeted me warmly and asked about Adaure and the family. I know he has been called of God for a great purpose.

One last note, I fear the rather somber tone of this letter may cause you concern. Don't worry. God is at the helm. He is strengthening His Saints and moving them to do His will. The more the opposition mounts, the more power He gives His people. In the book of Joel, chapter two, the Lord promises us that in the last days inspiration will rain down upon all the faithful. The Master says he will communicate His will through both visions and dreams. Even now, He or His servants are speaking to the minds and hearts of many as their heads lay upon their pillows. Remember, He guides this Church from the top to the bottom, from the First Presidency to each individual member.

All come under His guidance and love. Of course, He expects us to use our heads and do all we can, but when we have done our part, He will step in with the help we need. Now why am I telling you that? Your e-mails show me you and the members in your area know these things to be true.

Continue to spread the word.
With love,
Your Father
Chinedu

* * *

No! Dove cried silently into the emptiness. *No! I can't leave Benny.* The hellish light of a muzzle flash cracked across his memory; in the shock of memory, he could see each deadly bit of metal as it flew through the thickened air, as it tore and burrowed into Benny's back, and sent him crashing into the ochre dust. The scene repeated constantly, Dove frozen in place, pain keeping him immobile, unable to stop the shot, helplessly watching as Benny died again and again.

"Benny," he whispered, his voice threading out of a raw, parched throat. The name, screamed in his head, sounded thin and far away in his ears, lost in the gunshots roaring inside his head. Benny told him to run, Slick shouted an order, Pizarro's thick voice bellowed, the shotgun erupted, Benny fell in horrible slow motion, Dove cried his name. Slowly, a new sound wound its way into the catastrophic chaos inside Dove's head.

A woman's voice, low and sweet, speaking softly, calmly, the soothing cadences contrasting with the pandemonium ringing in his inner ears. He caught at the sound, turning toward it, grasping at it as if it were a lifeline in an ocean deeper than outer space.

". . . lend thy power to heal, to comfort, we pray." The words gradually took shape, forming out of the melody of her voice. "We thank Thee, and know that Thou knowest us, and we trust in Thy love and care. We say and ask in the name of thy Son, Jesus Christ, amen."

"Amen," a man's voice echoed. Deeper, rougher, but just as warm as hers, his voice took up the melody. "Gracious Father, we ask Thee to spare this, Thy son . . ."

The words faded, but the voice remained, drowning the sound of the gunshots and shouting in its deep rhythm. The horrible scene in his head faded slowly, darkening into a peaceful, rippling quiet that sucked him down and buried him in velvet unconsciousness.

The footsteps came closer, two—no, three—people, running, pursuing. Dove pulled himself awake, his heart pounding as if he'd been running too. *They're following! Get up, get going, keep going,* the adrenaline in his bloodstream shouted. *Run! Get away from Slick, from Pizarro, from Benny's empty, melancholy eyes. Move, move!*

Actually doing any of that, however, proved more than difficult. He took a breath and tried to move his arm, turn onto his side, get up—and promptly gave up the attempt, feeling as if knives had scored across his back, from his ribs to his shoulder.

"Mama!" a high, chirping voice exclaimed, "Mama!"

"Sh," Dove hissed, lifting his eyelids against the sandbag weights someone had attached to them. Under his lashes he made out a band of sunlight across a brightly colored, woven rug; the corner of a white-painted, wooden nightstand and the bright eyes of a tiny child who stood regarding him with much interest, a blanket in one hand and the fingers of the other in her mouth. The source of the siren-like cries retreating into the distance registered only as a momentary blur of blue and pink. Everything wavered, clear but insubstantial, like an underwater scene—and completely unexpected, totally unfamiliar.

He closed his eyes hard, opened them again. Nothing changed. He took a brief survey of the last memories he could reach: Rico and Cesare ambushing them, Butch gunning down Benny, the life fading from Benny's eyes, Slick shooting him, Butch's hot blood pouring over his arm, his own blood gushing over his side and leg, Pizarro's unmarked patrol car seeming to float under him, the tree looming out of the dusk. . . . Nope, none of that lined up with a tidy bedroom in a frame house, a comfortable bed for his decidedly uncomfortable body, and a little critter holding a blanket while staring at him.

Another attempt at getting up, however, told him that his body definitely remembered getting shot, and that hadn't changed. He stifled a groan and swallowed through a sandpapery throat, glancing at the little girl. "You got some tequila, *Chiquita?* I could use it."

"Tequila's the last thing you need." The woman's voice rippled through his aching memory, waking echoes of pleading, caring—and, inexplicably, love. She smiled at him, adding another comment that brushed past his ears without going in. She gently moved Blanket Girl aside to stand beside the bed. The elder girl, Siren, peered at him from behind her mother's skirt, suddenly shy.

Dove looked up at the woman, blinking blankly. Navajo—she'd spoken in Navajo. That fit with how she looked, her dark, clear skin unpainted, her soft, black hair swept back, silver earrings shining gently against its shadowy lengths.

She smiled again, shaking her head in apology, the silver earrings swinging with the motion. "Sorry. I assumed you were from the Rez," she said, in English. She poured a glass of water from the pitcher on the nightstand and sat carefully next to him, sliding one warm, competent hand under his unhurt shoulder. "Here, drink this. Water's better for you than tequila. You lost a lot of blood."

The water felt good going down, once Dove remembered how to swallow. "Sorry about the fountain," he muttered, trying to move again. This time he managed to get halfway up, gritting his teeth against the pain. "Thanks for the drink."

"Hold on," she ordered, gently catching him and forcing him back down. Much to his dismay, he couldn't resist even the mild pressure she exerted. "You've been shot, and you're in no shape to be wandering off."

"Yeah, you're in no shape to wander off," her skirt shadow piped up, giving him a saucy, bossy look before remembering that she was being shy.

Her sudden duck behind her mother made him chuckle, which in turn made him wince. "I remember getting shot. I just don't know where I am, or how I got here. The Rez, you said?" He looked at her, remembering the long drive into darkness. They'd been close to the border when the ambush took them. Had he driven north?

"Yes. You're on the Navajo Reservation—and in our home." She extended a hand. "Where, due to the unusual circumstances, I forgot to introduce myself. Renata Begay."

"*Hasbidì*—" he stopped, gathered his scattered thoughts, and started again. "I'm Salvatore Nakai."

"Dove," she translated, shooting him a curious look. "Interesting name."

"Benny—my brother Benicio—tagged it on me," he told her. Saying Benny's name brought the ambush crashing back into his mind. He tried to move again, fighting her restraining hand as well as he could. "Ms. Begay, thank you, but I've got to go. They'll be looking for me—"

"Let them look."

Dove jerked toward the sound of a man's voice, swearing almost inaudibly as the motion sent fire down his side and back. Through the haze of pain, he stared at the newcomer.

Navajo, like Renata, not tall but powerfully built, with big, capable hands and a broad, blunt face. His thick, black hair was cropped in a brush cut, and he wore a denim shirt over comfortable but clean jeans. The voice rang another bell in Dove's memory, a low, melodic chant through the darkness, driving out the horror of Benny's death, asking God to spare someone's son—had he meant Dove? Praying, the Rez, clean-cut family in an equally clean-cut house; one conclusion sprang to mind.

"You're Mormons," Dove said. "Some of those Navajo Mormons." He regretted how that sounded right after he said it.

"Guilty as charged," the Navajo man said, grinning. "I'm Sam Begay. Navajo, Mormon—second counselor in the bishopric, matter of fact—and a computer programmer."

But not a soldier, Dove thought, looking around at the pretty room, the pretty wife, the two pretty little kids getting brave enough to lean against the bed to look at him. He saw it all reflected in Slick's sunglasses, and this time he did manage to sit up. "Mr. Begay, Mrs. Begay, thanks for your help, but I gotta go now."

"No, you've got to stay here and get better," Renata said firmly.

This time, however, Sam's strong hands caught him by the shoulders. "Relax. Nobody's going to find you here. Is there anybody who's looking? Anybody who should know where you are?"

Dove leaned close, speaking quietly but intensely, trying to drive his point home without scaring the kids, "Nobody should know—but there's somebody looking. Somebody nasty, up from down south, and he's got the sheriff with him. You do not want to get messed up with these people."

"Neither do you. the southerners won't find you here, because they won't know where to look. There was nobody else on the road when I found you. The sheriff doesn't have jurisdiction on the Rez, so you're out of legal trouble unless you're wanted by the Navajo Tribal Police or maybe the FBI," Sam informed him, just as quietly but even more confidently. He looked into Dove's eyes, his gaze deep enough to go through the brown irises and into the younger man's soul. "Are you?"

Dove stared back, seeing more toughness and resolve than he expected from a computer geek—or a Mormon. That, plus the pain draining his strength away from his arms and legs, made it easier to say "No." Honesty, thanks to Benny, made him add, "Not by the Navajo Tribal Police—or the FBI."

Sam nodded, a half smile playing around his face. "But you've got the sheriff on your tail, and some mysterious Southerner. I'm going to be interested to hear this prodigal-son story."

A phone rang, startling Dove. Renata took it from Siren, who came running in waving the handset like a battle flag. She answered, listened for a moment, and smiled as she said, "Yes, he's finally awake—and trying to escape, too, just as you predicted. Here's Sam."

She passed the phone to her husband. He took it, said, "Joe, thanks for your help," patted Dove's unhurt shoulder, and left the room.

Renata smiled at Dove's questioning expression. "Joe—Joseph Gee—is the one who stitched you up after Sam found you. He works out at the hospital, when he's not making house calls."

"He made a house call here," Dove said. "Why?"

"You don't want to hear, 'because we called him,' do you?" Renata teased, then sobered. "Sam was driving home last night from a stake meeting, and saw that car off the side of the road. He pulled off to investigate and found you out cold against the steering wheel, bleeding but not from an accident. He called out to the hospital, but the ambulance crew was out on another call. Joe was there, though, and he came out to take a look at you. It wasn't as bad as it could've been; the bullet skimmed the top of your shoulder and ran down the muscles in your back instead of burrowing in." She swallowed against that thought, shook her head in sympathy. "Joe says you'll be fine; the main problem was that you'd bled so much. Once he got that stopped and stitched, and your ribs immobilized, it was pretty much okay. You were so far out that you probably don't even remember it; they said you were talking but didn't answer when they talked to you."

"So why am I not in the hospital, with an officer outside the room waiting to ask me about a bullet wound?" Dove asked, cutting to the most vital thing he was wondering about.

Renata looked at him, her head cocked to one side, as if she wondered about that, too. She rubbed Blanket Girl's back. "Sam said he had the strong impression that he should bring you home. And when he and Joe brought you in, I got the same feeling."

"Why?" Dove asked, blinking in disbelief.

"I don't know, exactly," she said, swinging Blanket Girl up into her arms. "For now, though, it's enough to know that you need help—'if you do it unto the least of these, ye have done it unto me.' And Sam is close enough for 'Samaritan.' Lie down, Salvatore. We'll take care of you. You'll be all right."

"Dove," he said softly, letting himself slowly relax against the pillow. "That's what my friends call me."

* * *

"So the real question is, can you trust your friends?" Garrett de Long smirked, as the extremely revealing (but, in this day and age, only mildly scandalous) candid shots of a film star's supposedly private birthday party faded from the screen behind him. The order number for the video scrolled beneath the screen, along with a summary of the *pro forma* lawsuit the star had filed against the distributors. "Back to you, Kathy. Have you got a birthday coming up?"

"Thanks, Garrett," the anchor said, giving the camera between them a flirtatious smile. "While we're on the subject, how trustworthy are you?"

Garrett giggled right on cue, fluttering his eyelashes. "Let's get together and talk about that later, Kathy darling—I'll bring my camera."

She laughed just long enough for the implication to register with the duller viewers out there in TV Land, then turned to the central camera again. "From entertainment to culture, you'll find it on Channel 8. A scandal has rocked the powerful Mormon Church, and its ripples are being felt worldwide. Will the Church's latest changes in leadership permanently damage the fastest-growing, most controversial religion in the world? Channel 8's religion specialist, Anne O'Neal, has the details, coming up. We'll be back after these messages." She kept her smile until the promos running along the sidebar expanded to fill the entire screen with the trailer for the star's upcoming film.

"And we're out," Monk informed her. He didn't bother to watch her leave the set, as he was deep in contract-negotiation talks with her agent on the other coast. Instead, he glanced at Kim, who had already started the cue-ups for the next segments while the ads rolled. "Ready with the live shot from Anne?"

Kim gave him the thumbs-up signal, flicking over a satellite relay and setting off the test signal.

"We're here," Anne responded, on cue.

"Yup, right here in Misery," Leon added.

Anne shot him a quelling look. She still couldn't quite believe that the promotion was real—from the local Channel 8 affiliate in San Diego to Channel 8's corporate third string was a huge jump. But here she stood, outside the Independence headquarters of The

Church of Jesus Christ of Latter-day Saints, ready to "work that ratings magic again" at Monk's command—and this time, as a full-fledged Channel 8 reporter.

While she'd always said she wouldn't stay in local news forever, actually getting the call from the legendary Monk had nearly put her into shock. Good shock, of course, but she'd almost asked him to repeat the part where he said that Corporate had been impressed by her interview with President Rojas and her coverage of the Mormon funeral for the San Diego office, and they wanted her to take on additional assignments on a national level. She'd recovered by the time they got to details (contract length, salary amount, benefits, copyright control)—just enough to ask that Leon come with her. Monk had agreed nonchalantly, telling her that was fine, as long as he signed his own contract. At the worldly tone in his voice, she'd hastened to reassure him that Leon was just her cameraman, not a boyfriend or otherwise "involved." Monk's unblinking statement that she didn't need to give him too much information had deflated her, made her feel like a complete hick for even bringing up the subject.

Then, as usual, Leon had almost torpedoed the whole thing, asking for a company car. Remembering that, she rolled her eyes at the camera man.

Leon grinned from behind the red light atop the camera. "That's a nice look to start the broadcast with. Shall I replay it when we get the on-air signal?"

"No," Anne sighed, stating the obvious. She glanced at her interview subjects, holding still while the makeup specialist dabbed on powder to eliminate light reflections from their foreheads and noses.

Suddenly aware of the makeup thickly painted on her own face, she practiced a smile, then a serious look, waiting for the endless set of commercials to finish. The soundtrack rippled in her ears, tie-ins to the last entertainment story giving way to a combination of ads aimed at Mormon and anti-Mormon audiences: Web-site editors and video-blocker software, family-vacation planning services, family-planning services, Web sites promising the "truth" about the Mormons for a small donation, upcoming Evangelical revivals and crusades. The combination struck Anne as odd, a Madison Avenue push-pull more likely to leave both sides off balance and put off than eager to purchase the products offered. She shrugged off the psychic dissonance—after all, what were ads for, if not capitalizing on each other, building "synergy?" The point was selling the product, not providing context or consistency. Look at the ads that had accompanied the previous story, touting both sales of a bootleg film and a law firm specializing in protecting intellectual property and privacy.

Kathy's overhyped intro trailed through her headset mostly as background noise, but Monk's signal brought her mind back to the present report. Leon gave her the signal, the red light blinked on, and she smiled. "I'm Anne O'Neal, live at the headquarters of The Church of Jesus Christ of Latter-day Saints in Independence, Missouri. It was here, a mere few months ago, that Richard M. Rojas was officially sustained as the Associate President of the Church—and became the center of a church-wide firestorm."

Clips of President Rojas standing with President Smith appeared beside Anne's image on the monitors, the two Mormon leaders walking into the Conference Center together, taking their places in the plush chairs on the dais. The peaceful footage disappeared in a flurry of images all montaged together, protests in California and Independence, anti-Mormon demonstrators joining anti-Rojas demonstrators, Mormon intellectuals declaring their deep aversion to *Rojas's* reactionary statements, Mormon fundamentalists loudly affirming that the mainstream church had gone off the rails into apostasy.

The scene pulled back to reveal Anne standing in front of the Church headquarters building once again. This time, the shot included the two interviewees, standing attentively to Anne's left. "I'm here with Dr. Sebastian Morrell, professor of civil-liberty studies at the University of Missouri, and Mr. LeVar Swenson, leader of a fundamentalist Mormon ward just outside of Independence." They looked remarkably easy in each other's company, given that they'd been chosen specifically to represent diametrically opposed sides of the Rojas issue.

"Actually, I prefer my true title of Bishop, Sister O'Neal," Swenson told Anne, with a paternal—and patronizing—smile. "And there is no such thing as a fundamentalist Mormon. Either you live the gospel as it was restored in these latter days, or you aren't a Mormon."

Anne let the "Sister O'Neal" go without correction—if the guy wanted to look goofy and sanctimonious on camera, more power to him, and more amusement for the viewers at home. "Then do you feel that the members of the current Church leadership are no longer Mormon?"

Swenson looked sorrowful. "I'm sorry to say that it appears that the leadership of the Restored Church has become apostate. It's been coming for several years, but this has confirmed the warnings and revelations that the faithful have been receiving."

"This meaning the appointment of Richard M. Rojas as the Associate President," Anne clarified. "However, Bishop Swenson, hasn't the office been used before? Hyrum Smith, the brother to the Church's founder, Joseph Smith, held the position of Assistant President in the first years of the Church."

"And the office died when Hyrum did," Swenson patiently informed her. "Like so many early missteps—polygamy, the united order, the Mountain Meadows Massacre—the office of Assistant President has served its purpose and is no longer part of the organization of the Church."

"And is it also true that your group objects to President Rojas on more personal grounds?" Anne asked.

Swenson frowned. "Personal? We don't object to anybody on personal grounds. We believe that we're all God's children, and He loves us all."

"But that doesn't mean everyone is equally qualified to be President of the Church," Anne pressed. "You're still concerned about President Rojas. Why is that?"

"We strongly believe that Richard Rojas, while an attractive figurehead and persuasive speaker, is not the Lord's true choice," Swenson told her. "He's a military man—he served in the Air Force for years, in South America. And, of course, he is not an American citizen. The Church of Jesus Christ of Latter-day Saints is an American church. The Book of Mormon tells us that the Lord's Church will be established in this land and will never be overcome until the Spirit of the Lord ceases to strive with us."

"Dr. Morrell may have a different assessment of the Church's staying power," Anne said smoothly, transitioning away from the fundamentalist quack at Monk's silent signal. Ratings only go up for so long with that kind of unintentional comedy.

"Indeed I do." Morrell, much more media savvy than Swenson, smiled at Anne. "In fact, given the growing opposition outside the Church and the division that Mr. Rojas's appointment has caused within its ranks, I think it's likely that we will see a major Mormon reformation in the next few years."

"Really?" Anne put in—he didn't need encouragement, but the viewers at home might.

Morrell nodded sagely. "Look at it this way, Anne. Martin Luther triggered the Protestant Reformation and subsequent fall of the monolithic Catholic Church by protesting the Church's abuses. That's exactly what we expect to see here." He waved away, toward the thin line of protesters circling in front of the headquarters' flowerbeds. "The monolithic Mormon Church has alienated its members and others with its unreasonable, reactionary stands on everything from a woman's right to an abortion to universal human rights for gay and lesbian citizens to encouraging women to have careers outside the confines of their homes."

Kim neatly inserted graphics to accompany his speech, for which he'd submitted suggestions when Anne contacted him about doing the interview. Images of happy, well-adjusted modern citizens (pretty women outside clinics, men holding hands with their life partners, groups enjoying a drink or toke in the local pub) contrasted with sober, straight-laced Mormons (harried housewife trying to juggle screaming children, stiff men in suits looking repressive, ancient photos of bonneted and corseted pioneer women).

"Mormonism has declared itself opposed to everything in today's scientific, logical, diverse, tolerant society," Morrell summed up. "It has put its members in the impossible position of choosing between their fundamental rights to live as free human beings and a huge list of irrational rules and regulations that decry everything progressive in modern society."

"What you call progressive, we call promiscuous!" Swenson broke in, giving the libertine academic the full, condemning glare of a righteous priesthood holder—and smartly picking up bonus points among the antiintellectual, antiatheist, Evangelical crowd.

The academic responded with a supercilious look of his own, the righteous upholder of tolerance rightfully despising the oppressor. "Fundamentalist religions—like Mormonism—breed depression, suicide, oppression of minorities, and a host of other social ills," he snapped. "The oppression and abuse that goes on in those systems eventually force the rational members to either leave or reform the institution into something more in line with modern ideals and realities. That will happen in the Mormon Church, now that the leadership has catalyzed the reform-minded people in its ranks."

"That, at least, we can agree on," Swenson said confidently. "The Church is going to split wide open."

"Thank you, Dr. Morrell, Bishop Swenson." Anne regained center screen. "Interesting predictions from both sides of the ongoing debate over Mormonism. Reverend Tommy Gibb, the noted Evangelical revivalist minister, has an equally dire forecast for the Church."

Tommy Gibbs appeared, walking quickly up the steps toward the magnificent, pillared façade of his Worldwide Revivals headquarters. His beautifully tailored trenchcoat billowed with the speed of his walk, but he wasn't moving too quickly for reporters to keep up. "I'm not surprised that the Mormon leadership has alienated the good people who've been blindly following them," he said in response to a reporter's gasped question. "And I think it's a good thing—Jesus sends all His true children a wake-up call. They just have to hear it." He paused at the doors, flashing his famous smile. "And it sounds like they have—this is just the last straw. Mormonism, like all counterfeits, can't stand up when you look at it in the true Light of Christ. We're looking forward to welcoming those lost sheep into the true fold when they realize how they've been deceived by the Enemy of all that is good."

"Confident words from the Evangelical side," Anne observed. "Unfortunately, President Rojas was unable to talk with me today, but I previously asked him for his views on the dire predictions for the Church. Here's what he had to say."

The scene shifted again, showing President Rojas in the hotel room in Hawaii. "Dire predictions? People have been predicting the end of this church since before it started, and they've all been disappointed—or converted," President Rojas laughed. His smile sobered, and he looked into the camera with a deep conviction that came clearly through the lens. "We're concerned about those who have let their testimony falter, whatever the reason. Worldly concerns, pride, confusion, hurt, lack of faith—they can all lead us astray, lead us into errors and misunderstandings if we're not careful to stay within gospel bounds. But no one, least of all the prophets or our Savior himself, said that following the gospel would be easy. What they did say is that the way would always be clear, and the Saints would always have leaders to guide them—and there would always be those that chose to go their own way. We've come to a time and place where it's more important than ever to follow that divinely appointed path. 'Choose ye this day whom you will serve.' It's time for all of us to choose which side we're on."

"And it looks like that's exactly what's happening," Anne followed up, standing before the Church's Missouri headquarters, protesters neatly framed in the background. "Mormons here in the United States and all over the world are choosing sides. The question is, will the Church survive the process? I'm Anne O'Neal, reporting for Channel 8 News, Independence, Missouri."

"Thank you, Anne," Kathy said.

"Slipping in a little of the opposition, huh?" Leon grinned at Anne as the audio feed went dead. "I'm pretty sure you were supposed to finish that little segment with Brother Gibb's lovely quote."

"It didn't seem fair, is all," Anne informed him. "We gave everybody else a chance to comment."

Leon's grin didn't waver. "You're letting these Mormons get under your skin."

She gave him an arch look. "I'm retaining my journalistic objectivity. Besides, Rojas is good for ratings."

The anchor finished her comments about Anne's story (neither Anne nor Leon paid any attention), then segued into the next story. "And now, in other news, the FDA has provisionally approved the new AllSafe vaccine for use in humans." Shots of jubilant patients quickly gave way to footage of angry protesters. "However, distribution of the vaccine will not begin for several months. Senator Howard

Garlick, sponsor of the Health and Safety Assurance bill currently under consideration in Congress, issued a strong statement condemning foot-dragging by the FDA and Center for Disease Control, calling delays irresponsible. Other groups, most notably Americans for Equal Health Care, warn that the vaccine could widen the gap between the medical haves and have-nots in this country. Senator Garlick is pushing the measure through to assure every American has ready access to the vaccine, and he vows to continue his fight to make it a mandatory measure."

Senator Garlick appeared on screen surrounded by elementary-school children, wind blowing his hair photogenically. "We must ensure that the rich do not assure their own health while disregarding the rights of the poor," he thundered. "We must ensure that each and every American citizen, regardless of economic status, race, gender, and sexual orientation, receives the vaccine to guard them, their families, and this great nation!"

"Over the top," Monk muttered, glancing at the ever-shifting ratings numbers in the corner of his console. "But they eat it up. How long are MedaGen and Garlick going to play this? I figure we've got about two more good humps on this camel, then it's time to fish or cut bait. What's up next? The big debut of the up-front MedaGen commercial, right?"

Kim nodded, keying in the ad, then hitting Play right after Kathy signed off.

CHAPTER 11

"Oh, shut *up!*" Merry exclaimed, hitting the mute button on the remote. Virginia's whispers abruptly cut off, leaving only the suggestive images of MedaGen's AllSafe sucker ad to flow and glitter across the screen in a stream of blue-green, pink, red, and white, ending with the ever-present MedaGen logo. "It's not even on the market yet—and it's not going to be!" She turned her attention to the phone's display, patiently indicating that it was waiting to make the connection at the other end of the line. "Come *on*—pick up, for crying out loud!"

"Channel 8, Lee Yuan," the voice finally said, sounding professional, detached—and vaguely wary.

"Mr. Yuan, this is Meredith Galen," she said, realizing even as he did that he already knew that; he'd have read her name and number off the ID display.

"Yes, Ms. Galen—Dr. Galen," he corrected himself, adding, "I heard about the other Dr. Galen—Chris—and that accident. I'm so sorry."

"Me too," Merry told him, taking a breath and suppressing the urge to throw the phone across the room, fall on the floor, and dissolve into screaming tears. She'd had a lot of practice doing that; maybe someday it would get easier. "Thank you. We were on our way to meet you when it happened—"

"I'm really sorry about that," he said.

"*C'est la vie*—or *la mort*, in this case," Merry assured him. The black humor of it did come easily. "I'm sorry I didn't get back to you sooner, but as you can imagine, things have been busy. But things have calmed down, and I still need to talk to you about MedaGen's vaccine. May we try this again?"

"Do you think it's safe?" he asked.

For a moment, Merry thought he was teasing her, which surprised her. It surprised her even more when she processed his tone and realized that he was at least partly serious. "As safe as anything in this world can be," she told him. "Which is to say, there are no guarantees. What are the odds of another drunk driver hitting us on the way to your office? I'm willing to risk it if you are. The alternative's a lot more dangerous."

"I'm not sure I would be willing," Yuan told her. "You're a brave person, Dr. Galen."

"But what?" she asked, picking up the hesitation on the reporter's end of the line.

He sighed. "Dr. Galen, I really hate to tell you this, but I just can't see a story on the AllSafe vaccine now. The FDA's approved it. Things have moved into the political arena now, and it's getting to be old news anyway. We could probably get a bump on it later, when the debate on mandatory vaccinations goes to the Senate, but there's just not a market for it right now."

"A market for it?" Merry repeated, blinking. "I'm not talking about selling something. I'm talking about a serious, severe, and ultimately deadly risk with that vaccine! I'm talking about a corporation using its political contacts to push the FDA to approve a cure that is literally worse than the disease—at least for everybody who doesn't already have AIDS or some other deadly plague! You're a journalist, for heaven's sake, someone who's supposed to be on the lookout for that kind of thing! The one who's supposed to uphold the people's right to know about threats to their lives, not just to get the dirt on celebrities! What do you mean, there isn't a *market* for it?" She realized that she had nearly been shouting into the phone and forced herself to calm down. Yelling at him wouldn't make him more inclined to listen to her. "Mr. Yuan, I'm sorry for getting heated, but—"

"I understand, Dr. Galen," he interrupted. "Just like I understand reality. We can say what we want about journalistic integrity, but reality is that news shows have got to compete just like everything else. We can't hold people down and make them listen. I can tell you really believe what you're saying. But I really can't see doing a story on the FDA approval of AllSafe without earth-shattering proof—or without an angle to hang it on. If you wanted to accuse MedaGen of arranging the accident, maybe, to shut your husband up, you could probably get on a couple of the tabloid shows. They usually do pretty well with young widows and corporate corruption—"

"That is ridiculous," Merry snapped. "I'm not interested in fifteen minutes of fame. AllSafe is anything *but* safe, and since MedaGen won't admit it, somebody's got to get the word out."

"Do you have absolutely solid proof?" Yuan asked, equally sharply. "Something that isn't just speculation, isn't just your word against theirs, isn't just jargon? Have you got hard data? Statistics? Memos? Pictures? Your husband mentioned a bunch of computer projections and experiment data that it would take another expert to understand, and even then, said it might not mean that AllSafe was actually a public-health risk. You may think it's ridiculous that MedaGen had anything to do with that accident, but they can kill my career if I go out on a limb with wild accusations that nobody can prove!"

Merry closed her eyes, opened them to see Missy tromping her dinosaur across the floor, then glanced at Virginia gyrating in the ad on the vid—the "newscast" replaying the ad over and over again behind their commentary on companies' use of celebrities to pitch products. "Would you defy MedaGen, get out on that limb to defend the public—or your own friends and family?"

"If there's really a threat, I'd listen," Yuan told her, adding before she asked, "and do the story, too."

"Then I'll get you your proof," she informed him. "I'll call you when I'm ready." She hung up. For the first time since the accident, she felt energetic, fury burning through the sticky cobwebs of grief. It didn't destroy the thick strands; instead it melted and hardened them into something strong enough to support her resolve.

"If God's leaving it up to me, I'll show Him!" she exclaimed aloud.

"Show 'im!" Missy chimed, then waved her dinosaur and growled. She didn't smile, however; she'd been annoyed with Merry, repeatedly asking Merry to produce her Dadadad, then crying when Merry didn't. Rational explanations, Merry found, didn't cut any ice with a debate partner who hadn't yet hit her second birthday. Chris always said that Missy's stubborn streak came right from her mama. Maybe, but right then it was yet another thing to be ticked off about.

Right on cue, the phone rang. The familiar number on the display communicated just one word: Sidney. The wave of righteous anger that Merry surfed crested right before she answered the phone—just a few seconds too late. She felt it curling into a cream-tipped trap as Sidney's clipped voice said, "Hello, Meredith."

"Hi, Sidney," Merry said, hiding a deflated sigh. Hearing her mother's voice hurt, as it always did. The loneliness flowed back, deeper and blacker than ever. "How are you?"

"Just fine. The conference went very well." Sidney hesitated, sounding like she might be hiding a sigh too. "Meredith, I'm sorry I couldn't make it to the funeral. You know what my schedule's been like—"

"I know what your schedule's been like," Merry assured her. Another wave of anger swelled out of the loneliness, this one rising from Sidney's absence at Chris's funeral—and practically Merry's entire life. "I know what it's always like. You've got to tear around the world trying to keep the Fourth Wave from collapsing in on itself. How could anything compete?"

The hidden sigh in Sidney's voice disappeared altogether, replaced by frosty disapproval. "I did not call to start that old argument again, but if it weren't for the vitally important work our organization has done, the women of your generation wouldn't—"

"Have all kinds of abandonment issues?" Merry interrupted again, hating herself for giving in to her adolescent rage but not quite able to stop the words from tumbling out. "Have to constantly fight their own instincts toward a normal family life? Feel that they were somehow betraying the sisterhood when they dare to fall in love or feel a career means less than having children?"

"If it weren't for the sisterhood, you wouldn't have the choice to make," Sidney informed her. "We proved that it's possible for a woman to have children and still have a successful career."

"Sure, it's possible—as long as you have a good nanny," Merry noted. "I understand and appreciate fighting for the vote, like the suffragettes did. I understand fighting for equal opportunities and pay at work, respect and autonomy in society. What I don't understand or appreciate is the idea that somehow women's rights got tied to the right to kill inconvenient babies, the push to forget all moral responsibilities, and support for any kind of lifestyle except hetero-sexual monogamy—"

This time, Sidney interrupted her, with equal heat. "Don't quote the chauvinistic Luddites who run that cult you're in at me! If they had their way, you'd be the sixth wife of some grotesque, lecherous old goat, kept ignorant, pregnant, and miserable until you died an early, painful death! I cannot understand how you can possibly hold on to your anachronistic, irrational belief in a 'church' that systematically denigrates, marginalizes, exploits, and abuses its female members!"

"The Church does not denigrate, marginalize, exploit, or abuse me," Merry shot back.

"It doesn't give you the respect you deserve, either," Sidney said. "It relegates you to secondary status, refusing you the leadership roles you could so easily and competently fill. But no, they tell you to stay home, tend babies, and give up your autonomy to that cabal of senile old men and their brainwashed, macho subordinates. Just another example of the eternal oppression of the patriarchy."

"So I should want to be Bishop as well as Relief Society President, have to tend the entire ward as well as my own family?" Merry asked.

"Yes!" Sidney exclaimed. "No man is expected to chain himself to domestic responsibilities. Why should a woman be any different?"

"Biology, maybe?" Merry hazarded, then spoke quickly to over-ride her mother's incipient objections. "And no, different doesn't mean inferior, no matter how much you'd like to believe it does. Mother isn't less than father. Woman isn't less than man. It's a question of different roles—not higher or lower, but partners, two people designed and assigned to work together to do the very best they can. I don't know why we got the roles we did, but I'm glad I got mine. The gospel offers answers, comfort, salvation, and responsibility to everyone, female, male, old, young, whatever. Humans discriminate, oppress, and use each other. God doesn't. I'm going to trust that He knows what He's doing."

"Hmm." Sidney said it flatly, no hint of either agreement or discension in her expression. "Even after you destroy your chances for a brilliant career, sacrifice your freedom on the altar of a degenerate religion, a freak accident kills the man you think is the love of your life. And all you can say is that you're trusting God?"

Silence filled the line, the faint humming of satellite relays almost audible.

"Yes," Merry said softly, choking down the crack in her voice. "Yes, I'm still trusting God." *And you'll never, ever know how hard it is for me*, she added silently.

"Meredith, I'm sorry," Sidney said, almost as quietly. "I'm sorry. That was over the line. I understand you're overwrought. I want you to know that whatever differences we have, I'm still your mother, and I love you."

"Are you allowed to do that, without betraying the ideals of feminism?" Merry asked, a faint smile breaking through her expression and warming her voice.

"Yes," Sidney said, a hint of amusement creeping into her tone, too. "I'm sure I read it in the bylaws somewhere. That's what feminism's all about, isn't it—having it all?"

"I'm going to find out," Merry told her. "Get ready to be proud of me, Sidney. I'm going back to work."

"Didn't Chris have insurance?" Sidney asked.

"What, depend on a man—a dead man at that—to provide for me?" Merry laughed. "Sidney, I'm shocked at the very thought! Yes, we had insurance. But insurance won't last forever at today's prices, not with Missy's college to pay for. And I feel I really have something to contribute to society." She didn't even consider telling Sidney about AllSafe; somehow, she just knew Sidney wouldn't see things the same way she did.

"Of course you do," Sidney said, a hint of wariness creeping into her voice. "I've always said so."

"The thing about having it all is that you've got to find somebody to tend part of it while you're gone," Merry said, reaching down and stroking Missy's wild curls. Missy glanced up at her, her eyes locking on the phone.

"Oh, you'll get used to it," Sidney said brightly. "It's just a matter of breaking old habits, getting used to new routines. We'll find you a nice nanny—Hector always did such a lovely job with your hair."

"Hector was great with hair," Merry agreed. The anger she thought Sidney's call had frozen came flooding back, cold and hard as steel. "And clothes, too. Just too bad that he was so comfortable with being gay that it took me years to believe that any man could fall in love with a mere girl like me."

Sidney's voice reflected the cool in Merry's voice, the momentary *détente* disappearing as quickly as the tension that prompted it. "I'm sorry you feel that way. What do you want me to do? Volunteer to babysit myself?"

"Why not?" Merry asked, recklessly. "You chose to have a child, and now your child needs you. Maybe it's time to put up or shut up."

"Was that supposed to be funny, Meredith?" Sidney asked, the ever-patient professional dealing with the tantrums of an unreasonable adolescent. "Please be reasonable. You're a grown woman, and you've always had potential. I really do want the very best for you, and I want to help. I'll be glad to help pay for Missy's daycare."

For a brief, luxurious second, Merry considered snarling and hanging up, but her sense of humor resurfaced. Missy shouldn't miss out on what was, after all, a family tradition. "That's very sweet. Thank you. I'll get her signed up and let you know what name to put on the check."

"I'll just send it to you," Sidney told her. "I'm off to New York tomorrow—"

"Have a grand time, Sidney," Merry told her, heading off the incipient explanation. "Thanks again. Do you want to say hello to Missy?" She got the answer she expected.

Missy looked hopeful as Merry broke the phone connection. "Hello?" she asked.

Merry kissed her forehead. "Sidney says hi, and that she'll wait to talk to you until you can carry on a coherent conversation." She picked up her daughter, swallowing against the old pain. "Count your blessings on that one. If you take after me, she might not talk to you until you're 40."

"Hello!" Missy repeated, reaching for the phone.

"Just a sec, sweetie." Merry dialed another number.

"Callatta's, Carmen here," Carmen answered in her usual bright lilt—but with an unmistakable glint of steel in it. "We're not buying anything."

"Luckily, I'm not selling anything," Merry informed her. "What happened?"

"Hey, Merry!" Carmen said. "Ah, the sales leeches are after us again. Giovanni used the cell phone for a new e-mail service to send Donna a birthday note, and they sucked our e-mail and phone number out of the database. I tell you, kids is kids is kids, and they never learn to stiff online surveys until they're the ones taking the turf-salesmen's calls! But you didn't call me to hear about my battles with telephone spam. What's up, honey?"

"Hello!" Missy shouted, grabbing for the phone. "Hello!"

"Missy, I'm talking to Carmen!" Merry exclaimed, putting Missy on the floor. "You wait a minute until it's your turn!"

Missy looked at Merry, looked at the phone, smacked Merry's leg, and burst into tears. Repeated cries of "Hello" alternated with furious wails.

Merry looked at her screaming baby, glanced across the kitchen at the family portrait hanging on the wall above the still-silent but flickering TV screen, and bonked her head against the wall. Her eyes filled with tears.

"That girl's quite the phone fan," Carmen noted, amusement bubbling in her voice. "You'd better sign up for a phone-company installment plan now, to lock in rates for later!"

"Right," Merry said, trying to pull herself together. "I'll get right on it."

Missy continued to scream and flail at her, jabbering furious nonsense. To Merry, it sounded like "I want Daddy! You're a terrible mama! I hate you!"

"How about you get right in your car and come over here?" Carmen suggested. She could translate desperate jabber, too—and the sound of tears in her friend's voice. "I've got a big batch of lasagna coming out of the oven, Gianni's bored out of his skull, and Tony needs help installing that new ChasteNet upgrade on our console."

"Carmen, I couldn't—" Merry began, reflexively pulling away, not wanting to be a bother, not wanting to admit even to Carmen that the end of her rope was a lot closer than she wanted it to be.

"Yes, you could, and you will," Carmen informed her. "Don't give me all that self-sufficient stuff. We're family! If I need help from you,

I'll ask, and you'll come running. Now, give Missy the phone and let her talk to me for a minute while you get your coats."

Merry didn't have a chance to get a syllable of renewed denial out.

"Uh! What did I say? The next voice I want to hear on this phone is Missy's—up close this time." Carmen said quickly, "Go, go, go!" After a second, she added, "Hey, little Miss!"

Missy told Carmen all about it, hardly pausing for breath, not knowing that Carmen was using her cell phone too and right then approaching Merry's drive. Carmen let Missy jabber until she could finally take advantage of proximity and sweep Missy right up and hug her breathless. Missy giggled—and finally surrendered the phone to Merry.

Merry smiled at Carmen, turning off the phone and tucking it into her purse. "Talk, talk, talk, all the way here. I can't imagine having to deal with her and a phone that was stuck to a wall!"

Carmen shifted Missy to one arm and grabbed Merry with the other. Her hug was as warm and enveloping as the smell of lasagna and golden light from the antique lamps in Callatta's entryway. Merry leaned against her shorter friend's shoulder, feeling the tight, frozen knot inside her loosen slightly.

Missy looked around Carmen's mane of dark curls and grinned at her mommy, ducking back around to play peek-a-boo. Merry smiled ruefully, then straightened herself, nosing Missy.

"All right, girls, looks like you're making up okay. Now, let's go in to dinner," Carmen said.

* * *

"It would be getting cold, if Carmen didn't believe in heating lasagna to volcanic temperatures," Tony contributed, appearing in the dining-room door with a linen-covered basket of bread in hand.

"It's the heat makes it good," Lucrezia told him, following her father into the dining room. "Hey, Merry. Hey, Missy! C'mere, big girl! You've gotten bigger since I tended you last, but I bet we can still do airplane rides." She held out her hands invitingly.

Missy considered the offer, glancing from Lucrezia to Carmen—and then to Merry. Much to Merry's surprise, Missy abandoned

Carmen's arms, not for Lucrezia's, but for her mother's. Merry hugged her. "Guess old mommy's not so bad, huh?"

"Come on, before Gianni starts—" Carmen began. An irritated holler interrupted her. "Oops. Too late. Come on, enough talking. Let's use these mouths for something more useful."

"Like demolishing lasagna," Donna suggested. "Come on—I've got the Tiny Terror corralled in his chair, but he's going to do an Incredible Hulk and bust out of there any second."

"Janni!" Missy called.

"Missy!" came the echoing shout.

"And we have contact," Tony noted. "All right, ladies, if you'd herd this way."

"Oh, *that's* a nice image, comparing us to a bunch of herd animals!" Carmen spatted his behind on her way past, collecting a semiapologetic kiss. Lucrezia and Donna demanded theirs too. Merry impulsively paused as she went past. She had just enough time to feel the potential awkwardness before Tony smiled, kissed her cheek, then nosed Missy's face as well.

Merry smiled back, grateful for . . . for not getting treated like an outsider, fragile creature, unexploded bomb—widow? She decided not to think about it and followed Donna to the table.

Tony brought up the rear of the line, taking his place at the table. "So, right after prayer, I get first dibs on conversation. So brush up on your ChasteNet answers, Merry."

She smiled, helping Missy into Carmen's spare high chair and settling between Missy and Lucrezia. "Actually, Chris usually does— did the software installing at our house. But I'm more than happy to take a stab at it. Prayer time, Missy."

Nobody started at her mention of Chris. Nobody even looked away at her correction to past tense, Merry realized a few minutes later. The conversation turned from computers to school to video games to movies, dinner pleasantly accompanied by easy teasing and conversation. Merry appreciated more than she'd imagined that she could actually talk about Chris without an awkward silence descending; Carmen and Tony shared their own Chris stories, and the girls took their cue from their parents. Missy seemed to relax as well, and aside from a brief tantrum after Merry and Carmen broke up a lasagna-noodle fight with Gianni, was happy throughout dinner.

"Well, that's certainly a paint job to remember!" Carmen laughed, surveying the two youngest members of their dinner party, their hair, faces, arms, hands, and shirts liberally Pollocked with marinara sauce.

"I'll take care of the remodeling," Tony announced, "while you two ladies deal with the computer. Girls, looks like you're on KP duty."

"It's your night for table clearing, Dad. And why aren't you installing the software? You're the software genius!" Lucrezia reminded him.

"Changing chore schedules is one of the perks of being a parent. You know we only had kids to get cheap labor," Tony assured her, spatting his daughter on her way to the kitchen with the first load of plates. "Besides, I'm an artiste—I create games, characters, entire universes! How do they expect me to sacrifice my creative vision to follow somebody else's installation interface?"

"That must be a very delicate creative vision, if an installer can bruise it," Merry laughed.

Donna grinned. "Yeah, turns out guys' creative visions are as delicate as their egos."

Tony blinked at her, faking hurt feelings. "See what support I don't get at home? No wonder I can't get a programming job! Besides, I'm going to chuck all that and go into construction. Carmen digs sweaty Italian guys in tank tops." He waggled his eyebrows at his wife.

"Better make that T-shirts, to cover your garments," Carmen told him.

"Oh, right," Tony said, glancing down at his shirt front, then smiling at his wife. "Speaking of wet shirts, we'd better get Gianni scrubbed. Does Miss Merry approve of her daughter joining our son in the tub?"

"Indeed I do," Merry agreed, moving to disentangle Missy from the high chair.

"No, no, let the delicate male handle this," Tony warned her off. "Don't want you getting red sauce all over. Go on, earn your dinner." He made growling noises, eliciting excited squeals from both babies, and dove into the potential maelstrom of lasagna smears.

"If that's all it takes to earn a full-course lasagna feast," Merry said a few minutes later, settling back in the office chair as ChasteNet files flowed from the LDS-oriented Web site into their proper places on the computer, "I may go into business as a software-installation consultant." She glanced sideways at Carmen, and smiled slightly. "Thanks for thinking up an excuse I could use to crash your family dinner."

Carmen shrugged, not quite admitting anything. "Hey, we love having you over. You, Chris, and Missy—you're all family around here."

"Speaking of family," Merry said, "how would you feel about getting another daughter?"

"Well, we've got a nice split now, two and two," Carmen said, eying her back. "And you're a little old for me. People'd think we were sisters. I'd always be having to correct them." She paused as Merry laughed, then leaned forward. "You mean Missy, right? What's up?"

Merry took a deep breath. "Carmen, I'm going back to work. It's not really for the money," she added quickly, to forestall Carmen's questions. "Chris made sure we'd be financially all right, and everything's fine as far as money's concerned. But I've got to find a way to get back into MedaGen."

"Why?" Carmen asked, blinking.

"Because Chris found out that the AllSafe vaccine is anything but," Merry told her. "He accidentally got access to some of the research files. The company did its human testing overseas, out of U.S. boundaries and rules, then shipped the results back to headquarters for analysis—and, it looks like, alteration." Columns of numbers, sparkling DNA strands, dire projection results all crowded into her memory as she sorted through the jargon and scientific formulas for the simplest explanation. "It looks like the vaccine protects against diseases by revving up the immune system. It's effective, but after a while, the body starts attacking itself. If you get that shot, you'll have to keep getting modified boosters of it to keep it from killing you."

"And they know this?" Carmen exclaimed. She didn't wait for an answer, reading all she needed in Merry's eyes. "Those rotten con artists! Drug researchers, my tail—drug pushers, more likely! And that slimy Senator in bed with them, pushing to make that vaccine mandatory! I wonder how much of a cut he's getting? Slime! It would be him—trying to get the Church declared a corporation, voting for laws to make tithing taxable—ooh! Where's the phone? Heck with the phone, gimme the computer! I'll give them a piece of my mind! Lying dogs!"

"Carmen, hold on." Merry caught Carmen's flailing hands. "Just sending e-mails isn't going to do what we need to do—it'll just put them on guard. I've got to get back there and pull the official report files they sent to the FDA, along with the original research files they got from their human tests. All Chris got was the raw data from a few of the tests. I've got to make sure that we're right."

"And when you find the proof?" Carmen asked.

Merry smiled at her, grateful for the "when," not "if." "Then I'll go to a reporter Chris and I have talked to at Channel 8 and show him what's going on, so he can get the word out."

"Him, huh? So it's not that Anne O'Neal person," Carmen said. "She seems like she'd listen—even if it's all an act for the camera. Are you sure this other guy will?"

"Pretty sure," Merry said. "I've already talked to him, and so has Chris. In fact, we were on our way to see him when the accident— happened." *Dumb, why start crying again now?* She thought furiously to herself.

Carmen rubbed her shoulder sympathetically. "Well, good. Sounds like we know what to do next, then."

"Right," Merry said, pulling herself together. "I update my resumé, I sign up Missy for daycare here—"

"Then we give the Beast a bellyache," Carmen finished smugly. "I've never liked MedaGen." She neatly co-opted the computer, bringing up Merry and Chris's Web page. "But you're not going to update your resumé alone, kiddo. That's something you should never do without somebody there to remind you how great you are."

"So, does anybody ever tell you how great you are?" Merry asked, taking over the data entry as she brought up her online resume form. She erased "Galen" and substituted "Anthony" (the name Sidney had chosen for them, after early feminist Susan B.; she'd choke if she knew that Merry considered it her "maiden name"). She felt a deep jab of sadness as the letters disappeared. *I'm sorry, Chris,* she thought silently. *I'll always be a Galen inside.*

"Oh, sure, Tony does," Carmen said. "But I'll take a compliment—or cash—from just about anybody."

* * *

Dear Chisom,

What I have heard and seen this week, including your Vid, has caused me to be awash with emotion. On the happy side, I am so pleased the work continues to progress in your area and that many have responded to the Church. The Brethren tell us that doors are being opened in the Far East because of our stand on the importance of the family. Regional leaders in southern China have extended overtures. Their interest is very good news.

On the sad side, I am stunned at the cruelty and inhumanity, especially that directed toward children, that covers so much of the world. Note what I said. I did not say the inhumanity that affects the children, but the inhumanity that abuses and exploits them. A broadcast on the news the other night showed the inhuman treatment of children both in South America and Central Europe—poor children, used and abused, dirty, tired, half naked, underfed, with no one willing to stand up for them. That is only the tip of the iceberg, the news said. Here in the U.S., child abuse and neglect cases have hit an all time, shocking high. Further, the U.S. has more children living in poverty than in any period in our history.

This ugly state is the result of prophetic warnings gone unheeded, especially those of the Savior. A few days before He died, He told his disciples that in the last days, because of abounding iniquity, the love of many would grow cold. We are seeing the results. The world has, by and large, lost its ability to love. That in turn has caused the loss of other virtues such as propriety, kindness, courtesy, balance, sensitivity, sympathy, self-control, a willing-

ness to sacrifice and, most disgracefully, a sense of shame. When there is no shame, people become brazen in their defiance of any moral code. For them, they boast, nothing is out of bounds. They are constrained only by power, and when that slackens, they take full advantage, especially of the weak or helpless.

Yes, the loss of love and its spiritual kin has produced a moral vacuum. Into it has rushed selfishness, thoughtlessness, greed, indulgence, bigotry, license, vanity, and meanness. These vices have produced a spiritually sick people who are past feeling. They cannot be touched by misfortune caused either by others or themselves. They cannot feel the sorrow, hurt, or distress of others, even the innocent. Many of these sordid souls have taken the next step becoming egocentric, obscene, nasty, vicious, and grossly immoral. Men sire children with no thought of ever getting to know let alone take care of them. What is worse, they don't care if their offspring suffer or even die. As long as they are not bothered and can continue to fornicate, these lecherous men are satisfied.

How did we get to this awful state? It seems to have started about middle of last century, shortly after the close of WWII. At that time, Satan mounted his greatest assault against the human family. His main thrust, the Lord showed His prophets, was directed at destroying the backbone of moral society, the nuclear family. Holy men, inspired by the Lord, knowing what the Father of Lies was about, took steps which we now see has prepared the Church for and protected it from the onslaught. The Western world, however, did not see what was coming and caved in at the first barrage. The cave-in began during the decade of the sixties.

A number of our historians have shown that this period saw the social matrix of the Western world, especially America, changed for the worse. Two factors were at the forefront. The first factor was the appearance, for the first time in history, of a large number of teenagers with a lot of leisure and even more spending money. Many of these teenagers, dubbed the baby boomers, were wealthy, spoiled, coddled, and undisciplined. They were easy targets for Babylon's satanically inspired propaganda. Polluted souls fed the young a damning but very appealing philosophy which they in turn embraced, refined, polished, spread, and eventually canonized. The world is now reeling under its painful consequences without benefit of anesthetic.

This philosophy unabashedly promoted self-absorption as the highest good. Selfishness became a pop religion. "Do your own thing, man," and "It's my bag," became, by the decade of the seventies, articles of faith by which the majority of the teens and young adults, if not others, lived. When anyone suggested that there might be rules to govern behavior, they asked the supposedly disarming question, "Just whose morals do you intend to impose on others?" The assumption undergirding the question (which was never intended as a question but as an answer) had been nourished and gaining strength for a decade. It was the belief that there were no absolutes; "truth" is neither real nor eternal. Out of this, moral relativism was born and, especially during the seventies, swept both high school and college campuses. Unfortunately, even many churches bowed to the "new morality," creating situation ethics as the only standard of evaluating the actions of self and others. Only a few brave, but largely ignored, souls (such as our Church leaders and missionaries) tried to offer counterpoint.

The older community, too preoccupied with materialism and tired from chasing it, paid little attention to their coddled brats and what Babylon was feeding them. Thus, they largely left the kids without moral guidance. It was easier for parents to do what they had been doing the previous decade—ignore them, buy them off, give into them, permit the little darlings to have their way. As a result, they allowed the new ethic, like a virulent weed, to take root. Its flower was the doctrine of relativism. Out of that came the intoxicating aroma that insisted "If it benefits me it's good. If it doesn't, it's bad. Through their lack of resistance, the larger community agreed, more tacitly than openly, that there were no absolutes. It also agreed, if unwittingly, that no one standard was better or worse than another.

The only exception, as I have noted, was the standard of selfishness, which was brazenly pushed from city to city, state to state, and nation to nation. This philosophy almost demanded self-indulgence and spiritual myopia. My good is everyone's good. If it requires me to sacrifice, put others first, or exercise self-restraint, then it is bad. The attitude promoted a disdain for authority—especially religious authority. The heady doctrine allowed the individual to become his own god, walking according to his own commandments and, somehow, feel holy doing so. What is the result? Just read the newspapers or look around.

Well, I've gone on too long, so I'll explain the other factor which helped change the world's social matrix for the worse in my next e-mail. Mom's sending some Vids. I hope you enjoy them. In the meantime, keep up the work. We enjoy seeing and reading about your experiences. Vids are wonderful! Know this (as I have said so often before), the work you and your fellow missionaries are doing is crucial to the salvation of this poor planet. Only as people come to believe in and live by eternal absolutes is there any hope. In the meantime, I hope the money and supplies the Church is sending to your area helps.

Love,
Your father,
Chinedu

* * *

"Anne, we'll take money and supplies from anybody who offers them without strings attached," the relief worker announced. The scene around her looked like the controlled chaos it was: workers bustling amid opened crates; sorting supplies into piles; preparing packets of food, clothing, and basic hygiene items; adding a soft toy, tiny mittens, or carefully tied quilt for each child into the bundles.

"You just can't understand what it's like here—and in so many other places around the world—until you've been here," the woman continued. "These kids need help, food, warm clothes, medicine— and they don't care where it comes from. Really, neither do we." She waved around the relief installation, directing the camera's attention to the lines of people patiently waiting outside the tent's flaps. "This is a war zone. These people, these kids, have suffered enough because people in their own areas can't grow up and get along. What does it matter that the quilts come from Mormons—or Buddhists, or Baptists, or atheists, for that matter? We're not trying to convert anybody here; we're trying to keep them from freezing. It's just infuriating that other people let their own personal differences get in the way of literally life-saving work!"

"Thank you, Helena Lebed, live from Columbia," Anne said. She reappeared on screen, standing in a huge warehouse full of crates. A forklift rumbled behind her as she said, "Clearly, the workers on the scene have very different ideas from the organizations contributing supplies and money to the worldwide relief efforts. Two major religiously based charities are threatening to boycott the effort to collect supplies for war orphans in Africa and South America, claiming that The Church of Jesus Christ of Latter-day Saints' participation taints the process. Official statements from relief organizations, however, urge potential contributors to give regardless of their objections to other contributors' philosophies. Still, it looks like another case of religious arguments getting in the way of the charitable service that all religions supposedly promote. Back to you, Kathy."

"The need for contributions for children's charities is only growing worldwide, as clashes continue between militias," Kathy took up the tale smoothly. Maps, casualty figures, and shots of burned, smoke-stained buildings flashed behind her, while the phone numbers and Web sites for a half-dozen different charities scrolled beneath.

"And, of course, it's always the littlest victims that tug at the heartstrings most." Images of ragged, shell-shocked children huddling in camps or wandering dazed among the ruins of their homes alternated with graphic footage of soldiers and guerillas blasting each other through city streets.

"Literally thousands of children have been orphaned or rendered homeless in the fighting that has engulfed entire regions." Now, the display showed maps, crimson markers indicating regions of civil war or invasion, spilling over the continents like a gush of blood. Refugee camps littered the edges of the war zones, picked out in tiny X's along the roads and rivers. The red tide had already engulfed many of them.

"In response, hundreds of volunteers, charitable organizations, and foundations have formed, all asking for donations to help support the tiny casualties of war." Logos and ads replaced the war-correspondents' footage—celebrities, ministers, and mothers asking for funds to help feed, clothe, and shelter needy children.

"Others have taken steps to do even more," Kathy noted. "The Mormon Church, in a move that sparked controversy among other charities, has gathered, shipped, and distributed 40,000 tons of supplies in South America alone, prompting accusations of unfair advantage and favoritism toward its own members." Pictures of chartered planes landing to deliver supplies gave way all too quickly to scenes of angry protesters.

"The Catholic Church's Modern Order has mobilized its priests to act as agents in the efforts to reunite families separated by conflicts." On-screen, male and female priests of the somewhat controversial new order appeared, interviewing weeping mothers and nervous children.

"In the Philippines, where fighting continues in the ongoing religious and ethnic war, the Ministry of Light has begun gathering up displaced orphans, providing a safe haven and an education for those who have lost parents and homes in the wars." Clean, smiling children appeared, dressed in neat uniforms, lining up to march into a classroom under the watchful eye of several young women. In the background, several hard-eyed teenagers lounged against the wall of the orphanage compound, watching the camera crew suspiciously.

"Unfortunately, there are more orphans in more places than any of us have resources to rescue," Kathy said, over images of running urban battles, uniformed soldiers, and ragged refugees in a rainbow of ethnic costumes. "Channel 8 correspondents all over the world report chaotic uprisings in Indonesia, Eastern Europe, northern China, Africa, and South America. Regional armies and warlords are springing up everywhere, and in may places, civil order has broken down. Even the United States and Canada aren't immune, with militia movements, growing regional frustration, and ethnic tensions. Is the United States headed for the kind of open warfare plaguing the rest of the world? Stay tuned for a Channel 8 in-depth report, 'Can It Happen Here?' right after these messages."

In the ads, pleas from war-orphan charities competed with pitches of new investment opportunities—especially in multinational companies specializing in transportation, heavy industry, and arms manufacturing. "Defending the American way for 200 years," breathed a buxom model, hefting a rocket launcher she couldn't hope to actually fire by herself. Without ChasteNet, you could see she wasn't wearing anything under her camo vest, but that didn't draw as much attention as Kathy's breathless teaser for the "special report."

* * *

"Can it happen here?" Perro mimicked, laughing at the screen. "Like, it *is* happening here! Wake up and smell the *frijoles*, Hairspray! That's us, right on your back porch!"

A round of catcalls, obscene suggestions about how they could make their presence known, laughter, and agreement met that assessment of the national situation—and Kathy's presentation. Nobody bothered to seriously address the idea that the United States had less and less claim on the name "united," nor to discuss the consequences of rampant corporate and private greed on the collective welfare of the citizenry, either.

Most of them didn't even think of it, actually; since Dove left, the philosophical level of the gang's conversations had pretty much disappeared. The silence of its disappearance echoed uncomfortably in a few ears, however. Calvin and Perro exchanged a momentary glance, neither saying anything aloud, both wondering what really happened to Dove. Rico had dropped some hints about Dove being dead or yellow and run off, but wouldn't say much more; neither Perro nor Calvin could really believe either of those, which left the uncomfortable suspicion that Rico had managed to trick him into trouble too deep even for him and Benny to talk their way out of. But then, what happened to Cesare? Nobody else mentioned him, or Dove or Benny, either; the unspoken consensus was that asking what happened to them would be a great way to find out—firsthand.

At the moment, aside from a few knowledgeable comments about the utility of the rocket launcher (and a few more speculative comments about the composition of the model's impressive bosom); however, the gang's consensus opinion was that they had endured enough news for the evening—or, as Slick's lieutenant Omerta put it, "Change the [bleeping] channel!"

Obediently, Perro got up and flipped through the available circuses. He finally landed on a "reality game show" featuring bare-knuckle boxing. "Welcome to the Ultimate Showdown!" the announcer roared, going on to list the stats for the various contestants. Disclaimers scrolling along the bottom of the broadcast noted that the contest was being broadcast live from Kenya, where local law-enforcement agencies saw nothing wrong with hosting a potentially fatal fight—as long as the promoters had laid out plenty of money (in cash, preferably American) for the privilege. Any international, national, or regional laws that might apply to the broadcast in the viewers' countries were strictly the viewers' own problem; neither the promoters nor the broadcasters accepted any liability for their pay-per-view special. The broadcast companies and satellite operators would assess the appropriate fees automatically and charge them to the viewers' bills (it was a pretty simple system—stop on the channel long enough, say 30 seconds, and the satellite company automatically recorded you as having watched the program, and billed you accordingly). The warnings that viewers could expect to see real blood shed, real bones broken, and possibly real fatalities appeared in much larger type—and in the announcer's overheated commentary.

The channel surfing stopped there, with several of the soldiers yelling the names of their favorite combatants ("Hey! El Toro!"

"Muhammad the Hammer!" "Man, Muhammad's dead—remember August?") and ordering Perro to leave it on. Two strutting human fighting cocks appeared in the iron-mesh cage, preening and flexing before the bell signaled them to start ripping into each other.

"Get those *chicos* outta there," Marco demanded of the screen. "Put in Lady Jane!"

"Chick fight!" echoed several others, pounding on the pool table.

The *chiquitas* lounging around the room smirked or pouted, depending on their self-inflicted roles. (The tough ones smirked. The delicate ones pouted.) Dolores split the difference, smacking Rico, then draping herself over him as he tried to line up a shot. It worked—the shot went wide, and she got his attention.

"Like they can hear you," Perro snorted, reaching for the remote again as the seconds ticked by. The stupid goons, yelling at the TV. He was acutely aware of Slick and two of the General's henchmen settled at a far table, watching *Abuelo's* gang with the condescending blankness of rich tourists taking in the picturesque locals. Their attitude made him angry, even as their cold eyes made him deeply nervous. The big guy, Butch, had disappeared the same time Cesare, Dove, and Benny did, but Omerta was still there, and others had arrived as well, shadowing Slick. They'd come around more, hanging at Mama Rosa's, laying out orders, even mouthing off to *Abuelo*.

Nobody said anything against them, either—especially not Rico, who grew three hat (or pants, depending on the commentator) sizes when they were around. He was worse than ever, and it looked like he was trying to prove something, not to the gang, but to Slick and the Southerners. Most of Benny's former shadows just transferred their allegiance to Rico (after a couple of negotiation sessions behind the restaurant that left them limping but loyal). Rico suddenly rose from the pool table and slapped Perro's hand away from the remote. "You deaf *and* stupid, Perrito? We said leave it there."

"We didn't pay for this one," Calvin noted, coming to Perro's defense. "*Abuelo* don't like that stuff showing up on his card—not on first run. Come on, Rico, we can hack into it later, get the backwash signal free. Dove can get—"

Rico hit him across the face, then grabbed him before he fell, pulling Calvin's aching face close to his as he snarled, "*Abuelo's* not here, see. And Dove's out of the gang. You want to follow where he went? Just take a bullet to put you there."

Calvin swallowed, limp in Rico's grip, like a wolf pup offering no resistance to the alpha male. "No."

"No, what?" Rico pressed.

"He don't know what," Perro interrupted, his voice cracking slightly as he overcame his own fear to try to save his buddy. "Calvin don't know nothing. Right, Cal?"

"Right," Calvin agreed. "Nothing."

Rico glanced from one boy to the other, noting the terror in their eyes. He grinned suddenly, sharply. "Keep it that way, *chiquitos*." He dropped Calvin, shoving Perro toward the kitchen, where Franklin watched disapprovingly. "Get me a beer, then fade."

Perro and Calvin hit the kitchen at warp speed, amid the laughter of Rico's friends. Franklin handed Perro a bottle of beer, which the boy delivered with a deep bow and (because his smart mouth always got ahead of his common sense) the announcement, "*Cerveza, Señor Rico.*" He got smacked again, but managed to retreat back into the kitchen without any serious damage to either his body or his junior-hood, jester-boy dignity.

Franklin shoved a plate of tortillas over to Perro and Calvin. "You get to doing your homework," he advised. "That Dove had the right idea there."

"And look where it got him," Perro grumped.

"We don't know where it got him," Calvin corrected heatedly. "We don't know nothing but what Rico says, and he won't say nothing right out. Dove's okay. Dove's gotta be okay. Probably Benny just took him off to go to school somewhere else. You know how Benny is. He probably asked *Abuelo*—"

"*Abuelo* don't know, neither," Perro interrupted him, a hint of worry creeping into his voice. "And you think Cesare went with them? He liked Benny about as much as a dog likes a cat." Perro shook his head, twisting a pencil in his fingers so hard that it broke. "Slick knows, and Rico, but *Abuelo* doesn't. And he won't ask, 'cause that makes Rico look big."

"And Rico's getting pretty big already," Franklin agreed, shooting a dark glance over the high counter into the dining room. His hands kept up their steady rhythm, chopping peppers as he spoke, but his voice dropped. "He's plenty confident about how big he is, long as that Slick's around. *Abuelo* knows that; whatever else he don't know, he knows that. 'S why he's not coming around so much. Don't want to face down Slick 'til he knows what's under them shades."

"What do we do?" Calvin asked, missing Dove's occasionally misguided or nutty but always rock-certain confidence. Even if Dove was wrong, and that wasn't often, he never let it get him down for long.

Franklin shrugged fatalistically. "What's anybody to do? Toss 'em out? Just as well set fire to the place myself. No, *chicos*, comes down to seeing which way the wind's blowing and getting set to bend that way."

"Great," Perro sighed, a sly smile breaking through his partly exaggerated melancholy. "Bending over for Rico. Just what we always wanted."

"Better him than Slick," Calvin said, missing the reference. He glanced over at the Southerner's mirror-lensed shades and shuddered.

Slick smiled from beneath the sunglasses, a show of teeth as cold and threatening as a row of needle-point icicles. He rose from the table and sauntered toward the kitchen—then, much to Calvin's relief, walked out the swinging doors, flicking on his phone.

"Northern command," he acknowledged the silent ring. He glanced around the quiet street, walking casually across Mama Rosa's parking lot as he listened to the voice of his High Commander beaming through the satellite link. "Yes, sir. Progressing nicely," he answered the general status-report question, glancing into the windows of Rico's cloth-topped Jeep. The General's next question pulled his attention away from consideration of the six most effective spots for a car bomb on that particular model. "We've destroyed four of the five major drug dealers in the borderlands region here. I sent the shipment volumes and runner routes to you via the usual channels. We have a treaty on with the last one. Should we finish him?"

The General told him to do what made the most sense—which earned another icicle smile. "The unaffiliated soldiers?" Slick shrugged, though the General couldn't see it. "Most are border trash, undisciplined thugs. They won't cause us any trouble."

"Including the half-breeds who caused you so much trouble with sweeping up the enforcer gangs in the area?" the General asked, his deep, slightly accented voice calm as always.

Slick didn't answer immediately, reading the potentially lethal reprimand in the matter-of-fact question. Suddenly, what had seemed a metaphorical walk in a meadow transformed into a jaunt through a quicksand swamp, and he felt the ground beginning to sink under the toes of his boots.

"We need talented men on our side," the General continued, his level tone sharpening to acid. "Or dead, gone, and forgotten. We do not need them running loose, spreading rumors, and rousing rabble against us. You botched one operation, which cost us time and treasure to cover up with the *federales*. How much time and treasure is this going to cost us?"

"The next leader of *Abuelo's* gang is with us already," Slick assured him, keeping his own voice cool and level with effort that he hoped didn't come through the link. He was telling the truth, after all. "I'll take care of the renegade talent problem, if I haven't already. One of them is dead, one has disappeared—and if he knows what's good for him, he'll never be back."

"Find him and make sure," the General ordered. His smile came through as clearly as the threat had as he quoted, "We shall overcome."

Slick clicked off the connection and walked back into the enchilada-scented light of Mama Rosa's, whistling.

* * *

Dear Chisom,

I have received an assignment from the Brethren that's going to take me out of town for awhile, so I thought I better write in case I don't get a chance until I get back. I'm going with Elder Rojas to do some public-relations work in the western states and then on to Central America.

I know your mother sent you the vid and pictures of our family reunion. It was delightful having the grandchildren around for awhile. Missouri is a long way from

Utah and California even by plane and that means it's too long between seeing the children.

Since your Mom is keeping you up to date on family matters, I'll share some current events with you. Our negotiations for recognition by and right to proselytize in southern China are moving ahead nicely. Working with their delegates here has kept me very busy. I find it interesting that in addition to all the structures that the great earthquake took down, it took the "bamboo curtain" down too. I did not realize it would affect our family directly, but, I must admit, I am rather excited about your new call to assist in spreading the word to mainland China. You, and the other Elders and Sisters who are being reassigned, are going to be a part of a historic moment. In a sad way, it may be good that the Church has been forced to consolidate and close a number of missions in Europe and the South Seas, because it frees missionaries for the Far East missions.

I am sorry to report that it is not just rejection of the gospel that is forcing our missions to close. It's escalating persecution and violence against us. I'll spare you the details this time, but let me say that even here in the States, opposition to the Church is growing. I should add, it's not just our Church that is being attacked. Organized religion, especially conservative Christianity, is also feeling the brunt of the hatred. Of course, we should expect this situation. An angel told Nephi that the "mother of abominations," as he calls Babylon, would "gather together multitudes upon the face of all the earth . . . to fight against the Lamb of God" (see 1 Nephi 14:13). Notice the angel's words. Babylon wars against the Lamb, not just the Saints. That means any and all who profess Him and work righteousness come under the censure of Babylon.

Which brings me back to the point I was making in my last letter. I mentioned that there were two major factors which helped change the social matrix of the West for the worse and which explain why conditions in much of the world are as bad as they are. Both of these were outgrowths of Satan's attack on the nuclear family, which he successfully launched in the decade of the sixties. As I mentioned last time, the first factor was the devil's success in promoting acute selfishness as a virtue along with the insistence that there were no absolutes. The second, which is the subject of this letter, was getting people to believe that children did just as well in single-parent homes as in double; therefore making marriage even less important to the world. Because people bought into that myth, the last of the deterrents to divorce was weakened and illegitimacy became unremarkable. As a result, both skyrocketed. Now fewer than thirty percent of all marriages last a lifetime. The real sadness is in the steep and shocking rise in illegitimacy. In 1950, five percent of the population was born out of wedlock, ten years later it doubled. In 1989, the figure rose to eighteen percent; by 1999, it escalated to thirty-three percent; by 2005 it was nearly half, and grows steadily worse. And what has been the result? More depression, crime, suicide and poverty. Thus, more children living at subsistence levels and in miserable social and psychological conditions.

These kids, by and large, have been raised, or better, not raised and disciplined, by an absentee parent. (Though I must admit, the same is true in too many two-parent homes.) Consider the fact that each year these children spend an average of only fourteen percent of their time at school in a year and four percent at other organized activities. That means they are spending eighty-two percent of their time elsewhere, and as some one said, "elsewhere" is not with an intact family. So where have they turned? Many to the gangs that are giving both local and national governmental leaders here and abroad so much trouble.

Organized and often smart, these gangs are taking over sections of cities and even counties. Gang wars are endemic. These people viciously persecute those who oppose them and refuse to give in to their wicked domination—and therefore, where they are the strongest, opposition to the Church is greatest and persecutions abound. Bought politicians, peace officers, judges, and lawyers protect these, the hit men of Babylon, from prosecution. Law enforcement is often ineffective and, in a few instances, allied with these elements. The lack of effectiveness comes due to resources stretched too thin, due to the poor economy, and heavy demands due to all the destruction nature is causing. Because of its need to protect the country from terrorists and its constant policing of other nations, the federal government itself has few resources to assist. Further, too many politicians and people with influence are not yet touched by the problems. They live in the suburbs and gated communities where they are immune from the sorrow, fear, and violence of the inner cities and such places as Amexica.

The above, however, are not the heart of the problem. Acute selfishness and lack of discipline have done far worse than produce cold love, divorce, abuse, and illegitimacy. They have produced a generation of cowards. You see, my son, the irreligious, undisciplined, and irresponsible have no moral backbone and nothing but their own selfish ends to fight for. Their souls are weak and this deprives them of the courage it takes to stand against the gangs or other forces that are, ironically, proving their very destruction. As a result, the social fabric is unraveling quite quickly now in Europe, northern China, South America, and the fraying is speeding up in America.

As crises hit, such as those triggered by the earthquake a few months ago and the twisters of this past summer, a nation's weakened moral fiber snaps. People refuse to work together because it demands sacrifice. Instead, uncaring and driven by selfishness, they take advantage of the situation and go on a rampage. Chaos and mob action such as that which the larger cities in Washington State and Louisiana (after the tornadoes hit) suffered this last half year ensues. And what will be the end? Again prophecy answers: the consumption decreed hath made "a full end of all nations" (see D&C 87:6).

I delight in the fact that our prophets prepared the Church members—beginning in the sixties let me stress—to meet these challenges. Admittedly, many people have left the Church, feeling it is too constraining, and I fear more will. However, those who have followed the guidelines of the prophets—keeping mothers at home unless absolutely necessary; making sure fathers preside in the home and take an active role in the nurturing process as well as providing for the family; having family home evening; practicing Sabbath worship; teaching the moral laws; having scripture study and family prayer—have been extremely resistant to the erosion of morality. Further, our people, for the most part, are productive, happy, successful, and well organized. There have been quite a number of reports lauding or berating the disproportionate number of Saints in top positions in various governments, businesses, and educational institutions. Of course, the Church's very successful Perpetual Educational Fund has contributed directly to this, providing a solid core of educated Latter-day Saints in poor countries who have risen to levels of influence. Thus, they have been and are in positions that have helped retard social decay especially in the Americas and sustained good governments elsewhere.

Thus, the Church continues to grow in spite of the opposition. Admittedly, the resistance has slowed Church growth a bit, but the quality of members, especially converts, has never been higher, but then, why am I telling you? The Wen family that you helped bring into the Church sounds like those about whom I am writing. The Lord is with His kingdom and it is becoming ever stronger.

Which brings me back to you and the importance of the work you are doing. There is little time. The world is polarizing at an ever-increasing rate. The people need your message, especially those in Taiwan and eventually south China. We are so glad you are the family's spokesman to the Taiwanese and Chinese and pray to the Lord for you each day.

Love,

Your father,

Chinedu

* * *

"Whistling girls and crowing hens always come to bad ends," Renata informed Abish, who'd skipped down the hall, trying to whistle but sounding more like a fast leak in a high-pressure tire. She topped off her admonition with an expertly whistled trill that sounded like Mozart from a mockingbird.

Abish laughed and air leaked some more. The proto whistle ended in a surprised squeak as she noticed Dove standing in the door of the guest room. She considered hiding behind her mother, but discarded that idea, replacing shyness with a saucy grin at their interesting houseguest. "Hello, Sleeping Beauty," she said.

"Hello, Siren Girl," Dove told her. She'd earned the name several times since their first meeting, when she went screaming through the house calling for her mama. Weren't little girls supposed to be quieter?

He leaned against the doorframe, breathing shallowly. The last two weeks had hurt more than he thought anything could—which scared him, because Joe the Doctor had told him that what the bullet did to him was considered "minor injuries" in triage terms. If cracked ribs and cut rib meat were minor, what were major injuries like? He was just glad that Sam was around; he didn't think he could've handled having to ask Renata for help getting up at all, let alone showering, dressing, and all the rest. *Not that the thought doesn't have a lot of off-limits appeal,* he thought, looking from Abish to her mama.

"How are you?" Renata asked, coming over from the vegetables she was chopping for dinner to look at him. She had a talent for divining truth from whatever he said, so he didn't bother to macho it. Plus, she still had that big old knife in her hand. *Never lie to somebody better armed than you are,* Benny had told him—*unless you're sure you can get away with it.*

"Same—stiff. Bored out of my skull." He tried to fidget, then gave it up when it twinged his ribs. "You guys got high-speed wireless Net connection here, and you don't even turn on the TV. What's with that?"

Abish's ears perked up at that. Dove's lobbying for TV privileges sounded way better than good to her. She got to see a couple of shows a week, carefully selected for their relative harmlessness and thoroughly analyzed in play-by-play commentary with her parents. Being all of nine years old, she considered herself practically a teenager in every way that counted—and she'd heard enough in school about all those shows she *didn't* get to see to have an extreme interest in getting a peek at them. (Even if she knew she probably wouldn't like what she saw.)

Renata looked from Dove to Abish and smiled. "I've told you what's with that. Most of the stuff on TV isn't worth the time it takes to download off the satellite. It's like the programs compete to see which ones can be stupider and nastier, let alone the ads. Besides, Sam needs full bandwidth for work. Come on, you two, and set the table. Busy hands, no boredom."

Abish and Dove exchanged a look and sighed, but did as they were told.

Setting the table for dinner—yet another strange experience. Just being there still felt weird to Dove; the peaceful, domestic routine seemed both utterly vivid and unreal, like something out of a mid-day dream. The combination of ancient memories and new strangeness still frequently threw him out of the moment. The smell of mutton stew summoned up images of his grandfather's weathered face and the feeling of hot afternoon dust, but the smooth surfaces of Renata's immaculate kitchen and the brightly colored toys scattered around the floor reminded him that the Begays' house was nothing like his grandfather's run-down hogan.

Sam and Renata didn't act like Benny and Dolores—or Marjorie, or Reiko, or any of the girls who'd been Dolores before Dolores got there—or like the traditional Navajos Dove had read about when he'd decided to get to know his Navajo cultural roots. (That attempt, like his brief but passionate Chivalry, Samurai, and Islam phases, hadn't given him the handle he was looking for to hang his life on; just left him vaguely depressed that he felt so distant from what his high-school teachers thought of as his heritage.) The movies and TV programs about normal people (civilians, as Benny called them, or sheep) he'd seen didn't fit them any better. Sam worked in the back office during the day, "crunching code for the greater glory of the Church and kingdom," he said. He came out for lunch and to play with Sariah or pick up Abish from school, to tell Renata about something that had come over the Web from another programmer, and to check on Dove. During the night, when the pain got worse in the dark, Sam was there to soothe him back down, give him a pain pill, shake him out of a nightmare. He wasn't only gentle, though. When Dove had moved abruptly and cut loose a blue streak at the pain, Sam had grabbed his face and told him never to use that kind of language in his house. He hadn't let go, either, until Dove had met his eyes, apologized, and promised not to do it again. Were civilians supposed to have that kind of tough edge to them?

Renata had a steel rod for a backbone, too, but she didn't show it as bluntly as Sam did. When Dove crossed a line, she just told him flat out, with complete certainty in her tone that he'd remember—and shape up—with the faint hint of unspeakable consequences lurking for him if he disobeyed. Like the time he'd turned on the TV in the living room (after Renata had explained the rules about watching only preapproved programs), looking for something to ease his boredom and take his mind off his back. Abish had come running in, and Dove caught her before she could yell. He grabbed her little face, covering her mouth, and shook his head at her. She'd nodded, catching on quickly, and settled down to watch with him, sneakiness and guilt chasing glee around her face.

They'd seen about half a show when Renata came in and turned off the set. She didn't shout, cry, or put them on a guilt trip. Instead, she coolly told Abish, "Go to your room. I'll talk to you in a minute."

Abish, her eyes already starting to tear up, whispered, "Sorry, Mama," and disappeared.

Renata looked at Dove, her even voice cutting his "Sorry, Renata" in half before he even got it out. "You know the rules, *Hasbìdì*. It's bad enough that you broke them. It's worse that you made a bad example for Abish by being dishonest." Her eyes looked through his, right to the back of his skull. It made his ears burn with embarrassment and shame. "Is that the kind of person you want to be?" And she left him sitting there—with the remote and TV—to think about it. He didn't turn on the TV. He had apologized later, and told Renata that she was a "different kind of *chica*." She'd laughed, and said that everybody was unique, including her.

Come to that, the Rez didn't live up to Dove's mental image of it, either. The Begays did live on the Navajo Reservation, in an ecologically built house instead of a traditional hogan. Sam was indeed a computer programmer, doing high-level digital work for the Church and a major software company over the DSL line that the tribe invested in years ago. Sam told him about the Reservation's history one night as Dove waited for the painkiller to kick in hard enough to let him sleep. The tribal leaders had finally pulled together, plowing the overdue and back pay and award funds from the BIA's long-overdue legal settlement into improving the reservation's power and digital infrastructure—and the career counseling programs that backed up the hardware with encouragement for high schoolers to get the training they needed to take advantage of it. It had been rough sledding at first, but with smart organization, community support, and (Sam noted with a grin) increasing influence from the Mormon contingent in the tribe, things had settled into a remarkably stable and decently profitable system.

"Sad thing is, once we got our act together, it looks like the rest of the world went to bits," Sam had said. He leaned back, stretched, and philosophized for awhile. He filled in the story, watching Dove's eyelids droop, then flicker back open as he breathed too deeply. The Navajo Nation had been watching the developments in the borderlands with deep suspicion; they'd managed to haul themselves out of the pit, and they were not interested in letting their neighbors drag them back down. Hence Sam and Renata's willingness to take Dove in.

"Anybody who'd hijacked a borderlands sheriff's patrol car couldn't be all bad," Sam noted.

Plus, Dove's delirious mutterings about ambushes and Southerners raised plenty of suspicions too, and during another long night, Sam asked him to fill in the details. Dove managed to keep the catch out of his voice as he told Sam about working for *Abuelo* (he left out the details of the work, but Sam's knowing look told him that his rescuer could fill in those details—correctly), skating on thin ice when he and Benny told everybody about Slick's viruses, how it got worse when they protested *Abuelo's* double-crossing the *Señor*—and then getting double crossed themselves. He had to stop for a moment when he came to the part about Benny dying and himself getting shot; somehow, remembering Rico and Cesare—even Pizarro—pulling their guns hurt worse than remembering Butch's laugh as he walked over to make sure that Dove and Benny were dead. *Benny couldn't be dead*, the plaintive child in Dove's heart whispered, *could he?*

Sam waited patiently, silent understanding filling the space between them, until Dove had regained control. Oddly, there didn't seem to be any disdain or discomfort in that silence; Sam didn't expect him to cry, but wouldn't condemn him if he did either. That made corralling the tears harder, but Dove's long training wouldn't let him break down in front of a stranger. He was grateful when Sam finally asked about the one who lead the ambush.

"Don't know the guy's name, but we call him Slick. He's working for a big-time boss named General Garza from down south. Not sure where, but probably Columbia, from rumors around," Dove said, stopping himself from shrugging.

That didn't surprise Sam. He reached over to adjust the pillow supporting Dove's unwounded shoulder. "That fits. We've been hearing things about gangs and drug lords moving in from down south."

"Hearing from who?" Dove's ears perked up, despite the growing haziness from the medication.

Sam's grin gleamed through that haze. "Let's just say that the Church isn't as otherworldly and innocent as people would like to make it. We've got a lot of good people down south, and they're worried about what's going on." Sam paused at the door, looking somberly at Dove. "Things are getting worse. We've got to make a stand somewhere. And to do that, we've got to know what's going on. Revelation's a phenomenal resource, but intelligence from the ground is always vital."

Or maybe that comment was part of the paranoid, violent dream Dove had slipped into when Sam finally left, advising him to sleep. It wasn't easy, with his back and ribs complaining, but he had to admit that he felt a lot better when he woke up.

He glanced around at Renata's kitchen as he handed Abish the stack of glasses. Talk of taking a stand, gathering intelligence, generals and drug runners didn't fit with the homey atmosphere. Sam, coming in from the office holding Sariah (she, in turn, was holding her ever-present blanket), didn't fit the image of a hardened soldier, either. Until you looked into his eyes—and Renata's. They held a surety that Dove had seen occasionally, in the older members of the gang, the ones who'd dedicated their lives to their leader. Only in this case, the leader they followed had scars on his hands and feet—and ran a protection racket that neither *Abuelo* nor the *Señor* could ever match. Follow *Abuelo*, you lived high enough to pick up a nice car and nicer gun; follow the Mormons' Jesus, you got to be a god.

Dove had heard Tommy Gibbs preaching against that kind of "blind, overwhelming arrogance," saying Mormons weren't real Christians and would burn if they didn't convert. Then again, Gibbs didn't hold out anything more logical or appetizing; why settle for being an angel through accepting Christ as your personal savior when you could do the same thing and wind up ordering angels around? If you believed what they did, anyway. He thought about what he'd heard about Mormons, off and on, all night, as the pain jabbed him into wakefulness again. The fact that they did believe made him jealous, which ticked him off. He'd been looking for something to really believe in all his life, but, aside from Benny, never found it. And even Benny couldn't smooth over the contradictions or make things come out all right. He shifted again, trying to get comfortable, trying not to think about Benny. It didn't work; he ended up crying again, for losing Benny, for never finding security.

* * *

"How can you take this stuff seriously?" Dove asked Renata the next morning, gingerly but restlessly pacing around the small sun room, dividing his time between staring out the window at the distant, brown hills rising above the desert floor and watching Renata's iron smooth across Sam's work shirts. (He worked at home, but still insisted that he was a professional and would dress like one. Besides, he noted, being able to loosen your tie and roll up your sleeves when you're "home" really helped draw the line between work and play time.)

"Oh, I don't really take it seriously," she assured him, spritzing steamy droplets onto the white cotton. "I just don't like wrinkles."

"Owooo," Sariah added, head flung back dramatically. The howl wasn't her attempt to contribute to the conversation; she'd picked up the coyote imitation a few days ago and used it at every opportunity.

"I didn't mean the shirt," Dove informed her, rolling his eyes.

What a teenage boy, Renata thought, suppressing a grin. "You should sit down, relax, give your back a rest, and help fold," she suggested.

"Rest and relax," he growled. "This keeps up, I'm going to start howling like Sariah Puppy Girl."

She glanced up at the sound of her name, regarded him solemnly for a moment, then repeated her howl.

"You're just bored and ornery," Renata informed him, passing over a basketful of sun-dried towels. "That's a good sign—shows you're getting better. So what's eating you now?"

"You guys," Dove told her flatly. "You Mormons, thinking you're so much better than the rest of the world. You got all that money, all that land, all the investments the news guys jabber about. You send missionaries all over the place, even to Catholic countries, and you're not even Christians."

"Wow. I never would've pegged you for a New American Baptist," Renata said, glancing at him as she flicked the ironed shirt off the board and wrapped it around a hanger.

"I'm not a Baptist," Dove informed her, needled by the accusation (why, he couldn't have said, but it went back to jealousy of people who thought they had a good bead on things) and the glint he saw in her eyes. "I know what Tommy Gibbs says about Mormons. They're cultists—deluded, reactionary, brainwashed, arrogant, thinking they've got all answers, looking down on everybody else—" His parroting of a TV program he didn't even like slowly wound down as she looked patiently at him, hands on her hips, iron steaming peacefully on the board beside her. Sariah watched him wide eyed from underneath. Finally, he stopped talking and shrugged, feeling like an idiot but ornery enough that he wasn't willing to admit it.

Renata sighed. "It's not a question of us being better than anybody. We're all brothers and sisters. Dove, we're not saying every other religion is bad, it's just that we have more of the truth—and anybody's welcome to it. Everybody's welcome to it! We'd love it if everybody in the entire world joined the Church."

"But you can't let them alone if they don't want to," Dove argued. "You've got to keep pushing stuff on everybody, making them think that if they don't do what your President says, they're all without hope. You don't believe in the Bible. You don't even believe that Jesus can save you."

"Oh, is that what we say? Is that what we believe?" Renata asked, fixing him with a stern look. "You've done a lot of investigating, talked to missionaries and other Mormons, and know that's all so?"

Dove looked back, then down at his bare feet, shifting them uncomfortably on her braided rug. He didn't want to fight with Renata—he wanted her to like him, to be impressed with him. "No," he finally said quietly. "Just what I've heard."

"Why don't you find out for yourself?" Sam's voice made Dove jump. He looked up to see Sam in the doorway, wearing one of those neatly pressed shirts and a half smile.

Oops, Dove thought, *woke up the big dog.* Aloud, he said, "Sorry for talking so loud."

"Daddy?" Sariah asked, peeking out from under the ironing board at him. Her expression finished the question: "Are you still at work, or can I tackle you?"

Sam grinned and held out a hand; his daughter ran over and jumped into his arms. He squeezed her, then shifted her to one side and looked back at Dove. "Looks like you're in the annoying stage of getting better," he observed. "You need something to keep you busy—and out of Renata's hair. She's got enough to deal with."

"I sure do," Renata laughed, as Sam handed Sariah back to her.

"Here," Sam said, pulling a well-thumbed book off the shelf and tossing it to Dove. "You're not a dumb thug. You read that, then we'll talk about what Mormons believe. And you can stop hassling my wife."

One look at the sharp edges of Sam's expression told Dove not to argue about his comparative thug status or whether he'd been "hassling" Renata or not. For all his nice-daddy habits, Sam had a lot of iron in him, and Dove had learned a long time ago to tell when you could push a man and when it was better to back off. Especially when the man could push back, hard. Besides, it was hard to snap at people he looked up to and wanted to like him back. "This is your Bible, isn't it?" Dove asked, reading the title on the worn cover.

"It's the Book of Mormon," Sam corrected. "It goes along with the Bible. They both testify of Jesus Christ. In my opinion, though, the Book of Mormon is a lot more straightforward about it. You can tell me what you think when you've read it—and the Bible. You know how to read, right?"

"Yeah, I know how to read! I've read the Bible," Dove told him with some heat. Sure, he mainly skimmed through it looking for the exciting bits and trying to decode the archaic language, but at least he'd read it once. That was more than a lot of those born-again types had done.

"Good. Settle down and read that," Sam ordered. "Don't get side-tracked by the Isaiah bits, either. I'll expect a full report tonight after dinner. Now, I've got code to crunch, and I don't want to hear any more arguing out of you until you've got something real to say."

"All right," Dove conceded, adding, "I'll get back to you when I've got some ammunition."

Sam just grinned, straightened his tie, and swaggered into his office. Dove got a smile from Renata, which made him feel like he'd have a supporter at the debate. He settled into the most approximately comfortable position he could find on the couch and opened the book. "The Book of Mormon. An account written by the hand of Mormon upon plates taken from the plates of Nephi. Wherefore, it is an abridgment of the record of the people of Nephi, and also of the Lamanites—Written to the Lamanites, who are a remnant of the house of Israel . . ."

CHAPTER 12

"And for all you adult-entertainment fans—and you know who you are," Garrett de Long smirked, the undulating graphic for Channel 8's Entertainment Report spinning behind him, "our next guest has something very interesting to say. Welcome a star who needs no introduction—Virginia!"

"No introduction," *Abuelo* growled, putting his half-empty bottle down beside the chair and glancing across at the TV screen blathering to itself in the corner. "Then what's with all the backup dancers? Turn it off already, Sasha." Over the writhing beat of Virginia's latest hit, a sound at the door drew his attention.

"Sasha's stepped out," Rico informed him. Marco's dark form bulked beside the doorway behind him, enforcing the woman's momentary absence.

"And you're her social secretary now?" *Abuelo* asked, sitting back in his chair and surveying his second in command coolly. Rico looked tight, tense, and high on something—a half shot of methamphetamine and his own ego. Bad combination. Definitely thought he had a tiger in his corner, and the confidence showed in his strut.

"I'm nobody's secretary," Rico snapped, then grinned.

"Nah, just Slick's lap dog," *Abuelo* said disdainfully, reaching down for the bottle. Rico's bright eyes instantly flicked to the motion. "You come to say something to me?"

"No," Rico shrugged, his grin widening. "I'm here to do something to you."

The roar of the shots drowned the TV's chatter. *Abuelo* got off the first one, the round from his shotgun cratering the doorframe where Rico had stood. He didn't get another shot. Splinters of wood falling around him, Rico dropped flat, shooting upward with deadly accuracy, as Marco returned fire from shoulder level. *Abuelo* slowly fell from the shattered chair and rolled to the floor. He didn't even look surprised. Sasha screamed obscenities from the porch, then dissolved into wracking sobs. Rico laughed, giddy, and grabbed Marco, pushing him out the door. Heedless of the crimson spatters winding their slow way down its face, the TV screen glowed in the dark room; the images reflected from *Abuelo's* empty eyes.

"I'm really talking to everybody, Garrett," Virginia said, sounding sincere and breathing deeply for the camera. "I think everybody should do what they can to help. Just look at all the terrible things that are going on in the world now—wars, diseases, intolerance, overcrowding. That's why I agreed to become the spokeswoman for AllSafe and MedaGen."

"Of course, the cushy paycheck didn't hurt either, did it?" Garrett de Long added, smirking. "I must say, if you bought that dress with it, it's a good investment. You're looking fabulous as ever, Virginia."

She smiled, flipping her hair away from the front of the dress, displaying the semidiscreet sequins of the MedaGen logo on her chest. "Don't be naughty, Garrett. Sure, the money's nice, but I really believe in this project. It's the goal we've been working for all these years. It's going to do away with all kinds of nasty diseases—starting with AIDS." She fluttered her glitter-laden lashes at the entertainment reporter. "I'm sure that's important to you, too."

"Sure is, Virginia," Garrett assured her. "And important to our viewers, too. Let's look at your appearance at a Brussels fundraiser—where you did a lot more than raise funds."

Footage from the charity bacchanal filled the screen, semiedited for early evening viewers. The editors hadn't bothered with trying to camouflage the content, though, which included a full-contact variation on the old-fashioned charity kissing booth.

"How'd she know the test results on Mr. Glamour Shot?" Monk barked in the control room. The network didn't want anybody to know that one of their anchor team had AIDS—it was company confidential until the brass decided whether to find some excuse for dumping de Long or to feature him as a brave survivor heroically battling a terminal disease. Ratings could go either way: viewers could either rally behind him to show their solidarity and support for alternative lifestyles, or they could boycott the network to protest Channel 8's corporate approval of said lifestyles—or lifestyle reporters; Garrett's snide on-air persona tended to polarize people, too.

Kim sent Monk's question through the network's instant-messaging link, with appropriate revisions, of course; very few employees at Channel 8 knew about Garrett's test results, so the message included only queries about contacts with Virginia's PR people and potential leaks of confidential personnel information. Possible answers and denials of responsibility poured in even before Monk had finished asking. Whatever had happened, nobody was going to take the fall for it, but everybody had someone else's name to suggest as the source of a possible indiscretion. Monk scanned through the responses while keeping an eye on the monitor still playing the interview. A few seconds later, he sat back and took a gulp from the steaming cup on the console. "Nobody here gave it to them." He grinned tightly. "But it looks like a bunch of our coworkers are out to skin each other. She must've got the test results straight from MedaGen. Apparently de Long's gone off the company's HMO list to get a fix for his little problem. Keep it playing. Chopping it now just lets her know she hit a nerve. Let's see where she goes with it."

Kim's hand relaxed away from the kill button that would've cut in another of de Long's prerecorded segments to cover the break as they informed Virginia that her interview was over.

Whatever he thought of that comment (and its skimming close to the truth), Garrett's professional mask didn't crack during the momentary pause. "You sure had a good time at that one!" he exclaimed, with his usual smirky innuendo. "Giving it your all, so to speak."

"Oh, honey, I'm doing a lot more than that," Virginia assured him—and, more importantly, the camera. "I'm doing my bit for humanity too. I'm donating my eggs to the vaccine research efforts. I want everybody to be able to have a little piece of me to brighten their day."

"Sad thing is that we don't get to choose which piece." Pause. "But Virginia, darling, really? All of them?" Garrett asked, on behalf of the audience. "That'll put an end to all those cute tabloid rumors about a bundle of joy on the way. What about passing along those fabulous genes of yours the old-fashioned way?"

"I can't even think about having kids—there are too many unwanted darlings in the world. How can anybody, really, with all that's going on?" Virginia waved away the question. "Besides, all that's too much work and responsibility for a party girl like me. There's too much fun out here, darling! Too many opportunities!" Another hair flip, and a well-glossed, seductive look. "And I want a shot at every one."

"I bet you do," Garrett agreed, with a wink. "Thanks, Virginia. Let's take a look at a preview of Kathy's upcoming special report on other women who want a shot at success. You'll be watching, won't you?"

"Oh, sure," Virginia smiled. "I'd love to watch."

The promo snippet Kim chose, to capitalize on the MedaGen connection, featured clips from an interview with MedaGen's own Ms. Zelik. The crawl across the bottom of the screen identified her as the COO—and one of the "10 Most Powerful Women" in the business world. "We've made great strides in infertility treatments," she noted, in response to Kathy's unheard question, then smiled. Even the warm lighting couldn't altogether disguise the ice in it. "But for many successful women, children aren't necessary for fulfillment or self-actualization. If you need something to love, get a cat." In the next sound bite, she gestured to the magnificent view outside the window of her elegant, top-floor office. "It's time for women to take their rightful place at the top of society. A bright, ambitious woman can contribute far more to society than a couple of extra mouths to feed. After all, women can do everything men can, and even better, which is why MedaGen does all it can to encourage young women to join the company."

* * *

"Welcome to the MedaGen Team, Meredith Anthony!" The voice attached to the visual equivalent of 100 percent cotton bond paper sounded professional rather than perky. Merry scanned the text of the message as the voice continued, "The Project Management Division of MedaGen, Incorporated, is pleased to accept your application for the position of Project Manager with the Research and Development Department. We're pleased to invite a candidate with your impressive qualifications to join our company. Please read the enclosed job description and contractual information. If you have any questions, contact Human Resources at the specified address. Remember that this offer of employment is contingent upon your completion of the necessary paperwork and final interview. We look forward to seeing you!"

Sure enough, Merry noted, the full contact information for the Human Resources department appeared in the letter, along with a picture and brief biography of the manager she needed to meet for her interview: Errol Humphrey. "Well, hello, Humphrey. Looks like I've got the right department," she said aloud.

"Hello!" Missy yipped, wandering over to hang on Merry's leg as she peered up at the screen. "Hello!"

"Hello, sweetie," Merry told her, giving her a quick squeeze. "It's just the computer, not the phone."

"Dadadad?" Missy asked skeptically, pointing at the picture.

"No, that's Humphrey. He worked with Daddy," Merry told her.

"Humf'ey," Missy tried the word, then gave it up for a more interesting one. "Ridiculous!" she exclaimed, then beamed happily at her mother. "Ridiculous!"

"What's ridiculous is that you can actually say that word," Merry said, giving her another quick squeeze before letting her go to unload a boxful of plastic dinosaurs by dumping it over her head. Seeing Missy smile again made her feel at least a little bit like things were going better. And Missy had finally seemed to forgive her for Daddy not coming home. Missy still asked where he was every day, though, and it still hurt Merry to tell her, "Daddy's in heaven helping Jesus," even if she honestly believed it herself. She usually added, "He'd rather be here with us, but sometimes you have to do things even if you don't want to."

Like project management, Merry thought, sighing as she read through the job description attached to the job offer. She did smile slightly, thinking of Sidney's reaction to her Ph.D. decorated daughter taking an administrative/clerical (emphasis, it appeared, on the "clerical" part) position instead of blazing into control of her own lab and revolutionizing the world of genetic medicine.

Originally, she thought about applying for the research openings—maybe even Chris's old job working on diabetes—but as she filled out the online application, another thought hit her. She didn't want to work for MedaGen, developing medicines for them; she wanted access to their confidential files, so she could find the proof she needed to show Yuan that AllSafe had some unsafe side effects. As a researcher, she'd be in Chris's shoes, with access only to her own research and very limited knowledge of what the other R&D labs were doing. Not helpful. She'd closed the application, wondering how to get what she needed and wishing (for the millionth time) that Chris were there. That thought broke her concentration; she gazed blankly at the MedaGen Web page, words and colors blurring into a mess of restrained, expensive color.

"All right, Chris, I'm going to do something. So what am I supposed to do?" she whispered, forcing herself to really look at what she was reading. That's when the "project manager" listing had jumped out at her from the Employment Opportunities screen.

After skimming the description and qualifications (project management, alias organizational nagging—keeping things moving, prodding slowpoke researchers to meet their deadlines, scheduling meetings, creating endless budgets and schedules), she grinned sharply. "Thanks, Chris."

She'd filled out the application, using a carefully incomplete version of her schooling and experience. Fortunately, lower-level administrative jobs didn't require the kind of tight background check that actual lab positions did, either, or she'd never get away with omitting an entire Ph.D. In this case, listing only her bachelor's degree and fudging her work experience as "lab manager" rather than "research fellow" would stand up to the cursory check MedaGen would do. The same privacy laws that protected the companies from disclosing the possibly illegal reasons why they fired or laid off employees worked in her favor this time: the university would confirm that she had indeed worked there, but it wouldn't say what she did or for whom. Accounting for the two-year gap between graduation and now wasn't difficult, either. She simply put in "freelance management/organization consultant," then filled the specifics with the tasks she'd become extremely familiar with: project management (putting together a nursery and baby trousseau for Missy was certainly a project), accounts management (she paid the bills and did the shopping), transportation coordinating (ever try to load a baby and a husband into the car for any extended trip without extensive planning?), and so on. Carmen had provided invaluable help—and plenty of giggles—as they re-engineered "housewife" into "professional project manager."

And it worked. Pending completion of an official interview and signing the actual contract, MedaGen hired Meredith Anthony—and in the process, gave her access to documents, schedules, and meetings, which was the point, after all. The idea of managing projects didn't appeal to her, but she was going there to get the dirt on them, not to climb the corporate ladder or find the career of her dreams. She'd found that already, being a mom to Missy and freelance consultant on Chris's projects.

Merry's smug smile faded slightly at that thought, but she pushed away the melancholy. "Well, Miss Missy, looks like your mama's got an official passport to the Dark Side. Let's go get Carmen—and however many of the other Callattas are available—and go celebrate."

* * *

The celebration, at a local ice-cream parlor conveniently located near a well-patrolled park, broke up early, amid many congratulations from Tony and Carmen (and sighs from both girls about how cute the waiter was). However, a nervous night meant that Merry felt rather sleep deprived when she and Missy got out of the car at Carmen's house the next morning.

"Hey, it's my favorite ladies!" Carmen exclaimed, throwing open the door.

Gianni ran over, squeaking happily. Beyond him, two other kids looked up from their colorful toys. One waved; the other continued chewing on a plastic hammer while pounding colorful nails into the plastic workbench with his fist. Missy returned Gianni's squeaks and wiggled to be let go. Merry set her down, smiling at Carmen. Overall, the place looked like a very happy war zone.

"Thanks so much for taking Missy, too," Merry told Carmen.

"Of course I would!" Carmen assured her. "Love her like my own. And love you, too. The little sister I never had to help me bat all those brothers into line." She straightened the collar of Merry's jacket— then wrinkled it again in an enthusiastic hug. "You look great, Merry. You'll do great, too. Don't worry about anything here. I'll take care of Missy while you go take care of the slime at MedaGen. Wonder Woman's got nothing on you."

"Well, with that kind of pep talk, how could I worry?" Merry laughed. She kept the smile despite the leaden weight in her stomach as she waved bye-bye to Missy—and Gianni, and Carmen, and the more friendly of Carmen's two charges.

As she drove away, through the early morning traffic on the roads and the random chatter of ads, news, and music on the radio, she heard Missy's "Bye, bye, Mama." What she saw, however, was the three-quarters finished cross-stitched sampler on the wall of Carmen's entryway: "On Judgment Day, if God should say, 'Did you clean your house today?' I shall say, 'I did not! I played with my kids, and I forgot!'"

Even a beautifully finished piece of needlework would've looked as out of place in MedaGen's slick, ultra-modern setup as a cactus in the bottom of a fishbowl—which the lobby now strongly resembled. Merry had come to the lab a couple of times, back when Benson Bioceuticals had owned the buildings, but MedaGen had put their own stamp on the place since then. She slowed before she got to the smoked-glass entryway, offering another silent prayer for help, guidance, and moral support. Then, squaring her shoulders and putting on a confident, no-nonsense expression, she presented the printout of her official job offer to the security guard standing imposingly beside the retinal scanner that Chris had told her about. He examined it, her ID, and her self (she met his look with the icy stare that she thought of as the one useful thing Sidney had taught her) before waving her in.

Inside the glass and steel lobby, Merry presented her credentials again, this time to Naomi behind the onyx reception desk. It felt odd to actually meet the receptionist, after hearing about her from Chris and seeing her picture on the company's Web site, and know that the other woman didn't know her from Eve—and couldn't, if she wanted to keep her cover. It all felt so strange, half familiar like something out of a recurring dream, seen half through her eyes and half through what she knew from talking with Chris. Naomi's smile was as genuine as she expected from Chris's stories, and Merry smiled warmly back, liking her because she'd been nice to Chris and he'd liked her. Still, Merry felt absurdly like an amateur spy as she took a seat on the smooth, leather bench beneath the metallic MedaGen logo to wait for her official interview.

From that vantage point, she watched various lab techs, administrators, guards, and visitors come and go, all with badges or temporary Visitor stickers. (The stickers not only marked outsiders as authorized guests, but even kept track of where they'd been. Sunlight changed the treated paper from white to blue, letting Naomi—and, more importantly, the guards—know that the visitors had been out of the building and back in without getting a new badge.) Benson Bioceuticals had been careful about guarding their intellectual property, but MedaGen took corporate paranoia to the next level. Every door had a scanner next to it, every employee had a badge with an electronic key, every turn required another set of secret signs and passwords. She watched half a dozen bonafide MedaGen researchers bow to the retinal reader guarding the doorway marked "Laboratory Wing." Were they nervous, wondering if the machine would suddenly decide they didn't have the right eyes to get back into their offices? A couple of them looked like doubts had crossed their minds, flinching slightly as they peered into the machine. Others adopted elaborately casual airs, barely pausing in their conversations to flourish their baby blues (or chocolate browns, or whatever) for the scanner's impartial, impersonal analysis. The only person who seemed utterly unfazed by the process was the elderly lady pushing a complicated mop bucket/cleaning cart arrangement—and she didn't even gaze deeply into the machine, stopping only long enough to slide a passkey through the slot under the scanner and key in a code. That made sense, since cleaning people were usually independent contractors or part-time employees with high turnover; keeping a retinal-scan database current for them would be more trouble than it was worth. (Merry couldn't quite tell from her angle, but it looked like the cleaning lady read the access code off a sticky note attached to the back of the passkey before carefully punching it into the keypad.)

So, how would someone without direct permission get into another team's lab? Merry wondered, partly out of amusement at indulging her spy-girl daydreams, and partly out of a half-formed conviction that she'd really need to know. *Bribe a guard?* One look at the hard-eyed musclemen in their dark uniforms exposed that thought for the silliness it was. Oh, sure, they'd take the money—then report you to the bosses, if they didn't help you fall down the stairs first. *Piggyback in on somebody else's entry, waiting for him to open the door, then slipping through right after him?* A few more minutes' observation gave her the answer to that one: no. Motion sensors on the doors let one person in at a time, and when two visitors attempted to go through the door too quickly, alarms went off, lights flashed, and the door closed with all the finality of a booby trap slamming into place in a B movie. It took two guards, five minutes, a hurried call from Naomi, and a personal inspection by a higher-level administrator to get things sorted back out and the important visitors (one of the guards addressed him as "Senator") on their way again.

"Ms. Anthony? Sorry for the wait. Mr. Humphrey can see you now," Naomi called.

Merry looked from the doorway to the receptionist and smiled. "Thanks." She rose, straightening her jacket and smoothing her skirt, taking a calming breath and testing the smile for tight edges. *Calm down. It's a job-confirmation interview. They won't have a lie detector in there—or a bare light bulb. You're just here for the project-management job.* Yeah, the gremlin voice inside her head shot back, *job interviews are stressful enough when you're not playing Spunky Girl Reporter Goes Undercover to Expose Corporate Corruption.*

"Right through there," Naomi said, pointing to the door that had taken a fit at the Senator's party.

"Is it safe?" Merry couldn't resist asking.

Naomi smiled, but said seriously, "I'll buzz you through. Don't touch the handle until it clicks. Humphrey's office is the fourth to your right."

Half expecting the sirens to go off again, Merry obediently waited until the door clicked open, then pushed through into the moister, warmer, more scientific-smelling atmosphere of the lab wing. Sure enough, the fourth door on the right was open. The room beyond was divided into several semi-open cubicles, with the solid glass wall of the lab itself at the far end of the room. The cubicle nearest the door was also the largest, with head-high partition walls and a sliding panel that gave the illusion of being a door. Currently, the panel was open, giving her an unobstructed view of perfectly coiffed hair above an expensive jacket as their owner spoke into a phone as sleek as he looked.

Merry waited for a moment, but the conversation—something to do with an office poll betting on the championship bout—continued, so she knocked firmly on the partition.

Humphrey slewed around in his chair—his front was as trendy and tailored as his back—stared at her for a moment, then grinned. "Hang it up, Bob," he said into the phone. "Something more interesting just came in." He flicked off the phone, smoothly adding, "I mean just came up, of course. Namely, a job interview. Please come in, have a seat. You can't make yourself comfortable, but that's only to be expected with mass-produced, modular furniture." The disdainful shrug went along with the offhanded gesture toward the guest chair.

Merry sat down in the chair. That put the desk between them, she in a slightly shorter seat, he in a position of power. She suppressed a snort—whether at his petty power-promoting *feng shui*, or at her own instant, Sidney-fueled analysis of it, she couldn't quite decide—and leaned back slightly in her own chair, acting comfortable and watching him watch her.

"Sorry about the delay," Humphrey finally said aloud, thinking there was something familiar about her. He didn't bring that up, though, gesturing around instead at the piles of reports, journals, and time lines that cluttered his double-wide cubicle and giving her another matinee-charming smile. "Things really pile up around here. You can see how much we need good project managers."

"I surely can," she agreed. "Sounds like you could use a good bookie, too," she added, before she thought about it. She about bit her tongue, embarrassed that she'd let her second-hand familiarity with (and simmering contempt of) Humphrey disable her internal editor.

He didn't even bother to pretend he missed the reference, leaning back casually. "Sure. You know one? If it's a woman, maybe we can get her in on the company's affirmative-action policy too."

"Affirmative action for bookies?" Merry asked innocently.

"Right." Humphrey matched her bland expression. "Especially if it's a female bookie."

"Sorry," Merry told him, shooting him a look with a warning dose of Sidney frost in it. "I don't know anyone like that."

"Too bad," he shrugged off both the frost and the topic of conversation—though he couldn't quite let it go without exhausting its leer potential. "But project managers meet a lot of people. Maybe we'll both get lucky."

"I'm more interested in getting this job offer signed than in getting 'lucky,'" Merry assured him.

"Back to business, huh? You're a slave driver, all right," Humphrey sighed. He glanced at the qualifications listed on her resumé, then looked at her again. This time, however, the frat-boy mischief in his eyes had disappeared. "You list experience managing three research projects at a university's genetics lab. What kinds of deadlines did you deal with? How big was the team, and what proportion of professionals to students did it have?"

Merry hoped her blink wasn't too noticeable as she switched gears to answer the barrage of surprisingly pointed questions that followed. The hardest part, she found, was not saying "we" (meaning herself and Chris), and not mentioning that one of the projects had been her own dissertation research. Other than that omission, she kept to the truth and nothing but the truth. And when his last question asked what she wanted to have accomplished in five years, she answered, "I hope to have made a real difference in promoting people's health and well being" with full confidence and conviction.

"Well, isn't that sweet?" Humphrey purred. The bored libertine was back, slithering in behind the competent administrator. "Did that go over big with the judges at the Strawberry Queen pageant?"

"I don't know if it would or not, but you're welcome to pass it along to any girlfriends who might want to try it instead of the usual 'world peace,'" she informed him coolly.

"Cute and quick," he noted. "What more could we ask for? Besides a female bookie."

"Can't think of a thing," she said. Despite the fact that this was a job interview and she really needed to get his signature, she was beginning to enjoy the banter, the feeling of knowing more about him than he knew about her, falling into the kind of disrespectful tone that Chris used when talking about Humphrey. "So, would you sign the paper and get somebody to show me my office?"

"And pushy." Humphrey shook his head, then pulled out the contract, signing it with a flourish. "All right, you're on. Until you get fired."

"Or until I leave for greener pastures." She took the contract and scribbled her own name across it (taking care to write "Anthony," not "Galen"—which hurt all over again). As she passed it back, she couldn't resist adding, "Just out of curiosity, do you ever worry about getting slapped—either literally or with a sexual harassment suit?"

"No," he said. "The one's assault, and the other's easy to beat in court. Community standards and courtesy just aren't what they used to be in this degenerate day and age."

"So I won't expect you to hold any doors for me," Merry said.

"Best way not to get hit with one," he agreed, standing up and yelling, "Lia! Get over here and show the new stopwatch monitor to her cell."

Merry rose as well. She didn't bother to offer to shake hands with Humphrey; instead, she claimed her copy of the contract and smiled at Lia. They left their manager back on the phone with Bob, looked over Merry's new home (shoulder-high partitions, computer, file cabinets, and enough space to turn around in—just barely), and agreed to meet for lunch with the rest of the team. Merry thanked Lia, then collapsed into the chair, which promptly sighed tiredly and sank four inches.

"You and me both," she told it. "Tired already." Silently, she added, *we'll just have to see if I'm any good at industrial espionage—or project management. Nothing like learning to swim by diving into the deep end!*

* * *

"How's our literate gang member?" Sam asked Renata.

She glanced into the front room, where Dove sat, dark head bent over the Book of Mormon. "He's taken to it like a fish to water." She smiled. "It'll be interesting to hear what he has to say when he finally resurfaces."

Sam looked toward Dove thoughtfully. "Resurfacing may be a bad thing."

"What?" Renata looked from Dove to Sam.

Her husband lowered his voice slightly. "Bishop Yazzie mentioned that there's been talk about strangers around—strangers asking about a Navajo kid turning up, somebody with no relatives. Nobody's called the Navajo Police for an official investigation, but somebody's looking for somebody who sounds a lot like Dove. Teenage kid, skinny, long hair, bad attitude, bullet wound—the whole picture."

"Looking for Dove?" Renata whispered, too. "Who is it?"

Sam shrugged. "Just strangers, that's all the word is. Probably not those Southerners Dove talked about, since they don't have accents."

"But the sheriff whose car he stole—" Renata filled in the gaps and came to the same conclusion Sam had. She looked up at him, worried. "Have they found out? Has anybody told them?"

"I don't think so, not yet." Sam rubbed her shoulder. "Nobody in the ward's going to talk about Dove, and nobody around here likes strangers much anyway."

"But they might say something, just for love of passing along news," Renata pointed out. "I wonder how long we've got before word gets back?"

"We'll see. And we'll just have to be ready for it when it happens," Sam said. "For now, we wait."

They didn't have to wait long for Dove's first reaction. He looked up from his plate at lunch and asked, "What happened to 'straightforward'? This book's got language as bad as the Bible."

"Let me guess, you've hit Second Nephi," Sam laughed. "That *is* Bible stuff, kid, a big, steaming slab of Old Testament poetry courtesy of Isaiah. Push on through, and things'll lighten up again so even you can handle it."

"Even me, huh?" Dove gave Sam—and Renata, who was smiling at him—a narrow-eyed look and inhaled his lunch. Nothing like a challenge to make a chore more interesting.

* * *

Determined to show Sam he wasn't a semiliterate thug, and because the mainline story had grabbed his attention like nothing had in a long time, he plowed on through ("beautiful feet" notwithstanding). Sure enough, once the story returned to the Nephites and Lamanites, the forests and rivers of Zarahemla and Nephi rose around him again. He didn't completely understand the heavy doctrine (the Son of God and God are the same God, but different and distinct?), but Ammon and General Moroni grabbed his attention—and his admiration. He could picture Moroni facing down the crowd on the street, waving the Title of Liberty ("In memory of our God, our religion, and freedom, and our peace, our wives, and our children"), winning incredible victories, as long as he didn't hit first. Amalickiah, Korihor, the endless stream of Gadianton robbers—they strutted in his mind's eye wearing the leather and designer sunglasses of rival gang leaders. The devastating earthquakes that almost pulled down the entire civilization flashed through his memory in telecast images of the fires burning in San Francisco and the flooded desolation of a Chinese village. The smoke from the burning of scriptures and believers burned his eyes and made his teeth gritty, like the cocaine smoke of a warehouse or the cordite stink of a gunfight. All the horrors resonated in him, touching scars in his own life.

But somehow, the love came through as well. Laman and Lemuel's psychotic hatred for Nephi made him love Benny all the more, the elder brother protecting him even from himself. Alma's blessings for his sons, even the one who'd desperately disappointed him, made Dove miss a father he'd never known. So did Mormon's sad but not despairing care for his own son, caught in an unwinnable war. Even more amazing, the growing point of light shining through the thick darkness, resolving into the image of the risen Savior, meant something to him for the first time in his life.

Dove had always heard of Jesus Christ—in all kinds of contexts. From default swear word to the best argument for getting early parole, he'd heard that name in all kinds of contexts. Television blathered that name incessantly, usually from robe-wearing reverends of the evangelical stripe, exhorting the sheep in their electronic congregations to accept Him as their personal Savior to assure their eternal salvation (though a $50 donation to the reverend's cause would really

312 Jessica Draper and Richard D. Draper

cement the deal). *Abuelas* and aunties prayed their rosaries not to Him, but to His sainted Mother, which amounted to the same thing. And sophisticated, successful commentators derided the entire idea of a mortal Son of God, while his young, socially progressive teachers derided Christianity and capitalism as the forces that destroyed his "indigenous culture." That had always rubbed a raw spot on Dove's psyche. He didn't have an "indigenous culture." He had vague memories of a Navajo grandfather who'd loved him but couldn't take care of him (death and poverty were good excuses, but it still hurt), much more recent memories of snide comments from everyone from lowlifes like Rico to full-blooded Native Americans deriding him as a border rat, and a sense that he'd never actually fit anywhere but where Benny was. No culture outside the gang, no history outside the few years he remembered, no family besides Benny, no heritage but a gun and the half-breed looks that let him blend into the sprawling slums and deserts of Amexica, no mission or morality past carrying out *Abuelo's* orders while maintaining any shred of honor or dignity he could scrounge out of a bunch of books written about ancient cultures so far removed from his reality that they might as well have described people on alien planets.

Which is probably why Mormon 7:2–10 hit him so hard: "Know ye that ye are of the house of Israel," he read. "Know ye that ye must come unto repentance, or ye cannot be saved. Know ye that ye must lay down your weapons of war, and delight no more in the shedding of blood, and take them not again, save it be that God shall command you. Know ye that ye must come to the knowledge of your fathers, and repent of all your sins and iniquities, and believe in Jesus Christ . . . And ye will also know that ye are a remnant of the seed of Jacob; therefore ye are numbered among the people of the first covenant."

My fathers, Dove thought. *Lamanites. Nephites. Prophets. Warriors. People who lived and loved and fought and died two thousand years ago. Dead and gone—but not forgotten, thanks to a line of rough and ready scribes and a New York farm boy.* And not gone forever, said Mormon, thanks to the Jesus that seemed more real in the pages of that beat-up book than any of the preachers' sermons. "By the power of the Father he hath risen again, whereby he hath gained the victory over the grave; and also in him is the sting of death swallowed up. And he bringeth to pass the resurrection of the dead, whereby man must be raised to stand before his judgment-seat."

"Benny," Dove whispered, through the lump in his throat. The last time he'd heard the word "resurrection," it had come from the bishop at the memorial service the ward had insisted on holding for Benny. The Navajo Tribal Police had picked up Benny's body where Slick had left him when he'd fallen and brought it to the small hospital; Dove had limped in to identify his brother. He didn't have to look long or closely—nor did he want to. He'd left with Benny's wallet and belt buckle, like souvenirs from the morgue. Then Renata had come into the guest room quietly, as if she expected to find him crying and didn't want to embarrass him, to tell him that they'd set up a memorial service for him the next day. That had surprised Dove. The gang wasn't much for funerals. If somebody ran out of luck, his comrades left him lying where he fell, got away as quickly as they could, and sometimes ordered a round of drinks to remember him by. He'd considered refusing Renata's invitation, but the look on her face made her soft "We'd like you to be there" an imperial command. The funeral itself had been short and small, with just their family, the bishop, Joe the doctor (present in both capacities, as counselor and medical officer), and Dove in a borrowed wheelchair at the simple graveside service. It all felt unreal to Dove at the time, the hymns and scriptures washing through him without finding any purchase on his grief-slick soul.

Now, however, he was reading through the tears in his eyes, as Mormon wrote of those long-dead people—his people, the ones who "believe in Christ, and are baptized, first with water, then with fire and with the Holy Ghost, following the example of our Savior, according to that which he hath commanded us," finishing, "it shall be well with you in the day of judgment." Would it be "well" with him? With Benny? Did the promise go that far, to cover a pair of orphan halfbreeds?

"You okay?" Sam asked, reaching over to turn on the lamp. Amber light filled the room, replacing the blue dusk that had dimmed the pages.

Dove opened his eyes, not acknowledging the tear on his cheek as he looked into Sam's bronze-sculpted face. "Who am I? Who are you? How can you be a Navajo and a Mormon?"

"Let the debates begin." A half smile broke Sam's concerned expression, but it didn't have any mockery in it. He sat down by Dove. "You're Salvatore Nakai, alias *Hasbidi* or Dove, and a kid with a lot more going for him than it looks like. I'm Samuel Begay, Sam to my friends, Mormon—and Navajo. And it's not that hard to be both."

"How?" Dove persisted. "Christian or Navajo—they don't go together."

"Sure they do," Sam told him, taking the book from him, slipping out the card that marked the page where Dove had stopped reading. "It's right here."

"On the bookmark?" Dove rolled his eyes, but he took the slip of closely printed card stock.

"They're the Articles of Faith," Sam clarified. "Take a look at number 13, especially that last bit."

"Praiseworthy, of good report?" Dove summarized.

"Right. It's all in accepting the good wherever you find it. Think God leaves his children to stumble around in the dark?" Sam shook his head. "He's given out a lot of truth over the centuries, to anybody who'd listen. Buddha, Mohammad, the Navajo ancestors—they all have good ideas, bits of light, that are worth keeping."

"Like the Navajos value family, community, harmony, and peace," Renata added, picking up one of Sariah's shoes from the floor as she came over to join Sam and Dove. "Those are completely compatible with Christ's teachings. Being members of the Church means we live by all the truth we can get."

"Truth," Dove repeated, looking at the Book of Mormon, trying to get his head around the idea that he might have found the answers he'd been looking for so long. Doubt, fear, cynicism, and a quivering flash of panic groped for an excuse to throw the whole thing away before it hurt him. "So what about the Gentle Savior? Those guys were fighting left and right—filling up rivers with casualties."

Renata shook her head before Sam could answer that one. "Don't get sucked into that 'Gentle Jesus' myth. This is the guy who took a whip to a bunch of traders in the Temple and stood up to the bosses of the whole country. Forgiving and turning the other cheek doesn't mean letting the bad guys run over you!"

"How about this," Sam said, reading into Dove's questions something deeper—and more personal. "It's not just being peaceful, it's being sorry when you can't be. Here's Moroni, one of the greatest generals ever, and it specifically says that 'he did not delight in the shedding of blood.' Ammon's people buried their weapons because they'd hurt innocent victims and would rather die than fall into that again. But their sons fought when their fathers couldn't—and they had divine approval."

"Repentance is always stronger than whatever you've done wrong," Renata said softly. "Dove, you need to trust what you're feeling."

"I'm feeling tired," Dove said. He stood up carefully, trying not to fight the pain in his back and side. Moving always hurt more when he was tense.

It wasn't as easy to fight the feeling slowly seeping through his chest. That strange, tingling internal pressure, not the aching in his hurt muscles and bones, kept him awake, staring at the ceiling. He didn't believe in ghosts—either the dead soldiers looking for revenge out at Blanca Hacienda or the *chindi* that haunted the night around Navajo hogans. Still, voices and faces hovered at the edges of his vision, in blood and smoke and dust. And beyond them, the roar of ancient battles mixed with prayers and a voice that shook the earth without hurting the ears. That voice finally pushed Dove out of bed and down the hall, navigating by moonlight to the Begays's bedroom door.

"Sam?" he whispered. The rustle of sheets told him that was enough; he stepped back to wait.

"What's up?" Sam asked. "You need another pill?"

"No." Dove hesitated, then took a breath and the plunge. "You know how to do a sweat bath? Grandfather used to say it was the best way to clear your head. Didn't work for his lungs, but helped him feel better."

Sam stood silent in the moonlit dark for a moment, then patted Dove's shoulder. "Yeah, I can help you with that. It might help—but praying, really praying, definitely will. Will you do that?"

"Yes," Dove said. "But I'm not sure how."

"I can tell you the basics," Sam assured him. "But it's not how you say it. What's important is that you mean it. And that you ask in Jesus' name."

* * *

Sitting in the hot, saturated air, feeling the thick steam on his skin and in his lungs, Dove let the heat melt his body away. He reached out into the darkness, searching blindly with his heart for the glimmer of light breaking through the vapor. The voices and faces around the edges of his memory grew louder and clearer. Cesare came into focus first, his thick, snarling face disappearing from Dove's gun sight, sweat-streaked in the firelight that filled the *Brujos*' warehouse, intent on a video game he was losing. Others followed: the Southern tech dying over a caseful of bomb, a Brujo banger crashing into a case of bananas, the assassin who'd targeted *Abuelo* falling from the roofline into the street (the bullet from Dove's gun, not the fall, had killed him). The hot-metal smell of shooting filled Dove's lungs, thick as the steam; the sickness he'd tried to deny and brush away after each battle swam into his gut. He swallowed against the nausea and sorrow. Guilt poured in too, with a slew of other, lesser memories: strutting down the main drag with *Abuelo's* gang; pushing civilians out of the way with a snarl and a threat; taking candy here, cold drinks there as "tribute"; bullying other gangs' soldiers and wannabes; lying to everybody but Benny. The entire parade of dishonorable garbage he'd done poured through his head and into the saturated air.

"I'm sorry," he whispered. "I've done wrong, and I'm sorry." Sam's instructions bubbled to the surface. "Father in Heaven, please hear me. I am so sorry." Dim memories of hearing a helpful *abuela* urging him to go to confession crept in next; he didn't know if it was "right" or not, but he figured that confession was good for the soul, and he didn't have anything to say that God didn't already know. He began listing the memories weighing on his mind, trivial, painful, serious, stupid, asking forgiveness for each one without offering excuses—just like he'd done with Benny, only more so. When his voice got too choked, he fell silent but kept up the litany in his mind. When the list of sins ran out, he found himself trying to put into words the rest of his life—searching for the truth, resenting Benny for drawing so many lines around him, feeling that he was stumbling in the dark without a guide, the horrible loneliness that crashed down on him when Benny died at the hands of someone who'd almost been a friend. Finally, he'd poured out everything. "Please, I ask You—Thee—to hear me. I want to do right. Please show me how." He took a breath, then said, as Sam had told him, "And I ask this in the name of the Savior, Jesus Christ."

Dove felt exhausted, limp but strangely light at the same time, like the leftover skin of a spent balloon. He opened his eyes, looking at the dark of the sweat bath, unbroken by even a glimmer of divine fire. Slowly, however, peace spread into the emptiness inside him, warm even in the heat of the steam. No pillar of light appeared, no angel descended, no voice spoke directly into his heart—but he knew, beyond all logic, that Someone had heard him. And, even more incredibly, that Someone cared. That hadn't happened before.

"You're there, aren't you?" he whispered into the silence. "And Benny's okay, isn't he?"

Nobody answered, but somehow it felt like the answer was yes.

"How'd it go?" Sam asked, helping Dove out of the dark and into the brightness of the desert dawn.

Dove took a deep breath, not even minding the twinge of pain in his back. "Not so good."

"What?" Sam blinked, his offer of a towel forgotten halfway through.

"Not so good," Dove repeated, taking the towel and mopping his face to hide a grin. "You know where I can find a prophet?"

"A prophet?" Sam gave him a suspicious look. "Why do you need a prophet?"

"Aren't they the ones that baptize people?" Dove asked.

"They could, but so can any ordained priest or elder," Sam told him.

Dove looked at him calculatingly. "That include you?"

"Yeah, that includes me, but there's more you've got to know before you can get dipped," Sam said. "I'll tell you plenty, but you better hear it from the professionals, too."

"I was afraid of that," Dove sighed. "You always got to make it hard, huh? Looks like I'm going to have to give up watching my afternoon soaps to talk to those missionaries of yours."

He didn't dodge when Sam thumped his shoulder. He didn't mind the hug from Renata, either—which she gave him right before she ran for the phone to make an appointment with the local elders.

The rodeo began that afternoon, shortly after the missionaries arrived. At least Sam viewed the whole thing as a rodeo, with Dove as the bronco intent on breaking for the far horizon (in this case, the baptismal font) while the elders, cowboy hats superimposed on their short haircuts, tried to slow him down long enough to get a doctrinal bit in his mouth. Sam stepped in only when Dove's incessant, argumentative questions and street-smart mouth threw Elder Crawford for a loop. Even then, Sam didn't tread on the missionaries' teaching role; he just smacked Dove lightly upside the head and reminding him to be polite. Sometimes it worked.

"Cracked, the whole thing," Dove declared, waving the Joseph Smith pamphlet at the elders. "God wants to set up His church, He tells some nothing and nobody fourteen-year-old kid? That's not how you build a gang. You get a strong leader, a real *capitan*, a *Señor* who'll run it right!"

Elder Puha, twice as wide as his companion, half again as tall, and as serenely sunny as the islands he'd grown up on, just grinned. "So He was setting up a gang? Check the scriptures again and tell me what the answer is on that one. Jesus wasn't a big *Señor* either."

Dove blinked, thinking of the radiantly haloed Savior holding court in the frescoes of the little Catholic church that Perro's *abuela* dragged them to when they visited her. It rocked his world to get into the Bible (under Elder Puha's expert, bantering direction) and read that Jesus didn't wander around glowing with divine fire, that He had "no beauty that men should desire him," and even got dissed in His own hometown.

"Heavenly Father's kingdom isn't the same as the kingdoms of this world," Elder Crawford assured him, stuttering slightly, the earnestness and sheer unshakable belief shining from his eyes. "He doesn't use worldly standards and tactics. By small and simple things are great things brought to pass, like revealing the restored gospel to a young, sincere boy like Joseph Smith."

"And like using a skinny white boy to spread the Word in the badlands?" Dove grinned at him.

By this time, Elder Crawford had caught on to Dove's teasing and managed a grin back.

"Okay, so maybe Jesus wasn't a big *Señor* either," Dove conceded. "But why not set up a church right?"

"What's right?" Elder Puha asked. "People need to believe in the Church, in the Holy Ghost, in their testimonies of the Savior, not in the guy at the pulpit. The Church isn't set up to impress the world. It's set up to help us come closer to our Heavenly Father through study, prayer, and serving each other. Faith's the important thing, your own relationship to Heavenly Father, not how well the Prophet's coming across on the TV."

"He comes across pretty well on the TV," Dove noted, thinking of President Rojas approvingly.

"Yeah, he does," Elder Puha conceded. "But it's not him—it's the Savior behind him. You ever read about Gideon's army, Dove?"

"No," Dove cocked his head at the big missionary, reaching for the battered Book of Mormon he'd hardly put down since he finished reading it the first time. "Where's it say he had an army of his own?"

"Not that Gideon," Elder Puha told him. "The one he was named for. In the Old Testament. I'll show you."

As Elder Puha had expected, the story of Gideon's ever-shrinking army and God's tests of the warriors' faith and readiness impressed Dove—especially the bit where they defeated their enemy despite absurd (and divinely engineered) odds. "See?" he asked. "It's not the leader. It's the leader's leader. Joseph Smith had the faith to ask the question first, and then the faith to keep following Heavenly Father's instructions, doing things the right way, even down to getting shot for what he believed in.

"He got the word out, he set the Church up by revelation, and he didn't put himself before God. If this were Joseph Smith's church, it would've died when he did," Elder Crawford chipped in.

"You read that again," Elder Puha told Dove, pointing at the pamphlet. "And the preface to the Book of Mormon, and the testimony in Joseph Smith History. Then you pray about it. Really pray about it. You promise?"

"I promise," Dove told him impatiently. " And then I can get baptized, right?"

"When they get through the discussions," Sam reminded Dove. "You've got to know what you're getting into before you jump in with both feet."

Dove reluctantly agreed and finally let the elders get on to their next appointment. He opened the account of the First Vision, half hearing Renata show the missionaries out, Elder Crawford saying, "Our District Leader still can't believe we've got somebody we're trying to commit to *wait* to get baptized."

At last, however, the wait was over. Dove easily answered the basic doctrinal questions Renata, Sam, and both elders shot at him—though he tended to favor the stories with a more violent edge. He had no problem committing to live the Word of Wisdom and the Law of Chastity (Benny hadn't let him smoke, drink, or sleep around anyway), or pay tithing (though Sam did have to remind him that you couldn't pay tithing on ill-gotten gains—or, come to that, do things that resulted in ill-gotten gains). And, as he admitted to Bishop Yazzie, while he still had questions, he was confident that he could find the answers one way or another.

"If it's not in the Book of Mormon," he said, "I'll ask Sam, or you, and pray about it. Then it'll come clear."

Confessing his sins to the bishop had been harder, not so much because he didn't want to talk about what he'd done as one of *Abuelo's* soldiers, but because Dove had worried that hearing about gang life would shock him.

"I'm an ex-Marine and a policeman, Salvatore," Bishop Yazzie had told him solemnly. "I think I can handle it. Please, though, don't start out with 'forgive me, Father.' That's the Catholics. You can just tell me whatever you think you need to."

They got through a somewhat toned-down version of Dove's gang career—and the background check the bishop also ran (no convictions in the Navajo Nation, no outstanding New Mexico warrants, surprisingly clean juvenile record—or not so surprising, since *Abuelo's Señor* had also owned the local sheriff). It had, however, led to a deadly serious talk about thieving, assault, extortion—and, most importantly, killing during war versus killing in self defense versus murder. To Bishop Yazzie's surprise, Dove had a finely graded and intensely thought-out set of distinctions between them already.

"I called it honor, before I knew about General Moroni," Dove told him. "I know that you fight for your home, family, and religion now, and not just because somebody tells you to. And I'll do that. I know the truth now. I know how to pray. I know God's listening to me. And I know what I need to do to listen to Him too. That's why I'm not pushing hard to get baptized now. It'll happen when He wants it to." Dove grinned. "Course, I hope that's not too much longer. You all can nearly talk me to death!"

"There's no doubting his testimony or desire," Bishop Yazzie told Sam, as they watched Dove walk over to tease the Elders.

"No," Sam agreed. "Whatever he does, he does big. There's no fence sitting with that kid."

"Angel or devil, huh?" the bishop asked, more to himself than Sam, then took a deep breath and straightened his shoulders. "All right, let's get him officially registered on our side, before Elder Puha's time is up."

Dove came out of the water feeling cleaner than any shower or sweat bath could make him. The weight of the hands on his head (Sam's chief among them) pressed the giddy excitement into a deeper, more heartfelt resolve. He didn't feel the Holy Ghost as fire, but as the strongest conviction his famous "instincts" had ever given him. This was right. He knew it to the marrow of his bones.

I'll do what You want me to do, he thought silently, pledging his own loyalty to the *Señor*, more powerful—and more loving—than he'd ever imagined. *Forever.*

He shook hands with Bishop Yazzie and the other counselor, hugged Sam, and grinned at the pale, skinny missionary while the big, Islander one slapped him on the back hard enough to help him remember he was not quite all the way healed

"You going to be OK. Now, remember not to get mixed up in more trouble, even though I'm going back home?" Elder Puha asked.

Dove shrugged nonchalantly. "Hey, now I've got religion pasted on me, you don't have to worry about me anymore. Mormons are my gang now."

* * *

Dear Chisom,
I know that you are anxious to get to China, and I am sorry your transfer has been delayed. Be patient and

continue to work where you are. Remember, these things go slowly. The Church has had a bit of a set back due to the work of our enemies, especially from a group in the Philippines headed by members of the "Ministry of Light." They have made the Church the main target for their wrath, it seems, because quite a number of our people have successfully opposed their leader on a number of fronts. His minions have succeeded in worrying some of the leaders in southern China about us. Even so, we have been able to answer our enemies' charges showing them to be the lies they are. Pres. Smith assures us that the Lord wants us in China and nothing will stop us from getting there; it will just take a little more time.

Your last transmission suggested that you believe that the Church must proselytize the world before the end comes, that we must have missionaries in every hamlet and village, including northern China, the Middle East, and the rest of Africa, before the Second Coming. That view is only partially correct. The scriptures are clear that the gospel will be preached in all the world and to every major language group (see JS—M 1:31 and D&C 133:37–38). That, however, is only part of the story. The scriptures do not say that the gospel will be preached to every person or even to a majority. In fact, they suggest there will be whole populations which shall not hear the gospel before the Second Coming. The scriptures refer to these as the heathen nations and the majority of the work for them will be done after the millennium begins. (See D&C 45:54; 90:9–11). It is unnecessary, therefore, for the missionaries to preach in every hamlet, village, or town, or even city. We may not even be much of a force in every nation before the Second Coming. We do know, however, that the gospel will be taught to every language group. It is your privilege to begin the work among the mainland Chinese. Others are taking it to the interior of Africa and still others to Turkey. We have been working among the Arabic speaking people for some time, though not yet officially in the Middle East. I'm yet unsure what will happen there.

Thus the Second Coming may be nearer than some suppose. The signs are very evident for those who have eyes to see. What is interesting is how many don't, or won't. This condition should not surprise us, however, for the Lord has forewarned us. A few days before His death, He told His disciples that the time just before His coming would echo that of Noah's day when nearly every person was blind to the signs of doom. They, like their modern kin, were eating and drinking, marrying and giving in marriage, totally unaware that the end was nigh. (See JS—M 1:41–43.) In spite of all warnings to the contrary, they stubbornly kept doing what was necessary to perpetuate their wicked society. Their obstinate insistence ended, as it will for their latter-day counterparts, when destruction took them all away. There is no doubt today's group will be caught in total surprise.

You, however, will be privileged to open the eyes of many. So let me leave you with one last thought. The Lord told the early missionaries that they were to preach nothing but repentance. When I first read those passages in the Doctrine and Covenants, I thought, Why emphasize one doctrine? Why should the process by which one's sins are forgiven supercede all others? That would become monotonous to hear and even more monotonous to preach. I have since learned, however, that repentance— deep, full, and total repentance—really describes everything a person must do to return to God. In fact, that is what the Hebrew word (shuv), translated repentance, means, to turn, return, or come back to where one was. Thus, the command to preach repentance is really a command to preach the plan of salvation and encourage people to accept and follow it. Getting one's sins forgiven is just a small part of what the doctrine of repentance is all about. The biggest part is how to become reunited with God in an eternal child-father relationship. When a person feels the cleansing power of God, is changed in the inner man, seeks to do righteousness, and finds the Spirit in his life, he has repented. We will have finally and fully repented only when we have returned to live with God. Until then, we must both practice and preach the principle. Do so with vigor to all those who will listen.

With love,
Your father,
Chinedu

* * *

"Don't you have anybody to meet up with? No gang to hang with? No friends?"

Merry started, slewing around in her chair from her computer to look at the woman who stood in the entrance (you couldn't call it a doorway) of her cubicle. The seating arrangement that put her back to people walking by tended to increase her paranoia. A wave of relief washed through her when she saw who it was this time, and she smiled. "Oh, hi, Olga. Anybody to meet up with?"

The cleaning woman smiled back, tucking her dusting cloth under the belt of her apron and comfortably leaning against the partition. "Well, sure—somebody to meet up with. A date, friends, somebody. What is a pretty young girl like you doing here late on a nice night like this?"

"Oh, you know, trying to catch up," Merry answered, gesturing vaguely around her paper-cluttered cubicle and the data blinking from the monitor. She discreetly touched the controls, hiding the data she'd been reading. The computer's clock caught her eye—rats! She'd stayed longer than she thought.

"If you ask me—which you won't, so I'll tell you—you just work way too much," Olga informed her, with a tolerantly disapproving head shake. "Why, you get more done than most everybody around here. Honey, you need a life. Get out and have fun, before you wind up old and dried out like me." She sighed theatrically, whipping out the rag to swipe half-heartedly at the small clear space on Merry's desk.

"I'd hardly call you dried out," Merry assured her, laughing. "You've still got plenty of juice."

Olga had frequently entertained her with tales of her wild life in Russia, her career as a backup dancer for various big-ticket pop-concert tours, her six husbands, her gaggle of assorted children (biological, adopted, picked up along the way), her habit of spending money like it was going out of style, and the vagaries of working as a janitor supervisor at a handful of high-tech firms around San Diego—including MedaGen. Now she tossed her head, brushing her hair back from her still-handsome face, and shot Merry the smile that had captivated audiences and casting agents alike.

"Oh, if you count sass and vinegar as juice," she allowed, shrugging carelessly. She flicked the dust rag at Merry. "But that's neither here nor there. Get out of here, go dancing, bundle up in bed with a cute boy or a box of ice cream. We need to vacuum, and we can't do it with your feet in the way."

"All right, I'm going." Merry had turned off her computer even before Olga threatened her with the rag. "And that ice cream idea sounds really good."

Olga gave her an arch smile. "And the cute boy?"

"Don't have one of those on hand," Merry said lightly. Memories of Chris, laughing, talking, thinking, sleeping, holding her, filled her head—and her eyes. She paid a lot of attention to detaching her purse from the file-cabinet drawer, intently searching for her keys.

"You will," Olga said gently, patting Merry's arm. "Somebody will turn up."

"Oh, somebody already has." Merry managed a smile, silently growling at her tears, threatening them with dire consequences if they dared creep past her lashes.

"Well, then you're set," Olga said. Self-absorbed as she was, she paid enough attention to pick up at least a hint of Merry's distress and left it at that. "Good night, Meredith."

"Good night, Olga," Merry said, making her escape. "Night, Lupe, happy birthday to DeShawn," she added, passing one of Olga's team on her way out of the offices.

Lupe waved and smiled. "Night, Ms. Anthony. He had a good evening."

Merry didn't bother to smile for the security camera that tracked her down the hall. The guard in the lobby didn't smile either; he just gazed impassively at her before turning back to the bank of monitors in the desk in front of him. Merry nodded politely anyway—just another corporate drone leaving for a few hours at home. At first, he'd watched her with deep suspicion, distrusting the new employee and her odd, late hours. Now, however, she was just another part of the daily routine, her late departures normal (and almost expected).

The rest of her work habits went along with the guard's—and now Humphrey's—expectations too. Everybody knew who Meredith Anthony was and what you could count on her to do, and Merry carefully cultivated an utterly unremarkable, totally dependable image. She'd jumped right into her project-management work, filling her cubicle with timelines, budgets, charts, and endless work-breakdown structures built with sticky notes and big sheets of presentation paper. She kept the teams assigned to her three projects on their toes with weekly updates. She took diligent notes at meetings, taking careful note of a host of tiny details (some project related and some most definitely not, but all potentially helpful). She pushed to bring in results on time and under budget. She asked for (and got) permission to come into the labs during off-work hours so she could "catch up on details" while the rest of the team was gone. And she convinced Humphrey and the tech-support supervisor that she could work that much more efficiently if she had access to the teams' network files, so she could instantly check on progress and update her reports. That had been a bit of an uphill battle, but they'd given in after she blinked innocently, explained how much more effective her idea would be than relying on team members' reports, and showed the data to prove it. Copying the projects' accountants on the message that pointed out the possible cost savings helped, too; they weighed in strongly in favor of expanding her computer access.

Humphrey had come into her cubicle with the news that her request for approval for permission to check the team's research files had been officially "escalated" to top management levels, and tossed a printout of the official e-mail he'd received asking for more information onto her desk.

She picked it up, read it, and smiled. "Oh, good! It got to people who can actually make that kind of decision. This will really help."

After a second, she looked up at Humphrey, who was still standing there, looking intently at her. "Yes? Something else?"

"Something else, all right," he said thoughtfully. "Something a lot slicker than I expected."

"Oh?" She maintained her bland expression, just like she'd done through all the meetings, working lunches, endless reports. She'd never fancied herself much of an actress, but she had always been very good at keeping a straight face, whatever she was feeling. Humphrey saw nothing of the rage, boredom, and sheer hostility bubbling up in her chest—she *so* did not care about any of this! The goal was to get the proof she needed, get the word out, and go back home to watch this entire crooked business go down in flames.

Humphrey couldn't see it, but he was too slick and practiced a corporate weasel to be completely oblivious to undercurrents either. He knew that something else lurked beneath Ms. Anthony's subdued perkiness and inhuman work ethic. Corporate weasel that he was, however, he misinterpreted the signs his instincts sniffed out. "You're pretty good at this."

"Thank you," she said modestly. "I have a talent for project management."

"And office politics," he shot back, leaning over her to look in to her eyes. "Copying Dell's money grubbers on that message was slick. The bosses noticed how good you are. You got their attention, and you'll probably get what you want. Slick."

"I sure did," she said calmly, thinking, *I got one step closer to getting access to the network files. I don't give a flying jump kick about what the bosses think, as long as they stay out of my way.*

Humphrey hovered for a few seconds more, and when she didn't shrink back, he stepped away. "You'll go far around here," he said approvingly, then warned, "Just watch your back—and who you try to step on. The right allies can make or break an ambitious executive."

"They sure can," Merry agreed. "One wrong step, and you end up owing your soul to the company."

To her surprise, Humphrey laughed at that barb. "Word to the wise, eh? Well, I like the cut of your jib—even if your skirt could be shorter—so I'll help you out here. Don't work too hard, Anthony." He strolled down the aisle to check on someone else.

Merry watched him go, made a mental note to make sure she stayed out of Humphrey's targeting sights until she'd found what she was looking for. She hoped that Humphrey's deciding to help her negotiate with the bosses would actually work. One more step, one more committee decision. That meant more time, which she didn't have to waste. MedaGen and Senator Garlick were still pushing for the ultimate goal of making AllSafe a country-wide security requirement. They'd begun giving the FDA-approved vaccine to "selected populations" already, to quiet the loudest protesters (those with the most immediate need to escape the health-related consequences of their actions and the money to make their voices heard). As far as Merry could tell—and in Carmen's vehement opinion—that meant they figured they could get the mandatory vaccination law passed within a year, since the first set of customers would start needing their boosters by then. The measure was a lot less likely to pass if everybody knew that AllSafe wasn't a one-time vaccination but a lifetime commitment.

With the metaphorical clock always ticking, Merry discreetly dug into the information she had access to whenever she thought she could get away with it. She poked around the edges of the research projects—and the buildings themselves—as much as possible, getting quite a reputation as a keen young thing spending long hours at work. Of course, staying late also meant meeting Olga and her crew.

Making friends with them had been one of the surprisingly pleasant aspects of her undercover operation; they weren't part of the Evil Empire, and they were more friendly and less driven than the other project managers Merry worked with (who spent most of their time trying to find ways to get ahead by stepping on each other and anybody else in their headlong rush up the corporate ladder). Merry took the time to chat with Olga, Lupe, and the other two janitors, learning about their lives, their kids, their routines, and the all-access passes and passages they used to get around MedaGen's paranoid security measures. With the relatively high turnover among the cleaning crew, it wasn't cost-effective to add their retinal scans to the MedaGen database, and MedaGen couldn't legally require them to submit to scans because they were actually employees of a professional cleaning company, rather than MedaGen's own. So, the cleaning company did the background checks and signed the security and nondisclosure agreements on behalf of their employees, and MedaGen's security guards checked them into the building and issued cards with the day's access code to them each night. Olga laughed about the arrangements ("What would we want to steal around here? Two-ton machines? It's silliness, just silliness."), but shrugged off the added hassle as part of working in today's corporate culture. She and her crew could get where they needed to go through the emergency-access doors anyway, and they had the freight elevator to use—as she showed Merry one night, when Merry helped her haul an especially bulky cart full of cleaning supplies to the basement parking garage. Merry had taken careful note of the route (you never knew when a back door would come in handy, right?), then left the building by her usual door, internally laughing at the guard who glared her on her way. Ancient corporate secret: you want a project to move, make friends with the secretary of the boss; you want to get a clean office and backdoor access, make friends with the janitors.

Her conscience did bother her a bit on that score; was she exploiting Olga's friendship for her own devious ends? That somehow felt more dishonest than simply taking MedaGen's pay while plotting against them. After all, she was giving them good value for the money, and getting the research files just *might* show that AllSafe really was all safe. However, she decided that she wasn't taking advantage of Olga by providing a listening ear and a friendly smile, and nothing Merry did with the research files would have dire consequences for the cleaning crew. After discussing it—and Carmen's urging her to pray about it—Merry felt justified in acquitting herself of the charge of janitorial exploitation.

Merry mercilessly exploited the business-world loophole known as the three-hour lunch to go home and see Missy during the day. Well, not exactly home, but to Carmen's, which was close. Missy was always glad to see her, telling her mama in Missy-ese all about the morning's activities (she made up in enthusiasm what she lacked in actual conversational skills). Merry read stories to her and put her down for her nap before leaving—"back to the old salt mine again," as Tony and Carmen put it—but couldn't stop the guilt from bubbling up every time she dropped Missy off. Carmen tried to reassure her that Missy still loved her and wouldn't hold it against her, when she had to leave: "It's not forever, and she knows you love her. Sometimes things just don't turn out. She'll understand." That helped, but it was almost more than Merry could take when Missy fell down and turned to Carmen to kiss her scraped knee better. Merry had helped put the bandage on (amazing how a bandage can perk up a kid), read another story, and finally left, more determined than ever to get back to being a mom again. How did Chris leave every day?

CHAPTER 13

"It takes a high level of personal and professional commitment to accomplish as much as you have here." Ms. Zelik surveyed Merry's chart-filled cubicle and favored her with a wintry smile. "You've made excellent progress in the short time you've been here. How long has it been?"

"Thank you. Just over three months," Merry smiled back, keeping her eyes modestly lowered. The Top Brass had suddenly descended on their lab area that morning, Humphrey leading the inspection parade. Merry had only a few minutes' warning—a brief message from Humphrey: "Brass coming. Impressed with you. Smile." She'd taken his advice, showing Ms. Zelik her project-management methods and progress reports, smiling again for the picture that the company's newsletter photographer had snapped of her and the COO.

"Impressive. The company always appreciates employees who really give their all to make their projects successful," Ms. Zelik said, mostly for the benefit of the company reporter who'd come to record the event for the edification of MedaGen employees all over the world. Merry's reputation, chart-covered cubicle, humble request for access, and savvy e-mail memo had given Humphrey a chance to grab the brass ring of corporate recognition: a personal visit by the top execs and a tasty spot in the company's year-end news wrap-up. Being a consummate politician with an eye out for the main chance at all times, Humphrey had indeed grabbed it. He'd get his name and face splashed over the newsletter, along with Merry's, and get in as much schmoozing as possible, too.

"That's exactly what I've tried to do," Merry agreed. "Which is why I requested additional access to network files."

Zelik gave her a narrow look. "And how exactly would that help? You couldn't understand the research itself, after all."

Merry swallowed a flash of "Oh, yeah?" and forced herself to nod. "Maybe not, but I could certainly tell when the reports had been updated, as well as overall progress on the research." She gestured to the Gantt charts showing the timelines for her projects. "I've found that one of the primary barriers to getting projects done on time is that the scientists on the research teams don't like to find time to report their progress. I understand why—they're busy, everybody is." She hesitated slightly, stealing a quick glance at Zelik's impassive face and remembering what she'd heard about the COO from Humphrey, then decided to go for it. "Or it could be that the team leads don't like having to account for their progress to a mere project manager—and a young woman on top of that. Most of them are men, after all, and very senior."

Zelik's face got even colder, if that were possible. "It's unfortunate that such Neanderthal attitudes still persist, but they certainly do." She glanced at Humphrey, who sorrowfully shook his head at such macho idiocy, at the company reporter, then back at Merry. She smiled again. "MedaGen certainly isn't a company to let outmoded attitudes stand in the way of progress. Ms. Anthony, you've not only pointed out a problem, but you've also suggested an excellent efficiency measure to solve it. I'll talk to the tech support department about getting you the access you need to the research files."

She was flicking out her phone as she spoke. The next few razor-edged words went straight to the office of the Chief Technology Officer. Pausing only to ask Merry her network ID, Zelik issued her orders, pausing again only long enough for the expected humble obedience before she hung up on the technician. "There. That's taken care of. And, in recognition of your proactive handling of this situation, you'll be promoted to Senior Project Manager grade."

"Thank you, Ms. Zelik!" Merry didn't have to fake the excitement in her voice—not for the promotion, but for the additional network access.

Zelik nodded regally, said something boilerplate about keeping up the good work, glanced at her watch, and swept out of the room.

Her flunkies hurried along in her wake. Humphrey somehow managed to come out in front, opening the door obsequiously and ushering them along.

Merry barely saw them go. She'd swirled her chair right back to her computer and tried her new network privileges. Sure enough, her password opened the previously restricted area of the network that stored the research data. In fact, it looked like a personal call from Zelik had rattled the technician so much that he (or she, be fair) had not just given Merry access to her own projects' files, but to the general R&D area. Yes! One step closer; now, she just had to unearth the files she needed without tipping anybody off to the search. Scrolling through the list was daunting—good heavens, how many projects did MedaGen have going on at once? And how could she find what she was looking for in that overwhelming mass of data?

A soft sound behind her made her jump. She quickly closed the directory, slewing around in her chair again—to see Humphrey slouch against her cubicle wall. He tossed a small, wood-and-brass plaque to her. "In official recognition . . . Senior Project Manager . . . [blank]." They hadn't had time to put her name on the generic award yet.

"Congratulations, you got a personal gold star from the Wicked Witch of the West Tower. Nice touch, accusing the R&D guys of dissing you because you're a woman. Of course, that promotion she gave you is mostly an administrative thing, to edge out a male competitor and look good on paper," Humphrey told Merry blithely. Apparently, the COO and her entourage had progressed to the next point on their royal tour. "She's paranoid about other women. You've been pigeonholed as a Senior Project Manager, and she can walk away feeling smug about derailing a potential rival."

"And how nice of you to tell me all of that," Merry shot back.

"Just here to help, kid," Humphrey assured her, giving her a glinting grin as he left. "Don't want you getting a swelled head."

"No swelled head at all," Merry said softly, tossing and neatly catching the small plaque commemorating her promotion. *Just a bigger title and that much more access.* She had to admit that she felt a little smug, too. More to the point, she felt very impatient for Humphrey to vanish, so she could dive back into her search.

Two hours later, however, both impatience and smugness had given way to gray weariness. There were just too many files! The information went on forever: studies on stem-cell cures for Parkinson's disease, research probing the possible link between fetal tissue and an Alzheimer's vaccine, animal trials for a DNA cocktail to fight the ravages of arteriosclerosis, results for preliminary simulation tests of what she recognized as Chris's Protocol 4 diabetes treatment. Merry sat almost sightlessly staring at the results scrolling down the screen—promising, actually, with the digital pancreatic cells responding positively to the genetic material that prompted them to begin manufacturing insulin in 8 cases of 10—before she lurched to her feet, blinking back tears of frustration and loneliness.

* * *

The security cameras weren't in tune enough to pick up the tears, but Carmen was. She patted Merry's shoulder sympathetically, helping her bundle Missy into the car. "Tough day?" she asked, as she set a dinner tray on the seat beside Missy's booster.

Merry gave her a sardonic grin. "Actually, I got a promotion. And the Wicked Witch of the Top Brass, Ms. Zelik herself, gave me access to the research files on the network."

Carmen whooped softly. "That's great!" She looked at Merry again and blinked. "Isn't it? I'm getting some mixed signals here, sweetie."

"It is great," Merry agreed, leaning against the side of the car. She glanced away, into the streetlight-spangled darkness of the neighborhood. Lights of distant houses climbed the low hills like an endless spider web of data points in a network. "It's just that there's so *much* of it there, and I don't really know where to start looking. I don't want to randomly poke around too much, because somebody's bound to notice, and I don't want to answer nosy questions." She sighed, feeling stupid, emotional, and weak, fighting the gnawing loss. Chris wasn't gone, he just wasn't *here*. "And while I was finding out how lost I am in the maze, I found Chris's research—the research Lia's been going on with. Looks like he just may have found a cure for diabetes after all."

"Of course he did," Carmen said staunchly, giving Merry an impulsive hug. "Trust the Galens to come up with the way to make it right, I always say."

"Yes, you always do," Merry smiled gratefully at her friend. "Whether it's warranted or not."

"It is," Carmen assured her, then glanced up at Merry thoughtfully, a hint of mischief dancing in her dark eyes. "Of course, sometimes even Galens need some help. Go home, Merry. Have some dinner, read a book with Missy—and then pray about it. He's always there to help us, you know. You just have to *ask* occasionally."

"Just have to ask occasionally," Merry repeated. The words had echoed between her ears all the way home. She smiled at Carmen's easy faith, wishing she were so sure—of anything reassuring—as she pulled Missy's bib over the baby's tousled curls. A soft chiming announced that the oven had finished warming up a dish of Carmen's superlative stir fry. "Dinner time, babykins."

"Jus ask," Missy advised solemnly, looking at her mother.

"You too, huh?" Merry asked her, carefully dishing rice and vegetables into Missy's bowl.

"Jus ask," Missy said again, then banged her spoon on her highchair tray. "Dinner time!"

"Speaking of asking," Merry caught the spoon. "How about you say blessing for us?"

That went over big, as it always did. Merry prompted, Missy ripped through an enthusiastic prayer mostly in English, but still partly in Missy-ese, and then equally enthusiastically demolished her bowl of stir fry.

Bathing Missy, reading the obligatory three bedtime stories (she didn't do voices as well as Chris, but she tried), and helping her say her prayers went by altogether too quickly. Despite her weariness, however, Merry ended up in the study instead of her bedroom, gazing at her computer screen. The original records scrolled by, chemical signatures for the genetic material in the vaccine, maps of the gene sequence where the mutated DNA should go, her own quick and dirty simulations of the effects of those snipped-off bits of genetic instructions. At the end of the column came partial accounts of off-shore human trials of the Corinth vaccine, safely removed from FDA observers, partial information on a half-hundred research subjects desperate enough (for cures or for money) to participate in testing an unknown drug. So many hints, so many subtle warnings that stood out like flashing Caution signs for anybody with the expertise to read them, but so little hard evidence that any of those unknown test subjects had needed another dose of the vaccine to keep their immune systems from eating them alive. It had to be out there, though. MedaGen *had* to have the hard data, whether it showed the results she and Chris expected—or whether it showed that the vaccine was as completely safe and effective as the company's marketing campaign claimed. From here, though, all the hints blurred together into a big, gray mess of speculation.

Merry sighed and turned off the screen, finally stumbling into the bedroom. She forced herself to concentrate on the words of the chapter of the Book of Mormon open in her lap; she opened to the place where she and Chris had left off in their study, and she still "heard" Amulek as a cultured Scotsman. It made her laugh through the ache in her throat. Angels and revelations, prophecies and visitations, faith and trials—the words gradually absorbed her into the meaning of the verses. At last, she put the book away, kneeling to say her own prayers. Yes, including a soft, heartfelt, "Please show me those files, Heavenly Father. Please tell me where to find them. What should I be looking for? Where should I look?" She didn't know whether to laugh or cry when nothing but the soft hum of the fan answered her.

* * *

"Well, lookee who I found." Pizarro grinned broadly, hooking his thumbs into his gun belt. The sheriff lounged against the freshly painted (and gilded) logo on the door of a brand-new vehicle.

Mercedes this time, Dove noted. Apparently, Pizarro had traded up since Dove drove off in his patrol car. The gigantic, shiny, four-wheel drive beast looked as out of place in the church parking lot as Pizarro himself did. He should've gone with his first instinct and run out the far door of the church the minute he spotted the glittering monstrosity out the doors. The sheer disbelief that Pizarro would face him down on a Sunday morning, at a Mormon chapel, had kept him from making a fast escape. He still had a hard time really believing the sheriff was standing there talking to him—weren't devils supposed to steer clear of holy sites? Nope, it was Pizarro, all right, and he didn't vanish into smoke as Dove paced over to trade stares with him.

The distinctions between murder, self-defense, and wartime (very finely distinguished in Dove's newly baptized black, white, and red conscience) spooled out in his memory, arguing against grabbing the gun cinched to that fat slob and blowing him away. One fast grab, two to the head, four to the torso, a spray of crimson, and the whole problem would hit the dirt—just like Benny had. A faint taste of metal and salt rose in the back of Dove's throat. He came to a halt in front of Pizarro, hate, conscience, and curiosity keeping him still as he faced the intruder.

Dove's silent gaze irritated the sheriff, who unhooked his thumb to poke Dove heavily in the chest. "Looks like the pigeon's flown the coop—but didn't fly far enough. Get your feathers together, kid, and get in. Don't kick up a fuss, and maybe you'll make it back to the station in one piece."

"What's up, sheriff?" Sam, decked out in his Sunday-suit civvies, walked over to make the third point of the triangle. Renata watched from the shadow of their car, holding both her girls close. She whispered in Abish's ear, patting her quickly toward the church.

Pizarro dismissed Sam after a single, raking glance. "Nothing you need to worry about, Reverend. This boy's wanted for questioning."

Just then, Abish came out of the doors, hauling Bishop Yazzie along. He spotted Pizarro even before the little girl pointed at him. A silent exchange of nods with Renata told him all he needed to know.

"Well, hey, Sheriff. What brings you this far out of your jurisdiction?" Bishop Yazzie asked, smiling even as all his cop hardness surfaced in his expression.

Pizarro returned the smile with equal lack of warmth. "Just here to take this boy in."

Bishop Yazzie discreetly gestured Sam's protest into silence. He surveyed the sheriff's vehicle, uniform, badge, and person with all the tender appreciation of a man examining a particularly slimy species of cockroach. "You have a warrant, you can take it up with the Navajo Tribal Police. If it's a valid charge, we'll handle it."

"Jurisdiction? Warrant?" Pizarro repeated. "Navajo Tribal Police?" He let a juicy hawk and spit tell the bishop exactly what he thought of jurisdictions, warrants, and the local law enforcement.

Bishop Yazzie bristled, all cop inside that bishopric suit.

Dove stepped in fast. "Me and the sheriff here go way back," he assured his leader. "He's not here to arrest me. All that warrant talk is just to scare me so I'll talk to him. Don't take account of how rude he is; he's just used to throwing his weight around. Right, *Gordo?*" He turned a sparkling smile on the sheriff.

That got him lowering looks from all three men, but Dove didn't pause. He patted Sam's arm, adding just a hint of push, and walked past Pizarro. "So we'll talk, and I'll be right back."

Sam and the bishop, looking skeptical, held their ground. Pizarro took the hint and stalked after Dove, around to the other side of the Mercedes. "Cooperative, huh?" he growled, swinging a heavy fist at Dove.

Dove caught the fist, hard, and threw it back at Pizarro. Fury lit his dark eyes as he spat a curse at the sheriff. "You want to find out how cooperative I feel like being? What are you doing here? Didn't get enough with watching Slick blow away Benny and me? Need more enemies around here? These people don't make deals with borderland scum like you."

"Just borderland scum like you?" Pizarro shot back, looking sly. "I heard you'd gone and went Mormon on us. Where's your black hat and side whiskers?"

"That's Amish—or Hasidic Jews," Dove retorted, unable to stop himself.

"Like it matters. You're still scum, and your hide's due for curing." Pizarro shrugged, glaring at Dove. "Things have changed back home, Nakai. You're in hot water now, and you got no more big guns behind you."

Dove swallowed, hoping Pizarro couldn't see the flush he felt on his cheeks. That meant *Abuelo* was out of the picture—either because he'd colluded with Slick on the ambush, or because Slick had arranged an ambush for him. Either way, the thought made Dove queasy.

Pizarro grinned again. "Oh, yeah, troubles just follow you like homing pigeons, Dovey. Think you can get away so easy? I found you easy enough, tracking that cruiser you stole. Even the Navajo Tribal Police can't cover up theft of law-enforcement vehicles, jurisdiction be stuffed. I start asking around, and there you are—some kid, shot up, hiding out with a nice little family." His gaze flicked to Sam and Renata, waiting tensely across the lot. "Be a real shame if anything happened to them."

"What would happen?" Dove asked, keeping his tone casual, careless—yet menacing. "And who'd do it?"

"Who knows? Been a lot of people hacked off at Mormons," Pizarro said noncommittally. "Course, some are more nasty than others. The General, for one. I've heard tell that Mormons got under his hide down south, and he's been ticked at them ever since." He held up a blunt hand, forestalling Dove's question. "Now, the General doesn't know where you are. Yet. But that could change, depending on whether you cooperate."

"I don't cooperate with anybody." Dove returned the sheriff's look silently, curiosity slamming into a psychic blank wall.

Pizarro suddenly leaned closer, as if proximity could add power to his drill-bit glare. "What does the General want you for, Nakai? What've you got that's got him and Slick combing the desert for you?"

Dove didn't flinch back. With one disdainful flick, he wiped away a trace of Pizarro's spit from his cheek. "Like I'd tell you anything. Slick wants to know, he can ask me himself. If he thinks he can catch me here. I know to look out for ambushes now."

"Slick'd like that answer," Pizarro told him, the glare deepening. "He doesn't like Mormons any more than the General. Any more than me. Think hard, Nakai. Things could go south pretty quick, you step the wrong way." He glanced around, at the chapel, the cars, the few families still waiting, the Begays. "Be a real pity if things started happening around here, like they did down at Deming, huh?"

"What do you want, *Gordo*?" Dove asked, as the sheriff turned away and opened the door of the brand-new land cruiser.

Pizarro looked back at him, shrugged. "I want the price of my cruiser taken out of your hide, if nothing else pans out. Before I skin you, though, I want to know about the General. What he's planning, what he's up to—what he's afraid of. You tell me why the General wants you caught, I may be able to help you."

"I don't need your help," Dove informed him, disgusted with the whole situation. "Like I could count on it—you'd sell me out just as fast as you're selling out the General. Whatever side your bread's buttered on, right, Pizarro? Just like Rico, selling your soul for any advantage you think you see. You got any honor? Any conscience? Any clue that the General's going to find out and kill you for a turn-coat—or just cause you got in his way?"

"I got plenty of clues," Pizarro said with infuriating, thick-headed calm. "Like, rumor's going 'round that Slick's expecting a big ship-ment of something from down south, coming in the end of this week. Rico's strutting around, promising everybody who'll listen to him that they're going to have to respect him or cough blood in two weeks' time. Sounds to me like they're planning their big move right now—and with how hard they're looking for you, sounds like they also moved up their timetable to beat whatever it is they figure you're going to do. Which ain't much, from what I can see."

The sheriff surveyed him scornfully, spitting into the dust beside Dove's borrowed Sunday shoes. "Looks like they don't have to worry about you doing much of anything useful, outside of trying to save what soul you got. You going to quote scripture to me some more, or you going to get smart and spill the important stuff? Speak up now, and I'll be able to offer you—and your little cult here—some protec-tion from whatever Slick's going to bring up here."

"I've got nothing to say to you," Dove informed him, hiding the cold, sick feeling that dropped like a ticking bomb into his gut. The end of the week? Rico telling everybody they had two weeks to decide to worship him? It was all Dove could do to stay impassive and suppress his urge to run for the truck; he concentrated on turning on his heel and stalking away. *At least I know that we've already got protec-tion better than anything you could offer*, he thought silently, *against you, Slick, the General and all the other devils.*

Pizarro reached for him—and his hand rebounded off Bishop Yazzie's shoulder. The sheriff and the Navajo cop glared at each other. Dove glanced over his shoulder when the gestures began, but kept walking. He'd made his exit, and now it looked like the bishop and Sam had a couple of their own points to make. He'd made it to the truck when Sam caught up.

"What did he want?" Renata asked, looking from Dove's set face to Sam's dark expression.

"He wanted to come up here, onto the Rez, and intimidate us," Sam growled, before Dove could answer.

"Well, shows he doesn't know much about us," Renata noted. She looked at Sam, raising her eyebrows. "Looks like Bishop Yazzie put him in his place—but if I know you, you had to put your two cents in too. How many sheep-camp words did you use when you told him what you thought of him?"

That question brought a half grin to Sam's face. Renata's campaign to clean up his language had been remarkably successful—around home, at least. "Just enough, I'd say, but Bishop Yazzie did most of the talking," he told her, then looked at Dove. "Get in, we're leaving. And I'll talk to you about your really bad taste in acquaintances when we finally get some dinner."

"I'm afraid that it's going to get a lot worse before it gets better," Dove warned him. "Sam, I think I just ran out of time."

Pizarro watched Dove climb into the back of Sam's pickup. The gleam of the windshield reflected in the sheriff's mirrored sunglasses as the truck drove past him and out of the church lot.

The fire that burned the church to the ground that night reflected in them, too, but both the sunglasses and their owner were gone long before sunrise. That left only the black smear of smoke to hang above the charred remains of the building—and the sooty, tired, and disbelieving rescue crew who'd arrived as soon as a half-drunk sheep herder reported seeing a "burning bush" up by the Mormon church. The volunteer fire department—and most of the male members of the ward—had arrived in time to fight a last-ditch, losing battle against the flames. They had to settle for making sure that the sparks didn't fly beyond the conflagration to light the dry vegetation beyond the parking lot. At least that effort worked; the building, however, was a total loss.

An arson investigator from the fire department hadn't even climbed out of his truck before he offered his formal diagnosis:

"Somebody doesn't like you guys much at all." That remark had prompted an ironic laugh from the small knot of weary, disbelieving civilians.

Sam wiped black off his face with a marginally less carbon-covered hand and sighed, surveying the damage. "This what your sheriff Pizarro uses as a subtle hint?"

"He's not my sheriff," Dove snapped. Fury ground so hard in his gut he felt sick. It just added to the weight that had kept him tossing and turning all night, despite Sam's argument that somebody else—the *federales*, the Border Patrol, the Army—would handle Slick and whatever the General was sending up. Dove listened, thought about it, and absolutely did not believe it for a second. Sam had finally told him to sleep on it, while he ran the whole virus scenario by Bishop Yazzie. They'd met the bishop in the morning, all right—just after midnight, in fact. Fighting the fire hadn't given them any time to broach the subject of stopping Slick's impending shipment, however.

"He's not your sheriff," Sam agreed.

"I'm sorry," Dove said, about the whole thing—snapping at Sam, the church burning down, Pizarro knowing about them in the first place.

"It's not your fault," Sam told him as the bishop and Joe came over to them. "Looks like that borderlands sheriff probably set this off."

"Think this has to do with him trying to pick you up yesterday?" Bishop Yazzie asked, wiping his own face with a bandana.

"Yeah, it's probably my fault," Dove told him.

Sam smacked him reprovingly.

"How's it your fault?" Joe asked.

The bishop sighed. "Sheriff Pizarro came out here yesterday hassling Dove, threatening me with 'agency' action if the Tribal Police didn't prosecute for 'theft of official property.' That was his patrol car you spotted, Joe. The sheriff's in bed with a bunch of drug runners, gang bangers, and that crazy General from down south. He was there when that flea-bitten Southerner ambushed Dove and his brother too."

"He's a ways out of his jurisdiction, isn't he?" Joe noted, a hard smile underlining the understatement.

"We don't have to put up with this," Sam said flatly. "Pizarro or his goons come back 'round here again, they'll eat lead."

"Hey, watch it with the vigilante talk," the bishop warned. He sighed. "I made a mistake not asking Dispatch to get a car out to shadow the sheriff out past the border—or doing it myself."

Sam shrugged. "If he shows up again, you will—now that we know what he's up to. This won't happen again."

"And what will happen?" Bishop Yazzie asked, weariness and bitterness washing through his tone like the smoke that turned his voice husky. "More goons show up, start burning houses instead of churches? We've got families, Sam. We're civilians, not soldiers. We can't start a war with drug dealers or crazy Generals."

"We won't start a war," Sam assured him. "Dove here's not the only one who's a fan of General Moroni. And we're not hung out to dry like the poor townies around the border. The Rez takes care of its own."

"That we do." The bishop grinned, straightening his shoulders. Weariness fell away as his usual confidence and determination won over a night's worth of no sleep. "And we will. The Tribal Police will increase patrols and spread the word—"

"And if Pizarro comes back, he'll find us waiting for him. That son of a conquistador has messed with the wrong bunch of Indians!"

Sam's heated pronouncement, loud enough to carry a fair ways, got a round of cheers and laughter from the weary group of firefighters and Church members. The enthusiastic reaction startled Sam for a second, but he recovered fast, giving them a fist-waving salute and grinning.

Eventually, Bishop Yazzie organized the crowd, strategy and plotting going on left and right. Dove's further explanation of what Pizarro said about Slick—and his own theory about the viruses the General was shipping north—only increased the tension.

"Viruses, now, eh? As if drugs and guns weren't bad enough, the gangs got to get into viruses now." Bishop Yazzie ran a hand over his hair, looking at Dove. "When is this going to happen?"

"End of the week," Dove said tightly. "That's when Pizarro said they were expecting it."

"Not a lot of time, especially for Homeland Security to get involved." The bishop closed his eyes, thinking about layers of bureaucracy. "And they're the ones who'd handle it. I'll get the wheels turning with the FBI. Maybe they've heard something too, through their sources—the ones who don't have their hands full with Arabs and Russians and whatever else. They might be able to jar the Mexican authorities loose on it too, get some help from across the border." He patted Dove's shoulder. "Thanks to the early warning, we just might be able to stop this."

Joe called for Bishop Yazzie, motioning him over to talk to the reporter who'd shown up. The bishop sighed, straightened his jacket, and headed over.

Sam and Dove got into the truck and headed for home, Sam articulating the arguments and suggestions he planned to give the bishop, the FBI, and anybody else who could be convinced that they had to get to the borders fast and put a stop to Slick—and whoever was helping him. He paused only long enough to pump Dove for specific information about what Pizarro was likely to do about it all.

"He's not quite in bed with the General," Dove told Sam. "He's lying back, watching which way the wind goes. The *Señor's* gone— that was him got car-bombed outside the bullfight a few weeks ago— so Pizarro's looking to see whether Slick's here to stay and what the General's going to do. He'd heard about the viruses, and Rico bragging around, and that made him wonder. That's why he was here. He thought I might know something more about it."

"Do you?" Sam asked.

"I'm not sure. I know that the General's got Slick up here gathering up all the enforcers in the area, taking over from the drug runners. I don't 100 percent for sure know, but I think that the General's messing around with bio-weapons—like I told the Bishop." Dove considered what else he knew, what his instincts (now heightened, he figured, with the additional wisdom of the Holy Ghost) were telling him, and finally added, "And I know I've got to stop Slick back down there. I've seen what that virus can do, and it just can't get loose. Especially not with Slick behind it."

Before Sam could say anything, Dove went on. "He's got to be stopped. What's the odds that the FBI, or Homeland Security, or whoever, is going to pay attention to a rumor coming out of the Navajo Reservation—especially when they find out it's some punk gang banger who's spreading it? The General's smart, Sam; what's the odds that there's been loose talk about his future plans? He's been using diseases to wipe out drug runners' bases down south, and nobody's pinned him for that. FBI, Army, all those guys want proof before they start blasting away within U.S. borders. Pizarro's not going to do it, and he's all the legal authority we've got back home."

Dove snorted, thinking over the status quo. "Him and *Abuelo's* gang. Nobody else said boo; they were just grateful not to have to dodge bullets every day. Things weren't real good with the *Señor* and Pizarro, but they were relatively smooth. Everybody knew how much to pay to keep from getting hassled. Slick's taken over, but he doesn't care about the guys who run the *taquerios* or the *abuelas* playing bingo. Without somebody in charge, keeping the real thugs like Rico in line, things are going to go bad fast. This church burns down here, the Rez will clamp down on outsiders, keep it from happening. Mama Rosa's burns down back home, people won't say two words—unless they've got somebody they think can beat Slick and Rico."

"And you think you can beat Slick and Rico where the Feds can't, huh?" Sam asked, skeptical. "Dove, we've got the legal authority and the right to kick Pizarro's fat behind if he sets foot on the Rez. We got nothing to say about what goes on down near the border. We're not soldiers, we're property owners and cops."

Dove gave him a hard smile. "No, you're not soldiers—but I know some people who are." He touched Sam's shoulder lightly. "Listen, it's not that I can do what the Feds can't, it's that they can't do it as fast as it has to happen. If they get in, great—but if they don't, it'll be too late before they get there. Nobody else knows about this; even Pizarro doesn't have the whole story. That's why he's up here. Pizarro doesn't care about you, and he doesn't want to start a war with the Navajo Nation. This was just a friendly warning, Amexica style. He wants to flush me out, find out what I know about Slick, so he can figure out which way to jump, which side he can play to make the biggest profit. I don't want Renata and the girls—or you—in the middle of a war, either. You don't deserve this. You're not in a position to fight outside your territory, but others are. And they don't have as much to lose—or worry about. Plenty of the guys in our gang didn't like Slick; they went along with it 'cause *Abuelo* did, or 'cause they were scared of Rico. I'll bet that I can convince a bunch of them to back me up, especially if they figure they can get rid of Slick."

"You're going to collect a bunch of juvenile delinquents to fight off a wannabe dictator?" Sam asked, giving him a look that added, "You've got to be kidding, or mental."

"The wannabe dictator's just got a bunch of overgrown juvenile delinquents on his side. That's why Slick recruited us. We're the soldiers of the borderlands revolution," Dove pointed out. He laughed. "The youth of today, like the newscast's always crying about. Teenagers with guns. Helaman had an army; why not us, too?"

Sam shook his head. "Helaman's army—that was a *real* war, Dove, not a—"

"Not a gang war? Or a war against drug dealers or crazy Generals?" Dove grinned at him, confidence and determination rapidly rising. "You can get just as killed in this war as in any other. I think this is the perfect chance to 'liken the scriptures unto us,' especially where it comes to protecting our religion, our families, and homes. I brought it down on you here, and you've got a handle on it. Slick's brought it down back home, and I'll take care of it."

"Don't pull a martyr act on me, *Hasbidí*," Sam warned.

"Getting killed is the last thing I'm planning," Dove assured him. "Like another crazy general said, the point isn't dying for your country—it's making the other guy die for *his* country. In this case, though, we'll settle for kicking them so hard their grandparents will hurt whenever they think about coming after Mormons—or coming up north with their viruses."

"You really think you can do it?" Sam asked, trying for skeptical but not quite completely doubting. Dove looked not just cocky but bone-deep confident, with the kind of assurance that probably meant either he really could successfully fight Pizarro, Slick, and this mysterious General Garza—or he was deluded enough to really believe he could. Sometimes, Sam had to admit silently to himself, that worked out to be the same thing.

"Yes," Dove said simply.

"Vigilante justice is still illegal," Sam reminded him. "You get hold of Pizarro around here and start pulling stunts like assault and battery, Bishop Yazzie will have to arrest you. Even if he thinks the guy deserved it, you are in Tribal Police jurisdiction, and the law still says that we've got to convict him before we can slap him around."

Dove grinned. "So I won't do anything in Navajo Tribal Police territory. I wasn't planning to anyway—the further away I get, the less likely they are to hurt you. I'm going back home—what was home. I'll check things out, see if Pizarro's telling the truth, and watch Slick. I'll let you know where I am, so the FBI can get hold of me when they come riding in like the Union Cavalry to save the day. If it looks like the *federales* are going to take care of it, I'll back right off. If it looks like they don't believe us, I'll find a way to get that virus away from Slick before he can use it. Either way, I'll be back when I've taken care of business there."

"Is there anything I can do to talk you out of this?" Sam asked, thinking of Renata. He had to ask, out of grown-up responsibility, even though the idea of gathering a bunch of gang members to hit Pizarro back sounded very appealing indeed in the bit of his brain that was still—and would probably always be—eighteen years old.

"No," Dove said.

"Is there anything I can do to help, besides helping the bishop get the word out to the legitimate authorities?" Sam finally conceded the inevitable. "Within tribal rules?"

"Getting the word out is great. I've got help on the foot-soldier stuff, or I will have," Dove answered, still with that strangely compelling confidence. He shot Sam a calculating look. "I might need some surveillance help, some missing-persons, police-files type stuff. If you think Bishop Yazzie would go for it, while we're waiting for the FBI guys."

Sam gave him a calculating look right back, then grinned. "I think we could arrange for a little inter-departmental cooperation. Just remember that you're a citizen deputy when you ask."

"Sure." Dove grinned, picturing himself with a badge and a hat. Never one to stop a winning streak, he added, "Also, I could use a ride down to Silver City. I can make my own way from there."

He got a shower first—as did Sam—and a good breakfast. And a furious argument from Renata; she pointed out the arrogance of his thinking the chapel burning was all his fault (there had been two others, after all, and one in Deming just two weeks ago), the stupidity of thinking he could face down a corrupt sheriff and a bent gang leader at once, the fact that he was just eighteen and in no way the next Julius Caesar. She didn't appreciate him saying he was only the backup plan, in case the *federales* didn't show, and that he intended to be more like a morally enlightened Pancho Villa, all things considered. (She also didn't appreciate Sam's refusal to jump into the argument on her side.) But even her most fierce mama threats couldn't dent Dove's resolve—and, finally, she hugged him hard and told him not to do anything stupid, to kick those slime dogs back to the Stone Age, and to come back to them in one piece this time. He returned the hug, patted both girls as they squeezed the stuffing out of him, and waved until they were out of sight behind Sam's truck. Then the second debate started, this one about tactics. Dove let Sam talk as the desert miles rolled by, reminiscing about his stint in the Army, pointing out the characteristics of gang leaders from the FBI profiles, reviewing divide-and-conquer tactics that the Nephites used so often, repeating the warning about trusting in the arm of the flesh, cautioning Dove about going on the attack or using underhanded tactics, the importance of prayer as a military tool, and anything else that came into his head.

"You sure about this?" Sam asked finally, leaning out the window of his truck as Dove shouldered the backpack Renata had insisted on putting together for him. "Nothing says you have to take this on."

"I'm sure," Dove said, for the hundredth time. He looked into Sam's eyes. "I know this is what I'm supposed to do. I *know* it. Do you really think I shouldn't?"

There is the rub, Sam thought. He sighed, checking his internal conscience compass again. "No. I really think you shouldn't. Be careful, Dove. Keep praying. We will be."

"I will," Dove said softly. "Love you—all of you."

"Call us when you can," Sam reminded him, for Renata—and for himself, too.

"Right. Now, get out of here before you blow my cover," Dove said gruffly. Goodbyes were bad. Not as bad as not getting to say goodbye, but bad. He started to turn away, but couldn't quite just leave. "Thanks again, Sam. Good hunting."

"You're welcome. It will be. Get going," Sam told him. The truck drove off, a thin trail of dust hanging in the still, warm air above the road.

An exorbitant cash down payment later, an invisible trail connected Dove through a satellite from the gas-station's uplink phone to Dolores's personal line. She always had her phone with her—trusting her boyfriend to pick up the tab. Dating Dolores was an expensive proposition. Dove personally thought Benny's assurance that she was "worth it" represented more wishful thinking and self-delusion than reality.

"Hey, Dolores," he said as she answered.

"Dove?" she yelped, after a moment's puzzled silence filled the connection. Her voice quickly dropped to a whisper. "Is that you?"

"Yeah, it's me," Dove told her. From the sound of the voice in the background, growling a question, Rico currently had the honor of paying Dolores's bills. The thought of Dolores kissing Rico made Dove gag. He fought down the snarl he felt rising in his throat. "I don't want to talk, Dolores. I just need Perro's number."

She hesitated, remembering Dove as the pesky kid always tagging after Benny, irritating but mostly harmless, giving her lip but always shoving over a plate in the morning, too. She regretted having to dump Benny, but a girl had to keep an eye on the direction the wind was blowing, and it had blown away from Benny pretty quick. *Nice guys finish last*, she reflected, *and Benny had been a very nice guy*. She'd taken it hard when he'd disappeared, but didn't let Rico see her cry when he bragged about Benny getting slagged. It could've been nostalgia, some spark of lingering affection, pique at Rico's insensitivity, or maybe a touch of guilt that prompted her to reel off a quick sequence of numbers, ending with "Don't call me."

"No fear," Dove muttered to the dead line. He dialed Perro's latest phone number. The gang got all of its electronic connections under the table, as part of their protection racket, so the numbers changed a lot. Dolores, with her addiction to yakking to her sister in Los Angeles and her habit of keeping a phone about her person at all times, acted as the gang's unofficial operator, keeping track of the pagers, beepers, phones, and PDDs that *Abuelo's*—now Slick's, Dove corrected himself—soldiers used. She was a better operator than girlfriend, even Dove had to admit. Though that wasn't really giving her a lot of credit.

"This is the big dog," his friend's voice said in his ear. From the sound of it, he and Calvin were tooling around town in the Dogmobile, and the muffler had gone out again. "Start barkin'."

"Big dog? More neutered Chihuahua, sounds like," Dove snorted.

"Dove!" Perro shouted. Dove could picture him practically climbing over the seat in surprise.

"Hey, Perrito," Dove laughed from the weird mix of relief, familiarity, and adrenaline that ran through him.

Perro's words tumbled over each other as he went into verbal over-drive. "*Hasbìdì!* Man, I knew you weren't dead! I knew it! Listen, Dove, you gotta come back. *Abuelo's* bit dust, Rico's taken over, thinks he's the big meat, but Slick's really running the game—bad game, like you said he would, too. They got something big going on. Some guys are in, but a lot of us *chiquitos* don't like what's up, like Franklin doesn't, neither. Serious, there's enough skinny going down here to curl your hair! You gotta come!"

"To tell you what to do, like always?" Dove asked, only half teasing.

"To tell me what to do, like always," Perro agreed. "Calvin, too. We gotta do something, and you always think of something smart to do. We need smart right now."

"Think the Dogmobile can make it to the Tesoro station just before the Silver City exit?" Dove asked.

"Baby, the Dogmobile be there in light speed," Perro agreed. "You have the master plan ready by then?"

"Yeah, I'll have the master plan ready," Dove assured him. "And my new buddies may get the FBI down on 'em, too. But even if the *federales* don't come through, we're not going to make it easy on 'em."

* * *

"Oh, please, don't make things easy on me," Merry growled. After a rough night full of dreams that had her looking everywhere for something she'd forgotten while Chris called to her to hurry, or they'd be late, the last thing she needed was more frustration at work. She'd been stuck in politically charged, boring meetings, got bad news that two projects were going to miss their deadlines by months, and had her lunch stolen out of the break-room refrigerator. The thought of another wrinkle in an already painful day made her cringe. But there it was, right in the middle of her tidy project-management task pile: a set of handwritten meeting notes (from a meeting she should've been invited to, by the way), with no identifying project name or number, and only a set of scrawled initials on them. "Well, thanks for making my day more interesting, XJT. Where's the fun in helping somebody else do her job so the whole team runs more smoothly?"

After a moment's time-out to bonk her head on the desk and feel silly about being so melodramatic, she set about comparing initials with team members on all likely projects. Actually, in this case, a match came up pretty quickly: Xavier Joseph Torres, working on the stem-cell lineage MedaGen had bought from a lab in Italy. She updated that project with the information Xavier had hastily written up. As she posted it, his unusual first name caught her eye—and pricked her memory. What's the odds of this happening? One of the trial subjects in Christoff's data had that first name too, but with an uncommon last name: Chaudry.

"Xavier Chaudry. I bet he doesn't run into a lot of duplicate phone book entries," Merry muttered, following the thought to its logical conclusion even as her fingers tapped the name into a network search.

The computer hummed and blinked, waiting for an answer as it sifted through mountains of records. After a subjective eternity, the computer chimed brightly. Four files gleamed in its match list, all buried deep in an eyes-only directory hidden in an obscurely named part of the system.

Merry shook her head at herself, as her hand quivered when she selected the first file. *Take a breath, girl. Be a scientist, for crying out loud! Cold-blooded objectivity, that's what we need here.* She took a deep breath, opened her eyes, and neatly opened all four documents. Her cold-blooded objectivity abruptly vanished. Data filled the screen: Xavier Chaudry, male, Hispanic/Indian, 28 years old, volunteer subject in the human trials for the Corinth vaccine. A black-and-white photo looked out at her, a youngish, sad-eyed man whose life had been reduced to a few lines in a subject file. Died of complications related to the trial, according to the cold note on the page. Merry flicked to the next document, the record of Xavier's actual treatment, dates and times of injections, careful notes about his progress—and then, when his number came up as part of the "initial treatment only" group, documenting his rapid decline and death. The cold-blooded objectivity of the descriptions ("fast-onset degradation of all connective tissue due to exaggerated immune response . . . hemorrhaging . . . hallucinatory effects") boiled down to one, horrifically calculated meaning: the researchers let him die to see if the immune system could readjust itself without the "booster." It didn't. Neither did those of the 19 other subjects whose files filled the same virtual file drawer as Xavier's.

They spread out on Merry's screen, file after file of cold facts (names, ages, ethnicities, etc.), starkly monochrome pictures—and detailed symptom descriptions garnishing the accounts of their horribly inevitable deaths. (Including the dosage amounts for the morphine that the researchers had administered to ease their human lab animals' descent into final darkness.) The files for the "follow-up" group, another twenty subjects temporarily luckier than their "initial treatment only" comrades, told a different story: the treatment's glowing success in curing their initial conditions, and the booster's glowing success in stopping the treatment from making chunky soup out of their insides. The treatment had proved just as effective with a group of volunteers who hadn't had any prexisting conditions—one dose of the vaccine, and no retrovirus or immune disease could take hold. The vaccinated volunteers showed no signs of infection or sickness six months after their exposure and inoculation; the volunteers in the control group had already developed symptoms or died. And the consent form, duly attached to each human guinea pig's file, mentioned only that "all subjects may not receive study medication," and that they might experience "some potentially adverse effects."

You could certainly look at death as a potentially adverse effect, Merry thought, stifling a reflexive laugh at the sick understatement of it. The fact that the consent forms were all in English, while the actual tests had taken place in South America using Spanish-speaking subjects, only added to the black villainy of it all.

With a crash of a trash can in another cubicle meeting Olga's mobile dumpster, current reality broke through her morbid fascination with the evidence that her hypothesis—their hypothesis—wasn't just a phantom born of bad data. She'd found the proof Yuan needed, all thanks to a strange last name and Xavier's laziness about taking proper minutes of meetings. It might not be the direct revelation she'd wished for last night, but she'd definitely take what she could get. Breathing a silent prayer of thanks, she directed the computer to copy the entire set of files. She had what she'd come for; now, she just had to grab it before anybody knew that she'd seen it. Get it, get it all, and get out! The machine hummed happily to itself as it extracted Christoff's incriminating data from its hiding place to a disc she could take with her.

She watched the progress bar creep along, dialing Carmen's number from her own phone—not the company-issued one on her desk. "Carmen? It's Merry. I know I'm late. I'm going to be a bit later." Swallowing against the quiver of excitement in her voice, she added, "Looks like that research project finally paid off."

Carmen's whoop came clearly through the phone. "Yes! Did I tell you? Oh, I wish Tony were here! I can't wait to see it! Wahoo!"

"It's not that pleasant to see," Merry cautioned, smiling at her friend's enthusiasm. "I'll be back as soon as I can. See you in a bit."

"Setting up an assignation?" Humphrey's voice chilled Merry to her bones. He leaned, casually as ever, against the entrance of her cubicle.

"You still here?" She managed a reasonably steady tone, stowing her phone in her purse and unhooking the heavy bag from its place hanging over her chair. For a moment, she considered trying to knock him out with it. Fortunately, the sheer silliness of that mental picture short-circuited the idea. Maybe he hadn't noticed. She itched to blank the screen, hide the tell-tale glow of the disk, but didn't dare move.

"No rest for the wicked," Humphrey assured her. He waved an electronic form in her direction. "I'm just here to double-check an anomaly in your resume. The whole Education section doesn't quite add up, now that we look at the numbers more carefully."

"Oh?" Merry blinked. "Why?"

"Why don't they add up? That's what I'm here to ask you," Humphrey said, stepping into her cubicle. "Why are we looking more carefully? Turns out getting a promotion isn't all cream and sugar, Anthony. Zelik ordered a background check when she boosted your network privileges." His eyes narrowed. "And it looks like that's not a bad idea. Copying a few files for light reading at home? Or just to trade with friends?"

Before she could stop him, he reached past her, hitting the Cancel command. The computer's reflexes were a bit quicker, however; it chimed that it was finished, and spit the disk into Merry's waiting hand. For a long second, they stared at each other, eyes locked over that thin piece of iridescent plastic. Determination replaced sheer panic in Merry's eyes; Humphrey's were unreadable, dark and still.

"Humphrey—Errol," Merry said softly, "they're killing people. Deliberately, in the offshore human trials. And they're setting up that vaccine to force people to pay for it again and again—or die. Badly."

"That's where I know you from," Humphrey said suddenly, snapping his fingers. "Galen's desk. He had a picture of a femme and a baby. You're her. The wife he told me not to talk about. Chris Galen—the original bleeding-heart Boy Scout." He shook his head, smiling bemusedly at the memory. "I thought you looked familiar when you came in to interview. Then, when your resumé seemed a little—well, the reverse of padded, more like there was stuff left off—I started checking and remembered where I'd seen you. In a picture. I just couldn't remember where the picture was. But it was on Galen's desk."

Merry stood up, moving carefully, as if the manager were a wild animal who might startle into attack at a sudden motion. The weight of the bag dragged against her shoulder. She wished that her martial-arts lessons had come with the Do-It-Yourself Spy Course she'd metaphorically signed up for.

Humphrey went on, half watching her. "He gave me that same line, about AllSafe not being safe, said he'd run into some files he shouldn't've seen. And now here you are, looking at those same files." His expression hardened. "I told him to forget it, to back off, to pay attention to his own stuff and keep his nose out, or he'd end up getting it cut off. You either go along with the Brass, or you end up as so much cat food. He didn't listen to me. Are you going to?"

"They're setting up the biggest extortion scheme in history," Merry said, praying silently for an opening, an inspiration, anything. "And they're trying to make it a law. That can't happen."

"Why not? It's going to." Cynical, weary lines settled onto his face. "They'll win. They always win. Put it down, Anthony—Galen. You're a smart kid. See reason. Put it down. I won't say anything, and we'll both get nice, fat bonuses at the end of the year to help us salve our consciences. Or yours, anyway. I don't have one anymore. I lost it along with my freedom and faith in humanity."

"The company doesn't own your soul, Errol." Merry edged toward the door, oozing cautiously around him. "Just your contract."

"Same thing." Humphrey watched her, his face completely still.

"I'm doing what I have to," Merry said, stepping into the passageway between the silent, empty cubicles. She looked at him once more, before whirling and running as fast as she could for the doors.

"So am I, just not as quick as I could," he said, more to himself than her. The cynical smile returned. "I'll consider this your resignation, effective immediately." He waited until she had disappeared through the armored doors of the lab room before he called Security to start the lockdown procedures.

Shortly, alarms rang in MedaGen's central security observation room—and on Ms. Zelik's personal phone. She hit the scene just seconds later, to see the late-shift security detail milling around in confusion.

"Where is she?" the head of security kept barking, as his frantic camera jockeys shifted from screen to screen. Empty corridors, a few executives and scientists working late hours, members of the cleaning crew—nowhere did the cameras capture the image of a former project manager pelting down the hallways toward the doors. The COO's sudden appearance only made his shouted questions more urgent.

She dropped a question of her own into the pandemonium. "What exactly is going on here?" Silence spread like ripples on the surface of a pond.

"We have a report of a potential network-security breach," the chief told her. "One of the lab managers called it in. Said he'd seen one of his team members download confidential files off the network.

She took off when he questioned her. We're scanning for her now, but we're not picking her up."

"Who is it?" Zelik asked, her calm tone coming not from understanding but from a predator's patience.

"Meredith Anthony," one of the security techs told her. "We're tracking her access. Her code's not registered on any of the door systems. We're watching all the doorways, so she can't tailgate out on anybody else. Not that there are many people to tailgate at this hour."

"She hasn't left the lab area yet," the security chief said confidently.

"Perhaps you should find where she is in the lab area, then." Zelik watched the security detail while they watched the screens, her freezing silence more effective than any additional shouting. There's nothing like imminent demise (personal or professional) to focus the attention.

At the moment, however, their attention was focused on the wrong thing. Merry had hit the double doors of the cubicle room, and instead of running like a nuclear-powered squirrel for the lab area's exit, she'd taken a fast left and jumped into the janitorial supply closet. As she'd expected, a couple of spare sets of coveralls hung on their hooks, and a huge cart full of supplies (three levels, mop bucket, squeegee tray, the works) filled most of the room's cramped floor space. By the time Humphrey got through to security, she'd shrugged into the coveralls, thrown her purse into the rag bag attached to the dusting equipment, put a kerchief around her hair, and strolled out of the closet pushing the cart down the hall. The camera—and the panicked security crew behind them—saw only a "PowerClean Crew" logo across the back of a gray coverall maneuvering a cleaning cart from doorway to doorway, neatly applying a squeegee to the narrow window in each office door.

Lupe, glancing up from vacuuming, blinked at seeing an unfamiliar janitor—and then blinked again when she saw that the unfamiliar janitor looked a lot like Meredith Anthony. Merry glanced at her, smiled, and winked, hoping Lupe would take the hint. Lupe smiled back, shrugged ("Whatever floats your boat, honey") and went back to her vacuuming.

Merry, breathing a silent sigh of relief—and a quick prayer that everything else would go that well—continued down the hall, forcing herself to move casually. *Project conscientious boredom: dip, swipe, wipe. Next window. Dip, swipe, wipe. Three more doors to the service entrance at the end of the line of offices.* At long last, she got to the door—and realized she didn't have the all-purpose passkey to open it. No! Panic filled her head, roaring like a stormy ocean—or like a vacuum.

"Lupe!" she called, hoping the corridor cameras didn't have audio pickups as well as visual. "Lupe!"

Lupe looked up at last, giving her a curious glance, the vacuum still rhythmically gliding across the short-pile carpet. Every step brought her closer to Merry, but just not quickly enough.

"Could you let me through?" Merry asked. She didn't gesture toward the door, leaning casually against the cart as she explained. "I don't have the key for this door. Would you swipe me through with your access card?"

"All right," Lupe shrugged, pulling the vacuum along behind her until she came level with Merry and the hijacked cart. "Why?"

"I need to get out of the building," Merry told her quietly. "Lupe, I'm in trouble with Security, and they're probably looking for me. I have to get out before they realize this is me they're seeing on their cameras."

Lupe's expression didn't change. She simply shrugged again, swiped her card through the door's reader, and keyed in the day's code. Then she turned back to her vacuuming, as if Merry were just another lint-headed coworker who'd forgotten to pick up her card.

"Thanks, Lupe," Merry said to her back. "Don't let them get you or DeShawn with that vaccine."

"I won't," Lupe said. The words blended with the growling of the vacuum. "Good luck."

Merry maneuvered the cart through the door, growling to herself at the thing's stubborn, inanimate-object awkwardness. Finally, she found herself in the maintenance elevator, and gratefully hit the button for the parking garage. She watched the numbers counting down, feeling her heart pounding. Now, she just had to get her car out of here. The question was how to get to the car. The cleaning cart and coverall that gave her perfect camouflage upstairs would stand out like a skunk in a snowfield in the garage. Olga had spent an enraged half hour complaining about getting attitude from an uppity security monkey telling her that the executives' garage was off-limits to the janitorial staff—and their junker cars. Okay, fine. Time to dump the janitor outfit, go back to her natural coloration, and hope that the word hadn't spread clear down here about *who* caused the security breach. *Cover me, please,* she thought toward an authority a lot higher than the security office on the top floor, as she peeled out of her coveralls and retrieved her purse.

She strolled out of the freight elevator and calmly walked under the eye of the camera pointed at the passenger elevators, all executive confidence and slightly impatient savoir faire. The chrome sheen of the elevators reflected her unremarkable appearance—and the kerchief still covering her hair. She quickly snatched it off and stuffed it into her jacket pocket as she headed for her car. The weight of the data disc, light as it was, seemed to pull the purse heavily against her shoulder. Glancing casually at her watch provided an excuse for keeping her head down, as did rummaging for her keys in her pocketbook. Of course, her hands had to forget how to insert a key into a lock, but she got it after a couple of tries. She didn't know whether to laugh at herself or scream in frustration when the ignition threatened to give her trouble too. Finally, the engine turned over, and the car slid smoothly out of its spot toward the gate.

Much to her horror, she saw a puzzled-looking gate guard hanging up the phone beside the gate bar. "They want a lockdown," he informed his partner in the booth.

"A lockdown?" she repeated, sliding up to the gate arm. "What's up, Nick?"

"Oh, hi, Ms. Anthony," the guard smiled at her. The garage guards, lower in status than the lobby guards, had a correspondingly higher friendliness level. "Yeah, we got word from upstairs that there's a general security alert on. They want us to shut the gate and not let anybody in—or out."

"Can I slip out?" Merry asked, not having to fake worried concern. "Missy's been at the babysitter's all day, and it's already late . . . " She let her appeal trail off into a sweetly pleading expression.

Bambi eyes worked as she'd hoped (of course, saying hello to Nick every night helped too). "Well, sure, don't see any harm in that. It's not like you're an outsider spy," he said. "Lift the bar, Phil," he called.

The gate arm rose slowly, its red-and-yellow length humming up out of the way as the steel teeth set in the concrete floor retracted.

"Stop her!" Ms. Zelik's voice echoed through the cement cave. She appeared in Merry's rearview mirror, leading a contingent of security guards—lobby guards, all hard looks and square jaws and unsympathetic eyes.

Nick, startled at their sudden appearance, slewed around in the booth, his hand reflexively going to the pistol at his belt. Phil, equally startled but more sedentary, just blinked, standing there with his hand on the switch. The lobby guards didn't hesitate, however. They ran forward like MedaGen-uniformed cheetahs, pulling out some decidedly un-cheetahlike sidearms as they came.

Merry looked from the rearview mirror to the windshield, smiled apologetically at Phil, and gunned the car forward. Sparks flew from the tailpipe as she bounced over the speed dip at a much higher velocity than the engineers (and the parking signs) recommended. Sparks also flew from the exposed steel beams as bullets ricocheted after Merry's retreating tail lights.

"Enough!" Zelik shouted over the fading engine noise and painfully amplified gunshots.

The lobby guards held their fire but didn't holster their weapons; instead, they leveled the hot barrels at Nick and Phil.

Zelik turned a furious glare on them, which for sheer threat put the guns to shame. "Why didn't you idiots stop her?"

Nick couldn't quite flash back at Zelik, so he glared at the guards instead. The "idiots" comment stung almost as much as the lobby guards' treating them like criminals. "She was gone before you told us it was her you wanted to stop! You want us to stop somebody, you tell us who to stop!"

"What could we do?" Phil asked, gesturing helplessly up the ramp.

"It seems we've issued you sidearms," Zelik observed, her tone dripping acid and poison. "Did you assume they were for decoration? Or to enhance your masculinity? Or to make it easier for you to commit suicide to atone for taking up valuable space and air on this planet?"

Neither gate guard had a response. Phil settled for looking at his shoes and mentally cleaning out his locker. Nick ground his teeth. He couldn't shoot a woman—not a woman he knew and liked, like Merry—but decided he wouldn't mind shooting Ms. Zelik at the moment. His fingers itched where they rested on his pistol.

Fortunately for Nick's continued existence, Zelik finished her tirade with a cold, "You're both fired. Get out of my sight." She turned, snarling a command to the lobby guards, "Escort these two idiots to their lockers, then throw them out in the street. When you're done, get back to your stations—and bring me Humphrey."

She stalked away, snatching out her phone. Senator Garlick's number, of course, was already programmed in. "Get me the senator," she ordered. "Yes, I am well aware of the time. Are you equally well aware of who I am? Then you know that it is in the senator's best interest to give me what I want. Yes, I will settle for your security specialist." She waited impatiently, her sharp-toed shoe tapping on the carpeted floor of the express elevator as it rose smoothly back into the executive levels. Repeated reflections of her long, sleek, ice-cold form echoed the movements, glittering like mantises in glass cages.

The reflections followed her as she glided down the glass and brass corridors of the executive suite, followed like the shadows of the rivals who wanted to pull her down. She thought of Abbott and suppressed a scream. First thing, her name came off the memo promoting that snake Anthony—and off the work order authorizing expanded network access. The tech who made the change had a choice: forget what happened in return for a nice bonus, or remember what happened on his way to the unemployment line. Visualizing the chaos she could inflict on the unfortunate tech's future employment possibilities slightly soothed the homicidal fury spinning in her head.

"I want a phone tap on Meredith Anthony," she said, as soon as the Senator's chief bodyguard came online and asked with his usual smooth politeness what he could do for her. She hadn't admitted it to the secretary, but he was actually a better tool for what she needed. He had the senator's access, power, and contact with the mob enforcers that Garlick so enjoyed flaunting to enhance his prestige. He also had a stoic competence that appealed to Zelik. She should hire him away from Garlick as soon as possible. After all, the Senator was an unreliable ally. Why leave a valuable security man in his stable? "She's an employee—former employee," Zelik corrected, "who we believe has stolen confidential information about human trials for the AllSafe vaccine."

She threw open the door to her outer office. "Yes, I understand that a breach of security could adversely affect the senator's legislation and chances of being appointed head of Homeland Security. Do you understand that I don't care if the senator lives or dies? I want that data back because if it gets out before we're ready to release it, the mindless public reaction to it will hurt my company. That little witch is going to call somebody to sell that data, and I want to know when she does."

The voice in her ear didn't bother to soothe, jabber, or equivocate. Instead, he simply told her that as soon as she uploaded the company's files on the subject, he would arrange for tracking Meredith Anthony—and for apprehending her. Did Ms. Zelik have any recommendations about what should happen to Ms. Anthony when their agents had her in custody?

A subdued glint from the secretary's desk caught Zelik's eye as the senator's agent talked; she snatched up the "I Love Mommy" coffee mug from which it came. "I don't care what you do with her—if the disc has some blood on it, oh well. We'll break out the disinfectant. This is what you can tell the senator and your goon boys: I want the data back, I want the leak permanently plugged, and I want this fire out *now*!" The mug smashed very satisfactorily as she threw it against the wall.

CHAPTER 14

Dear Chisom,

We are busy here at the Central Stake. Even though Church growth has slowed quite a bit world wide over the last five years, we find there is still more than enough to do. In fact, I'm glad growth has slowed because it gives us a chance to strengthen our local leadership and make sure the branches and wards are in capable hands. Please don't get me wrong. I really wish people were repenting and coming into the Church in droves. That would give me great hope that maybe the terrible prophecies I have written you so much about may not happen.

They are, in fact, provisional. (It is only the good prophecies that are unconditional: the gathering of Israel, the expansion of the kingdom of God into the entire world, the restoration of the tribes of Israel, the establishment of Zion, and the coming of the Lord.) All the ugly stuff need not come to pass if only people will turn to God. Unfortunately, they won't. For that reason, I expect the worst.

One of the great signs that shows how desperate people are to continue their immoral and perverse life styles is the craze over a new vaccine called AllSafe. According to all we hear, it guarantees complete safety against any and all infections. The "porn industry" and other immoral elements of society are rallying behind it. The religious gay community (yes, there is one), answering the charge that AIDS was God's curse against their perversion, is boasting that AllSafe is the divine sign that God accepts their lifestyle. I am fascinated by how many put God's name on their cause.

Speaking of being busy, I have a trip coming up. I will be accompanying Elder Nabil to a conference dealing with cancer research. He was heading a project working on the molecular level of cancer inhibition just before God called him as a member of the Twelve. As it turns out, his team was able to prove his theories correct. The breakthrough promises a great advance in cancer prevention. As a result, he has been invited to present the team's findings at a conference in Atlanta, Georgia. The reason I am going is that the last time Doctor Nabil attended one of these, he was swamped with questions about the Church and unable to take full advantage of the interest shown by some of his colleagues. We hope that with me there, we can better use the opportunity for good.

May I say in closing, I love the Lord's work. The kingdom, in spite of opposition, is growing stronger not only in numbers but also in righteousness. As the world polarizes and becomes more dark (physically and spiritually by all the signs), the Church's pure beacon reaches ever further. Some, because the light hurts their spiritually weak eyes, want to extinguish it, but others find the light soothing and reassuring and want the safe harbors it promises. You and your fellow missionaries are the flame of that beacon. Shine brightly that others may see your good works and be drawn to God. Never let the fire go out.

With love,
Your father,
Chinedu.

* * *

"For the moment, the fire is out." Anne stood in the hot sunlight, the last few trails of smoke from the burned-out chapel rising in lazy, black wisps behind her. "As you can see, the congregation is already making plans to rebuild." The shot panned left to show a bulldozer in the parking lot and a group of hard-hatted workers clustered around it, discussing demolition plans. A couple of kids (older elementary to middle school, by the look of them) cavorted and mugged for the camera in the middle distance.

Anne reappeared on screen, concerned and sincere. "But how can a community rebuild the trust destroyed by a rash of hate crimes? Six Mormon churches have burned here in New Mexico, the worst series of arsons in the country since the vandalism ring in Missouri last year." A map grew along beside her, marking the fires that had dotted the New Mexico desert. "What makes the situation even more complicated are claims that the hate crimes weren't just directed at Mormons, but at Navajos, too."

"Of course it's a hate crime!" A large, emphatic woman appeared in a prerecorded interview. Her silver and turquoise necklace bounced as she gestured. "These guys aren't after Mormons—they're after Navajos, and all Native Americans. It's the White Knights, an Aryan Nations offshoot. They've moved into this area, claiming that they're going to finish off what the cavalry started with the Trail of Tears."

"It's because those churches mainly served immigrants," another man said softly, the anger in his eyes belying his calm tone as he spoke to Anne, stroking his mustache. "Many of our Hispanic citizens are Mormons here. It's a symptom of the intolerance in our society—and the breakdown of law and order. There are gangs, outlaws just like the old Wild West, skinheads or drug runners, all over the region. They take over the little towns, terrorize anybody who speaks Spanish, and they get away with it. These guys think they can do anything, and the police just look the other way."

"As you can see, there are plenty of theories about the source of these problems, but few solutions," Anne said, reappearing against the desert hills and brilliant blue sky. "The Navajo Tribal Police are investigating this latest incident, since it took place on the Navajo Reservation. The FBI spokesperson issued a statement leaving the investigation in their hands; the FBI has determined that the fire was not related to terrorist activity."

Leon neatly shifted the camera angle, catching Anne again against the charred remains of the chapel. "But is terrorist activity the only problem? And how do we define terrorist activity? The Church of Jesus Christ of Latter-day Saints experienced its own share of terrorism two centuries ago, when it was driven out of the eastern United States by mobs. Will the general breakdown of law and order in the borderlands, as some speculate, result in the same thing happening here? The church's members are valuable members of this community, and the church itself has provided both personnel and assistance to the Navajo Nation's efforts to jump on the high-tech bandwagon. Are these fires the result of prejudice against Mormons or Navajos—or reprisals against citizens who won't play along with extortion or criminal activity? At this rate, only time will tell."

The scene shifted to watch the bulldozer take a first run at what was left of the outside wall of the church. Bricks collapsed in a cloud of sooty dust. "The rebuilding begins. But will they be able to rebuild their community as well? This is Anne O'Neal, Channel 8 News, reporting from the Navajo Reservation."

* * *

The blue light from the TV flickered over the mound under the sheets. The mound shuddered suddenly, the snoring that had emanated from it choking off. There is nothing in the world colder than the muzzle of a gun that hasn't been fired—yet.

"Hey, *Gordo*, looks like you made the news," Dove said softly, shifting the muzzle from Pizarro's neck to his forehead as the sheriff turned over to blink at him through wide eyes.

"Nakai?" Pizarro held very still, glancing up at the hand just inches from his nose.

"Got it in one," Dove agreed. "As you can see, I'm back in town. So you don't have to burn any more churches. Fact, it's best if you don't show yourself up 'round the Rez anymore. That might get you scalped."

"That church fire wasn't me," Pizarro growled. "I'm no firefly. So you can get that popgun out of my face."

"Will do, soon as I tell you that four other people know where I am." Dove waited for Pizarro to react.

He did—with what he imagined was heavy sarcasm. "Oh, you warning me that if you don't come back, somebody's going to report your disappearance? And who're they gonna tell? The deputy on desk duty tonight. And who's he gonna tell? Me. And I'll already know."

"No," Dove said patiently. "I'm telling you so you'll realize that if I disappear, somebody else is going to get in the same way I did, and he won't bother to wake you up before he shoots you."

"That a threat?" Pizarro growled, but at about half the confidence he'd just had. His eyes flicked to the window, the drapes, the door.

"It's a promise." Dove withdrew the gun, held it casually—but still pointed at the sheriff's nose. "Sit up, would you? And cover up. I'm seeing way too much hairy hide. If you didn't burn that church, who did?"

"Like I know—and like I'd tell you." Pizarro sat up, pulling the sheet over his torso. With what he imagined was slick subtlety, he used the sheet motion to hide his reach for the nightstand. "Probably skinheads, like the Navajo activists keep yelling."

"Don't!" Dove's sharp order stopped the sheriff in mid-reach. He looked over to see the glint of the gun at eye level. "Think sense, *Gordo*. You know I won't miss this close. I shot Cesare through the eye from ten times this distance. And he was a friend, in a way. Think I'd hesitate shooting you?"

"You shoot me, you're dead before you get out of this hotel." Pizarro glared at the young man, trying not to sweat visibly. He'd never liked Dove—or that too-smart brother of his—and the kid's freakishly calm smile just kept reminding him of all the reasons why.

"Dying doesn't really bother me," Dove assured him, with a confidence that chilled Pizarro's expansive gut even more than the gun muzzle had. "But I've got things that I'd like to get done before I check out. Let's get down to business here."

"If that means you'll shut up and get out of here faster, fine with me." Pizarro glanced toward the bathroom door. The light was still on, meaning Lillian still hadn't finished that endless bubble bath she insisted on taking every time he got a free night to bring her to the hotel. It was almost tradition: they got to the room, he sacked out on the bed for some much-needed shut eye, she hit the tub, they went out to a late dinner, and then came back to the room to make a night of it. Pizarro suspected that there was something wrong about having to wait for his own mistress to finally decide to wander into the bedroom, but he seemed to have a talent for picking pushy broads. First his wife, now her. He didn't want to think about that. He turned his attention back to Dove before Dove prodded him with that blasted gun again.

Dove just grinned at him, following his glance. "You let yourself in for all kinds of trouble, Sheriff. But that's not my problem. This is: you stay away from Mormons or Navajos—"

"I told you, I didn't torch that place," Pizarro interrupted.

"And stay away from Slick, too," Dove went on, overriding the interruption.

"You on Slick's side now?" Pizarro asked, jolted into really listening. Why would the kid threaten him on Slick's behalf? Was Dove working for the General after all?

"Oh, *Gordo*, you can do better than that." Dove leaned over, the TV picture reflecting in his eyes. Since there was a fire-insurance commercial playing at the moment, the flames only added to the effect on the sheriff. "I'm going to take Slick down. He and his General are moving up here, taking over the gangs, pushing out the dust runners so they can sell the drugs themselves. They're also messing with germs and bio-weapons. The Navajos have called the FBI already. And if the FBI's too busy, like they usually are until the disaster hits the rich neighborhoods, I'm going to stop Slick and his General. You can help, or you can get out of the way."

Bio-weapons—that fit the rumors that had filtered out of the southern law-enforcement agencies, and Rico's boasts of some big thing that would make everybody swear allegiance to Slick (and, vicariously, to Rico). If Dove could prove it, no wonder Slick wanted him caught and silenced. The FBI ignored church burnings, but they wouldn't ignore biological weapons moving into the borderlands. Not for long, anyway. The drug runners' disappearance, that was fine, and actually pretty common, coyotes ending up dead when a bigger wolf moved in. But germs, real military maneuvers—why did it have to hit his tidy little fiefdom? And why did a whacked-out gang enforcer with mystical leanings have to get involved in it? And worse, bust in to his hotel room and get him involved in it? Pizarro's laugh came out more strained than hearty, but at least it came out. "You're gonna take Slick out. That's good. And here I didn't think you had a sense of humor, Nakai."

"I do. And I'm going to take Slick out." Dove smiled, but his voice remained coolly confident and deadly serious. "Help or get out of the way."

"I'm staying out of it," Pizarro informed him. "I'd stay out of it anyway. It's none of my business what you psychos do to each other."

"That's right—or really wrong." Dove got up, keeping a bead on Pizarro as he walked to the door. He shook his head sadly. "Mostly wrong, you being the sheriff. But very smart of you for now. You'll be safe for the moment—as long as you stay out of the crossfire."

"Hey, Nakai," Pizarro called. Dove paused, his hand on the door latch. "How'd you get in here? I got guards in the hallway. They wouldn't take your money."

Dove's smile glinted white in the dark. "No money. I treated 'em to a drink, *Gordo*. It's one of the oldest tricks in the book—and it still works."

The two guards were still sprawled in their chairs on either side of Pizarro's door. Dove stepped around them, not feeling a bit sorry for the hiding Pizarro was going to give them when they came out of their drug-assisted sleep. He loped down the hall, taking the back stairs down to the service entrance.

"Thanks, Josef," he called, tossing the all-access electronic key back to the room-service boy. "Happy last day at work."

Josef neatly caught the key, pulling off the bills wrapped around it and stowing both in his coverall. "Any time, Dove—or it would be, if I was ever coming back here again."

"Might be a good idea not to," Dove told him. They exchanged a grin, and Dove disappeared into the windy darkness of the alley beside the parking lot. He glanced up at the hotel just once, seeing that bright yellow lamplight had replaced the blue of the TV shining through the crack in Pizarro's curtains.

* * *

"Privacy laws escaped another challenge today," Kathy stated. She continued oblivious through Pizarro's torrent of profanity. "The Supreme Court ruled that libraries may not ban access to any Web or broadcast materials to any patron, regardless of content. The American Library Association issued a statement lauding the decision, while several conservative and church groups strongly condemned it."

After the obligatory shots of protesters, gratified lawyers, and half-censored examples of the offensive material saved from the filter (with adverts explaining how viewers could order the material to judge for themselves, of course), Kathy went on. "In a related story, the Better Business Bureau and Consumer Alert Council have once again issued a warning to the general public about identity theft."

A buttoned-down consumer analyst appeared on the other side of the screen, and began his spiel. "It's important to remember that while privacy laws may protect your video-rental records, it's your credit-card numbers that identity thieves really want." Scenes of criminals passing false IDs and credit cards accompanied his well-rehearsed public-service announcement. Privacy laws are strict, with the exception of the wide latitude given the Office of Homeland Security, he assured viewers, but many large companies have legal exceptions to check up on their employees, and thieves can break into almost any database. Electronic records make it easier for both businesses and consumers, but sometimes carelessness also makes it easier for thieves.

"So, everyone should remember to shred their receipts, transmit their credit-card numbers only over secure lines, and not print their social-security numbers on checks," Kathy finished the announcement in a bored sing-song. It was the same warning, over and over again; in her opinion, anybody who got caught in this day and age probably deserved it. Besides, warnings like that were always a ratings loser; she heard Monk ordering them to pick it up through her headset.

Her voice lost its bored overtone, however, as she continued to the next story, accompanied by a splashy graphic of shadowy figures haunting dark streets. "But while some people get their identities stolen, others willingly disappear. Some choose to go off the grid to escape apprehension for crimes, some to escape their debts. And what about a related problem: the growing number of people who have dropped out of the grid voluntarily? Thousands of American citizens—and illegal aliens—have no digital identity to steal. They exist on the fringes, in a shadowy cash-only economy, unwilling or unable to join the rest of society. Clara Cortez has this report from the barrios of Los Angeles."

"Thank you, Kathy." Clara appeared on-screen, surrounded by dirty, graffiti-covered walls and carefully chosen derelicts. Channel 8's advance team knew better than to let the actual inhabitants of the place get within grabbing distance of their reporter—or, more to the point, their camera equipment. "As you can see, I am standing in an area known as *La Iglesia*, or the Churchyard, where the homeless come for shelter against the cold of the night—and the predators who prowl the darkness . . ."

* * *

The streetlights were gone, Merry realized. Not just out, not just out of service, but literally gone. Beyond the light poles with their jaggedly broken tops, multistory tenements, run-down shops, and litter-filled parking lots loomed out of the darkness into her headlights, then disappeared into the shadows that filled her rearview mirror. The fat ellipse of the rust-colored moon rode above it all, an alien satellite above an equally alien horizon. She slowed the car, and tried not to hear the flapping of the blown-out tire above the soft purr of the engine, fighting the pull of the steering wheel against the unequal forces. No good—the poor car couldn't go on like this. Echoes of Sidney's voice from her first flat-tire incident rippled through her memory: "Never run a car on the rims, Meredith, even if you think it's not very far from home. Now you've damaged the rims, and we'll have to pay twice as much as a tow truck would've charged."

Driving the car home on the rims—not likely, now. She'd gunned it out of MedaGen's parking garage in something close to blind panic, and her only (semi-coherent) thought had been that she mustn't lead them back home, to Missy. They'd *shot* at her! The realization threatened to bring the panic back, but she fought it back with hard determination and black humor. They hadn't just shot at her, they'd managed to do what security guards in the movies never managed and actually knocked out one of her tires. She smiled tiredly at that thought; they weren't movie guards, and she definitely wasn't a movie heroine. In fact, now that common sense had reasserted itself, she realized two important things: One, MedaGen knew where she lived already; all they had to do was check her personnel records. In fact, they had probably already called the police to pick her up as a corporate spy. Two, in her attempt to elude possible pursuers (who, as far as she could tell, hadn't materialized), she'd taken four or five unfamiliar turnings. That was enough to put her in a part of town she didn't recognize. Well, wasn't familiar with anyway. She recognized it pretty easily as the sort of neighborhood that she definitely didn't belong in.

The dim glow of a tube station sign gleamed through the darkness, even its canary yellow looking grimy. Merry hesitated, then stopped the car. *Any port in a storm, right?* She got out of the car, swinging the purse over her head and around her shoulder, just like the travel advisories showed. *That way, if a purse snatcher grabbed it, he'd have a better chance of breaking her neck.* She shook her head to clear the cynical thought. Black humor was fine when it helped, but if her internal jester kept going this way, she'd have to put a tight lid on it. Automatically, she locked the doors, hoping against all evidence that the poor car wasn't going to be stripped within minutes, and ran for the concrete stairs that led down into the fluorescent-lit cave of the subway.

Virginia writhed and mouthed silently to her as she reached the platform. The newly installed monitors hung safely behind an impervious, thin-mesh grid. The older speakers, however, didn't have that protection, and hung out of the walls in tangles of burnt wires and blown circuitry. Apparently somebody—maybe the same one or ones who had killed the streetlights—didn't appreciate hearing an endless barrage of commercials while waiting for the train. The two surveillance cameras in the station had suffered the same fate, or one similar; from the look of the walls around them, they'd been shot several times rather than pulled out and dismembered. The shattered cameras and cracked, starred look of the bullet marks on the concrete chilled Merry, then sent an irrational wave of relief through her. Fugitive, outlaw, criminal, that was her now. It all seemed so bizarre, so incredible—and so terribly, immediately real.

"Just get home. Please, just help me get home," she whispered the order and the prayer under her breath as she paced down the uninhabited platform. "Please, God, please help me get home. Help me. Help Missy."

The sign on the heavy grille of the revolving door brought her up short. An aimless breeze blew a swirl of paper wrappers around her legs as she read the notice: "Trains Stop 7:00 A.M.–9:00 P.M." The clock beyond the bars, like her watch, told her that she'd missed the last train by an hour and a half.

Voices jarred her out of her sick contemplation of the sign and the empty tracks beyond the gate. She glanced aside, acutely aware of her pretty cloth coat, tailored suit, professional shoes—and the purse with its vital information riding heavily on her neck and shoulder. A pair of young boys, elaborately ragged and much too young to be out so late in any better part of town, chased each other down, then back up the stairs, shouting something about cigarettes. Merry whispered another prayer and followed the two boys back up the stairs onto the street. She felt more exposed, but staying in the station couldn't help, either, and it was a dead end. Here, at least, she could keep moving. And the phone reception was better.

A flicker of doubt assailed her as she stopped by the disabled car again and pulled her phone out of her purse. Fugitive using a phone, letting the police track her—wasn't that one of the classic blunders? She sighed, silently cursing the disappearance of the old-fashioned pay phones, and clamped down on her nerves again. That applied to fugitives from the police, or the FBI, or some government agency with access. MedaGen was a private company, and private companies didn't get to slap traces on people's phone conversations. *Didn't they?* her doubts whispered as she dialed Carmen's number. *Are you sure?*

"No, I'm not sure!" she snarled aloud. "But it's not like I have a choice here!"

"What? Merry, is that you?" Carmen asked, adding in a New York accent. "Hey! You talking to me?"

"No, just to myself." Merry looked at the subway sign again. "Carmen, I'm in trouble here. I really need a ride, and I need it quick."

"You got it," Carmen said instantly. "I'm even in the van. Just dropped off Lucrezia. Donna's watching Missy. Where are you?"

Gratitude (and, to her horror, tears) welled up. "I'm at the Rosemont Street subway station."

"Wow." Surprise and concern colored Carmen's always expressive voice. "Rosemont. I've heard of it. Let's see—" the words faded into a rustling as she consulted her well-thumbed street map.

The words tumbled out of Merry before she could stop them. "Yes, and the car's out of commission, and I've got the—stuff, and they were shooting at me, and I've got to get out of here!"

"I'm there." Carmen didn't waste any time in reassurances or recriminations. "You get out of sight, somewhere with your back to a good wall, and watch for me. I'll be right there."

"Right. Thank you, Carmen." Merry listened to the dial tone for a moment, went to put the phone back into her purse—and stopped. "Why not?" she asked, dialing the towing-assistance hotline number her insurance company provided. She'd made one call, so if somehow MedaGen could monitor her phone, she was already toast. One more call couldn't hurt, and she owed it to her car. The poor thing had taken her through altogether too many years of high school, college, and graduate school before it got shot. She really couldn't just leave it here to get cannibalized—or found by the police or MedaGen's guards. Besides, the thought of a wrecker crew pulling up in a big, solid, tow truck with high-beam headlights sounded really good right now.

"I'm sorry, where?" The dispatcher asked, then continued without waiting for Merry to repeat her location, "I'm sorry, we don't send crews into that area after dark. Company policy."

"But you'll leave me here after dark, with no car?" Merry asked. No answer from the dispatcher; just the click and hiss of a dead connection.

A soft, metallic jingle pulled Merry's attention away from the phone—before a tattooed hand pulled the phone away from her. She looked up, from the phone to the broad hand wrapped around it (dark skinned under the black, writhing tattoos, thick copper bracelet surrounding the thick wrist that in turn disappeared into a brown-leather sleeve) to the reflective sunglasses. The thought of running never occurred to her. You never do that with predators; if you take off, they think you're prey, and they chase you. Of course, standing stock still and staring isn't always a good tactic, either. It certainly doesn't help rabbits faced with weasels.

Or foxes, with sharp, glittering canines—like the ones in the corner of the smile the gang leader flashed at her as he removed the glasses. He had cat-slit eyes (either contacts or cosmetic surgery, but totally appropriate). She felt more than saw the other four predators surround her, and dared a quick, sidelong glance left and right. No kids here, no teenagers or juveniles. These guys—correction, three guys and one woman—were full-grown adults, poised on the balls of their feet, with all the assured confidence of hyenas in the veldt. They might be scavengers, but they were very, very good at it. (Lions got their reputation as king of beasts because they stood over their kill as the sun came up, with the hyenas crouching in a ring around them. What the humans didn't know is that the hyenas had brought down the deer bleeding on the ground, before the lionesses had driven them away and given the lion the opportunity to strike the heroic pose.) There weren't any lions here, just plenty of grinning hyenas. She wondered suddenly if they could hear her heartbeat.

The leader hefted her phone, bringing it to his spangled ear. (The plastic surgery that sculpted it into a point only increased his resemblance to a four-footed carnivore.) "Lookee this nice thing—clear as bells. Got a good rate plan, *sheila?*"

"Decent," Merry heard herself say. *Amazing*, she thought. *I actually sound calm.* "It's a standard personal-service plan. Base minutes on subscription, additional services at premium. But I wouldn't use it, if I were you."

That got a laugh from him, low but genuinely amused. His pack echoed the sound. "Why? You going to hurt me if I do?"

Merry felt a hand brush down her sleeve, feeling the nap of the velvet and the flesh of her arm as if checking a piece of fruit for ripeness. The leader stepped closer to Merry, holding the phone toward her mockingly. The smell of smoke, musk, and sweat loosed another flash of panic. She stepped back involuntarily, only to bounce off the chest of the hyena behind her, the one she couldn't see but could smell—more tobacco, or something stronger (the chemical scent reminded her of the labs she'd worked in), with a harsh cologne that caught in her throat. This time, though, the hands that rose to grab her didn't provoke panic. They touched the strap of her purse— and provoked exactly the response Sidney's personal-defense specialist had programmed into her: stomp on the instep, elbow to the solar plexus, back of knuckles to nose. The hands dropped away, along with the body behind her, but the others closed in immediately, blocking her retreat. She whirled, the ring of snarling faces spinning around her, unbroken darkness behind them. *Please, God,* she cried silently, *please help me!*

Pain lanced through her head from the hand wrapped in her hair. The lead hyena pulled hard, twisting her around. Feral eyes stared into hers. "That why you're slumming down in Rosemont, little girl? Teasing the animals? Gonna beat up some dregs?"

"No," Merry said, praying desperately that he'd believe her, that it would make a difference. She felt the female hyena pulling the purse off her shoulder. "No!" She caught herself, stopping the reflexive grab for the purse, holding absolutely still in his grip. "I'm here because the security guards at MedaGen shot the tires out of my car, and this is as far as I got."

The mention of shooting got their attention. Out of the corner of her eye, she saw them glance at each other. "Why did Corp gorillas lay lead on you?" her captor asked, a trace of real interest behind his sarcastic tone.

She went on, keeping her voice calm, reminding herself not to talk too quickly or use too much jargon. "Because I found out that their AllSafe vaccine has some side effects they don't want anybody to know about. The first dose does what they say it does—it'll cure you if you already have AIDS or some other disease, and it'll stop you from getting sick later."

"That's a bad thing?" The woman—girl, really, under her hard expression and peacock hair—laughed harshly. "We seen all that on the vids already."

"No, that's not the bad thing." Merry didn't look away from the gang leader's eyes. "The bad thing is what happens a year later. If you don't go back to MedaGen for another shot, your body starts to self destruct. AllSafe revs up your system to fight infections as hard as it can. When it doesn't have any more infection to fight, it starts taking you apart, from the inside out. That disc," she pointed without looking, indicating the translucent plastic object in the woman's hands, "shows what happened to forty-five volunteers who took the first shot and didn't get the second. The first died in four days after the reaction set in. The last one died in three months."

"Lucky dog, that one," another banger noted. His chains rattled as he coughed around a cigarette.

"No, the first one was lucky," Merry said softly but clearly. "The last one went to pieces bit by bit. He died drowning in his own blood when his immune system finished eating his lungs."

The soft click of the disk dropping back into her purse punctuated the silence. She didn't drop her stare, though, or the silent litany of prayer in her head. "Please, take the rest of the purse if you need to, but please give me the disk and let me go. I need to get the word out. I need to make sure that nobody—and nobody's babies—get eaten up by their own blood."

Merry watched his eyes, so angry, cold, hungry, and alien to everything she thought she knew of reality. Same planet, different worlds. But AllSafe—and the callous, greedy company behind it— threatened both. Would he understand? Could he? Gradually, a light grew in his eyes, but it wasn't the dawning of a new understanding. It wasn't even metaphorical. His pupils contracted as the brilliant white beams of headlights splashed over his face, illuminating all of them as they turned toward the source of the sudden interruption.

A long, low, glossy car pulled up to the curb behind Merry's forlorn little vehicle. The doors opened, all four of them in smoothly coordinated unison, and a half-dozen flashily dressed thugs sprang out.

"Dancer?" The gang looked to their leader.

He grinned again, his gilded canines sparkling. "Payday," he announced.

Merry caught her balance as he tossed her away—then caught her purse as the peacock girl tossed it to her. She scrambled out of the way, diving into the shadows of the street as more bodies erupted out of the darkness to converge on the car and its cargo of rich victims.

Armed, rich victims, she amended, as the first shot crashed down the street. Only two more followed, the sound of shouts, curses, and blows with blunt objects taking their place. She continued running back the way she'd come, not looking back. She didn't want to see what was going on behind her; she'd seen enough to know that the guys who'd pulled up and pulled their guns weren't MedaGen security guards. The government parking pass on the car glinted in her mind's eye. They'd found her, traced her call—through their government contacts. Senator Garlick, standing in front of the FDA building, advocating AllSafe as a mandatory security measure, a senior United States politician, safely in MedaGen's pocket. She couldn't go home. She couldn't call from her phone.

Her feet screamed protests, and her lungs seconded the motion. She couldn't run much more, not in these shoes. Fortunately, she didn't have to. A minivan came barreling up the street, as out of place in that post-apocalyptic neighborhood as a polar bear on Long Beach, and a million times more welcome. Merry ran into the street, waving frantically. It screeched to a halt beside her, the door flinging open.

Carmen leaned out. "Boy, this is a bad part of town to get stuck in! You know, the lights are out all the way back to Meadow Road— had a heck of a time reading the street signs. With Tony out interviewing in Independence, I didn't even have my semitrusty navigator. Ended up just going on a prayer and taking the turns whenever the angel tapped me on the shoulder. What are you waiting for? Get in!"

Merry hadn't waited for the invitation; by the time Carmen asked what she was waiting for, she'd already buckled herself in. "I'm in. Let's go!"

"We're gone," Carmen agreed, hitting the gas and heading for lighter, if not higher, ground.

"Just don't get pulled over," Merry advised. The thought of a policeman pulling over a speeding minivan and arresting them both for high-stakes industrial espionage released a sudden wave of utterly inappropriate giggles. Clamping both hands over her mouth didn't help—in fact, the knowledge that she was probably about this close to hysterical only made the situation funnier.

Carmen glanced at Merry. *Poor kid looks like Tony did when he got laid off the first time*, she thought. *Can't decide whether to laugh, cry, or break something.* Laughing, in Carmen's opinion, was the best option just about every time. So she shot Merry a theatrically conspiratorial look and cockily announced, "Them coppers ain't got a shot at us, boss! They'll never take us alive!"

Merry did laugh at that, but it sounded healthier—even with the little hiccup sob at the end. She sobered quickly, reaching over to give her friend a one-armed hug. "Thanks, Carmen. Thanks for the joke, thanks for coming to get me, thanks for taking care of Missy—"

"Hey, enough already," Carmen interrupted. "You're going to make me blush, all that gratitude. You want to thank me, tell me what happened. It's not every day that I end up in Gangster Town making a pickup. I feel like something out of a spy movie."

"I'm never going to watch a spy movie again." Merry pulled the disc out of her purse, just to make sure it was still there, then put it back. She laid her hand over the thin, hard shape. "I got it, Carmen. Ms. Zelik herself gave me top-level network access, and I found Christoff's evaluations and full information on the human trials."

"And?" Carmen prompted, expertly skinning through a light on burnt orange and speeding up the ramp onto the freeway. She breathed a silent sigh of relief herself, as the familiar gray road stretched before them. Being on a known road was like being halfway home.

"And Chris was right." Merry tapped the disc; she had the weird impression that it felt cold from the uncaring greed that filled it, even through the leather of the purse. "AllSafe is anything but safe. Yes, it works, but then you've got to get another shot to keep it under control, or it goes berserk. Everybody in the group that didn't get the 'booster' shot died—most of them miserably. Just like the computer simulations we made showed."

"This is the stuff they want to give to kids?" Carmen exploded, pounding the steering wheel. The van swerved, but she caught it before it crossed the line. "Those greedy—" she paused, thinking furiously, then snorted. "Dang—I hate it when I can't think of a word bad enough!"

"I can think of plenty," Merry said grimly. "Murderers, for one. They killed those people, Carmen. Just as surely as if they'd put guns to their heads. And why? So they could sell their 'vaccine' to a captive audience. They're literally turning blood into money."

"They're trying to," Carmen corrected. "But they're not going to do it. Merry, are you all right?"

Merry thought about it, taking careful stock of her emotional state. She was slightly surprised at the final result. "I'm all right. No bullet holes, other than in my car, no bad consequences from running headlong into a whole wolf pack of muggers, no sign of police lights in the rearview mirror." She gave Carmen a brief rundown of her evening, starting with getting the network access she needed, through Humphrey's half-and-half betrayal, to her masquerade as a janitor, over her first experience with an actual shootout, and ending with the hyenas' leader letting her go. "That had to be divine intervention, and I don't care what anybody else has to say about it!"

"Amen!" Carmen agreed, her eyes wide. "I can see why you don't think you'll be in the mood for a James Bond flick anytime soon!"

Merry rubbed her face wearily, slumping back into the well-worn seat. "Now I just need to get the disc to Yuan—the reporter we talked to, the one who needed proof."

Carmen grinned wolfishly. "Well, you've got that. What can I do to help?"

"Well, I definitely can't go home now. That's the first place they'll look. I hate to ask, but could I borrow your credit card to book a motel room?" Merry's lips pulled into a wry half smile. "I just found out that MedaGen can trace phone calls—probably got the favor from that senator of theirs—and if they can do that, they can trace credit cards too. The police can, for sure, and they'll be on my tail, too."

"No, you absolutely may *not* borrow my credit card!" Carmen exclaimed.

"Wh—" Merry began, stunned.

"Don't be goofy, girlfriend!" Carmen reached over, grabbing Merry's shoulder and giving her an affectionate shake. "You're absolutely right about not going home. You're coming right home with me. And you'll stay as long as you need to."

"I don't want you in trouble," Merry said, worried.

Carmen snorted. "Me, in trouble? And how are they going to figure out you're with me? Nobody knows that we even know each other—we live ten miles away, in totally different neighborhoods. I've never gone to your work, none of your neighbors know who I am, and the Church doesn't sell its membership lists."

"I do call you a lot," Merry pointed out. "If they pull my phone records—"

"Let 'em," Carmen shrugged that off. "So they come around, asking about you. I'm just the babysitter, don't know a thing about you other than that you have a cute, catastrophically precocious daughter. I'll play dumb and speak Spanish at them until they go away. Tony will totally back us up. By the time they figure it out, that reporter will have spilled their little secret on TV, and the whole game will be over. You'll get a medal."

"Better make it Italian, to fit your last name," Merry suggested, worry battling relief in her stomach. "Carmen, are you sure? This could be dangerous, if they send more of the kind of thugs I saw back there."

"Am I ever not sure?" Carmen flipped her hair over her shoulder as she pulled the van to a stop in the driveway. "Like I said, it'll all be over by the time they even realize I'm Italian instead of Mexican. Now, let's get inside and you call that reporter buddy of yours. Let's get this show on the road!"

"Mamama!" Missy shouted, as Merry followed Carmen into the kitchen. The tiny, curly-topped missile crashed into her mommy's legs and squeezed. Merry bent over and squeezed her right back, swooping her up to snuggle her the minute Missy let go. "Miss Missy!"

Donna shrugged, smiling apologetically. "Sorry, Mom. She just wouldn't lie down. Kept saying she wanted to wait for Merry to come home."

"'S alright," Carmen assured her, considering the enthusiastic welcome, and the way Merry held Missy tight, her face buried against the baby's hair. "I think she knew what her mama needed tonight. Turn on the computer, Donna. We're going to need to transfer some data."

* * *

"Got it," Yuan said later, as the last of the files slid down the line through the anonymous-mail Web server and into place in his computer. Merry heard him whistle softly through the phone. "These are legit? The real files from the company's human-trial experiments? Is this all you've got?"

"No," Merry assured him. "I have copies of what I sent you, plus the chemical and medical specs for the vaccine itself—and the booster shot."

"You didn't send those?" the reporter sounded disappointed.

"They do put the cap on the evidence," Merry admitted, "but I'd rather not just broadcast them. That kind of information is much too dangerous to chance it falling into anybody else's hands. The point is to tell everyone that the FDA approval was rigged, and that the vaccine is dangerous, not to tell everybody else in the world how to make the stuff. You've got enough to get the word out to people who will listen. When we've got the legitimate authorities on our side, I'll be able to give them the rest of the data."

"This is freaking amazing," Yuan muttered, as the case studies, complete with mug shots and gory deaths, scrolled across his screen. The silver MedaGen logo glowed from each page.

"It's horrible, and we need to make sure that nobody else gets killed to line MedaGen's pockets," Merry informed him. "Please, Yuan—"

"I'll review it," he promised quickly. "Give me a day. Where can I contact you?"

"I'll call you," Merry corrected. "I'm using a friend's phone now, but I don't know where I'll be later."

She had to repeat that in several different ways before he finally accepted it and hung up. (Admittedly, the fascination of the files gleaming from his computer did distract him from his determination to pry Merry's whereabouts from her.) "Well, that's it, then," she told Carmen, shivering slightly.

"That's it," Carmen agreed. She hugged Merry. "Tony's going to be ticked-off that he's missed all the excitement! Now, we just hole up, get some rest, and watch the news for Yuan's story of the century."

* * *

"Sasha's holed up *here?* Man, it's a nunnery!" Perro stared at the elegant lancet windows piercing the old church's gray stone walls. The paper lanterns strung from pillar to pillar cast brightly colored anti-shadows over the walls and the brilliantly colored murals in place of the traditional, more sedate plaques and memorials. A many-armed *bodhisattva* had replaced the traditional painting of the Virgin; she gestured in sixteen directions while smiling benevolently down at him. His eyes drifted from her sweetly serene smile—that still resembled the images of Mary he was used to—to her decidedly riper curves, then jerked away. You weren't supposed to think about a goddess like that, right? "No matter what it looks like," he added uncertainly.

Dove grabbed and shoved him as his eyes drifted down Kuan-yin's bodice again. "Keep up."

They hustled after the preternaturally serene woman gliding down the smaller corridor in front of them. Her saffron robes and bald head under its diaphanous veil didn't even faintly resemble the black gown and wimple of the sisters who had once swept through the cool hallways—and handled the "behavior problems" at the elementary school where Dove had met Perro—but she definitely had that whole nun presence down cold. The Catholic Church had put the building up for sale when the last member of the Sisters of Benevolent Charity had died (and the ever-spiraling costs of defending against lawsuits had meant the local diocese required an instant infusion of cash). A group of Buddhist do-gooders eventually bought it and moved in, their golden nuns replacing the black ones, Kuan-yin replacing Mary, and nothing replacing the same old problem with lack of funds and lack of commitment. The convent, run by a bunch of California Buddhists as a tax write off, finally applied for and got government funding as a hospice for indigent, terminally ill patients. Whatever the bosses' intentions were, however, the women who ran the place had a good reputation—and the charity to take in a former gang leader's girlfriend who'd come to the sharp end of her gilded but altogether too short rope.

"Look at that!" Perro exclaimed, stopping dead as a huge, gold statue of Buddha loomed before them in a small chapel where a Presence lamp had once hung. He puffed out his cheeks and laughed. "Whoa, look at that! All hail to the fat man!"

This time, Dove punched him. "Lay off it, Perro. They really believe, and they're doing good. You can talk when you have something to talk about."

"Yes, Father," Perro muttered sarcastically.

Dove shot him a grin. "That's 'elder'—or will be, when I get ordained."

"Ordained?" Perro yipped. A glance from the nun made him drop his voice. "You're kidding me! You said you'd gone Mormon, not that you were aiming to be a priest!"

"I'll be a priest too," Dove assured him, just to watch his face.

It was worth it—until a low cough distracted them both.

"Here." The nun opened a small, wooden door. "Be gentle. She is near to passing into the next cycle."

The cough came again, harsher without the thin panel to soften it. Sasha looked harsher too. Without the makeup, heavy jewelry, and deep-cut clothes she'd always worn as *Abuelo's* old lady (and thus the first lady of the gang), the boys would've barely recognized her; the disease underneath the cough made her a disconcertingly familiar stranger. Her slender frame had turned bony, her eyes sunk back into her skull. The hair that had curled luxuriantly around her shoulders hung flat and thin against her neck. She managed a smile before another coughing fit hit her so hard it looked like it would tear her apart.

Perro cringed back, until he remembered that showing fear wasn't macho, and tried to turn his retreat into a casual move to lean against the doorway.

Dove stepped forward, catching her shoulders, easing her down onto the hard, wooden chair beside the flat, narrow bed. She felt like a birdcage under his hands, a frail framework caging a fluttering, desperate life. "Hey, Sasha," he said quietly, when the fit had passed. "How you doing?" It was a stupid question, but nothing else came to mind.

"Better than you, *Hasbidi*," she husked, with the ghost of a laugh. "You're supposed to be dead. Rico's been bragging it up and down, how he killed you and Benny for getting in his way." Her eyes darkened within their deep sockets, flashing with the dark light of rage. "Like he killed my Jaime. But he really did that."

"*Abuelo?*" Dove asked. *Abuelo's* name was Jaime? He'd never even thought about *Abuelo* having an actual name.

Sasha let out one racking cough, then ruthlessly suppressed its cousins. She leaned forward, jabbing one finger at him. (Her nails hadn't changed, but now the skeletal thinness of her fingers made them look even longer.) "*Sì, Abuelo.* That's how you knew him. That's how you all knew him."

Her gaze flashed over Perro, shrinking him against the doorframe again. "As the old man, bitter, tired. He was tired. You know why? Because he never had a minute's peace, never! Always looking out for you, always having to bow to the *Señor*—whoever had the big house that year—always having to watch his back against punks like Rico who took his protection and came gunning for him."

The cough came back, with reinforcements. The violent spasms shook her so hard that she nearly fell off her chair. Dove reached out, but she waved him away. "No," she choked, stumbling to the bed. "Don't touch."

Once again, she conquered the cough through sheer force of will. "Listen. Both of you—Perrito, prick your ears for once. That Slick, he came to Jaime, he promised everybody millions and all the ammo they could shoot if Jaime would help him, go over to that General of his. They burned out the *Señor*, killed all his bodyguards. They've brought in more junk from down south than the *Señor* let in, sucking money back down to the General. Jaime was a soldier, not a dust runner! He thought about it, but then he started hearing things, from down south, from California—the General's not to be trusted."

Her voice faded, breath failing. She swallowed hard. "After Rico strutted into Mama Rosa's and spilled what happened—that Slick killed Benny, shot you, Dove—Jaime told Slick to buzz off." The darkness in her eyes deepened, tears making them black pools. "Why couldn't you take the hint and go? Just go?"

"Benny wouldn't leave *Abuelo*," Dove told her softly. "We're family."

"Family." Sasha managed to roll her eyes in a fair imitation of her old aristocratic hauteur. "You didn't run, Rico came back, and Jaime closed the door on Slick." The cough returned. This time, she didn't have the strength to suppress it. When the spasm passed, she lay on the bed, a husk of what she had been. "Slick sent Rico. Backstabber. Shot Jaime, grinning like a loon, proving himself to Slick. Thought they'd shoot me, too, but they didn't. Not with a gun. Slick stabbed me with a needle, told me I wouldn't miss Jaime long. That son of a—"

The hate in her voice started another coughing fit. When it passed, she decided to forego profanity in favor of saving her breath for the main point. "Just smiling at me, that bloody cold smile, talking about 'vectors' and 'noncommunicable forms' telling me there's weapons of mass destruction and weapons of assassination. 'Sometimes, you want to kill many as quickly as possible,' he says, casual as Saturday, 'sometimes you only want to kill one,' and stabs me in the throat with the needle."

Her eyes fluttered closed, pain crossing her drawn face. "Felt like fire taking my head off. Blacked out. When I came 'round, they had me locked in my bedroom with Dolores. I couldn't hardly move, and that slut just kept bawling and blaming me for Rico letting Slick put her in there. As a test, he said, to make sure I wasn't contagious. Guess I wasn't, 'cause Dolores didn't get more'n a bellyache from bawling, and I started coughing blood by nightfall." Another cough bubbled through her control; it sounded deeper this time, with gravel in it.

She swallowed against it, dragging in as much breath as she could get, her eyes fixed on Dove's face. "Slick came for us, brought us out with the whole gang there, showing me off like a coyote he'd skinned, Dolores standing there limp like a beat dog. I couldn't hardly hear, him telling them all about how the General could touch this one and leave the other healthy—did they want to rule the world? Then he gives me another needle, tells everybody to come back in a couple days. I figured they'd killed me, but I got better for awhile—so he could show everybody that his General's got the cure for it too. Hauled me out again, made me run in place to show everybody how much better I was feeling." Her eyes blazed with remembered humiliation. "So he offers them all a chance to prove how loyal they are—take the first shot, get the second to show they trusted the General. Were they brave enough? Got 'em cheering each other on, like idiots. Got Rico, too, taking the shot himself like it was Black Mass Communion. Slick stabbed him with the antidote needle and promised the General would keep him healthy as long as he behaved himself—and all the rest of them lined up to prove how macho they were."

A bitter smile crossed her ravaged face. "Rico's a fool to trust him, but he told him the truth. The antidote works—for awhile. But now Slick's decided he don't need me, with all the idiots to use as guinea pigs. He tossed me out. So it's killing me, the poison the General sent north, but nobody else. Yet." Her clawed hand reached for Dove, then withdrew. "I never liked you, the righteous boy who always looked down on us. But now you're the only one left. Kill them, Dove, *Hasbìdì*. Kill them for *Abuelo*. Your family."

"I'll stop them," Dove said softly. "I'll stop Slick and his General. For our freedom and our families."

"Righteous—" This time, the cough ripped through her answer. A crimson trickle of blood ran out of her mouth. Breath bubbled up in more red gouts.

"Sister—nun—whatever!" Perro called out the door, panic cracking the words in ragged halves.

The nun came in, at high speed but seeming as unrushed as always. Two more saffron-robed women followed. The three of them converged on the convulsing scarecrow on the bed. Dove and Perro found themselves pushed unceremoniously out the door and down the hall by the sudden crowd and by their own helplessness in the face of imminent death.

"Wow." Perro looked up at the serene smile of Kuan-yin and shuddered. "Never thought Sasha'd go down like that. I always figured her for shopping herself to death—if *Abuelo* didn't strangle her first, just to shut her up."

"They killed her as an experiment and an example." Dove finished a silent prayer for Sasha—for whatever she'd let God do for her. "Come on, Perro. Let's get out of here. They killed her to test their disease."

"The virus thing?" Perro asked, feeling chilled all over again despite the hot sunlight that poured over them after they left the shadowy confines of the church.

"The virus thing," Dove agreed. "It killed her, and it'll kill the ones who gave it to her. One way or another, this is going to bring the General down."

"You're going to get the General sick?" Perro looked at Dove, raising his eyebrows. "I don't figure the FBI will go for that."

"No." Dove rolled his eyes. "We're going to get to everybody that Slick and his boss want to screw over, and we're going to put together our own army."

"You and whose army?" Perro quoted, grinning as he opened the Dogmobile's door. "You mean the real Army? You heard back from those Navajo cop buddies of yours yet? They called, right, last night? Late."

Dove sighed. "No—I mean, yes, I heard from Sam. He says Bishop Yazzie passed the word along, but the *federales* gave him the runaround. They said they'd look into it as soon as possible—but they're checking out a suicide-bomb cult in San Jose, then they have to run down rumors about a bunch of Heaven's Gaters trying to poison a reservoir in Colorado, and who knows what else. We're on the list. That's what they said. We're on the list. Maybe they'll come through. Maybe they won't. But we don't have time to wait for them. Slick's gonna get his big case in another few days, and we're the only ones taking it seriously right now."

"And you don't even look surprised. Great," Perro echoed the sigh. "So it's just us."

"Buck up, Perrito. Did we really think they'd listen? Bunch of border rats and Navajo cops telling the FBI how to do their job? So now it's just us and our army—the army I'm going to gather up around here. Slick's got enemies that'll help us. They've just got to get to know each other, realize that together they're tougher than he is." Dove slid into the car.

"Enemies, huh?" Perro looked at him skeptically. "Like who? Besides you and me and Calvin, I mean."

"Let's start with the *Brujos* and work up from there," Dove said. "They know about Slick's ammo dumps."

"*Brujos?* There aren't any of them left above ground—or anywhere but deep cover. Slick sent us gunning for them right up front. How're we going to hunt them down?"

Dove shot him a grin, tapping the side of Perro's head with a thin sheet of printout. "That phone call wasn't all bad news. We got Johnny Law on our side for once. Turns out I have something Slick doesn't—fugitive-tracking information from the Navajo Tribal Police."

"You got the skinny from the cops. You know, hanging with you just gets weirder and weirder," Perro noted appreciatively. The Dogmobile peeled away from the curb in a cloud of scorched rubber and burning oil.

CHAPTER 15

"The clouds are heavier around the Big Sister region because of the increase in dust from the ongoing eruptions. They get suspended in the air and give the clouds tiny seeds to form around," Hideyoshi explained to the video monitor. "That's contributing to the strange weather patterns you've seen in the Western United States, Eastern Russia, and Japan." Pictures filled the screen in four quadrants: a thin sprinkling of snow in Los Angeles, drought in Washington State, a huge waterspout tornado whirling like a column of dirty glass out of the Pacific just off Okinawa, torrential rains tearing down huge trees on Sakhalin. The shots of extreme weather shrank, split to the four corners of the screen, leaving Hideyoshi in the center.

"Of course, the dust and greenhouse gases from the eruptions aren't the only cause of the strange weather. The increased volcanic activity has directly contributed to the growing number of earthquakes up and down the fault regions." A spinning globe, Earth as seen from the International Space Station, glowed softly from a monitor. It grew, focused on the region where the volcano had abruptly thundered into life. As Hideyoshi spoke, outlining the faults of the region, brilliant red, orange, and yellow spots appeared, vividly marking the earthquakes that shook the coastlines and seafloor. "As you can see, the pressure from the tectonic activity under these faults is increasing, causing the plates to shift. Up here, that looks like a sudden deformation in the Earth's surface. Down where you are, it feels like somebody's trying to shake you off your feet."

"Or out of bed," the science reporter suggested brightly. "It always seems to happen at night."

Hideyoshi smiled. "It may feel like that, but statistically, there's no difference. An earthquake doesn't care what time it is."

The reporter, however, wasn't done yet. She giggled. "Well, Dr. Hideyoshi, you can make the earth move for me anytime."

"I can't take any credit. It's all the fault of the faults." Hideyoshi maintained his professional smile while Ivana rolled her eyes at him from off camera. The new science reporter wasn't any better than the other one. How did they always manage to miss the main idea (the earth is rolling over in its unquiet sleep, and that meant physical and financial damage for thousands, if not millions, of people) and focus on the stupidest things (let's joke with the cute astronaut!). Hideyoshi hid a sigh and gently prompted, "I think you've got Andre Becker on the line from the Big Sister area."

"Take the hint, Bambi," Monk growled into his headphones at the starry-eyed reporter. "She's as bad as the last idiot. At least she polls better with the young-male demographic. All that blondeness. And, we're over."

Kim switched the feed to the camera set up in Becker's observation post as the science reporter (whose name wasn't Bambi but that really didn't matter anyway) managed a fast transition. "So what does an earthquake feel like for you, Dr. Becker?"

Becker, less proper than Hideyoshi and endowed with far more wag-capable eyebrows, gave her a grin. "Well, I'd like to tell you, but I haven't been home in a long time."

"Oh!" The reporter giggled again. Another aural jab from Monk brought her back to the subject at hand. "Our contacts at the Space Station told us that we could expect even more shaking going on."

"Whole lotta shaking going on, to be precise." Becker grinned again, this time at the audible groans from his research team. The lure of science brought him quickly back to the subject at hand. "Yes, from what we've been able to tell from our instruments, it looks like we're in for several more significant seismic events." He held up a small device, shaped a lot like a land mine, with wires trailing from it. "These are seismographs. In addition to the InSAR system on the Space Station, we've got these little beauties buried all around this region. They're so sensitive that they transmit the signals back to our computers at the slightest shake of the ground. That lets us map—

and sometimes predict—the way the volcano's evolving. It's the first time we've been able to use modern scientific observation methods on an incipient volcano."

A faint wobble shook the image of Becker's enthusiastic face. "Dr. Becker!" a voice from off camera called tensely. "Dr. Becker, we have an event—"

"No kidding!" Becker yelled back. The movement rapidly progressed from a wobble to a severe shaking. The camera bucked. Becker leaned in, his face filling the screen as he grabbed for the power switch. "As you can see, we can *sometimes* predict an event. It's science in motion around here. We'll be back."

The screen went dark. Kim quickly flipped to the feed from the studio camera.

"Nice," Monk said, pleased. "Got a ratings spike there. Play it up, Bambi. Scientists in danger from an erupting volcano. Kim, see if there's reports of local damage, especially in cities. Small-town stuff is fine, if it's Grandpa's truck getting run off the road, but try for the dramatic scenes—schools, churches, grocery stores if nothing else. And get Becker back as soon as you can. Meantime, hit the secondary screen with the footage from the SanFran quake and the shots of the volcano blowing. That'll keep 'em glued 'till we get casualty and damage shots."

"Got a press conference requesting live access," Kim pointed out, as Bambi breathlessly told viewers to hang on for the latest updates on the fate of Becker and his team.

"Politics!" Monk swore. "Is it more welfare jabber, or something good, like a terrorist warning?"

"Halfway between. Press conference about AllSafe." Kim keyed up the description. "Bosses put a green light on this one. Looks like it's paid for."

Monk took a drag on his cigarette, glaring at the order, then shrugged fatalistically. "They want to blow ratings on a bribe package, they'll do it. They just better not come down on my review when we lose points. Roll it."

* * *

The august façade of the Capitol filled the background, Senator Garlick standing on a flag-draped podium in front of it, positively glowing with patriotic triumph. The current Director of Homeland Security stood beside the podium, in her rival's literal and figurative shadow, keeping a camera-ready smile on her face as her eyes screamed political murder. A carefully selected crowd milled and cheered in front of the dignitaries.

"We are here to make an announcement that will improve the lives of every American citizen!" Senator Garlick beamed at the camera. "The House has passed the Garlick-Benyanny Health and Security Bill! This is the first dramatic step to making the AllSafe vaccine freely available to all citizens—and mandatory for all who work in high-risk areas or have contact with the public." He went on to extol the virtues of both the bill and the courage of the representatives who (due to overwhelming pressure from MedaGen propaganda and Senator Garlick's office) took the patriotic step of passing it.

Abbott and Zelik, standing with the corporate officers assembled before the cameras at MedaGen headquarters to virtually participate in the triumph of the Health and Security Bill, smiled blandly, applauding at the scripted moments for the viewers watching the secondary feed. They'd long since mastered the technique of conducting discreet conversations without drawing attention; it was a basic survival skill at top corporate levels.

"Have you got rid of our second pest problem yet?" Abbott's wide smile bore absolutely no resemblance to his whip-crack tone.

"We're working on it," Zelik said calmly through her own Mona Lisa expression. "The house is empty. No one's used the phone. The mother hasn't been helpful—just complained about how she knew her daughter would do something radical sooner or later. Anthony's been messed up with the Mormon Church for awhile. The neighbors just know her as a strange Mormon girl; none of them know where she's gone. The good news is that the termites are from the same hive. Ms. Anthony is also Mrs. Galen."

"Mrs. Galen," Abbott repeated, glancing at his COO. "As in the Galen who conveniently 'offed' himself a few months ago before we had to do it for him?"

"As in that Galen." A faint hint of snarl crept into Zelik's good-citizen face. "We'll find her and make sure she follows her dearly departed."

"Do it fast. Garlick's upset about losing her trail—and losing a crack team of made men to a pack of street thugs." Abbott focused a diamond-drill gaze on the back of the Senator's head. "He threatened to send more of them in to take care of things."

"Like they did at the subway station?" Zelik asked, with a sub-vocal snort. "This calls for finesse, not Tommy guns and concrete shoes. All I want from him is access to the Homeland Security moni-tors. He can keep his Guidos to himself while I figure out which Mormons she's hiding out with."

"Finesse it, then," Abbott advised. "Finesse it well and thoroughly. Too bad the database doesn't list Mormons as potential threats to government security. It probably should." He looked thoughtful for a moment, then returned to his previous thought. "Find out who she's talked to, who she's trying to sell it to. Squash her and contain anybody she's infected. And do it *now*."

"I've got a possible lead, rumors about somebody asking technical questions, but I don't think she's selling it." Zelik applauded the Senator's plastic declaration of love for every citizen in the United States and Puerto Rico, mentally wiping sweat off her brow in relief. The tech-support drone had erased her name off the authorization fast enough that Abbott's spies, trolling for the daily dirt on all his rivals (especially her), hadn't picked it up. She had planted a little misinformation she was making sure Abbot would find, and someone else would take the fall. Indeed, whatever nasty consequences he arranged for Errol Humphrey weren't her problem.

"Not selling it?" Abbott's hands faltered for a moment. He rolled his eyes as the implications hit (not selling it, giving it away, or possibly keeping it for a "good cause"), and groaned. "Mormons. Boy Scouts."

"Girl scout, in this case," Zelik corrected. Despite the situation, she couldn't help feeling a bit smug as she added, "Doing what the boys couldn't. But don't worry about our little Brownie spreading nasty gossip too far. I'll handle it."

* * *

"You said you'd handle it!" Merry shouted furiously into the phone. She wanted to rail, scream, kick the machine across the room, shake an explanation out of Yuan herself, but she couldn't do anything more aggressive than leave an eardrum-busting voice-mail message.

"Actually, he said he'd review it. Want to use a police whistle on the next one?" Carmen suggested, unable to suppress a grin at the sight of her friend yelling at the absent reporter, despite her sympathy for Merry's frustration.

"The stupid system probably has a decibel-leveling feature anyway," Merry sighed. She hung up the phone with exaggerated care—then ruined the effect by knocking her forehead on the wall. "What is going on, Carmen? We weren't supposed to see a happy press conference with Garlick announcing that AllSafe was practically mandatory! We were supposed to see them all hauled off to jail in chains while the entire scientific community officially renounced the vaccine as a vicious corporate ploy!"

Carmen caught Merry's head. "Hey, don't knock yourself out."

"He hasn't answered," Merry went on, whirling around to plant her back against the wall instead, her arms clenched across her chest. "He doesn't answer the phone, he doesn't answer e-mail. Doesn't he believe me? Has he lost the files I sent? Doesn't he realize this is important?" *Chris,* she thought, *Chris, we didn't count on him not listening, not acting on it. What do I do now?*

"Janny!" Missy shouted from the other room, demanding her playmate's instant presence. "Janny, Janny, Janny!" A bang accompanied each repetition of Gianni's name, as she applied a spoon to the pan she'd liberated from one of Carmen's cupboards.

Gianni, down to his last nerve from living constantly with the original Queen Bee for a week (and a tense week at that), shot a hunted glance at the doorway and promptly hid behind his mother's legs. Carmen patted him.

Merry stalked into the kitchen to gaze down at her daughter from her full annoyed-mommy height. "Missy, yelling at Gianni from the other room isn't doing anybody any good. If you want his attention, you can go to where he is and talk nicely to him."

Missy looked up at her mother with an equally annoyed-baby expression. "No!" She liked the sound of that, and added it as the vocal track to her drum solo. "No!" Bang! "No!" Bang! Much to her surprise, her mother didn't react to this outright display of defiance.

Instead, Merry looked at the ceiling for a moment, then turned on her heel and headed for the coat closet. "Carmen, I'm going to confront him myself. He's there—I know he is. He hasn't changed his answering machine message to say he's on vacation. He's just not taking my calls. And if he's not there, I'll get his home number out of the secretary. Even if I have to claim I'm his sister to do it!"

"You'd be more believable claiming to be his girlfriend," Carmen noted, grinning.

"Whatever," Merry waved away the need to think up a cover story. She'd take care of that later—if she needed to do it. "Could you call a cab for me?" She brushed briskly at a fluff of lint on her suit-jacket lapel. Not being able to get back to her house even to pack a suitcase hadn't been as bad as Merry had feared it would be, especially since Donna had very generously offered to share her wardrobe (Gianni hadn't been consulted, but Missy looked fine in blue and soccer-ball motifs). Fortunately, she'd had to make her initial escape in a sharp business suit. She couldn't see facing down Yuan wearing jeans and a "Tabernacle Choir Tour" T-shirt that Tony had designed as a joke.

"No," Carmen said decisively, sweeping up Gianni. "I'll drive you down there myself." She raised a hand to forestall Merry's objection. "Tony and I talked to you already, Merry. Mum's the word, until we know where we stand. I'd rather not even have a cabbie know where you are. MedaGen hasn't called the cops, Merry. Nobody's said boo about this. That means they're handling this themselves. And *that* means all bets are off."

"Carmen," Merry flapped her hands ineffectively in the face of Carmen's determination. "Much as I appreciate Tony's borderline paranoid protectiveness—and yours too—doesn't it seem a little over the top for a major genetic-medicine company to lurk around cab companies, like they were putting out a hit on somebody?"

"They shot at you in the garage, then sent thugs after you that night," Carmen pointed out implacably, tucking Gianni's feet into his shoes. "And you're the one who's found proof that they're not beyond killing people to get that vaccine of theirs out. I always did think that Dr. Christoff person died a little too suddenly too."

"I just so don't want to live in a world where that's true," Merry said softly, staring at the button on her jacket—and through it, at Zelik's hate-frozen face under the garage lights, at Humphrey's cynical smile, at Chris's gentle expression. She sighed. "Let's go save the world."

They pulled up a block away from the elegant high rise with Channel 8's logo prominently gilded onto the wall—and subtly tiled into every element of the building's design and decoration, almost subliminally filling the eye with 8s and infinity symbols. Carmen looked around the street, taking in the elegantly businesslike mixture of functional (wide sidewalks, bus shelters, glass entryways) and "urban design" (trees in wrought-iron containers, fancy stones built into the sidewalk, open spaces between skyscrapers), and nodded. "Yup, this looks good. We'll stay here and play by that little fountain. You go make sure Yuan's going to cooperate."

Merry agreed, helping extract the babies from their car seats. Missy, however, decided not to cooperate. "No!" she shrieked, as Merry kissed her and rose to walk away. "No! Mamamam! Me go! Go! No! Go with!"

Merry, feeling suddenly exposed in hostile territory, quickly picked her up. "Hush!"

Missy, satisfied, smiled and said more quietly. "Good. Go, Mamamam."

"Honey, this is not the time to go on a separation-anxiety jag. I'm going to talk to a grown-up man about boring things," Merry told her. "Stay here with Carmen and Gianni. See, you can splash in the water."

The moment Missy's feet neared the ground, she started shrieking again. A couple of suited executives glanced over as they passed, smilingly superior to the young-mother type struggling to leave her overindulged offspring with the nanny. Carmen, knowing Missy's stubborn streak—and her mother's—didn't try to intervene.

"All right," Merry growled, capitulating in the face of contrary fate. She'd never prided herself on her ability to read people, but she knew one of Missy's stubborn streaks when she saw one beginning.

"But if you get bored and start causing a fuss, I'm going to put you in a recycling bin and let you stay there until I'm done."

"Bin," Missy agreed calmly.

"You just have no clue," Merry told her, planting a brusque kiss on her forehead. How could she love anybody so much and have so little control?

"It'll be fine," Carmen assured her, figuring that the decision had been made. She smiled. "Might even help. Make you look less suspicious."

"Right." Merry shifted Missy to her hip and tugged at the jacket to align it for baby carrying. "Here goes."

"Good luck. I'll pray for you," Carmen said quietly.

"I'll do that too." Merry took a breath, sent up a fervent prayer for help, and headed down the sidewalk.

Missy happily waved to Gianni over Merry's shoulder. She also waved to the receptionist, who smiled and told Merry that Yuan was in. Another happy wave and she helpfully suggested that she could buzz Merry through (their security wasn't as tight as MedaGen's, but it wasn't open access, either) so they wouldn't have to wait around in the lobby. Merry gratefully accepted and stepped into the elevator while Missy played with their Visitor badge.

Yuan just blinked when Missy waved at him, obviously having a hard time deciding how to react to a young woman and a baby suddenly appearing in his cluttered cubicle of an office. The confusion evaporated immediately when Merry held out a hand and introduced herself; panicked, apologetic sneakiness replaced it.

"Nice to meet you in person, Dr. Galen," Yuan managed.

"Is it?" Merry pinned him with a baleful eye, then relented slightly. "I thought you'd have a story out by now. What happened? Did you run into questions about the data? Was it too hard to understand?"

"No, it was pretty clear." Yuan's eyes kept sliding away from hers. "Listen, Dr. Galen, MedaGen's one of Channel 8's biggest sponsors. The files you sent are really great—I mean, really important—but we can't just run with it without getting official confirmation. And when I asked our program director about it, kind of generally, you know, not outright, he said that we didn't have a place for it."

"You didn't have a place for it?" Merry stared at him. So did Missy. "You don't have a place for warning people that a vaccine that's supposed to protect them is actually going to make them sick or *dead?*"

"Eventually, over months and months, and not even then if they get the second shot," Yuan said defensively. "According to you. The FDA's passed it. Everybody's high on it right now. Nobody wants to hear that the miracle cure of the century has problems." He deflated slightly, hearing the hypocrisy in his own words. The next sentence didn't do anything to alay the sobbing ghosts of journalism school, shreds of idealism gibbering about ethics in reporting. "It's really technical stuff. It'll need a lot of digesting to make it understandable to our target audiences. Besides, the program director says medical stories just don't play to ratings during playoff season, so we should wait a few months."

"Few months," Missy echoed, wiggling slightly. This wasn't as entertaining as she'd hoped. The main thing, however, was that she'd managed to come with her mommy. She was heartily sick of being left behind.

Merry shifted Missy slightly at the interruption, giving the baby a new angle of view. "In a few months, there won't be any point." Her tone sounded thin and bewildered before she shook the shock out of her vocal chords. "People will already have the vaccine running amok in their bodies. It won't be news that they'll have to get boosters to keep it from killing them—MedaGen will tell everybody themselves, so they can sell more shots!"

Yuan brightened up. "That could be an angle—they'll say they didn't know, and we can show they did!" *Perfect solution*, he congratulated himself. That would give the accountants time to get another major sponsor. It would also make him the hero who exposed government and corporate corruption after the fact, instead of the goat who spoiled AllSafe for everybody.

"Show they knew?" Merry thought she'd given him an incredulous stare before; it seemed positively jaded compared to the one she could feel on her face now.

Why'd she have to look at him that way? Yuan looked back, slamming his reporter cool back into place. "Sorry. It's not that your idea isn't a good one. The timing's just not right."

Silence spread between them, diluted with the bustling noise of the newsroom. Voices called instructions and speculations to each other, discussed stories, cracked jokes—and failed to distract Merry from her steady, dumbfounded concentration on the reporter. Yuan gave up on eye contact altogether and started organizing the random stacks of stuff on his desk in a businesslike fashion that he hoped would let her know that the interview had come to an end. (More like crashed to a halt.)

Realizing he wouldn't act even if he did believe her (or fully understand the implications she'd tried to explain), Merry swallowed the lump of fury and frustration in her throat. What could she do, threaten to beat him up unless he went on the air immediately? And then threaten to beat up his boss? And the boss's boss? "I'm sorry too."

"Oh! Hi!" Missy moved against her shoulder, her arm coming up to wave happily down the passageway.

Merry's head whipped around, in time to see four figures coming out of the elevator. The woman in front of the group had the tired, impatient, aristocratic expression of a top-level manager, handling an unpleasant duty she couldn't delegate to anybody else. The other three were all men, one bald, one with a flat-top, and one blond, sleek in their suits, their thick arms swinging at their wide shoulders, pulling their jackets open enough for Merry to catch a glimpse of brown leather and black metal. The gun registered before the next flash of recognition hit her like a bolt of cold lightning: she'd last seen the bald, mustached leader in a MedaGen uniform, glaring down at her as she entered the company's lobby.

Now, he glared at her over the top of the cubicles, then smiled. It was the first time she'd seen him smile, and it had been worth waiting for—worth waiting forever for, as a matter of fact. She felt, more than saw, the three of them brush past the Channel 8 administrator as she turned to run. Yuan's face was a blur of surprise and apology as he rose, babbling something she couldn't take time to hear. She just hoped he'd get in their way.

Cubicle walls, shoulder high, made a rat maze around them. Merry left Yuan's office and made a sharp right, trying to crouch and run in her dress shoes, clutching Missy close. Missy ducked and grabbed, her little hands closing on Merry's blouse in a death grip.

Merry bounced off the opposite wall as she took another turn too fast, then rebounded into another narrow, gray passageway. She risked a quick groundhog-bounce to look above the cubicles. Baldie was right behind her, taking the sharp turn with the grace of a trained athlete. Flattop's dark head showed above the line of cubicles on her right. And Blondie appeared in front of her, springing out of a cross-corridor to grab for her. Merry backpedaled, nearly falling as her smooth-soled shoes slipped on the thin carpeting. Her clumsy lurch made his reach go wide; she ducked under his arm and took another fast turn, only to come face-to-face with a young woman carrying files between the offices. Merry used her as an anchor to take the next turn, holding her arm long enough to help make the tight corner. A straightaway opened in front of her, just a few startled media hounds between her and a long bank of windows.

A shriek and fountain of papers behind her warned Merry that Blondie hadn't avoided a collision with the intern with the folders. That might slow him down, but now Baldie and Flattop had broken from the maze too. Praying that they wouldn't actually shoot, Merry kicked off her shoes and ran for the far end, scattering reporters and clerks in her wake. The pursuit had finally started causing enough commotion for the office's inhabitants to start stirring; the passageways were getting choked with milling, questioning bodies. *Please, God, please, show me the way out*, Merry pleaded, dodging through the crowd, running parallel to the windows, hoping for a cross-wall that would lead her back to the elevators. A few Channel 8 citizens tried to stop her, babbling questions or orders, but not firmly enough to do more than slow her down momentarily. She still had the lead, surfing the edge of the crowd wave that thickened behind her.

A fast glance back showed that Blondie and Baldie had abandoned all pretense of politeness, shoving their way through the crowd with sheer force. Blondie and Baldie—where was Flattop? A hard wall and wooden doors loomed suddenly before her; she thudded into one, guarding Missy with her shoulder, rolled along it, and kept running. How big could this place possibly be? Her breath burned in her chest, pressed against her hammering heart. She couldn't keep this up much longer. She half stumbled on a trailing bit of plastic sheeting trailing from the emergency exit, then backed sharply as she saw the ladder filling the doorway. The repairman perched on top of it gawked at her, fish-eyed as she sped up again. Another corner—that's three, she should be heading back where she came in. Yes! The green of the ficus trees guarding the elevators flashed across her vision.

So did the hard, obsidian gleam of Flattop's pistol as he stepped around one of the trees. He gave her a Doberman smile, leveling the weapon at her head. "Got something to say to a reporter, little lady?"

"Gun!" she managed to shriek to anyone who'd listen. "Terrorists! Please help!" Missy added a heartbreaking, terrified wail.

Chaos plunged into pandemonium. Flattop's finger convulsed on the trigger as the first wave of the earthquake rolled beneath them. The shot went wide, sizzling past Merry's head to blast a hole in one of the video monitors. Sparks cascaded down while cubicle walls threatened to collapse like dominoes.

Merry's field of vision narrowed to a sheet of plastic, white in the stark illumination of the emergency lights that seemed to be vibrating, then suddenly jumping. She clawed back along the wall, feeling the building sway lightly on its foundations as it rode out the tremors. Ducking under the rocking ladder in the emergency-exit doorway, she looked up in time to see the large air-conditioning panel the repairman had been working on come loose from its half-fastened frame and tumble in impossible slow motion to the floor. Bits of the crushed ladder spanged into the walls around her, skittering across the metal and concrete steps as she pelted down them. One more shiver, then the steps went still under her feet. Her legs threatened to give way, but somehow kept going. Twelve, ten, six, three—the lobby door gave way to her frantic shove. She stumbled out into the crowded reception area, accompanied by a low cloud of dust.

"She's got a baby!" An authoritative voice broke through the commotion. "Let her through!"

Strong hands—the receptionist's, Merry realized—caught her shoulder, guiding her through the crowd. "It's okay, it's over. Are you all right? Is your little girl all right?"

"I'm fine," Merry gasped, catching her breath and smiling at the woman. "I'm fine. So's Missy."

"Fine," Missy quavered, blinking uncertainly.

"Whoo, what a ride," Merry told her, trying to head off a melt-down—for both of them. "Did Mommy ever run down those stairs!"

"Run," Missy agreed, perking up at Merry's bright tone. She coughed.

"Thanks so much," Merry told the receptionist, striking out for the door. "She'll be fine. I just need to get her out into the fresh air."

In the street, people had recovered from their initial surprise, and (since the damage appeared to be minimal or nonexistent) were either shakily comparing notes or getting back about their business with the blasé attitude of Californians used to the Earth's little tantrums. A couple of bystanders glanced at Merry with her Sheetrock-dusted jacket, but most had their own business to attend to. She concentrated on putting one foot in front of the other (this pair of nylons was destined for the trash), hugging Missy, and sending a fervent prayer of thanks.

"Did you do that?" Carmen's voice startled her out of her almost painful relief.

"No, but God may have. I'm very glad it happened when it did." Merry panted and then took a deep breath, trying to calm her heart. "Carmen, they sent security guards after me. MedaGen did. They chased me all over that office—had me cornered—and the earthquake hit."

"Divine intervention again," Carmen said decisively. "Now, let's not waste it. Come on—in the van, before they come after you!"

Merry didn't hesitate, tucking Missy into her car seat and collapsing gratefully into the passenger seat. "I don't think they'll be coming soon. The elevators all lock down during an emergency, and there was this big air-conditioning thing that fell across the emergency exit."

"Right after you got past it?" Carmen asked rhetorically. "Yup, divine intervention."

The idea made Merry feel strangely significant, and altogether too spotlighted. That wasn't the way her world worked. In her world, drunk drivers crashed into cars, and people died. "It's not who does it, it's that it gets done," Chris's voice said softly in her memory. She shrugged off the paralyzing debate threatening to start in her head. Whether it was divinely assisted luck or the direct hand of God, she and Missy had gotten out safely. They still had their original problem, however. "Yuan's not going to run the story. Channel 8 doesn't want to ruin its ratings, go out on a limb, or offend MedaGen. We're back at square one, Carmen. Except that now I know I need to start an exercise program, if I have to keep running like this!"

Carmen laughed, as Merry hoped she would, then concentrated on getting them out of the downtown traffic before the emergency vehicles arrived.

Merry sighed, rubbing her eyes. She had to find a way to keep as many people from getting the "vaccine" as possible, but without Yuan, how could they get the word out wide enough and fast enough?

* * *

"In here," Calvin's voice came softly through the thin wooden panel, barely louder than the backroom echo of the pounding beat that always filled Carlito's.

Dove stood at the head of the short conference table in the well-lit room, trying for casual confidence but radiating intense, focused purpose. Trujo, the strip club's huge, tattooed bouncer, pulled the door open for a small group of apprehensive merchants and shopkeepers. They looked even more surprised when they recognized Dove.

"Aren't you supposed to be dead?" Chavez, the owner of the race-track and *Abuelo's* something-cousin, broke the momentary silence.

"Yes. But as you see, I'm not." Dove gestured for them to take seats around the table.

"So what do you want from us, since you're not dead?" Chavez leaned on the back of a chair, not sitting. "You come collecting protection money again? Slick's already sent his boys. We got nothing to give you."

"I want your help to run Slick and his General out of here," Dove said simply.

The businessmen exchanged looks: incredulous, nervous, angry, and vaguely hopeful.

"Do you like the way Slick's running things?" Dove asked, looking from one face to another.

That broke their silence in a torrent of furious imprecations and complaints. Where *Abuelo* had hit them up for protection money on the *Señor's* behalf, he'd at least come through with his end of the deal. "I paid up, I didn't see you clowns again for a month, unless some jackass tried to knock over my shop" as Escobedo, the tobacco seller, put it. That, they could put up with, even respect. The *Señor* and *Abuelo* provided the security, peace, and protection that the police had long since given up trying to enforce (in fact, most of them were Pizarro's men, or sold out directly to the *Señor*). But Slick didn't uphold the contract. He was bleeding the town dry, letting Rico (whom they described with a level of profanity that won Perro's grudging admiration) lead the southern dregs doing whatever they wanted.

"They busted up my store, even after I paid them!" Escobedo shouted indignantly—and everybody else had a similar story. *Abuelo's* gang had been part of the community (if a disreputable and often resented part), but Slick's troop of thugs, drug runners, and coyotes swaggered through the town, treating it like conquered territory. They made everybody nervous, scared off legitimate customers, and beat up anybody who crossed their path, making life impossible for "honest businessmen," as the men around the table described themselves.

Dove listened intently, asking a question here and there not so much for information as to help them remember the full extent of the outrages Slick and Rico had committed. "It's been bad," he agreed, breaking into the litany of abuses when they started repeating themselves. The confidence and prophetic foreboding in his tone caught their attention. "It's going to get worse."

"How worse?" Chavez asked. "What's worse than having my shop busted up every other week?"

"How about having your shop busted up every day?" Dove suggested. "Or burned down entirely, to make room for something else? Or left perfectly all right, but under new management—because you came down with a bad case of the Plague?"

"Plague?" Escobedo asked. The others muttered, exchanging haunted looks.

"Plague," Dove affirmed. "You've all heard rumors about that farm out by Blanca Hacienda. It's not Recho Ojo's ghosts killing people there, *Señores*, just like it's not ghosts killing the drug towns down south. It's the General putting down people who get in his way.

He doesn't even waste bullets on them. He's sent Slick up from the South, looking for money to funnel back down there, putting down the *Señors* and runners, so he can take over their operations."

"And how do we know all this isn't just you spouting off?" Chavez demanded. "Cause you're mad at Rico for shooting your leader and trying to off you?"

Dove met his gaze steadily. "You can look at what's going on. You think Slick's just settling in as the new *Señor*, taking over from *Abuelo*, and things'll go back to normal as soon as he's done flexing? You want to trust Slick to take care of you? Think about what you've heard. And think about this: why would Slick want to kill me? Why would he kill Benny? It's 'cause I've seen the disease he's spreading first hand, and he doesn't want that getting out before he's ready to tell it. You're not safe with Slick. He's not here to settle, he's here to make money for his boss. You're low-hanging fruit for him to squeeze dry and throw away. And that's the best-case scenario."

"So what do you want us to do? Pay another round of that phone tax your little buddy went 'round collecting yesterday? Pay some other protection money?" The others looked to Martel, the landlord who owned most of Main Street and a half share of Pizarro. He didn't say much, but when he did, everybody listened. He'd negotiated the terms with the former *Señor*, but hadn't made any headway with Slick. "Or you want something else from us now? You say Slick's working for this General, who's got his own business down south and the weapons to back it up. You want us to stand up to them? You want us to stop them? How?"

Angry, nervous commentary ran through the half-dozen businessmen. "Yeah, they're so tough, we're supposed to do what?" "Why you telling us all this?" "We're dead, that what you're saying?"

Dove brought his hands down on the table with a report that brought everybody's attention back to him. "No, I don't want you to stop them. I'll do that," he glanced at Perro and Calvin, then amended, "we'll do that. What you've got to do is make sure there's no way he can get back in."

"How do we do that?" Martel asked. He left the question of how Dove thought he could stop the General hanging in the air. Somehow, he believed the kid could do it.

"The reason *Abuelo*—and the *Señor* behind him—could hit you up for protection money is that you let them." Dove held up his hands, raising his voice to overcome the immediate flood of denial and argument. "No, listen! You say the cops wouldn't protect you, that they were dirty. Right. They are. So hire your own. Elect a sheriff who'll work *for* you. If you all stand together, if you convince everybody in town with a stake in security to work together, you can close the crack the snakes use to get in. Thing is, you all have to work together. If one of you bails, that'll leave a hole. You've got to watch each other's backs, and you've got to be willing to defend yourselves from the coyotes. You either be your own pack of wolves, or you'll end up skinned like sheep."

"Easier said than done," Escobedo snorted. "You learn all that social-theory crap in high school, kid?"

"In history class," Dove shot back. "And on the job. You used to hand me five grand a month, Escobedo, because you didn't dare stand up to *Abuelo* with nobody to protect your back."

Martel stood, cutting off the mutters that followed Escobedo's challenge—and Dove's blunt assessment of their behavior. "So we hang together, defend ourselves against the coyotes, close ranks against the snakes you're talking about. Who says that works?"

"Albuquerque does," Dove told them. "The Navajo Nation does. White Sands does. Slick's just a nastier, better backed version of the usual gangs and runners we've got all over the borderlands. They're not hitting the big cities, the military bases, the places where the legitimates stand up to them. They need you to be afraid of them, to be weak and isolated. They're parasites, not predators—they'll hit you hard to make you knuckle under, but they don't want a real war, can't support an actual occupation. You stand together, you don't give in, you hit them back hard, and they'll find easier targets. It'll cost you blood, too, but if you knock their teeth out, they're not going to come back. Remember, I was one of those guys. I know."

Martel stared at him under lowering brows for a long moment. The atmosphere in the room crystallized suddenly as he grinned. "You talk a good line, kid. Come back when you're 21, and we just might elect you sheriff. For now, you got things to do. Go put a wrench in Slick's machine. We'll talk about how to keep another one from driving into town." He gestured sharply as Escobedo started to object. The other businessmen fell into calculating silence, watching Martel as Dove nodded (almost regally, one commander to another) and strode to the door. Trujo opened it, and the three boys disappeared into the light-shot darkness of Carlito's. Behind them, a furious debate erupted, voices raised in argument and negotiation.

"Bet General Moroni never had a strategy meeting in a strip club," Dove muttered to himself.

"General who?" Perro shrugged it off, batting at Calvin as Calvin hauled him along, avoiding the main room with its two tiny stages and handful of noon-time regulars. "Dove, what was that? Why you wasting time talking to the suits? They can't help us!"

"That's called securing our flank, Perrito," Dove told him. "We want to stop the bad guys, we're going to need a lot of backup—and we can't waste time trying to defend a bunch of sheep who roll over when the next wolf pack comes into town."

"Think there'll be another wolf pack?" Calvin asked.

"There always will be, until the end," Dove assured him. "And it's just going to get meaner from here for awhile. Things are getting tight. It's down to the part where the good guys have to choose sides and stick together or get run over." A flash of white caught his eye— and he caught a young man wearing the shirt.

The young missionary blinked, his eyes going from Dove to Calvin to Perro (grinning maliciously as always), then to his companion. His companion, more familiar with the area, recognized the guys confronting them from his own days as a greenie. It was a true testament to his faith and strength of personality that he managed to plaster a smile onto his face. "What can we do for you gentlemen?" he asked.

Dove smiled at him, genuine warmth suddenly blazing from his dark eyes. "You can keep up the good work, Elders. And, next few days, you can keep your heads down. There's going to be some shooting going on. Don't want you caught out in the lead rain. Let the local branch know too. Get down, stay tight, and pray."

"Right. Will do," the missionary blinked.

Dove patted his shoulder approvingly, thumped the other affectionately, and strode off down the street.

"Who were those gringos?" Perro asked, blinking in disbelieving incomprehension.

"God's Army," Dove told him, and laughed. "The regular troops. Come on, Perrito, pick up your feet—let's get the reserves called up."

Calling the reserves took longer, with a lot more stealth built in. The first official strategy meeting took place in Franklin's back room. Mama Rosa's was no longer the gang's hangout of choice—that dubious honor belonged to Benny's house. Perro assured Dove that using the restaurant as a base of operations was a good idea—they'd been doing their homework there anyway, so Rico knew the gang's junior members would be there. Perfect cover, right?

"If Franklin's okay with it," Dove had conditionally agreed. "Let's ask him first."

The old cook grinned hugely when Dove appeared at his back door. "Well, 'pears the rumors of your death have been highly exaggerated, or whatever that Mark Twain character said!" he drawled. "You come back to set things right?" he asked, motioning Dove in with a bandaged arm.

"I've come back to set things right," Dove told him solemnly. He glanced around at the kitchen, noting the freshly patched holes in the walls, the broken fan over the big stove. It looked like it had been dented by a bowling ball—or a skull. "You okay with us using your back room to do it from? It could be dangerous."

"Dangerous!" Franklin's eyes darkened. He stirred the frijoles fiercely. "Back room, front room, wherever. That southern cockroach, strutting around like he owns the place—and Rico! That idiot, shooting *Abuelo* and bragging about it! I let them know their kind ain't welcome 'cross this threshold no more."

"Is that how you broke your arm?" Dove asked quietly.

Franklin snorted. "My arm and my nose—but the nose's come back quicker. Would've had me in my own oven, 'cept that bull Marco butts in. He tells Rico I'm just an old man, not worth the time, and starts smacking me around, tossing me into things until I hit the floor and don't get up. Then he's standing over me, arguing that if they shoot me, he won't get his enchilada fix no more. Who's gonna cook for him? They crack some Mammy jokes, tell me they'll set fire to my place if I don't pay them protection like everybody else, rob my till, and leave."

"I'm sorry, Franklin." Dove closed his eyes, shoving down the rage that boiled up in him. *Don't get mad, just stop them.*

"Ain't your fault, kid." Franklin spared him a world-weary glance and sighed. "It's just the way life goes."

"For now it is," Dove looked at the old cook, "but it won't be forever. And we'll be there to help it."

"Hey, Dove!" Perro and Calvin slipped through the door, Perro grinning brightly. "You know how you said we had a communication problem? Well, not anymore. Just call me Ma Bell!" He upended his backpack. A couple dozen small, sleek PDDs (personal digital devices—pagers, instant messengers, phones, computers, all in tiny, and mostly designer, cases) scattered over the surface of Franklin's heavy work table like a scatter of glittering, multicolored beetles.

Dove picked up one of the plastic jewels, flicked it open and watched its tiny screen light up. He looked at Perro, unable to suppress a grin. "This what Martel was talking about, the 'phone tax' thing?"

Perro utterly failed to look contrite. "Hey, I got these before we decided to go Lone Ranger. And now, well, we need them for the fight."

"Commandeering necessary materiel and supplies," Calvin clarified.

"What've you commandeered?" Dove asked, noting Calvin's bulging backpack.

"Nothing." He set the heavy bag on the table, unzipping it to pull out a heart-stoppingly familiar jacket.

"Benny's coat," Dove said softly, taking it.

"Yeah," Calvin rummaged in the bag. "I stopped by your old house, you know, checking in, making an appearance for Rico, catching up with Boris and Scruffy. Figured I'd get Dolores to give me a couple things; said I needed some more clothes. She gave me most of everything Rico hadn't taken or torn up. Most of your clothes were okay. You're lucky Rico's too caught up in Slick's big plans to go through the closet."

Dove looked up from the almost-comforting jacket (it still smelled like Benny, making his eyes swim with tears). "You asked Dolores for these? Was that smart, Calvin?"

Calvin met his eyes easily, even as he shrugged. "Things have changed since you've been gone, *Hasbidí*. Dolores, too. It's been bad. She might even help us, if she could stab Rico a good one."

"Maybe." Dove fell silent, thinking about Benny's ex-girlfriend cozying up to Cesare, moving to Rico when it looked advantageous—then getting used as a canary in Slick's disease coal mine and watching Sasha cough herself to death. "Let's concentrate on more sure bets for now," he suggested.

They did, gathering small groups of potential allies together in meetings. Perro and Calvin quietly spread the word to the junior members of the gang, the ones who'd been part of Dove's posse before Rico staged his coup. They sent younger brothers or sisters or girl-friends to deliver discreet invitations to others, based on recommendations from trustworthy recruits: the rougher but good-hearted guys from the alternative school; the young border rats that used to knuckle under to *Abuelo's* gang, hoping to get in; junior members of the gangs Slick had taken over, the ones without the status to share in the booty while they took the risks; biker cliques that hired themselves out for extra enforcement work without actually belonging to the gangs; even a few roustabouts and roughnecks working the oil rigs and mines, the ones who came around for Franklin's molé at Mama Rosa's and stayed for the card games.

Perro hadn't exaggerated when he told Dove that things had changed—but in this case, the changes worked to their advantage. *Abuelo* had run his gang as a bizarre version of a family, a family of criminals, true, but a family nonetheless, one that took care of its members and looked out for the kids who tagged along. Slick had wiped out the patriarch of the family, but he hadn't taken his place. He ran the gang like a mercenary troop, with little patience for personal loyalties between the soldiers—and even less for their dependents. Weakness—broadly defined in Slick's handbook to include any lingering evidence of morals, emotional attachment, or simple aversion to blindly following orders—instantly rendered a man unfit for the borderlands detachment of the General's army. If the man in question were lucky, it didn't render him dead as well. (Women never even got as far as being evaluated for "weakness"—their gender automatically disqualified them as anything but tools, decorations, or victims.) Rico's coterie fit in well with the select crew of hardened drug runners, assassins, guerillas, and southern rebels that Slick recruited for his personal strike force.

The other members of *Abuelo's* gang, and the two or three other enforcer bands who'd shared the *Señor's* patronage in that area of the borderlands, found themselves suddenly cast adrift, if not actively liquidated. Thus, Dove's discreet call for volunteers found plenty of takers. They trickled into Mama Rosa's back room at all hours of the night, under cover of Calvin's all-night study sessions—and Perro's eternal parties. Dove ducked into the bathroom when Marco looked in twice, casually smacked Perro down and gave the rest of the kids the evil eye, reminding them that Rico still "owned" them, now that *Abuelo* was gone. He growled at them until Franklin set up a fuss about Marco scaring away his customers. "The racket these flea-bit pups are making doesn't scare 'em, I'm not going to," the big man snorted—but he stalked out.

The silence lasted until the sound of his footsteps died away outside the back door. Then the incessant salsa music—and the intense discussion that used the music as cover—started up again. The meetings followed the same basic pattern each time; only the small group across the work table changed. The venting session always came first. Most comments, whispered, growled, or said aloud (in a few bold cases) dwelled on how things had changed for the worse since *Abuelo's* death.

Talking to potential guerillas, Dove dispensed with the social-cohesiveness theory he'd used with Martel and the merchants in favor of laying out what Slick and the General were up to—and the potential risks versus rewards for the soldiers who threw their lot in with Slick and Rico.

"You think working for Slick sounds good? You've all heard stories about how he pays off his own guys with a bullet if they mess up. Take a look at what happened to the *Brujos.* He used them up, blew them up—and then when he got another gang, he tore them up. Down to the last man. Paco here can tell you about that." Dove gestured to the limping Brujo.

Paco took a deep drag on his cigarette before telling the audience (sometimes incredulous, sometimes suspicious, always attentive) about what happened when the General decided he didn't need them anymore. "He called a meeting, just like usual—only when we got there, he had Rico's boys there, plus some Southerners I didn't know from before. Cut us down like rabbits, as we came in the door. I got hit in the first wave, went down, played dead. Saw them laughing, shooting at my posse like it was some game. Even the girls. They cut Maria's throat, to stop her crying." The story got worse from there: Slick ordered all of the *Brujos* eliminated, down to their mamas and babies. "'For failing,' he said." Only Paco and a few others had escaped, all wounded, and all shell shocked, hating Slick with a bitter, bone-freezing passion.

Calvin quickly learned to tune out when Paco started talking, to sit back and watch the others' reactions. Perro just put himself on lookout duty.

Dove listened, his eyes wet every time. The tears didn't show in his voice, though, when he told them about the coyote gang dead at Blanca Hacienda, the farmers who caught the plague scavenging from the dead, Sasha coughing her life out because Slick wanted to test a new kind of poison, the ambush that killed Benny and wounded him, *Abuelo* dying in a hail of bullets from his own lieutenant. It wasn't all Dove talking, either; Slick had already gained a reputation for liquidating anybody who disappointed him.

"You're not safe with Slick," he finished. "He's got no honor, doesn't play by the rules, isn't interested in earning your loyalty. And if he thinks you're a threat, even if he doesn't need you anymore, he'll kill you. Like he did *Abuelo*. Like he did my brother Benny, for standing up to him. Like he tried to do to me."

"Rico said he shot you." Sometimes the statement came out as a challenge, sometimes as a question, but it always came: Rico had bragged about shooting Dove and Benny for mouthing off to him, promising the same to anybody else who crossed him.

"No, Slick shot me, while Rico yelled for Cesare and Marco to do his work for him." Dove pulled off his shirt, turning to show the scar that ran down his back, from shoulder to lower ribs. "But it didn't kill me. And now I'm back, like a ghost they can't shake, to stop them for good."

He swept them with that intense, confident look. "You can help. You can fight to keep yourselves safe, keep your families safe, drive Slick and his thugs out of here. We have a plan, we have weapons, we just need you to show you have the backbone it takes to keep breathing. We're fighting on our home territory here, for our honor, for our families. Slick and Rico are weaker than they think they are, because they've squeezed too hard, spread themselves too thin. We can stop them, if we hit them hard and fast, before they realize that we're coming. Are you with us?"

Calvin watched the faces change, doubt morphing into determination as Dove spoke, their answers coming in shouts, growls, or whispers, but always "yes." Dove had always been persuasive—that's why he was always getting himself in trouble, talking about honor and stirring up questions in the gang. But now, he had even more of *it* than he ever had, coming back from the dead with a light in his eyes that hadn't been there before. When he talked, you believed he could face down Slick—and that you could do it too. More importantly, the effect lasted even after the meeting broke up. Mostly, Dove told him, because they always gave everybody something to do, whether it was spreading rumors about Slick's General, gathering up ammunition and weapons caches the various gangs had stashed, or keeping an eye on the Southerners' movements. Each team got a PDD, linked to send messages, rumors, and reports to each other—and to get orders from headquarters. Dove also assigned each team in twos and threes so they could look after each other, and because having a buddy depending on you made it harder to duck off and sell them out to Slick. Of course, the altogether too plausible warning that spilling word of the conspiracy to Slick would earn the messenger a bullet between the eyes (if not something worse) carried a lot of weight.

"That scar on your back's pretty cool too," Perro noted, as they slipped into the back of Mama Rosa's for a follow-up meeting with Calvin and Perro's original recruits from *Abuelo's* gang. "It's way better than just a missing toe or something. Too bad you didn't get swiped across the face, to make it more dramatic."

"Thanks for the thought, Perro." Dove rolled his eyes, then grinned at the familiar faces around the table. "Hey, Boris, Natasha, Scruffy, you came. Calvin said we could trust you, that you'd be smart."

"Yeah, smart," Boris snorted. "Last two days, it's like somebody stuck a stick in a hornet's nest. Been hearing rumors you're back,

Dove, dead or alive or whatever. It's spread through town like fire ants. I mean, I'm glad it's true." His face softened slightly, then hardened again. "But it's got us nervous that Slick's going to hear. Rico caught Scruffy here and about choked him, trying to shake out what he knows."

"Did you spill?" Perro asked.

Scruffy rolled his eyes. "Duh, Perro. You see Rico here? With his hands around my neck, I just flopped around and gacked. If he'd thought about it, he'd've let go of my throat enough to make me answer. Finally let me go, kicked me out."

Natasha nodded. He'd earned his nickname because his real handle, an Eastern European nightmare of consonants, hadn't flown trippingly from the gang's tongues—and because, between his height, black hair, thick accent, and his buddy Boris's name, it was pretty much inevitable that somebody would come up with a "Boris and Natasha" gag. Perro started it, expecting a fight, but Natasha had just grinned, said something guttural in Serbian, and answered to it. He still did, even after the accent had faded into a weird pastiche of Serbian, Spanish, and Valley American. "Rico's freaked, but he still thinks we're just dumb kids. What everybody else is saying, though, is that you're a ghost or something. They all want to know if it's true that you're going to hit Slick, for offing *Abuelo*."

"We're going to hit Slick," Dove confirmed, "but not just for offing *Abuelo*. We've got to stop him from bleeding this whole place dry to feed his General down south, from killing everybody worth anything. And then using the area as a hole to bring his plague through."

"Whatever, as long as we're going to hit him." Boris shrugged. "That'll buy us a lot of karma points. He hit *Abuelo*, and that's enough for me. Rico's been threatening to shoot everybody who doesn't swear loyalty to him—and take a shot from Slick to prove it. The —— with that. You got something better, we can get six more guys in on it. Think you can work up some money too?"

"I've got something better." Dove settled onto a stack of bean sacks. "Even if I can't offer them money, I can offer them a chance to hit Slick and drive him back where he came from at least. I've been talking to Paco—"

"That Brujo?" Natasha asked, snorting. Old prejudices died hard.

"Yes." Dove waved away the incipient objection, quickly sketching outlines over the table as he talked. "Slick used them first, since they were running drugs up for the Shonjiri cartel. Paco said the General wants the money from the drug trade to send back south. He was planning to stage a big fight with the cartel guys around here, to secure the markets in California and points north. That means he needs soldiers—but he's sent ammo and weapons already. Remember that warehouse we burned up, the one the *Brujos* were guarding? That wasn't just the cocaine that burned so hot, but the *Brujos* got most of their materiel out of there beforehand. They moved it out to SkateTown. Now, we grab all we can from there and destroy the rest. That gives us the firepower we need to go against Slick."

"And how do we plan to do that?" Boris leaned back, crossing his arms.

"Slick likes staging ambushes," Dove grinned tightly. "Let's see if he can take it as well as he can dish it out. We'll make him chase us out to a good place, then turn it all on him."

"We're going to have to move fast," Boris warned, leaning forward again. "Listen, nobody's outright spilled yet, but there's word going 'round that something's happening. They're going to find out—"

"They have!" Everybody froze at Scruffy's frantic announcement. He'd been watching the dining room through the swinging doors. "Marco's coming!"

"Marco's here!" Perro corrected, as the big man shoved through the flimsy doors.

Habit instantly kicked in. Junior bucks never got in the top lieutenants' way—even when they weren't plotting treason. Boris, Natasha, and Scruffy sprang out of their chairs, launching themselves toward Mama Rosa's back door. One of the overturned chairs flipped hard, skittering across the floor and tripping Perro, sending him sprawling into Calvin and bringing them both to the floor. Their flailing bodies crashed into the door, closing it hard behind the three escapees.

Cursing, Marco lunged toward Perro and Calvin—and came up short as Dove stepped in front of him.

"Hey, Marco," he said casually. He kicked back, connecting with some soft part of either Perro or Calvin. The writhing mass stilled, either too scared to move or taking Dove's hint.

"Dove," Marco managed, surprise blunting the hard edge in his voice. He shook off the shock (and uncomfortable flash of guilt), glowering darkly at the younger man. "I heard you got back—and heard you got to stirring up problems again." He spat in disgust. "Boris and Scruffy. Figures they'd come sniffing around."

"They've always been smart kids," Dove agreed, smiling. "Boris, Scruffy, and Natasha. They can see what's right, when you put it in front of them."

Behind him, Calvin swatted Perro off; the two of them settled warily, backs against the door, watching Dove and Marco. The shine of the gun in Marco's hand sent them into retreat mode again. They rose to their feet in unison, both reaching for the handle at the same time.

"Cut it out," Dove advised them, rolling his eyes. Those eyes came back around to focus on Marco again. "Marco's not going to shoot us."

"I'm not?" Marco snarled.

"No." Dove laughed, drawing stares from the others. He walked toward Marco. "You're not. You didn't shoot me when Rico and Slick ambushed us. Remember? You stood there, watching Rico, not wanting to shoot me—or Benny. It was Cesare who shot at us when Rico told him to. Remember what happened to him?"

Marco tried to hide a flinch, which made him angry. He brought the gun up to point between Dove's eyes. "You keep talking, same thing's gonna happen to you."

"It won't," Dove assured him. "Because there are three of us and one of you," his hand slashed out, neatly snatching the gun out of Marco's grip, "and you're unarmed." He tossed the gun behind him. It skittered across the floor to stop between Calvin's feet.

Marco wasted just a second staring at his empty hand, before he roared and charged head down at Dove. It took Perro and Calvin longer to process the implications, but insurrection was an easy habit to acquire. Calvin snatched the gun, bringing it to bear on Marco as Dove whirled quickly out of the big man's way. Marco crashed into the wall and bounced off. He slewed around, clawing the strings of dried peppers away from his shoulders. A motion from Perro caught his eye, just before one of Franklin's pots caught him upside the head. Stars erupted behind Marco's eyes, and Dove landed on his back.

* * *

By the time the stars cleared, Marco found himself hogtied, lying folded in an uncomfortably tight space. He looked up at Calvin, pointing his own gun at his head, then at Perro grinning like a runt kid who's managed to put one over on a notorious bully. Perro's grin faded slightly as he met their captive's glare.

"Untie me, or I'll eat your guts—fried, with onions," Marco rumbled. *I'm in the trunk*, he realized. *I'm in the trunk of that sorry wreck they drive. Those uppity coyotes knocked me out and put me in their trunk!*

"Not yet," Dove said. He leaned casually against the Dogmobile's side panel and looked down at Marco before glancing at the sky. "I figure we've got a couple of hours before Rico starts wondering where you are."

"What?" Marco blinked at him. "I went looking for Boris, tracking down rumors."

"And the rumors turned out to be true." Dove asked. "You found me, plotting against Slick—and Rico."

"My lucky day," Marco grunted.

Perro laughed. "Whoa, Marco, I didn't think you were smart enough to be sarcastic!" He startled, but didn't skitter back as Marco lunged against the side of the trunk, spitting a blue streak about Perro's parentage. Ten years of ducking under blows aimed at his head boiled up in a flash; Perro snarled and lashed out, his fist striking Marco's cheekbone with a dull crack.

Dove caught his arm before he delivered the second blow. "Easy, Perro. Don't turn into a bully the minute you get the chance to hit somebody who can't hit you back."

"What do you want?" Marco asked, interrupting Perro's hot retort.

"We want you to help us," Dove told him.

"Help you?" Marco gave him an incredulous look, then burst into laughter. His guffaws slowly died away, however, under three deadly sober stares. (Emphasis on "deadly"—at least in Perro's case.) He stared from one to the other, ending with Dove. "You serious?"

"I'm serious." Dove leaned down to look deeply into Marco's eyes. "Here's the deal, Marco. You agree to help us, we untie you right now, and you live past Sunday. I promise we'll do everything we can to protect you."

"If I don't help?" Marco glared back at Dove.

Dove sat back and shrugged. "I close the trunk, and we drive the Dogmobile around the back roads long enough for Rico—and, more importantly, Slick—to realize you're missing. We'll dump you out to walk home. By the time you get back, there'll be a new rumor around, all about how you found me and told me all about Slick's ammo dumps."

"He's not gonna believe that," Marco informed him, with something less than perfect confidence.

"Not at first," Dove conceded. "But after we've hit SkateTown and blown up everything we don't take, he might see things differently."

"How do you know about SkateTown?" Marco asked—and belatedly bit his tongue.

"Paco told me. One of the few *Brujos* who survived landing on Slick's bad side." Dove flicked out his knife, casually testing the edge on his thumb. "So, Marco, what'll it be? Do I cut you loose now or after the raid? You want to take your chances with Rico and Slick, or with us?"

Marco weighed his options. Even though nobody (including himself) took him for an intellectual heavyweight, he'd managed to land on his feet through fifteen years of borderland skirmishes. That had a lot to do with his size, strength, and basic fearlessness, but it also came from his ability to pick a competent leader and follow him unquestioningly. Lately, however, questions had started bubbling under his thick skull. He'd respected *Abuelo*, but Rico seemed to have more juice despite his macho attitude and hot temper. Marco had Rico figured for the gang's next leader and eagerly accepted the position as his left-hand man. Then things went south—literally—when Slick started in, filling Rico's head with big ideas and encouraging him to get even crazier than he was before. Marco hadn't liked the idea of ambushing Benny and Dove; you just didn't stab your own guys in the back like that. If Rico had a problem with them, he should've challenged them to a fair fight—Dove and Benny against Rico (which meant Rico, Cesare, and Marco).

It just got worse from there. He'd tried to stop Rico from turning on *Abuelo*. He shut up fast, though, when Rico turned on him, snarling that if he didn't want to obey Rico, he could take his chances with Slick. And Slick just looked at him behind those mirror shades and gave him that crocodile grin. Since then, he'd seen that ice-cold smile way too often, usually glinting over the sprawled bodies of the gang bangers or dust runners who turned down the opportunity to join Slick's operation. It was pretty clear that Rico wasn't running things anymore, if he ever had. Rico figured he was Slick's second in command, but Marco couldn't see any two-way relationship there: Slick said shoot, and Rico did.

So what would Slick say when Marco came in with a story about seeing Dove, talking to him, but not telling him anything? A sharp chill ran down his sweating back as he realized it wouldn't matter; Slick would as likely shoot him for letting three boys catch him as for telling them about his ammo dump out at SkateTown. He was already skating thin ice, defending that idiot Franklin out of stupid sentimentality. (It was hard to forget the free tortillas and beans Franklin had fed him when his uncle kicked him out to fend for himself or starve. Food and a kind word meant a lot to a beat-up twelve-year-old—enough to remember a dozen years later.)

Marco looked up at Dove, trying to listen to his instincts through the adrenaline tightening his gut. The kid was nuts, in a different way from Rico, always going on about honor. He sighed. "All right, let me up. I'll take my chances with you."

Dove nodded, unsurprised, and reached toward the clothesline bonds around Marco's arms.

"He said he'd help us," Dove said simply. He rested the hair-splittingly sharp blade against the rope—and against Marco's wrist. "And we're going to trust him just like he's going to trust us. We hold each other's lives. I'd like to appeal to a higher argument, but practical survival's going to have to do it for now."

The ropes fell away as Marco surged out of the trunk. Perro spat a curse and stepped back as Marco reached for him. When the big man's hand landed, however, it delivered an open-palmed clap on Perro's back. Marco grinned, the setting sun glinting off the gold caps on his eyeteeth. "You can trust me, Perrito. Dove's loco, but he's not psycho like Slick. I'll help you boys out." He looked them over, his eyes calculating as he noted that Calvin's steady aim hadn't wavered.

"You're smarter than they give you credit for," Dove told Marco, slapping him on the back and grinning. He sobered quickly, handing over a folded paper. "Get back fast, Marco. Gather up Boris and the others, give them this to let them know you're on our side, help keep them quiet. Don't make any move until I send word through Boris that we're ready to go."

"Better be quick," Marco advised. "Rumors have started flying around already." He took the gun from Calvin's reluctant but yielding hand.

"It'll be quick," Dove said, watching Marco lumber away. He patted Perro's shoulder reassuringly.

Perro shrugged off the touch, turning a hot glare on Dove. Years of casual abuse from Marco still stung hard. "How do you know we can trust him?"

"We don't." Calvin's flat statement surprised Perro. He shrugged. "That's why we didn't tell him anything but what he already knew—about Boris and the guys, about Dove being back. He didn't get anything else, and what he doesn't know, he can't tell Rico. That's why we've been meeting with everybody separate. Nobody knows who's on our side but us."

Dove grinned. "You got it. Understand, Perro? If we can trust Marco, we've got a good ally. If we can't, he can't give away our plans."

"Except the raid on the ammo dump," Perro reminded them.

"Which we're pulling tonight. Now, let's go get Boris and the guys, to let them know what's up. They can keep an eye on Marco for us, but I don't think they'll have to." He stretched, then opened the Dogmobile's door. "Marco's dependable, as long as we don't push him too far, or leave him to think about it too long. We've got to have somebody on the inside who knows how to handle himself in a fight, and give orders to the younger guys. Come on, let's get out of here.

We've got a couple more things to do before we're ready to take Slick on, and we're not the only ones spreading the word."

CHAPTER 16

"The most vital thing—the very most important thing we can do in this life, brothers and sisters, the one thing that can really make a difference in this sad, sorry world of ours—is spreading the good Word of the Lord!" Tommy Gibbs's elegantly down-home voice came through Carmen's van speakers with the rolling, thrilling cadences of a professional evangelist.

Merry rolled her eyes, but Carmen just grinned. "I know, you don't approve of Brother Gibbs and his never-ending crusade, but I kind of get a kick out of his speeches. They're so over the top, compared to the button-down calm we get from our General Authorities—though President Rojas tends to mix it up a little. Besides, it's listen to this or keep scanning stations trying to find one that's not playing Virginia's latest MedaGen jingle."

"You're driving, you get final say about the radio," Merry shrugged, smiling at Carmen. "I'm just glad you *are* driving!" She checked the rearview mirrors for the hundredth time, but no sinister sedan trailed their unlikely getaway vehicle. Reassured, she fell back into staring at (but not really through) the windshield, wracking her brains for a way to spread a totally different kind of truth as quickly as possible.

"Everywhere you go, testify!" Tommy urged. "Testify of Jesus' divine mercy, testify of the Savior's sweet love, testify of the righteous judgments of God! But you say, Brother Tommy, I don't know how to testify! I can feel my Savior's love in my heart, but when I try to testify, my tongue gets all tied up. How can I know what to say, to reach my precious brothers and sisters? What words can I use to rebuke the Devil? Well, you don't need to fret over that any more. Jesus has provided the answer in His scriptures, and we've taken those precious gospel truths and distilled them right down to their purest essence in a set of simple, easy, and above all, understandable lessons! Don't search for words, humble follower of Christ, use ours! Yes, right now, you can order these quick, easy, and indispensable teaching tools, for only a tiny donation—"

"Donation!" Missy exclaimed from the back seat. She waved a French fry happily. Any day Missy got french fries was by definition a good day—and stopping by the local Greaseteria to get the kids lunch to keep them quiet on the drive back from Channel 8's headquarters had saved Carmen's and Merry's sanity.

"Yeah, donation," Carmen sighed. "It always comes down to that, doesn't it? Sorry, Tommy, much as I like some of what you say, you just keep crossing the line." She reached for the scan button as Tommy spelled out the directions to his Web page yet again.

"Wait!" Merry sat up straight, animation flooding back into her face.

"What? You don't have that Web site memorized yet?" Carmen asked, blinking.

"Not his Web site, any Web site. Everything's online these days. Everybody's got a Web site—and everybody's got an electronic discussion group, including a whole bunch of geneticists," Merry exclaimed. "Yuan won't broadcast a simple explanation to everybody in general, but we can still get the data out. Carmen, how do we get to the library from here?"

"Conspiracy theorists, too, and MedaGen's competitors, and government watchdogs." A slow smile spread over Carmen's face. "All just waiting for a nice, anonymous posting."

* * *

"Why wait when there's other boys out there?—that's what I told Holly," Donna said into the phone tucked against her shoulder as she opened the Callattas' front door. She blinked at the two neatly dressed figures on the doorstep. "Okay, listen, somebody's at the door," she said, slightly more quietly. "I don't know, maybe Jehovah's Witnesses or something. I'll call you back."

Clicking off the phone, she smiled and returned to normal-conversation levels. "Hi. We're not interested in school fund-raisers, we're happy with our current security system, and we don't need to be saved. So, other than that, what can we do for you?"

The woman, a middle-aged, middle-sized, pleasant-looking person who strongly resembled Donna's second-grade teacher, smiled at her. "Well, you're forthright, aren't you?"

Donna smiled back, not budging an inviting inch from the doorway. "Mom says it saves time to get all the excuses out of the way up front. That's good for everybody. So, what's up?"

"Is this the Callatta residence?" This time the man asked the question. He had the same nicely nondescript businesslike wardrobe as the woman, but he looked younger, trimmer—and hungrier.

"Sure is," Donna affirmed. "You could've gotten that off the mailbox. What do you want?"

The woman shot her companion a quelling glance. "We're actually here on official business, dear. Is your mother home? We'd like to talk to her."

"Mom's gone for the day. Sorry." Donna took a step back, ready to close the door.

"Then maybe you can help us," the woman said hurriedly.

The man stepped forward, like he wanted to catch the door. He backed off when Donna's stare sharpened into a silent but clear warning.

"Maybe I can, if you'll tell me what your 'official business' is. And maybe I can't, if you're trying to pull something. Mom's not home, but we've got a dog, a deadbolt, and a phone with 9 and 1 buttons on it." She showed them the phone, flicking it on with a practiced thumb.

"Oh, dear, don't worry! It's nothing like that!" The woman's hands fluttered reassuringly, but her flustered act never made it to her eyes. "I'm Ms. White, and this is Mr. Cornell. We're just here to find out if your mother could help us find out about a coworker of ours, Ms. Meredith Anthony."

"Merry?" Donna blinked. "What about her? Do you work at MedaGen too?"

"Yes, we work at MedaGen. In fact, we work with Merry. She hasn't come to work in the last few days, and she hasn't called. That's really unlike her, so we got concerned." Ms. White leaned in confidentially. "Since she's a widow, all alone in the world, nobody to watch out for her, our manager, Mr. Humphrey, asked us if we would check up on her. So we can help, if we need to."

"We got your mom's name from a neighbor," Mr. Cornell added. He wasn't as good at playing harmless. "They said she babysat Ms. An—Merry's little girl?"

"Oh, sure," Donna smiled. "Yeah, we tend Missy. We run a daycare, guaranteed certified and everything. Missy's a little sweetie—and really smart, too."

"Takes after her mommy," Ms. White noted. (The barest hit of venom gilded the words.) "Do you know where Merry is—where she's been?"

"Sure," Donna smiled. The phone belled in her hand. "Just a sec." She held up the other toward the MedaGen people, turning sideways. "Hello? Oh, hi, Mom. Susanna hasn't come by to pick up the Visiting Teaching stats yet. When she does, can I take the car? When are you coming home?" After a pause, she added, "Okay. There's a couple of people here looking for Merry. She's gone to visit her mom, right? Okay, love you. Bye."

"Gone to visit her mom?" Mr. Cornell asked when Donna clicked off.

"Sorry—didn't mean to eavesdrop," Ms. White said sweetly.

"How could you help it? I'm standing right here," Donna shrugged, popping her gum. "No problem. So, anyway, Merry told us she wouldn't need us to tend Missy for a couple of weeks. She said she was going to take some vacation days to jet off to Belgium or somewhere like that to visit her mom. How would that be? My mom never goes further than Portland."

"Are you sure she's gone to visit her mother?" Mr. Cornell asked, leaning in slightly. His expression was as suspicious as his voice.

Donna looked at him, at Ms. White, then back. The famous Callatta temper flashed in her dark eyes. "No, I'm not sure. I know what Mom told me, and she said Merry's gone to visit her mother. Why is it my problem to be sure? Since when am I in charge of keeping track of our kids' parents? Maybe Merry didn't tell you where she was going because she doesn't like nosy coworkers prying into her personal business!"

That didn't set well with Cornell, but Ms. White stepped in front of him. Her smile had come back, unshakable as a coat of paint. "Sorry. Really, dear, we were just worried. If she's gone to visit her mom, that's wonderful. Her vacation-request form probably just got lost in the shuffle. We'll let Mr. Humphrey know that all's well. Thank you so much." She herded Cornell off the porch, then paused, turning back as if a thought had just occurred to her. "You wouldn't happen to have a phone number for her, would you?"

"All I've got is her personal phone number," Donna said. "The one she's always had. If she's not answering that, it sounds like she really is on vacation. Maybe she doesn't want to have to be tied to the office on her days off."

"Can't blame her a bit," Ms. White said. "Well, thank you again, dear. Hope you have a good day."

"You too," Donna said politely. Her smile lasted until the door shut. "You witch. The neighbors told you, my tail." The ring signal from Carmen's phone buzzed in her ear. "Come on, Mom, pick up."

* * *

The phone rang once, twice. "Operator," Calvin said crisply.

Perro rolled his eyes. "You and your old movies."

Dove looked up from the map of SkateTown and grinned, punching Perro's arm. "Let Calvin handle the communications however it works. Pay attention to this, Perrito." He tapped the map, cocking his head toward Paco and the other two fugitive *Brujos* across the table. "It's here, the main stash?"

"Yeah, it's there." *And you think knowing that's going to help you?* Paco thought, glancing from Calvin to Perro and back to Dove. The other two, Boris and Scruffy, just sat silently at the table, Boris trying for casual, Scruffy vibrating with half-suppressed excitement.

Paco coughed, took another drag on his cigarette to cover the pause. What did these kids think they could do against Slick? Unless they had more help they hadn't bothered to tell him about, it looked like they were headed for a long walk off a short cliff. Still, every time the Two Stooges had him thinking he'd backed the wrong horse, this Dove kid managed to come up with a smart maneuver that almost convinced Paco they had a chance. And either way, it worked for him. They lost, he disappeared again, the situation didn't change; they won, Slick went down, he got revenge. From his point of view, there was no way to lose—so long as he didn't get caught talking to the Junior Marines. He pulled his attention back to the matter at hand, leaning over Dove's map.

"Right there, under the main concession. There's a couple of cement-block rooms, used to be the storerooms, equipment repair, that kind of thing, before the park went out of business." Paco paused to light another cigarette and continued with a cough. "Slick's got guns and ammo stocked down there—plus detonators, plastique explosive, a couple cases of grenades, and what looked like a rocket launcher. It's not all he's got, but it's a pile. Called it the 'rainy day fund,' the first shipment up from that General down south. Had us put it there 'cause the cement bunker's secure, just two doors—and 'cause nobody could see it from the air, or with sonar snoopers. Guy always talked like he was fighting a war, or planning one."

"I think they are, but they're going to get it sooner than they expect." Dove regarded the map soberly. "So, we wait until shift change, when Slick's guys get the night off and Rico's take over guarding the bunker."

"Yeah, always giving us the gut work they're too good for," Perro growled. "Night shift."

"Don't get too sympathetic," Dove reminded him. "They're not 'us' anymore. We're going to have to hit them hard if your cocktail doesn't work. Then we'll have to move fast, pulling out everything we can before anybody comes around checking on things."

"They will," blurted Paco's companion, a thin, jumpy man Paco had introduced as Speedy. His words flooded out, occasionally tripping over each other; no mystery where he got his nickname. "They're always coming around, always rousting you out, always with the boot in the back. Slick thinks he's some kind of psycho sergeant or something. Do this, do that, faster, slower, be careful you idiots! Do it again, do it again, can't even think with him hanging over my shoulder, and he wants it faster, faster. You don't go fast with explosives! You just don't. You take your time, set it up, do it right, sit back and think a minute if you have to. Working for the Rat wasn't like that, he'd give you some time to kick back. Wouldn't shoot you for no reason but feeling like it, neither—" Speedy's monologue trailed off under Paco's steady, smoke-veiled stare.

"We may need to move pretty fast," Dove told him gently. "We'll want to blow up what we don't take."

"Why? Waste a lot of good hardware that way!" Speedy objected.

"Two reasons," Dove said quickly, before the man could take off on another verbal walkabout. "First, we don't want Slick to know what we've got—I want him thinking we just blew it all up, like we didn't need it, like we got backing already. Second, we don't want to leave it for him to use it on us. Understand?"

"Yeah, sure, I understand." Speedy twitched, tossing his long, lank hair out of his eyes. "I'm not dumb."

"No, you're not." Dove kicked Perro under the table before he could say anything; now wasn't the time for one of Perro's smart-apple jokes. "That's why Paco brought you down here. You're the best demolitions guy around. Now we just need you to show us how to rig the place so it'll go up after we get out of there."

"Show you how. Tonight." Speedy's eyes darted from Dove to Paco (who nodded) back to Dove, then to the backpack beside him on the floor.

"Yes, tonight." Dove shot a glance at Calvin, who gave him a thumbs-up gesture, still glued to the phone. "Before midnight, actually."

"Four hours." Speedy's eyebrows climbed even further into the bangs covering his face. He contemplated the ceiling (decorated with a restaurant lifetime's worth of smoke and sauce stains), sighed deeply, and pulled the backpack onto the table. "Better get started, then."

"Pay attention," Dove told Scruffy. "You're the one with the hot fingers."

Scruffy leaned forward, reaching toward the components Speedy pulled out of the pack. He quickly leaned back again, as Speedy whacked his hand away. "Don't touch until you know what you're doing. These here, these are fuses. They've got these wires that—"

"Transfer the charge from the detonators to the plastique," Scruffy finished the sentence. "Man, they're just like the diagrams on the Web. So, you tuck the wire in here, set it there—"

This time, Speedy didn't slap him away, just snorted about "Web amateurs" and showed him how it really went. Dove grinned, watching Scruffy's curly head bent over high-octane destruction. With all the homemade fireworks that kid had put together, it was only his attachment to a "lucky" T-shirt (getting more ragged every month) and aversion to shaving that got him tagged "Scruffy" instead of "Sparky."

"We got three trucks plus Natasha's buggy and the Dogmobile," Calvin announced, clicking off the phone, "and ten more bodies for sure. Half can bring their own guns. We can kyfe the rest there."

"Everything goes right, they'll need gloves more than guns," Dove said. He looked at Paco. "We could use a steady head and hand there."

"You sure could," Paco agreed, acknowledging the implied request only enough to turn it down flat. "How're yours?"

"No shakes here." Dove held out his hands, rock still until he flexed hard, then stretched. "But we're not relying on these arms. We got better backing. God's with us."

"So am I." Speedy waved away the surprised looks from the others (especially Paco). "All right, black-powder boy here's got potential. But there's no way you wet puppies can take care of that bunker." An evil expression crossed his thin face. "And I been wanting to put a match to Slick's fuse for a long time now."

"Party's on!" Perro exclaimed.

"Party's on," Dove agreed, a thrill of adrenaline flashing through him, cold and hot at once. "Operator, let 'em know. It's time."

Tiny, glittering beetles chirped, whistled, rang, and vibrated in the hot dusk. The message appeared across their matte-plastic stomachs: "Party at Perro's. 11:30. BYOG."

* * *

Instant Messaging, E-mail, and Web Browsing. All patrons are responsible to monitor their usage of electronic materials. The sign above the row of public terminals stated the library's official policy on censorship. The National Library Association still stood as the proud citadel of the last of the free-range libertarians, fighting suppression of information in any form. (If that meant defending pornography, anarchy, and occasionally treason, so be it; the library association had fought the government to a Supreme Court standstill on the issue of providing information services to any and all who wanted them—for any and all reasons.) The terminals themselves were open to the public for research and e-mail, anonymous in a way that nothing else was since pay phones went the way of the dinosaurs. If Merry used Carmen's computer, MedaGen's watchdogs could trace the connection back to its owner. Using one of the library's connections let her log right on with her own account, under her own name, which she knew MedaGen would pick up. However, logging in from a public computer gave Zelik's hounds nothing real to latch onto.

"Can you get on from here?" Carmen asked, surveying the row of computers.

"No problem," Merry assured her.

"Good." Carmen nodded decisively, taking Missy's diaper bag and Missy herself from her mother. "I'm going to take these two to the facilities—they're both less than fresh. Then we'll hit the children's section while you bring down the Great Wall of MedaGen."

"Sounds good." Merry caught Carmen's arm as another thought occurred to her. "But, Carmen, make it quick. We may have to leave fast. The library's computer may not be mine, but it's got a permanent address. If they realize what I'm posting, they'll know where I'm posting from in the next second."

"They can do that?" Carmen looked impressed.

"After they traced my cell phone?" Merry twitched her shoulders, trying to hide or dismiss the goosebumps that sprang out on her arms at the thought. "I'd say they can do anything they want, with a Senator in their pocket. Besides, the Web hasn't been a wide-open frontier for a long time now."

"Okay, kidlets, get ready for the world's fastest diaper change," Carmen ordered, herding her two small charges toward the bathroom.

Merry settled onto a dilapidated chair in front of one of the public-access screens and clicked the MedaGen data into the terminal. While the library's electronic immune system sniffed her data for computer viruses and other nasty surprises, she quickly signed onto several genetics discussion groups (she already belonged to most of them, as MGalen). A quick survey of the current topics surprised her; a couple of skeptics still held out among the adoring comments about AllSafe, but they were definitely voices crying in the wilderness.

"What you've got to ask yourself is what aren't they telling us!" An emphatic (colored, capitalized, and blinking) statement from a member signing herself (or himself) GeneDoc caught Merry's eye.

She smiled grimly as she created a new message. "You don't have to ask what MedaGen's hiding anymore, GeneDoc. It's all right here. AllSafe's not safe at all."

The machine hummed, sending her message—and all the data on her disk—into the electronic ether. Duplicate messages flashed along the lines to a half dozen discussion boards as Merry copied her original posting. The indication bar crawled at a lame snail's pace, feeding case studies, treatment projections, and computer simulations to servers all over the world.

Faster, faster, faster, Merry silently urged it, prickles of paranoia rippling down her spine. She glanced behind her back reflexively, but the small group of teenage girls scoping out the equally small (but less shrill) group of teenage boys weren't paying any attention to her. Neither was the older man slouched half asleep in one of the worn chairs beside the newspaper rack. The librarian assigned to tech-support duty hid a yawn and turned another page of her magazine.

* * *

She didn't see the sleepy tech in MedaGen's subterranean data-center suddenly jerk into full alert, staring at his own screen through a litter of chip bags and half-empty drink cups. "MGalen," he muttered, staring at the ALERT graphic blinking and beeping at him from the computer.

"GeneticArts discussion board, AllSafe, MGalen," he read aloud. "File uploads. Confidential—oh, man!"

The chip packets fluttered to the floor as he grabbed for the phone. A cup fell over as he stabbed the buttons, the remaining sugar sludge in the bottom of it escaping to pool under his keyboard. "This is Sean, in tech support," he gasped into the receiver. "Security alert! I just picked up MGalen—Meredith Anthony posting on a forum! It looks like she's uploading those stolen files!" His voice cracked as he made the dramatic announcement; then he slumped in his chair as he hit the bureaucratic wall. "Sure, I can hold for Ms. Zelik."

* * *

The online reaction to Merry's message, on the other hand, came immediately—and dishearteningly. Three boards returned her post and its accompanying files, unceremoniously dumping them back onto the terminal with a curt explanation that the board moderators had set rules against posting large documents, unproved studies, or attacks against sponsors. Three more, however, not only accepted her data but promptly posted it in the general discussion area.

"Good to hear from you again, MGalen." The words flickered across the screen, as a geneticist from Cambridge, D. Breckinridge, noticed Merry's name on the "Active" list (it instantly showed all members who were logged in at the time). "Looks like you've been busy!"

"You can say that again," Merry sent back. She and Chris had never met Donna Breckinridge face to face, but they'd exchanged greetings and experimental data often since graduate school. She was a regular on the discussion forums, and well respected in her own field (using gene therapies to prevent congenital birth defects). "So's MedaGen. AllSafe's a lot more than they've been advertising. Check the case studies. The vaccine's lethal in every case, unless the subjects get a booster shot to mitigate its effects."

"Where'd you get this?" another member demanded, signing in as BobWright. "These files have MedaGen's Confidential stamp on them. Posting confidential research files on a public forum is illegal!"

"Marketing a harmful product using false advertising is illegal AND immoral," Merry retorted.

"AllSafe passed the FDA's approval process, including human trials," BobWright pointed out.

Merry gritted her teeth and pounded out her response. "AllSafe passed under heavy pressure on the FDA from MedaGen and Senator

Garlick, both of whom have everything to gain from a quick approval—and mandatory vaccinations! Don't argue with me. Look at the data—it's all there."

"This is extremely troubling, if it's true," Donna wrote.

"It's MedaGen's data, with their stamp on it," Merry pointed out. "There's no way to fake that mark."

"Where did you get—" Donna's posting abruptly cut off.

A new message scrolled across Merry's screen. "MGalen, you have violated the rules of this forum. Your membership has been terminated. Any further postings will be blocked, and your previous postings will be deleted. If you feel you have been terminated in error, contact the moderator of the forum."

In quick succession, the moderators of the other two boards chopped Merry's access, sending nearly identical form letters.

* * *

Sean, in MedaGen's tech-support center, looked from the rapidly clearing boards to the woman standing behind his chair. Sean had still been on hold with her secretary when she came into the room, scaring him half to death. The adrenaline hadn't subsided much since his initial startle. Zelik inspired instant fear in small, furry creatures—and computer techs. "There. The moderators nuked her account. She won't be able to post to those boards again unless she totally changes her user profile and moves out of state."

"Not likely," Zelik said softly. The tips of her teeth showed in her smile. "Where is she?"

"I'm not—" Sean's demurral cut off when he met the COO's eyes. "I'll find out."

"Do that," Zelik advised, then into her phone, "Prepare a team for clean-up duty."

Sean hunched over the keyboard, listening to her instructions to somebody else as his computer tracked Merry's message through the maze of the Web and right back to the public library.

* * *

"That can't be good," Carmen noted, glancing over Merry's shoulder. Gianni and Missy leaned against her legs, each clutching a brightly colored book.

"It's not." Merry stared at the screen. "I've been kicked out. I tried to tell them what's going on, and the moderators kicked me out. They're deleting the files I sent." After a few seconds, the program automatically timed out, flashing back to its standard program of news clips, prepress notices for genetics articles—and an advertisement for AllSafe.

Virginia's full-lipped smile swam in front of Merry's eyes, the MedaGen logo blurry with tears of anger, worry, and sheer frustration. "Please, help," she whispered. "Please." There had to be a way to get the word out, to warn everybody in time to stop millions of innocent—or at least decent and undeserving of death—people from taking that vaccine! She felt Missy lean against her and gathered up the baby, holding her close.

"So, we tried the usual idiot box and the digital one. No dice. Fine." Carmen rubbed Merry's back bracingly. "There's always another way. We've made it this far. You even got an earthquake! We're going to get the word out to everybody who needs to hear it. Buck up, kiddo. If anybody can save the world, you can."

"You and Chris, the eternal optimists. Carmen, you'll be handing out Band-Aids and organizing a cleanup crew the day after Armageddon!" Merry informed her, smiling despite herself. She sat up and rubbed her eyes with her free hand, looking up at her friend over Missy's head. Her friend, Carmen—her former visiting teacher, the one time in her life where the formula for instant friendship had actually worked. Her visiting teacher. "That's it!"

"What's it?" Carmen asked. "Band-Aids for Armageddon?"

"Band-Aids," Missy repeated hopefully.

Gianni grinned and exclaimed "Boo-boo!" showing his own bandaged elbow.

"No. Visiting teachers—and home teachers and bishops and stake presidents and General Conferences and messages from the Brethren," Merry informed her. "Maybe we can't save the world—but we can get the word out to the Church, internally at least! And they've got clout, political pull, access to the media, members all over the place. They can get the word out!" The manic gleam in her eyes dimmed slightly. "Can we do that? How do we start?"

Carmen whistled softly. "There's an idea. I don't know where to start—but we can find out. Start with the bishop," she said decisively. "If he doesn't know, he'll find out who does."

Merry brightened. She paused only long enough to bump noses with Missy before handing her off to Carmen, then opened the messaging program again. She didn't bother with the discussion boards this time. She half noticed Carmen's quiet "Darn!" as she fired off a final message, telling the bishop that she needed to get in touch with someone who could put the word through the Church—someone who could evaluate medical-research data, and who would understand her when she explained it. She signed off with Carmen's number, saying that she, Carmen, and Tony needed to meet with him as soon as possible.

"That's it," Merry said, as the message disappeared.

"That's what?" Carmen asked.

The tone in her voice caught Merry's full attention—and so did the expression on her face. "I just sent word to the bishop that we'd like to meet him tonight. Carmen, what's wrong?"

"Good idea—if we meet at his place. Donna's been trying to call—I had my phone off so Gianni could play with it." Carmen shook her head, brushing away the reasons and her own reaction to her lapse in security. "Two of MedaGen's goons came by the house today, asking about you. She told them you'd gone to Sidney's."

"Sidney's?" The preposterousness of that concept made Merry pause even in that situation, but she got through it fast. "That means they've found your house! Carmen, I'm so sorry!"

"No harm done," Carmen assured her. "Donna's a smart girl—and always has been able to lie with a straight face. Much to my sorrow and shame, of course, but it came in handy this time. Now, let's get ourselves out of here, just in case those security goons manage to figure out which library we're at. Besides, we've got a couple of kidlets here who could use the rest. It's been a big day."

"They look like they could go for a couple more hours, especially with new stories," Merry said, sweeping up Missy and glancing at Gianni as they sprinted for the exit.

"I meant us," Carmen told her. "All this saving the world stuff takes a lot of energy!"

The van pulled away from the library's parking lot, exchanging a brisk honk with the occupants of a long, dark sedan that careened around the corner to screech to a halt in the Handicapped stall in front of the library. None of the three dark-suited and slightly dusty men (blond, bald, and flat-topped) who got out looked disabled. The ragged man slumped against the library's steps glared at them as they went by.

* * *

Ochoa, leaning against the concrete wall, glared at Perro. Great. He was stuck on guard duty, and one of the goobers showed up. "What the blue streak you want?"

"Hey, is that any way to talk to somebody come all the way out here to bring you some tea and sympathy?" Perro asked, mocking wide-eyed innocence as he held up both hands. The shapes of the bottles showed clearly through the plastic bags. "Stuck out here all night sitting on concrete until your butts fall asleep, while the Southerners sleep nice and comfy? Few of us figured that don't seem fair, and Marco finally took pity on you. Us locals, we got to stick together."

"Up the Brotherhood," Spanish grinned, his metal caps glinting in the light from the lantern. He set his rifle down and motioned Perro closer. "Marco's a good ——, when he gets 'round to it. Gimme a shot of that tea."

"Slick catches us drinking on duty—" Ochoa began.

His half-hearted objection promptly drowned in a barrage of abuse from Spanish and the other three sentries, who'd drifted over to find out what the excitement was. He didn't bother to try again. He also didn't turn down a cup of the rotgut Perro liberally dished out— along with the latest gossip (whose girlfriend was sleeping with which of Slick's Southern buddies), weather reports (tonight was going to be miserable), and the inevitable stand-up routine that Perro couldn't help delivering (most of the jokes dirty).

"So she says, 'Honey, I thought that *was* you,'" Perro finished, pouring out the last of the liquor for Spanish. He grinned at the guffaws, trying to hide the off-key twitch in his head.

Somehow, telling dirty jokes felt weird after watching Dove drop
to his knees and say a prayer that sounded more like one of those old-
time warrior priests going into battle than his old buddy *Hasbìdì*.
He'd blessed them all, not to be safe, but to have clear minds and
obey the orders of the Spirit to do what they had to do. Perro didn't
know if anybody else felt the prayer like he did, but even as he teased
Dove about "Hey, they say prayers before football games, right? Why
not now?" he couldn't shake the impression that Somebody was
looking over him—not over his shoulder, not watching him like a
spook, more just watching over the whole scene. He'd never put
much stock in the church—the nuns who taught him to read in grade
school had been scary, but in a ruler-and-knuckles way; the guitar-
playing, long-haired priest who came to the detention center on
"youth outreach" missions just made him laugh; the old, dusty-black
padre in the mission church stood by like a sorrowful mummy
regarding the folly of the young from the inside of a tomb. Dove
hadn't paid much attention to them, either, saying that they didn't
have the truth he was looking for. Now, though, he'd found the truth
with those Mormon Navajos out on the Rez, and the light in his eyes
almost made Perro believe too. Dove told him bits and pieces—like
the story in that book of his that landed Perro serving drinks to
Ochoa and the guys—and threatened to drag him to church as soon
as they put Slick down. Perro resisted, of course, knowing his
curiosity would drag him in as much as Dove would.

Right now, though, he had more immediate concerns. Watching
Spanish yawn, Perro reached back to a half-remembered night with
his mother patiently leaning over him. "Dear Jesus, Mother Mary,
keep us safe—and help *them* sleep sound." He had a feeling that he
hadn't got the words right.

The effects, however, whether from the novice prayer or the heavy
dose of Sasha's sedatives they'd mixed into the booze, were all he hoped for.
One by one, the sentries dropped into silence and stillness, their eyes
growing heavy, then drifting closed. Ochoa lurched to his feet, swaying as
he leaned on his rifle, but a yawn almost big enough to split his head interrupted his angry "What the blue streak is going on? What'd you give us?"

Perro caught him before he fell and woke himself back up, easing
the unconscious man to the ground. He brushed off a yawn himself, a

manic grin breaking out on his face as he surveyed the five snoring guards. "Enter Sandman," he said gleefully, pulling out his beetle-com. "And the rest of us."

The three trucks—plus Natasha's cobbled-together Frankenstein of a dune buggy—pulled up to the bunker a few minutes later, maneuvering around the half-pipes and swimming-pool sized skating craters. Bodies piled out of all four vehicles, rapidly converging on Perro.

"Man, it worked!" Scruffy exclaimed, staring at the sprawling sentries.

"Yeah, it worked," Dove poked him. "Now, you get to work. Think you can wire it?" he asked Speedy.

Speedy surveyed the half-submerged concrete box in front of them. "Sure enough. You get us in, me and Scruff there will turn it into a fireball. You just better be a ways away when it blows, unless you want to get brained by a chunk of flying cement. Cement's good for insulation, good for hiding stuff, but it's mainly brittle. Set the right charge in the right place, you get a blast wave that hits all the faults and brings the wall down. Sometimes, if you're real good, you can set a charge that powders cement right back to sand, but that's tough. Need training for that, get into a professional demolitions company, like the ones that take down those big buildings—"

"Hey, Dove, it's locked," Boris called, interrupting Speedy's stream-of-consciousness monologue. He hefted a thick, silver padlock securing the door.

"No problem." Perro put a hand against Dove's chest as Dove started forward. "You go organize the pack mules, Fearless Leader. I'll take care of this little problem."

"You've learned lock picking in the last couple months?" Dove asked.

"The best method there is," Perro assured him, pulling a pistol from its place under his jacket. "High-speed lead. Works every time."

"Discreet." Dove grinned at him and moved off to organize the pack mules.

The lock, an insult to the integrity of the (currently out cold) guards, was indeed no match for Perro's locksmithing techniques. He pushed the door open, and everybody filed into the room under the stark light of a pair of bare bulbs. It was small, cool, and full of the smell of desert-thin damp, metal, old wooden crates, and gun oil. Dove moved the loose lid of a long, narrow box by the door. Under a layer of packing material, the dull black sheen of an automatic rifle gleamed back at him. He pulled the gun out, blew dust flecks off it, and hefted it lightly. He'd used one once, when *Abuelo* got a couple of them as a bribe—or rather, personal gift— from a gun runner needing safe passage through the borderlands and into Mexico. He'd headed for Chiapas. The gang headed for the hills and tried their hands at spray-and-pray shooting.

Rico had that gun now, Dove thought. *That one and the other four. But he and Slick won't have these. We will.* A chill of apprehension instantly followed the excited rush at that idea. *We'll have them. And we'd better be ready to use them,* His thoughts wandered to the consequences if he failed: *Slick and the General taking over, spreading their virus to anyone opposing them—like Perro and the guys, Sam and Renata.* The vision of little Abish coughing like Sasha had hit him hard, making the burden heavier, reinforcing his nerves.

"Get everything you can." Dove set the gun into a corner, just to be safe, snugged its mates back into their container, then pulled the lid down tight over it. "Take everything that looks good, but pull the guns and bullets first. Stow it and lash it down—we've got a bumpy ride out to Blanca Hacienda."

"Blanca Hacienda?" Natasha hesitated, thin arms wrapped around a couple of ammo boxes. "We're taking the stuff out there? Isn't it dangerous?"

"It's going to be dangerous to Slick." Dove patted his shoulder.

"There's ghosts out there," Natasha reminded him.

"We're going out there to lay some ghosts." Dove thought about the drifting spirits of those dead banditos, wondering for an irrational moment if they'd help him against Slick or go after both sides impartially. He shook off the distraction. Ghosts weren't their problem— though something equally invisible might be, if they didn't succeed. For now, the important thing was that the reports about the farmers who'd died of the infection (after stealing the banditos' truck) said that the virus couldn't live for long outside a host. It couldn't survive on dry bones and blowing dust. The dead man's family had already sold the farm to another set of ambitious and determinedly non-superstitious immigrants, and they were still healthy, despite the dire-sounding teasers for the news reports he'd pulled up from the library's archives. ("Two months ago, everyone in this farmhouse died mysteriously. Now, a new family has moved in. Will they suffer the same horrible fate? Tune in at 10:00!")

He pulled his attention back to the moment and grinned reassuringly at Natasha. "Don't worry about old Recho Ojo—we've got something even scarier on our tail. Think of Slick, and put on some speed!"

"Right," Natasha hiked up the ammo boxes and disappeared out the door at something close to a lope.

The room was rapidly emptying, the raiding party resembling a troupe of ambitious ants as they hustled the cases out to the vehicles. Scruffy and Speedy worked the edges of the room, a thickly insulated crate of Slick's explosives open between them as they positioned charges and strung detonator wires.

Dove deposited a half-pilfered crate of bullets into the bed of one of their trucks, then started as his beetle-com went off. "COMPANY!!!" flashed on the tiny screen. He glanced up at Calvin's shadow rapidly descending the framework of the SkateTown sign he'd skinned up as a lookout.

"We're blown!" he yelled, shoving the ammo box into place. "Everybody, hit your rides. Drop it if you can't stow it. Drivers, got your maps? Get out—everybody go a different direction. Make sure you're not followed! Meet at the rendezvous, as planned. Last one in has to make breakfast!"

They scattered, stowing the boxes they were carrying, jumping into the trucks. Dove ran through the haze of flying dust that the rapidly spinning tires kicked up. "Speedy! You done yet? They're coming!"

"Always with the hurry up," the *Brujos'* demolitions man complained. The chatter didn't slow his fingers, however, which flew just as quickly among the components. "Can't hurry good work—you get bad results. Gimme that wire, Scruff. Do the other one like this, turn, so. Got it?"

"Sorry about the rush," Dove snapped, grabbing the gun he'd put aside, expertly snapping its clip into place and tucking two more full clips into his pockets, "but we've got Slick's goons about two minutes away. How much time do you need?"

"Five minutes," Speedy declared. "Five minutes." He didn't add anything else—or look away from the wires he was inserting into their places so fast that his hands blurred.

"Minute you're done, hit the Dogmobile," Dove told him, and raced back outside. "Perro! Calvin! Delaying party! Come on!"

They grabbed their own recently liberated guns and fell in step with him. The three of them ran, dodging around the concrete barriers rising out of the ground like the frozen waves of a massive earthquake. The park spread around them in a moonscape of cracked cement, steel and stone slopes sculptured for surfing and carving without either water or snow. Dove dashed up the stairs of the main bowl, throwing himself flat on its spectator platform. Below, at the front gates, two heavy-duty land rovers trundled up the park's entranceway. Their headlights blazed across the rusted barriers as they turned into the single access road.

"Please, God, help us protect Your children," he whispered, then added aloud, "Now!"

The headlights went out, one shattered, the others turned off from the inside. Bodies boiled from the trucks and headed for the cover of the overhanging cement walls. Flashes marked the origins of the bullets that suddenly whined and buzzed around the boys' heads and pinged off the metal railing around the bowl's top. The echoing of the gunshots multiplied into shards of echoes. Voices echoed too—shouts, questions, orders, curses.

Perro contributed one of the latter, as a bullet struck close to his head, showering him with high-velocity bits of concrete. He oozed up again, raking the trucks below with another stream of lead.

"What do we do?" Calvin asked tightly, slapping another clip into place. "We've got 'em pinned, but we can't get to 'em from here, either."

"Pinned is all we need," Dove told him, "just long enough for Speedy and Scruff to finish."

"We need more than that," Perro contradicted. "I think a couple of 'em are coming up alongside, left. Couldn't get a clear look, but thought I saw bodies moving."

"Doesn't matter," Dove told him. "Left's okay. We just don't want anybody going right." His beetle-com buzzed. "Fire in the hole!" it announced. "They've got it done!" At least, he hoped that's what it meant, but since the explosion didn't instantly follow, it seemed like a safe assumption. "Let's get out of here!"

With one more raking barrage on the trucks, they slithered backward, rising only when they couldn't see over the edge. Bullets pinged and cracked into the concrete behind them, as they hit the stairs on the far side of the bowl, the noise covering the clatter of their feet on the rusted metal stairs. Their feet hit the ground in puffs of dust, which left thin trails behind them as they ran around the far side of the bowl and into the winding maze of the park's walkways again. The gunshots trailed off behind them, fading into the sounds of furious pursuit.

"Run, run, as fast as you can." Perro grinned, his teeth glinting in the rusty moonlight. "Can't catch me, I'm the gingerbread man!"

The bullet that narrowly missed his ear as he came around the corner of a looming half pipe wiped off the grin and nearly made a liar of him. He dove one way, shooting reflexively as he rolled; Dove and Calvin went the other direction, hitting the shadow of the walls. They exchanged glances across the open walkway, holding fire until they could figure out where the enemy was.

"I'm not just going to catch you." Slick's voice floated, cool as ever, in the silence. "I'm going to catch you, then skin you. That'll teach you to stay dead. I assume I'm talking to Salvatore Nakai?"

"You can assume that," Dove called back, looking around the convoluted cement horizon around them. The walkway lay clear, rails, bowls, and the thick bulk of a half pipe casting shadows. Where was Slick?

"Rico said you wouldn't dare show your face around here again, after what happened to your brother." Slick's voice echoed slightly, bouncing off the stark walls. "It's not the first time Rico's been wrong. I wonder if he's wrong about how stupid you are too?"

Dove didn't answer, concentrating on matching the direction of Slick's voice with the shadows—and the feather-light touch of his instincts pointing him toward the overhang of the half-pipe.

"Let's find out," Slick went on. "How about this for a proposal? The General can use ambitious men who aren't afraid to take chances. You fit that category pretty well. You just need to learn what chances to take. We'll teach you that, help you put those leadership skills of yours to good use. How does a commission sound, Nakai? You can go from border rat to captain in an army that's going to sweep the dregs out of the borderlands."

"Why do you need an army? You've got viruses." A flicker of motion caught Dove's eye. A bird, startled out of its nest, flew out from under the walkway around the half-pipe.

Slick laughed. "Rico said you'd figured that out. *Abuelo* knew it, too. You just couldn't keep your mouth shut. That's going to get you in more trouble unless you learn to control yourself. Yes, we've got viruses. I'm expecting the next shipment of it to come in tomorrow, actually, enough to last us while we finish off a few pests. And when we finish a deal the General's got cooking, we'll have even better ones. But we don't want to have to use them too much. What good is conquering an empty country? The General doesn't want to kill everybody. He's offering the last chance for real peace and order. Governments are failing left and right. They don't have the strength, determination, or skill to rule. The General does."

"Is this the part where you tell me your whole nefarious plan?" Dove asked. He gestured to Perro. One more, coming up alongside, on top of the half-pipe. "Next, you'll tie me to a big laser that'll cut me in half, then laugh and walk away, right?" From behind, the sounds of pursuit got louder, as the rest of Slick's men broke cover and charged into the park.

"How about I give you the chance to accept our offer, then tell you if you don't, I'm going to wipe out every last one of your border-rat buddies, a piece at a time, then go after every Mormon I can find in a hundred-mile radius?" The smooth tone disappeared; Slick's voice was made of poison-dipped razor blades. "They've got a lot of kids, I hear, but not a lot of guns. Be good target practice, picking off martyrs. Especially cute little Navajo girls."

"I'll think about it," Dove said. Another flicker of movement, the flash of moonlight on a gun sight. Got him. He motioned to Perro and Calvin—that way, then straight ahead. On three. Shoot straight ahead. Perro cursed as Dove walked out of the shadow into the walkway.

"I've thought about it." Sure enough, from this angle, he could see Slick, standing in the shadow of the half-pipe. Both their guns came up, mirroring each others' motions, as he finished. "You'll have to kill us first."

Gunshots ripped through the air. Slick's first barrage barely missed Dove, who whirled aside at the last second. He aimed his own shots not for Slick, but for Omerta crouching on the catwalk above them. The man grunted, his gun slipping from his fingers, then fell slowly backward, sliding bonelessly down the slippery slope of the skate ramp behind him. Slick dodged as well, ducking back into the cover of the half-pipe as Calvin and Perro filled the air around him with whining projectiles.

"Come on!" Dove charged forward, using his last clip in indiscriminate cover fire before and behind. Perro and Calvin ran on either side of him, weaving and ducking, shooting wildly behind them as they retreated.

They came around the corner and nearly hit the Dogmobile at warp speed. Perro scrambled down the length of the car and fell into the back seat. Calvin and Dove bounced off the hood, recovered, and piled into the back seat in a tangle of guns and bodies. A crack appeared in the windshield a second before the sound of the shot.

"Go, go, go!" Perro shouted, scattering diamond bits of safety glass as he lurched up to kneel on the seat.

Scruffy slewed the car around, its overtaxed emissions system belching thick smoke at the figures tearing up behind it. Dust billowed up as well, partly obscuring their taillights as the car screeched down the access road, away from the bunker. A few bullets spanged into the trunk of the car, but the pursuers had other things on their minds—primarily, gathering their forces for the long, lonely run down the desert road, where the four-wheel trucks could easily overtake the Dogmobile.

"Set it off!" Dove shouted to Speedy.

Speedy, hunched over a duct-taped detonator in the front seat, shrugged off Dove's order. "Not yet. Not yet. Not yet. Not yet."

"When? They're coming!" Perro yelled from his perch on the seat. "One of the trucks just pulled up to Slick. When's 'yet'? The other one's gone around it. They just passed the big half-pipe—"

"Now." Speedy clicked the switch.

Nothing happened. "We're toast. They're passing the bunker. What the—" Perro's incipient complaint disappeared in a flash of actinic fire.

The shockwave from the expertly placed charges rippled through the unforgiving structure of the concrete bunker. Pressure built, cement cracked, shards and chunks of shredded concrete blew outward in an expanding wave of heat and missiles, like an avalanche from Hades. It engulfed the lead truck, demolishing it and its passengers, throwing rubble across the road, embedding bits of rebar and girders in the cement walls of the half-pipe beside it. Far above, the rusted scaffold of the SkateTown sign groaned, leaned, and finally toppled, crashing down in a ringing heap of twisted iron and broken plastic.

The second truck slewed to a halt, especially far-flung boulders battering its front and side. The windows shattered under the hail of heated gravel. Omerta, peering over the edge of the ramp, lay there and bled, watching for any sign of movement. He wasn't sure if he was disappointed or relieved when the door finally opened and Slick stumbled out, wavering for just a moment before pulling himself into square-shouldered fury.

Rico wasn't relieved. He turned from chasing the remains of the first truck with an obscene exclamation to find himself looking into the barrel of Slick's pistol. "Hey, what's up?"

The other guys, the ones who'd trailed along after the ambush, ran up, yelling questions and curses, staring at the wreck. Slick kept a bead on Rico's head. "That's what I want to know. Find the guards," he ordered.

"In that mess?" one of the Southerners asked, eying the rubble skeptically.

"Find them or the pieces of them," Slick rapped out. "Move!"

As it turned out, finding them was easy; Boris's team had moved Ochoa and the others into the shelter of the half-pipe across from the bunker, mostly to keep from tripping over them. The sentries were just starting to come around, groggily staring at the Southerners dragging them out of the shelter that had saved their lives.

"Whoa, what happened?" Spanish slurred, blinking at the crater where the bunker had been, at the smashed remains of the first truck.

"What *did* happen?" Slick asked, standing over them. "Why were you asleep?"

Somewhere in the thick fog filling the back of Ochoa's head, alarm bells started going off.

"Must've been stronger than we thought," Spanish muttered.

"What was?" Slick asked, all steel-tipped patience. Fury burned in his eyes, froze his face into sculpted calm under the thin layer of cement dust.

Rico contributed a heavy kick at Spanish's ribs and a flow of invective-laced questions.

"Perro came, gave us the tequila you sent," Spanish babbled, squirming away from Rico's boot. "Payback for standing night shift. Thought it tasted funny . . . then everything went black—"

Everything went black again, permanently this time, as Slick shot him point-blank in the head. Ochoa had just enough time to try to dodge before a bullet ended his sentry career as well. The other three died in a narcotic fog. The gun swung up again, its single eye glaring at the space between Rico's.

"Wait! What—" The click of a hammer striking home on an empty chamber cut off his question but left him breathing hard and raggedly.

"You sent one of those boys with refreshments for the sentries?" Slick asked, never breaking his icy calm as he reholstered his empty pistol.

"No! I didn't send nothing to the sentries!" Rico heard himself babbling like a scared girl and choked it off in fury. The sentries were weak; they deserved what they got. Rico was strong—and one day, he'd show Slick what it felt like to stare down a gun barrel. Then the General would promote Rico to the command he deserved. For now, though, that meant staying alive while he gave the psycho Southerner enough rope to hang himself.

"Dove did it," he said flatly. "That Navajo coyote tricked 'em." He cracked a grin, motioning to the still bodies. "It won't happen again."

"Obviously," Slick agreed. The dying inferno from the explosion reflected in his eyes—and like the fires of Hades itself in the back of his head, as he thought about the General's assessment of the situation and his own, extremely short, future when he told the General (or someone else did) that the Navajo kid who'd faced him down at the warehouse and nearly put a wrench in their "recruiting" efforts had managed to get over him again—and destroy an entire arms cache this time. *Hasbìdì.* Dove. Birdbrain, definitely, thinking he and two of his juvenile delinquent buddies could take on Slick and have any hope of winning, let alone coming out with their hides intact. No, they'd shortly learn exactly what it meant to cross Slick. So Salvatore Nakai wanted to play savior, huh? Fine. Time to put out a decoy and catch the little squab using his own over-inflated *noblesse oblige* as the net. Perfect.

Slick suddenly grinned back at Rico, showing his teeth like a tiger's. They glinted in the headlights of another truck.

Marco got out, holding his hands out, looking from one tense face and gun barrel to another, then beyond them to the ruins. "It's me," was all he said.

Slick took the keys from his hand. "Clean up the mess," he directed Rico, as he climbed into Marco's truck. "Make it look like a meth-lab explosion, fireworks, whatever. Disappear the bodies. It doesn't have to be real, just plausible enough. I'll tell Pizarro the story for his deputies. And Rico—find Nakai." He didn't have to add "or else." Everything he did had an "or else" attached to it.

Rico watched the taillights disappear, then rounded on Marco. "Where have you been, you dumb ox?"

"Out in town," Marco evaded. "Dolores said you came out here, then I heard the explosion—" His explanation cut off as Rico punched him in the face.

He backed off, shaking his head as Rico ripped into him, blaming him for everything that had gone wrong with the gang, with the sentries, with the entire operation—up to and including Slick's birth.

"Should shoot you myself," Rico spat for a finish. "But you're still almost smart enough to be useful. Get them working on cleanup."

Marco nodded as silently as he'd taken the gang boss's tirade. As he turned away, he dropped Dove's note back into his pocket. He'd deliver it later—to Boris.

CHAPTER 17

"We know they're delivered." Sean winced as he said it, his eyes locked on the display above the Web cam beside his computer so he didn't have to look at Ms. Zelik's face when he gave her the news. "I got the moderators of the boards to wipe out the versions of the files on the mail servers, but we can't be sure how many users downloaded the files in the little while they were posted."

"Aren't sure, or have no idea whatsoever?" The COO's voice practically left frost on the speakers.

"No idea whatsoever," Sean admitted, mentally calculating how long his savings would last, assuming he could get another job and wasn't blackballed out of the entire high-tech industry. Zelik's reputation preceded her in tech-support circles. Sean's predecessor likened working for the Ice Queen to stealing a dragon's treasure hoard: success brought mind-boggling rewards, and failure meant you didn't have to worry about life's minor problems anymore. (Sean's predecessor also moonlighted as Zorg the Impaler in the online multiplayer game "Realms of Mysteria.")

"Get an idea—an accurate idea," Zelik ordered, much to Sean's amazement and relief. "And while you're at it, make sure our fifth column starts circulating posts on those boards about what a great idea AllSafe is, the necessity of some pain for progress, the trustworthiness of MedaGen, the whole party line. Send the usual message, with the usual pay scale—plus a 20 percent bonus for anybody whose posts get quoted by major media outlets."

She clicked off the connection in the middle of Sean's stuttered acknowledgment. Her frozen calm disappeared the instant the skinny tech's face did. Rising from her chair in one smooth spring, she paced her office, wall to window to wall, her sharp heels making no sound on the smooth nap of the beige carpet. Her thoughts, however, made more than enough racket. Wilson's security specialists hadn't caught Anthony at Channel 8—because of an earthquake, of all the stupid things! Of course, the Senator's Mob goons hadn't had any better luck with their attempt at direct apprehension, getting cut to pieces by a mob of street thugs. Surprising that a bunch of "made men" would go down so easily, but at heart, they were no better than the wolf pack that finished them off. So much for the Senator's underground connections. A sickle of icy smile scythed across her face. Then again, if organized crime were better organized, it wouldn't still be crime, would it?

Her own organization's failures quickly erased the smile, however. Wilson's team had missed Anthony at the library as well, even after a direct tip. She rolled her eyes, remembering the team leader's idiot face as he told her they'd searched the library in vain, then scouted the parking lot but hadn't been able to find her car. She acidly reminded him that Anthony had abandoned the car outside a tube station miles and days away from the library! With help like that, who needed enemies? The point was, how could a single woman be so overwhelmingly lucky—including the perfect timing of that blue-streaking earthquake?

Anthony—Galen, she reminded herself, hating the taste of the name but forcing herself to think the whole blasted thing to focus on her failure—Meredith Anthony Galen had more help than Zelik had thought possible. The search had seemed promising at first. Her mother was a nightmare of self-centered arrogance, more concerned about Meredith tossing away a golden corporate opportunity than covering for her; she had no husband, wife, brothers, sisters, or lover listed on her insurance records to whom she could turn for help; her coworkers half admired her work and half resented her for setting the bar too high; none of them had any reason to stick their necks out for her, even if she'd asked them for help. But she hadn't. She'd told her babysitter she was going to her mother's and vanished. There—that was the rub. Meredith Galen hadn't turned to any potentially vulnerable contacts for assistance. Instead, she'd vanished into the blasted Mormon underground!

"Are we getting our exercise for the day, or are we deeply worried about something?" Abbott stood in the doorway, smiling benevolently.

Zelik came to a graceful halt, inwardly cursing the secretary for letting him in without announcing him first. "Are we here to chat about feelings, or do we have actual business to conduct?" she inquired.

Abbott sauntered into the office, surveying the furnishings appraisingly, well aware that he didn't belong in this room. Its stark, neutral color scheme, spare, modern lines and Zen-like emptiness were the perfect setting for Zelik's sleek, angular, rational presence. Mahogany, deep carpeting, and *objets d'art* suited his own robustly handsome frame and personality. *The perfect yang to her yin,* he thought. *Fire and ice, forming an uneasy alliance in a precise balance of power. Is this the shift that will tilt that balance in my favor? Wait and see.* His smile widened. "Still having difficulties solving your pest problem?"

"*Our* pest problem," she reminded him smoothly. "And it has become a major infestation. Garlick has already called, threatening unspecified but of course bitter consequences if anyone uses the leaked information to 'kick up a fuss' on his Homeland Security initiative—"

"Not to mention what the stockholders will do if they feel it threatens their precious investments," Abbott finished for her. He casually ran a hand along the rim of an angular vase, supporting a single branch of perfectly crafted glass-blown cherry blossom. "Did she get enough to prove it?"

"Yes." Zelik matched his directness. "She uploaded the case files for the human trials, formula simulations, and computer projections for dosage effects to three discussion boards. The boards have been wiped, but we have no information on who downloaded the information locally—or how much they got." She finished her recitation, furious at having to admit a failure, hating even more that she had to admit it to *him.*

"Awkward," Abbott observed. "And really galling, isn't it, to think that a little homemaker managed to outwit Wilson's—your—expert security team? I wonder if all Mormon *hausfraus* are so surprisingly competent?" He turned that avuncular smile on her. "Fortunately, I'm prepared to clean up after you."

That earned him a poisonous look, but she didn't give him the satisfaction of an argument. "Really? How?"

"We'll just have to step up our campaign for the KeepSafe booster." Abbott shrugged. "I've already got the creatives in Marketing working on the next line. Virginia looks just luscious, by the way."

"Like a dish of wax fruit," Zelik noted. "And just as natural."

"Now, now," Abbott reprimanded gently. "She's vital to the success of the public-relations campaign."

"And what about the more intelligent members of the public?" Zelik asked. "The ones unlikely to be swayed by wax—or rather silicone—peaches?"

Abbott grinned, appreciating that image. "Three of the research team have kindly consented to admit to making errors in their zeal to save the wonderful citizens of this country from the terrible effects of bio-terrorism. The Senator's people are already spinning KeepSafe into a new security campaign—no one who's not certified 100 percent red, white, and blue gets the booster. It's all part of the master plan, to keep America and Americans one step ahead of the radical nutballs out there in the world."

He glanced out the windows at the magnificent view, only slightly marred by the volcanic haze lending a copper wash to the upper atmosphere. "And, of course, I've talked to Ken over at Channel 8. I think the network people understand that as MedaGen's CEO and one of their top clients, I'm very interested in seeing stories on Mormons—specifically, how fundamentalist, scientifically illiterate, backward, reactionary, and ignorant they are. He said he'd pass the word right along to Monk, their chief producer."

"Sounds like interesting programming," Zelik agreed.

"Yes, I'm sure it will be." Abbott strode to the door, pausing to shoot her a look completely stripped of his usual hearty charm. The corporate raptor gazed out of his eyes. "Don't spend any time watching the tube, Zelik. You have homework to do. Put your great brain into finding our little Mormon mouse—use Senator Garlick's access if you have to, but keep his goons out of it. I want this pest problem terminated before it spreads any further."

So do I, Zelik thought silently, watching him go. *Even more than you do.* She turned back to her desk, picking up the phone to start the next phase of the mouse hunt. She'd use Senator Garlick's access, all right. And maybe he could tuck a new law in his Homeland Security initiative requiring Mormons to register with the State as potential hazards to corporate—and national—security.

* * *

"They can't tell we're Mormons by looking at us, sure—but Mormons ain't the most discreet bunch of *hombres* around, either," Dove laughed at Sam's comment that all Navajos look alike to white guys. He sobered, however, as he went on. "I don't know if it's threat or promise, Sam, but Slick said he'd set his sights on Mormons if I didn't go to the 'dark side' with him."

"And you didn't," Sam finished. "No surprise there, Dove."

"No surprise," Dove agreed. "But Sam, watch out. Tell Bishop Yazzie about it, so the tribal cops know. And could you get him to phone the mission president and bishop around here, too? I mean, I could call out of the blue, tell 'em that Slick's guys might start hacking up trouble, but who am I?"

"You're a good kid—a good man, Salvatore Nakai," Renata interrupted. "You remember that."

"I will," Dove promised. "Sam, Renata, spread the word?"

"You got it," Sam said. The sound of fingers tapping keys came through the connection. "Be careful."

"Hey, speaking of spreading words," Perro said, as Dove clicked off the phone. "Somebody says he's got something to spread to you." He pointed at the grubby street urchin shifting from foot to foot in the thin, striped shade of Blanca Hacienda's sagging porch. "He looks plenty contagious to me. Want me to spray him down?"

"Nah, leave him be, Perro." Dove surveyed the messenger, agreed with Perro's assessment of his overall hygiene, and motioned him over.

The kid stepped forward, his eyes darting around, taking in the tumble-down ranch house, the discreet lack of obvious habitation, the hot emptiness of the place, the trio of tough-looking guys watching him right back. He didn't see any ghosts—or the dried-out, grisly skeletons of the banditos. The *Santos Soldados* had buried them last night. Nobody wanted to sleep under the gaze of those empty eye sockets.

They'd come up with the name last night too. Natasha insisted that they couldn't have a gang without a name. How'd you know who the *Brujos* were, otherwise, or the Rodeo Rattlers? They'd been *Abuelo's Chicos* before, what were they now? The others had agreed, tossing out suggestions and arguing over them as they stowed the weapons and ammunition: Rebels. No, too redneck. Disciples. Closer, but too common; there's sixteen Disciple Whatever gangs between L. A. and Albuquerque already. Cowboys? Redskins? The brainstorming (or brain spewing) had gotten goofier as they got into the spirit of things.

Calvin had stopped it all with a quiet observation: "Dove said we're a holy army. God's army."

"Just the reserves," Dove added quickly, half regretting the joke, which seemed close to blasphemy now that he thought about it in the hot light of the day after a firefight—and before more shooting.

"No," Calvin shook his head. "You're right. We're the good guys, fighting the bad guys."

"First time ever, us with the white hats," Perro laughed, but the joke wasn't mocking; thinking about it, he felt surprisingly good about the idea. "Onward, Christian soldiers!"

"*Santos Soldados*," Calvin said. "That's us."

"Not good Spanish, but a cool logo," Boris said thoughtfully. "We're the SS."

"Take it back from the Nazis," Natasha suggested, "and give it a good twist."

Now, the messenger kid's eyes settled on the first draft of an SS logo, which Butch had spray painted on the wall of the hacienda, half hidden under the broken awning. Painted angels (leather-jacketed and hefting machine guns, but angels from their halos to their gilded wings), clouds (lightning included), and Jacob's Ladder light beams surrounded the initials, which sported little halos of their own. He grinned, suddenly feeling more at home with an outfit that painted their walls. The grim-faced fighters who'd taken over *Abuelo's* gang couldn't be bothered with that kind of touch. "Nice spray work there," he told Dove. "Lots better decoration than those big cement things in the yard."

"Water troughs, kid. We hauled them around from the back and placed them very carefully right where they are. You don't like 'em, you don't have to look. Besides, you an art critic or a messenger?" Dove grinned. Who knew plotting had so many long, boring stretches? The painting had given Boris and the guys something to do besides sit, sweat, and worry; they really did feel better once they had their identities straight and a symbol to focus on. They'd even approved of Dove's suggestion that they work the Title of Liberty into the design—and they'd all agreed that General Moroni was a leader worth following, once Dove had told them about him.

"Both," the kid shot back, returning the grin. "Marco sent me to tell you. He says Slick's big ammo dump is in Benny Nakai's old house; he's using it as his headquarters." He paused, judging Dove's reaction to that. The Navajo guy's face had gone still, but he didn't look really mad. "Marco says the Southerners just hauled in a big, black case that he don't like the look of."

"Sounds like more virus," Dove said. "Like what Rico took, maybe, so the rest of the gang can prove how loyal they are by taking a dose of it and selling out to Slick for the antidote."

Perro groaned. "What's with this guy and getting sick? Gimme bullets over bugs every time."

"You'll get them sooner than later. Keep going," Dove told the messenger, who'd listened to their exchange with calculating eyes.

The kid shrugged. "Sure. Not much else. Your friend Marco wants you to know that your enemy wants you to know it too. So you'll have to pay off two messengers."

"Two messengers?" Calvin asked.

"Yeah, and one's a lot cheaper." The kid winked, gesturing to the drive.

On cue, the sound of an engine came through the still air, the dust plume visible down the hacienda's long, rock- and bush-bounded drive. A few moments later, a dirty little coupe pulled into the ranch's dusty front yard, screeching to a halt in an ochre cloud. Dolores kicked the door open and got out, surveying the scene with her hands on her hips. Hard sunlight glittered on her jewelry and gilded nails.

"You're the expensive one, right?" Perro asked the kid, who just grinned at him.

Dove tossed him a folded bill and stood up. "Hey, Dolores."

She didn't spare a glance for the messenger, who skirted her car and retrieved his dirt bike from its spot beneath the dried-out lilacs. The thin whine of its engine faded down the drive before she returned the greeting. "Hey, Dove. You're looking more like a coyote than ever."

Dove glanced down at his sweat-soaked shirt and dusty jeans. "Thanks, Dolores. You got anything else to say? Like how you knew to look for us here, and who knows you came?"

"Ooh, you're tough all of a sudden." She tossed her hair disdainfully, looking down her nose at him. "This the same little Dovey who kept coming into his big brother's room? Just had to wake him up for the big earthquake? Always with something he just *had* to talk about?"

"I did that mainly to bug you, 'cause I knew it would." Dove shrugged. "We've never liked each other, Dolores. Maybe that's my fault. Maybe I wasn't fair to you. I'm sorry. So why are you here?"

"I was looking for Calvin, not you. He came 'round the other day, scavenging for your clothes. Marco told me where he was." Dolores shrugged back at him. "I came to tell him that Slick's going to be out of Benny's house tonight, but since you're here, I'll tell you right off. They're celebrating down at Carlito's tonight, getting blasted on the General's dime and telling themselves how great they're gonna be. They've got big plans, talking about running drugs and guns up into California and Nevada. Rico says they got a package last night that'll make everybody stand up and salute, or else. It's not guns, either; smaller, more like a hard-side music case or something." She hesitated, about to say more, then shut her mouth and gave Dove an impatient look. "So, if you want the rest of your stuff—and what's left of Benny's—you better send one of your boys to get it tonight."

"Thanks for the head's up." Dove tilted his head back, looking at her steadily. "Why tell me all that?"

"Because Rico's a lying, nasty scrub who's treating me mean and won't give me any money," Dolores said, her tone flat and vindictive. "Benny was good, but didn't have the money; one of these days, I'm gonna learn to go for good and forget the cash."

"That's a good idea," Dove agreed solemnly. "Here's another one, Dolores: disappear but good. Rico's not going to give you money or treat you better for telling him where I am—and he's going to kill you if he finds out you didn't tell him."

"Think I don't know that?" Suddenly, the strain showed on Dolores's proud face. She blinked hard, forcing back tears. "I been through more than you know. Bye, Dove. Say hi to Benny when you see him." She slammed the door, ground the engine into life, and lurched out of the yard.

They watched the dust settle, listened to the sound of her car's engine throb away down the drive. The rocks dampened the sound when she turned onto the dirt road.

"Sounds like a trap." Perro leaned against the wall. "They're trying to get us to come out to the house."

"Sure does," Calvin agreed.

"It's perfect." Dove waved off the instant objections from the other two. "No, listen. It's perfect. They want us to raid the house, so we'll raid the house—and we'll set a trap for the hunters. We'll trip their alarms, and they'll chase us. We'll lead them out here and ambush them. And we'll do it tonight." He checked the idea that blossomed in his mind. It still looked good—so crazy that it just might work. Slick, though psycho for sure, wasn't really crazy enough to believe they'd actually stand and fight him.

Dove grinned at Calvin. "All right, Operator—spread the word. Tonight's the night we're going to put a stop to Rico, Slick, and the General's invasion plans."

* * *

"Got a cockroach invasion? Call us to rout out the little devils!" the Aussie-accented mascot for Down Under Exterminators drawled from the radio. Tony flicked off the commercial as the didgeridoo jingle started.

Through the windshield of his car, Merry's house sat quiet behind the two small trees in the front yard. Other than a general air of vague neglect—the lawn too long, long creepers of bindweed showing in the flower bed, those stupid free newspapers in an untidy pile on the front step—it looked just like it had last week. He got out of the car, whistling (out of nervousness, hoping it sounded casual), and headed up the front walk like he belonged there.

He did, of course. He'd come to pick up a few necessary things for Merry and Missy, since it looked like her emergency stay at their house wasn't the short-term thing they'd originally thought. It still felt impossible, Merry a fugitive, stealing confidential files from a major medical-research company—files that showed the company had deliberately created a vaccine with fatal side effects and knowingly marketed it. He'd wondered, when Carmen first told him about it, if Merry hadn't fallen into a strange version of what he called the Bereaved Syndrome (the mother whose toddler drowned in a wading pool makes it her life's work to make wading pools illegal to save other toddlers from a similar fate, for instance), but the minute he'd seen those files for himself, he'd realized that it was a lot more serious than that.

So there he was, walking up the driveway, rehearsing the story he'd prepared in case agents from MedaGen jumped out of the bushes to question him. Merry asked him to go over, mow the lawn, look after things while she went to stay with her mother. He checked out the scenery, like a character in one of his own espionage video games. The street looked quiet as he looked in the stuffed mailbox, pulling out the pile of miscellaneous envelopes and flyers, casually going through it as he scanned the street. An expensive sedan parked under the shade of a spreading tree across the street caught his eye. On the other side, a woman relaxed in a lawn chair on her front porch, reading a magazine. He shot a hard glance at her as he sorted through the junk mail. Was it his video-game design mind-set making him paranoid? Sure, that might just be normal for her, but why would anybody sit on the porch during a colder than normal autumn? Merry might know whether she had a polar bear for a neighbor—or whether that sedan belonged across the street.

No use speculating on insufficient evidence, Tony decided. The lock turned easily around the key; no suspicious, bomblike clicks or beeps greeted the door's opening. He laughed at himself for expecting a full-on fireball. The house itself looked undisturbed, uninhabited, unsearched. Either they were very discreet, or they hadn't actually gotten in. Still, any outfit that managed to monitor her phone calls— and be there when she met with that guy at Channel 8—wasn't likely to miss something as obvious as her home address. He turned the puzzle over in his mind, thinking of the way he'd handle the machinations of a global corporate villain in a video game. Plotting, dialogue, and character designs filled his head as he grabbed a few clothes for

Merry and Missy, gathered the important papers Merry had asked for (insurance, title to the house, bank statement, marriage license, all tucked into the drawer she'd told him to check), and on impulse added Merry and Chris's wedding picture to the small pile. Sentimental? Sure—that was part of why Carmen loved him.

Now, how to carry all that out of here without looking too obvious? Suitcase? No, that'd be a dead giveaway. Laundry bag? Merry had a washer in the basement—and why would he need to haul laundry when nobody was here? He opened closets, looking for likely alternatives. Too bad he hadn't brought Gianni with him. Diaper bags were the ultimate all-purpose stuff carriers, and nobody really wanted to search them, for obvious reasons. Ha—there it was, in the hall closet. He folded the clothes tightly around the picture, bent the papers into shape, and crammed it all into the bowling bag Chris got years ago at a ward white-elephant Christmas party.

"Anybody asks, I'm just a semi-larcenous bowling nut borrowing a neighbor's equipment," he announced.

Nobody asked, but as he pulled out of the driveway and headed down the street, the expensive car casually pulled out of the shade to fall in a discreet block behind him. After three turns, including a last-minute run at the freeway entrance, it seemed pretty clear that he'd acquired a tail. Bizarre.

"Okay, Tony boy, what do you do?" he muttered under his breath. He considered making a run for it, but even though he'd programmed plenty of chase games, he realized that a true high-speed chase wasn't up his alley. Images flashed through his head: fishtailing and weaving through traffic, bouncing off the guard walls, the sedan screeching behind, glued to his tailpipe as they knocked innocent bystanders off the walkways and blasted through construction zones at 100 miles an hour. Yeah, right. More like hit the accelerator, dodge around a semi, and rear-end some poor grandma from Long Beach. Even if he managed to pull off a pretty good imitation of a professional stunt driver, and assuming the guy behind the sedan's wheel knew his stuff too, the most a chase would buy would be a visit from the Highway Patrol. Besides, Carmen always told him not to do anything that would get him on the 10 o'clock news. The thought made him smile, despite the sedan hovering in his rearview mirror.

Then again, he thought, *why do anything? They already know where I live, and I haven't done anything sneaky—other than borrowing a bowling ball without asking first. Carmen and Merry aren't home, so there isn't anybody to catch. Why not just play it cool, and see what they do?*

They didn't do anything. Tony got home, parked in the garage, and walked into the house—where he and Donna watched the car pull across the street and settle down to watch them.

"This is bogus!" Donna finally declared. "Dad, what if Lucrezia and I pretend one of us is you, put on your cap, and take the car. We can lead them away, so you can go meet Mom at the bishop's."

"Veto." Tony shook his head, holding up his hands to forestall her protests. "Donna girl, I appreciate that you want to help—and that you're bored. But we don't know what they're going to do."

"They just asked me a bunch of questions before," Donna pointed out.

"They did. And they also killed 52 people testing that vaccine. And pulled a gun on Merry." Tony squeezed her shoulder. "Baby, we're not going to give them a chance to get any of us alone."

"People shouldn't just be able to besiege other people in their own houses, sitting in their cars like a real stakeout," Donna complained.

"Darn right." Suddenly, Tony grinned and picked up the phone. "Baby, what's the license on that car?"

Donna read it out, giving him a quizzical look. Her puzzlement turned to a wicked laugh as he phoned the police to report a car with those plates stolen from Merry's neighborhood.

"Here." He handed the phone to her. "Wait a couple minutes, then call them again. I'll get a suitcase and diaper bag packed for Merry and Missy."

She did—and sold it too, breathlessly informing the dispatcher that she'd seen a bunch of teenagers speeding down their road in an expensive sedan, blowing through stop signs, and generally scaring the kids, pets, and old folks.

Tony rolled his eyes. "Over the top a little?"

Donna shrugged. "Cops always like busting teenagers. The important thing is to get them here, right?"

"Right," Tony hugged her. "Here comes the cavalry." A few minutes later, he added, "Eventually."

A half-hour later, Tony, Donna, and Lucrezia pulled out of their driveway and drove right past the expensive sedan—and the officer questioning its two occupants. Donna waved to Ms. White.

* * *

Perro waved in the last truck, pointing them down the access way toward the crater where SkateTown's central bunker had stood. The oil rigger behind the wheel waved back, a good-naturedly obscene salute.

"That's it," Perro called to Scruffy. "Close the gate—well, you know what I mean." They each grabbed an end of the pile of girders that had been part of SkateTown's sign until last night, pivoting it screechingly into place across the road. It wouldn't hold a determined assault, but it didn't have to—just give them warning and delay any snoops long enough to set up a welcoming party.

"You're on," he told the messenger kid—Dove had christened him Mercury, for reasons that were still unclear to Perro—and tossed him a beetle-com. "Keep your eyes open."

"Ah, and I see so much better with 'em shut," Mercury teased, catching the beetle-com out of the air. He settled himself more comfortably on the tall walkway up to the park's main observation deck, disregarding the dark stain of Omerta's blood on the metal.

"And don't shoot yourself with that thing," Perro added, pointing to the gun that the kid cradled in both arms. (His concern came mainly out of an altogether too vivid memory of what a hoser he'd been when he first got issued a firearm, rather than anything specific Mercury had done.)

"Go to your meeting, Grandpa," Mercury advised, much to Scruffy's amusement. "I'll stay here and make sure you don't get another finger shot off. Old guy like you needs all the . . . digits he has."

Perro growled and showed him an eloquent gesture, but it was obvious he wasn't angry when he had to turn away to hide a grin. He and Scruffy slid into the back ranks lining the slick sides of a shallow bowl.

From the bottom of the bowl, Dove and Calvin surveyed the crowd. It looked good—everybody who they'd seriously recruited had come, about 25 altogether. *A motley crew,* Dove thought, some *Brujos,* some of *Abuelo's* gang, some of the young bucks from school, a bunch of roughnecks who got sick of Slick trying to put the muscle on them. They lounged, huddled, and crouched on the bowl's surface in small groups, casually sizing each other up, discussing rumors and counter rumors, a few of them offering odds on beating Slick. The odds estimates weren't as bad as they could be; the sheer size of the crater outside the bowl had impressed them, as planned. Dove figured it would be a psychological boost to hold the meeting at the site of a victory for the *Santos Soldados*—plus, it made security sense. Unlikely as it might be, Dove didn't want anyone wondering about a convoy of vehicles crossing the border to Blanca Hacienda quite yet, and he didn't know whether Rico had contacts among the border patrol—or whether Pizarro would pass the word along. He'd stayed out of Dove's way so far, but how far could he trust the fat sheriff? Holding the strategy meeting at SkateTown had another advantage as well; he knew that Slick's forces wouldn't be hanging around there, because SkateTown was no use to them anymore. (Or anybody else, since the original owners had gone bankrupt and defaulted to the county; the single insurance adjuster who'd checked the site for the county hadn't spent more than fifteen minutes casing the damage, and the local reporters hadn't even bothered to show up.)

Dove did a slow visual inspection around the half circle of audience in front of him, doing his best to project an air of commanding confidence, nodding to this one or that one, letting them look him over in return. He just hoped they respected what they saw. Movement caught his eye—Marco walking down the slope toward him. Boris and Natasha broke off at the top of the bowl, settling beside Perro and Scruffy.

"Hey, Marco," Dove said softly as the big man stopped beside him. "Glad you came."

"Hey, Dove. Bet you are," Marco returned with a sharp smile. "So you know, we've got twelve. Including me." He waited a moment, to make sure that sank in, then went on. "Those two puppies—Boris and Natasha—came in late yesterday, about blew your cover with Rico. They said they were out tagging—good cover for all the back-splatter on them—what'd you do, have 'em repaint the hacienda?"

"No, that was their idea," Dove told him, smiling despite the potential seriousness of the situation. "I had 'em moving cattle troughs into the front as cover."

"Not bad," Marco nodded. "Might work. Better work. I gotta get back, so here's the fast version. I'm officially out helping those two idiots freshen up Rico's tags and teaching them not to come in late. We'll get back 'round midnight. That gonna give us time to get ready for the party?"

"Plenty of time, since the party begins just before dawn." Dove glanced up at the moon, showing copper on the horizon through a thin haze of blood-colored clouds. The sun had just finished setting in a molten-iron inferno. "If Dolores didn't come back and tell Rico all about Blanca Hacienda."

Marco shook his head. "Rico don't know about Blanca Hacienda, except it's one of the places I told Slick that Perro and Calvin maybe bunked off to. Said I'd check it out tomorrow—if they don't catch you tonight. And they better not, kid. Slick's about ready to spit nails right through your skull for what you did here—and Rico's even more hacked off, since without you to skin, Slick's been spitting nails at him. You better plan a real good ambush."

"Thanks for the advice." Dove glanced around the bowl again. Just about time to start talking; they looked like they'd nearly hit the point where curiosity turned to restlessness. They'd recognized Marco, though, and that caught their attention. "They still think it's just me, Perro, and Calvin?"

"They figure you bought a bomb expert too, or got real lucky." Marco looked over to where Speedy sat, rocking back and forth, carrying on an animated one-way conversation at nobody in particular. "But far as they know, they just got to worry about you three boys." He clapped Dove on the shoulder suddenly, grinning. "You got a helluva reputation, *Hasbidi* Nakai. Smart, but crazy enough to take 'em on with nobody but a clown and a geek. Rico wants you stuffed. Slick wants you dead—or on the General's payroll. Me, I'm just glad you're not that psycho. We got your back tonight. *Hasta la vista, Capitan.*" Much to Dove's surprise—and gratitude—he stepped back and snapped off a crisp salute.

"*Vaya con Dios.*" Dove returned the salute.

The assembled reserves watched Marco leave, gathering the other two in his wake. The last few mutters of conversation died, as all eyes came back to rest on the lone figure at the bottom of the bowl.

Dove stood for a moment, his head bowed. One last time, he offered a silent prayer, asking for final word, final approval of what they were about to do. Bishop Yazzie's deep voice played in his head. "Study it out in your mind, decide on your course of action, then ask God if it's right. If it isn't, you'll feel it as doubt and confusion. If it is, dig in and get it done." He took stock of what he felt: excitement, fear, apprehension, exhilaration. No doubt. No confusion. He opened his eyes and stepped forward, into the waiting silence.

"This is it. Tonight, we pull Slick into a trap and take him out. Neutralize him, like the Army says. And like the Army does, this is going to be real. Not a quick raid, not a beat down, not a smash job. It's a hot war with real standing and shooting, to stop Slick and his General from taking over the borderlands—our borderlands—with Southern soldiers and traitors like Rico. And that's not all they've got. They fight with poison too, diseases that they'll spread to anybody who stands up to them, anybody who gets in their way." Dove's gaze swept the circle, catching their eyes, driving the point home.

He continued, speaking clearly, the slope of the concrete bowl amplifying his voice and adding deeper echoes. "This isn't about turf or protection money or drugs. This is about defending everything you've got from total domination and destruction. You're already marked, because you haven't joined up already. If Slick wins, he can't leave you standing. You'll have one choice: knuckle under to him, or die. Or, like the *Brujos* found out, knuckle under to him *and* die."

A low growl swept through the gathered men, glances flicking to Paco, Speedy, and the handful of *Brujos* looking grim-faced and silent beside them.

"Will you lie down, or take a stand? Will you stand for your *chicos*, your comrades, your families, your freedom?" Dove made it a personal challenge, shot point blank at each one of them. "Will you stand and fight?"

The words hung in the charged air, vibrating in the silence. Dove hardly dared breathe, waiting for their reaction. He didn't have to wait long.

Calvin unfolded his skinny length from where he leaned on the concrete and said quietly, "I will."

"Me too." Perro jumped to his feet, without even adding an irreverent crack.

For a moment, the decision hung in the balance. Then Paco tossed his cigarette aside and rose as well. "Better to die on our feet than live on our knees—as long as we'd live. You need a crip, you got one."

"Somebody's gotta manage the dynamite," Speedy noted, a wicked grin carving across his thin face. "I'd get on my knees to Slick just long enough to stategically place a stick—"

He didn't have to finish the sentence. A roar of approval and agreement flashed around the bowl as all two dozen lurched to their feet, shouting their commitment to the cause—and to putting Slick and Rico at least six feet under (and in as many pieces as possible). The uproar died away almost as quickly as it had erupted, leaving a charge of adrenaline and determination behind it.

"*Hai, Santos Soldados!*" Perro crowed. "What are we gonna do to those coyotes, *Capitan?*"

"We're going to do what they tried to do to Benny and me," Dove told them, "but we're going to do it right. Here's the deal: Slick and Rico still think that they're just facing me, Calvin, and Perro—"

"That's enough to scare 'em out of their boots without all you yahoos," Perro assured them—and got roundly dissed for it.

Dove waited for the laughter to die down and continued, "Marco's gone back to spread the word that I'm going to take the bait they used Dolores to toss me: that Slick's got a new virus shipment, and he's going to be so busy celebrating that he's left it unguarded."

Another round of catcalls met that statement, most of them demeaning Slick's intelligence for thinking that Dove would be that stupid—and a few comments about Dove's likelihood of doing exactly that.

"Yeah, maybe I would," Dove grinned at them. "That's what we're going to let Slick believe, anyway, that we're that stupid. Tonight, the three of us—"

"Hey! Who's stupid?" Perro yipped at that, until Calvin poked him.

"—will get out there," Dove continued without stopping, "and pretend to case the joint. We'll plant a couple of Speedy's bombs to blow the place—to get Slick's attention."

"Portable explosives again," Speedy muttered. "More hurrying up and hurrying up again." Everybody else liked the sound of that idea, however.

"We'll stick around just long enough for Slick to get a bead on us," Dove shot a warning look at Perro, who didn't say anything this time. "Then we'll hike the Dogmobile as fast as it can fly out to Blanca Hacienda, with Slick and the guys in hot pursuit—right into an ambush. That's where you come in."

Cheers at that, along with dark mutterings about the fate of anybody who fell into any ambush they set up.

"You saw the crater out there." Dove motioned toward the devastation where the bunker had been. "It used to be full of Slick's weapons and ammo—which you'll turn right back on him. You'll be waiting for him, rifles ready, out at Blanca Hacienda."

"Recho Ojo's old place?" one of the roughnecks asked. "The ranch house down off the border?"

"Right," Dove agreed. "Slick's used it once as a hideout for his banditos, and he knows I know about it. It's got a nice, controlled approach corridor, big rocks at the entranceway, rough ground out beyond. Cross-country travel out there is okay for a good dirt bike, but it's virtually impossible for a truck, even a four wheeler, to go 'round the back. Recho Ojo had good reason to choose it as his hideout. And, it's better than having a shootout in town; we don't have to worry about civilians getting in the way—or the cops stepping in."

That got another laugh, and then the questions started. *Would* the cops step in? Dove told them that Pizarro had promised to stay out of it. How much ammo did they have? Enough to get the job done, but they should make every shot count. How did they know Slick would follow them out there? Pride and anger—they'd already raided and destroyed one of his caches, and now they were going to blow up his headquarters. How could he let that go? Plus, he didn't know that he'd be heading toward the jaws of a bear trap; he thought he was chasing three psycho kids, not facing an Amexican Special Forces unit. They liked that description.

"Everybody got it?" Dove asked. "Anybody want out?"

"Out? And miss seeing Slick's face when we blow him away?" Perro yelled.

A general roar of agreement met that sentiment. Scruffy started a chant of "*Santos Soldados*," which quickly caught on.

Holy soldiers, fighting saints. Dove closed his eyes, stretching his hands toward the sky. Around him, the chant faded into silence. "Oh, God, we know You can hear us. We know that with Your power behind us, we can win this fight. We ask You to forgive us, guide us as Your servants this night. Defend us from evil as we defend the innocents. In the name of the Savior Jesus, Amen."

As he spoke, the silence deepened. Far from religious as they were, most still had at least a distant respect for the church their *abuelas* had taught them about when they were tiny; more immediately, the force of Dove's sincere belief drove deep into their minds and hearts. One by one, the *Santos's* heads bowed; first two, then most of them, dropped to their knees. When the prayer finished, they rose with grim determination and a strange, light confidence.

The meeting broke up in virtual silence, Dove catching each of the team individually, bidding them farewell with a word and touch—and a beetle-com. Headlights scattered into the night, taking different paths across the desert to the border and to Blanca Hacienda, to distribute weapons and dig in.

"Here we go," Perro said. Excitement bubbled through his attempt at a casual, bored tone.

"Here we go," Calvin nodded. He touched Dove's shoulder, smiling almost shyly. "You got 'em, Dove. They listened. They went for it."

"He got 'em, Calvin." Dove said, feeling a rush of gratitude that almost brought tears to his eyes. *Gonna pull an Ammon here, Hasbídí?* he thought wryly to himself. *Cry and faint? No time. Later. Plenty of time later.* "Now, let's get going. We got a whole bunch of *Santos Soldados* to hide."

The Dogmobile pulled away from SkateTown, one more set of headlights heading for the border and the battle.

CHAPTER 18

"Headlights pulling into the driveway," Carmen announced from her discreet post beside Bishop Michelsen's front window. "It's Tony—and the girls!"

Merry laughed softly, at the panic she felt about headlights, then the intense relief that hit when the car contained allies instead of enemies. "Paranoid," she muttered, running her hands over her arms to smooth down the goose bumps. It all seemed so unreal, like an intense dream, too impossible but altogether too plausible at once.

"I should say!" Carmen exclaimed. "And with good reason. Merry, they've been chasing us! That guy pulled a *gun* on you! They showed up at my house—my house!—grilling Donna for information! Not that they got anything useful out of her." She smiled, all mama-tiger pride.

Her smile only widened as she jumped into Tony's arms when he came in the door. Donna and Lucrezia tumbled in after him, talking at once about calling the cops on White and Cornell, driving right past them, then taking a deliberately loopy path to the bishop's house.

Tony kissed Carmen, then smiled at Merry, offering the bowling bag. "Here. Sorry about the bag—it was the most discreet thing I could grab. I hope I got the right stuff."

"As long as you've got plenty of diapers and remembered garments for me, it's perfect," Merry assured him. "Oh, and Missy's lucky green sleepsuit, of course." She laughed as Tony's face fell, and gave him a big hug. "Just kidding, Tony. Thank you."

Sister Michelsen, unperturbed at the sudden influx of hyperactive bodies, calmly replenished the cookie plate and retreated into the kitchen to finish feeding dinner to her own kids. Gianni and Missy had already eaten their french-fry depleted suppers and crashed on the Michelsen's bed.

"Did you hear that, Merry? The cops pulled them over." Lucrezia helped herself, waving the cookie to punctuate her point. "So, we know the cops aren't in on it. See? The uniform on the street's still dependable. Not everybody's corrupt—"

"Or everybody's corrupt, but they're not all in MedaGen's pocket yet," Donna interrupted.

Fortunately, Bishop Michelsen came in at that moment, short-circuiting the incipient argument. He shrugged off his jacket as he came through the door, spotting Merry right off. "Well, it looks like you were right. Elder Nabil understood—"

The five conspirators (Merry hid a smile at that mental description) turned simultaneously to look at him. He started slightly, feeling the pressure of ten eyes all boring into him at once, and lost his train of thought.

"Elder Nabil?" Carmen repeated.

"Oh—right! The one who's a doctor," Lucrezia nodded, satisfied.

"The Apostle?" Carmen asked, her eyes wide.

"Yes, Sweetheart, the Apostle," Tony's patronizing tone brought Carmen out of her momentary star-struck stare. She smacked his arm and grinned.

"What did Elder Nabil say?" Merry asked cautiously.

"He checked the files you gave me to send and said he wanted to talk to you as soon as possible. Just like that. He said he'd start smoothing the way, and asked if you can get to Salt Lake City. Elder Nabil's there this week, and it's closer than Independence." Bishop Michelsen looked a bit amazed himself as he relayed the message.

"Salt Lake City?" Merry repeated, trying to process the idea of talking to an Apostle about AllSafe. The trained scientist side snorted at the idea; the faithful Latter-day Saint side responded with "Well, of course! Who else?"

"That's a plane ticket." Carmen nodded decisively. "Donna, grab my purse. We'll book a seat right now."

"Carmen, I can cover—" Merry protested, grabbing for her own wallet.

Tony gently caught her hand. "Merry, airlines don't take cash. And you can't use your credit card."

"They might trace it," Lucrezia finished the obvious connection.

"Oh, sure, cops aren't corrupt, but credit-card companies are?" Donna shot back.

"Utterly! Is there any outfit less corrupt than credit-card companies?" Merry laughed, rubbing Donna's shoulder. "Actually, your mom's right. We're not fighting the credit-card people or the cops, but it looks like Senator Garlick's thrown his access keys to Ms. Zelik. As second in line to Homeland Security, he's got the 800-pound gorilla status to get her any information she wants. Including credit-card numbers, and phone records."

"That is just so not right." Donna and Lucrezia exchanged a completely sympathetic glance.

"Hush," Carmen waved her free hand at them. "Yes, I'd like to buy a ticket for Salt Lake City. As soon as possible—it's a family emergency."

* * *

"Talk about family emergency," Merry muttered, leaning back across the seat as she tried to retrieve Missy's sippy cup from the floor. Missy continued to scream, kicking her feet against the car seat furiously, and promptly threw the cup across the van when Merry handed it back to her. Missy hadn't appreciated getting rousted out of a sound sleep, hustled into a new outfit, and rushed out to the car to catch a plane leaving in just two and a half hours. The tension screaming up and down Merry's nerves hadn't helped matters.

She was on her way to a city she didn't know, on the run from literally deadly enemies, with nothing but a bowling bag full of underwear, important documents—and a wedding photo that had brought her to tears. *Chris!* she'd sobbed silently, while Bishop Michelsen sent them off with a heartfelt prayer for protection, success, and inspiration. *I'm not a spy! I'm not an agent! I hate traveling!* The thoughts kept spiraling around in her head, echoing Missy's furious shrieks and sobs, drowning the sound of the late-night traffic on the road to the airport and the jets thundering above them.

"Fine!" she nearly shouted to herself as the cup went flying again. "Be that way, then!" The motion of the van suddenly slowing grabbed her attention. The sheer ridiculousness of the situation made her want to laugh—or cry. "Now, see what you've done? We've fought so much Carmen's stopping the car."

Carmen didn't laugh or cry—or even roll her eyes at Merry's frustrated quip. She just sat there, gazing straight ahead, at the security guards manning the gates of the airport entrance as the thin stream of cars passed by.

"Carmen?" Merry said softly, touching her friend's shoulder. "Are you all right?" Missy, distracted by the stop and the abrupt change in the emotional temperature, hiccupped to a stop.

"Merry, how do you feel about doing this?" After a long moment, Carmen looked at her.

"Terrified," Merry said honestly. "Tired. Stressed. My mind's spinning a million miles an hour. Why?"

"I just really feel like we shouldn't go in there." Carmen waved at the brightly lit gateway.

"Why?" Merry asked, surprised.

"Not sure," Carmen said, more confident now. "But it's not thinking, it's feeling. Don't think about it, Merry, just try to listen."

Merry surveyed the gate, with the usual complement of guards and guns, but no more unwelcoming than usual. *Don't think, just feel.* She tried to quiet the jabbering in her mind, to get to the feeling trying to make itself heard through her tight planning and wild adrenaline rush, staring at the gate and past it. As she looked, the flicker of aversion she'd put down to preflight nerves grew stronger.

"Why wouldn't this be a good idea?" she asked aloud, then amended the question and answered it herself. "Because I have to fly under my own name, and while MedaGen shouldn't be able to get passenger lists, they might. Especially with a powerful Senator's name on the request."

"Right." Carmen nodded. "And because I figure the Holy Ghost just stepped up to the microphone with the whole 'still, small voice' thing. We are so out of here."

Carmen put the van into gear and hit the accelerator, pulling off the side of the road and into a wide U-turn away from the gate. She and Merry caught sight of the demurely sleek, silver car speeding up the airport road toward them at the same time. The driver slowed and honked, clearly annoyed at having to brake for a minivan lumbering through a turn. Beside him, in the bright lights of the airport's gate, Ms. Zelik frowned, staring past the obstruction at the airport beyond.

Her face imprinted itself on Merry's retinas—and Merry ducked below the dashboard, hoping the shadows had hidden her well enough. Carmen tossed Zelik's driver an apologetic smile and wave as she drove by. She successfully resisted the urge to duck too; they didn't know what she looked like, and how suspicious would it look for the driver to suddenly disappear? Still, she breathed a sigh of relief as she checked her rearview mirrors and saw the taillights of the silver car speed away toward the airport gate.

"Curses! Foiled again!" Merry muttered, using Chris's terrible movie-Russian accent. She stayed down, her face against her knees, until she got the tears under control.

"Curses!" Missy repeated. She kept saying it too, which made Tony laugh despite the situation when Carmen called him.

He sobered fast, however, when she told him that they'd had a very near miss, passing the word along to the rest of the conspirators.

"What do we do now?" Carmen rubbed Merry's back, addressing the question to all and sundry through Tony. "We've got to get Merry to Salt Lake, and we've got to keep her under MedaGen's radar."

"And keep any of you from getting on MedaGen's hit list," Merry added, pulling herself together. *Please, God, don't let me go to pieces now—and please help!* "I'm so sorry, Carmen. I didn't mean to get you all mixed up in something this amazingly, stupidly complicated!"

"Merry's trying to apologize for getting us involved," Carmen told Tony, then nodded. "Nope, I won't let her." She grinned at Merry. "Tony and I—and the girls too—got into it because we love you. And because it's our chance to strike a blow for truth, justice, and the American way. No apologies. We're going to stop the bad guys and save the good guys, and that's just it. Now, we just have to figure out how to smuggle you to Salt Lake without getting caught by the MedaGen goons."

Silence descended, broken by the noise of the van rushing along the highway, Missy singing random words on one side of the connection, and the sound of a distant TV news report and frantic brain wracking on the other.

Sister Michelsen's voice came clearly through the phone. "It sounds like compassionate service to me."

The silence lasted a second longer, with a distinct component of stunned to it. Then the van and house erupted in hopeful pandemonium. Tony kept asking Carmen if she'd heard, Carmen crowed that it took a Relief Society president to think so practically, and Sister Michelsen squeaked as the bishop swept her up in a hug.

An hour and a blizzard of phone calls later, Carmen pulled the van into a church parking lot. A few minutes later, another minivan pulled into the lot and parked beside them.

"Hi!" the woman who got out of the van smiled apologetically. "Sorry it took so long—I had to drop the kids off at my sister's. Hope you haven't been waiting long."

"Not long at all," Merry assured her. "Thank you so much for coming out so late, Sister—"

"Call me Margie," Margie instructed firmly, helping Carmen transfer Missy's car seat from one vehicle to the other. "And don't worry a bit about it. It's exciting, getting an emergency call that doesn't involve having to get four people to make funeral potatoes before noon tomorrow."

Merry winced at the thought of funeral potatoes, hugging Missy close. The poor kid had finally given up and fallen asleep again. Carmen kissed her cheek anyway, petting her curls. "You be good, little Miss Missy, just like always. Don't forget us."

"Neither of us will!" Merry leaned into Carmen's maternal bear hug. "I'll call as soon as I get there. Watch out, be safe, give Tony and the girls hugs for me!"

"I will, I will!" Carmen helped her snug Missy into the car seat and practically lifted Merry into Margie's van. "Don't you worry about a thing. Get going, tell Elder Nabil all about it, and throw a big old wrench into MedaGen's nasty plans!" She waved vigorously until the van's taillights disappeared down the road. It took a few minutes for her eyes to clear enough to hit the road for the long drive home.

"You just look all in," Margie told Merry. "Go ahead and recline that seat—it goes all the way back—and get some rest."

"Thanks," Merry managed a rueful smile. "I'm exhausted, but I'm too wired to sleep."

"Well, in that case," Margie shot her an encouraging glance, "tell me about what's going on. I'm just dying of curiosity, and it'll sure pass the time. It's not every day that I get called to pick somebody up in the middle of the night at the church and drive her over to a different one just to meet somebody else waiting to do the same thing! What's going on? Is it top secret?"

"It's not top secret at all," Merry assured her. "In fact, please tell everybody you can about it! You know those commercials you've been seeing for the AllSafe vaccine?"

The story lasted through the drive—and through half of the next one, with an equally curious, charitable, and (by the end of her tale) outraged Compassionate Service leader as chief witness-smuggler and her wide-eyed teenage son as chauffeur. After answering their questions between jaw-cracking yawns, Merry finally fell asleep, her head against Missy's seat. She woke in the thin light of predawn to see yet another car waiting, this time in a driveway. It wasn't going anywhere immediately, however.

"Hi, Sister Galen? I'm Pedro Hernandez, and this is my wife, Gloria." The man helped Merry out of the back seat as his wife neatly extracted Missy from her restraints. "Come on in—it looks like you could use a chance to freshen up and get some breakfast before we take off for Salt Lake."

"I sure could," Merry agreed. Her eyes filled with tears (equal parts exhaustion, tension, and gratitude). "Thank you. Thank you so much."

"Glad to do it." Pedro grinned. "We're just here to help."

* * *

"Why are we here again?" Perro whispered, as he and Dove oozed through the thin line of scrubby shrubs that divided Benny's house—Rico's headquarters, Dove reminded himself, swallowing against the sick loneliness thickening his throat—from the neighbor's. The neighbor had planted the bushes right after Benny bought the house, and had asked the nursery man to give him the fastest-growing plants available. Apparently, even though they sprang up to nearly head high in just five years, and so thick that the wall of spiky branches was about as impenetrable as a stone wall, they hadn't grown fast enough for the neighbor. He'd had a For Sale sign outside the house for almost as long before he finally gave up and moved out without finding a buyer. The bushes appealed to Benny too, because they afforded extra privacy and protection from everybody but little kids and dogs. Dove knew about a well-hidden gap in the hedge only because he'd seen one of the neighborhood kids suddenly burst into the backyard after an errant baseball.

"We're here to get the new shipment of virus serum that Dolores said Slick's just got from the General, and being too stupid or naïve or whatever to realize we're walking into a trap." Dove scoped out the house—quiet, dark, and seemingly uninhabited, just as Dolores had said.

"No, I mean for us, not for Slick." Perro rolled his eyes, pausing to very carefully disentangle the strap of the backpack he carried from one of the stubborn bushes. He wasn't about to go jerking a bagful of plastique loose.

"We're here to get Slick's attention, make him madder than he already is, run from him fast enough that we don't lose him, lead him out to Blanca Hacienda, and ambush his—" Dove paused, glancing back toward the street, where Calvin waited in the Dogmobile. He thought he saw a flicker of motion, off to the left behind the bushes they'd just crawled through. "And we'd better hurry, because it looks like his trap might be better than I expected."

The bullet that whined past his shoulder sharply seconded that impression. He and Perro ran toward the house, abandoning all pretense of stealth. Dove hoped it looked like their only thought was to get to cover as quickly as possible—and didn't quite admit to himself just how close that was to the truth. They hit the wall and slipped around the corner as shouts and more shots broke out. Floodlights came on like permanent lightning, so stark that each blade of dry grass in the neglected lawn stood out with flashbulb clarity. Benny hadn't installed floodlights—especially not floodlights just at the rim of the eaves, protected by little metal-mesh cages.

"Tell me Benny had a secret back door put in," Perro told Dove, looking frantically around for any escape that didn't involve running across the brilliantly lit shooting gallery of the yard.

"Sorry," Dove shot back—literally, pulling his pistol and hitting the ground, then rolling to fire around the corner at ankle level. Chips of siding showered over him from overhead, as the bullets tore into the spot where they expected his head to be. Out in the bushes, a yell and string of curses told him that one of Slick's guys would need a new pair of shoes (and maybe a new foot, too). "How 'bout you set the bomb instead of asking so many questions?"

"Right, give me the tough job," Perro muttered, trying to shrink into the peeling paint of the wall as he carefully brought out the wad of plastique and wires. At least in this glare he wouldn't need the flashlight he'd brought. How had Scruffy showed him?

"You want to trade?" Dove asked, ducking back into the dubious shelter of the house to slap a new clip into his gun. They couldn't keep this up long—he hadn't counted on having to hold them off this soon, or from two directions. Speaking of which . . . He rose fluidly to his feet, shooting down the length of the house to discourage the second contingent from barreling around the far corner.

"One, and two, and green, and blue," Perro chanted, finishing the assembly of the crude but effective bomb Scruffy had showed him. They'd chosen Perro as the demolitions man over Speedy's initial objections, but he'd finally relented when Scruffy pointed out that Dove was a better shot, and besides, Perro was already missing a toe. Might give him a leg up, so to speak, with the bomb gods. So far, it seemed to be working. "Got it, got it, got it! Let's go!"

"Ready to run?" Dove asked, gesturing out into the bare yard. A fusillade of shots smashed into the wall of the house, a running track of splintered holes crashing toward Dove's chest. He threw himself flat again, taking Perro with him.

Perro groaned. "This is really stupid!"

"On the bright side, we've definitely fooled Slick into thinking we're idiots." Dove knew the laugh that accompanied his words was more than a touch hysterical, but at the moment he didn't care. Dirt showered over him from the other direction, where the second contingent had arrived. "Hit the detonator, Perro, and then we'll run."

"Scruffy said to run, *then* hit the detonator," Perro yelped.

"Scruffy didn't know we'd be pinned." Dove squeezed off another shot; the head that had peeked around the near side of the house disappeared abruptly. Two gun barrels took its place. Dove grabbed Perro's hand and squeezed it around the detonator. The red light went on, blinked once.

Dove sprang up and dragged Perro with him.

The red light blinked twice.

Dove and Perro sprinted across the dry yard toward the bushes, zigzagging and weaving crazily. A horizontal hail of bullets followed and outstripped them.

The red light blinked for the third time.

Dove felt a hard blow glance off the side of his leg as the back side of the house dissolved in a roar of light and flame, replacing the harsh white of the floodlights with an inferno of yellow and red. An overwhelming force hit Dove's back, lifting him off his feet and throwing him into the bushes. Perro hit the branches a few feet away so hard that he crashed through onto the other side, landing hard and rolling. He opened his eyes in time to see something flying at his head and ducked aside. A half-melted floodlight smacked into the ground where he'd lain, still sizzling. Lights. The thought occurred too late, making him bonk his head on the ground in chagrined realization. They should've shot out the lights! He didn't have time to meditate on past mistakes or his near miss with lobotomy by light fixture before Dove grabbed him and pulled hard.

"Come on, Perro—time to fly!" He spared a glance for the figures picking themselves up off the ground all around the flaming ruin of the house (home?), and the reinforcements pouring out of the neighbor's abandoned property. "Fly!" he repeated, and ran for the street, where the headlights of the Dogmobile suddenly flared into view. His leg shook slightly, but held under him as they raced across the yard, avoiding a couple of small fires.

They hit the car's doors and more fell than climbed in; Calvin hit the accelerator before Perro's second foot had lifted off the ground. The Dogmobile belched its customary cloud of diesel exhaust, jumped the curb like a veteran steeplechaser, and fishtailed away. Like hounds after a fox—or, given the desert setting, like coyotes after a rabbit—five big SUVs roared to life, gathering their cargoes of armed, cursing men as they sped after their prey.

Perro looked out the spiderweb of cracked glass where the back window had been, then slumped down in his seat, rummaging for the gun and ammunition boxes they'd stashed there. "Dove, maybe we *are* idiots."

"Second that," Calvin said tightly, taking a corner—and clipping a light pole—at speeds no highway engineer would recommend.

"Maybe we are." Dove pulled off his jacket, ducking as shots rang out behind. Another bit of the Dogmobile's back window disappeared in a cloud of crystal splinters. The side of his leg felt like it was on fire, hot and slick with blood. It still moved though, still supported his weight as he moved. Breathing a silent prayer of thanks and begging for continued help, he shrugged out of his shirt, ripped the sleeves off, and tied them tight around the wound.

Calvin skidded around another corner, throwing Dove into the door and Perro into him.

"Wow!" Perro held up a hand, feeling the sticky wet on his fingers. "Either I'm in shock so bad I don't know where I got hit, or they got you, *Hasbìdì*."

"It's only a flesh wound," Dove assured him, laughing again as he pulled himself up and retrieved his gun. "Calvin, get out of town *now*—they're shooting at us!"

Calvin's reply (translation: No, duh!) was unprintable, as was Perro's comment as the Dogmobile bashed a large hole through a white picket fence on its way to clearer pastures. The lead SUV took out the rest of the fence.

"There goes the neighborhood," Perro commented, watching the fence's owners run out of the house to investigate—and run right back in when they saw four more SUVs bearing down on them. He leveled his own gun at the headlights behind them.

Dove caught his hand. "Not yet. You might hit somebody—some civilian. Wait until we get out of town."

Perro gave him a look of blank disbelief, but held his fire.

Two more creatively interpreted turns, however, and they broke free of the last residential streets. Scrub, rock, and desert stretched around the road, which curved and looped around a few low hills. Around the first high-banked turn, Dove nodded at Perro, and the two of them knelt on the back seat, firing back at the oncoming glint of the SUVs' headlights. An occasional bullet thumped into the trunk, burying itself in the sandbags hidden there as primitive bullet-proofing. They were heavy, but as Calvin pointed out, the weight could actually help with road grip—and it's not like they needed to worry about long-distance gas mileage.

"You know what you said about being slow enough for them to follow? How about being fast enough for them not to catch us?" Perro asked a few minutes later.

"That'd be a good idea too," Dove admitted. "Calvin?"

"Working on it," Calvin patted the dashboard and tried a prayer of his own.

"Work real good, cause if you don't, Slick's going to feed us our livers." Perro shuddered.

The lead SUV was gaining rapidly, loaded as it was. Calvin shifted and slithered over both lanes of the road, desperately trying to keep ahead of Slick's vehicle and keep it from coming up along-side. The roar of an air horn startled both drivers; they fought to get out of the way as a semi appeared around the curve ahead of them. The SUV slewed left, running off the road in a cloud of moonlit dust, then forcing its way back to the blacktop in a squeal of tires and complaining brakes. The driver yanked the wheel, keeping it from going into an all-out spin—and lost the effort, as one of the wheels abruptly came apart. The SUV slewed in a circle, staying upright only by luck. The other four vehicles swerved madly to avoid a collision with the spinning former leader. Two roared off the road in their own clouds of dust; one came to a whiplash stop. The last, initially at the end of the line, took up the lead, but it had lost a lot of ground.

"Yes, Marco!" Calvin crowed. "Way to go!"

"Go right!" Dove shouted, as the border checkpoint loomed in front of them. They hit the Exit lane, screaming past the startled border patrol. The wooden gate arm splintered across the Dogmobile's hood.

One of the more quick-acting members of the border patrol pulled his rifle, getting off a shot that put out the Dogmobile's one remaining taillight. The others, not so quick acting but quicker thinking, dove out of the way as the four SUVs blew through the checkpoint, slowing only enough to return fire when the hot-headed patrolman whirled to aim at the more immediate threat.

Past the momentary distraction at the border checkpoint, the SUVs steadily gained ground. The huge stones marking the entrance to Blanca Hacienda loomed out of the half-lit darkness, then receded into the background. Calvin pushed the Dogmobile to its red-line limit, the smoke from burning oil combining with the dust from the long dirt drive in a protective curtain that hung between them and Slick. The dust caught up to them, wafting around the car in a whirl of hot particles as they screeched to a final halt in the dusty yard just seconds before Slick and Rico's forces arrived. Dove, Perro, and Calvin abandoned the Dogmobile, racing to take cover behind the big, cement water troughs they'd hauled into the front from the cattle yard.

The SUVs pulled up as well, forming a half-circle around the front of the old ranch house, blocking the drive. In a well-organized rush, their passengers piled out and took cover behind the big vehicles.

For a long moment, the scene stilled under the red eye of the moon: four well-armed SUVs packed with hard-eyed Southerners and *Abuelo's* ex-gang members, armed to the teeth, facing three teenage boys cowering behind the rough cover of a couple of cement water troughs.

"If you surrender now, nobody has to get hurt," Dove called.

"Oh, but we *want* somebody to get hurt." Slick grinned, all cold-blooded shark, and motioned to a bandaged Omerta. "Finish them off."

Omerta nodded, stepped forward, and raised his hand. At his signal, a hail of bullets erupted out of the old hacienda, out of the cover of the lilacs—even out of the ground, as the *Santos* who'd literally buried themselves under tarps and a thin layer of dust sat up and cut the Southerners to bits. All over the yard, men screamed and fell, some scrambling to get back into the trucks, others taking cover and returning fire.

Slick, spitting curses, crawled into the back of his SUV, ducking the spattering glass shards as the second round of shots from the hacienda shattered the windows. In the semi dark, he found a case of grenades and ripped off the lid. Whirling around, he used the heavy lid to clock a gibbering, bleeding soldier across the head to get him out of the way. The man fell back out of the truck where he'd tried to hide, screaming again as two more bullets hit him. Slick noted the direction he fell and slipped around the truck on the other side.

"Omerta!" he shouted, tossing a grenade to his lieutenant with one hand, while pulling the pin out of the second with his teeth. The heavy globe arced toward the cattle troughs.

Calvin caught Slick's motion out of the corner of his eye, looked up to see the incoming explosive as a darker blot against the black sky. "Move!" he screamed at Perro and Dove—but there was nowhere to go but out into the hail of bullets. Without thinking, he lurched forward, catching the grenade as it fell. It registered as a heavy, improbably cold weight in his hand, finally triggering a thought— grenade!—before he threw it as hard as he could out and away.

The grenade exploded overhead at the same moment Omerta's grenade hit the ranch house, blowing a huge hole in it and starting a fire that ran like liquid heat over the ancient, desiccated wood inside the adobe walls.

The *Santos* dove out—some leaping from rickety second-story windows as the flames spread—and ran for the dubious cover of the run-down sheds. Dove noted with a flush of almost paternal pride that over half of them kept up their covering fire even as they ran.

"Back at ya!" The shout, along with a few choice obscenities, came through the momentary lull in the firefight, as both sides tried to adjust to a burning house in the middle of the conflict. With that warning, Speedy and Scruffy returned the explosive favor, tossing a few captured grenades themselves from the secondary cache hidden in the shed. One of the trucks shuddered with the sudden retreat of two of Rico's men as a grenade clattered on the roof and came to a rest on the hood, then went up in a fireball.

"You said he was alone!" Rico yelled at Slick—who couldn't hear him from across the yard, but who made an ideal target for Rico's desperate rage and denial of responsibility for the mess. They were in trouble here, three trucks left, facing an enemy who knew the lay of the land better than they did. Ambushed by Dove Nakai! He spat, adding motivational curses to saliva, shouting at his men to keep shooting or by all the saints and demons he'd shoot them himself.

Another flash of light caught Rico's attention. Headlights, two pair, coming down the long drive at high speed. These weren't Slick's fancy Mercedes models, but the jacked-up jobs that *Abuelo* used, complete with poacher lights. Marco—finally! Rico laughed aloud. "Marco!" he yelled.

"Marco!" Rico's gang set up a cheer that quickly spread to the Southerners. The cheer redoubled when they realized that the *Santos's* fire had trickled down. Scared—probably running like rabbits. Rico laughed again, waving his arms at the oncoming trucks.

As he expected, Marco, Boris, and the rest of the junior members of his gang piled out of the trucks and fanned out behind the SUVs, guns at ready. "What took you blue streaking lazy tails so freaking long to get here? Did you get lost? Or—"

Rico's taunting welcome cut off abruptly as Marco grinned back—and turned his gun toward Slick and Rico. Boris didn't grin as he followed suit; he and the others looked like grimly determined death.

"Shoot them!" Rico screamed at them. "Shoot these stupid *Santos*!"

Marco's grin just got bigger—and harder. "We *are* the *Santos*."

Setting his teeth against the wave of nausea and pain that hit when he put weight on his leg, Dove rose to his feet. "You're surrounded. Surrender, and we'll guarantee your safety. Just put your guns down."

Another eternal moment passed in the fading, rusty moonlight, this one punctuated by the bodies sprawled in the dust, the black puddles of blood spreading around them, the sobbing of the wounded.

Omerta glanced at Slick, who nodded tightly, then looked at Dove and the hard eyes of the *Santos* in the flickering light of the gathering fire. Omerta stepped forward, letting his gun swing around his finger to dangle harmlessly before he dropped it into the dust. With a rush of relief that sounded like a sigh, the rest of the southerners did the same, adding their weapons to the pile. Rico's men followed a few seconds later, ducking under Rico's blazing stare. He didn't put his gun down; Marco jabbed his own gun into Rico's throat and took it from him, tossing it onto the pile.

Slick, last of all, stepped forward and coolly offered his pistol to Dove. In a voice that could freeze alcohol, he said, "You have our guns. Now, let us go."

"If you promise to leave, go back to your General, and tell him to stay away from the borderlands forever—him, his troops, his drugs, and his viruses." Dove met his eyes unflinchingly, the steel in his voice meeting and matching the ice in Slick's.

A sickle of shark's smile flicked across Slick's face. He took off his mirror shades, tucking them carefully into his pocket. "No demand for a cut of the drug money? No maneuvering to replace us in the General's advance guard? All right, we'll leave. You're an honorable man, Nakai. It's almost an honor to lose to you." He offered his hand to seal the deal.

Dove extended his own hand, feeling dizzy with relief (and blood loss)—until the sharp glitter on Slick's sleeve brought the dark world into crystal clarity. He brought up the pistol in his left hand, shooting Slick through the chest at close range. Close enough to see the surprise in Slick's eyes turn to fury, the fury to terror, and the terror to vacant blackness. Close enough to feel the hot spatter of blood over his chest and face as Slick's heart convulsed and seized to a halt. Close enough that the full weight of Slick's lurching, empty corpse hit him and brought him down to the dust.

"Dove!" Calvin's voice resolved out of the pandemonium of shouts, cries, and questions. "Are you dead?"

"No, Calvin," Dove said quietly. "But Slick is. Help me get him off."

Calvin, with Marco's help, rolled Slick's corpse off Dove.

"He had something up his sleeve," Dove told them, swallowing hard. He stood, with Calvin's help, shaking with reaction. He couldn't bring himself to touch the gun lying where it fell. Not yet.

Marco's big hand groped around the dead Southerner's arm, then raised high, a glittering shard of summer-proof ice shining in it. "All right! Shut up! Nobody's going to shoot you—unless you pull something like this." He displayed the syringe to the panicked prisoners, to the shocked *Santos.*

"It's one of the viruses," Omerta said into the silence, stepping forward. He glanced down at his fallen leader, then focused on Dove. "Slick was dead anyway; the General was going to kill him if he didn't stop you. Rico's not the only one the General used the virus on—as loyalty insurance."

The words hit Rico like a meteor, destroying all his grand hopes and dreams. He felt the toxins washing through him like acid, eating away his future and his sanity. He lurched forward with an inarticulate cry, grabbed Dove around the throat, and began throttling him. The crushing force on Dove's windpipe released abruptly, however, as two bullets tore into Rico, pre-empting the virus.

Dove pulled away, gasping for breath, staring at Marco over the barrel of his smoking pistol—then beyond Marco, to the second gun that put Rico down, a gun with the glint of a sheriff's badge behind it. A line of deputies walked out of the broken country behind the burning hacienda, facing the former combatants.

"Well, lookee here. Arrived just in time for the last dance. Good thing we decided to come out to keep an eye on things." Pizarro swept the *Santos* and their prisoners with a sunglassed, impartial look. "Round 'em up, boys," he ordered. He amended the order to "Only Slick's men, you idiots," when the *Santos's* gun sights and gimlet stares converged on him.

The deputies, much relieved, moved in to relieve the *Santos* of their prisoners, slapping cuffs on Slick's men and forcing them to the ground.

"So you show up after the shooting's over, *Gordo?*" Dove asked, rubbing his throat, feeling light headed and heavy hearted.

Pizarro grinned. "I got in the one shot that counts, Pigeon." He surveyed the scene smugly. "Got a call that a bunch of desperados had blown through the border without showing the proper papers—or bothering to stop. Got a patrolman with a bullet in his butt too. Can't have that kind of thing going on. We're just here to preserve order, after all. Doing the People's business."

Calvin snorted at that, but Dove let it go, giving Pizarro a hard look instead. "You'd better pay a lot more attention to preserving order, Pizarro, or you'll get in a situation where you can't change sides fast enough to keep from getting burned. Spread the word to watch out for the General's troops, and make sure the snakes can't crawl back in. And Pizarro, while you're on snake patrol, stay clear of the *Santos*—us and the Latter-day Saints."

"Don't harass the Mormons, huh?" Pizarro spat on the blood-flecked dust. "'Cause you're protecting them?"

"No, because God is—and if He doesn't use me, He'll use somebody else." Dove met the sheriff's stare.

"Just get your boys out of here before the *federales* show up," Pizarro advised. "I'm not putting my neck on the block to cover for them."

"Looks like we need three paddy wagons and an ambulance," a deputy reported, coming over to the sheriff. His uniform had a hint of color to it in the growing light. Behind him, a van with a satellite transmitter atop the roof lumbered up the drive. A pair of sleek sedans followed, clearly official from the deep window tint to the lack of decals on their doors.

Good advice, even if it came out of malice. "Let's fade," Dove told Calvin. He strode away until the approaching lights of the reporter's video camera absorbed Pizarro's attention. Then he leaned against Calvin.

Perro caught him from the other side, the rest of the *Santos* falling in around them as they headed for their concealed vehicles. Calvin, much to Dove's surprise, hugged him hard, then let him go just as abruptly. "I'm getting the Dogmobile," he announced.

Dove watched Calvin climb into the battered car and slowly back it around. Weariness descended like lead into his bones. He followed it to the ground, kneeling in the brightening light of dawn. "Thank You, God," he whispered. "Thank You for delivering our enemies into our hands. Thank You for sparing your people. Please, help them to always choose to trust You. And please forgive us—forgive me." He finished the prayer silently when tears clotted his voice too much to speak.

"Amen."

The word, said in many voices, jerked Dove's attention back to the world outside his head—and the *Santos*, who stood around him. He rose as Perro pulled him up. "Thank you, too—all of you," he said, pulling his emotions under control. "You really came through. I don't know what to say."

"How about you tell us what to do next?" Marco suggested. "Like everybody go back to town, get cleaned up, and meet at Mama Rosa's to celebrate?"

A cheer met that suggestion. Dove managed a smile. "All right, it's a plan. I'll meet you there." His smile got stronger (and more wicked) as he added, "And no alcohol this time."

Good-natured grumbling and complaints met his stipulation, but no one kicked up a serious fuss. They scattered, dividing up among the various dented, dusty cars and trucks, roaring off into the sunrise.

The Dogmobile pulled up in front of Perro and Dove. "It'll make the drive back," Calvin assured them, patting the steering wheel affectionately. "And it's still got one window left." When he rolled up the driver's side window, however, it fell to pieces around a bullet hole that had gone through the outer panel of the door.

"Never mind," Perro said, laughing at Calvin's long face. "We'll get her fixed. Better than ever—with a new mural on the hood. The *Santos Soldados*, right, *Hasbìdì*?"

"Right, Perro." Dove eased onto the front seat. "Remind me not to get shot again."

"Will do." Perro leaned forward, patting Dove's shoulder. "You did it. You took Slick down for Benny."

"No," Dove told him, as Calvin urged the Dogmobile back onto the long drive between the lilacs, "Benny's all right. He's really all right. We took Slick down for Renata, Sam, the kids, and anybody else Slick and the General would've hurt." He looked back, watching Blanca Hacienda's huge sentinel boulders recede behind them. "And it's not over. The fight's only beginning, Perro."

"The fight can wait until we've got a patch on that leak in your leg and you actually eat something. Fasting's fine, but geez, Dove, moderation in all things, right?" Calvin sighed. "Except your big ideas. I knew you'd have to start something else. So now what? You better have a plan, 'cause the rest of the *Santos* are going to want to know what to do tomorrow—especially if you won't let them get drunk tonight."

"Well, we have to organize the people in town—all around here—to stand up to whoever follows Slick, and to Pizarro," Dove thought aloud, then grinned and poked Perro. "And we gotta get you both baptized."

"Calvin and me? Oh, yeah, they'd love us walking in the church door," Perro laughed.

"Well, you'd have to shower first." Dove grinned as he leaned his head against the torn-up seat back and closed his eyes. He could see Benny grinning too, through the brilliant light of sunrise shining through his eyelids—and the dark clouds massed along the horizon.

CHAPTER 19

"Oh, bright!" Missy exclaimed, squinting her eyes against the glare of the evening sun gleaming from the mirror-like windows of the Church Administration Building.

"Very bright," Merry agreed. "Can you wave to Sister and Brother Valados?" Missy did, enthusiastically. Merry added a more sedate wave, smiling at the kind couple who'd picked them up in Saint George, Utah, and driven them though the afternoon to Salt Lake City.

"Oh, we have grandbabies in the neighborhood who we should go see anyway," Sister Valados had assured her. "It's no trouble at all."

It hadn't been any trouble at all for any of the intrepid volunteers who'd shuttled Merry and Missy from car to car, town to town, taking handoffs in church parking lots. People with nothing in common but their membership in the Church had passed Merry along through the night, taking her from San Diego to Salt Lake without even once using her own phone or credit cards. *If Ms. Zelik could use Senator Garlick's access to phone records to track their progress through the virtual maze of seemingly random late-night conversations between their chauffeurs,* Merry thought, *she deserves to catch us!* Apart from a roadblock at the Nevada border set up to catch drug runners or illegal aliens, however, they'd breezed across the desert like the thin wind out of the clear, black sky. They'd stopped in Springville for a quick lunch and as much brushing up as Merry could manage (it worked better for Missy than it did for her). And now she stood here, at the very far end of business hours, outside what had been the primary headquarters of The Church of Jesus Christ of Latter-day Saints until the recent move to Jackson

County. Merry blinked up at the building, at the mountains rising beyond it, and took a deep breath of the dry, autumn-warm air.

"All right, Miss Missy, this is it," she said aloud, hiking the diaper bag on her shoulder. She sternly squelched the flash of embarrassment at catching sight of herself in the glass doors, wishing she was wearing something more, well, professional than Donna's jeans and sparkly T-shirt. Her ponytail, sneakers, and Missy's diaper bag completed the picture of a weary, harried, young mother out running errands. A sudden thought of Chris's reaction to her current costume made her laugh; he'd probably tell her she looked just like the girl next door—and then nuzzle her while telling her she made it easy to love his neighbor.

The door opened, breaking her reflection and momentary melancholy. A pleasant, unremarkable looking young man looked at her, smiled, and extended his hand. "Dr. Galen? I'm Jonathan Crow." Missy cawed softly, hearing the man's last name; one of her favorite cartoons featured a crow character. "Sister Valados called and said you'd arrived. Elder Nabil asked me to bring you right up."

Several people glanced at them as they walked through the elegant lobby, but they smiled. Missy happily waved at everyone, exclaiming over the mural decorating the lobby wall. "Jesus, Mommy! Jesus!"

"Yes, that's Jesus," Merry agreed.

"We go see Jesus?" Missy asked. "Crow? We go see Jesus?"

Jonathan coughed suddenly, to cover a laugh. When he answered, "No, you're going to see Elder Nabil," his voice was thoroughly under control, answering her question politely. He even helped Missy pronounce "Nabil" as they signed in with the indulgently smiling security guard.

Brownie point for you, Brother Crow, Merry thought.

He introduced them both to Elder Nabil with the same pleasant courtesy. "Elder Nabil, this is Dr. Meredith Galen, and her daughter, Melissa Galen."

"Thank you so much for letting us come—especially so late in the day," Merry began. "I know it's an imposition—"

"Imposition! I am only too happy to meet with you, at any time!" Elder Nabil didn't so much shake Merry's hand as engulf it in both of his, smiling warmly. "Such an adventure you have had, dear lady! So good to meet you here, in person, safe and sound. And with your charming daughter equally safe." His voice was even more lovely in person than in the General Conference broadcasts, deep, rich, and lightly accented. He smiled at Missy, offering a long, dark hand.

Missy, well trained by her father, promptly slapped the Apostle's palm. "Five!" she announced.

"I'm so sorry," Merry began, blushing furiously. She didn't finish the apology.

A broad smile crept across Elder Nabil's elegant, aquiline features. He gently slapped Missy's offered palm in return. "I see your daddy has trained you well!"

"Dadadad," Missy agreed.

"Indeed." Elder Nabil sobered, compassion replacing amusement in his face. "The other Dr. Galen. Sorely missed, I am sure. I would have loved to have met him. But come, tell me what the two of you have found. The information in the files you sent was horrible almost beyond belief. Sadly, though, we must believe that such wickedness is only too common in these last days we live in. We need to talk, Dr. Galen."

Turning away, he called to a comfortably professional woman sitting behind an immaculately organized desk. "Connie, would you please help Jonathan entertain our young Miss Galen? With your permission, of course," he added, nodding to Merry.

"Will you play with Crow and Connie while I talk to Elder Nabil?" Merry asked Missy.

"Mamamam come back?" Missy caught Merry's face between her hands.

"Yes, I will most definitely come back. I'm just going to be in that office right there," Merry pointed.

Missy considered the possibility, sizing up the two potential babysitters. Connie, veteran of the homemaking wars, tipped the balance with a welcoming smile and a bagful of tiny crackers. In short order, Missy was happily ensconced in Jonathan's rolling chair, snarfing crackers and peppering them both with questions.

Elder Nabil smiled. "That is a little girl who knows her mind. Rather like her mother, I think. Please." He ushered Merry into his well-appointed, book-filled office. A computer screen shone from the wall above the desk, Xavier Chaudry's thin, expressionless mug shot staring out at them. Below it, statistics and computer projections showed the inevitable deterioration as his over-hyped immune system turned against him.

"Please, be seated. Be comfortable—as much as possible." Elder Nabil gestured Merry to a soft leather chair and settled in his own chair (beside the visitor chair, not across the desk from it). They regarded the screen together in silence as Merry gathered her thoughts.

"The AllSafe vaccine isn't safe," she said into the strangely comfortable silence. "It enhances the human immune system to fight off any current infection, and it does guard against infections thereafter. However, unless the patient receives a booster shot to control the initial vaccine's effects, the immune system eventually goes into overdrive. It begins attacking the patient's own healthy cells. Fatally, in every case during the human trials. Elder Nabil, please—you must help me warn—well, *everyone* not to take it! Unless they get that booster, it will kill them. And MedaGen absolutely owns the booster. I couldn't even get to the files that contained the formulas for it."

"A dire threat indeed." Elder Nabil sat quietly for a long moment, regarding Merry, then looking out the window at the mountains gleaming under the sun. His gaze came back to Merry, sharpened and purposeful. "Show me, here in the files, what you've found. And tell me the entire story, from the beginning. How you found what you did, why you began to suspect, what MedaGen did to stop you—and I have it on very good authority that they felt the situation warranted desperate measures indeed."

"It started with a computer glitch—well, really, it started when we heard about MedaGen's reputation for stem-cell experiments," Merry began, moving to the monitor. "Then Chris accidentally got access to a set of very confidential files for the Corinth project . . ."

Four hours, much discussion, two glasses of water, and the arrival of a napping Missy later, Elder Nabil sat back in his chair with a sigh. "And so Satan moves in the hearts of men." His pensive pose broke, however, as he stood suddenly. "Thank you, Meredith. I understand—and I am most grateful to you for all the risks you took to get this information to us. We will indeed trumpet this word from the rooftops. Pending the approval of the First Presidency, of course, but I feel that they will give it quickly. Jonathan!"

Jonathan appeared instantly at the door.

"Jonathan, we need to get Dr. Galen a lawyer," he ordered.

"A lawyer?" Merry asked, taken aback.

"Yes, my dear." Elder Nabil nodded decisively. "To my understanding, you qualify for Federal protection from prosecution—and persecution—under Federal whistle-blower laws. Making that official should keep MedaGen's wolves from your door. Also, Jonathan, we need to find these two lovely ladies a place to stay. They're going to need a nice apartment to live in while Dr. Galen turns her formidable talents to finding the antidote to MedaGen's opportunistic poison."

"Finding the antidote?" Merry repeated, feeling like a goose rather than an intrepid corporate spy/adventurer. "I didn't know the Church sponsored research in genetic medicine."

"We don't," Elder Nabil winked at her, patting her shoulder bracingly. "But we have several influential and wealthy members who run programs that do—or can. The Lord directs us to seek truth wherever we find it, to educate ourselves in all needful things, and a wide variety of things are becoming more needful as time goes on. We will warn our people against the consequences of seeking medicine to give them consequence-free lives, but we will also, with divine help, prepare to combat the aftereffects of MedaGen's ambition. As my grandmother said, 'Trust in Allah, but tie up your camel.' Divine intervention is always possible, but it's usually up to us to do the legwork."

"Legwork." Merry heard herself repeat his words for the third time and suddenly laughed. "I'm sorry. I feel like such a ditz. Thank you, Elder Nabil. I am more than happy to help all I can in tying up this particular camel. 'I will go and do,' to trade one good quote for another."

Elder Nabil looked at her, his eyebrow quirked.

Merry laughed again. "Oops. Another slip. When we read the Book of Mormon, Chris always used a thick Austrian accent for Nephi. Big and strong for his age, you see." It occurred to her too late that an Apostle might not take the same freewheeling approach to characterizing prophets (ancient or modern) as Chris did.

To her relief, however, Elder Nabil laughed too. "Quite a unique individual, that other Dr. Galen. I shall look forward to meeting him some day. For now, however, I must take my leave. You have given us all much to think about—and to do." He strode off down the hall, already dialing his phone. "Yes, it is almost good morning, Richard. I apologize for calling at this late hour, but we do indeed need to talk." The elevator door closed behind him.

Merry turned to Jonathan. "Well, since we're being so self reliant and dealing with our own camels, I'll take responsibility for my own lodgings. I do have a place to stay in the area—well, more or less. My in-laws live down in Provo. May I use your phone to call them?"

"Absolutely," Jonathan said, offering her the receiver from Connie's desk. "But before you very self-reliantly head off to Provo, please, let me treat you all to at least a midnight snack."

After a tearful (on Merry's part) and gleeful (on Missy's) reunion with Grandma and Grandpa Galen, a snack, and the drive to Provo, the tight knot inside Merry's chest finally loosened enough to let her sleep. She made sure that Missy had her blanket, jammies, and dinosaur at the ready, then crashed hard, diving so deeply asleep that even dreams of guns and MedaGen goons couldn't follow her. By the time she resurfaced, it was sunset again.

"There you are, awake at last," Grandma Galen smiled at her, as Missy barreled into her legs, happily jabbering greetings. "Just in time to see the latest wrinkle in your saga, as Chris would say."

Merry followed her gesture to the TV screen, where Abbott, suave and cool behind an impressive bank of audio pickups, gently defused a reporter's heated question. "Of course, we at MedaGen are aware of the rumors surrounding our upcoming rollout of the revolutionary AllSafe vaccine. We can say with utter confidence, however, that the vaccine's effects are exactly as designed. It is the ultimate break-through in managing epidemics that present such a dire threat to public health. It is also based on completely safe, well understood science that has been with us since Dr. Salk introduced the polio vaccine—which really was the AllSafe of its day, defusing a horrible scourge that threatened the lives and health of millions of people all over the world. AllSafe is a vaccine, with a vaccine's impressive successes, and, inevitably, some of its drawbacks. The need for peri-odic booster shots is one of them. No vaccine can reliably immunize a person forever with just one dose. And MedaGen is determined to work with the government—particularly the progressive, forward-looking lawmakers, such as Senator Howard Garlick, who truly have the best interests of the people at heart—to make the boosters, as well as the vaccine itself, easily accessible to everyone. It has become a sadly dangerous world—and we deplore the ignorance, if not outright malice, that prompts some individuals and organizations to fight against progress. Thank you all. With your help, we will win the war against bio-terrorism in all its forms."

"Well, Chris, we tried," Merry thought, watching Abbott's smug face fade from the screen. Unexpectedly, however, her heart failed to drop into her shoes. Instead, she heard Chris say, *We succeeded, sweetheart. And this is just round one.* She knew better than to whirl around looking for him; it was just her subconscious talking. The strangely comforting feeling, on the other hand, definitely came from outside, accompanied by a strangely comforting green-gold warmth.

* * *

"I think in these uncertain times, people take comfort wherever they can find it," said a dapper-looking man. The crawl at the bottom of the screen identified him as a well-respected evolutionary psychologist. "Even when they're looking in completely irrational places."

"How can you say believing in the existence of God is irrational?" another man—this one a reverend and noted creationist—shot back. "It's your insane belief in the vagaries of evolution that's irrational!"

The panel, a group of hand-picked scientific chauvinists and rabid evolutionists, erupted into cross-talk and argument, contradicting, insulting each other, flinging aspersions and inflammatory statements across the table.

"Hammer and tongs," Monk observed, nodding sagely. "That's public debate for you. Successful public debate, anyway. And we hit the previews—now."

"Well, we've certainly had a lively discussion today," the panel's moderator slid into the frame, replacing the intellectual combatants throwing the ideological equivalent of chairs at each other. "I hope you heard something that got you thinking. Tune in next week for more thought-provoking dialogue, when CrossTalk takes on another controversial topic: religion and medicine. We'll look at fundamentalist fulminations against organ transplants, Christian Scientist refusal of all treatment—and, most dramatically, Mormon opposition to stem-cell research and the great advances that come from it."

"Great lead-in. Cue the next segment." Monk relaxed into his chair. "Anne O'Neal. Sell it, baby."

"This is Anne O'Neal, reporting live from Independence, Missouri." Leroy framed Anne neatly, the massive headquarters of the Church on one side, a mob of sign-waving protesters on the other. "Demonstrators have converged here to protest the latest controversial statement by the Church's leadership. This time, The Church of Jesus Christ of Latter-day Saints has used its Web site, well-organized network of local parishes, and extensive contacts in business, government, and military to issue a directive to its members. And that directive, in a letter from the First Presidency of the Church advises Church members—and anyone else who will listen—not to take the AllSafe vaccine. The letter raises several concerns about the vaccine's safety, hinging on the as yet unpublished reports by whistle-blower Dr. Meredith Galen."

A picture of Merry—her ID portrait from MedaGen's files—appeared on the screen beside Anne. "MedaGen has blocked the release of the contested reports as a Senate panel debates the extension of Federal protection to Dr. Galen. Another Senate panel has convened to discuss the political implications of Senator Howard W. Garlick's proposal for mandating the vaccine as part of a Homeland Security program."

Senator Garlick appeared on a clip of archival footage, waving to reporters as he hustled through the microphone-waving mob and into a meeting with his fellow politicians. He disappeared, replaced by a silver-haired, handsome evangelist who pounded the pulpit while declaiming his own views to a stadium full of devotees. "In the meantime, well-known evangelist Reverend Tommy Gibb has jumped into the fray," Anne continued, "even going so far as to call the AllSafe vaccine the 'Mark of the Beast.' While public-opinion polls still show that over 60 percent of Americans think AllSafe *is* safe and plan to take the vaccinations as soon as they become widely available, MedaGen reports that first-quarter sales haven't met projections. It appears that many non-Mormons have followed the LDS Church's lead." A brief shot of Abbott and Zelik smiling at a shareholder meeting faded from the screen.

Anne, with the inevitable protesters still flailing signs behind her, reappeared. "At the same time, some analysts suspect that the Senator's congressional support is fading as well. We'll all be watching closely to see how it goes. Stay tuned for an in-depth report from Channel 8's own science specialist, explaining how AllSafe works. This is Anne O'Neal, Channel 8 News." As she signed off, a sepia-toned, nostalgia-wrapped ad replaced her, the narrator recounting the horrors of polio in the early 1900s and the heroic efforts of doctors to create an effective vaccine—just like MedaGen today, discovering an effective solution for a wide spectrum of humanity's ills. The lilting strains of Virginia's latest record, a sweetly melancholy ballad, wound around and through the images.

"Think Garlick's really gonna get minced on this one?" Leroy asked, wrapping up cables.

Anne replied thoughtfully, ignoring the bad culinary pun. "I don't know. He's been good at landing on his feet before, and MedaGen's already spinning it." She thought of President Rojas, calm in the spotlight, taking heat from inside and outside for the Church's reaction to the AllSafe decision. "All I know for sure is that the Church has made some very powerful enemies on this one, and they're not going to forget it—or take it lying down."

* * *

Dear Chisom,

As I walked into my study a few minutes ago to begin this e-mail, I happened to look out the window. To this moment I am transfixed by what I see and don't see. I must admit that I don't like either. I haven't seen the stars for months. Tonight the moon is full, but rather than shimmering in silver brightness, it hangs like a dull ball of blood. Its sanguine hue, speckling the landscape, seems to touch everything with the promise of death. I know that's melodramatic, but I can't help feeling vulnerable. Of course the events of the last couple of weeks have probably put me in this mood.

I have been telling you that Babylon is alive and well riding her seven horned beast across the lands. Little have I realized how true, how close to home, and how immediate she really was. I am amazed how close one of her beast's horns came to enslaving the human race. I suspect you know I'm talking about the MedaGen scandal. In light of what Elder Nabil has told us and what the news reports say, I fear I have greatly underestimated the power of the Mother of Harlots. I just wonder how many other "horns" there are out there biding their time but ready to strike. We were very blessed this time. Just think, MedaGen would have gotten away with its nefarious scheme if it were not for some sharp, faithful, and very brave, Latter-day Saints, Elder Nabil's knowledge of biochemistry, Pres. Smith's ability to mobilize our people, and a lot of help from the Divine. What that company tried to do (and is still trying to do, by the way, we haven't seen the last of it), shows the Mahanic principle (the turning of human life into property, remember?) is alive, well, and being put into practice even as I write. The question is, in how many other places and in how many other forms will it appear? Will we again be so blessed?

I fear one of Babylon's "horns" is General Garza. We found out he's an Italian. Indeed, he grew up in Rome. When I heard that I was immediately reminded of the book of Revelation. There John describes Babylon's beast as the Seven Hills of Rome. I'm wondering if one of its sons may be pushing the whore's cause in our day. From what we hear, it is good we warned the Saints away from him, for many others have been seduced into joining his ranks and been enslaved. He has been able to amass a small but well supplied army and is intimidating the weaker nations in South America and flexing his muscles against Central America as well. A few brave leaders—

primarily faithful members of the Church—have taken stands against him, but they are outnumbered and may fall to his political maneuverings and professional assassins. Many of the Saints are either hiding or fleeing to other areas to get away from him and his organized and disciplined thugs. It is terrible down south. What is also frightening is that he is continually looking further northward.

He is not, however, the only "horn" the Brethren tell us we need to fear. The scriptures speak of another, this one described as a two-horned lamb. (See Revelation 13.) The lamb is the Antichrist, working miracles, teaching false doctrines, and promising salvation. It is also called "the false prophet" by John. Its greatest power comes from its deceptive abilities. It is the greatest of the latter-day persecutors of the Saints. When this false prophet, this wolf in lamb's clothing, comes, the devil will have his last emissary in place. Mark my words, Chisom, when that lamb appears—that powerful and seductive false prophet—the world will be headed nonstop for Armageddon.

Stay faithful and help the Saints build their spiritual defenses. We are all going to need them.

Your loving father,
Chinedu

ABOUT THE AUTHORS

JESSICA DRAPER is unaccustomed to writing about herself in the third person. She is also an avid reader, Primary teacher, big sister, trained librarian, amateur needleworker, cat owner, and possessor of a rich fantasy life (obviously). She currently works at the Center for Instructional Design at Brigham Young University, after spending many years writing software documentation (which often qualifies as speculative fiction).

RICHARD D. DRAPER is a professor of ancient scripture at BYU and was recently appointed as Director of the Religious Studies Center. He holds a PhD in Ancient History. Brother Draper is a best-selling author of several books and talk tapes, and has written numerous articles for the *Ensign* and other publications. He has been a popular lecturer at *Know Your Religion* and Education Week for many years.

Richard and his wife, Barbara, are the parents of six children and reside in Lindon, Utah.

Damage Noted _Slight water damage_

Date _7-8-15_ Initials _MH-RIV_